THE VIKING PORTABLE LIBRARY

ENLIGHTENMENT READER

ISAAC KRAMNICK was born in 1938 and educated at Harvard University, where he received a B.A. degree in 1959 and a Ph.D. in 1965, and at Peterhouse, Cambridge. He has taught at Harvard, Brandeis, Yale, and Cornell, where he is now professor of government. He is married to Miriam Brody and lives in Ithaca, New York. Among his publications are *Bolingbroke and His Circle, The Rage of Edmund Burke*, and numerous articles on eighteenth-century topics. He has edited *The Federalist Papers*, William Godwin's *Enquiry Concerning Political Justice*, Thomas Paine's *Common Sense*, and the *Thomas Paine Reader* for Penguin Classics. Most recently he is the author, with Barry Sheerman, M.P., of *Laski: A Life on the Left.*

Each volume in The Viking Portable Library either presents a representative selection from the works of a single outstanding writer or offers a comprehensive anthology on a special subject. Averaging 700 pages in length and designed for compactness and readability, these books fill a need not met by other compilations. All are edited by distinguished authorities, who have written introductory essays and included much other helpful material.

The Portable
ENLIGHTENMENT READER

Edited and with an Introduction by

ISAAC KRAMNICK

PENGUIN BOOKS

To the Memory of Judith N. Shklar (1928–1992)
Teacher, scholar, friend: A philosophe *for our age*

PENGUIN BOOKS
Published by the Penguin Group
Penguin Books USA Inc., 375 Hudson Street, New York, New York 10014, U.S.A.
Penguin Books Ltd, 27 Wrights Lane, London W8 5TZ, England
Penguin Books Australia Ltd, Ringwood, Victoria, Australia
Penguin Books Canada Ltd, 10 Alcorn Avenue, Toronto, Ontario, Canada M4V 3B2
Penguin Books (N.Z.) Ltd, 182–190 Wairau Road, Auckland 10, New Zealand

Penguin Books Ltd, Registered Offices: Harmondsworth, Middlesex, England

First published in Penguin Books 1995

10

Grateful acknowledgment is made for permission to reprint the following copyrighted works:
"The Human Mind Emerged from Barbarism" by Jean Le Rond d'Alembert, translated by Stephen J. Gendzier. By permission of Stephen J. Gendzier.
"The Beautiful and Sublime" from *Observations on the Feeling of the Beautiful and Sublime* by Immanuel Kant, translated and edited by John Goldthwait. Copyright © 1960 The Regents of the University of California. By permission of the University of California Press.
"The New Science" from *The New Science of Giambattista Vico: Unabridged Translation of the Third Edition (1744) with the addition of "Practic of the New Science,"* translated by Thomas Goddard Bergin and Max Harold Fisch. Copyright © 1984 by Cornell University. Used by permission of the publisher, Cornell University Press.
"The Rights of Woman" by Olympe de Gouges from *Women in Revolutionary Paris* edited by Darline G. Levy, et al. © 1979 by the Board of Trustees of the University of Illinois. Used with permission of the author and of the University of Illinois Press.

LIBRARY OF CONGRESS CATALOGING IN PUBLICATION DATA
Kramnick, Isaac.
The portable Enlightenment reader/Isaac Kramnick.
p. cm.
Includes bibliographical references.
ISBN 0 14 02.4566 9 (pbk.)
1. Enlightenment. 2. Philosophy, Modern—18th century.
I. Title.
B802.K73 1995
940.2'53—dc20 95-16720

Printed in the United States of America Set in Bembo

CONTENTS

INTRODUCTION

FEW HAVE CAPTURED the spirit of the Enlightenment, its intellectual and social agenda, as has Mozart in his operas. *The Magic Flute*, with its secular priests presiding over Temples of Wisdom, Reason, and Nature, is a series of variations on the triumph of light over darkness, of sun over moon, of day over night, of reason, tolerance, and love over passion, hate, and revenge. Masonic imagery and symbolism abound in the opera, as the Freemasons Mozart and his librettist, Emanuel Schikaneder, bring the disdain for superstition and mystery in church and state, which so marked this most radical of Enlightenment groups, into their musical and literary texts. Similarly, *The Marriage of Figaro* is a rendering of Enlightenment social ideals, a lyrical hymn to the individualistic claims of self-made assertive men who achieve their place through hard work, skill, and talent, as opposed to aristocrats who are simply born to privilege. What have you done to earn your fortune, rank, and position? Figaro asks the great nobleman Almaviva. He answers his own question: "You took the trouble to get born, and no more."

It was the assumed triumph of these ideals that led the French philosopher D'Alembert to call his eighteenth century *l'age des lumieres*, the age of splendid illumination, of light and enlightenment. He and his fellow intellectuals, he assumed, would realize the project begun by the Renaissance: to lift the darkness that fell with the Christian triumph over the virtues of classical antiquity. While it is French eighteenth-century thought that is conventionally depicted as best embodying Enlightenment principles, with the writings of the *philosophes* and their magisterial seventeen-volume *Encyclopédie* given pride of place, the Enlightenment was, in fact, an intellectual movement that knew no national boundaries. The *philosophes* themselves saw three Englishmen as the prophets of Enlightenment, and they dedicated their *Encyclopédie* to Bacon, Locke, and Newton. Jefferson, an American disciple of the Enlightenment, agreed, ordering for his library in 1789 a composite portrait of the same three Englishmen. They had, he wrote to a friend, laid the foundation for the physical and moral sciences of modernity and were "the three greatest men that have ever lived, without any exception."[1]

The Enlightenment was an international movement that included French, English, Scottish, American, German, Italian, Spanish, and even Russian schools. Voltaire and Montesquieu visited England and wrote extensively about its institutions. Franklin and Jefferson visited England and France and were well connected with writers in both countries. The intellectual ferment was transnational. John Adams wrote his *Defense of the Constitution of the United States of America* in response to criticism from the *philosophe* Turgot, and Smith's *Wealth of Nations* was translated into French by Condorcet. Mozart's operas as Enlightenment icons epitomize the internationalism of the movement as well. The Austrian composer used Figaro, a literary invention of the Frenchman Beaumarchais, who, in addition to writing *Le mariage de Figaro* in 1778, had been involved in secret French munitions deals to help the revolutionary Americans. Beaumarchais's play was immediately translated into English by Thomas Holcroft, Enlightenment novelist and close friend of Enlightenment philosopher William Godwin. Mozart's librettist for *Figaro*, Lorenzo da Ponte, was an Italian who lived in London in the 1790s and became, finally, a professor of Italian literature at Columbia University in New York City.

Dating an intellectual movement like the Enlightenment is never precise, but a rough guide would emphasize the hundred-plus years from the 1680s to the 1790s. The beginnings are marked in Britain by the Glorious Revolution in 1688, which provided a constitutional arrangement repudiating Stuart autocracy and ushering in religious toleration, as well as by the writings of Locke and the publication in 1687 of Newton's *Principia.* The French beginnings are signaled by the Revocation of the Edict of Nantes in 1685 and the writings in the 1680s of Bayle and Fontonelle. The end of the Enlightenment is best linked to the realization of its ideals in the revolutionary fervor that swept through America, France, and even England in the last quarter of the eighteenth century, which in turn produced the romantic and conservative reactions of the early nineteenth century.

The initiating events of the 1680s provide glaring evidence of the differing political contexts in which the Enlightenment occurred in its French and British settings. In the liberal atmosphere of Augustan and Georgian Britain, religious toleration and freedom of publication generally flourished. Louis XIV's decision in 1685 to revoke the limited toleration given French Protestants in 1598, on the other hand, ushered in a century of illiberal and autocratic rule in that country, with first the persecution and then the flight of the Huguenots. Royal and clerical control and censorship of publication led to the arrest of writers like Voltaire, as well as the condemnation and suppression at various times of works by Helvétius, Diderot, d'Holbach, Montesquieu, and of the *Encyclopédie* itself in 1759. Performances of Beaumarchais's *Le mariage de Figaro* were proscribed in the 1780s by royal decree. In turn, French writers like Montesquieu and Diderot, in order to avoid suppression, often resorted to using observations from fictional foreigners to criticize French political institutions or the Catholic Church. The harsher realities of repression and persecution understandably give the writings of the French Enlightenment a tone that is more bitter and less compromising than is found in the British. Not that despotism, when freed from religious zeal, was utterly incompatible with enlightenment. For several of the *philosophes*—Voltaire, Diderot, and Helvétius, for example, the political ideal was the "enlightened despotism" of a reforming monarch, like Frederick in Prussia or Catherine in Russia, who, while sponsoring religious toleration, was committed to the rational reform of political, legal, and economic life befitting an age of reason.

These political differences notwithstanding, the intellectuals of the French and British Enlightenment operated in relatively similar settings. They shared the profound transformation of Western life brought by commerce and industrialization and, with it, the emergence of middle-class Figaros as the new cultural ideal. Far from being alarmed at this great change, they generally embraced the new commercial civilization and its values, seeing it as a progressive, reforming force that would undermine the dead hand of aristocratic privilege and religious fanaticism. Theirs was also an age of increasing literacy, as for the first time in history reading ceased to be a monopoly of the very few, the rich, and the clergy. It was also an age when intellectuals eagerly wrote for and to this wider audience of new readers, not yet having become alienated from the philistine public in a posture of romantic weariness.

What was the message of these Enlightenment intellectuals? What were their ideals? They believed that unassisted human reason, not faith or tradition, was the principal guide to human conduct. "Have courage to use your own reason—that is the motto of Enlightenment," Kant wrote in 1784.[2] Everything, including political and religious authority, must be subject to a critique of reason if it were to commend itself to the respect of humanity. Particularly suspect was religious faith and superstition. Humanity was not innately corrupt as Catholicism taught, nor was the good life found only in a beatific state of otherworldly salvation. Pleasure and happiness were worthy ends of life and realizable in this world. The natural universe, governed not by the miraculous whimsy of a supernatural God, was ruled by rational scientific laws, which were accessible to human beings through the scientific method of experiment and empirical observation. Science and technology were the engines of progress enabling modern men and women to force nature to serve their well-being and further their happiness. Science and the conquest of superstition and ignorance provided the prospect for endless improvement and reformation of the human condition, progress even unto a future that was perfection. The Enlightenment valorized the individual and the moral legitimacy of self-interest. It sought to free the individual from all varieties of external corporate or communal constraints, and it sought to reorganize the political, moral, intellectual, and economic worlds to serve individual interest.

Central to the Enlightenment agenda was the assault on religious superstition and its replacement by a rational religion in which God became no more than the supreme intelligence or craftsman who had set the machine that was the world to run according to its own natural and scientifically predictable laws. This deism, so reminiscent of the cosmic outlook of the ancient Stoics, was inherently anticlerical and deeply suspicious of religious fanaticism and persecution. More than anyone else, Voltaire and his motto *Ecrasez l'infâme* symbolized the war against torture and persecution bred by the infamy of religious fanaticism. But virtually all the Enlightenment theorists followed the lead of Locke in demanding religious toleration. Religion removed from public life and public authority would be reserved for the private sphere of individual preference and individual practice. Public matters in a commercial society involved markets and property, not the saving of souls. So Voltaire approvingly described the Royal Exchange in London as the place where "the Jew, the Mahometan, and the Christian transact together, as though they all professed the same religion, and give the name of infidel to none but bankrupts."[3] Jefferson, in turn, rendered the same liberal, tolerant theme in simple American folk wisdom: "The legitimate powers of government extend to such acts only as are injurious to others. But it does me no injury for my neighbor to say there are twenty gods, or no God. It neither picks my pocket nor breaks my leg."[4]

If religion was the principal villain of the Enlightenment, then science was its hero. The eighteenth century began the Western love affair with science and technology that only now shows signs of being broken up by environmentalism and certain strands of postmodernism. Science embodied reason, and a scientific worldview embodied a rational perspective freed from religion and superstition. Moreover, science, a very practical science, would ameliorate human life, providing the comfort that accompanied happiness in this world. Many of the Enlightenment writers were themselves scientists. Locke, Hartley, and La Mettrie were doctors; Voltaire, Montesquieu, and Diderot were authors of scientific papers; d'Alembert, Richard Price, and Condorcet were mathematicians; Priestley, Buffon, and Franklin were world-famous scientists; and even Tom Paine was the inventor of the iron bridge.

Science was in the service of reform. According to Priestley, science would "overturn in a moment . . . the old building of error and superstition." It would "be the means, under God, of extirpating all error and prejudice, and of putting an end to all undue and usurped authority." Science also fueled millennial fervor in the Enlightenment. It was the basis for an unbounded faith in progress, a belief in perfectibility and the imminent elimination of pain and suffering. Priestley, Condorcet, and Turgot assumed that science would create a people "more easy and comfortable," who would "grow daily more happy." "Whatever was the beginning of the world, the end will be glorious and paradisiacal."[5] Science might even eliminate mortality, as Franklin wrote to Priestley:

> The rapid progress the sciences now make, occasions my regrets sometimes that I was born so soon. It is impossible to imagine the heights to which may be carried in a hundred years, the power of man over matter. . . . All diseases may by sure means be prevented or cured, not excepting even that of old age, and our lives lengthened at pleasure even beyond the antediluvian standard.[6]

Progress was a leitmotiv of the Enlightenment, but not only in the dreams of scientists like Priestley and Franklin. It was central, for example, to the writers in the Scottish Enlightenment and their sociological "histories" of the stages of social development. Smith, Ferguson, Miller, and Kames wrote of the four stages of human progress—the hunting, pasturage, agricultural, and commercial—and they saw this evolutionary process as moving humanity from "rude" simplicity to "civilized" complexity. Like Mandeville, Hume, and Voltaire, and unlike Rousseau, they accepted and defended the luxury of contemporary "civilized" commercial society. Condorcet, in turn, read a clear-cut egalitarian political message in the patterns of scientific and commercial progress. His optimistic hope for the "future condition of the human race" was "the abolition of inequality between nations, the progress of equality within each nation, and the true perfection of mankind."[7]

Such faith in progress required a jaundiced view of the past, and once again Voltaire was the Enlightenment's guide. History, he wrote in 1754, was "little else than a long succession of useless cruelties" and "a collection of crimes, follies, and misfortunes."[8] Progressive, perfectible humanity disdained the superstitious past and traditions in general, for it could not pass the skeptical test of reason. The American *philosophe* Jefferson summed up well this Enlightenment ideal in a letter to his friend Priestley, attacking what the former labeled "the Gothic idea," which has one "look backwards instead of forwards for the improvement of the human mind." Just as Priestly had insisted that "those times of revered antiquity have had their use and are now no more," so Jefferson agreed that Americans would have nothing to do with such errors:

> To recur to the annals of our ancestors for what is most perfect in government, in religion, in learning, is worthy of those bigots in religion, and government, by whom it is recommended, and whose purpose it would answer. But it is not an idea which this country will endure.[9]

One clear feature of the Enlightenment's idea of the "true perfection of mankind" was that humanity be comfortable and happy. Maximizing public happiness was a central theme in the utilitarian politics of Helvétius, Beccaria, Priestley, and Bentham. The Enlightenment was convinced, as Bayle wrote, that basic to the human temperament was "our natural inclination to seek pleasure."[10] In reaction to the religious view that in this life and under its veil of tears a virtuous person lived a life of self-denial and privation, Enlightenment writers emphasized enjoyment and happiness, not the least of which was sensual pleasure. How better to ridicule the asceticism and self-denial preached by religion than to mock it in sexual fantasy. So it was that the eighteenth century is the fountain of modern pornography, be it the Marquis de Sade or John Cleland's *Fanny Hill.* Montesquieu, Diderot, and even Franklin wrote their share as well. In his *Encyclopédie* entry on "Enjoyment" (*jouissance*),

Diderot praised sexual pleasure as the most noble of passions. To the "perverse man" who takes offense at this praise "I would evoke Nature before him, I would make it speak, and Nature would say to him: why do you blush to hear the word pleasure pronounced, when you do not blush to indulge in its temptations under the cover of night."[11]

Happiness was an explosive political ideal as well, for it was closely linked to the new world of individualism and the legitimacy of self-interest. Jefferson knew exactly what he was doing when he changed Locke's trilogy "life, liberty, and property" to "life, liberty, and the pursuit of happiness." Property, and the individual's right to it, was but one expression of the larger human right to individual happiness. The emphasis is properly on the individual's happiness, for the Enlightenment's revolutionary objective, enshrined in Jefferson's text for the Declaration of Independence, was to place at the heart of politics the sacredness of each separate individual's own quest for happiness and the good life. No longer was there assumed to be a Christian conception of the good life or the moral life, which the church and state defined and to whose common values it led all men and women. The Enlightenment assumption was that each individual pursued his or her own happiness and their own individual sense of the good life—so long, that is, that in doing this they did not interfere with other people's life, liberty, or pursuit of happiness—or as Jefferson put it, so long as "it neither picks my pocket, nor breaks my leg."

There is a profoundly radical individualism at the heart of Enlightenment thought. Its rationalism led Enlightenment philosophy to enthrone the individual as the center and creator of meaning, truth, and even reality. Descartes had doubted everything, but he could not doubt himself. He as the I, the irreducible thinking being, existed at the core of reality. This epistemological and ontological focus on the individual provided by Descartes's *cogito ergo sum* was reinforced in Enlightenment thought by Lockean sensationalism. The mind as a "blank slate" received sensations from the external world. That individual mind imperially ordered chaotic sensory experience, constructing, therefore, its own meaning for the world. This Lockean portrayal of individuals as sole intellectual creators of their universe dominates the eighteenth century, from the writings of his disciples Hartley and Condillac to Helvétius, Beccaria, and Condorcet. No wonder, then, that Diderot and d'Alembert dedicated the *Encyclopédie* in part to Locke.

It wasn't only Locke's *Essay on Human Understanding*, however, that held the Enlightenment in thrall. It was also the political liberalism of his *Second Treatise on Civil Government*. Indeed, it is in its basic assumptions about society, so heavily influenced by Locke, that one sees best the linkage of the Enlightenment's ideals and liberal individualism. Enlightenment liberalism set the individual free politically, intellectually, and economically. The political universe was demystified, as the magical power of thrones, scepters, and crowns was replaced by rational acts of consent. The individual (understood, of course, in the Enlightenment as male and property-owning) did not receive government and authority from a God who had given his secular sword to princes and magistrates to rule by his divine right. Nor did the individual keep any longer to his subordinate place in a divinely inspired hierarchy, in which kings and noblemen had been placed above him as "your highnesses" who were society's natural governors. Government was voluntarily established by free individuals through a willful act of contract. Individuals rationally consented to limit their own freedom and to obey civil authority in order to have public protection of their natural rights. Government's purpose was to serve self-interest, to enable individuals to enjoy peacefully their rights to life, liberty, and property, not to serve the glory of God or dynasties, and certainly not to dictate moral or religious truth.

Enlightenment liberalism freed the individual in the intellectual and moral world as well. Here, too, Locke provided the basic text with his *Letters on Toleration* and his argument that governments were only concerned with the worldly matters of life and property, not with immaterial things like salvation of souls. No *summum bonum*, no unquestioned and absolute truths were to be enforced on the individual by public authority, be it secular or spiritual. If men and women were not to slaughter each other in religious wars, then matters of belief and moral conviction had to be reserved for the private realm, where each individual was free to believe as he wished. Public law no longer enforced God's higher truths nor any ideal of the moral life; it merely kept order. What individuals privately believed seldom stole property or injured others. Clerical or royal censorship and persecution of free individual minds was the lightning rod for Enlightenment contempt.

As Enlightenment liberalism would free the individual from intellectual constraint, so it would also liberate that individual from economic restraints on private initiative. Rejected were the ideas of a moral economy in which economic activity was perceived as serving public moral ends of justice, whether these be realized through church-imposed constraints on wages and prices, or through magistrates setting prices and providing relief to insure that the poor not starve. Church, state, and guilds were no longer to superintend economic activity; individuals would be left alone to seek their own self-interest in a free voluntary market, which through "an invisible hand" would produce the good of all. These Enlightenment ideals are associated principally with Adam Smith and the French physiocrats Turgot and Quesnay, but they pervade the era and are found in writers as disparate as Voltaire, Priestley, and Jefferson. So too, we should also note the fundamental unity of the Enlightenment's message, for the economic liberals, the Smiths and the physiocrats, were as strongly committed to the principles of political and intellectual individualism as were the rest of the Enlightenment intellectuals.

Indeed, it is Smith who weaves together all the social strands of Enlightenment individualism with his striking insights into human nature. In commercial societies, Smith suggested, the individual was ever ambitious and striving. Every individual "seeks to better his own condition." This ambition, Smith writes, is "a desire which comes with us from the womb and never leaves us until we go into the grave." Life, he wrote, was "a race for wealth and honors and preferments." Life is no longer a hierarchal ladder or chain of being. In commercial society, life is a race. This race should be fair; each and every runner in it should have an equal opportunity to win. Each competitor will "run as hard as he can, and strain every move and every muscle, in order to outrun all his competitors." Interfering with other runners or seizing special advantages is "a violation of fair play."[12] But merit, talent, virtue, and ability are, alas, no sure indicators of success, because the church, the state, and the aristocracy are too involved in the race. By reserving offices, power, and authority for the privileged, they tilt the competition in favor of an idle aristocracy devoid of the talent and virtue of a Figaro—or a Mozart, for that matter.

We have here the powerful Enlightenment liberal ideal of equal opportunity and social mobility for self-made individuals. Figaro and his middle-class friends would use these ideals to storm the hierarchical bastions of privilege, and they would realize the universal Enlightenment ideal of a "career open to the talented" with the subversive egalitarian potential that would be realized in the American and French revolutions. But one must be careful in assessing the extent of the Enlightenment's commitment to equality, of the *philosophe*'s real attitude to the people.

There were class, gender, and racial restrictions in "the race of life." An occasional uneducated poor man might make it into the competition, but strict barriers kept virtually all women and people of color from the starting line. Even the enlightened Mozart, for example, has racist and patriarchal themes in *The Magic Flute.*

The ideal of equality of opportunity at its origins was both an effort to reduce inequality and to perpetuate it. It appeared egalitarian because it lashed out at the exclusiveness of aristocratic and clerical privilege, but it sought to replace that secular and spiritual elite with a new meritocratic elite, albeit one more broadly based in talent and merit. Equality of opportunity is not really a theory of equality but one of justified and morally acceptable inequality. What can legitimize some having more than others? Only that all have had an equal opportunity to have more. Equality for Enlightenment liberalism really means fairness, no rigging of life's rewards by priests or princes. Let all men who are not of color have an equal chance to win in the social competition that is the race of life, just as all claimants to truth compete freely in the marketplace of ideas.

Equal opportunity and a boundless optimistic faith in progress found their eighteenth-century home in America and her revolution, which appeared to many contemporaries to embody the Enlightenment in action. Her politics, after all, were utterly secular. While the Articles of Confederation gives credit to "the Great Governor of the world," the Constitution has no mention of God whatsoever. Jefferson and Madison sought to evict religion from public life, while Anti-Federalist opponents of the Constitution unsuccessfully criticized the new order as falsely based on the religion of nature and reason, neglectful of Christian virtue and morality. Condorcet described America as of all nations "the most enlightened, the freest and the least burdened by prejudices."[13] Its respect for human rights, he wrote, was a lesson for all the peoples of the world. He offered what would be the characteristic praise of America, where there were "no distinctions of class" and where property was secure and industry and hard work encouraged. There was no spiritual or political aristocracy in America, he wrote, "to hold a part of the human race in a state of humiliation, simplicity, and misery."[14] Diderot, in turn, saw America as "offering all the inhabitants of Europe an asylum against fanaticism and tyranny."[15] For Turgot the American people were "the hope of the human race, they may well become its model."[16] Tom Paine joined the chorus, writing that the cause of America was "the cause of all mankind." Free of clerical and political tyranny, America was "an asylum for mankind."[17]

If America was the embodiment and natural home of the Enlightenment, according to Europe's advanced thinkers, then the American who best personified the Enlightenment ideal was Benjamin Franklin. A veritable cult of Franklin developed: English baby boys were named Benjamin and French artists painted Franklin as Turgot had described him: "He seized fire from the heavens and the scepter from the tyrant's hand." More than anyone, Franklin brought together Enlightenment politics and science. After his death Benjamin West gave his fellow Americans a mythic Franklin on canvas, which is used for the cover of this book. The heroic philosopher-scientist with his calculations in his left hand, his simple laboratory equipment in the corner, reaches his right arm to the kite string and the key while lightning shoots from the sky and the key to Franklin's fist. Nature is harnassed by the hand of rational humanity, assisted as always at such meta-historic moments by helpful and hardworking cherubs.

Tocqueville later saw in America the realization of the Enlightenment spirit that he traced to Descartes. Like Descartes, he wrote, Americans instinctively doubted tradition and subjected the truth of all opinions to individual reason and judgment. For others, America represented a happy marriage of Enlightenment religious and social ideals. A close friend of Priestley wrote in 1784 that "the people of America have a saying—that God Almighty is Himself a mechanic, the greatest in the universe; and He is respected and admired more for the variety, ingenuity and utility of his handiwork than for the antiquity of His family."[18] To reinforce this Enlightenment conviction, there is also Jefferson writing in 1788 that "there is not a crowned head in Europe whose talents or merits would entitle him to be elected a vestryman by the people of any parish in America."[19]

European crowned heads would fall in the years immediately following Jefferson's boast, and in the French Revolution much of the Enlightenment's agenda seemed to be realized, in some cases with a bloody vengeance. Parliamentary institutions and the Declaration of the Rights of Man replaced the politics of the aristocratic and monarchical old order. Feudal restrictions on individual economic activity were removed. Primogeniture, tithes, and obligatory service to the lord of the manor were replaced by new economic ideals focused on individual property rights and free-market principles. The state took over church property and schools and made the clergy civic employees. The revolutionaries waged a vigorous campaign to "de-Christianize" France, culminating in the replacement of Catholic dogma and clerical fanaticism by Temples of Reason in which the Supreme Being, the God of Nature, would be worshiped.

Rousseau, Voltaire, Montesquieu, and the contributors to the *Encyclopédie* were by no stretch of the imagination political revolutionaries, but they have nonetheless been pilloried for creating a climate of intellectual distrust for traditional authority that made Revolution, and its excesses, possible. Rather unfairly, in fact, much of the debate over the Enlightenment these last two hundred years has focused on assessing its role in producing the French Revolution, as if that were the only basis for evaluation. Burke and de Maistre set forth the terms of discourse. The Revolution, according to Burke, was produced by a conspiracy of men of letters. He was proud that the British were "not the converts of Rousseau, not the disciples of Voltaire; Helvétius has made no progress amongst us. Atheists are not our preachers."[20] He prepared the ground for the nineteenth-century romantic assault on the Enlightenment with his suggestion that the power of reason in men was small and that they needed to be guided by feelings, emotion, historical tradition, custom, and a reverence for old ideas (prejudice) and old institutions (prescription). Deference to political hierarchy and established religion were restored as worthy social ideals by this gravedigger of the Enlightenment. The French clergyman de Maistre echoed Burke in his plea for respecting power and ideas that "have been established from time immemorial." Like Burke he ridiculed the abstractions of Enlightenment thought, its tendency to invoke a priori ideals like the rights of man. The Enlightenment, for de Maistre, was guilty of the satanic sin of pride, seeking to give to man the power and insights of God. The "mad *philosophes*," de Maistre wrote, sought with their "presumptuous wisdom . . . to guide the universe."[21] These apostles of tolerance, humanity, intelligence, virtue, and reason, he thundered, had left France littered with corpses and tombs.

In the nineteenth century the battle continued. Liberals paid homage to the Enlightenment and invoked its individualistic vision of citizens voluntarily consenting to government, acting freely in the marketplace and thinking, publishing, and believing what they wanted to, without interference from church or state. Science and its seemingly unbounded power to tame nature, to ameliorate the human condition, and to fuel progress kept alive a vital part of the Enlightenment legacy. Conservatives, on the other hand, insisted on respect for the very authority the Enlightenment ridiculed, while the romantics replaced what they took to be the Enlightenment's flawed and limited ideal of human reason with the richer potential of feeling, intuition, imagination, and spirit. Marxism was ambivalent about the Enlightenment. Marx and Engels were themselves products of Enlightenment optimism, with their assumptions about inevitable historical progress, their self-proclaimed scientism, and their dismissal of religion. Yet they also offered a full-blown critique of the Enlightenment, for the "kingdom of reason," Engels wrote, "was nothing more than the idealized kingdom of the bourgeoisie."[22]

The twentieth century, with two cataclysmic wars, the madness of the Holocaust and Stalin's *gulags*, has tragically tried the Enlightenment liberal's faith in reason and optimistic belief in progress. The writings and work of Freud and his disciples have in their own way contributed to disenchantment with Enlightenment assumptions about rationality. Some, like Carl Becker and J. L. Talmon, have criticized the Enlightenment as an unrealistic quest for earthly perfection. For Becker, this is reminiscent of older Christian utopianism, simply substituting infinite terrestrial progress for the paradisiacal afterlife. For Talmon, the secular perfectionism of the Enlightenment is a dangerous anticipation of the social messianism he finds writ large in modern totalitarian movements. Becker and Talmon are, in their own ways, repeating the Burkian reaction John Adams felt on first reading Condorcet's *Outline of a Historical View of the Progress of the Human Mind*:

> The public mind was improving in knowledge and the public heart in humanity, equity, and benevolence; the fragments of fuedality, the Inquisition, the rack, the cruelty of punishments, Negro slavery, were giving way etc. But the philosophers must arrive at perfection *per saltum*. Ten times more furious than Jack in *The Tale of a Tub*, they rent and tore the whole garment to pieces and left not one whole thread in it. They have even been compelled to resort to Napoleon, and Gibbon himself became an advocate for the Inquisition. What an amiable and glorious Equality, Fraternity, and Liberty they have now established in Europe.[23]

The twentieth century's critique of the Enlightenment has been most subtly expressed by Theodore Adorno and Max Horkeimer, who, in their *Dialectic of Enlightenment*, lament that "the fully enlightened earth radiates disaster triumphant."[24] Following Adorno, a series of different thinkers argued against the Enlightenment's faith in progress, instrumental reason, science, and human liberation. Writing from a Marxist perspective, Adorno, Horkeimer, and their later disciple Herbert Marcuse connected the project of the Enlightenment with late-capitalist "administered society." The Enlightenment's venerable claim to have demystified the world, argue Adorno and Horkeimer, was ultimately transformed into bourgeois domination. The critical edge of reason became "instrumental reason" or rationalization; the liberal society became the total system. The Enlightenment's "disenchantment" of nature, Adorno and Horkeimer suggest, bore its final fruit in Auschwitz.

This Germanic Marxist critique was echoed by the Parisian avant garde, particularly Michael Foucault and Jean-François Lyotard. Foucault's writings are punctuated by a deflation of the Enlightenment's program for liberation and tolerance. In *Madness and Civilization*, Foucault argues both that Enlightenment "reason" was articulated by a careful "silencing" of what he calls "unreason," and that nominally progressive modes of treatment were in fact dissimulated efforts of control. In *Discipline and Punish*, Foucault situates Enlightenment humanism in terms of the emergence of the modern prison system. He argues that the individual is not a subject of study or liberation but an effect of knowledge produced in "disciplinary" organizations (prisons, schools, the army, and so forth). Whereas Foucault takes aim at humanism and rationalism, Lyotard's *The Post-Modern Condition* trumpets that the postmodern age has dispensed with all "myths of progress." The Enlightenment (under which was subsumed Marxism as well), he claims, foundered on a specious "grand narrative."

These often dire pronouncements are by no means identical, nor are they without complexity. Adorno's understanding of the Enlightenment, after all, labors over what he calls a dialectical contradiction, in which the searching and critical projects of the Enlightenment (to which he is indebted) are inseparable from instrumental and dominating reason. Likewise Foucault's later work, especially an essay on Kant's *What Is Enlightenment*, reconsiders his summary dismissal of the Enlightenment. Perhaps most significant, however, Adorno's heterodox student Jurgen Habermas has recast the Enlightenment as "an unfinished project" and has theorized at length on the possibility of rational democratic speech communities.

Postmodernist, feminist, and certain strands of communitarian thought reject in general what they take to be the Enlightenment's inadequate conception of selfhood and individuality, with its ideal of a central autonomous self defined by its isolation and separateness. This Enlightenment self is uninvolved with relationships to others, its critics claim, and is mistakenly held to be the creative center of its world and of meaning. This solitary self is an empty self, unencumbered and unsituated, an autonomous master of its own destiny through self-generated voluntary agency, by which it dominates reality. In place of this false unique self, presumed by Enlightenment liberalism, these schools offer instead individuals as socially constructed, as never solitary but always involved in social relationships, selves shaped by history, tradition, and aspects of identity that society and social classes construct and over which individuals have little control. Rejection of the Enlightenment's rampant individualism leads some of these critics, like pornography-censorship advocates, to call for shifting attention away from individual rights to a greater concern for community or group rights. With their insistence on complex webs of relationships, and the inevitably constraining power of community, tradition, and social construction over individuals, these most recent critics of the Enlightenment, whether they intend to or not, ironically often end with depictions of a social world that in some respects Enlightenment liberals had set out to destroy.

Not that the Enlightenment has lacked its vigorous defenders in recent decades. Peter Gay, for example, has not only deftly disposed of Becker's indictment of the Enlightenment's "heavenly city," he has also offered a magisterial two-volume study that is an Enlightenment *apologia* for our times. More recent criticisms of the Enlightenment from conservatives and communitarians or from leftist postmodernists and feminists have been answered by a vigorous new school of neoliberals, which continues to plead for the Enlightenment liberal values of tolerance, individualism, and respect for rights.[25]

This brings us a long way from Mozart's Temples of Wisdom, Reason, and Nature and from his Figaro insisting that Almaviva and his kind dance to the new tune that he and his self-made friends were playing. But Mozart's Temples and his Figaro are, of course, still very much with us, as are the Enlightenment ideas and ideals he codified. How we respond to them, how we evaluate them today, ought not to be shaped, however, by how well authorities like Burke, Becker, Adorno, Talman, Habermas, or Gay have understood the Enlightenment. In the spirit of the Enlightenment itself, any assessment of it must be grounded on how each new reader responds on his or her own to the writings of the Enlightenment, which is why we offer this anthology.[26]

NOTES TO INTRODUCTION

1. *Papers of Thomas Jefferson*, ed. Boyd, et al. (Princeton, 1950), Jefferson to John Trumbull, 15 February 1789, vol. XIV, 561.
2. See this book, page 1.
3. See this book, page 133.
4. See this book, page 160.
5. Priestley, *Reflections on the Present State of Free Inquiry in This Country* (London, 1785), 101; F. W. Gibbs, *Joseph Priestley* (New York, 1967), 62.
6. See this book, page 74.
7. See this book, page 27.
8. See this book, pages 371, 375.
9. *Works of Thomas Jefferson*, ed. Ford (New York, 1905), vol. IX, 102; Priestley, *Lectures on History and General Policy* (London, 1782), 349.
10. See this book, page 77.
11. See this book, page 266.
12. See this book, page 508, and *Theory of Moral Sentiments* (Edinburgh, 1759), vol. I, 188.
13. See this book, page 27.
14. See Nicholas Capaldi, *The Enlightenment* (New York, 1968), 268.
15. Cited in Peter Gay, *The Enlightenment: An Interpretation* (New York, 1977), 577.
16. Ibid., 556.
17. T. Paine, *Common Sense*, ed. Kramnick (London, 1976), 120, 100.
18. T. Cooper, *Some Information Respecting America* (London, 1794), 230.
19. *The Political Writings of Thomas Jefferson*, ed. E. Dumbauld (New York, 1955), 172.
20. Burke, *Reflections on the Revolution in France*, ed. T. Mahoney (New York, 1955), 97.

21. Cited in William F. Church, *The Influence of the Enlightenment on the French Revolution* (Boston, 1964), 17.
22. Cited in Jack Lively, *The Enlightenment* (New York, 1966), 105.
23. Cited in Brinton, *The Age of Reason* (New York, 1956), 622.
24. *Dialectic of Enlightenment* (New York, 1969), 3.
25. See the writings of Don Herzog, Stephen Holmes, Amy Guttman, and Nancy Rosenblum.
26. The editor would like to thank Jim Fuerst and Louis Ayala for their help in preparing this Reader. Jonathan Brody Kramnick made important contributions to the introduction and Kimberley Shults and Michael Busch were invaluable in translating my handwriting to the printed page.

SUGGESTIONS FOR FURTHER READING

Adorno, T., and M. Horkheimer. *The Dialectics of Enlightenment* (1947).

Becker, C. L. *Heavenly City of the Eighteenth Century Philosophers* (1932).

Bryson, G. *Man and Society: The Scottish Inquiry of the Eighteenth Century* (1945).

Bury, J. B. *The Idea of Progress* (1955).

Cassirer, E. *The Philosophy of the Enlightenment* (1951).

Caton, H. *The Politics of Progress* (1988).

Cobban, A. *In Search of Humanity* (1960).

Commager, H. S. *The Empire of Reason: How Europe Imagined and America Realized the Enlightenment* (1977).

Crocker, L. *An Age of Crisis: Man and World in Eighteenth Century Thought* (1959).

Ferguson, M. *First Feminists: British Women Writers 1578–1779* (1985).

Frankel, C. *The Faith of Reason: The Idea of Progress in the French Enlightenment* (1948).

Gay, P. *The Enlightenment: An Interpretation*, 2 vols. (1966, 1969).

———. *The Party of Humanity: Essays in the French Enlightenment* (1964).

Gillispie, C. C. *The Edge of Objectivity: An Essay in the History of Scientific Ideas* (1960).

Goodman, D. *The Republic of Letters: A Cultural History of the French Enlightenment* (1994).

Harrison, P. *Religion and the "Religious" in English Enlightenment* (1990).

Hazard, P. *The European Mind, 1680–1715* (1953).

———. *European Thought in the Eighteenth Century* (1954).

Hont, I., and M. Ignatief, eds. *Wealth and Virtue: The Shaping of Political Economy in the Scottish Enlightenment* (1983).

Jacob, M. *Living the Enlightenment* (1981).

———. *The Radical Enlightenment* (1981).

Kramnick, I. *Republicanism and Bourgeois Radicalism* (1991).

Laski, H. J. *The Rise of European Liberalism* (1937).

Lough, J. *The Encyclopédie* (1971).

Lovejoy, A. O. *Essays in the History of Ideas* (1952).

Manuel, F. E. *The Age of Reason* (1951).

______. *The Prophets of Paris* (1962).

May, H. *The Enlightenment in America* (1976).

Meek, R. L. *Social Science and the Ignoble Savage* (1976).

Payne, H. C. *The Philosophes and the People* (1976).

Porter, R., and M. Teich. *The Enlightenment in National Context* (1981).

Raccvskis, K. *Post-Modernism and the Search for Enlightenment* (1993).

Rendall, J. *The Origin of the Scottish Enlightenment* (1978).

Shklar, J. *After Utopia* (1957).

Smith, P. *The Enlightenment* (1934).

Spencer, S. I., ed. *French Women and the Age of Enlightenment* (1984).

Talmon, J. L. *Political Messianism* (1961).

______. *The Rise of Totalitarian Democracy* (1952).

Venturi, F. *Italy and the Enlightenment* (1972).

Vyverburg, H. *Historical Pessimism in the French Enlightenment* (1958).

Wade, I. O. *The Structure and Form of the French Enlightenment* (1977).

Willey, B. *The Eighteenth Century Background.*

Yolton, J., et al., eds. *The Blackwell Companion to the Enlightenment* (1991).

The Portable
ENLIGHTENMENT READER

"We are not afraid to follow truth wherever it may lead,
nor to tolerate any error so long as reason is left free to combat it."
—Thomas Jefferson

PART I

THE ENLIGHTENMENT SPIRIT: AN OVERVIEW

WHAT IS ENLIGHTENMENT?

Immanuel Kant

In this short essay written in 1784, the great German philosopher Immanuel Kant (1724–1804), whose writings are still central to any serious study of philosophy, declares the Enlightenment's creed: Sapere aude! *"Dare to know!"*

Enlightenment is man's release from his self-incurred tutelage. Tutelage is man's inability to make use of his understanding without direction from another. Self-incurred is this tutelage when its cause lies not in lack of reason but in lack of resolution and courage to use it without direction from another. *Sapere aude!* "Have courage to use your own reason!"—that is the motto of enlightenment.

Laziness and cowardice are the reasons why so great a portion of mankind, after nature has long since discharged them from external direction (*naturaliter maiorennes*), nevertheless remains under lifelong tutelage, and why it is so easy for others to set themselves up as their guardians. It is so easy not to be of age. If I have a book which understands for me, a pastor who has a conscience for me, a physician who decides my diet, and so forth, I need not trouble myself. I need not think, if I can only pay—others will readily undertake the irksome work for me.

That the step to competence is held to be very dangerous by the far greater portion of mankind (and by the entire fair sex)—quite apart from its being arduous—is seen to by those guardians who have so kindly assumed superintendence over them. After the guardians have first made their domestic cattle dumb and have made sure that these placid creatures will not dare take a single step without the harness of the cart to which they are confined, the guardians then show them the danger which threatens if they try to go alone. Actually, however, this danger is not so great, for by falling a few times they would finally learn to walk alone. But an example of this failure makes them timid and ordinarily frightens them away from all further trials.

For any single individual to work himself out of the life under tutelage which has become almost his nature is very difficult. He has come to be fond of this state, and he is for the present really incapable of making use of his reason, for no one has ever let him try it out. Statutes and formulas, those mechanical tools of the rational employment or rather misemployment of his natural gifts, are the fetters of an everlasting tutelage. Whoever throws them off makes only an uncertain leap over the narrowest ditch because he is not accustomed to that kind of free motion. Therefore, there are only few who have succeeded by their own exercise of mind both in freeing themselves from incompetence and in achieving a steady pace.

But that the public should enlighten itself is more possible; indeed, if only freedom is granted, enlightenment is almost sure to follow. For there will always be some independent thinkers, even among the established guardians of the great masses, who, after throwing off the yoke of tutelage from their own shoulders, will disseminate the spirit of the rational appreciation of both their own worth and every man's vocation for thinking for himself. But be it noted that the public, which has first been brought under this yoke by their guardians, forces the guardians themselves to remain bound when it is incited to do so by some of the guardians who are themselves capable of some enlightenment—so harmful is it to implant prejudices, for they later take vengeance on their cultivators or on their descendants. Thus the public can only slowly attain enlightenment. Perhaps a fall of personal despotism or of avaricious or tyrannical oppression may be accomplished by revolution, but never a true reform in ways of thinking. Rather, new prejudices will serve as well as old ones to harness the great unthinking masses.

For this enlightenment, however, nothing is required but freedom, and indeed the most harmless among all the things to which this term can properly be applied. It is the freedom to make public use of one's reason at every point. But I hear on all sides, "Do not argue!" The officer says: "Do not argue but drill!" The tax collector: "Do not argue but pay!" The cleric: "Do not argue but believe!" Only one prince in the world says, "Argue as much as you will, and about what you will, but obey!" Everywhere there is restriction on freedom.

Which restriction is an obstacle to enlightenment, and which is not an obstacle but a promoter of it? I answer: The public use of one's reason must always be free, and it alone can bring about enlightenment among men. The private use of reason, on the other hand, may often be very narrowly restricted without particularly hindering the progress of enlightenment. By the public use of one's reason I understand the use which a person makes of it as a scholar before the reading public. Private use I call that which one may make of it in a particular civil post or office which is intrusted to him. Many affairs which are conducted in the interest of the community require a certain mechanism through which some members of the community must passively conduct themselves with an artificial unanimity, so that the government may direct them to public ends, or at least prevent them from destroying those ends. Here argument is certainly not allowed—one must obey. But so far as a part of the mechanism regards himself at the same time as a member of the whole community or of a society of world citizens, and thus in the role of a scholar who addresses the public (in the proper sense of the word) through his writings, he certainly can argue without hurting the affairs for which he is in part responsible as a passive member. Thus it would be ruinous for an officer in service to debate about the suitability or utility of a command given to him by his superior; he must obey. But the right to make remarks on errors in the military service and to lay them before the public for judgment cannot equitably be refused him as a scholar. The citizen cannot refuse to pay the taxes imposed on him; indeed, an impudent complaint at those levied on him can be punished as a scandal (as it could occasion general refractoriness). But the same person nevertheless does not act contrary to his duty as a citizen when, as a scholar, he publicly expresses his thoughts on the inappropriateness or even the injustice of these levies. Similarly a clergyman is obligated to make his sermon to his pupils in catechism and his congregation conform to the symbol of the church which he serves, for he has been accepted on this condition. But as a scholar he has complete freedom, even the calling, to communicate to the public all his carefully tested and well-meaning thoughts on that which is erroneous in the symbol and to make suggestions for the better organization of the religious body and church. In doing this, there is nothing that could be laid as a burden on his conscience. For what he teaches as a consequence of his office as a representative of the church, this he considers something about which he has no freedom to teach according to his own lights; it is something which he is appointed to propound at the dictation of and in the name of another. He will say, "Our church teaches this or that; those are the proofs which it adduces." He thus extracts all practical uses for his congregation from statutes to which he himself would not subscribe with full conviction but to the enunciation of which he can very well pledge himself because it is not impossible that truth lies hidden in them, and, in any case, there is at least nothing in them contradictory to inner religion. For if he believed he had found such in them, he could not conscientiously discharge the duties of his office; he would have to give it up. The use, therefore, which an appointed teacher makes of his reason before his congregation is merely private, because this congregation is only a domestic one (even if it be a large gathering); with respect to it, as a priest, he is not free, nor can he be free, because he carries out the orders of another. But as a scholar, whose writings speak to his public, the world, the clergyman in the public use of his reason enjoys an unlimited freedom to use his own reason and to speak in his own person. That the guardians of the people (in spiritual things) should themselves be incompetent is an absurdity which amounts to the eternalization of absurdities.

But would not a society of clergymen, perhaps a church conference or a venerable classis (as they call themselves among the Dutch), be justified in obligating itself by oath to a certain unchangeable symbol in order to enjoy an unceasing guardianship over each of its members and thereby over the people as a whole, and even to make it eternal? I answer that this is altogether impossible. Such a contract, made to shut off all further enlightenment from the human race, is absolutely null and void even if confirmed by the supreme power, by parliaments, and by the most ceremonious of peace treaties. An age cannot bind itself and ordain to put the succeeding one into such a condition that it cannot extend its (at best very occasional) knowledge, purify itself of errors, and progress in general enlightenment. That would be a crime against human nature, the proper destination of which lies precisely in this progress; and the descendants would be fully justified in rejecting those decrees as having been made in an unwarranted and malicious manner.

The touchstone of everything that can be concluded as a law for a people lies in the question whether the people could have imposed such a law on itself. Now such a religious compact might be possible for a short and definitely limited time, as it were, in expectation of a better. One might let every citizen, and especially the clergyman, in the role of scholar, make his comments freely and publicly, i.e., through writing, on the erroneous aspects of the present institution. The newly introduced order might last until insight into the nature of these things had become so general and widely approved that through uniting their voices (even if not unanimously) they could bring a proposal to the throne to take those congregations under protection which had united into a changed religious organization according to their better ideas, without, however, hindering others who wish to remain in the order. But to unite in a permanent religious institution which is not to be subject to doubt before the public even in the lifetime of one man, and thereby to make a period of time fruitless in the progress of mankind toward improvement, thus working to the disadvantage of posterity—that is absolutely forbidden. For himself (and only for a short time) a man can postpone enlightenment in what he ought to know, but to renounce it for himself, and even more to renounce it for posterity, is to injure and trample on the rights of mankind.

And what a people may not decree for itself can even less be decreed for them by a monarch, for his lawgiving authority rests on his uniting the general public will in his own. If he only sees to it that all true or alleged improvement stands together with civil order, he can leave it to his subjects to do what they find necessary for their spiritual welfare. This is not his concern, though it is incumbent on him to prevent one of them from violently hindering another in determining and promoting this welfare to the best of his ability. To meddle in these matters lowers his own majesty, since by the writings in which his subjects seek to present their views he may evaluate his own governance. He can do this when, with deepest understanding, he lays upon himself the reproach. *Caesar non est supra grammaticos.* Far more does he injure his own majesty when he degrades his supreme power by supporting the ecclesiastical despotism of some tyrants in his state over his other subjects.

If we are asked, "Do we now live in an *enlightened age*?" the answer is, "No," but we do live in an *age of enlightenment.* As things now stand, much is lacking which prevents men from being, or easily becoming, capable of correctly using their own reason in religious matters with assurance and free from outside direction. But, on the other hand, we have clear indications that the field has now been opened wherein men may freely deal with these things and that the obstacles to general enlightenment or the release from self-imposed tutelage are gradually being reduced. In this respect, this is the age of enlightenment, or the century of Frederick.

A prince who does not find it unworthy of himself to say that he holds it to be his duty to prescribe nothing to men in religious matters but to give them complete freedom while renouncing the haughty name of *tolerance*, is himself enlightened and deserves to be esteemed by the grateful world and posterity as the first, at least from the side of government, who divested the human race of its tutelage and left each man free to make use of his reason in matters of conscience. Under him venerable ecclesiastics are allowed, in the role of scholars, and without infringing on their official duties, freely to submit for public testing their judgments and views which here and there diverge from the established symbol. And an even greater freedom is enjoyed by those who are restricted by no official duties. This spirit of freedom spreads beyond this land, even to those in which it must struggle with external obstacles erected by a government which misunderstands its own interest. For an example gives evidence to such a government that in freedom there is not the least cause for concern about public peace and the stability of the community. Men work themselves gradually out of barbarity if only intentional artifices are not made to hold them in it.

I have placed the main point of enlightenment—the escape of men from their self-incurred tutelage—chiefly in matters of religion because our rulers have no interest in playing the guardian with respect to the arts and sciences and also because religious incompetence is not only the most harmful but also the most degrading of all. But the manner of thinking of the head of a state who favors religious enlightenment goes further, and he sees that there is no danger to his lawgiving in allowing his subjects to make public use of their reason and to publish their thoughts on a better formulation of his legislation and even their open-minded criticisms of the laws already made. Of this we have a shining example wherein no monarch is superior to him whom we honor.

But only one who is himself enlightened, is not afraid of shadows, and has a numerous and well-disciplined army to assure public peace can say: "Argue as much as you will, and about what you will, only obey!" A republic could not dare say such a thing. Here is shown a strange and unexpected trend in human affairs in which almost everything, looked at in the large, is paradoxical. A greater degree of civil freedom appears advantageous to the freedom of mind of the people, and yet it places inescapable limitations upon it; a lower degree of civil freedom, on the contrary, provides the mind with room for each man to extend himself to his full capacity. As nature has uncovered from under this hard shell the seed for which she most tenderly cares—the propensity and vocation to free thinking—this gradually works back upon the character of the people, who thereby gradually become capable of managing freedom; finally, it affects the principles of government, which finds it to its advantage to treat men, who are now more than machines, in accordance with their dignity.

THE HUMAN MIND EMERGED FROM BARBARISM

JEAN LE ROND D'ALEMBERT

In these two selections d'Alembert (1717–1783), French mathematician, philosopher, and a principal editor of the Encyclopédie, *provides a splendid summary of Enlightenment attitudes. The first is from the introduction he wrote for the first volume of the* Encyclopédie, *and the second, a stirring defense of his fellow French* philosophes, *is a 1760 essay, "Reflections on the Present State of the Republic of Letters."*

When the human mind emerged from barbarism, it found itself in a kind of childhood, eager to accumulate ideas yet incapable at first of acquiring those of a certain order because the intellectual faculties had been for so long in a sluggish state. . . .

While certain adversaries, either men of small attainments or of evil intent, openly made war on philosophy, the philosophic spirit itself took refuge in the writings of some great men. Without desiring to tear the blindfolds from the eyes of their contemporaries, they worked silently in the remote background to prepare the light of reason which gradually and by imperceptible degrees was to illuminate the world.

At the head of these illustrious personages must be placed the immortal Chancellor of England, Francis Bacon, whose works are so justly esteemed, and more esteemed than they are known, so that they deserve to be read even more than praised. If we consider the sound and extensive views of this great man, the multitude of subjects which his mind entertained, the boldness of his style which united everywhere the most sublime images with the most rigorous precision, we would be tempted to regard him as the greatest, the most universal, and the most eloquent of the philosophers. Bacon, who was born in the depths of dark night, felt that philosophy was not yet possible, although many people without a doubt flattered themselves that they excelled in it. For the coarser the century, the more men consider themselves learned in everything that can be known. He began, therefore, by considering with a general view the diverse objects of all the natural sciences. He divided these sciences into different branches of which he made the most exact enumeration possible. He investigated what was already known about each one of these subjects, and he made an immense catalogue of what remained to be discovered. This was the goal of his admirable work *De dignitate et augmentis scientiarum* [the final version of *The Advancement of Learning*]. In the *Novum Organum* he perfected the views that he had given in his first work, extending them even further, pointing out the necessity of scientific experimentation, a new idea at that time. An enemy of systems, he only considered philosophy as that part of our knowledge which must contribute to making us better and happier. He seems to have limited it to the science of useful things and at all times recommended the study of Nature. His other works were conceived with the same plan in mind. Everything, even the titles, announce the man of genius, the mind that sees things on a large scale. He collects facts, compares experiments, and indicates a great many that have to be performed. He invites men of learning to study and perfect the arts which he considers the most exalted and essential part of human knowledge. He states with noble simplicity *his conjectures and his thoughts* on the different subjects which are worthy of interesting mankind, and he could have said, like the venerable old Terence, that nothing concerning man was a matter of indifference to him: knowledge of economics, morality, nature, politics, in fact everything seemed to have fallen within the province of this luminous and profound mind. We do not know what we should admire the most, his rich intuitive views on all subjects or the dignified tone of his style. His writings can be compared only with those of Hippocrates on medicine; and they would be neither less admired nor less read if the cultivation of the mind were as dear to the human race as the conservation of health. But only the writings of leading sectarians can achieve a certain vogue; Bacon was not one of them, and his philosophic method was opposed to this: it was too judicious to astonish anyone. Scholasticism, which prevailed at that time, could only be overthrown by bold and new opinions; and it was not likely that a philosopher satisfied with saying to men: "Here is the little bit that you have learned; this is what remains to be investigated," was destined to make a great stir with his contemporaries. We would even venture to reproach Chancellor Bacon for having been perhaps too timid, if we did not know that prudence and in a way even devotion must be exercised in judging such a sublime genius. Although he acknowledges that the scholastics emasculated the sciences with their trifling questions, and that the mind must sacrifice the study of general things for the investigation of particular objects, it nevertheless seems that by the frequent use he made of medieval terms, sometimes even of scholastic principles, as well as the divisions and subdivisions which were then quite fashionable, that he showed a little too much caution and deference to the dominant taste of his century. This great man, after having destroyed so many fetters, was still held back by chains which he was unable or did not dare to break.

We now declare that we owe our tree of knowledge mainly to Chancellor Bacon. You will find it at the end of the *Discourse*. We have already acknowledged this several times in the *Prospectus;* we will recall it to your attention again; and we would not miss any opportunity to repeat it. Despite the fact that we recognize this great man as our master, we did not feel obligated to follow him point by point. . . .

Chancellor Bacon was followed by the illustrious Descartes. This extraordinary man, whose fortunes have varied so much in less than a quarter of a century, had the wherewithal to change the general lines of philosophy: a powerful imagination, an extremely rational mind, knowledge derived from himself more than from books, a great deal of courage to combat the most widely held prejudices, and an independence which gave him the freedom to criticize. He therefore experienced, even in his own lifetime, what happens as a rule to all men whose influence is too conspicuous. He had some enthusiastic followers and many determined enemies. Either because he knew his country or simply distrusted it, he took refuge in a completely free country in order to meditate in more favorable conditions. Although he thought much less of making disciples than of deserving them, persecution sought him out even in his retreat; and the secluded life which he led could not protect him. In spite of all the sagacity he employed to prove the existence of God, he was accused of denying it by clergymen who perhaps did not have any faith at all. Tormented and slandered by foreigners, shabbily treated by his compatriots, he went to die in Sweden without in any way presuming that his opinions would one day have such brilliant success.

Descartes can be considered either as a geometrician or as a philosopher. Although he seemed to have attached rather little value to mathematics, it is nevertheless the most solid and the least contested part of his reputation today. Algebra, created in a way by the Italians and prodigiously enlarged by our illustrious Vieta, was further developed at the hands of Descartes. One of the most notable contributions is his method for indeterminate equations, a rather ingenious and subtle device which has since been applied to a great number of subjects. But what has especially immortalized the name of this great man was his application of algebra to geometry, one of the most far-reaching and felicitous ideas which the human mind ever had, and which will always be the key to the most profound research, not only in sublime geometry but also in all the physico-mathematical sciences.

As a philosopher he was perhaps as great but not so fortunate. Geometry, which by the nature of the subject must always gain rather than lose ground, could not fail to make rather perceptible and evident progress when practiced by so great a genius. Philosophy, in a much different state, was just beginning: and how great is the effort required to make the first steps in any discipline? The merit of having taken small ones excuses people for not proceeding even further. If Descartes, who pointed the way for us, did not go as far as his followers would have us believe, it is, on the other hand, not true that the sciences owe him as little as his adversaries maintain. His method alone would have been sufficient to make him immortal; his *Dioptrics* is the greatest and most beautiful application yet made of geometry to physics. Finally we see in his works, even those least read today, the constant sparkle of inventive genius. If you judge without bias his solar vortex, which has become almost ridiculous today, you will agree, I dare say, that it was impossible to imagine anything better at the time. The astronomical observations used to destroy this idea were still imperfect or hardly recorded. Nothing was more natural than to assume the existence of a fluid which transports the planets. Only a long stream of phenomena, reasonings, and calculations, therefore a long sequence of time, could force people to renounce such an attractive theory. Moreover it had the singular advantage of explaining the gravitation of bodies by the centrifugal force of the vortex itself. And I do not hesitate to maintain that this explanation of gravity is one of the most beautiful and ingenious hypotheses that philosophy has ever conceived. For physicists to abandon it they had to be tempted almost in spite of themselves by the theory of central forces and by experiments performed much later. Let us therefore admit that Descartes, forced to create a completely new physics, was not able to make it any better; that it was necessary, so to speak, to pass by means of the vortices to arrive at the true system of the earth; and that if he was mistaken about the laws of movement, he was at least the first to guess that there had to be some.

His metaphysics, as ingenious and new as his physics, had approximately the same fate; and it is with approximately the same reasons that we can justify it. For such is today the fortune of this great man that after having had countless followers he is practically reduced to a few apologists. He was without doubt mistaken in assuming the existence of innate ideas: but if he had retained from the peripatetic sect [the Aristotelians] the only truth that they taught about the origin of ideas in the senses, perhaps the errors, which would dishonor this truth because of its association with it, would have been much more difficult to eradicate. Descartes dared at least to teach good minds how to shake off the yoke of scholasticism, public opinion, and authority; in a word, certain prejudices and barbaric attitudes. From this revolt, whose fruits we are now reaping, philosophy received from him a service much more difficult perhaps to render than all those which it owes to his illustrious successors. We can consider him as the head of a group of conspirators, the first to have the courage to rise against a despotic and arbitrary power, and while preparing a brilliant revolution, to have laid the foundations of a more just and valid government which he was unable to see established. If he finally believed that he had explained everything, at least he began by doubting everything; and the arms that we use to combat him do not belong to him any the less because we turn them against him. Moreover, when absurd opinions have become inveterate, we are sometimes forced to replace them with other errors (if we can do no better) in order to disabuse the human race. The uncertainty and vanity of the mind are such that it must always entertain an opinion: it is a child that must be presented with a toy so that we can take away a dangerous weapon; he will lay aside the toy himself when the age of reason is attained. In putting philosophers, or those who believe they are, on a false scent, we teach them at least to mistrust their own understanding, and this disposition is the first step toward the truth. Consequently Descartes was persecuted in his lifetime as if he had come to bring the truth to mankind.

Newton, whose path had been prepared by Huygens, finally appeared and gave to philosophy a method it seems obliged to retain. This great genius saw that it was time to banish from physics all vague conjectures and hypotheses, or at least to attribute to them only what they were worth, and that this science had to be submitted exclusively to experiments and to geometry. It is perhaps with this point of view that he first invented the calculus and the method of infinite series, whose uses are so widespread in geometry itself and even more so in calculating the complex operations observed in nature, where everything seems to comply with a kind of infinite progression. The experiments with gravity and the observations of Kepler made this English philosopher discover the force which holds the planets in their orbits. At the same time he taught how to distinguish the various causes of their movements and how to calculate them with an accuracy that could only be demanded of work which had been carried on for several centuries. Creator of a completely new system of optics, he made light known to mankind by decomposing it. What we would be able to add to the praise of this great philosopher would be far beneath the universal testimony that is given today to his almost innumerable discoveries and to his genius, which was at the same time expansive, judicious, and profound. In enriching philosophy with a great quantity of real assets, he deserved without doubt all of its gratitude. But perhaps he did more than that by teaching it to be prudent, to restrict into the proper limits that sort of audacity which circumstances had forced upon Descartes. His Theory of the World (for I do not mean his System) is so generally accepted today that people are beginning to dispute the author's right to this discovery, because they begin by accusing great men of being mistaken and finally treat them as plagiarists. . . .

Some scientists thought that they reproached Newton in a much more justifiable manner when they accused him of having brought back into physics the *occult qualities* of the scholastic and ancient philosophers. These two words, devoid of meaning in medieval works, were intended by the scholastics to designate something which they believed they understood. But are the scientists just mentioned really sure that the *occult qualities* of the ancient philosophers denoted anything more than the modest expression of their ignorance? Newton, who had studied Nature, did not imagine that he knew more than they about the first cause which produced the phenomena of Nature; but he did not use the same language for fear of shocking some contemporaries who would not have failed to misinterpret him. He was content to prove that Descartes' vortices could not explain the movements of the planets; that phenomena as well as the laws of mechanics united in overthrowing them; and that there is a force which induces the planets mutually to attract one another and whose principle is entirely unknown to us. He did not reject the theory of momentum; he merely asked scientists to use it more profitably than they had done in the past to explain planetary motion: his desires have not yet been fulfilled and perhaps will not be for a long time. After all, what harm did he do philosophy when he led us to think that matter could have certain properties which we did not suspect, and also when he disabused us of our ridiculous faith in the assumption that we already knew all of its properties?

In addition, Newton seems not to have entirely neglected the study of metaphysics. He was too great a philosopher not to feel that it is the foundation of our knowledge and that we must search in it for clear and exact notions of everything. From the works of this profound geometrician it even appears that he succeeded in creating such notions about the principal subjects which preoccupied him. Nevertheless, he was either not very happy with his progress in other aspects of metaphysics, or he believed it difficult to give to the human race satisfactory or extensive knowledge about a science which is contentious and very often unreliable. Finally, he might have feared that within the shadow of his authority people might abuse his metaphysics as they had abused Descartes' in order to maintain dangerous and mistaken opinions. In any case, he refrained almost entirely from discussing it in those of his works which are most well-known; and we barely learn what he thought about different subjects of that area of learning save through the works of his disciples. Because he did not cause any revolution on this question, we shall therefore refrain from considering this aspect of his work.

What Newton had not dared or would not perhaps have been able to do, Locke undertook and executed with success. We can say that he created metaphysics almost as Newton had created physics. He understood that abstractions and ridiculous questions that had until then been debated, and even comprised the very essence of philosophy, had to be especially forbidden in its practice. He looked for the principal causes of our errors in these abstractions and in the abuse of symbols, and found them there in abundance. In order to know our mind, its ideas and affections, he did not study books, because they would have instructed him poorly: he was satisfied with examining himself intently; and after having contemplated himself for a long time, he merely offered to mankind in his *Essay Concerning Human Understanding* the mirror in which he had seen himself. In a word, he reduced metaphysics to what it must as a matter of fact be, the experimental science of the mind, a kind of science which is rather different from that of natural bodies, not only because of the subject, but also because of the manner in which it is considered. In the latter field unknown phenomena can be and often are discovered; in the former the facts, which are as ancient as the world, exist to the same extent in all men: so much the worse for anyone who believes that he has seen new ones. Rational metaphysics, like experimental science, can only consist of collecting all of the facts with great care, of arranging them into a body of knowledge, of explaining certain ones by others, and of distinguishing those of primary importance which serve as a foundation. In a word, the principles of metaphysics, as simple as axioms, are the same for philosophers and laymen. But the small amount of progress which this realm of knowledge has accomplished in such a long period of time demonstrates how rare is the successful application of these principles, either because of the difficulty which such work entails or perhaps because of the natural impatience which prevents people from exercising self-restraint. Nevertheless, the title of metaphysician or even of great metaphysician is still rather common in our century; for we love to lavish praise on everything: but few people are truly worthy of this name! How many are there who earn it only because of their unfortunate talents in obscuring clear ideas with a great deal of subtlety and in preferring the extraordinary to the true, which is always simple? We must not be astonished now when most of those who are called "metaphysicians" set little value on each other. I do not doubt that this title will soon become an insult for our men of intelligence, just as the name sophist, which nevertheless means "sage," was debased in Greece by those who bore it and finally became rejected by true philosophers.

Let us conclude from all this history that England owes to us the origins of that philosophy which we received back from her. There is perhaps a greater distance from substantial forms to vortices than from vortices to universal gravitation; as there is perhaps a greater interval between pure algebra and the idea of applying it to geometry than between Barrow's small triangle and differential calculus.

These are the principal geniuses that the human mind must regard as its masters and for whom the Greeks would have erected statues, even if they were obliged to make more space by demolishing the monuments of some conquerors.

• • •

Moral philosophers are fond of asking how men lived in what is called a state of *pure nature*, before there were organized societies and laws, and whether such a state was one of peace or war. They have written on this question endlessly, as on all questions where the pros or the cons can be maintained at will, without danger of being contradicted by actual experience. From all these dissertations one can learn what one can usually learn from metaphysical discussions—that is, nothing.

Yet there is, it seems to me, a shorter way to decide the question; that is, to examine the way in which men of letters have behaved throughout the centuries. For the man of letters is in relation to other men of letters almost in that state of pure nature about which we talk so much without really knowing what we are talking about. They struggle for renown much as, it is maintained, men without laws and government struggled, or would have struggled, for their food acorns. But in society no one has the right to live to the complete detriment of his fellows; therefore the laws regulate, at least roughly, the distribution of acorns—that is, the bare necessities of life—among men. On the contrary, in the best regulated society it is possible to live without renown, and often, indeed, to live more happily without it. Those who made the laws, therefore, have left this phantom to be disputed over by those who prize it.

Literary renown is then the reward of the first to take it: the scepter belongs to him who seizes it, or who has the skill to have it offered him. Passed endlessly from hand to hand, it is the prize of the strongest or the cleverest. Usually the cleverest enjoys it but briefly, for it comes back to the strongest and stays in his possession.

To gain this scepter, or at least to snatch off a few ornaments from it, men of letters write and intrigue, praise or tear to pieces. Some of them indeed protest that they scorn renown, all the while desiring it very much. But no one is the dupe of their protests, which do not prevent their getting renown if they deserve it, and which make them ridiculous only if they disdain it without deserving it.

Among men of letters there is one group against which the arbiters of taste, the important people, the rich people, are united: this is the pernicious, the damnable group of *philosophes*, who hold that it is possible to be a good Frenchman without courting those in power, a good citizen without flattering national prejudices, a good Christian without persecuting anybody. These *philosophes* believe it right to make more of an honest if little-known writer than of a well-known writer without enlightenment and without principles, to hold that foreigners are not inferior to us in every respect, and to prefer, for example, a government under which the people are not slaves to one under which they are.

This way of thinking is for many people an unpardonable crime. What shocks them most of all, they say, is the tone the *philosophes* use, the tone of dogmatism, the tone of the master who knows. I admit that those of the *philosophes* who do indeed deserve this reproach would have done well to avoid deserving it. When it is necessary to hurt with what is said, it is wrong to hurt still more by the tone in which it is said. The writer is always master of his tone, his way of saying things. Truth can hardly be too modest. Truth indeed, just by being truth, runs always a sufficiently great risk of being rejected. But after all, this truth, so feared, so hated, so insulted, is so rare and precious, it seems to me, that those who tell it may be pardoned a little excess of fervor. The writer who wants to write more than ephemerally has got to be right. Form is in itself of little importance—it is something for the moment, for the passing generation, but nothing for the next one, still less for distant posterity. If a dogmatic tone, one that tells the truth crudely, shocks our delicate judges, they will do well never to open geometry books; they won't find more insolent ones.

The *philosophes*, they say, are enemies of authority. This is a more serious reproach and deserves a serious reply. The *philosophes* respect authority in the monarch, to whom it belongs, and whose love of truth and justice they recognize. They would respect power in the hands of those to whom he confided it, even though it were abused. What would they gain by attacking such power? Who would guarantee them against oppression? Who would take their part? A thousand voices would be raised to overwhelm them, and not one to defend them. What resolution can they take, save to obey and keep silent? What prerogative have they to claim to be dispensed from obedience? If they were persecuted, they would at most defend themselves. To protest is not to revolt. No, no, if legitimate authority has in these days been weakened under attack, it has not been from attacks by men of letters or *philosophes*, but rather by those who most openly declare themselves the enemies of the *philosophes*.

Let us speak without disguise or constraint. If those men we call *philosophes* haunted more often the antechambers of ministers, courted ladies of well-known piety, put themselves forward as advocates of persecution and intolerance, they would not be the targets for all the insults that are hurled at them. But they honor the great and flee them; they revere true piety and detest persecuting zeal; they believe the first of Christian duties is charity; and finally, as has been said elsewhere (for there are truths good to repeat for certain ears), they respect that which they ought to, and prize that which they can. This is their real crime.

"ENCYLOPÉDIE"

Denis Diderot

Along with d'Alembert, the major force behind the Encylopédie *was Denis Diderot (1713–1784), philosopher, scientist, and man of letters who in this entry for the word "encyclopédie" described the ambitions of its editors.*

ENCYCLOPÉDIE, f. n. (*Philosophy*). This word means the *interrelation of all knowledge;* it is made up of the Greek prefix *en*, in, and the nouns *kyklos*, circle, and *paideia*, instruction, science, knowledge. In truth, the aim of an *encyclopédie* is to collect all the knowledge scattered over the face of the earth, to present its general outlines and structure to the men with whom we live, and to transmit this to those who will come after us, so that the work of past centuries may be useful to the following centuries, that our children, by becoming more educated, may at the same time become more virtuous and happier, and that we may not die without having deserved well of the human race. . . .

We have seen that our *Encyclopédie* could only have been the endeavor of a philosophical century; that this age has dawned, and that fame, while raising to immortality the names of those who will perfect man's knowledge in the future, will perhaps not disdain to remember our own names. We have been heartened by the ever so consoling and agreeable idea that people may speak to one another about us, too, when we shall no longer be alive; we have been encouraged by hearing from the mouths of a few of our contemporaries a certain voluptuous murmur that suggests what may be said of us by those happy and educated men in whose interests we have sacrificed ourselves, whom we esteem and whom we love, even though they have not yet been born. We have felt within ourselves the development of those seeds of emulation which have moved us to renounce the better part of ourselves to accomplish our task, and which have ravished away into the void the few moments of our existence of which we are genuinely proud. Indeed, man reveals himself to his contemporaries and is seen by them for what he is: a peculiar mixture of sublime attributes and shameful weaknesses. But our weaknesses follow our mortal remains into the tomb and disappear with them; the same earth covers them both, and there remains only the total result of our attributes immortalized in the monuments we raise to ourselves or in the memorials that we owe to public respect and gratitude—honors which a proper awareness of our own deserts enables us to enjoy in anticipation, an enjoyment that is as pure, as great, and as real as any other pleasure and in which there is nothing imaginary except, perhaps, the titles on which we base our pretensions. Our own claims are deposited in the pages of this work, and posterity will judge them.

I have said that it could only belong to a philosophical age to attempt an *encyclopédie;* and I have said this because such a work constantly demands more intellectual daring than is commonly found in ages of pusillanimous taste. All things must be examined, debated, investigated without exception and without regard for anyone's feelings. . . . We must ride roughshod over all these ancient puerilities, overturn the barriers that reason never erected, give back to the arts and sciences the liberty that is so precious to them. . . . We have for quite some time needed a reasoning age when men would no longer seek the rules in classical authors but in nature, when men would be conscious of what is false and true about so many arbitrary treatises on aesthetics: and I take the term *treatise on aesthetics* in its most general meaning, that of a system of given rules to which it is claimed that one must conform in any genre whatsoever in order to succeed. . . .

It would be desirable for the government to authorize people to go into the factories and shops, to see the craftsmen at their work, to question them, to draw the tools, the machines, and even the premises.

There are special circumstances when craftsmen are so secretive about their techniques that the shortest way of learning about them would be to apprentice oneself to a master or to have some trustworthy person do this. There would be few secrets that one would fail to bring to light by this method, and all these secrets would have to be divulged without any exception.

I know that this feeling is not shared by everyone. These are narrow minds, deformed souls, who are indifferent to the fate of the human race and who are so enclosed in their little group that they see nothing beyond its special interest. These men insist on being called good citizens, and I consent to this, provided that they permit me to call them *bad men*. To listen to them talk, one would say that a successful *encyclopédie*, that a general history of the mechanical arts, should only take the form of an enormous manuscript that would be carefully locked up in the king's library, inaccessible to all other eyes but his, an official document of the state, not meant to be consulted by the people. What is the good of divulging the knowledge a nation possesses, its private transactions, its inventions, its industrial processes, its resources, its trade secrets, its enlightenment, its arts, and all its wisdom? Are not these the things to which it owes a part of its superiority over the rival nations that surround it? This is what they say; and this is what they might add: would it not be desirable if, instead of enlightening the foreigner, we could spread darkness over him or even plunge all the rest of the world into barbarism so that we could dominate more securely over everyone? These people do not realize that they occupy only a single point on our globe and that they will endure only a moment in its existence. To this point and to this moment they would sacrifice the happiness of future ages and that of the entire human race.

They know as well as anyone that the average duration of empires is not more than two thousand years and that in less time, perhaps, the name *Frenchman*, a name that will endure forever in history, will be sought after in vain over the surface of the earth. These considerations do not broaden their point of view; for it seems that the word *humanity* is for them a word without meaning. All the same, they should be consistent! For they also fulminate against the impenetrability of the Egyptian sanctuaries; they deplore the loss of the knowledge of the ancients; they accuse the writers of the past for having been silent or negligent in writing so badly on an infinite number of important subjects; and these illogical critics do not see that they demand of the writers of earlier ages something they call a crime when it is committed by a contemporary, that they are blaming others for having done what they think it honorable to do.

These *good citizens* are the most dangerous enemies that we have had. In general we have tried to profit from just criticism without defending ourselves, while we have simply ignored all unfounded attacks. Is it not a rather pleasant prospect for those who have persisted stubbornly in blackening paper with their censure of us that if ten years from now the *Encyclopédie* has retained the reputation it enjoys today, no one will read or even remember their opinions; and if by chance our work is forgotten, their abusive remarks will fall into total oblivion!

I have heard it said that M. de Fontenelle's rooms were not large enough to hold all the works that had been published against him. Who knows the title of a single one of them? Montesquieu's *Spirit of Laws* and Buffon's *Natural History* have only just appeared, and the harsh criticism against them has been entirely forgotten. We have already remarked that among those who have set themselves up as censors of the *Encyclopédie* there is hardly a single one who had enough talent to enrich it by even one good article. I do not think I would be exaggerating if I should add that it is a work the greater part of which is about subjects that these people have yet to study. It has been composed with a philosophical spirit, and in this respect most of those who pass adverse judgment on us fall far short of the level of their own century. I call their works in evidence. It is for this reason that they will not endure and that we venture to say that our *Encyclopédie* will be more widely read and more highly appreciated in a few years' time than it is today. It would not be difficult to cite other authors who have had, and will have, a similar fate. Some (as we have already said) were once praised to the skies because they wrote for the multitude, followed the prevailing ideas, and accommodated their standards to those of the average reader, but they have lost their reputations in proportion as the human mind has made progress, and they have finally been forgotten altogether. Others, by contrast, too daring for the times in which their works appeared, have been little read, hardly understood, not appreciated, and have long remained in obscurity, until the day when the age they had outstripped had passed away and another century, to which they really belonged in spirit, overtook them at last and finally gave them the justice their merits deserved.

DEFINITION OF A *PHILOSOPHE*

CESAR CHESNEAU DUMARSAIS

This description of the philosophic spirit is attributed to Cesar Chesneau Dumarsais (1676–1756), French grammarian and philosopher who provided this entry for "philosopher" in the Encyclopédie.

Reason is to the philosopher what grace is to the Christian.

Grace causes the Christian to act, reason the philosopher.

Other men are carried away by their passions, their actions not being preceded by reflection: these are the men who walk in darkness. On the other hand, the philosopher, even in his passions, acts only after reflection; he walks in the dark, but by a torch.

The philosopher forms his principles from an infinity of particular observations. Most people adopt principles without thinking of the observations that have produced them: they believe that maxims exist, so to speak, by themselves. But the philosopher takes maxims from their source; he examines their origin; he knows their proper value, and he makes use of them only in so far as they suit him.

Truth is not for the philosopher a mistress who corrupts his imagination and whom he believes is to be found everywhere; he contents himself with being able to unravel it where he can perceive it. He does not confound it with probability; he takes for true what is true, for false what is false, for doubtful what is doubtful, and for probable what is only probable. He does more, and here you have a great perfection of the philosopher: when he has no reason by which to judge, he knows how to live in suspension of judgment. . . .

The philosophic spirit is, then, a spirit of observation and exactness, which relates everything to true principles; but the philosopher does not cultivate the mind alone, he carries his attention and needs further. . . .

Our philosopher does not believe in exiling himself from this world, he does not believe that he is in enemy country; he wishes to enjoy with wise economy the goods which nature offers him; he wishes to find pleasure with others, and in order to find it, he must make it: thus he tries to be agreeable to those with whom chance and his choice have thrown him, and at the same time he finds what is agreeable to him. He is an honest man who wishes to please and to make himself useful.

The majority of the great, whose dissipations do not leave enough time to meditate, are savage towards those whom they do not believe to be their equals. The ordinary philosophers who meditate too much, or rather who meditate badly, are savage towards everybody; they flee men, and men avoid them. But our philosopher who knows how to strike a balance between retreat from and commerce with men, is full of humanity. He is Terence's Chrémès who feels that he is a man, and that humanity alone is interested in the good and bad fortune of his neighbor. *Homo sum, humani a me nihil alienum puto.*

It would be useless to remark here how jealous the philosopher is of everything calling itself honor and probity. Civil society is, so to speak, a divinity for him on earth; he burns incense to it, he honors it by probity, by an exact attention to his duties, and by a sincere desire not to be a useless or embarrassing member of it. The sentiments of probity enter as much into the mechanical constitution of the philosopher as the illumination of the mind. The more you find reason in a man, the more you find in him probity. On the other hand, where fanaticism and superstition reign, there reign the passions and anger. The temperament of the philosopher is to act according to the spirit of order or reason; as he loves society extremely, it is more important to him than to other men to bend every effort to produce only effects conformable to the idea of the honest man. . . .

This love of society, so essential to the philosopher, makes us see how very true was the remark of Marcus Aurelius: "How happy will the people be when kings are philosophers or philosophers are kings!"

LE MARIAGE DE FIGARO

PIERRE AUGUSTIN CARON DE BEAUMARCHAIS

Mozart's opera of the same name was based on the play written in 1778 by the Frenchman Beaumarchais (1732–1799). This selection is the famous denunciation in Act V by the self-made valet, Figaro, of his aristocratic employer and tormentor, Almaviva, with whom Figaro is vying for the affections of Susanah.

FIGARO *(Alone, walking in the darkness, speaks in somber tones):* . . . No, Monsieur le Comte, you shan't have her! You shan't have her. Because you are a great noble, you think you are a great genius! Nobility, a fortune, a rank, appointments to office: all this makes a man so proud! What did you do to earn all this? You took the trouble to get born—nothing more. Moreover, you're really a pretty ordinary fellow! While as for me, lost in the crowd, I've had to use more knowledge, more brains, just to keep alive than your likes have had to spend on governing Spain and the Empire for a century. And you want to contest with me— Someone's coming, it's she—no, nobody— The night is black as the devil, and here I am plying the silly trade of husband, though I'm only half a husband. *(He sits down on a bench)* Is there anything stranger than my fate? Son of I don't know whom, kidnapped by robbers, brought up in their ways, I got disgusted with them, and tried to follow an honest career; and everywhere I met with rebuffs. I learned chemistry, pharmacy, surgery, and all the credit of a great noble barely succeeded in putting a veterinary's lancet in my hand! Tired of making sick beasts sadder, I turned to a very different trade, and threw myself into the life of the theater. What a stone I hung around my neck that time! I sketched a comedy about harem life; being a Spanish writer, I assumed I could be irreverent towards Mohammed without any scruples: but at once an Envoy from somewhere complained that my verses offended the Sublime Porte, Persia, a part of India, all Egypt, the kingdoms of Barca, Tripoli, Tunis, Algiers and Morocco; and there was my comedy burned, to please some Mohammedan princes not one of whom I suppose knows how to read, and who keep cursing away at us all as "Christian dogs"—not being able to degrade the human spirit, they take revenge by abusing it. A question came up about the nature of wealth: and since it isn't necessary to own a thing to reason about it, I, penniless, wrote on the value of money and the *produit net:* at once I saw, from the inside of a cab, the lowered drawbridge of a fortress prison at the entrance to which I left hope and liberty! *(He gets up)* How I'd love to get one of these powerful men of four days' standing, so ready with such penalties, just after some good disgrace had fermented his pride! I'd tell him—that printed foolishness has no importance, except for those who try to suppress it; that without freedom to blame, there can be no flattering eulogies; and that only little men fear little writings. *(He sits down again)* Tired of feeding an obscure boarder, they let me out of prison. I was told that during my economic retreat, there had been established in Madrid a system of free sale of products which included even the press. To profit by this sweet liberty, I announced a periodical, and, thinking to offend no one, I called it *The Useless Journal.* Whew! I had a thousand poor devils of scribblers rise up against me: I was suppressed; and there I was once more among the unemployed. I began almost to despair; I was thought of for a government post, but unfortunately I was qualified for it. They needed an accountant: a dancer got the job. All that was left for me was stealing; I set up a faro game; and now, good folk, I supped in society, and people known as *comme il faut* opened their houses to me politely, on condition they kept three-quarters of the profits. I might have gone pretty far, for I was beginning to understand that to gain wealth it is better to have know-how [*savoir-faire*] than to have knowledge [*savoir*]. But as everybody about me stole, while insisting I stay honest, I should have failed once more. I should have left this world and put a watery grave between me and it, but a kindly God recalled me to my first condition. I took up once more my barber's case and my English leather strop. I traveled about, shaving, from town to town, living at last a carefree life.

THE MAGIC FLUTE

Wolfgang Amadeus Mozart

In these two selections from The Magic Flute *by Mozart (1756–1791) he and his librettist, Emanuel Schikaneder (1751–1812), distill the intellectual spirit of the Enlightenment. In the first, Tamino has just arrived at the Temple of Wisdom, which is flanked by the Temple of Reason and the Temple of Nature. In the second, Sarastro and his fellow secular priests proclaim first from their holy pyramid and then from the Temple of the Sun their triumph over the Queen of the Night, the victory of light over darkness.*

TAMINO: Where am I now? What will happen to me?
Is this the domain of the Gods?
These portals, these columns prove
That skill, industry, art reside here;
Where action rules and idleness is banished
Vice cannot easily gain control.
I will boldly pass through that portal;
Its design is noble, straightforward, pure. . . .

CHORUS OF PRIESTS: O Isis and Osiris, what bliss!
Dark night retreats from the rays of the sun.
Soon the noble youth will feel a new life,
Soon he will be wholly dedicated to our order.
His spirit is bold, his heart is pure,
Soon he will be worthy of us. . . .

• • •

SARASTRO: The rays of the sun
Drive away the night;
Destroyed is the hypocrite's
Surreptitious power.

CHORUS:

Hail to the initiates!
You have penetrated the night.
Thanks to thee, Osiris,
Thanks, Isis, be thine!
Vigor has overcome,
And crowns as reward
Beauty and wisdom
With its eternal diadem!

THE FUTURE PROGRESS OF THE HUMAN MIND

MARQUIS DE CONDORCET

No more vivid picture of the Enlightenment's utopian vision exists than this selection from Marie-Jean-Antoine-Nicholas de Caritat, marquis de Condorcet (1743–1794). It is the tenth and final stage of his Sketch for a Historical Picture of the Human Mind, *written shortly before his death.*

If man can, with almost complete assurance, predict phenomena when he knows their laws, and if, even when he does not, he can still, with great expectation of success, forecast the future on the basis of his experience of the past, why, then, should it be regarded as a fantastic undertaking to sketch, with some pretence to truth, the future destiny of man on the basis of his history? The sole foundation for belief in the natural sciences is this idea, that the general laws directing the phenomena of the universe, known or unknown, are necessary and constant. Why should this principle be any less true for the development of the intellectual and moral faculties of man than for the other operations of nature? Since beliefs founded on past experience of like conditions provide the only rule of conduct for the wisest of men, why should the philosopher be forbidden to base his conjectures on these same foundations, so long as he does not attribute to them a certainty superior to that warranted by the number, the constancy, and the accuracy of his observations?

Our hopes for the future condition of the human race can be subsumed under three important heads: the abolition of inequality between nations, the progress of equality within each nation, and the true perfection of mankind. Will all nations one day attain that state of civilization which the most enlightened, the freest and the least burdened by prejudices, such as the French and the Anglo-Americans, have attained already? Will the vast gulf that separates these peoples from the slavery of nations under the rule of monarchs, from the barbarism of African tribes, from the ignorance of savages, little by little disappear?

Is there on the face of the earth a nation whose inhabitants have been debarred by nature herself from the enjoyment of freedom and the exercise of reason?

Are those differences which have hitherto been seen in every civilized country in respect of the enlightenment, the resources, and the wealth enjoyed by the different classes into which it is divided, is that inequality between men which was aggravated or perhaps produced by the earliest progress of society, are these part of civilization itself, or are they due to the present imperfections of the social art? Will they necessarily decrease and ultimately make way for a real equality, the final end of the social art, in which even the effects of the natural differences between men will be mitigated and the only kind of inequality to persist will be that which is in the interests of all and which favors the progress of civilization, of education, and of industry, without entailing either poverty, humiliation, or dependence? In other words, will men approach a condition in which everyone will have the knowledge necessary to conduct himself in the ordinary affairs of life, according to the light of his own reason, to preserve his mind free from prejudice, to understand his rights and to exercise them in accordance with his conscience and his creed; in which everyone will become able, through the development of his faculties, to find the means of providing for his needs; and in which at last misery and folly will be the exception, and no longer the habitual lot of a section of society?

Is the human race to better itself, either by discoveries in the sciences and the arts, and so in the means to individual welfare and general prosperity; or by progress in the principles of conduct or practical morality; or by a true perfection of the intellectual, moral, or physical faculties of man, an improvement which may result from a perfection either of the instruments used to heighten the intensity of these faculties and to direct their use or of the natural constitution of man?

In answering these three questions we shall find in the experience of the past, in the observation of the progress that the sciences and civilization have already made, in the analysis of the progress of the human mind and of the development of its faculties, the strongest reasons for believing that nature has set no limit to the realization of our hopes.

If we glance at the state of the world today we see first of all that in Europe the principles of the French Constitution are already those of all enlightened men. We see them too widely propagated, too seriously professed, for priests and despots to prevent their gradual penetration even into the hovels of their slaves; there they will soon awaken in these slaves the remnants of their common sense and inspire them with that smoldering indignation which not even constant humiliation and fear can smother in the soul of the oppressed.

As we move from nation to nation, we can see in each what special obstacles impede this revolution and what attitudes of mind favor it. We can distinguish the nations where we may expect it to be introduced gently by the perhaps belated wisdom of their governments, and those nations where its violence intensified by their resistance must involve all alike in a swift and terrible convulsion.

Can we doubt that either common sense or the senseless discords of European nations will add to the effects of the slow but inexorable progress of their colonies, and will soon bring about the independence of the New World? And then will not the European population in these colonies, spreading rapidly over that enormous land, either civilize or peacefully remove the savage nations who still inhabit vast tracts of its land?

Survey the history of our settlements and commercial undertakings in Africa or in Asia, and you will see how our trade monopolies, our treachery, our murderous contempt for men of another color or creed, the insolence of our usurpations, the intrigues or the exaggerated proselytic zeal of our priests, have destroyed the respect and goodwill that the superiority of our knowledge and the benefits of our commerce at first won for us in the eyes of the inhabitants. But doubtless the moment approaches when, no longer presenting ourselves as always either tyrants or corrupters, we shall become for them the beneficent instruments of their freedom.

The sugar industry, establishing itself throughout the immense continent of Africa, will destroy the shameful exploitation which has corrupted and depopulated that continent for the last two centuries.

Already in Great Britain, friends of humanity have set us an example; and if the Machiavellian government of that country has been restrained by public opinion from offering any opposition, what may we not expect of this same spirit, once the reform of a servile and venal constitution has led to a government worthy of a humane and generous nation? Will not France hasten to imitate such undertakings dictated by philanthropy and the true self-interest of Europe alike? Trading stations have been set up in the French islands, in Guiana and in some English possessions, and soon we shall see the downfall of the monopoly that the Dutch have sustained with so much treachery, persecution and crime. The nations of Europe will finally learn that monopolistic companies are nothing more than a tax imposed upon them in order to provide their governments with a new instrument of tyranny.

So the peoples of Europe, confining themselves to free trade, understanding their own rights too well to show contempt for those of other peoples, will respect this independence, which until now they have so insolently violated. Their settlements, no longer filled with government hirelings hastening, under the cloak of place or privilege, to amass treasure by brigandry and deceit, so as to be able to return to Europe and purchase titles and honor, will now be peopled with men of industrious habit, seeking in these propitious climates the wealth that eluded them at home. The love of freedom will retain them there, ambition will no longer recall them, and what have been no better than the counting houses of brigands will become colonies of citizens propagating throughout Africa and Asia the principles and the practice of liberty, knowledge and reason, that they have brought from Europe. We shall see the monks who brought only shameful superstition to these peoples, and aroused their antagonism by the threat of yet another tyranny, replaced by men occupied in propagating amongst them the truths that will promote their happiness and in teaching them about their interests and their rights. Zeal for the truth is also one of the passions, and it will turn its efforts to distant lands, once there are no longer at home any crass prejudices to combat, any shameful errors to dissipate. . . .

The progress of these peoples is likely to be more rapid and certain than our own because they can receive from us everything that we have had to find out for ourselves, and in order to understand those simple truths and infallible methods which we have acquired only after long error, all that they need to do is to follow the expositions and proofs that appear in our speeches and writings. If the progress of the Greeks was lost to later nations, this was because of the absence of any form of communication between the different peoples, and for this we must blame the tyrannical domination of the Romans. But when mutual needs have brought all men together, and the great powers have established equality among societies as well as among individuals and have raised respect for the independence of weak states and sympathy for ignorance and misery to the rank of political principles, when maxims that favor action and energy have ousted those which would compress the province of human faculties, will it then be possible to fear that there are still places in the world inaccessible to enlightenment, or that despotism in its pride can raise barriers against truth that are insurmountable for long?

The time will therefore come when the sun will shine only on free men who know no other master but their reason; when tyrants and slaves, priests and their stupid or hypocritical instruments, will exist only in works of history and on the stage; and when we shall think of them only to pity their victims and their dupes; to maintain ourselves in a state of vigilance by thinking on their excesses; and to learn how to recognize and so to destroy, by force of reason, the first seeds of tyranny and superstition, should they ever dare to reappear amongst us.

In looking at the history of societies we shall have had occasion to observe that there is often a great difference between the rights that the law allows its citizens and the rights that they actually enjoy, and, again, between the equality established by political codes and that which in fact exists amongst individuals: and we shall have noticed that these differences were one of the principal causes of the destruction of freedom in the ancient republics, of the storms that troubled them, and of the weakness that delivered them over to foreign tyrants.

These differences have three main causes: inequality in wealth; inequality in status between the man whose means of subsistence are hereditary and the man whose means are dependent on the length of his life, or, rather, on that part of his life in which he is capable of work; and, finally, inequality in education.

We therefore need to show that these three sorts of real inequality must constantly diminish without, however, disappearing altogether: for they are the result of natural and necessary causes, which it would be foolish and dangerous to wish to eradicate; and one could not even attempt to bring about the entire disappearance of their effects without introducing even more fecund sources of inequality, without striking more direct and more fatal blows at the rights of man.

It is easy to prove that wealth has a natural tendency to equality, and that any excessive disproportion could not exist, or at least would rapidly disappear, if civil laws did not provide artificial ways of perpetuating and uniting fortunes; if free trade and industry were allowed to remove the advantages that accrued wealth derives from any restrictive law or fiscal privilege; if taxes on covenants, the restrictions placed on their free employment, their subjection to tiresome formalities, and the uncertainty and inevitable expense involved in implementing them did not hamper the activity of the poor man and swallow up his meager capital; if the administration of the country did not afford some men ways of making their fortune that were closed to other citizens; if prejudice and avarice, so common in old age, did not preside over the making of marriages; and if, in a society enjoying simpler manners and more sensible institutions, wealth ceased to be a means of satisfying vanity and ambition, and if the equally misguided notions of austerity, which condemn spending money in the cultivation of the more delicate pleasures, no longer insisted on the hoarding of all one's earnings.

Let us turn to the enlightened nations of Europe, and observe the size of their present populations in relation to the size of their territories. Let us consider, in agriculture and industry, the proportion that holds between labor and the means of subsistence, and we shall see that it would be impossible for those means to be kept at their present level, and consequently for the population to be kept at its present size, if a great number of individuals were not almost entirely dependent for the maintenance of themselves and their family either on their own labor or on the interest from capital invested so as to make their labor more productive. Now both these sources of income depend on the life and even on the health of the head of the family. They provide what is rather like a life annuity, save that it is more dependent on chance; and in consequence there is a very real difference between people living like this and those whose resources are not at all subject to the same risks, who live either on revenue from land, or on the interest on capital, which is almost independent of their own labor.

Here then is a necessary cause of inequality, of dependence and even of misery, which ceaselessly threatens the most numerous and most active class in our society.

We shall point out how it can be in great part eradicated by guaranteeing people in old age a means of livelihood produced partly by their own savings and partly by the savings of others who make the same outlay, but who die before they need to reap the reward; or, again, on the same principle of compensation, by securing for widows and orphans an income which is the same and costs the same for those families which suffer an early loss and for those which suffer it later; or again by providing all children with the capital necessary for the full use of their labor, available at the age when they start work and found a family, a capital which increases at the expense of those whom premature death prevents from reaching this age. It is to the application of the calculus to the probabilities of life and the investment of money that we owe the idea of these methods which have already been successful, although they have not been applied in a sufficiently comprehensive and exhaustive fashion to render them really useful, not merely to a few individuals, but to society as a whole, by making it possible to prevent those periodic disasters which strike at so many families and which are such a recurrent source of misery and suffering.

We shall point out that schemes of this nature, which can be organized in the name of the social authority and become one of its greatest benefits, can also be the work of private associations, which will be formed without any real risk, once the principles for the proper working of these schemes have been widely diffused and the mistakes which have been the undoing of a large number of these associations no longer hold terrors for us. . . .

So we might say that a well-directed system of education rectifies natural inequality in ability instead of strengthening it, just as good laws remedy natural inequality in the means of subsistence, and just as in societies where laws have brought about this same equality, liberty, though subject to a regular constitution, will be more widespread, more complete, than in the total independence of savage life. Then the social art will have fulfilled its aim, that of assuring and extending to all men enjoyment of the common rights to which they are called by nature.

The real advantages that should result from this progress, of which we can entertain a hope that is almost a certainty, can have no other term than that of the absolute perfection of the human race; since, as the various kinds of equality come to work in its favor by producing ampler sources of supply, more extensive education, more complete liberty, so equality will be more real and will embrace everything which is really of importance for the happiness of human beings.

It is therefore only by examining the progress and the laws of this perfection that we shall be able to understand the extent or the limits of our hopes.

No one has ever believed that the mind can gain knowledge of all the facts of nature or attain the ultimate means of precision in the measurement, or in the analysis of the facts of nature, the relations between objects and all the possible combinations of ideas. Even the relations between magnitudes, the mere notion of quantity or extension, taken in its fullest comprehension, gives rise to a system so vast that it will never be mastered by the human mind in its entirety, that there will always be a part of it, always indeed the larger part of it, that will remain forever unknown. People have believed that man can never know more than a part of the objects that the nature of his intelligence allows him to understand, and that he must in the end arrive at a point where the number and complexity of the objects that he already knows have absorbed all his strength so that any further progress must be completely impossible.

But since, as the number of known facts increases, the human mind learns how to classify them and to subsume them under more general facts, and, at the same time, the instruments and methods employed in their observation and their exact measurement acquire a new precision; since, as more relations between various objects become known, man is able to reduce them to more general relations, to express them more simply, and to present them in such a way that it is possible to grasp a greater number of them with the same degree of intellectual ability and the same amount of application; since, as the mind learns to understand more complicated combinations of ideas, simpler formulae soon reduce their complexity; so truths that were discovered only by great effort, that could at first only be understood by men capable of profound thought, are soon developed and proved by methods that are not beyond the reach of common intelligence. If the methods which have led to these new combinations of ideas are ever exhausted, if their application to hitherto unsolved questions should demand exertions greater than either the time or the capacity of the learned would permit, some method of a greater generality or simplicity will be found so that genius can continue undisturbed on its path. The strength and the limits of man's intelligence may remain unaltered; and yet the instruments that he uses will increase and improve, the language that fixes and determines his ideas will acquire greater breadth and precision, and, unlike mechanics, where an increase of force means a decrease of speed, the methods that lead genius to the discovery of truth increase at once the force and the speed of its operations.

Therefore, since these developments are themselves the necessary consequences of progress in detailed knowledge, and since the need for new methods in fact only arises in circumstances that give rise to new methods, it is evident that, within the body of the sciences of observation, calculation and experiment, the actual number of truths may always increase, and that every part of this body may develop, and yet man's faculties be of the same strength, activity and extent.

If we apply these general reflections to the various sciences, we can find in each of them examples of progressive improvement that will remove any doubts about what we may expect for the future. We shall point out in particular the progress that is both likely and imminent in those sciences which prejudice regards as all but exhausted. We shall give examples of the manner and extent of the precision and unity which could accrue to the whole system of human knowledge as the result of a more general and philosophical application of the sciences of calculation to the various branches of knowledge. We shall show how favorable to our hopes would be a more universal system of education by giving a greater number of people the elementary knowledge which could awaken their interest in a particular branch of study, and by providing conditions favorable to their progress in it; and how these hopes would be further raised if more men possessed the means to devote themselves to these studies, for at present even in the most enlightened countries scarcely one in fifty of the people who have natural talents receives the necessary education to develop them; and how, if this were done, there would be a proportionate increase in the number of men destined by their discoveries to extend the boundaries of science.

We shall show how this equality in education and the equality which will come about among the different nations would accelerate the advance of these sciences whose progress depends on repeated observations over a large area; what benefits would thereby accrue to mineralogy, botany, zoology and meteorology; and what a vast disproportion holds in all these sciences between the poverty of existing methods, which have nevertheless led to useful and important new truths, and the wealth of those methods which man would then be able to employ.

We shall show how even the sciences in which discovery is the fruit of solitary meditation would benefit from being studied by a greater number of people, in the matter of those improvements in detail which do not demand the intellectual energy of an inventor but suggest themselves to mere reflection.

If we turn now to the arts, whose theory depends on these same sciences, we shall find that their progress, depending as it does on that of theory, can have no other limits; that the procedures of the different arts can be perfected and simplified in the same way as the methods of the sciences; new instruments, machines and looms can add to man's strength and can improve at once the quality and the accuracy of his productions, and can diminish the time and labor that has to be expended on them. The obstacles still in the way of this progress will disappear, accidents will be foreseen and prevented, the insanitary conditions that are due either to the work itself or to the climate will be eliminated.

A very small amount of ground will be able to produce a great quantity of supplies of greater utility or higher quality; more goods will be obtained for a smaller outlay; the manufacture of articles will be achieved with less wastage in raw materials and will make better use of them. Every type of soil will produce those things which satisfy the greatest number of needs; of several alternative ways of satisfying needs of the same order, that will be chosen which satisfies the greatest number of people and which requires least labor and least expenditure. So, without the need for sacrifice, methods of preservation and economy in expenditure will improve in the wake of progress in the arts of producing and preparing supplies and making articles from them.

So not only will the same amount of ground support more people, but everyone will have less work to do, will produce more, and satisfy his wants more fully.

With all this progress in industry and welfare, which establishes a happier proportion between men's talents and their needs, each successive generation will have larger possessions, either as a result of this progress or through the preservation of the products of industry; and so, as a consequence of the physical constitution of the human race, the number of people will increase. Might there not then come a moment when these necessary laws begin to work in a contrary direction; when, the number of people in the world finally exceeding the means of subsistence, there will in consequence ensue a continual diminution of happiness and population, a true retrogression, or at best an oscillation between good and bad? In societies that have reached this stage, will not this oscillation be a perennial source of more or less periodic disaster? Will it not show that a point has been attained beyond which all further improvement is impossible, that the perfectibility of the human race has after long years arrived at a term beyond which it may never go?

There is doubtless no one who does not think that such a time is still very far from us; but will it ever arrive? It is impossible to pronounce about the likelihood of an event that will occur only when the human species will have necessarily acquired a degree of knowledge of which we can have no inkling. And who would take it upon himself to predict the condition to which the art of converting the elements to the use of man may in time be brought?

But even if we agree that the limit will one day arrive, nothing follows from it that is in the least alarming as far as either the happiness of the human race or its indefinite perfectibility is concerned. If we consider that, before all this comes to pass, the progress of reason will have kept pace with that of the sciences, and that the absurd prejudices of superstition will have ceased to corrupt and degrade the moral code by its harsh doctrines instead of purifying and elevating it, we can assume that by then men will know that, if they have a duty towards those who are not yet born, that duty is not to give them existence but to give them happiness; their aim should be to promote the general welfare of the human race or of the society in which they live or of the family to which they belong, rather than foolishly to encumber the world with useless and wretched beings. It is, then, possible that there should be a limit to the amount of food that can be produced, and, consequently, to the size of the population of the world, without this involving that untimely destruction of some of those creatures who have been given life, which is so contrary to nature and to social prosperity. . . .

Organic perfectibility or deterioration amongst the various strains in the vegetable and animal kingdom can be regarded as one of the general laws of nature. This law also applies to the human race. No one can doubt that, as preventive medicine improves and food and housing become healthier, as a way of life is established that develops our physical powers by exercise without ruining them by excess, as the two most virulent causes of deterioration, misery and excessive wealth, are eliminated, the average length of human life will be increased and a better health and a stronger physical constitution will be ensured. The improvement of medical practice, which will become more efficacious with the progress of reason and of the social order, will mean the end of infectious and hereditary diseases and illnesses brought on by climate, food, or working conditions. It is reasonable to hope that all other diseases may likewise disappear as their distant causes are discovered. Would it be absurd, then, to suppose that this perfection of the human species might be capable of indefinite progress; that the day will come when death will be due only to extraordinary accidents or to the decay of the vital forces, and that ultimately the average span between birth and decay will have no assignable value? Certainly man will not become immortal, but will not the interval between the first breath that he draws and the time when in the natural course of events, without disease or accident, he expires, increase indefinitely? Since we are now speaking of a progress that can be represented with some accuracy in figures or on a graph, we shall take this opportunity of explaining the two meanings that can be attached to the word *indefinite.*

In truth, this average span of life, which we suppose will increase indefinitely as time passes, may grow in conformity either with a law such that it continually approaches a limitless length but without ever reaching it, or with a law such that through the centuries it reaches a length greater than any determinate quantity that we may assign to it as its limit. In the latter case such an increase is truly indefinite in the strictest sense of the word, since there is no term on this side of which it must of necessity stop. In the former case it is equally indefinite in relation to us if we cannot fix the limit it always approaches without ever reaching, and particularly if, knowing only that it will never stop, we are ignorant in which of the two senses the term *indefinite* can be applied to it. Such is the present condition of our knowledge as far as the perfectibility of the human race is concerned; such is the sense in which we may call it indefinite.

So, in the example under consideration, we are bound to believe that the average length of human life will forever increase unless this is prevented by physical revolutions; we do not know what the limit is which it can never exceed. We cannot tell even whether the general laws of nature have determined such a limit or not.

But are not our physical faculties and the strength, dexterity and acuteness of our senses, to be numbered among the qualities whose perfection in the individual may be transmitted? Observation of the various breeds of domestic animals inclines us to believe that they are, and we can confirm this by direct observation of the human race.

Finally may we not extend such hopes to the intellectual and moral faculties? May not our parents, who transmit to us the benefits or disadvantages of their constitution, and from whom we receive our shape and features, as well as our tendencies to certain physical affections, hand on to us also that part of the physical organization which determines the intellect, the power of the brain, the ardor of the soul or the moral sensibility? Is it not probable that education, in perfecting these qualities, will at the same time influence, modify and perfect the organization itself? Analogy, investigation of the human faculties and the study of certain facts, all seem to give substance to such conjectures, which would further push back the boundaries of our hopes.

These are the questions with which we shall conclude this final stage. How consoling for the philosopher, who laments the errors, the crimes, the injustices which still pollute the earth, and of which he is often the victim, is this view of the human race, emancipated from its shackles, released from the empire of fate and from that of the enemies of its progress, advancing with a firm and sure step along the path of truth, virtue and happiness! It is the contemplation of this prospect that rewards him for all his efforts to assist the progress of reason and the defense of liberty. He dares to regard these strivings as part of the eternal chain of human destiny; and in this persuasion he is filled with the true delight of virtue and the pleasure of having done some lasting good, which fate can never destroy by a sinister stroke of revenge, by calling back the reign of slavery and prejudice. Such contemplation is for him an asylum, in which the memory of his persecutors cannot pursue him; there he lives in thought with man restored to his natural rights and dignity, forgets man tormented and corrupted by greed, fear, or envy; there he lives with his peers in an Elysium created by reason and graced by the purest pleasures known to the love of mankind.

PART II
REASON AND NATURE

THE NEW SCIENCE

FRANCIS BACON

In this selection from his 1620 book, Novum Organum, *Francis Bacon (1561–1626), English philosopher of science, essayist, and statesman, spells out the scientific methodology that would so influence the Enlightenment.*

Man, being the servant and interpreter of Nature, can do and understand so much and so much only as he has observed in fact or in thought of the course of nature: beyond this he neither knows anything nor can do anything.

Neither the naked hand nor the understanding left to itself can effect much. It is by instruments and helps that the work is done, which are as much wanted for the understanding as for the hand. And as the instruments of the hand either give motion or guide it, so the instruments of the mind supply either suggestions for the understanding or cautions.

Human knowledge and human power meet in one, for where the cause is not known the effect cannot be produced. Nature to be commanded must be obeyed; and that which in contemplation is as the cause is in operation as the rule.

The subtlety of nature is greater many times over than the subtlety of the senses and understanding; so that all those specious meditations, speculations, and glosses in which men indulge are quite from the purpose, only there is no one by to observe it.

The logic now in use serves rather to fix and give stability to the errors which have their foundation in commonly received notions than to help the search after truth. So it does more harm than good.

The syllogism is not applied to the first principles of sciences, and is applied in vain to intermediate axioms; being no match for the subtlety of nature. It commands assent therefore to the proposition, but does not take hold of the thing.

The syllogism consists of propositions, propositions consist of words, words are symbols of notions. Therefore if the notions themselves (which is the root of the matter) are confused and overhastily abstracted from the facts, there can be no firmness in the superstructure. Our only hope therefore lies in a true induction.

There is no soundness in our notions whether logical or physical. Substance, Quality, Action, Passion, Essence itself, are not sound notions: much less are Heavy, Light, Dense, Rare, Moist, Dry, Generation, Corruption, Attraction, Repulsion, Element, Matter, Form, and the like; but all are fantastical and ill defined.

The conclusions of human reason as ordinarily applied in matter of nature, I call for the sake of distinction *Anticipations of Nature* (as a thing rash or premature). That reason which is elicited from facts by a just and methodical process, I call *Interpretation of Nature.*

Anticipations are a ground sufficiently firm for consent; for even if men went mad all after the same fashion, they might agree one with another well enough.

For the winning of assent, indeed, anticipations are far more powerful than interpretations; because being collected from a few instances, and those for the most part of familiar occurrence, they straightway touch the understanding and fill the imagination; whereas interpretations on the other hand, being gathered here and there from very various and widely dispersed facts, cannot suddenly strike the understanding; and therefore they must needs, in respect of the opinions of the time, seem harsh and out of tune; much as the mysteries of faith do.

In sciences founded on opinions and dogmas, the use of anticipations and logic is good; for in them the object is to command assent to the proposition, not to master the thing.

Though all the wits of all the ages should meet together and combine and transmit their labors, yet will no great progress ever be made in science by means of anticipations; because radical errors in the first concoction of the mind are not to be cured by the excellence of functions and remedies subsequent.

It is idle to expect any great advancement in science from the superinducing and engrafting of new things upon old. We must begin anew from the very foundations, unless we would revolve forever in a circle with mean and contemptible progress.

The honor of the ancient authors, and indeed of all, remains untouched; since the comparison I challenge is not of wits or faculties, but of ways and methods, and the part I take upon myself is not that of a judge, but of a guide.

This must be plainly avowed: no judgment can be rightly formed either of my method or of the discoveries to which it leads, by means of anticipations (that is to say, of the reasoning which is now in use); since I cannot be called on to abide by the sentence of a tribunal which is itself on its trial.

The doctrine of those who have denied that certainty could be attained at all, has some agreement with my way of proceeding at the first setting out; but they end in being infinitely separated and opposed. For the holders of that doctrine assert simply that nothing can be known; I also assert that not much can be known in nature by the way which is now in use. But then they go on to destroy the authority of the senses and understanding; whereas I proceed to devise and supply helps for the same.

The idols and false notions which are now in possession of the human understanding, and have taken deep root therein, not only so beset men's minds that truth can hardly find entrance, but even after entrance obtained, they will again in the very instauration of the sciences meet and trouble us, unless men being forewarned of the danger fortify themselves as far as may be against their assaults.

There are four classes of Idols which beset men's minds. To these for distinction's sake I have assigned names—calling the first class *Idols of the Tribe;* the second, *Idols of the Cave;* the third, *Idols of the Market Place;* the fourth, *Idols of the Theater.*

The formation of ideas and axioms by true induction is no doubt the proper remedy to be applied for the keeping off and clearing away of idols. To point them out, however, is of great use; for the doctrine of Idols is to the Interpretation of Nature what the doctrine of the refutation of Sophisms is to common Logic.

The Idols of the Tribe have their foundation in human nature itself, and in the tribe or race of men. For it is a false assertion that the sense of man is the measure of things. On the contrary, all perceptions as well of the sense as of the mind are according to the measure of the individual and not according to the measure of the universe. And the human understanding is like a false mirror, which, receiving rays irregularly, distorts and discolors the nature of things by mingling its own nature with it.

The Idols of the Cave are the idols of the individual man. For everyone (besides the errors common to human nature in general) has a cave or den of his own, which refracts and discolors the light of nature; owing either to his own proper and peculiar nature; or to his education and conversation with others; or to the reading of books, and the authority of those whom he esteems and admires, or to the differences of impressions, accordingly as they take place in a mind preoccupied and predisposed or in a mind indifferent and settled; or the like. So that the spirit of man (according as it is meted out to different individuals) is in fact a thing variable and full of perturbation, and governed as it were by chance. Whence it was well observed by Heraclitus that men look for sciences in their own lesser worlds, and not in the greater or common world.

There are also Idols formed by the intercourse and association of men with each other, which I call Idols of the Market Place, on account of the commerce and consort of men there. For it is by discourse that men associate; and words are imposed according to the apprehension of the vulgar. And therefore the ill and unfit choice of words wonderfully obstructs the understanding. Nor do the definitions or explanations wherewith in some things learned men are wont to guard and defend themselves, by any means set the matter right. But words plainly force and overrule the understanding, and throw all into confusion, and lead men away into numberless empty controversies and idle fancies.

Lastly, there are Idols which have immigrated into men's minds from the various dogmas of philosophies, and also from wrong laws of demonstration. These I call Idols of the Theater; because in my judgment all the received systems are but so many stage plays, representing worlds of their own creation after an unreal and scenic fashion. Nor is it only of the systems now in vogue, or only of the ancient sects and philosophies, that I speak; for many more plays of the same kind may yet be composed and in like artificial manner set forth; seeing that errors the most widely different have nevertheless causes for the most part alike. Neither again do I mean this only of entire systems, but also of many principles and axioms in science, which by tradition, credulity, and negligence have come to be received.

MATHEMATICAL PRINCIPLES OF NATURAL PHILOSOPHY

ISAAC NEWTON

Sir Isaac Newton (1642–1727), professor of mathematics at Cambridge University, personified science and its rationalist ideals for the eighteenth century. The following is an excerpt from his monumental Principia, *written in Latin in 1687.*

DEFINITIONS

Definition I

The quantity of matter is the measure of the same, arising from its density and bulk conjointly.

Thus air of a double density, in a double space, is quadruple in quantity; in a triple space, sextuple in quantity. The same thing is to be understood of snow, and fine dust or powders, that are condensed by compression or liquefaction, and of all bodies that are by any causes whatever differently condensed. I have no regard in this place to a medium, if any such there is, that freely pervades the interstices between the parts of bodies. It is this quantity that I mean hereafter everywhere under the name of body or mass. And the same is known by the weight of each body, for it is proportional to the weight, as I have found by experiments on pendulums, very accurately made, which shall be shown hereafter.

Definition II

The quantity of motion is the measure of all the same, arising from the velocity and quantity of matter conjointly.

The motion of the whole is the sum of the motion of all the parts; and therefore in a body double in quantity, with equal velocity, the motion is double; with twice the velocity, it is quadruple. . . .

Definition IV

An impressed force is an action exerted upon a body, in order to change its state, either of rest, or of uniform motion in a right line.

This force consists in the action only, and remains no longer in the body when the action is over. For a body maintains every new state it acquires, by its inertia only. But impressed forces are of different origins, as from percussion, from pressure, from centripetal force. . . .

Definition VI

The absolute quantity of a centripetal force is the measure of the same, proportional to the efficacy of the cause that propagates it from the center, through the spaces round about.

Thus the magnetic force is greater in one loadstone and less in another, according to their sizes and strength of intensity.

Definition VII

The accelerative quantity of a centripetal force is the measure of the same, proportional to the velocity which it generates in a given time.

Thus the force of the same loadstone is greater at a less distance, and less at a greater: also the force of gravity is greater in valleys, less on tops of exceedingly high mountains; and yet less, at greater distances from the body of the earth; but at equal distances, it is the same everywhere; because (taking away, allowing for, the resistance of air), it equally accelerates all falling bodies, whether heavy or light, great or small. . . .

Axioms, or Laws of Motion

Law I

Every body continues in its state of rest, or of uniform motion, in a right line, unless it is compelled to change that state by forces impressed upon it.

Projectiles continue in their motions, so far as they are not retarded by the resistance of the air, or impelled downwards by the force of gravity. A top, whose parts by their cohesion are continually drawn aside from rectilinear motions, does not cease its rotation, otherwise than as it is retarded by the air. The greater bodies of the planets and comets, meeting with less resistance in freer spaces, preserve their motions both progressive and circular for a much longer time.

Law II

The change of motion is proportional to the motive force impressed; and is made in the direction of the right line in which that force is impressed.

If any force generates a motion, a double force will generate double the motion, a triple force triple the motion, whether that force be impressed altogether and at once or gradually and successively. And this motion (being always directed the same way with the generating force), if the body moved before, is added to or subtracted from the former motion, according as they directly conspire with or are directly contrary to each other; or obliquely joined, when they are oblique, so as to produce a new motion compounded from the determination of both.

Law III

To every action there is always opposed an equal reaction: or, the mutual actions of two bodies upon each other are always equal, and directed to contrary parts.

Whatever draws or presses another is as much drawn or pressed by that other. If you press a stone with your finger, the finger is also pressed by the stone. If a horse draws a stone tied to a rope, the horse (if I may say so) will be equally drawn back towards the stone; for the distended rope, by the same endeavor to relax or unbend itself, will draw the horse as much towards the stone as it does the stone towards the horse, and will obstruct the progress of the one as much as it advances that of the other. If a body impinge upon another, and by its force change the motion of the other, that body also (because of the equality of the mutual pressure) will undergo an equal change, in its own motion, towards the contrary part. The changes made by these actions are equal, not in the velocities but in the motions of the bodies; that is to say, if the bodies are not hindered by any other impediments. For, because the motions are equally changed, the changes of the velocities made toward contrary parts are inversely proportional to the bodies. . . .

Rules of Reasoning in Philosophy

Rule I

We are to admit no more causes of natural things than such as are both true and sufficient to explain their appearances.

To this purpose the philosophers say that Nature does nothing in vain, and more is in vain when less will serve; for Nature is pleased with simplicity, and affects not the pomp of superfluous causes.

Rule II

Therefore to the same natural effects we must, as far as possible, assign the same causes.

As to respiration in a man and in a beast; the descent of stones in *Europe* and in *America;* the light of our culinary fire and of the sun; the reflection of light in the earth, and in the planets.

Rule III

The qualities of bodies, which admit neither intensification nor remission of degrees, and which are found to belong to all bodies within the reach of our experiments, are to be esteemed the universal qualities of all bodies whatsoever.

For since the qualities of bodies are only known to us by experiments, we are to hold for universal all such as universally agree with experiments; and such as are not liable to diminution can never be quite taken away. We are certainly not to relinquish the evidence of experiments for the sake of dreams and vain fictions of our own devising; nor are we to recede from the analogy of Nature, which is wont to be simple, and always consonant to itself. We no other way know the extension of bodies than by our senses, nor do these reach it in all bodies; but because we perceive extension in all that are sensible, therefore we ascribe it universally to all others also. That abundance of bodies are hard, we learn by experience; and because the hardness of the whole arises from the hardness of the parts, we therefore justly infer the hardness of the undivided particles not only of the bodies we feel but of all others. That all bodies are impenetrable, we gather not from reason but from sensation. The bodies which we handle we find impenetrable, and thence conclude impenetrability to be a universal property of all bodies whatsoever. That all bodies are movable, and endowed with certain power (which we call the inertia) of persevering in their motion, or in their rest, we only infer from the like properties observed in the bodies which we have seen. The extension, hardness, impenetrability, mobility, and inertia of the whole, result from the extension, hardness, impenetrability, mobility, and inertia of the parts; and hence we conclude the least particles of all bodies to be also all extended, and hard and impenetrable, and movable, and endowed with their proper inertia. And this is the foundation of all philosophy. Moreover, that the divided but contiguous particles of bodies may be separated from one another, is matter of observation; and, in the particles that remain undivided, our minds are able to distinguish yet lesser parts, as is mathematically demonstrated.

But whether the parts so distinguished, and not yet divided, may, by the powers of Nature, be actually divided and separated from one another, we cannot certainly determine. Yet, had we the proof of but one experiment that any undivided particle, in breaking a hard and solid body, suffered a division, we might by virtue of this rule conclude that the undivided as well as the divided particles may be divided and actually separated to infinity.

Lastly, if it universally appears, by experiments and astronomical observations, that all bodies about the earth gravitate towards the earth, and that in proportion to the quantity of matter which they severally contain; that the moon likewise, according to the quantity of its matter, gravitates towards the earth; that, on the other hand, our sea gravitates towards the moon; and all the planets one towards another; and the comets in like manner towards the sun; we must, in consequence of this rule, universally allow that all bodies whatsoever are endowed with a principle of mutual gravitation. For the arguments from the appearances concludes with more force for the universal gravitation of all bodies than for their impenetrability; of which, among those in the celestial regions, we have no experiments, nor any manner of observation. Not that I affirm gravity to be essential to bodies: by their *vis insita* I mean nothing but their inertia. This is immutable. Their gravity is diminished as they recede from the earth.

Rule IV

In experimental philosophy we are to look upon propositions inferred by general induction from phenomena as accurately or very nearly true, notwithstanding any contrary hypotheses that may be imagined, till such time as other phenomena occur, by which they may either be made more accurate, or liable to exceptions.

This rule we must follow, that the argument of induction may not be evaded by hypotheses.

THE NEW PHYSICS

Roger Cotes

English astronomer and mathematician Roger Cotes (1682–1716) wrote the preface to the second edition of Newton's Principia *in 1713, from which this section is taken.*

Those who have treated of natural philosophy may be nearly reduced to three classes. Of these some have attributed to the several species of things specific and occult qualities, on which, in a manner unknown, they make the operations of the several bodies to depend. The sum of the doctrine of the Schools derived from Aristotle and the Peripatetics is herein contained. They affirm that the several effects of bodies arise from the particular natures of those bodies. But whence it is that bodies derive those natures they don't tell us; and therefore they tell us nothing. And being entirely employed in giving names to things, and not in searching into things themselves, we may say that they have invented a philosophical way of speaking, but not that they have made known to us true philosophy. . . .

There is left then the third class, which profess experimental philosophy. These indeed derive the causes of all things from the most simple principles possible; but then they assume nothing as a principle that is not proved by phenomena. They frame no hypotheses, nor receive them into philosophy otherwise than as questions whose truth may be disputed. They proceed therefore in a twofold method; synthetical and analytical. From some select phenomena they deduce by analysis the forces of nature, and the more simple laws of forces; and from thence by synthesis show the constitution of the rest. This is that incomparably best way of philosophizing, which our renowned author most justly embraced before the rest; and thought alone worthy to be cultivated and adorned by his excellent labors. Of this he has given us a most illustrious example, by the explication of the System of the World, most happily deduced from the Theory of Gravity. That the virtue of gravity was found in all bodies, others suspected, or imagined before him; but he was the only and the first philosopher that could demonstrate it from appearances, and make it a solid foundation to the most noble speculations.

Therefore that we may begin our reasoning from what is most simple and nearest to us, let us consider a little what is the nature of gravity with us on Earth, that we may proceed the more safely when we come to consider it in the heavenly bodies that lie at so vast a distance from us. It is now agreed by all philosophers that all circumterrestrial bodies gravitate towards the Earth. That no bodies really light are to be found is now confirmed by manifold experience. That which is relative levity is not true levity, but apparent only, and arises from the preponderating gravity of the contiguous bodies.

Moreover, as all bodies gravitate towards the Earth, so does the Earth again towards bodies. That the action of gravity is mutual, and equal on both sides, is thus proved. . . .

This is the nature of gravity upon Earth; let us now see what it is in the Heavens.

That every body perseveres in its state either of rest, or of moving uniformly in a right line, unless insofar as it is compelled to change that state by forces impressed, is a law of nature universally received by all philosophers. But from thence it follows that bodies which move in curve lines, and are therefore continually going off from the right lines that are tangents to their orbits, are by some continued force retained in those curvilinear paths. Since then the planets move in curvilinear orbits, there must be some force operating by whose repeated actions they are perpetually made to deflect from the tangents. . . .

From what has been hitherto said, it is plain that the planets are retained in their orbits by some force perpetually acting upon them; it is plain that that force is always directed towards the centers of their orbits; it is plain that its efficacy is augmented with the nearness to the center, and diminished with the same; and that it is augmented in the same proportion with which the square of the distance is diminished, and diminished in the same proportion with which the square of the distance is augmented. . . .

Because the revolutions of the primary planets about the Sun, and of the secondary about Jupiter and Saturn, are phenomena of the same kind with the revolution of the Moon about the Earth; and because it has been moreover demonstrated that the centripetal forces of the primary planets are directed towards the center of the Sun, and those of the secondary towards the centers of Jupiter and Saturn, in the same manner as the centripetal force of the Moon is directed towards the center of the Earth; and since besides, all these forces are reciprocally as the squares of the distances from the centers, in the same manner as the centripetal force of the Moon is as the square of the distance from the Earth; we must of course conclude that the nature of all is the same. Therefore as the Moon gravitates towards the Earth, and the Earth again towards the Moon; so also all the secondary planets will gravitate towards their primary, and the primary planets again towards their secondary; and so all the primary towards the Sun; and the Sun again towards the primary.

Therefore the Sun gravitates towards all the planets, and all the planets towards the Sun. . . .

That the attractive virtue of the Sun is propagated on all sides to prodigious distances, and is diffused to every part of the wide space that surrounds it, is most evidently shown by the motion of the comets; which coming from places immensely distant from the Sun, approach very near to it; and sometimes so near, that in their perihelia they almost touch its body. The theory of these bodies was altogether unknown to astronomers, till in our own times our excellent author most happily discovered it, and demonstrated the truth of it by most certain observations. So that it is now apparent that the comets move in conic sections having their foci in the Sun's center, and by radii drawn to the Sun describe areas proportional to the times. But from these phenomena it is manifest, and mathematically demonstrated, that those forces, by which the comets are retained in their orbits, respect the Sun, and are reciprocally proportional to the squares of the distances from its center. Therefore the comets gravitate towards the Sun; and therefore the attractive force of the Sun not only acts on the bodies of the planets, placed at given distances and very nearly in the same plane, but reaches also to the comets in the most different parts of the heavens, and at the most different distances. This therefore is the nature of gravitating bodies, to propagate their force at all distances to all other gravitating bodies.

The foregoing conclusions are grounded on this axiom which is received by all philosophers; namely that effects of the same kind, that is, whose known properties are the same, take their rise from the same causes and have the same unknown properties also. For who doubts, if gravity be the cause of the descent of a stone in Europe, but that it is also the cause of the same descent in America? . . .

Since then all bodies, whether upon Earth or in the heavens, are heavy, so far as we can make any experiments or observations concerning them; we must certainly allow that gravity is found in all bodies universally. And in like manner as we ought not to suppose that any bodies can be otherwise than extended, moveable or impenetrable, so we ought not to conceive that any bodies can be otherwise than heavy. The extension, mobility, and impenetrability of bodies become known to us only by experiments; and in the very same manner their gravity becomes known to us. All bodies we can make any observations upon are extended, moveable, and impenetrable; and thence we conclude all bodies, and those we have no observations concerning, to be extended and moveable and impenetrable. So all bodies we can make observations on we find to be heavy; and thence we conclude all bodies, and those we have no observations of, to be heavy also. If anyone should say that the bodies of the fixed stars are not heavy because their gravity is not yet observed, they may say for the same reason that they are neither ex,tended nor moveable nor impenetrable, because these affections of the fixed stars are not yet observed. In short, either gravity must have a place among the primary qualities of all bodies, or extension, mobility and impenetrability must not.

ON BACON AND NEWTON

François-Marie Arouet de Voltaire

More than any other philosophe, *Voltaire (1694–1778) helped to popularize English writers and science in general to his French readers. The following excerpts are from his* Letters Concerning the English Nation, *published in 1733.*

It is not long since the ridiculous and threadbare question was agitated in a celebrated assembly; who was the greatest man, Caesar or Alexander, Tamerlane or Cromwell? Somebody said that it must undoubtedly be Sir Isaac Newton. This man was certainly in the right; for if true greatness consists in having received from heaven the advantage of a superior genius, with the talent of applying it for the interest of the possessor and of mankind, a man like Newton—and such a one is hardly to be met with in ten centuries—is surely by much the greatest; and those statesmen and conquerors which no age has ever been without, are commonly but so many illustrious villains. It is the man who sways our minds by the prevalence of reason and the native force of truth, not they who reduce mankind to a state of slavery by brutish force and downright violence; the man who by the vigor of his mind, is able to penetrate into the hidden secrets of nature, and whose capacious soul can contain the vast frame of the universe, not those who lay nature waste, and desolate the face of the earth, that claims our reverence and admiration.

Therefore, as you are desirous to be informed of the great men that England has produced, I shall begin with the Bacons, the Lockes, and the Newtons. The generals and ministers will come after them in their turn.

I must begin with the celebrated baron Verulam, known to the rest of Europe by the name of Bacon, who was the son of a certain keeper of the seals, and was for a considerable time chancellor under James I. Notwithstanding the intrigues and bustle of a court, and the occupations incident to his office, which would have required his whole attention, he found means to become a great philosopher, a good historian, and an elegant writer; and what is yet more wonderful is that he lived in an age where the art of writing was totally unknown, and where sound philosophy was still less so. This personage, as is the way among mankind, was more valued after his death than while he lived. His enemies were courtiers residing at London, while his admirers consisted wholly of foreigners. When Marquis d'Effiat brought Princess Mary, daughter of Henry the Great, over to be married to King Charles, this minister paid Bacon a visit, who being then confined to a sick bed, received him with close curtains. "You are like the angels," said d'Effiat to him; "we hear much talk of them, and while everybody thinks them superior to men, we are never favored with a sight of them."

You have been told in what manner Bacon was accused of a crime which is very far from being the sin of a philosopher, of being corrupted by pecuniary gifts; and how he was sentenced by the house of peers to pay a fine of about four hundred thousand livres of our money, besides losing his office of chancellor, and being degraded from the rank and dignity of a peer. At present the English revere his memory to such a degree that only with great difficulty can one imagine him to have been in the least guilty. Should you ask me what I think of it, I will make use of a saying I heard from Lord Bolingbroke. They happened to be talking of the avarice with which the duke of Marlborough had been taxed, and quoted several instances of it, for the truth of which they appealed to Lord Bolingbroke, who, as being of a contrary party, might, perhaps, without any trespass against the laws of decorum, freely say what he thought. "He was," said he, "so great a man that I do not recollect whether he had any faults or not." I shall, therefore, confine myself to those qualities which have acquired Chancellor Bacon the esteem of all Europe.

The most singular, as well as the most excellent, of all his works, is that which is now the least read, and which is at the same time the most useful; I mean his "*Novum Scientiarum Organum.*" This is the scaffold by means of which the edifice of the new philosophy has been reared; so that when the building was completed, the scaffold was no longer of any use. Chancellor Bacon was still unacquainted with nature, but he perfectly knew, and pointed out extraordinarily well, all the paths which lead to her recesses. He had very early despised what those square-capped fools teach in those dungeons called *Colleges*, under the name of philosophy, and did everything in his power that those bodies, instituted for the cultivation and perfection of the human understanding, might cease any longer to mar it, by their "quiddities," their "horrors of a vacuum," their "substantial forms," with the rest of that jargon which ignorance and a nonsensical jumble of religion had consecrated.

This great man is the father of experimental philosophy. It is true, wonderful discoveries had been made even before his time; the mariner's compass, the art of printing, that of engraving, the art of painting in oil, that of making glass, with the remarkably advantageous invention of restoring in some measure sight to the blind; that is, to old men, by means of spectacles; the secret of making gunpowder had, also, been discovered. They had gone in search of, discovered, and conquered a new world in another hemisphere. Who would not have thought that these sublime discoveries had been made by the greatest philosophers, and in times much more enlightened than ours? By no means; for all these astonishing revolutions happened in the ages of scholastic barbarity. Chance alone has brought forth almost all these inventions; it is even pretended that chance has had a great share in the discovery of America; at least, it has been believed that Christopher Columbus undertook this voyage on the faith of a captain of a ship who had been cast by a storm on one of the Caribbee islands. Be this as it will, men had learned to penetrate to the utmost limits of the habitable globe, and to destroy the most impregnable cities with an artificial thunder, much more terrible than the real; but they were still ignorant of the circulation of the blood, the weight and pressure of the air, the laws of motion, the doctrine of light and color, the number of the planets in our system, etc. And a man that was capable to maintain a thesis on the "Categories of Aristotle," the *universale a parte rei*, or such-like nonsense, was considered as a prodigy.

The most wonderful and useful inventions are by no means those which do most honor to the human mind. And it is to a certain mechanical instinct, which exists in almost every man, that we owe far the greater part of the arts, and in no manner whatever to philosophy. The discovery of fire, the arts of making bread, of melting and working metals, of building houses, the invention of the shuttle, are infinitely more useful than printing and the compass; notwithstanding, all these were invented by men who were still in a state of barbarity. What astonishing things have the Greeks and Romans since done in mechanics? Yet men believed, in their time, that the heavens were of crystal, and the stars were so many small lamps, that sometimes fell into the sea; and one of their greatest philosophers, after many researches, had at length discovered that the stars were so many pebbles, that had flown off like sparks from the earth.

In a word, there was not a man who had any idea of experimental philosophy before Chancellor Bacon; and of an infinity of experiments which have been made since his time, there is hardly a single one which has not been pointed out in his book. He had even made a good number of them himself. He constructed several pneumatic machines, by which he discovered the elasticity of the air; he had long brooded over the discovery of its weight, and was even at times very near to catching it, when it was laid hold of by Torricelli. A short time after, experimental physics began to be cultivated in almost all parts of Europe. This was a hidden treasure, of which Bacon had some glimmerings, and which all the philosophers whom his promises had encouraged made their utmost efforts to lay open. We see in his book mention made in express terms of that new attraction of which Newton passes for the inventor. "We must inquire," said Bacon, "whether there be not a certain magnetic force, which operates reciprocally between the earth and other heavy bodies, between the moon and the ocean, between the planets, etc." In another place he says: "Either heavy bodies are impelled toward the center of the earth, or they are mutually attracted by it; in this latter case it is evident that the nearer falling bodies approach the earth, the more forcibly are they attracted by it. We must try," continues he, "whether the same pendulum clock goes faster on the top of a mountain, or at the bottom of a mine. If the force of the weight diminishes on the mountain, and increases in the mine, it is probable the earth has a real attracting quality."

This precursor in philosophy was also an elegant writer, a historian, and a wit. His moral essays are in high estimation, though they seem rather calculated to instruct than to please; and as they are neither a satire on human nature, like the maxims of Rochefoucauld, nor a school of skepticism, like Montaigne, they are not so much read as these two ingenious books. His life of Henry VII passed for a masterpiece; but how is it possible some people should have been idle enough to compare so small a work with the history of our illustrious M. de Thou? Speaking of that famous impostor Perkin, son of a Jew convert, who assumed so boldly the name of Richard IV, king of England, being encouraged by the duchess of Burgundy, and who disputed the crown with Henry VII, he expresses himself in these terms: "About this time King Henry was beset with evil spirits, by the witchcraft of the duchess of Burgundy, who conjured up from hell the ghost of Edward IV, in order to torment King Henry. When the duchess of Burgundy had instructed Perkin, she began to consider with herself in what region of the heavens she should make this comet shine, and resolved immediately that it should make its appearance in the horizon of Ireland." I think our sage de Thou seldom gives in to this gallimaufry, which used formerly to pass for the sublime, but which at present is known by its proper title, "bombast." . . .

• • •

A Frenchman who arrives in London will find philosophy, like everything else, very much changed there. He had left the world a *plenum*, and he now finds it a *vacuum*. At Paris the universe is seen composed of vortices of subtle matter; but nothing like it is seen in London. In France it is the pressure of the moon that causes the tides; but in England it is the sea that gravitates towards the moon; so that when you think that the moon should make it flood with us, those gentlemen fancy it should be ebb, which, very unluckily, cannot be proved. For to be able to do this it is necessary the moon and the tides should have been enquired into at the very instant of the Creation.

You'll observe farther that the sun, which in France is said to have nothing to do in the affair, comes in here for very near a quarter of its assistance. According to your Cartesians, everything is performed by an impulsion, of which we have very little notion; and according to Sir Isaac Newton, it is by an attraction, the cause of which is as much unknown to us. At Paris you imagine that the earth is shaped like a melon, or of an oblique figure; at London it has an oblate one. A Cartesian declares that light exists in the air; but a Newtonian asserts that it comes from the sun in six minutes and a half. The several operations of your chemistry are performed by acids, alkalies and subtile matter; but attraction prevails even in chymistry among the English.

The very essence of things is totally changed. You neither are agreed upon the definition of the soul nor on that of matter. Descartes, as I observed in my last, maintains that the soul is the same thing with thought, and Mr. Locke has given a pretty good proof of the contrary.

Descartes asserts farther, that extension alone constitutes matter, but Sir Isaac adds solidity to it.

How furiously contradictory are these opinions!

Non nostrum inter vos tantas componere lites.
VIRGIL, ECLOG. III.

'Tis not for us to end such great Disputes.

This famous Newton, this destroyer of the Cartesian system, died in March Anno 1727. His countrymen honored him in his lifetime, and interred him as though he had been a king who had made his people happy.

The English read with the highest satisfaction, and translated into their tongue, the elogium of Sir Isaac Newton which Mr. de Fontenelle spoke in the Academy of Sciences. Mr. de Fontenelle presides as judge over philosophers; and the English expected his decision as a solemn declaration of the superiority of the English philosophy over that of the French. But when it was found that this gentleman had compared Descartes to Sir Isaac, the whole Royal Society in London rose up in arms. So far from acquiescing with Mr. de Fontenelle's judgment, they criticized his discourse. And even several (who, however, were not the ablest philosophers in that body) were offended at the comparison, and for no other reason but because Descartes was a Frenchman.

It must be confessed that these two great men differed very much in conduct, in fortune, and in philosophy.

Nature had indulged Descartes a shining and strong imagination, whence he became a very singular person both in private life and in his manner of reasoning. This imagination could not conceal itself even in his philosophical works, which are everywhere adorned with very shining, ingenious metaphors and figures. Nature had almost made him a poet; and indeed he wrote a piece of poetry for the entertainment of Christina, Queen of Sweden, which, however, was suppressed in honor to his memory.

He embraced a military life for some time, and afterwards becoming a complete philosopher, he did not think the passion of love derogatory to his character. He had by his mistress a daughter called *Froncine*, who died young and was very much regretted by him. Thus he experienced every passion incident to mankind.

He was a long time of the opinion that it would be necessary for him to fly from the society of his fellow creatures, and especially from his native country, in order to enjoy the happiness of cultivating his philosophical studies in full liberty.

Descartes was very right, for his contemporaries were not knowing enough to improve and enlighten his understanding, and were capable of little else than of giving him uneasiness.

He left France purely to go in search of truth, which was then persecuted by the wretched philosophy of the Schools. However, he found that reason was as much disguised and depraved in the universities of Holland, into which he withdrew, as in his own country. For at the time that the French condemned the only propositions of his philosophy which were true, he was persecuted by the pretended philosophers of Holland, who understood him no better, and who, having a nearer view of his glory, hated his person the more, so that he was obliged to leave Utrecht. Descartes was injuriously accused of being an atheist, the last refuge of religious scandal; and he who had employed all the sagacity and penetration of his genius in searching for new proofs of the existence of a God was suspected to believe there was no such Being.

Such a persecution from all sides must necessarily suppose a most exalted merit as well as a very distinguished reputation, and indeed he possessed both. Reason at that time darted a ray upon the world through the gloom of the Schools and the prejudices of popular superstition. At last his name spread so universally that the French were desirous of bringing him back into his native country by rewards, and accordingly offered him an annual pension of a thousand crowns. Upon these hopes Descartes returned to France, paid the fees of his patent, which was sold at that time, but no pension was settled upon him. Thus disappointed, he returned to his solitude in North Holland, where he again pursued the study of philosophy, whilst the great Galileo, at fourscore years of age, was groaning in the prisons of the Inquisition, only for having demonstrated the earth's motion.

At last Descartes was snatched from the world in the flower of his age at Stockholm. His death was owing to a bad regimen, and he expired in the midst of some *literati* who were his enemies, and under the hands of a physician to whom he was odious.

The progress of Sir Isaac Newton's life was quite different. He lived happy and very much honored in his native country, to the age of fourscore and five years.

It was his peculiar felicity not only to be born in a country of liberty, but in an age when all Scholastic impertinencies were banished from the world. Reason alone was cultivated, and mankind could only be his pupil, not his enemy.

One very singular difference in the lives of these two great men is that Sir Isaac, during the long course of years he enjoyed, was never sensible to any passion, was not subject to the common frailties of mankind, nor ever had any commerce with women; a circumstance which was assured me by the physician and surgeon who attended him in his last moments.

We may admire Sir Isaac Newton on this occasion, but then we must not censure Descartes.

The opinion that generally prevails in *England* with regard to these two philosophers is that the latter was a dreamer and the former a sage.

Very few people in England read Descartes, whose works indeed are now useless. On the other side, but a small number peruse those of Sir Isaac, because to do this the student must be deeply skilled in the mathematics, otherwise those works will be unintelligible to him. But notwithstanding this, these great men are the subject of everyone's discourse. Sir Isaac Newton is allowed every advantage, whilst Descartes is not indulged a single one. According to some, it is to the former that we owe the discovery of a vacuum, that the air is a heavy body, and the invention of telescopes. In a word, Sir Isaac Newton is here as the

Hercules of fabulous story, to whom the ignorant ascribed all the feats of ancient heroes.

In a critique that was made in London on Mr. de Fontenelle's discourse, the writer presumed to assert that Descartes was not a great geometrician. Those who make such a declaration may justly be reproached with flying in their master's face. Descartes extended the limits of geometry as far beyond the place where he found them as Sir Isaac did after him. The former first taught the method of expressing curves by equations. This geometry, which, thanks to him for it, is now grown common, was so abstruse in his time that not so much as one professor would undertake to explain it; and Schotten in Holland, and Format in France, were the only men who understood it.

He applied this geometrical and inventive genius to dioptrics, which, when treated of by him, became a new art. And if he was mistaken in some things, the reason of that is, a man who discovers a new tract of land cannot at once know all the properties of the soil. Those who come after him, and make these Lands fruitful, are at least obliged to him for the discovery. I will not deny but that there are innumerable errors in the rest of Descartes's works.

Geometry was a guide he himself had in some measure fashioned, which would have conducted him safely through the several paths of natural philosophy. Nevertheless he at last abandoned this guide, and gave entirely into the humor of forming hypotheses; and then philosophy was no more than an ingenious romance, fit only to amuse the ignorant. He was mistaken in the nature of the soul, in the proofs of the existence of a God, in matter, in the laws of motion, and in the nature of light. He admitted innate ideas, he invented new elements, he created a world; he made Man according to his own fancy; and it is justly said that the Man of Descartes is in fact that of Descartes only, very different from the real one.

He pushed his metaphysical errors so far as to declare that two and two make four for no other reason but because God would have it so. However, it will not be making him too great a compliment if we affirm that he was valuable even in his mistakes. He deceived himself, but then it was at least in a methodical way. He destroyed all the absurd chimaeras with which youth had been infatuated for two thousand years. He taught his contemporaries how to reason, and enabled them to employ his own weapons against himself. If Descartes did not pay in good money, he however did great service in crying down that of a base alloy.

I indeed believe that very few will presume to compare his philosophy in any respect with that of Sir Isaac Newton. The former is an essay, the latter a masterpiece. But then the man who first brought us to the path of truth was perhaps as great a genius as he who afterwards conducted us through it.

Descartes gave sight to the blind. These saw the errors of antiquity and of the sciences. The path he struck out is since become boundless. Rohault's little work was during some years a complete system of physics; but now all the transactions of the several academies in Europe put together do not form so much as the beginning of a system. In fathoming this abyss no bottom has been found. We are now to examine what discoveries Sir Isaac Newton has made in it.

THE RAT

Comte de Buffon

Classification, minute observation, and factual description are essential to scientific inquiry. Georges Louis Leclerc, comte de Buffon (1707–1788), was a French naturalist recognized as a master of this genre. The following is an excerpt from his Natural History of Animals, Vegetables and Minerals, *written in 1767.*

If we descend by degrees from the great to the small, from the strong to the weak, we shall find that Nature has uniformly maintained a balance; that, attentive only to the preservation of each species, she creates a profusion of individuals, and is supported by the numbers which she has formed of a diminutive size, and which she has denied weapons, denied either strength or courage; and that she has not only taken care that these inferior species should be in a condition to resist, or to maintain their ground by the abundance of their own number, but has likewise provided a supplement, as it were, to each, by multiplying the species which nearly resemble or approach them. The rat, the mouse, the *mulot*, or field-mouse, the water-rat, the *campagnol*, or little field rat, the *loir*, or great dor-mouse, the *lerot*, or middle dor-mouse; the *muscardin*, or small dor-mouse, the *musaraigne*, or shrew-mouse, with many others which I shall not enumerate here, as they are strangers to our climate, form so many distinct and separate species, but yet so little varied, that should any of the others fail, they might so well supply their places that their absence would be hardly perceptible. It is this great number of approximate species that first gave naturalists the idea of *genera*; an idea which can never be employed unless when we view objects in the gross, and which vanishes when we come to consider Nature minutely, and as she really is.

Men began by appropriating different names to things which appeared to them absolutely distinct and different, and at the same time they gave general denominations to such as seemed to bear a near resemblance to each other. Among nations rude and unenlightened, and in all infant languages, there are hardly any but general names, that is to say, vague and unformed expressions of things which, though of the same order, are yet in themselves highly different. Thus, the oak, the beech, the linden, the fir, the yew, the pine, had at first no name but that of tree; afterwards the oak, the beech, the linden, were all three called *oak*, when they came to be distinguished from the fir, the pine, and the yew, which in like manner would be distinguished by the name of *fir*. Particular names proceeded solely, in process of time, from the comparison and minute examination of things. Of these the number was encreased in proportion as the works of Nature were more studied, and better understood; and the more we shall continue to examine and compare them, the greater number there will be of proper names, and of particular denominations. When in these days, therefore, Nature is presented to us by general denominations, that is, by genera, it is sending us back to the ABC, or first rudiments of all knowledge, and to the infant-darkness of mankind. Ignorance produced *genera*, and science produced, and will continue to produce, proper names; nor of these shall we be afraid to increase the number, whenever we shall have occasion to denote different species.

Under the generical name of rat, people have comprised and confounded several species of little animals. This name we shall solely appropriate to the common rat, which is black, and lives in our houses. Each of the other species shall have its particular denomination; for as neither of them couple together, each is, in reality, different from all the rest. The rat is well enough known by the trouble he gives us. It generally inhabits barns, and other places where corn and fruit are stored; and from these it proceeds, and invades our dwellings. This animal is carnivorous, and even, if the expression is allowable, *omnivorous*. Hard substances, however, it prefers to soft ones: it devours wool, stuffs, and furniture of all sorts; eats through wood, makes hiding places in walls, thence issues in search of prey, and frequently returns with as much as it is able to drag along with it, forming, especially when it has young ones to provide for, a magazine of the whole. The females bring forth several times in the year, though mostly in the summer season; and they usually produce five or six at a birth. They search for warm places; and in winter they generally shelter themselves about the chimnies of houses, or among hay and straw.

In defiance of the cats, and notwithstanding the poison, the traps, and every other method that is used to destroy these creatures, they multiply so fast as frequently to do considerable damage. In old houses in the country especially, where great quantities of corn are kept, and where the neighboring barns and haystacks favor their retreat, as well as their multiplication, they are often so numerous that the inhabitants would be obliged to remove with their furniture, were they not to devour each other. This we have often by experience found to be the case when they have been in any degree straitened for provisions; and the method they take to lessen their numbers is for the stronger to fall upon the weaker. This done, they lay open their skulls, and first eat up the brains, afterwards the rest of the body. The next day hostilities are renewed in the same manner; nor do they suspend their havoc till the majority are destroyed. For this reason it is that after any place has for a long while been infested with rats, they often seem to disappear of a sudden, and sometimes for a considerable time. It is the same with the field-mice, whose prodigious encrease is checked solely by their cruelties towards each other, when they begin to be in want of food. Aristotle attributes this sudden destruction to the rain; but rats are not exposed to the weather, and field-mice know well how to secure themselves from it, their subterranean habitations being never even moistened.

The rat is an animal as salacious as it is voracious. They have a kind of yelp when they engender; and when they fight, they cry. They prepare a bed for their young, and provide them immediately with food. On their first quitting the hole, she watches over, defends, and will even fight the cats, in order to save them. A large rat is more mischievous, and almost as strong, as a young cat. Its foreteeth are long and strong; and as the cat does not bite so hard, as she can do little execution except with her claws, she must be not only vigorous, but well experienced to conquer. The weasel, though smaller in size, is yet a more dangerous enemy to the rat, and is more feared by it, because he is capable of following it into its hiding-places. The combat between these two animals is generally sharp and long; their strength is at least equal, but their manner of fighting is different. The rat cannot inflict any wounds but by snatches, and with its foreteeth, which, however, being rather calculated for gnawing than for biting, have but little strength; whereas the weasel bites fiercely with the force of its whole jaw at once, and instead of letting go its hold, sucks the blood through the wound. In every conflict with an enemy so formidable, it is no wonder, therefore, that the rat should fall a victim.

There are many varieties in this as in every other species of which the individuals are very numerous. Beside the common black rat there are some which are brown, and some almost black; some which are grey, inclining to white or red, and some altogether white. The white rat, like the white mouse, the white rabbit, and all other animals which are entirely of that color, has red eyes. The white species, with all its varieties, appears to belong to the temperate climates of our continent, and have been diffused in much greater abundance over hot countries than cold ones. Originally they had none in America; and those which are to be found there in such numbers at this day are the produce of rats which accidentally obtained a footing on the other side of the Atlantic with the first European settlers. Of these the increase was so great that the rat was long considered as the pest of the colonies; where indeed it had hardly an enemy to oppose it but the large adder, which swallows it up alive. The European ships have likewise carried these animals to the East Indies, into all the islands of the Indian Archipelago, as well as into Africa, where they are found in great numbers. In the North, on the contrary, they have hardly multiplied beyond Sweden; and those which are called Norway rats, in Lapland, etc., are animals different from our rats.

THE UTILITY OF SCIENCE

Marquis de Condorcet

Condorcet was a distinguished mathematician as well as political activist and writer. In the ninth stage of his Sketch for a Historical Picture of the Human Mind *(1794), he offered a veritable hymn to science and its usefulness in human affairs.*

We may endeavor more especially to trace that practice of genius in the sciences which at one time descends from an abstract and profound theory to learned and delicate applications; at another, simplifying its means, and proportioning them to its wants, concludes by spreading its advantages through the most ordinary practices; it plunges into the most remote speculations, in fear of resources which the ordinary state of our knowledge must have refused.

We may remark that those arguments which are made against the utility of theories, even in the most simple arts, have never shown any thing but the ignorance of the declaimers. We may prove that it is not to the profundity of these theories, but, on the contrary, to their imperfection, that we ought to attribute the inutility or unhappy effects of so many useless applications.

These observations will lead us to one general truth, that in all the arts the results of theory are necessarily modified in practice; that certain sources of inaccuracy exist, which are really inevitable, of which our aim should be to render the effect insensible, without indulging the chimerical hope of removing them; that a great number of data relative to our wants, our means, our time, and our expenses, which are necessarily overlooked in the theory, must enter into the relative problem of immediate and real practice; and that, lastly, by introducing these requisites with that skill which truly constitutes the genius of the practical man, we may at the same time go beyond the narrow limits wherein prejudice against theory threatens to detain the arts, and prevent those errors into which an improper use of theory might lead us.

Those sciences which are remote from each other cannot be extended without bringing them nearer and forming points of contact between them.

An exposition of the progress of each science is sufficient to show that in several the intermediate application of numbers has been useful, as, in almost all, it has been employed to give a greater degree of precision to experiments and observations; and that the sciences are indebted to mechanics, which has supplied them with more perfect and more accurate instruments. How much have the discovery of microscopes, and of meteorological instruments, contributed to the perfection of natural history? How greatly is this science indebted to chemistry, which, alone, has been sufficient to lead to a more profound knowledge of the objects it considers, by displaying their most intimate nature, and most essential properties—by showing their composition and elements; while natural history offers to chemistry so many operations to execute, such a numerous set of combinations formed by nature, the true elements of which require to be separated, and sometimes discovered, by an imitation of the natural processes; and, lastly, how great is the mutual assistance afforded to each other by chemistry and natural philosophy; and how greatly have anatomy and natural history been already benefited by these sciences.

But we have yet exposed no more than a small portion of the advantages which have been received, or may be expected, from these applications.

Many geometers have given us general methods of deducing, from observations of the empiric laws of phenomena, methods which extend to all the sciences; because they are in all cases capable of affording us the knowledge of the law of the successive values of the same quantity, for a series of instants or positions; or that law according to which they are distributed, or which is followed by the various properties and values of a similar quality among a given number of objects.

Applications have already proved, that the science of combination may be successfully employed to dispose observations, in such a manner, that their relations, results, and sum may with more facility be seen.

The uses of the calculation of probabilities foretell how much they may be applied to advance the progress of other sciences; in one case, to determine the probability of extraordinary facts, and to show whether they ought to be rejected, or whether, on the contrary, they ought to be verified; or in calculating the probability of the return of those facts which often present themselves in the practice of the arts, and are not connected together in an order, yet considered as a general law. Such, for example, in medicine, is the salutary effect of certain remedies, and the success of certain preservatives. These applications likewise show us how great is the probability that a series of phenomena should result from the intention of a thinking being; whether this being depends on other co-existent, or antecedent phenomena; and how much ought to be attributed to the necessary and unknown cause denominated chance, a word the sense of which can only be known with precision by studying this method of computing.

The sciences have likewise taught us to ascertain the several degrees of certainty to which we may hope to attain; the probability according to which we can adopt an opinion, and make it the basis of our reasonings, without injuring the rights of sound argument, and the rules of our conduct—without deficiency in prudence, or offense to justice. They show what are the advantages or disadvantages of various forms of election, and modes of decision dependent on the plurality of voices; the different degrees of probability which may result from such proceedings; the method which public interest requires to be followed, according to the nature of each question; the means of obtaining it nearly with certainty, when the decision is not absolutely necessary, or when the inconveniences of two conclusions being unequal, neither of them can become legitimate until beneath this probability; or the assurance beforehand of most frequently obtaining this same probability, when, on the contrary, a decision is necessary to be made, and the most feeble preponderance of probability is sufficient to produce a rule of practice.

Among the number of these applications we may likewise state, an examination of the probability of facts for the use of such as have not the power, or means, to support their conclusions upon their own observations; a probability which results either from the authority of witnesses, or the connection of those facts with others immediately observed.

How greatly have inquiries into the duration of human life, and the influence in this respect of sex, temperature, climate, profession, government, and habitudes of life; on the mortality which results from different diseases; the changes which population experiences; the extent of the action of different causes which produce these changes; the manner of its distribution in each country, according to the age, sex, and occupation—how greatly useful have these researches been to the physical knowledge of man, to medicine, and to public economy.

How extensively have computations of this nature been applied for the establishment of annuities, tontines, accumulating funds, benefit societies, and chambers of assurance of every kind.

Is not the application of numbers also necessary to that part of the public economy which includes the theory of public measures, of coin, of banks and financial operations, and lastly, that of taxation, as established by law, and its real distribution, which so frequently differs, in its effects on all the parts of the social system.

What a number of important questions in this same science are there, which could not have been properly resolved without the knowledge acquired in natural history, agriculture, and the philosophy of vegetables, which influence the mechanical or chemical arts.

In a word, such has been the general progress of the sciences, that it may be said there is not one which can be considered as to the whole extent of its principles and detail, without our being obliged to borrow the assistance of all the others.

In presenting this sketch both of the new facts which have enriched the sciences respectively, and the advantages derived in each from the application of theories, or methods, which seem to belong more particularly to another department of knowledge, we may endeavor to ascertain what is the nature and the limits of those truths to which observation, experience, or meditation, may lead us in each science; we may likewise investigate what it is precisely that constitutes that talent of invention which is the first faculty of the human mind, and is known by the name of genius; by what operations the understanding may attain the discoveries it pursues, or sometimes be led to others not sought, or even possible to have been foretold; we may show how far the methods which lead to discovery may be exhausted, so that science may, in a certain respect, be at a stand, till new methods are invented to afford an additional instrument to genius, or to facilitate the use of those which cannot be employed without too great a consumption of time and fatigue.

If we confine ourselves to exhibit the advantages deduced from the sciences in their immediate use or application to the arts, whether for the welfare of individuals or the prosperity of nations, we shall have shown only a small part of the benefits they afford. The most important perhaps is, that prejudice has been destroyed, and the human understanding in some sort rectified; after having been forced into a wrong direction by absurd objects of belief, transmitted from generation to generation, taught at the misjudging period of infancy, and enforced with the terrors of superstition and the dread of tyranny.

All the errors in politics and in morals are founded upon philosophical mistakes, which, themselves, are connected with physical errors. There does not exist any religious system, or supernatural extravagance, which is not founded on an ignorance of the laws of nature. The inventors and defenders of these absurdities could not foresee the successive progress of the human mind. Being persuaded that the men of their time knew everything they would ever know, and would always believe that in which they then had fixed their faith; they confidently built their reveries upon the general opinions of their own country and their own age.

The progress of natural knowledge is yet more destructive of these errors, because it frequently destroys them without seeming to attack them, by attaching to those who obstinately defend them the degrading ridicule of ignorance.

At the same time, the just habit of reasoning on the object of these sciences, the precise ideas which their methods afford, and the means of ascertaining or proving the truth, must naturally lead us to compare the sentiment which forces us to adhere to opinions founded on these real motives of credibility, and that which attaches us to our habitual prejudices, or forces us to yield to authority. This comparison is sufficient to teach us to mistrust these last opinions, to show that they were not really believed, even when that belief was the most earnestly and the most sincerely professed. When this discovery is once made, their destruction becomes much more speedy and certain.

Lastly, this progress of the physical sciences, which the passions and interest do not interfere to disturb; wherein it is not thought that birth, profession, or appointment have given a right to judge what the individual is not in a situation to understand; this more certain progress cannot be observed, unless enlightened men shall search in the other sciences to bring them continually together. This progress at every step exhibits the model they ought to follow; according to which they may form a judgment of their own efforts, ascertain the false steps they may have taken, preserve themselves from pyrrhonism as well as credulity, and from a blind mistrust or too extensive submission to the authorities even of men of reputation and knowledge.

The metaphysical analysis would, no doubt, lead to the same results, but it would have afforded only abstract principles. In this method, the same abstract principles being put into action, are enlightened by example and fortified by success.

Until the present epoch, the sciences have been the patrimony only of a few; but they are already become common, and the moment approaches in which their elements, their principles, and their most simple practice will become really popular. Then it will be seen how truly universal their utility will be in their application to the arts, and their influence on the general rectitude of the mind.

THE ORGANIZATION OF SCIENTIFIC RESEARCH

Joseph Priestley

One of the Enlightenment's greatest scientists was the Englishman Joseph Priestley (1733–1804), the discoverer of oxygen. Convinced that America was the natural home of the scientific spirit, Priestley emigrated there and is today buried in Northumberland, Pennsylvania. The selection that follows, his proposal for systematic scientific research, is from his History and Present State of Electricity *(1767).*

The business of [natural] philosophy is so multiplied, that all the books of general philosophical transactions cannot be purchased by many persons, or read by any person. It is high time to subdivide the business, that every man may have an opportunity of seeing everything that relates to his own favorite pursuit; and all the various branches of philosophy would find their account in this amicable separation. Thus the numerous branches of a large overgrown family, in the patriarchical ages, found it necessary to separate; and the convenience of the whole, and the strength and increase of each branch were promoted by the separation. Let the youngest daughter of the science set the example to the rest, and show that she thinks herself considerable enough to make her appearance in the world without the company of her sisters.

But before this general separation, let each collect together everything that belongs to her, and march off with her whole stock. To drop the allusion; let histories be written of all that has been done in every particular branch of science, and let the whole be seen at one view. And when once the entire progress, and present state of every science shall be fully and fairly exhibited, I doubt not but we shall see a new and capital era commence in the history of all the sciences. Such an easy, full, and comprehensive view of what has been done hitherto could not fail to give new life to philosophical enquiries. It would suggest an infinity of new experiments, and would undoubtedly greatly accelerate the progress of knowledge; which is at present retarded, as it were, by its own weight, and the mutual entanglement of its several parts.

I will just throw out a farther hint, of what, I think, might be favorable to the increase of philosophical knowledge. At present there are, in different countries in Europe, large incorporate societies, with funds for promoting philosophical knowledge in general. Let philosophers now begin to subdivide themselves, and enter into smaller combinations. Let the several companies make small funds, and appoint a director of experiments. Let every member have a right to appoint the trial of experiments in some proportion to the sum he subscribes, and let a periodical account be published of the result of them all, successful or unsuccessful. In this manner, the powers of all the members would be united and increased. Nothing would be left untried, which could be compassed at a moderate expense, and it being *one person's business* to attend to these experiments, they would be made, and reported without loss of time. Moreover, as all incorporations in these smaller societies should be avoided, they would be encouraged only in proportion as they were found to be useful; and success in smaller things would excite them to attempt greater.

I by no means disapprove of large, general, and incorporated societies. They have their peculiar uses too; but we see by experience, that they are apt to grow too large, and their forms are too slow for the dispatch of the *minutiæ* of business, in the present multifarious state of philosophy. Let recourse be had to rich incorporated societies, to defray the expense of experiments, to which the funds of smaller societies shall be unequal. Let their transactions contain a summary of the more important discoveries, collected from the smaller periodical publications. Let them, by rewards, and other methods, encourage those who distinguish themselves in the inferior societies; and thus give a general attention to the whole business of philosophy.

I wish all the incorporated philosophical societies in Europe would join their funds (and I wish they were sufficient for the purpose) to fit out ships for the complete discovery of the face of the earth, and for many capital experiments which can only be made in such extensive voyages.

Princes will never do this great business to any purpose. The spirit of adventure seems to be totally extinct in the present race of merchants. This discovery is a grand desideratum in science; and where may this pure and noble enthusiasm for such discoveries be expected but among philosophers, men uninfluenced by motives either of policy or gain? Let us think ourselves happy if princes give no obstruction to such designs. Let them fight for the countries when they are discovered, and let merchants scramble for the advantage that may be made of them. It will be an acquisition to philosophers if the seat of war be removed so far from the seat of science; and fresh room will be given to the exertion of genius in trade, when the old beaten track is deserted, when the old system of traffic is unhinged, and when new and more extensive plans of commerce take place. I congratulate the present race of philosophers on what is doing by the English court in this way; for with whatever view expeditions into the South Seas are made, they cannot but be favorable to philosophy.

Natural Philosophy is a science which more especially requires the aid of wealth. Many others require nothing but what a man's own reflection may furnish him with. They who cultivate them find within themselves everything they want. But experimental philosophy is not so independent. Nature will not be put out of her way, and suffer her materials to be thrown into all that variety of situations which philosophy requires, in order to discover her wonderful powers, without trouble and expense. Hence the patronage of the great is essential to the flourishing state of this science. Others may project great improvements, but they only have the power of carrying them into execution.

Besides, they are the higher classes of men which are most interested in the extension of all kinds of natural knowledge; as they are most able to avail themselves of any discoveries, which lead to the felicity and embellishment of human life. Almost all the elegancies of life are the produce of those polite arts, which could have had no existence without natural science, and which receive daily improvements from the same source. From the great and the opulent, therefore, these sciences have a natural claim for protection; and it is evidently their interest not to suffer promising enquiries to be suspended for want of the means of prosecuting them.

But other motives, besides this selfish one, may reasonably be supposed to attach persons in the higher ranks of life to the sciences; motives more exalted, and flowing from the most extensive benevolence. From Natural Philosophy have flowed all those great inventions, by means of which mankind in general are able to subsist with more ease, and in greater numbers upon the face of the earth. Hence arise the capital advantages of men above brutes, and of civilization above barbarity. And by these sciences also it is, that the views of the human mind itself are enlarged, and our common nature improved and ennobled. It is for the honor of the species, therefore, that these sciences should be cultivated with the utmost attention.

And of whom may these enlarged views, comprehensive of such great objects, be expected, but of those whom divine providence has raised above the rest of mankind. Being free from most of the cares peculiar to individuals, they may embrace the interests of the whole species, feel for the wants of mankind, and be concerned to support the dignity of human nature.

Gladly would I indulge the hope, that we shall soon see these motives operating in a more extensive manner than they have hitherto done; that by the illustrious example of a few, a taste for natural science will be excited in many, in whom it will operate the most effectually to the advantage of science and of the world; and that all kinds of philosophical enquiries will, henceforward, be conducted with more spirit, and with more success than ever.

Were I to pursue this subject, it would carry me far beyond the reasonable bounds of a preface. I shall therefore conclude with mentioning that sentiment, which ought to be uppermost in the mind of every philosopher, whatever be the immediate object of his pursuit; that speculation is only of use as it leads to *practice*, that the immediate use of natural science is the power it gives us over nature, by means of the knowledge we acquire of its laws; whereby human life is, in its present state, made more comfortable and happy; but that the greatest, and noblest use of philosophical speculation is the discipline of the heart, and the opportunity it affords of inculcating benevolent and pious sentiments upon the mind.

A philosopher ought to be something greater, and better than another man. The contemplation of the works of God should give a sublimity to his virtue, should expand his benevolence, extinguish everything mean, base, and selfish in his nature, give a dignity to all his sentiments, and teach him to aspire to the moral perfections of the great author of all things. What great and exalted beings would philosophers be, would they but let the objects about which they are conversant have their proper and moral effect upon their minds! A life spent in the contemplation of the productions of divine power, wisdom, and goodness, would be a life of devotion. The more we see of the wonderful structure of the world, and of the laws of nature, the more clearly do we comprehend their admirable uses, to make all the percipient creation happy: a sentiment, which cannot but fill the heart with unbounded love, gratitude and joy.

Even everything painful and disagreeable in the world appears to a philosopher, upon a more attentive examination, to be excellently provided, as a remedy of some greater inconvenience, or a necessary means of a much greater happiness; so that, from this elevated point of view, he sees all temporary evils and inconveniences to vanish, in the glorious prospect of the greater good to which they are subservient. Hence he is able to venerate and rejoice in God, not only in the bright sunshine, but also in the darkest shades of nature, whereas vulgar minds are apt to be disconcerted with the appearance of evil.

LETTER TO JOSEPH PRIESTLEY

BENJAMIN FRANKLIN

Internationally renowned as a scientist, statesman, and writer, Franklin (1706–1790) in this letter articulates the quintessential Enlightenment utopian vision of science as the handmaiden of progress.

PASSY, Feb. 8, 1780.

DEAR SIR,

Your kind letter of September 27 came to hand but very lately, the bearer having stayed long in Holland. I always rejoice to hear of your being still employed in experimental researches into nature, and of the Success you meet with. The rapid Progress *true* Science now makes, occasions my regretting sometimes that I was born so soon. It is impossible to imagine the height to which may be carried, in a thousand years, the power of man over matter. We may perhaps learn to deprive large masses of their gravity, and give them absolute levity, for the sake of easy transport. Agriculture may diminish its labor and double its produce; all diseases may by sure means be prevented or cured, not excepting even that of old age, and our lives lengthened at pleasure even beyond the antediluvian standard. O that moral science were in as fair a way of improvement, that men would cease to be wolves to one another, and that human beings would at length learn what they now improperly call humanity!

I am glad my little paper on the *Aurora Borealis* pleased. If it should occasion further enquiry, and so produce a better hypothesis, it will not be wholly useless. I am ever, with the greatest and most sincere esteem, dear sir, yours very affectionately

B. FRANKLIN.

PART III

REASON AND GOD

ON SUPERSTITION AND TOLERANCE

PIERRE BAYLE

The writings of the French Protestant scholar Pierre Bayle (1647–1706) anticipated and inspired the philosophes, *especially with respect to religion. These selections are from his* Miscellaneous Thoughts on the Comet of 1680 *(1682) and* Philosophical Commentary on the Words of Jesus Christ, "Compel Them to Come In" *(1686–1687).*

Now let us undertake the task of considering whether or not the general agreement among ancients and moderns that comets are evil omens should bear much weight. Again I say, it is pure illusion to claim that a notion that has passed from one century to the next, from generation to generation, cannot be entirely false. If only we examine the causes of the establishment of certain opinions in the world about us, we readily see that nothing is less reasonable than such a claim. You will certainly grant me that it is easy to persuade the people of certain false opinions which are in accordance with the prejudices of childhood or the desires of the heart, as are all the so-called rules in regard to omens. That is all I ask, for that admission is enough to perpetuate such opinions forever; for except for a few philosophical minds, no one thinks of submitting to examination what is universally held to be true. We assume that the ancients once examined it and were sufficiently on their guard against error; and therefore we teach it in our turn to our children as infallible fact. If you remember, too, what I have said elsewhere about man's intellectual indolence and the pains that must be taken for thorough reconsideration, you will see that we will not say, with Minucius Felix, "Everything is uncertain in human affairs, but the more uncertain it is, the more reason to be astonished that some, disgusted with the exacting search for the truth, prefer rashly to embrace the first opinion that lies at hand, rather than take the time and the care that deep thought requires"; we should rather say, "The more uncertain everything is, the less reason we have to be astonished at such a solution." The author of the *Art of Thinking* observes very judiciously that most men decide to accept one notion rather than another because of certain superficial and extraneous traits which they consider to be more in conformity with truth than with falsehood and which are easily discernible; whereas solid and essential reasons which reveal truth are difficult to come by. Hence, since men are prone to follow the easier course, they almost always take the side on which these superficial traits are apparent.

It is a common occurrence to see people avoid marriage in the month of May, because it has been believed from time immemorial that May weddings bring bad luck; and I have no doubt that this superstition, which came down to us from ancient Rome and was founded on the fact that the festival of evil spirits, or Lemuralia, was celebrated in May, will subsist among Christians until the end of time. For it will be kept alive in a family, if only it is remembered that some grandfather or uncle took such precautions. And the reasoning becomes invincible and all the more impressive when we see intelligent people observe the same practice. In fact many persons, not superstitious themselves, delay or speed up their marriage to avoid the month of May, because it is important that the belief should not be spread around that they have courted misfortune. In this society of ours, all precautions should be taken. A merchant can become truly unlucky just because people entertain the ridiculous idea that he is threatened with bad luck; for no one will be willing to extend him credit or associate in business with him. If anyone wanted to seek out all the reasons for popular misconceptions, it would be an unending task. . . .

That man is a reasoning animal, we are all agreed; it is no less true that he almost never acts in accordance with his principles. He is well able, in speculative matters, to avoid drawing false conclusions, for in this field he sins much less through the ease with which he entertains false principles than through the false suppositions that he derives from them. But in questions of moral conduct, it is an entirely different matter.

Almost never yielding to false principles and almost always retaining in his conscience ideas of natural equity, he nevertheless almost always concludes to the advantage of his unbridled desires. Tell me, please, how it happens that although there exists among men a prodigious diversity of opinion concerning the manner of serving God and living according to the laws of propriety, we see nonetheless that certain passions constantly hold sway in all countries and have done so through all ages; that ambition, avarice, envy, the desire for vengeance, indecency, all the crimes that satisfy these passions are everywhere apparent; that the Jew, the Mohammedan, the Turk, and the Moor, Christian and infidel, Indian and Tartar, continentals and islanders, noblemen and commoners, all these kinds of people who, in other respects, we might say have only their humanity in common, are so alike in respect to these passions that we would think they copy one another? How can all that be true unless we admit that the true principle of all our actions (I except those in whom the grace of the Holy Spirit is fully operative) is our temperament, our natural inclination to seek pleasure, the taste that we acquire for certain objects, the desire to please someone, a habit contracted in dealing with our friends, or some other disposition which arises from the depths of our natures, in whatever country we may be born, and with whatsoever knowledge our minds may be imbued?

That must be so, since the ancient heathen, overwhelmed with an unbelievable multitude of superstitions, perpetually busy appeasing the anger of their gods, terrified by an infinity of prodigies, imagining that the gods were dispensers of adversity and prosperity according to the lives that they had led, did not fail to commit all crimes imaginable. And if that were not so, how would it be possible that Christians, who know so clearly through a revelation upheld by so many miracles that they must renounce vice in order to be eternally happy and not to be eternally damned; who have such excellent preachers to present to them in these matters the most vivid and pressing exhortations possible; who have all around them so many zealous and learned directors of conscience and so many books of devotion; how would it be possible, I say, that in the midst of all that, Christians could lead, as they do, the most sinful of lives? . . .

The charge has sometimes been made against Christians that the principles of the Gospel are not suited to safeguarding the commonwealth, because they undermine courage and inspire horror for blood and all the violence of war. . . .

Evangelical courage only makes us despise the insults of poverty, the persecution of tyrants, prisons, torture, and all the throes of martyrdom. It quite properly makes us brave with heroic patience the most inhuman rage of persecutors of the faith. It resigns us to the will of God in the most painful of maladies. In that consists the courage of the true Christian. That is enough, I confess, to convince infidels that our religion does not undermine courage and inspire cowardice. But that does not prevent them from being able to say with reason that if we take the word courage in its commonly accepted sense, the Gospel is not apt to foster it. It is understood that by a courageous man we mean a man who makes it a point of honor not to suffer the least insult, who avenges himself gloriously and at the peril of his life for the slightest offense given him; who loves war, seeks the most perilous occasions to dip his hands in the blood of enemies, who is ambitious and wants to shine above all other men. It would be completely nonsensical to say that the counsels and precepts of Jesus Christ inspire us with that spirit; for it is a notorious conviction among all who know the first elements of the Christian religion that it recommends above all else that we suffer insults, walk humbly, love our neighbor, seek peace, and render good for evil, and abstain from every semblance of violence. I defy all living men, no matter how expert they may be in the military arts, ever to make good soldiers of an army in which are found only men resolved to follow punctually all these maxims. The best that could be expected would be that they would not be afraid to die for their country and their God. But I leave it to those who know what war is to decide if that is sufficient to qualify as a good soldier and if men who want to succeed in that calling must not inflict all possible harm on the enemy, outguess him, take him by surprise, put him to the sword, burn his supplies, reduce him to starvation and destitution. . . .

It may be said that if the principles of Christianity were truly followed, we would see no conqueror among Christians nor offensive war, and we would restrict ourselves to a defense against the invasions of infidels. That being so, how many nations in Europe would we see enjoying a profound peace for very long who because of that would be the least fit of all peoples in the world to wage war? It is therefore true that the spirit of our holy religion does not make us warlike: and yet there are no more warlike nations on the face of the earth than those which make a profession of Christianity. . . .

We Christians daily improve upon the art of war by inventing an infinite number of machines to make sieges more deadly and horrible; and from us Christians infidels learn to use better weapons. I know very well that we do not do that because we are Christians, but because we are more skillful than infidels: for if they were clever and valorous enough to wage war better than Christians they would do so without fail. Nevertheless I find here a very convincing argument to prove that in daily life we do not follow the principles of our religion, since I show that Christians employ all their knowledge and passions in improving upon the art of war, without the slightest hindrance from a knowledge of the Gospel in pursuing this cruel design.

• • •

If a multiplicity of religions is harmful to the State, that is only because one religion will not tolerate the other but wants rather to swallow it up by dint of persecution. *Hinc prima mali labes,* that is where trouble begins. If each religion adopted the spirit of tolerance that I recommend, there would be the same concord in a state with ten religions as in a city in which different artisans and craftsmen mutually support one another. The most that could happen would be honest rivalry in outdoing one another in piety, good conduct and knowledge; each religion would take pride in proving its favored share of God's love by exhibiting a firmer attachment to moral conduct; all would boast of greater love for their country, if the sovereign protected them all and through his justice held them in balance. Such handsome emulation would give rise to innumerable blessings; consequently toleration is of all things the most conducive to the return of the golden age and the formation of a concert and harmony of a number of voices and instruments of different tones and notes as agreeable at the very least as the uniformity of a single voice. What then prevents this beautiful concert composed of such different voices and tones? It is only because one of two religions wants to exercise cruel tyranny over men's minds and force others to act against their conscience; because kings foment this unjust partiality and lend secular force to the furious and tumultuous desires of a populace of monks and clerics; in short the whole disorder springs not from toleration but from non-toleration. . . .

It is impossible in our present condition to know with certainty whether or not what appears to us to be the truth (I am speaking of the particular truths of religion and not of the properties of numbers or the first principles of metaphysics or the demonstrations of geometry) is absolute truth; the best we can do is to be fully convinced that we hold to absolute truth, that we are right and other people are wrong, all very dubious indications of truth, since they can be found among pagans and the most damnable of heretics. It is therefore certain that there is no trustworthy indication which will enable us among our beliefs to distinguish the true from the false. This distinction cannot be deduced from evidence; for on the contrary everyone says that the truths of God's revealed word are profound mysteries which require us to surrender our intelligence in obedience to the Faith. This is not because of incomprehensibility, for what is more false and altogether incomprehensible than a squared circle, than an essentially vicious first principle, than God a father through carnal generation, as Jupiter was among the pagans? Nor is it to satisfy our conscience, for a Papist is as satisfied with his religion, and a Turk and a Jew with theirs, as we are with ours. Nor is it because of the courage and zeal that belief inspires, for the falsest of religions have their martyrs, their incredible austerities, their spirit of proselytism which very often overcomes the charity of true believers, and their unshakable attachment to superstitious ceremonies. Nothing in short can assure a man of the distinction between truth and falsehood. Thus it is asking too much of him to hope that he can make this distinction. The best he can do is to judge certain questions under examination by their appearances, whether or not they seem true or false to him. He can then be asked to see to it that those that are true appear to him to be true; but whether he succeeds in this or whether the false seem to him to be true, he must follow his own persuasion. . . .

This consideration, if it were carefully weighed and thoroughly meditated upon, would surely reveal the truth of what I am here claiming: which is that, in man's present condition, God is content to demand that he seek the truth as diligently as possible and when he thinks he has found it that he cherish it and make it the rule of his life. As everyone can see, this proves that we are obliged to have the same respect for presumptive as for real truth. Whence it follows that all the objections that can be brought to bear on the difficulty of examination disappear like idle phantoms, since each individual is surely capable of finding a meaning in what he reads or hears, and of feeling that that meaning is true; and thus his particular brand of truth is established. It is enough that every man consult sincerely and in good faith the light that God gives him and seize accordingly upon the idea that seems to him the most reasonable and the most conformable to God's will. In this way he is a true believer in respect to God, although through a flaw for which he cannot be blamed his thoughts may not be a faithful image of reality, just as a child is a true believer in taking for his father his mother's husband, of whom he is not the son. The important consideration is then to act virtuously; thus everyone should try as hard as he can to honor God through prompt obedience to moral precepts. In this respect, that is, in respect to the knowledge of our moral obligations, the light of revelation is so clear that few can mistake it if only they seek it in good faith. . . .

Whence I conclude that ignorance founded on good faith is excusable in the most criminal of cases, such as robbery or adultery, and that thus ignorance in every domain is excusable, to the extent that a heretic of good faith or even an infidel will be punished by God only for evil acts that he has committed knowing well that they were evil. As for acts committed in all good conscience, a conscience, I say, that he has not himself maliciously stultified, I cannot be convinced that they constitute a crime. . . .

Judging by our ideal of a man most accomplished in wisdom and justice, we believe that if, after leaving an order with his servants as he departed on a long journey he found upon his return that they understood it differently and that while they were all agreed that their master's will was their sole guide, they disagreed only on what that was, he would declare that they were all equally respectful of his orders; but that some were more intelligent than others in their understanding of the real meaning of his instructions. Certainly, we would clearly and distinctly expect that to be his pronouncement; therefore Reason requires that God should declare likewise in regard to both true believers and conscientious heretics.

A LETTER CONCERNING TOLERATION

JOHN LOCKE

John Locke (1632–1704), the patron philosopher of liberalism, would profoundly influence Enlightenment thought with his Letters Concerning Toleration *(1689–1693), in which he sought "to distinguish exactly the business of civil government from that of religion."*

The toleration of those that differ from others in matters of religion, is so agreeable to the Gospel of Jesus Christ, and to the genuine reason of mankind, that it seems monstrous for men to be so blind as not to perceive the necessity and advantage of it in so clear a light. I will not here tax the pride and ambition of some, the passion and uncharitable zeal of others. These are faults from which human affairs can perhaps scarce ever be perfectly freed; but yet such as nobody will bear the plain imputation of, without covering them with some specious color; and so pretend to commendation, whilst they are carried away by their own irregular passions. But, however, that some may not color their spirit of persecution and unchristian cruelty with a pretense of care of the public weal and observation of the laws; and that others, under pretense of religion, may not seek impunity for their libertinism and licentiousness; in a word, that none may impose either upon himself or others, by the pretenses of loyalty and obedience to the prince, or of tenderness and sincerity in the worship of God I esteem it above all things necessary to distinguish exactly the business of civil government from that of religion, and to settle the just bound that lie between the one and the other. If this be not done, there can be no end put to the controversies that will be always arising between those that have, or at least pretend to have, on the one side, a concernment for the interest of men's souls, and, on the other side, a care of the commonwealth.

The commonwealth seems to me to be a society of men constituted only for the procuring, preserving, and advancing their own civil interests.

Civil interests I call life, liberty, health, and indolency of body; and the possession of outward things, such as money, lands, houses, furniture, and the like.

It is the duty of the civil magistrate, by the impartial execution of equal laws, to secure unto all the people in general, and to every one of his subjects in particular, the just possession of these things belonging to this life. If any one presume to violate the laws of public justice and equity, established for the preservation of those things, his presumption is to be checked by the fear of punishment, consisting of the deprivation or diminution of those civil interests, or goods, which otherwise he might and ought to enjoy. But seeing no man does willingly suffer himself to be punished by the deprivation of any part of his goods, and much less of his liberty or life, therefore is the magistrate armed with the force and strength of all his subjects, in order to the punishment of those that violate any other man's rights.

Now that the whole jurisdiction of the magistrate reaches only to these civil concernments, and that all civil power, right, and dominion, is bounded and confined to the only care of promoting these things; and that it neither can nor ought in any manner to be extended to the salvation of souls, these following considerations seem unto me abundantly to demonstrate.

First, because the care of souls is not committed to the civil magistrate, any more than to other men. It is not committed unto him, I say, by God; because it appears not that God has ever given any such authority to one man over another, as to compel anyone to his religion. Nor can any such power be vested in the magistrate by the consent of the people, because no man can so far abandon the care of his own salvation as blindly to leave to the choice of any other, whether prince or subject, to prescribe to him what faith or worship he shall embrace. For no man can, if he would, conform his faith to the dictates of another. All the life and power of true religion consist in the inward and full persuasion of the mind; and faith is not faith without believing. Whatever profession we make, to whatever outward worship we conform, if we are not fully satisfied in our own mind that the one is true, and the other well pleasing unto God, such profession and such practice, far from being any furtherance, are indeed great obstacles to our salvation. For in this manner, instead of expiating other sins by the exercise of religion, I say, in offering thus unto God Almighty such a worship as we esteem to be displeasing unto him, we add unto the number of our other sins those also of hypocrisy, and contempt of his Divine Majesty.

In the second place, the care of souls cannot belong to the civil magistrate, because his power consists only in outward force; but true and saving religion consists in the inward persuasion of the mind, without which nothing can be acceptable to God. And such is the nature of the understanding, that it cannot be compelled to the belief of anything by outward force. Confiscation of estate, imprisonment, torments, nothing of that nature can have any such efficacy as to make men change the inward judgment that they have framed of things.

It may indeed be alleged that the magistrate may make use of arguments, and thereby draw the heterodox into the way of truth, and procure their salvation. I grant it; but this is common to him with other men. In teaching, instructing, and redressing the erroneous by reason, he may certainly do what becomes any good man to do. Magistracy does not oblige him to put off either humanity or Christianity; but it is one thing to persuade, another to command; one thing to press with arguments, another with penalties. This civil power alone has a right to do; to the other good-will is authority enough. Every man has commission to admonish, exhort, convince another of error, and, by reasoning, to draw him into truth; but to give laws, receive obedience, and compel with the sword, belongs to none but the magistrate. And upon this ground, I affirm that the magistrate's power extends not to the establishing of any articles of faith, or forms of worship, by the force of his laws. For laws are of no force at all without penalties, and penalties in this case are absolutely impertinent, because they are not proper to convince the mind. Neither the profession of any articles of faith, nor the conformity to any outward form of worship (as has been already said), can be available to the salvation of souls, unless the truth of the one, and the acceptableness of the other unto God, be thoroughly believed by those that so profess and practice. But penalties are no way capable to produce such belief. It is only light and evidence that can work a change in men's opinions; which light can in no manner proceed from corporal sufferings, or any other outward penalties.

In the third place, the care of the salvation of men's souls cannot belong to the magistrate; because, though the rigor of laws and the force of penalties were capable to convince and change men's minds, yet would not that help at all to the salvation of their souls. For there being but one truth, one-way-to-heaven, what hope is there that more men would be led into it if they had no rule but the religion of the court, and were put under the necessity to quit the light of their own reason, and oppose the dictates of their own consciences, and blindly to resign themselves up to the will of their governors, and to the religion which either ignorance, ambition, or superstition had chanced to establish in the countries where they were born? In the variety and contradiction of opinions in religion, wherein the princes of the world are as much divided as in their secular interests, the narrow way would be much straitened; one country alone would be in the right, and all the rest of the world put under an obligation of following their princes in the ways that lead to destruction; and that which heightens the absurdity, and very ill suits the notion of a Deity, men would owe their eternal happiness or misery to the places of their nativity.

These considerations, to omit many others that might have been urged to the same purpose, seem unto me sufficient to conclude that all the power of civil government relates only to men's civil interests, is confined to the care of the things of this world, and hath nothing to do with the world to come.

Let us now consider what a church is. A church, then, I take to be a voluntary society of men, joining themselves together of their own accord in order to the public worshiping of God in such manner as they judge acceptable to him, and effectual to the salvation of their souls.

I say it is a free and voluntary society. Nobody is born a member of any church; otherwise the religion of parents would descend unto children by the same right of inheritance as their temporal estates, and everyone would hold his faith by the same tenure he does his lands, than which nothing can be imagined more absurd. Thus, therefore, that matter stands. No man by nature is bound unto any particular church or sect, but everyone joins himself voluntarily to that society in which he believes he has found that profession and worship which is truly acceptable to God. The hope of salvation, as it was the only cause of his entrance into that communion, so it can be the only reason of his stay there. For if afterwards he discover anything either erroneous in the doctrine or incongruous in the worship of that society to which he has joined himself, why should it not be as free for him to go out as it was to enter? No member of a religious society can be tied with any other bonds but what proceed from the certain expectation of eternal life. A church, then, is a society of members voluntarily uniting to that end.

It follows now that we consider what is the power of this church, and unto what laws it is subject.

Forasmuch as no society, how free soever, or upon whatsoever slight occasion instituted, whether of philosophers for learning, of merchants for commerce, or of men of leisure for mutual conversation and discourse, no church or company, I say, can in the least subsist and hold together, but will presently dissolve and break in pieces, unless it be regulated by some laws, and the members all consent to observe some order. Place and time of meeting must be agreed on; rules for admitting and excluding members must be established; distinction of officers, and putting things into a regular course, and such-like, cannot be omitted. But since the joining together of several members into this church-society, as has already been demonstrated, is absolutely free and spontaneous, it necessarily follows that the right of making its laws can belong to none but the society itself; or, at least (which is the same thing), to those whom the society by common consent has authorized thereunto. . . .

The end of a religious society (as has already been said) is the public worship of God, and, by means thereof, the acquisition of eternal life. All discipline ought therefore to tend to that end, and all ecclesiastical laws to be thereunto confined. Nothing ought nor can be transacted in this society relating to the possession of civil and worldly goods. No force is here to be made use of upon any occasion whatsoever. For force belongs wholly to the civil magistrate, and the possession of all outward goods is subject to his jurisdiction. . . .

Concerning outward worship, I say, in the first place, that the magistrate has no power to enforce by law, either in his own church, or much less in another, the use of any rites or ceremonies whatsoever in the worship of God. And this, not only because these churches are free societies, but because whatsoever is practiced in the worship of God is only so far justifiable as it is believed by those that practice it to be acceptable unto him. Whatsoever is not done with that assurance of faith is neither well in itself, nor can it be acceptable to God. To impose such things, therefore, upon any people, contrary to their own judgment, is in effect to command them to offend God, which, considering that the end of all religion is to please him, and that liberty is essentially necessary to that end, appears to be absurd beyond expression. . . .

In the next place: As the magistrate has no power to impose by his laws the use of any rites and ceremonies in any church, so neither has he any power to forbid the use of such rites and ceremonies as are already received, approved, and practiced by any church; because, if he did so, he would destroy the church itself: the end of whose institution is only to worship God with freedom after its own manner.

You will say, by this rule, if some congregations should have a mind to sacrifice infants, or (as the primitive Christians were falsely accused) lustfully pollute themselves in promiscuous uncleanness, or practice any other such heinous enormities, is the magistrate obliged to tolerate them, because they are committed in a religious assembly? I answer, No. These things are not lawful in the ordinary course of life, nor in any private house, and therefore neither are they so in the worship of God, or in any religious meeting. But, indeed, if any people congregated upon account of religion should be desirous to sacrifice a calf, I deny that that ought to be prohibited by a law. Meliboeus, whose calf it is, may lawfully kill his calf at home, and burn any part of it that he thinks fit. For no injury is thereby done to anyone, no prejudice to another man's goods. And for the same reason he may kill his calf also in a religious meeting. Whether the doing so be well-pleasing to God or no, it is their part to consider that do it. The part of the magistrate is only to take care that the commonwealth receive no prejudice, and that there be no injury done to any man, either in life or estate. And thus what may be spent on a feast may be spent on a sacrifice. But if peradventure such were the state of things that the interest of the commonwealth required all slaughter of beasts should be forborne for some while, in order to the increasing of the stock of cattle that had been destroyed by some extraordinary murrain, who sees not that the magistrate, in such a case, may forbid all his subjects to kill any calves for any use whatsoever? Only it is to be observed that, in this case, the law is not made about a religious, but a political matter; nor is the sacrifice, but the slaughter of calves, thereby prohibited.

By this we see what difference there is between the church and the commonwealth. Whatsoever is lawful in the commonwealth cannot be prohibited by the magistrate in the church. Whatsoever is permitted unto any of his subjects for their ordinary use, neither can nor ought to be forbidden by him to any sect of people for their religious uses. If any man may lawfully take bread or wine, either sitting or kneeling in his own house, the law ought not to abridge him of the same liberty in his religious worship; though in the church the use of bread and wine be very different, and be there applied to the mysteries of faith and rites of divine worship. But those things that are prejudicial to the commonweal of a people in their ordinary use, and are therefore forbidden by laws, those things ought not to be permitted to churches in their sacred rites. Only the magistrate ought always to be very careful that he do not misuse his authority to the oppression of any church, under pretense, of public good. . . .

Thus far concerning outward worship. Let us now consider articles of faith.

The articles of religion are some of them practical and some speculative. Now, though both sorts consist in the knowledge of truth, yet these terminate simply in the understanding, those influence the will and manners. Speculative opinions, therefore, and articles of faith (as they are called) which are required only to be believed, cannot be imposed on any church by the law of the land. For it is absurd that things should be enjoined by laws which are not in men's power to perform. And to believe this or that to be true, does not depend upon our will. But of this enough has been said already. But (will some say) let men at least profess that they believe. A sweet religion, indeed, that obliges men to dissemble and tell lies, both to God and man, for the salvation of their souls! If the magistrate thinks to save men thus, he seems to understand little of the way of salvation. And if he does it not in order to save them, why is he so solicitous about the articles of faith as to enact them by a law?

Further, the magistrate ought not to forbid the preaching or professing of any speculative opinions in any church, because they have no manner of relation to the civil rights of the subjects. If a Roman Catholic believe that to be really the body of Christ, which another man calls bread, he does no injury thereby to his neighbor. If a Jew do not believe the New Testament to be the word of God, he does not thereby alter anything in men's civil rights. If a heathen doubt of both Testaments, he is not therefore to be punished as a pernicious citizen. The power of the magistrate and the estates of the people may be equally secure whether any man believe these things or no. I readily grant that these opinions are false and absurd. But the business of laws is not to provide for the truth of opinions, but for the safety and security of the commonwealth, and of every particular man's goods and person. And so it ought to be. For the truth certainly would do well enough is she were once left to shift for herself. She seldom has received, and I fear never will receive, much assistance from the power of great men, to whom she is but rarely known, and more rarely welcome. She is not taught by laws, nor has she any need of force to procure her entrance into the minds of men. Errors indeed prevail by the assistance of foreign and borrowed succors. But if truth makes not her way into the understanding by her own light, she will be but the weaker for any borrowed force violence can add to her. Thus much for speculative opinions. Let us now proceed to practical ones.

A good life, in which consists not the least part of religion and true piety, concerns also the civil government; and in it lies the safety both of men's souls and of the commonwealth. Moral actions belong therefore to the jurisdiction both of the outward and inward court; both of the civil and domestic governor; I mean both of the magistrate and conscience. Here, therefore, is great danger, lest one of these jurisdictions intrench upon the other, and discord arise between the keeper of the public peace and the overseers of souls. But if what has been already said concerning the limits of both these governments be rightly considered, it will easily remove all difficulty in this matter.

Every man has an immortal soul, capable of eternal happiness or misery; whose happiness depending upon his believing and doing those things in this life which are necessary to the obtaining of God's favor, and are prescribed by God to that end. It follows from thence, first, that the observance of these things is the highest obligation that lies upon mankind, and that our utmost care, application, and diligence ought to be exercised in the search and performance of them; because there is nothing in this world that is of any consideration in comparison with eternity. Secondly, that seeing one man does not violate the right of another by his erroneous opinions and undue manner of worship, nor is his perdition any prejudice to another man's affairs, therefore, the care of each man's salvation belongs only to himself. But I would not have this understood as if I meant hereby to condemn all charitable admonitions, and affectionate endeavors to reduce men from errors, which are indeed the greatest duty of a Christian. Anyone may employ as many exhortations and arguments as he pleases, towards the promoting of another man's salvation. But all force and compulsion are to be forborne. Nothing is to be done imperiously. Nobody is obliged in that matter to yield obedience unto the admonitions or injunctions of another, further than he himself is persuaded. Every man in that has the supreme and absolute authority of judging for himself. And the reason is because nobody else is concerned in it, nor can receive any prejudice from his conduct therein. . . .

These things being thus explained, it is easy to understand to what end the legislative power ought to be directed, and by what measures regulated; and that is the temporal good and outward prosperity of the society; which is the sole reason of men's entering into society, and the only thing they seek and aim at in it. And it is also evident what liberty remains to men in reference to their eternal salvation, and that is, that everyone should do what he in his conscience is persuaded to be acceptable to the Almighty, on whose good pleasure and acceptance depends their eternal happiness. For obedience is due, in the first place, to God, and afterwards to the laws.

But some may ask, What if the magistrate should enjoin anything by his authority that appears unlawful to the conscience of a private person? I answer, that if government be faithfully administered, and the counsels of the magistrates be indeed directed to the public good, this will seldom happen. But if, perhaps, it do so fall out, I say, that such a private person is to abstain from the action that he judges unlawful, and he is to undergo the punishment which it is not unlawful for him to bear. For the private judgment of any person concerning a law enacted in political matters, for the public good, does not take away the obligation of that law, nor deserve a dispensation. But if the law indeed be concerning things that lie not within the verge of the magistrate's authority (as for example, that the people, or any party amongst them, should be compelled to embrace a strange religion, and join in the worship and ceremonies of another church), men are not in these cases obliged by that law, against their consciences. For the political society is instituted for no other end, but only to secure every man's possession of the things of this life. The care of each man's soul, and of the things of heaven, which neither does belong to the commonwealth nor can be subjected to it, is left entirely to every man's self. Thus the safeguard of men's lives, and of the things that belong unto this life, is the business of the commonwealth; and the preserving of those things unto their owners is the duty of the magistrate. And therefore the magistrate cannot take away these worldly things from this man or party, and give them to that; nor change propriety amongst fellow-subjects (no not even by a law), for a cause that has no relation to the end of civil government, I mean for their religion, which whether it be true or false does no prejudice to the worldly concerns of their fellow-subjects, which are the things that only belong unto the care of the commonwealth.

ON ENTHUSIASM

Earl of Shaftsbury

In this selection from his famous Characteristics of Men, Manners, Opinions, Times, etc. *(1699), Anthony Ashley Cooper, third earl of Shaftsbury (1671–1713), offers a sober plea for reason and moderation to replace superstition and enthusiasm, by which he meant religious zeal and fanaticism.*

If the knowing well how to expose any infirmity or vice were a sufficient security for the virtue which is contrary, how excellent an age might we be presumed to live in! Never was there in our nation a time known when folly and extravagance of every kind were more sharply inspected, or more wittily ridiculed. And one might hope, at least from this good symptom, that our age was in no declining state; since whatever our distempers are, we stand so well affected to our remedies. To bear the being told of faults is in private persons the best token of amendment. 'Tis seldom that a public is thus disposed. For where jealousy of state, or the ill lives of the great people, or any other cause, is powerful enough to restrain the freedom of censure in any part, it in effect destroys the benefit of it in the whole. There can be no impartial and free censure of manners where any peculiar custom or national opinion is set apart, and not only exempted from criticism, but even flattered with the highest art. 'Tis only in a free nation, such as ours, that imposture has no privilege; and that neither the credit of a court, the power of a nobility, nor the awfulness of a Church can give her protection, or hinder her from being arraigned in every shape and appearance. 'Tis true, this liberty may seem to run too far. We may perhaps be said to make ill use of it. So every one will say, when he himself is touched, and his opinion freely examined. But who shall be judge of what may be freely examined and what may not? Where liberty may be used and where it may not? What remedy shall we prescribe to this in general? Can there be a better than from that liberty itself which is complained of? If men are vicious, petulant, or abusive, the magistrate may correct them: but if they reason ill, 'tis reason still must teach them to do better. Justness of thought and style, refinement in manners, good breeding, and politeness of every kind can come only from the trial and experience of what is best. Let but the search go freely on, and the right measure of everything will soon be found. Whatever humor has got the start, if it be unnatural, it cannot hold; and the ridicule, if ill-placed at first, will certainly fall at last where it deserves.

I have often wondered to see men of sense so mightily alarmed at the approach of anything like ridicule on certain subjects; as if they mistrusted their own judgment. For what ridicule can lie against reason? or how can any one of the least justness of thought endure a ridicule wrong placed? Nothing is more ridiculous than this itself. The vulgar, indeed, may swallow any sordid jest, any mere drollery or buffoonery; but it must be a finer and truer wit which takes with the men of sense and breeding. How comes it to pass, then, that we appear such cowards in reasoning, and are so afraid to stand the test of ridicule? O! say we, the subjects are too grave. Perhaps so: but let us see first whether they are really grave or no: for in the manner we may conceive them they may, peradventure, be very grave and weighty in our imagination, but very ridiculous and impertinent in their own nature. *Gravity* is of the very essence of imposture. It does not only make us mistake other things, but is apt perpetually almost to mistake itself. For even in common behavior, how hard is it for the grave character to keep long out of the limits of the formal one? We can never be too grave, if we can be assured we are really what we suppose. And we can never too much honor or revere anything for grave, if we are assured the thing is grave, as we apprehend it. The main point is to know always true gravity from the false: and this can only be by carrying the rule constantly with us, and freely applying it not only to the things about us, but to ourselves; for if unhappily we lose the measure in ourselves, we shall soon lose it in everything besides. Now what rule or measure is there in the world, except in the considering of the real temper of things, to find which are truly serious and which ridiculous? And how can this be done, unless by applying the ridicule, to see whether it will bear? But if we fear to apply this rule in anything, what security can we have against the imposture of formality in all things? We have allowed ourselves to be formalists in one point; and the same formality may rule us as it pleases in all other.

'Tis not in every disposition that we are capacitated to judge of things. We must beforehand judge of our own temper, and accordingly of other things which fall under our judgment. But we must never more pretend to judge of things, or of our own temper in judging them, when we have given up our preliminary right of judgment, and under a presumption of gravity have allowed ourselves to be most ridiculous and to admire profoundly the most ridiculous things in nature, at least for aught we know. For having resolved never to try, we can never be sure.

This, my lord, I may safely aver, is so true in itself, and so well known for truth by the cunning formalists of the age, that they can better bear to have their impostures railed at, with all the bitterness and vehemence imaginable, than to have them touched ever so gently in this other way. They know very well, that as modes and fashions, so opinions, though ever so ridiculous, are kept up by solemnity; and that those formal notions, which grew up probably in an ill mood and have been conceived in sober sadness, are never to be removed but in a sober kind of cheerfulness, and by a more easy and pleasant way of thought. There is a melancholy which accompanies all enthusiasm. Be it love or religion (for there are enthusiasms in both) nothing can put a stop to the growing mischief of either, till the melancholy be removed and the mind at liberty to hear what can be said against the ridiculousness of an extreme in either way.

It was heretofore the wisdom of some wise nations to let people be fools as much as they pleased, and never to punish seriously what deserved only to be laughed at, and was, after all, best cured by that innocent remedy. There are certain humors in mankind which of necessity must have vent. The human mind and body are both of them naturally subject to commotions: and as there are strange ferments in the blood, which in many bodies occasion an extraordinary discharge; so in reason, too, there are heterogeneous particles which must be thrown off by fermentation. Should physicians endeavor absolutely to allay those ferments of the body, and strike in the humors which discover themselves in such eruptions, they might, instead of making a cure, bid fair perhaps to raise a plague, and turn a spring-ague or an autumn-surfeit into an epidemical malignant fever. They are certainly as ill physicians in the body-politic who would needs be tampering with these mental eruptions; and under the specious pretense of healing this itch of superstition, and saving souls from the contagion of enthusiasm, should set all nature in an uproar, and turn a few innocent carbuncles into an inflammation and mortal gangrene.

We read in history that Pan, when he accompanied Bacchus in an expedition to the Indies, found means to strike a terror through a host of enemies by the help of a small company, whose clamors he managed to good advantage among the echoing rocks and caverns of a woody vale. The hoarse bellowing of the caves, joined to the hideous aspect of such dark and desert places, raised such a horror in the enemy, that in this state their imagination helped them to hear voices, and doubtless to see forms too, which were more than human: whilst the uncertainty of what they feared made their fear yet greater, and spread it faster by implicit looks than any narration could convey it. And this was what in after-times men called a *panic.* The story indeed gives a good hint of the nature of this passion, which can hardly be without some mixture of enthusiasm and horrors of a superstitious kind.

One may with good reason call every passion panic which is raised in a multitude and conveyed by aspect or, as it were, by contact of sympathy. Thus popular fury may be called panic when the rage of the people, as we have sometimes known, has put them beyond themselves; especially where religion has had to do. And in this state their very looks are infectious. The fury flies from face to face; and the disease is no sooner seen than caught. They who in a better situation of mind have beheld a multitude under the power of this passion, have owned that they saw in the countenances of men something more ghastly and terrible than at other times is expressed on the most passionate occasion. Such force has society in ill as well as in good passions: and so much stronger any affection is for being social and communicative.

Thus, my lord, there are many panics in mankind besides merely that of fear. And thus is religion also panic; when enthusiasm of any kind gets up, as oft, on melancholy occasions, it will. For vapors naturally rise; and in bad times especially, when the spirits of men are low, as either in public calamities, or during the unwholesomeness of air or diet, or when convulsions happen in nature, storms, earthquakes, or other amazing prodigies: at this season the panic must needs run high, and the magistrate of necessity give way to it. For to apply a serious remedy, and bring the sword, or *fasces*, as a cure, must make the case more melancholy, and increase the very cause of the distemper. To forbid men's natural fears, and to endeavor the overpowering them by other fears, must needs be a most unnatural method. The magistrate, if he be any artist, should have a gentler hand; and instead of caustics, incisions, and amputations, should be using the softest balms; and with a kind sympathy entering into the concern of the people; and taking, as it were, their passion upon him should, when he has soothed and satisfied it, endeavor, by cheerful ways, to divert and heal it.

This was ancient policy: and hence (as a notable author of our nation expresses it) 'tis necessary a people should have a *public leading* in religion. For to deny the magistrate a worship, or take away a national church, is as mere enthusiasm as the notion which sets up persecution. For why should there not be public walks as well as private gardens? Why not public libraries as well as private education and home-tutors? But to prescribe bounds to fancy and speculation, to regulate men's apprehensions and religious beliefs or fears, to suppress by violence the natural passion of enthusiasm, or to endeavor to ascertain it, or reduce it to one species, or bring it under any one modification, is in truth no better sense, nor deserves a better character, than what the comedian declares of the like project in the affair of love.

Not only the visionaries and enthusiasts of all kinds were tolerated, your lordship knows, by the ancients; but, on the other side, philosophy had as free a course, and was permitted as a balance against superstition. And whilst some sects, such as the Pythagorean and latter Platonic, joined in with the superstition and enthusiasm of the times; the Epicurean, the Academic, and others, were allowed to use all the force of wit and raillery against it. And thus matters were happily balanced; reason had fair play; learning and science flourished. Wonderful was the harmony and temper which arose from all these contrarieties. Thus superstition and enthusiasm were mildly treated, and being let alone they never raged to that degree as to occasion bloodshed, wars, persecutions, and devastation in the world. But a new sort of policy, which extends itself to another world and considers the future lives and happiness of men rather than the present, has made us leap the bounds of natural humanity; and out of a supernatural charity has taught us the way of plaguing one another most devoutly. It has raised an antipathy which no temporal interest could ever do; and entailed upon us a mutual hatred to all eternity. And now uniformity in opinion (a hopeful project!) is looked on as the only expedient against this evil. The saving of souls is now the heroic passion of exalted spirits; and is become in a manner the chief care of the magistrate, and the very end of government itself.

If magistracy should vouchsafe to interpose thus much in other sciences, I am afraid we should have as bad logic, as bad mathematics, and in every kind as bad philosophy, as we often have divinity, in countries where a precise orthodoxy is settled by law. 'Tis a hard matter for a government to settle wit. If it does but keep us sober and honest, 'tis likely we shall have as much ability in our spiritual as in our temporal affairs: and if we can but be trusted, we shall have wit enough to save ourselves, when no prejudice lies in the way. But if honesty and wit be insufficient for this saving work, 'tis in vain for the magistrate to meddle with it: since if he be ever so virtuous or wise, he may be as soon mistaken as another man. I am sure the only way to save men's sense, or preserve wit at all in the world, is to give liberty to wit. Now wit can never have its liberty where the freedom of raillery is taken away: for against serious extravagances and splenetic humors there is no other remedy than this.

We have indeed full power over all other modifications of spleen. We may treat other enthusiasms as we please. We may ridicule love, or gallantry, or knight-errantry to the utmost; and we find that in these latter days of wit, the humor of this kind, which was once so prevalent, is pretty well declined. The crusades, the rescuing of holy lands, and such devout gallantries, are in less request than formerly: but if something of this militant religion, something of this soul-rescuing spirit and saint-errantry prevails still, we need not wonder, when we consider in how solemn a manner we treat this distemper, and how preposterously we go about to cure enthusiasm.

I can hardly forbear fancying that if we had a sort of inquisition, or formal court of judicature, with grave officers and judges, erected to restrain poetical license, and in general to suppress that fancy and humor of versification; but in particular that most extravagant passion of love, as it is set out by poets, in its heathenish dress of Venuses and Cupids: if the poets, as ringleaders and teachers of this heresy, were, under grievous penalties, forbid to enchant the people by their vein of rhyming; and if the people, on the other side, were, under proportionable penalties, forbid to hearken to any such charm, or lend their attention to any love tale, so much as in a play, a novel, or a ballad—we might perhaps see a new Arcadia arising out of this heavy persecution: old people and young would be seized with a versifying spirit: we should have field-conventicles of lovers and poets: forests would be filled with romantic shepherds and shepherdesses: and rocks resound with echoes of hymns and praises offered to the powers of love. We might indeed have a fair chance, by this management, to bring back the whole train of heathen gods, and set our cold northern island burning with as many altars to Venus and Apollo, as were formerly in Cyprus, Delos, or any of those warmer Grecian climates.

THE ARGUMENT FOR A DEITY

Isaac Newton

In these two selections, which anticipate much of Enlightenment deism, Newton insists that the design apparent everywhere in nature proves the existence of an intelligent and omnipresent Supreme Being. The first excerpt is from Newton's Opticks *(1704), and the second is from a letter written in 1692 to the Reverend Dr. Richard Bentley.*

The main business of natural philosophy is to argue from phenomena without feigning hypotheses and to deduce causes from effects, till we come to the very first cause, which certainly is not mechanical; and not only to unfold the mechanism of the world, but chiefly to resolve these and suchlike questions. What is there in places almost empty of matter, and whence is it that the sun and planets gravitate toward one another, without dense matter between them? Whence is it that nature does nothing in vain, and whence arises all that order and beauty which we see in the world? To what end are comets, and whence is it that planets move all one and the same way in orbs concentric while comets move all manner of ways in orbs very eccentric, and what hinders the fixed stars from falling upon one another? How came the bodies of animals to be contrived with so much art, and for what ends were their several parts? Was the eye contrived without skill in optics and the ear without knowledge of sounds? How do the motions of the body follow from the will, and whence is the instinct in animals? Is not the sensory of animals that place to which the sensitive substance is present and into which the sensible species of things are carried through the nerves and brain, that there they may be perceived by their immediate presence to that substance? And these things being rightly dispatched, does it not appear from phenomena that there is a Being, incorporeal, living, intelligent, omnipresent, who in infinite space, as it were in his sensory, sees the things themselves intimately and thoroughly perceives them, and comprehends them wholly by their immediate presence to himself, of which things the images only carried through the organs of sense into our little sensoriums are there seen and beheld by that which in us perceives and thinks? And though every true step made in this philosophy brings us not immediately to the knowledge of the first cause, yet it brings us nearer to it, and on that account is to be highly valued.

• • •

SIR,

When I wrote my Treatise about our System, I had an Eye upon such Principles as might work with considering Men, for the Belief of a Deity, and nothing can rejoice me more than to find it useful for that Purpose. But if I have done the Public any Service this way, it is due to nothing but Industry and patient Thought.

As to your first Query, it seems to me that if the Matter of our Sun and Planets, and all the Matter of the Universe, were evenly scattered throughout all the Heavens, and every Particle had an innate Gravity towards all the rest, and the whole Space, throughout which this Matter was scattered, was but finite; the Matter on the outside of this Space would by its Gravity tend towards all the Matter on the inside, and by consequence fall down into the middle of the whole Space, and there compose one great spherical Mass. But if the Matter was evenly disposed throughout an infinite Space, it could never convene into one Mass, but some of it would convene into one Mass and some into another, so as to make an infinite Number of great Masses, scattered at great Distances from one to another throughout all that infinite Space. And thus might the Sun and fixt Stars be formed, supposing the Matter were of a lucid Nature. But how the Matter should divide itself into two sorts, and that Part of it, which is fit to compose a shining Body, should fall down into one Mass and make a Sun, and the rest, which is fit to compose an opaque Body, should coalesce, not into one great Body, like the shining Matter, but into many little ones; or if the Sun at first were an opaque Body like the Planets, or the Planets lucid Bodies like the Sun, how he alone should be changed into a shining Body, whilst all they continue opaque, or all they be changed into opaque ones, whilst he remains unchanged, I do not think explicable by mere natural Causes, but am forced to ascribe it to the Counsel and Contrivance of a voluntary Agent.

The same Power, whether natural or supernatural, which placed the Sun in the Center of the six primary Planets, placed *Saturn* in the Center of the Orbs of his five secondary Planets, and *Jupiter* in the Center of his four secondary Planets, and the Earth in the Center of the Moon's Orb; and therefore had this Cause been a blind one, without Contrivance or Design, the Sun would have been a Body of the same kind with *Saturn*, *Jupiter*, and the Earth, that is, without Light and Heat. Why there is one Body in our System qualified to give Light and Heat to all the rest, I know no Reason, but because the Author of the System thought it convenient; and why there is but one Body of this kind I know no Reason, but because one was sufficient to warm and enlighten all the rest. For the *Cartesian* Hypothesis of Suns losing their Light, and then turning into Comets, and Comets into Planets, can have no Place in my System, and is plainly erroneous; because it is certain that as often as they appear to us, they descend into the System of our Planets, lower than the Orb of *Jupiter*, and sometimes lower than the Orbs of *Venus* and *Mercury*, and yet never stay here, but always return from the Sun with the same Degrees of Motion by which they approached him.

To your second Query, I answer, that the Motions which the Planets now have could not spring from any natural Cause alone, but were impressed by an intelligent Agent. For since Comets descend into the

Region of our Planets, and here move all manner of ways, going sometimes the same way with the Planets, sometimes the contrary way, and sometimes in cross ways, in Planes inclined to the Plane of the Ecliptick, and at all kinds of Angles, 'tis plain that there is no natural Cause which could determine all the Planets, both primary and secondary, to move the same way and in the same Plane, without any considerable Variation: This must have been the Effect of Counsel. Nor is there any natural Cause which could give the Planets those just Degrees of Velocity, in Proportion to their Distances from the Sun, and other central Bodies, which were requisite to make them move in such concentrick Orbs about those Bodies. Had the Planets been as swift as Comets, in Proportion to their Distances from the Sun (as they would have been, had their Motion been caused by their Gravity, whereby the Matter, at the first Formation of the Planets, might fall from the remotest Regions towards the Sun) they would not move in concentrick Orbs, but in such eccentrick ones as the Comets move in. Were all the Planets as swift as *Mercury*, or as slow as *Saturn* or his Satellites; or were their several Velocities otherwise much greater or less than they are, as they might have been had they arose from any other Cause than their Gravities; or had the Distances from the Centers about which they move, been greater or less than they are with the same Velocities; or had the Quantity of Matter in the Sun, or in *Saturn*, *Jupiter*, and the Earth, and by consequence their gravitating Power been greater or less than it is; the primary Planets could not have revolved about the Sun, nor the secondary ones about *Saturn*, *Jupiter*, and the Earth, in concentrick Circles as they do, but would have moved in Hyperbolas, or Parabolas, or in Ellipses very eccentrick. To make this System therefore, with all its Motions, required a Cause which understood, and compared together, the Quantities of Matter in the several Bodies of the Sun and Planets, and the gravitating Powers resulting from thence; the several Distances of the primary Planets from the Sun, and of the secondary ones from *Saturn*, *Jupiter*, and the Earth; and the Velocities with which these Planets could revolve about those Quantities of Matter in the central Bodies; and to compare and adjust all these Things together, in so great a Variety of Bodies, argues that Cause to be not blind and fortuitous, but very well skilled in Mechanicks and Geometry.

To your third Query, I answer, that it may be represented that the Sun may, by heating those Planets most which are nearest to him, cause them to be better concocted, and more condensed by that Concoction. But when I consider that our Earth is much more heated in its Bowels below the upper Crust by subterraneous Fermentations of mineral Bodies than by the Sun, I see not why the interior Parts of *Jupiter* and *Saturn* might not be as much heated, concocted, and coagulated by those Fermentations as our Earth is; and therefore this various Density should have some other Cause than the various Distances of the Planets from the Sun. And I am confirmed in this Opinion by considering, that the Planets of *Jupiter* and *Saturn*, as they are rarer than the rest, so they are vastly greater, and contain a far greater Quantity of Matter, and have many Satellites about them; which Qualifications surely arose not from their being placed at so great a Distance from the Sun, but were rather the Cause why the Creator placed them at great Distance. For by their gravitating Powers they disturb one another's Motions very sensibly, as I find by some late Observations of Mr. *Flamsteed*, and had they been placed much nearer to the Sun and to one another, they would by the same Powers have caused a considerable Disturbance in the whole System.

To your fourth Query, I answer, that in the Hypothesis of Vortices, the Inclination of the Axis of the Earth might, in my Opinion, be ascribed to the Situation of the Earth's Vortex before it was absorbed by the neighboring Vortices, and the Earth turned from a Sun to a Comet; but this Inclination ought to decrease constantly in Compliance with the Motion of the Earth's Vortex, whose Axis is much less inclined to the Ecliptick, as appears by the Motion of the Moon carried about therein. If the Sun by his Rays could carry about the Planets, yet I do not see how he could thereby effect their diurnal Motions.

Lastly, I see nothing extraordinary in the Inclination of the Earth's Axis for proving a Deity, unless you will urge it as a Contrivance for Winter and Summer, and for making the Earth habitable towards the Poles; and that the diurnal Rotations of the Sun and Planets, as they could hardly arise from any Cause purely mechanical, so by being determined all the same way with the annual and menstrual Motions, they seem to make up that Harmony in the System, which, as I explained above, was the Effect of Choice rather than Chance.

There is yet another argument for a Deity, which I take to be a very strong one, but till the Principles on which it is grounded are better received, I think it more advisable to let it sleep.

I am,

Your most humble Servant

to command,

Cambridge, Is. NEWTON.

Decemb. 10, 1692.

A DISCOURSE OF FREE-THINKING

ANTHONY COLLINS

A friend of John Locke, Anthony Collins (1676–1729) was perhaps England's most outspoken foe of religion in the eighteenth century. His recurring theme in this essay of 1713 is the inability of religious believers and priests to agree on creedal truth.

The Subjects of which Men are deny'd the Right to think by the Enemys of *Free-Thinking*, are of all others those of which Men have not only *a Right to think*, but of which they are oblig'd in duty to think; *viz*. such as *of the Nature and Attributes of the Eternal Being* or *God, of the Truth and Authority of Books esteem'd Sacred*, and *of the Sense and Meaning of those Books*; or, in one word, *of Religious Questions*.

1*st*. A right Opinion in these matters is suppos'd by the *Enemys of Free-Thinking* to be absolutely necessary to Mens Salvation, and some Errors or Mistakes about them are suppos'd to be damnable. Now where a right Opinion is so necessary, there Men have the greatest Concern imaginable to think for themselves, as the best means to take up with the right side of the Question. For if they will not think for themselves, it remains only for them to take the Opinions they have imbib'd from their Grandmothers, Mothers or Priests, or owe to such like Accident, for granted. But taking that method, they can only be in the right by chance; whereas by Thinking and Examination, they have not only the mere accident of being in the right, but have the Evidence of things to determine them to the side of Truth: unless it be suppos'd that Men are such absurd Animals, that the most unreasonable Opinion is as likely to be admitted for true as the most reasonable, when it is judg'd of by the Reason and Understanding of Men. In that case indeed it will follow, That Men can be under no Obligation to think of these matters. But then it will likewise follow, That they can be under no Obligation to concern themselves about Truth and Falshood in any Opinions. For if Men are so absurd, as not to be able to distinguish between Truth and

Falshood, Evidence and no Evidence, what pretense is there for Mens having any Opinions at all? Which yet none judg so necessary as the Enemys of *Free-Thinking.*

2dly. If the surest and best means of arriving at Truth lies in *Free-Thinking,* then the whole Duty of Man with respect to Opinions lies only in *Free-Thinking.* Because he who *thinks freely* does his best towards being in the right, and consequently does all that God, who can require nothing more of any Man than that he should do his best, can require of him. And should he prove mistaken in any Opinions, he must be as acceptable to God as if he receiv'd none but right Opinions. . . .

On the other side, the whole Crime of Man, with respect to Opinions, must lie in his not *thinking freely.* He who is in the right by accident only, and does but suppose himself to be so without any *Thinking,* is really in a dangerous state, as having taken no pains and used no endeavors towards being in the right, and consequently as having no Merit; nay, as being on the same foot with the most stupid *Papist* and *Heathen.* For when once Men refuse or neglect to think, and take up their Opinions upon trust, they do in effect declare they would have been *Papists* or *Heathens,* had they had *Popish* or *Heathen* Priests for their *Guides,* or *Popish* or *Heathen* Grandmothers to have taught them their Catechisms.

3dly. Superstition is an Evil, which either by the means of Education, or the natural Weakness of Men, oppresses almost all Mankind. And how terrible an Evil it is, is well describ'd by the ancient Philosophers and Poets. TULLY says, *If you give way to Superstition, it will ever haunt and plague you. If you go to a Prophet, or regard Omens; if you sacrifice or observe the Flight of Birds; if you consult an Astrologer or Haruspex; if it thunders or lightens, or any place is consum'd with Lightning, or such-like Prodigy happens (as it is necessary some such often should) all the Tranquillity of the Mind is destroy'd. And Sleep it self, which seems to be an Asylum and Refuge from all Trouble and Uneasiness, does by the aid of Superstition increase your Troubles and Fears.*

Horace ranks Superstition with Vice; and as he makes the Happiness of Man in this Life to consist in the practice of Virtue and Freedom from Superstition, so he makes the greatest Misery of this Life to consist in being vicious and superstitious. *You are not covetous,* says he; *that's well: But are you as free from all other Vices? Are you free from Ambition, excessive Anger, and the Fear of Death? Are you so much above* Superstition, *as to laugh at all Dreams, panick Fears, Miracles, Witches, Ghosts, and Prodigys?*

This was the state of Superstition among the Antients; but since

Uncharitableness and damning to all eternity for Trifles, has (in opposition both to Reason and Revelation) come into the World, the Evil of Superstition is much increas'd, and Men are now under greater Terrors and Uneasiness of Mind than they possibly could be when they thought they hazarded less.

Now there is no just Remedy to this universal Evil but *Free-Thinking*. By that alone can we understand the true Causes of things, and by consequence the Unreasonableness of all superstitious Fears. *Happy is the Man,* says the Divine VIRGIL, *who has discover'd the Causes of Things, and is thereby cured of all kind of Fears, even of Death it self, and all the Noise and Din of Hell.* For by *Free-Thinking* alone Men are capable of knowing, that a perfectly Good, Just, Wise and Powerful Being made and governs the World; and from this Principle they know, that he can require nothing of Men in any Country or Condition of Life, but that whereof he has given them an opportunity of being convinc'd by Evidence and Reason in the Place where they are, and in that Condition of Life to which Birth or any other Chance has directed them; that an honest and rational Man can have no just reason to fear any thing from him: nay, on the contrary, must have so great a Delight and Satisfaction in believing such a Being exists, that he can much better be suppos'd to fear lest no such Being should exist, than to fear any harm from him. And lastly, That God being incapable of having any addition made either to his Power or Happiness, and wanting nothing, can require nothing of Men for his own sake, but only for Man's sake; and consequently, that all Actions and Speculations which are of no use to Mankind, [as for instance, Singing or Dancing, or wearing of Habits, or Observation of Days, or eating or drinking, or slaughtering of Beasts (in which things the greatest part of the Heathen Worship consisted) or the Belief of *Transubstantiation* or *Consubstantiation*, or of any Doctrines not taught by the *Church of England*] either signify nothing at all with God, or else displease him, but can never render a Man more acceptable to him.

By means of all this, a Man may possess his Soul in peace, as having an expectation of enjoying all the good things which God can bestow, and no fear of any future Misery or Evil from his hands; and the very worst of his State can only be, that he is pleasantly deceiv'd.

Whereas superstitious Men are incapable of believing in a perfectly just and good God. They make him talk to all Mankind from corners, and consequently require things of Men under the Sanction of Misery in the next World, of which they are incapable of having any convincing

Evidence that they come from him. They make him (who *equally beholds all the Dwellers upon earth*) to have favorite Nations and People, without any Consideration of Merit. They make him put other Nations under Disadvantages without any Demerit. And so they are more properly to be stil'd *Demonists* than *Theists.* No wonder therefore if such Wretches should be so full of Fears of the Wrath of God, that they are sometimes tempted (with the Vicious) to wish there was no God at all; a Thought so unnatural and absurd, that even *Speculative Atheists* would abhor it. These Men have no quiet in their own Minds; they rove about in search of *saving Truth* thro the dark Corners of the Earth, and are so foolish as to hope to find it (if I may so say) hid under the Sands of *Africa*, where *Cato* scorn'd to look for it: and neglecting what God speaks plainly to the whole World, take up with what they suppose he has communicated to a few; and thereby believe and practice such things, in which they can never have Satisfaction. For suppose Men take up with a Religion which consists in Dancing or Musick, or such-like Ceremonys, or in useless and unintelligible Speculations; how can they be assur'd they believe and perform as they ought? What Rule can such Men have to know whether other Ceremonys, and useless and unintelligible Speculations, may not be requir'd of them instead of those they perform and believe? And how can they be sure that they believe rightly any unintelligible Speculations? Here is a foundation laid for nothing but endless Scruples, Doubts, and Fears. Wherefore I conclude, that every one, out of regard to his own Tranquility of Mind, which must be disturb'd as long as he has any Seeds of Superstition, is oblig'd to *think freely* on *Matters of Religion.*

4*thly.* The infinite number of Pretenders in all Ages to Revelations from Heaven, supported by Miracles, containing new Notions of the Deity, new Doctrines, new Commands, new Ceremonys, and new Modes of Worship, make thinking on the foregoing Heads absolutely necessary, if a Man be under an obligation to listen to any Revelation at all. For how shall any Man distinguish between the true Messenger from Heaven and the Impostor, but by considering the Evidence produc'd by the one, as *freely* as of the other? . . .

It is objected, *That to allow and encourage Men to think freely, will produce endless Divisions in Opinion, and by consequence Disorder in Society.* To which I answer,

1. Let any Man lay down a Rule to prevent Diversity of Opinions, which will not be as fertile of Diversity of Opinions as *Free-Thinking;* or

if it prevents Diversity of Opinions, will not be a Remedy worse than the Disease; and I will yield up the Question.

2. Mere Diversity of Opinions has no tendency in nature to Confusion in Society. The *Pythagoreans*, *Stoicks*, *Scepticks*, *Academicks*, *Cynicks*, and *Stratonicks*, all existed in *Greece* at the same time, and differ'd from one another in the most important Points, *viz.* concerning the Freedom of human Actions, the Immortality and Immateriality of the Soul, the Being and Nature of the Gods, and their Government of the World: And yet no Confusion ever arose in *Greece* on account of this Diversity of Opinions. Nor did the infinite Variety of Religions and Worships among the Antients ever produce any Disorder or Confusion. Nay, so little *Polemick Divinity* was there among them, and so little mischief did the Heathen Priests do, that there are no Materials for that sort of History call'd *Ecclesiastical History*. And the true reason why no ill effect follow'd this Diversity of Opinions, was, because Men generally agreed in that mild and peaceable Principle of allowing one another to *think freely,* and to have different Opinions. Whereas had the common practice of Calumny us'd among us prevail'd among them, or had they condemn'd one another to Fire and Faggot, Imprisonment and Fines in this World, and Damnation in the next, and by these means have engag'd the Passions of the ignorant part of Mankind in their several Partys; then Confusion, Disorder, and *every evil Work* had follow'd, as it does at this day among those who allow no Liberty of Opinion. We may be convinc'd of this by our own Experience. How many Disputes are there every where among Philosophers, Physicians, and Divines; which, by the allowance of free Debate, produce no ill effects? Further, let any man look into the History and State of the *Turks*, and he will see the influence which their tolerating Principles and Temper have on the Peace of their Empire. . . . So that it is evident Matter of Fact, that a *Restraint upon Thinking* is the cause of all the Confusion which is pretended to arise from Diversity of Opinions, and that *Liberty of Thinking* is the Remedy for all the Disorders which are pretended to arise from Diversity of Opinions.

"IF THERE IS A GOD . . ."

BARON DE MONTESQUIEU

In his Persian Letters, *published in 1721, Charles de Secondat, baron de la Brède et de Montesquieu (1689–1755), offers a penetrating critique of French life through imagined letters home from two Persians traveling in France. The following selections are from Letters 83 and 85.*

If there is a God, my dear Rhedi, he must necessarily be just; for if he were not, he would be the most wicked and imperfect of all beings.

Justice is a true relation between two things: this relation is always the same, no matter who examines it, whether it be God, or an angel, or lastly, man himself.

It is true that men do not always perceive these relations; often even when they do perceive them, they turn away from them, and their self-interest is what they perceive most clearly. Justice cries aloud, but her voice can hardly be heard above the tumult of the passions.

Men can commit unjust acts because it is to their advantage to do so and because they prefer their own contentment to that of others. They always act from selfish motives: no man is evil gratuitously: there must be a determining cause, and that cause is always selfishness.

But God cannot possibly commit an unjust act: once we assume that he perceives what is just he must of necessity act accordingly, for since he is self-sufficient and in need of nothing, he would otherwise be the most wicked of beings, since he has no selfish interests.

Thus if there were no God, we would still be obliged to venerate justice, that is, we should do everything possible to resemble that being of whom we have such an exalted notion and who, if he exists, would necessarily be just. Free though we might be from the yoke of religion, we should never be free from the bonds of equity.

That, Rhedi, is what makes me think that justice is eternal and does not depend on human conventions. And if it did depend on them, that would be a terrible fact that we should hide from ourselves.

We are surrounded by men stronger than we are: they can harm us in a thousand different ways; three times out of four, they can do it with impunity. What a relief for us to know that there is in the hearts of all men an inner principle fighting in our behalf and protecting us from their attempts.

Without that principle, we could live only in a state of constant alarm; we would walk among men as among lions; and we could never be assured for a moment of our goods, our honor, or our lives.

These thoughts always stir me up against those theologians who represent God as a being who makes tyrannical use of his power; who make him do things that we would not do for fear of offending him; who burden him with all the imperfections that he punishes us for: and represent him, quite contradictorily, sometimes as an evil being, sometimes as a being who hates evil and punishes it.

When a man looks within himself, what a satisfaction it is for him to find that his heart is just! This pleasure, no matter how austere, should delight him: he sees himself as far above those lacking in this quality as he is above tigers and bears. Yes, Rhedi, if I were always sure of following inviolably the justice that I perceive, I would consider myself the first among men.

• • •

You know, Mirza, that a number of ministers of Shah-Soliman had formed the project of forcing all the Armenians in Persia to leave the realm or become Mohammedans, with the idea that our empire would be polluted as long as it kept these infidels in our midst.

That would have meant the end of the grandeur of Persia, if blind devotion had been heeded on this occasion.

It is not known why the project failed. Neither those who proposed it nor those who rejected it knew what the consequences thereof would have been: chance played the part of reason and policy and saved the empire from a risk greater than it could have run from the loss of a battle and the capture of two cities.

By proscribing the Armenians, the ministers were on the verge of destroying in a single day all the merchants and nearly all the artisans of the kingdom. I am sure that the great Shah-Abbas would have preferred to cut off his two arms rather than sign such an order, and that by sending to the Mogul and other kings of India his most industrious subjects, he would have believed he was giving away half of his States.

The persecutions that our zealous Mohammedans have inflicted upon the Parsees obliged a multitude of them to flee into India and deprived Persia of a population devoted to agriculture which alone was capable by dint of labor to overcome the sterility of our soil.

Religious devotees had only to make a second attempt and ruin industry; as a result of which the empire would have toppled, and with it, as a matter of course, the very religion that they had sought to strengthen.

All prejudice aside, I do not know, Mirza, if it is not a good thing to have several religions in a State.

It is notable that those who adhere to tolerated religions ordinarily render more useful services to their country than do those who are members of the dominant religion, because, since they are kept from honored positions and can gain distinction only through opulence, they are led to acquire wealth by their toil and embrace the most arduous of society's tasks.

Besides, since all religions entertain socially useful precepts, it is good to have them zealously observed. And what is more apt than a multiplicity of religions to inspire zeal?

Rival religions grant each other nothing. Their jealousy is shared by their individual members: all are on their guard and are afraid of doing things that would dishonor their sect and expose it to the contempt and unpardonable censure of the opposite sect.

It has also always been observed that the introduction of a new sect into a State has been the surest means of correcting the abuses of the older sect.

In vain we say that it is not in the interests of the prince to tolerate several religions within his State: even if all the sects in the world should happen to be brought together, no harm would result, because there is not one of them which does not prescribe obedience and preach submission.

I confess that histories are replete with religious wars: but on close examination, it is apparent that they were caused, not by a multiplicity of religions, but by the spirit of intolerance that ran rife in the religion that considered itself dominant.

The cause was that spirit of proselytism which the Jews took over from the Egyptians and which passed from them, like a common epidemic disease, to Mohammedans and Christians.

It was indeed a kind of madness, the progress of which can be looked upon only as a total eclipse of human reason.

For even if it were not inhuman to afflict the consciences of other peoples, even if there were none of the evil results that are counted by the thousands, it would be madness even to consider it. The man who wants to make me change my religion surely does so only because he would not change his, even if forced: he thinks it strange, then, that I do not do something he would not do himself perhaps for the whole world.

OF MIRACLES AND THE ORIGIN OF RELIGION

DAVID HUME

In these two selections the Scottish philosopher and historian David Hume (1711–1776) turns his philosophical skepticism on religious faith and the history of religion. The first is from Essays and Treatises on Several Subjects *(1768), and the second is from* The Natural History of Religion *(1757). This second selection, "The Origin of Polytheism," contains an interesting discussion of the psychology of religion.*

A miracle is a violation of the laws of nature; and as a firm and unalterable experience has established these laws, the proof against a miracle, from the very nature of the fact, is as entire as any argument from experience can possibly be imagined. Why is it more than probable, that all men must die; that lead cannot, of itself, remain suspended in the air; that fire consumes wood, and is extinguished by water; unless it be, that these events are found agreeable to the laws of nature, and there is required a violation of these laws, or in other words a miracle to prevent them? Nothing is esteemed a miracle, if it ever happen in the common course of nature. It is no miracle that a man, seemingly in good health, should die on a sudden: because such a kind of death, though more unusual than any other, has yet been frequently observed to happen. But it is a miracle, that a dead man should come to life; because that has never been observed in any age or country. There must, therefore, be a uniform experience against every miraculous event, otherwise the event would not merit that appellation. And as a uniform experience amounts to a proof, there is here a direct and full *proof*, from the nature of the fact, against the existence of any miracle; nor can such a proof be destroyed, or the miracle rendered credible, but by an opposite proof, which is superior.

The plain consequence is (and it is a general maxim worthy of our attention), "That no testimony is sufficient to establish a miracle, unless the testimony be of such a kind, that its falsehood would be more miraculous than the fact which it endeavors to establish; and even in that case there is a mutual destruction of arguments, and the superior only gives us an assurance suitable to that degree of force, which remains, after deducting the inferior." When anyone tells me, that he saw a dead man restored to life, I immediately consider with myself, whether it be more probable, that this person should either deceive or be deceived, or that the fact, which he relates, should really have happened. I weigh the one miracle against the other; and according to the superiority, which I discover, I pronounce my decision, and always reject the greater miracle. If the falsehood of his testimony would be more miraculous than the event which he relates; then, and not till then, can he pretend to command my belief or opinion.

In the foregoing reasoning we have supposed, that the testimony, upon which a miracle is founded, may possibly amount to an entire proof, and that the falsehood of that testimony would be a real prodigy: But it is easy to show, that we have been a great deal too liberal in our concession, and that there never was a miraculous event established on so full an evidence.

For *first*, there is not to be found, in all history, any miracle attested by a sufficient number of men, of such unquestioned good sense, education, and learning, as to secure us against all delusion in themselves; of such undoubted integrity, as to place them beyond all suspicion of any design to deceive others; of such credit and reputation in the eyes of mankind, as to have a great deal to lose in case of their being detected in any falsehood; and at the same time, attesting facts performed in such a public manner and in so celebrated a part of the world, as to render the detection unavoidable: All which circumstances are requisite to give us a full assurance in the testimony of men.

Secondly. We may observe in human nature a principle which, if strictly examined, will be found to diminish extremely the assurance which we might, from human testimony, have in any kind of prodigy. The maxim, by which we commonly conduct ourselves in our reasonings, is, that the objects of which we have no experience, resemble those of which we have; that what we have found to be most usual is always most probable; and that where there is an opposition of arguments, we ought to give the preference to such as are founded on the greatest number of past observations. But though, in proceeding by this rule, we readily reject any fact which is unusual and incredible in an ordinary degree; yet in advancing farther, the mind observes not always the same rule; but when anything is affirmed utterly absurd and miraculous, it rather the more readily admits of such a fact, upon account of that very circumstance, which ought to destroy all its authority. The passion of *surprise* and *wonder*, arising from miracles, being an agreeable emotion, gives a sensible tendency towards the belief of those events, from which it is derived. And this goes so far, that even those who cannot enjoy this pleasure immediately, nor can believe those miraculous events, of which they are informed, yet love to partake of the satisfaction at second-hand or by rebound, and place a pride and delight in exciting the admiration of others.

With what greediness are the miraculous accounts of travelers received, their descriptions of sea and land monsters, their relations of wonderful adventures, strange men, and uncouth manners? But if the spirit of religion join itself to the love of wonder, there is an end of common sense; and human testimony, in these circumstances, loses all pretensions to authority. A religionist may be an enthusiast, and imagine he sees what has no reality: he may know his narrative to be false, and yet persevere in it, with the best intentions in the world, for the sake of promoting so holy a cause: or even where this delusion has not place, vanity, excited by so strong a temptation, operates on him more powerfully than on the rest of mankind in any other circumstances; and self-interest with equal force. His auditors may not have, and commonly have not, sufficient judgment to canvass his evidence: what judgment they have, they renounce by principle, in these sublime and mysterious subjects: or if they were ever so willing to employ it, passion and a heated imagination disturb the regularity of its operations. Their credulity increases his impudence: and his impudence overpowers their credulity.

Eloquence, when at its highest pitch, leaves little room for reason or reflection; but addressing itself entirely to the fancy or the affections, captivates the willing hearers, and subdues their understanding. Happily, this pitch it seldom attains. But what a Tully or a Demosthenes could scarcely effect over a Roman or Athenian audience, every Capuchin, every itinerant or stationary teacher can perform over the generality of mankind, and in a higher degree, by touching such gross and vulgar passions.

The many instances of forged miracles, and prophecies, and supernatural events, which, in all ages, have either been detected by contrary evidence, or which detect themselves by their absurdity, prove sufficiently the strong propensity of mankind to the extraordinary and the marvelous, and ought reasonably to beget a suspicion against all relations of this kind. This is our natural way of thinking, even with regard to the most common and most credible events. For instance: There is no kind of report which rises so easily, and spreads so quickly, especially in country places and provincial towns, as those concerning marriages; insomuch that two young persons of equal condition never see each other twice, but the whole neighborhood immediately join them together. The pleasure of telling a piece of news so interesting, of propagating it, and of being the first reporters of it, spreads the intelligence. And this is so well known, that no man of sense gives attention to these reports, till he find them confirmed by some greater evidence. Do not the same passions, and others still stronger, incline the generality of mankind to believe and report, with the greatest vehemence and assurance, all religious miracles?

Thirdly. It forms a strong presumption against all supernatural and miraculous relations, that they are observed chiefly to abound among ignorant and barbarous nations; or if a civilized people has ever given admission to any of them, that people will be found to have received them from ignorant and barbarous ancestors, who transmitted them with that inviolable sanction and authority which always attend received opinions. When we peruse the first histories of all nations, we are apt to imagine ourselves transported into some new world; where the whole frame of nature is disjointed, and every element performs its operations in a different manner from what it does at present. Battles, revolutions, pestilence, famine and death, are never the effect of those natural causes, which we experience. Prodigies, omens, oracles, judgments, quite obscure the few natural events that are intermingled with them. But as the former grow thinner every page, in proportion as we advance nearer the enlightened ages, we soon learn, that there is nothing mysterious or supernatural in the case, but that all proceeds from the usual propensity of mankind towards the marvelous, and that, though this inclination may at intervals receive a check from sense and learning, it can never be thoroughly extirpated from human nature.

It is strange, a judicious reader is apt to say, upon the perusal of these wonderful historians, *that such prodigious events never happen in our days.* But it is nothing strange, I hope, that men should lie in all ages. You must surely have seen instances enough of that frailty. You have yourself heard many such marvelous relations started, which, being treated with scorn by all the wise and judicious, have at last been abandoned even by the vulgar. Be assured, that those renowned lies, which have spread and flourished to such a monstrous height, arose from like beginnings; but being sown in a more proper soil, shot up at last into prodigies almost equal to those which they relate.

• • •

We are placed in this world, as in a great theater, where the true springs and causes of every event are entirely concealed from us; nor have we either sufficient wisdom to foresee, or power to prevent, those ills with which we are continually threatened. We hang in perpetual suspense between life and death, health and sickness, plenty and want, which are distributed amongst the human species by secret and unknown causes, whose operation is oft unexpected, and always unaccountable. These *unknown causes*, then, become the constant object of our hope and fear; and while the passions are kept in perpetual alarm by an anxious expectation of the events, the imagination is equally employed in forming ideas of those powers on which we have so entire a dependence. Could men anatomize nature, according to the most probable, at least the most intelligible philosophy, they would find that these causes are nothing but the particular fabric and structure of the minute parts of their own bodies and of external objects; and that, by a regular and constant machinery, all the events are produced, about which they are so much concerned. But this philosophy exceeds the comprehension of the ignorant multitude, who can only conceive the *unknown causes*, in a general and confused manner; though their imagination, perpetually employed on the same subject, must labor to form some particular and distinct idea of them. The more they consider these causes themselves, and the uncertainty of their operation, the less satisfaction do they meet with in their researches; and, however unwilling, they must at last have abandoned so arduous an attempt, were it not for a propensity in human nature, which leads into a system that gives them some satisfaction.

There is an universal tendency among mankind to conceive all beings like themselves, and to transfer to every object those qualities with which they are familiarly acquainted, and of which they are intimately conscious. We find human faces in the moon, armies in the clouds; and, by a natural propensity, if not corrected by experience and reflection, ascribe malice or good-will to every thing that hurts or pleases us. Hence the frequency and beauty of the *prosopopœia* in poetry, where trees, mountains, and streams, are personified, and the inanimate parts of nature acquire sentiment and passion. And though these poetical figures and expressions gain not on the belief, they may serve, at least, to prove a certain tendency in the imagination, without which they could neither be beautiful nor natural. Nor is a river-god or hamadryad always taken for a mere poetical or imaginary personage, but may sometimes enter into the real creed of the ignorant vulgar; while each grove or field is represented as possessed of a particular *genius* or invisible power, which inhabits and protects it. Nay, philosophers cannot entirely exempt themselves from this natural frailty; but have oft ascribed to inanimate matter the horror of a *vacuum*, sympathies, antipathies, and other affections of human nature. The absurdity is not less, while we cast our eyes upwards; and, transferring, as is too usual, human passions and infirmities to the Deity, represent him as jealous and revengeful, capricious and partial, and, in short, a wicked and foolish man in every respect but his superior power and authority. No wonder, then, that mankind, being placed in such an absolute ignorance of causes, and being at the same time so anxious concerning their future fortune, should immediately acknowledge a dependence on invisible powers, possessed of sentiment and intelligence. The *unknown causes* which continually employ their thought, appearing always in the same aspect, are all apprehended to be of the same kind or species. Nor is it long before we ascribe to them thought, and reason, and passion, and sometimes even the limbs and figures of men, in order to bring them nearer to a resemblance with ourselves.

In proportion as any man's course of life is governed by accident, we always find that he increases in superstition, as may particularly be observed of gamesters and sailors, who, though of all mankind the least capable of serious reflection, abound most in frivolous and superstitious apprehensions. The gods, says Coriolanus in Dionysius, have an influence in every affair; but above all in war, where the event is so uncertain. All human life, especially before the institution of order and good government, being subject to fortuitous accidents, it is natural that superstition should prevail everywhere in barbarous ages, and put men on the most earnest inquiry concerning those invisible powers, who dispose of their happiness or misery. Ignorant of astronomy and the anatomy of plants and animals, and too little curious to observe the admirable adjustment of final causes, they remain still unacquainted with a first and a Supreme Creator, and with that infinitely Perfect Spirit, who alone, by his almighty will, bestowed order on the whole frame of nature. Such a magnificent idea is too big for their narrow conceptions, which can neither observe the beauty of the work, nor comprehend the grandeur of its author. They suppose their deities, however potent and invisible, to be nothing but a species of human creatures, perhaps raised from among mankind, and retaining all human passions and appetites, together with corporeal limbs and organs. Such limited beings, though masters of human fate, being each of them incapable of extending his influence everywhere, must be vastly multiplied, in order to answer that variety of events which happen over the whole face of nature. Thus every place is stored with a crowd of local deities; and thus polytheism has prevailed, and still prevails, among the greatest part of uninstructed mankind.

REFLECTIONS ON RELIGION

François-Marie Arouet de Voltaire

More than any of the other philosophes, *Voltaire has been identified as the archenemy of supernatural religion. These selections are principally from his* Philosophical Dictionary, *published in 1764. The next to last is a letter of 1770 to Frederick the Great, and the last, "On the Presbyterians," is from his* Letters Concerning the English Nation *(1733), which contains his famous evocation of religious tolerance at London's Royal Exchange.*

The Ecclesiastical Ministry

The institution of religion exists only to keep mankind in order, and to make men merit the goodness of God by their virtue. Everything in a religion which does not tend toward this goal must be considered alien or dangerous.

Instruction, exhortation, threats of torments to come, promises of immortal beatitude, prayers, counsels, spiritual help, are the only means ecclesiastics may use to try to make men virtuous here below, and happy for eternity. All other means are repugnant to the liberty of reason, to the nature of the soul, to the unalterable rights of conscience, to the essence of religion, to that of the ecclesiastical ministry, and to the rights of the sovereign.

Virtue supposes liberty, as the carrying of a burden supposes active force. Under coercion there is no virtue, and without virtue there is no religion. Make a slave of me, and I shall be no better for it. The sovereign, even, has no right to use coercion to lead men to religion, which in its nature presupposes choice and liberty. My thought is subject to authority no more than is sickness or health.

In order to disentangle all the contradictions with which books on canon law have been filled, and to clarify our ideas on the ecclesiastical ministry, let us investigate, amid a thousand equivocations, what the Church really is.

The Church is the assembly of all the faithful summoned on certain days to pray in common, and at all times to do good actions.

The priests are persons established under the authority of the sovereign to direct these prayers and all religious worship.

A numerous Church could not exist without ecclesiastics; but these ecclesiastics are not the Church.

It is no less evident that if the ecclesiastics, who are part of civil society, have acquired rights which might trouble or destroy society, these rights should be suppressed.

It is still more evident that, if God has attached to the Church prerogatives or rights, neither these rights nor these prerogatives should belong exclusively either to the chief of the Church or to the ecclesiastics, because they are not the Church, just as the magistrates are not the sovereign, in either a democratic state or in a monarchy.

Finally, it is quite evident that it is our souls which are under the clergy's care, solely in spiritual matters.

Our soul acts internally. Internal acts are thought, volition, inclinations, acquiescence in certain truths. All these acts are above coercion, and are within the ecclesiastical minister's sphere only in so far as he must instruct, but never command.

The soul also acts externally. External actions are under the civil law. Here coercion may have a place; temporal or corporal penalties maintain the law by punishing those who infringe it.

Obedience to ecclesiastical order must consequently always be free and voluntary: no other should be possible. Submission to civil order, on the other hand, may be compulsory and compelled.

For the same reason, ecclesiastical punishments, always spiritual, reach only those here below who are convinced inwardly of their fault. Civil pains, on the contrary, accompanied by physical ill, have their physical effects, whether or no the guilty person recognizes their justice.

From this it results, obviously, that the authority of the clergy is and can be spiritual only; that the clergy should not have any temporal power; that no coercive force is proper to its ministry, which would be destroyed by force.

It follows from this further that the sovereign, careful not to suffer any partition of his authority, must permit no enterprise which puts the members of society in external and civil dependence on an ecclesiastical body.

Such are the incontestable principles of real canon law, of which the rules and decisions should be judged at all times by the eternal and immutable truths which are founded on natural law and the necessary order of society.

FANATICISM

Fanaticism is to superstition what delirium is to fever and rage to anger. The man visited by ecstasies and visions, who takes dreams for realities and his fancies for prophecies, is an enthusiast; the man who supports his madness with murder is a fanatic. Jean Diaz, in retreat at Nuremberg, was firmly convinced that the Pope was the Antichrist of the Apocalypse, and that he bore the sign of the beast; he was merely an enthusiast; his brother, Bartholomew Diaz, who came from Rome to assassinate his brother out of piety, and who did in fact kill him for the love of God, was one of the most abominable fanatics ever raised up by superstition.

Polyeucte, who goes to the temple on a solemn holiday to knock over and smash the statues and ornaments, is a less dreadful but no less ridiculous fanatic than Diaz. The assassins of the Duke François de Guise, of William, Prince of Orange, of King Henri III, of King Henri IV, and of so many others, were fanatics sick with the same mania as Diaz'.

The most detestable example of fanaticism was that of the burghers of Paris who on St. Bartholomew's Night went about assassinating and butchering all their fellow citizens who did not go to mass, throwing them out of windows, cutting them in pieces.

There are coldblooded fanatics: such as judges who condemn to death those who have committed no other crime than failing to think like them; and these judges are all the more guilty, all the more deserving of the execration of mankind, since, unlike Clément, Châtel, Ravaillac, Damiens, they were not suffering from an attack of insanity; surely they should have been able to listen to reason.

Once fanaticism has corrupted a mind, the malady is almost incurable. I have seen convulsionaries who, speaking of the miracles of Saint Pâris, gradually grew impassioned despite themselves: their eyes got inflamed, their limbs trembled, madness disfigured their faces, and they would have killed anyone who contradicted them.

The only remedy for this epidemic malady is the philosophical spirit which, spread gradually, at last tames men's habits and prevents the disease from starting; for, once the disease has made any progress, one must flee and wait for the air to clear itself. Laws and religion are not strong enough against the spiritual pest; religion, far from being healthy food for infected brains, turns to poison in them. These miserable men have forever in their minds the example of Ehud, who assassinated King Eglon; of Judith, who cut off Holofernes' head while she was sleeping with him; of Samuel, who chopped King Agag in pieces. They cannot see that these examples which were respectable in antiquity are abominable in the present; they borrow their frenzies from the very religion that condemns them.

Even the law is impotent against these attacks of rage; it is like reading a court decree to a raving maniac. These fellows are certain that the holy spirit with which they are filled is above the law, that their enthusiasm is the only law they must obey.

What can we say to a man who tells you that he would rather obey God than men, and that therefore he is sure to go to heaven for butchering you?

Ordinarily fanatics are guided by rascals, who put the dagger into their hands; these latter resemble that Old Man of the Mountain who is supposed to have made imbeciles taste the joys of Paradise and who promised them an eternity of the pleasures of which he had given them a foretaste, on condition that they assassinated all those he would name to them. There is only one religion in the world that has never been sullied by fanaticism, that of the Chinese men of letters. The schools of philosophers were not only free from this pest, they were its remedy; for the effect of philosophy is to make the soul tranquil, and fanaticism is incompatible with tranquility. If our holy religion has so often been corrupted by this infernal delirium, it is the madness of men which is at fault.

Religion

Tonight I was in a meditative mood. I was absorbed in the contemplation of nature; I admired the immensity, the movements, the harmony of those infinite globes which the vulgar do not know how to admire.

I admired still more the intelligence which directs these vast forces. I said to myself: "One must be blind not to be dazzled by this spectacle; one must be stupid not to recognize the author of it; one must be mad not to worship Him. What tribute of worship should I render Him? Should not this tribute be the same in the whole of space, since it is the same supreme power which reigns equally in all space? Should not a thinking being who dwells in a star in the Milky Way offer Him the same homage as the thinking being on this little globe where we are? Light is uniform for the star Sirius and for us; moral philosophy must be uniform. If a sentient, thinking animal in Sirius is born of a tender father and mother who have been occupied with his happiness, he owes them as much love and care as we owe to our parents. If someone in the Milky Way sees a needy cripple, if he can help him, and if he does not do so, he is guilty in the sight of all globes. Everywhere the heart has the same duties: on the steps of the throne of God, if He has a throne; and in the depth of the abyss, if He is an abyss."

I was plunged in these ideas when one of those genii who throng the interplanetary spaces came down to me. I recognized this aerial creature as one who had appeared to me on another occasion, to teach me how different God's judgments were from our own, and how a good action is preferable to an argument.

He transported me into a desert, covered with piles of bones; and between these heaps of dead men there were walks of evergreen trees, and at the end of each walk there was a tall man of august mien, who regarded these sad remains with pity.

"Alas! my archangel," said I, "where have you brought me?"

"To desolation," he answered.

"And who are these fine patriarchs whom I see sad and motionless at the end of these green walks? They seem to be weeping over this countless crowd of dead."

"You shall know, poor human creature," answered the genie from the interplanetary spaces. "But first of all you must weep."

He began with the first pile. "These," he said, "are the twenty-three thousand Jews who danced before a calf, with the twenty-four thousand who were killed while lying with Midianitish women. The number of those massacred for such errors and offenses amounts to nearly three hundred thousand.

"In the other walks are the bones of the Christians slaughtered by each other in metaphysical quarrels. They are divided into several heaps of four centuries each. One heap would have mounted right to the sky, so they had to be divided."

"What!" I cried. "Brothers have treated their brothers like this, and I have the misfortune to be of this brotherhood!"

"Here," said the spirit, "are the twelve million Americans killed in their native land because they had not been baptized."

"My God! why did you not leave these frightful bones to dry in the hemisphere where their bodies were born, and where they were consigned to so many different deaths? Why assemble here all these abominable monuments to barbarism and fanaticism?"

"To instruct you."

"Since you wish to instruct me," I said to the genie, "tell me if there have been peoples other than the Christians and the Jews in whom zeal and religion wretchedly transformed into fanaticism have inspired so many horrible cruelties."

"Yes," he said. "The Mohammedans were sullied with the same inhumanities, but rarely; and when one asked *amman*, pity, of them and offered them tribute, they were merciful. As for the other nations, there has not been a single one, from the beginning of the world, which has ever made a purely religious war. Follow me now." I followed him.

A little beyond these piles of dead men, we found other piles; they were composed of sacks of gold and silver, and each had its label: "Substance of the heretics massacred in the eighteenth century, the seventeenth, and the sixteenth." And so on in going back: "Gold and silver of Americans slaughtered," etc., etc. And all these piles were surmounted with crosses, mitres, croziers, and triple crowns studded with precious stones.

"What, my genie! Do you mean that these dead were piled up for the sake of their wealth?"

"Yes, my son."

I wept. And when, by my grief, I was worthy of being led to the end of the green walks, he led me there.

"Contemplate," he said, "the heroes of humanity who were the world's benefactors, and who were all united in banishing from the world, as far as they were able, violence and rapine. Question them."

I ran to the first of the band. He had a crown on his head, and a little censer in his hand. I humbly asked him his name. "I am Numa Pompilius," he said to me. "I succeeded a brigand, and I had to govern brigands. I taught them virtue and the worship of God, but after me they forgot both more than once. I forbade that there should be any image in the temples, because the Deity which animates nature cannot be represented. During my reign the Romans had neither wars nor seditions, and my religion did nothing but good. All the neighboring peoples came to honor me at my funeral; and a unique honor it was."

I kissed his hand, and I went to the second. He was a fine old man about a hundred years old, clad in a white robe. He put his middle finger on his mouth, and with the other hand he cast some beans behind him. I recognized Pythagoras. He assured me he had never had a golden thigh, and that he had never been a cock; but that he had governed the Crotoniates with as much justice as Numa governed the Romans, almost at the same time; and that this justice was the rarest and most necessary thing in the world. I learned that the Pythagoreans examined their consciences twice a day. The honest people! How far we are from them! But we, who have been nothing but assassins for thirteen hundred years, we call these wise men arrogant.

In order to please Pythagoras, I did not say a word to him, and I passed on to Zoroaster, who was occupied in concentrating the celestial fire in the focus of a concave mirror, in the middle of a hall with a hundred doors which all led to wisdom. (Zoroaster's precepts are called *doors*, and are a hundred in number.) Over the principal door I read these words which are the sum of all moral philosophy, and which cut short all the disputes of the casuists: "When in doubt if an action is good or bad, refrain."

"Certainly," I said to my genie, "the barbarians who immolated all these victims had never read these beautiful words."

We then saw Zaleucus, Thales, Anaximander, and all the sages who had sought truth and practiced virtue.

When we came to Socrates, I recognized him very quickly by his flat nose. "Well," I said to him, "so you are one of the Almighty's confidants! All the inhabitants of Europe, except the Turks and the Tartars of the Crimea, who know nothing, pronounce your name with respect. It is revered, loved, this great name, to the point that people have wanted to know those of your persecutors. Melitus and Anitus are known because of you, just as Ravaillac is known because of Henry IV; but I know only this name of Anitus. I do not know precisely who was the scoundrel who calumniated you, and who succeeded in having you condemned to drink hemlock."

"Since my adventure," replied Socrates, "I have never thought about that man, but seeing that you make me remember it, I pity him. He was a wicked priest who secretly conducted a business in hides, a trade reputed shameful among us. He sent his two children to my school. The other disciples taunted them with having a father who was a currier, and they were obliged to leave. The irritated father did not rest until he had stirred up all the priests and all the sophists against me. They persuaded the council of five hundred that I was an impious fellow who did not believe that the Moon, Mercury, and Mars were gods. Indeed, I used to think, as I think now, that there is only one God, master of all nature. The judges handed me over to the poisoner of the republic. He cut short my life by a few days: I died peacefully at the age of seventy, and since that time I have led a happy life with all these great men whom you see, and of whom I am the least."

After enjoying some time in conversation with Socrates, I went forward with my guide into a grove situated above the thickets where all the sages of antiquity seemed to be tasting sweet repose.

I saw a man of gentle, simple countenance, who seemed to me to be about thirty-five years old. From afar he cast compassionate glances on these piles of whitened bones, across which I had had to pass to reach the sages' abode. I was astonished to find his feet swollen and bleeding, his hands likewise, his side pierced, and his ribs flayed with whip cuts. "Good Heavens!" I said to him, "is it possible for a just man, a sage, to be in this state? I have just seen one who was treated in a very hateful way, but there is no comparison between his torture and yours. Wicked priests and wicked judges poisoned him. Were priests and judges your torturers?"

He answered with much courtesy: "Yes."

"And who were these monsters?"

"They were hypocrites."

"Ah! that says everything. I understand by this single word that they must have condemned you to death. Had you proved to them then, as Socrates did, that the Moon was not a goddess, and that Mercury was not a god?"

"No, these planets were not in question. My compatriots did not know what a planet is; they were all arrant ignoramuses. Their superstitions were quite different from those of the Greeks."

"You wanted to teach them a new religion, then?"

"Not at all. I said to them simply: 'Love God with all your heart and your fellow creature as yourself, for that is man's whole duty.' Judge if this precept is not as old as the universe; judge if I brought them a new religion. I did not stop telling them that I had come not to destroy the law but to fulfill it. I observed all their rites; circumcised as they all were, baptized as were the most zealous among them. Like them I paid the Corban; I observed the Passover as they did, eating, standing up, a lamb cooked with lettuce. I and my friends went to pray in the temple; my friends even frequented this temple after my death. In a word, I fulfilled all their laws without a single exception."

"What! these wretches could not even reproach you with swerving from their laws?"

"No, not possibly."

"Why then did they reduce you to the condition in which I now see you?"

"What do you expect me to say! They were very arrogant and selfish. They saw that I knew them for what they were; they knew that I was making the citizens acquainted with them; they were the stronger; they took away my life: and people like them will always do as much, if they can, to anyone who does them too much justice."

"But did you say nothing, do nothing that could serve them as a pretext?"

"To the wicked everything serves as pretext."

"Did you not say once that you were come not to bring peace, but a sword?"

"It is a copyist's error. I told them that I brought peace and not a sword. I never wrote anything; what I said may have been changed without evil intention."

"You therefore contributed in no way by your speeches, badly reported, badly interpreted, to these frightful piles of bones which I saw on my road in coming to consult you?"

"It is with horror only that I have seen those who have made themselves guilty of these murders."

"And these monuments of power and wealth, of pride and avarice, these treasures, these ornaments, these signs of grandeur, which I have seen piled up on the road while I was seeking wisdom, do they come from you?"

"That is impossible. I and my followers lived in poverty and meanness: my grandeur was in virtue only."

I was about to beg him to be so good as to tell me just who he was. My guide warned me to do nothing of the sort. He told me that I was not made to understand these sublime mysteries. But I did implore him to tell me in what true religion consisted.

"Have I not already told you? Love God and your fellow creature as yourself."

"What! If one loves God, one can eat meat on Friday?"

"I always ate what was given me, for I was too poor to give anyone food."

"In loving God, in being just, should one not be rather cautious not to confide all the adventures of one's life to an unknown being?"

"That was always my practice."

"Can I not, by doing good, dispense with making a pilgrimage to St. James of Compostella?"

"I have never been in that region."

"Is it necessary for me to imprison myself in a retreat with fools?"

"As for me, I was always making little journeys from town to town."

"Is it necessary for me to take sides either for the Greek Church or the Latin?"

"When I was in the world, I never differentiated between the Jew and the Samaritan."

"Well, if that is so, I take you for my only master." Then he made me a sign with his head which filled me with consolation. The vision disappeared, and a clear conscience stayed with me.

SECT

Every sect, of every kind, is a rallying point for doubt and error. Scotist, Thomist, Realist, Nominalist, Papist, Calvinist, Molinist, and Jansenist are only pseudonyms.

There are no sects in geometry. One does not speak of a Euclidean, an Archimedean. When the truth is evident, it is impossible for parties and factions to arise. There has never been a dispute as to whether there is daylight at noon. The branch of astronomy which determines the course of the stars and the return of eclipses being once known, there is no dispute among astronomers.

In England one does not say: "I am a Newtonian, a Lockian, a Halleyan." Why? Those who have read cannot refuse their assent to the truths taught by these three great men. The more Newton is revered, the less do people style themselves Newtonians; this word supposes that there are anti-Newtonians in England. Maybe we still have a few Cartesians in France, but only because Descartes' system is a tissue of erroneous and ridiculous speculations.

It is the same with the small number of matters of fact which are well established. The records of the Tower of London having been authentically gathered by Rymer, there are no Rymerians, because it occurs to no one to assail this collection. In it one finds neither contradictions, absurdities, nor prodigies; nothing which revolts the reason, nothing, consequently, which sectarians strive to maintain or upset by absurd arguments. Everyone agrees, therefore, that Rymer's records are worthy of belief.

You are a Mohammedan; therefore there are people who are not; therefore you might well be wrong.

What would be the true religion if Christianity did not exist? The religion in which there were no sects, the religion in which all minds were necessarily in agreement.

Well, to what dogma do all minds agree? To the worship of a God, and to honesty. All the philosophers of the world who have had a religion have said in all ages: "There is a God, and one must be just." There, then, is the universal religion established in all ages and throughout mankind. The point in which they all agree is therefore true, and the systems through which they differ are therefore false.

"My sect is the best," says a Brahmin to me. But, my friend, if your sect is good, it is necessary; for if it were not absolutely necessary you would admit to me that it was useless. If it is absolutely necessary, it is for all men. How, then, can it be that all men have not what is absolutely necessary to them? How is it possible for the rest of the world to laugh at you and your Brahma?

When Zoroaster, Hermes, Orpheus, Minos, and all the great men say: "Let us worship God, and let us be just," nobody laughs. But everyone hisses the man who claims that one cannot please God unless one is holding a cow's tail when one dies; or the man who wants one to have the end of one's prepuce cut off; or the man who consecrates crocodiles and onions; or the man who attaches eternal salvation to dead men's bones carried under one's shirt, or to a plenary indulgence which may be bought at Rome for two and a half sous.

Whence comes this universal competition in hisses and derision from one end of the world to the other? It is clear that the things at which everyone sneers are not very evidently true. What would we say of one of Sejanus's secretaries who dedicated to Petronius a bombastic book entitled: "The Truths of the Sibylline Oracles, Proved by the Facts"?

This secretary proves to you, first, that it was necessary for God to send on earth several sibyls one after the other; for He had no other means of teaching mankind. It is demonstrated that God spoke to these sibyls, for the word sibyl signifies *God's counsel.* They had to live a long time, for persons to whom God speaks should have this privilege, at the very least. They were twelve in number, for this number is sacred. They had certainly predicted all the events in the world, for Tarquinius Superbus bought three of their books from an old woman for a hundred crowns. "What incredulous fellow," adds the secretary, "will dare deny all these obvious facts which happened in a corner in the sight of the whole world? Who can deny the fulfillment of their prophecies? Has not Virgil himself quoted the predictions of the sibyls? If we have no first editions of the Sibylline Books, written at a time when people did not know how to read or write, have we not authentic copies? Impiety must be silent before such proofs." Thus did Houttevillus speak to Sejanus. He hoped to have a position as augur which would be worth an income of fifty thousand francs, and he had nothing.

"What my sect teaches is obscure, I admit it," says a fanatic; and it is because of this obscurity that it must be believed; for the sect itself says it is full of obscurities. My sect is extravagant, therefore it is divine; for how should what appears so mad have been embraced by so many peoples, if it were not divine?" It is precisely like the Koran, which the Sunnites say has an angel's face and an animal's snout. Be not scandalized by the animal's snout, and worship the angel's face. Thus speaks this mad fellow. But a fanatic of another sect answers: "It is you who are the animal, and I who am the angel."

Well, who shall judge the case? Who shall decide between these two fanatics? Why, the reasonable, impartial man who is learned in a knowledge that is not that of words; the man free from prejudice and the lover of truth and justice—in short, the man who is not the foolish animal, and who does not think he is the angel.

Sect and *error* are synonymous. You are a Peripatetic and I a Platonist; we are therefore both wrong; for you combat Plato only because his fantasies have revolted you, while I am alienated from Aristotle only because it seems to me that he does not know what he is talking about. If one or the other had demonstrated the truth, there would be a sect no longer. To declare oneself for the opinion of one or the other is to take sides in a civil war. There are no sects in mathematics, in experimental physics. A man who examines the relations between a cone and a sphere is not of the sect of Archimedes: he who sees that the square of the hypotenuse of a right angled triangle is equal to the square of the two other sides is not of the sect of Pythagoras.

When you say that the blood circulates, that the air is heavy, that the sun's rays are pencils of seven refrangible rays, you are not either of the sect of Harvey, or the sect of Torricelli, or the sect of Newton; you merely agree with the truth as demonstrated by them, and the entire world will always be of your opinion.

This is the character of truth: it is of all time, it is for all men, it has only to show itself to be recognized, and one cannot argue against it. A long dispute means that *both parties are wrong*.

Superstition

The superstitious man is to the rogue what the slave is to the tyrant. Further, the superstitious man is governed by the fanatic and becomes a fanatic. Superstition born in paganism, and adopted by Judaism, invested the Christian Church from the earliest times. All the fathers of the Church, without exception, believed in the power of magic. The

Church always condemned magic, but she always believed in it: she did not excommunicate sorcerers as madmen who were mistaken, but as men who were really in communication with the devil.

Today one half of Europe thinks that the other half has long been and still is superstitious. The Protestants regard the relics, the indulgences, the mortifications, the prayers for the dead, the holy water, and almost all the rites of the Roman Church, as evidences of superstitious dementia. Superstition, according to them, consists in taking useless practices for necessary practices. Among the Roman Catholics there are some more enlightened than their ancestors, who have renounced many of these usages formerly considered sacred; and they defend themselves against the others who have retained them, by saying: "They are unimportant, and what is merely unimportant cannot be an evil."

It is difficult to set the limits of superstition. A Frenchman traveling in Italy finds almost everything superstitious, and he is right. The Archbishop of Canterbury maintains that the Archbishop of Paris is superstitious; the Presbyterians direct the same reproach against His Grace of Canterbury, and are in their turn treated as superstitious by the Quakers, who are the most superstitious of all in the eyes of other Christians.

In Christian societies, therefore, no one agrees as to what superstition is. The sect which seems to be the least attacked by this malady of the intelligence is that which has the fewest rites. But if, with few ceremonies, it is still strongly attached to an absurd belief, this absurd belief is equivalent alone to all the superstitious practices observed from the time of Simon the magician to that of Father Gauffridi.

It is therefore clear that it is the fundamentals of the religion of one sect which are considered as superstition by another sect.

The Moslems accuse all Christian societies of it, and are themselves accused. Who will judge this great matter? Will it be reason? But each sect claims to have reason on its side. It will therefore be force which will judge, while awaiting the time when reason can penetrate a sufficient number of heads to disarm force.

Up to what point can statecraft permit superstition to be destroyed? This is a very thorny question. It is like asking to what depth should one make an incision in a dropsical person, who may die under the operation. It is a matter for the doctor's discretion.

Can there exist a people free from all superstitious prejudices? This is equivalent to asking: Can there exist a nation of philosophers? It is said that there is no superstition in the magistracy of China. It is probable that some day none will remain in the magistracy of a few towns of Europe.

Then the magistrates will stop the superstition of the people from being dangerous. These magistrates' example will not enlighten the mob, but the leading citizens of the middle class will hold the mob in check. There is perhaps not a single riot, a single religious outrage in which the middle classes were not once involved; because these same middle classes were then the mob. But reason and time will have changed them. Their softened manners will soften those of the lowest and most savage populace. We have had striking examples of this in more than one country. In a word, less superstition, less fanaticism; and less fanaticism, less misery.

Tolerance

What is tolerance? It is the natural attribute of humanity. We are all formed of weakness and error: let us pardon reciprocally each other's folly. That is the first law of nature.

It is clear that the individual who persecutes a man, his brother, because he is not of the same opinion, is a monster. There is no difficulty here. But the government! But the magistrates! But the princes! How do they treat those whose religion is other than theirs? If they are powerful foreigners, it is certain that a prince will make an alliance with them. François I, most Christian, will unite with Mussulmans against Charles V, most Catholic. François I will give money to the Lutherans of Germany to support them in their revolt against the Emperor; but, in accordance with custom, he will start by having Lutherans burned at home. For political reasons he pays them in Saxony; for political reasons he burns them in Paris. But what happens? Persecutions make proselytes. Soon France will be full of new Protestants. At first they will let themselves be hanged, later they in their turn will hang. There will be civil wars, then will come St. Bartholomew's Eve, and this corner of the world will be worse than all that the ancients and moderns have ever told of hell.

Madmen, who have never been able to worship the God who made you! Miscreants, whom the examples of the learned Chinese, the Parsees, and all the sages have never been able to lead! Monsters, who need superstitions as crows' gizzards need carrion! It has been said before, and it must be said again: if you have two religions in your land, the two will cut each other's throats; but if you have thirty religions, they will dwell in peace. Look at the Great Turk. He governs Guebres, Banians, Greek Christians, Nestorians, Romans. The first who tried to stir up tumult would be impaled; and everyone is at peace.

Of all religions, the Christian is without doubt the one which should inspire tolerance most, although up to now the Christians have been the most intolerant of all men. The Christian Church was divided in its cradle, and was divided even in the persecutions which it sometimes endured under the first emperors. Often the martyr was regarded as an apostate by his brethren, and the Carpocratian Christian expired beneath the sword of the Roman executioners, excommunicated by the Ebionite Christian, while the Ebionite was anathema to the Sabellian.

This horrible discord, which has lasted for so many centuries, is a very striking lesson that we should pardon each other's errors. Discord is the great ill of mankind, and tolerance is the only remedy for it.

There is nobody who does not agree with this truth, whether he meditates soberly in his study, or peaceably examines the truth with his friends. Why then do the same men who in private advocate indulgence, kindness, and justice, vise in public with so much fury against these virtues? Why? Can it be that their own interest is their god, and that they sacrifice everything to this monster which they worship?

I possess a dignity and a power founded on ignorance and credulity; I walk on the heads of the men who lie prostrate at my feet; if they should rise and look me in the face, I am lost; I must bind them to the ground, therefore, with iron chains. Thus have reasoned the men whom centuries of bigotry have made powerful. They have other powerful men beneath them, and these have still others, who all enrich themselves with the spoils of the poor, grow fat on their blood, and laugh at their stupidity. They all detest tolerance, as partisans grown rich at the public expense fear to render their accounts, and as tyrants dread the word liberty. And then, to crown everything, they hire fanatics to cry at the top of their voices: "Respect my master's absurdities, tremble, pay, and keep your mouths shut."

It is thus that a great part of the world was long treated; but today when so many sects make a balance of power, what course shall we take with them? Every sect, as one knows, is a ground of error; there are no sects of geometers, algebraists, arithmeticians, because all the propositions of geometry, algebra, and arithmetic are true. In every other field of knowledge one may be deceived. What Thomist or Scotist theologian would dare say seriously that he is sure of his case?

If it were permitted to reason consistently in religious matters, it would be clear that we all ought to become Jews, because Jesus Christ our Savior was born a Jew, lived a Jew, died a Jew, and said expressly that he was accomplishing, that he was fulfilling the Jewish religion. But it is clearer still that we ought to be tolerant of one another, because we are all weak, inconsistent, liable to fickleness and error. Shall a reed laid low in the mud by the wind say to a fellow reed fallen in the opposite direction: "Crawl! as I crawl, wretch, or I shall petition that you be torn up by the roots and burned"?

To Frederick William, Prince of Prussia

Monseigneur, the royal family of Prussia has excellent reasons for not wishing the annihilation of the soul. It has more right than anyone to immortality.

It is very true that we do not know any too well what the soul is: no one has ever seen it. All that we do know is that the eternal Lord of nature has given us the power of thinking, and of distinguishing virtue. It is not proved that this faculty survives our death: but the contrary is not proved either. It is possible, doubtless, that God has given thought to a particle to which, after we are no more, He will still give the power of thought: there is no inconsistency in this idea.

In the midst of all the doubts which we have discussed for four thousand years in four thousand ways, the safest course is to do nothing against one's conscience. With this secret, we can enjoy life and have nothing to fear from death.

There are some charlatans who admit no doubts. We know nothing of first principles. It is surely very presumptuous to define God, the angels, spirits, and to pretend to know precisely why God made the world, when we do not know why we can move our arms at our pleasure.

Doubt is not a pleasant condition, but certainty is an absurd one.

What is most repellent in the *System of Nature* [of Holbach]—after the recipe to make eels from flour—is the audacity with which it decides that there is no God, without even having tried to prove the impossibility. There is some eloquence in the book: but much more rant, and no sort of proof. It is a pernicious work, alike for princes and people:

"Si Dieu n'existait pas, il faudrait l'inventer." [If God did not exist, it would be necessary to invent him.]

But all nature cries aloud that He does exist: that there *is* a supreme intelligence, an immense power, an admirable order, and everything teaches us our own dependence on it.

From the depth of our profound ignorance, let us do our best: this is what I think, and what I have always thought, amid all the misery and follies inseparable from seventy-seven years of life.

Your Royal Highness has a noble career before you. I wish you, and dare prophesy for you, a happiness worthy of yourself and of your heart. I knew you when you were a child, monseigneur: I visited you in your sick room when you had smallpox: I feared for your life. Your father honored me with much goodness: you condescend to shower on me the same favors which are the honor of my old age, and the consolation of those sufferings which must shortly end it. I am, with deep respect, etc.

On the Presbyterians

The Church of England is confined almost to the kingdom whence it received its name, and to Ireland, for Presbyterianism is the established religion in Scotland. This Presbyterianism is directly the same with Calvinism as it was established in France and is now professed at Geneva. As the priests of this sect receive but very inconsiderable stipends from their churches, and consequently cannot emulate the splendid luxury of bishops, they exclaim very naturally against honors which they can never attain to. Figure to yourself the haughty Diogenes, trampling under foot the pride of Plato. The Scotch Presbyterians are not very unlike that proud though tattered reasoner. Diogenes did not use Alexander half so impertinently as these treated King Charles the Second; for when they took up arms in his cause, in opposition to Oliver, who had deceived them, they forced that poor monarch to undergo the hearing of three or four sermons every day; would not suffer him to play, reduced him to a state of penitence and mortification; so that Charles soon grew sick of these pedants, and accordingly eloped from them with as much joy as a youth does from school.

A Church of England minister appears as another Cato in presence of a juvenile, sprightly French graduate, who bawls for a whole morning together in the divinity schools, and hums a song in chorus with ladies in the evening: But this Cato is a very spark when before a Scotch Presbyterian. The latter affects a serious gait, puts on a sour look, wears a vastly broad-brimmed hat, and a long cloak over a very short coat; preaches through the nose, and gives the name of the whore of Babylon to all churches where the ministers are so fortunate as to enjoy an annual revenue of five or six thousand pounds, and where the people are weak enough to suffer this and to give them the titles of my lord, your lordship, or your eminence.

These gentlemen, who have also some churches in England, introduced there the mode of grave and severe exhortations. To them is owing the sanctification of Sunday in the three kingdoms. People are there forbid to work or take any recreation on that day, in which the severity is twice as great as that of the Romish church. No operas, plays or concerts are allowed in London on Sundays; and even cards are so expressly forbid, that none but persons of quality and those we call the genteel play on that day; the rest of the nation go either to church, to the tavern, or to see their mistresses.

Though the Episcopal and Presbyterian sects are the two prevailing ones in Great Britain, yet all others are very welcome to come and settle in it, and live very sociably together, though most of their preachers hate one another almost as cordially as a Jansenist damns a Jesuit.

Take a view of the Royal Exchange in London, a place more venerable than many courts of justice, where the representatives of all nations meet for the benefit of mankind. There the Jew, the Mahometan, and the Christian transact together as though they all professed the same religion, and give the name of Infidel to none but bankrupts. There the Presbyterian confides in the Anabaptist, and the Churchman depends on the Quaker's word. At the breaking up of this pacific and free assembly, some withdraw to the synagogue, and others to take a glass. This man goes and is baptized in a great tub, in the name of the Father, Son, and Holy Ghost: That man has his son's foreskin cut off, whilst a set of Hebrew words (quite unintelligible to him) are mumbled over his child. Others retire to their churches, and there wait for the inspiration of heaven with their hats on, and all are satisfied.

If one religion only were allowed in England, the government would very possibly become arbitrary; if there were but two, the people would cut one another's throats; but as there are such a multitude, they all live happy and in peace.

PROFESSION OF FAITH OF A SAVOYARD VICAR

JEAN-JACQUES ROUSSEAU

Always somewhat at odds with his fellow philosophes, *Jean-Jacques Rousseau (1712–1778) offers a deism much more reflective of heartfelt religious sensibility. This profession of faith is from his 1762 novel,* Emile.

I believe, therefore, that the world is governed by a wise and powerful *Will.* I see it, or rather I feel it; and this is of importance for me to know. But is the world eternal, or is it created? Are things derived from one self-existent principle, or are there two or more, and what is their essence? Of all this I know nothing, nor do I see that it is necessary I should. In proportion as such knowledge may become interesting I will endeavor to acquire it: but further than this I give up all such idle disquisitions, which serve only to make me discontented with myself, which are useless in practice, and are above my understanding.

You will remember, however, that I am not dictating my sentiments to you, but only explaining what they are. Whether matter be eternal or only created, whether it have a passive principle or not, certain it is that the whole universe is one design, and sufficiently displays one intelligent agent: for I see no part of this system that is not under regulation, or that does not concur to one and the same end; viz., that of preserving the present and established order of things. That Being, whose will is his deed, whose principle of action is in himself—that Being, in a word, whatever it be, that gives motion to all parts of the universe, and governs all things, I call GOD.

To this term I affix the ideas of intelligence, power, and will, which I have collected from the order of things; and to these I add that of goodness, which is a necessary consequence of their union. But I am not at all the wiser concerning the essence of the Being to which I give these attributes. He remains at an equal distance from my senses and my understanding. The more I think of him, the more I am confounded. I know of a certainty that he exists, and that his existence is independent of any of his creatures. I know also that my existence is dependent on his, and that every being I know is in the same situation as myself. I perceive the deity in all his works, I feel him within me, and behold him in every object around me: but I no sooner endeavor to contemplate what he is in himself—I no sooner enquire where he is, and what is his substance, than he eludes the strongest efforts of my imagination; and my bewildered understanding is convinced of its own weakness.

For this reason I shall never take upon me to argue about the nature of God further than I am obliged to do by the relation he appears to stand in to myself. There is so great a temerity in such disquisitions that a wise man will never enter on them without trembling, and feeling fully assured of his incapacity to proceed far on so sublime a subject: for it is less injurious to entertain no ideas of the deity at all, than to harbor those which are unworthy and unjust.

After having discovered those of his attributes by which I am convinced of his existence, I return to myself and consider the place I occupy in that order of things, which is directed by him and subjected to my examination. Here I find my species stand incontestibly in the first rank; as man, by virtue of his will and the instruments he is possessed of to put it in execution, has a greater power over the bodies by which he is surrounded than they, by mere physical impulse, have over him. By virtue of his intelligence, I also find, he is the only created being here below that can take a general survey of the whole system. Is there one among them, except man, who knows how to observe all others? to weight, to calculate, to foresee their motions, their effects, and to join, if I may so express myself, the sentiment of a general existence to that of the individual? What is there so very ridiculous then in supposing everything made for man, when he is the only created being who knows how to consider the relation in which all things stand to himself?

It is then true that man is lord of the creation, that he is, at least, sovereign over the habitable earth; for it is certain that he not only subdues all other animals, and even disposes by his industry of the elements at his pleasure, but he alone of all terrestrial beings knows how to subject to his convenience, and even by contemplation to appropriate to his use, the very stars and planets he cannot approach. Let anyone produce me an animal of another species who knows how to make use of fire, or hath faculties to admire the sun. What! am I able to observe, to know other beings and their relations; am I capable of discovering what is order, beauty, virtue, of contemplating the universe, of elevating my ideas to the hand which governs the whole; am I capable of loving what is good and doing it, and shall I compare myself to the brutes? Abject soul! it is your gloomy philosophy alone that renders you at all like them. Or, rather, it is in vain you would debase yourself. Your own genius rises up against your principles; your benevolent heart gives the lie to your absurd doctrines, and even the abuse of your faculties demonstrates their excellence in spite of yourself.

For my part, who have no system to maintain, who am only a simple, honest man, attached to no party, unambitious of being the founder of any sect, and contented with the situation in which God hath placed me, I see nothing in the world, except the deity, better than my own species; and were I left to choose my place in the order of created beings, I see none that I could prefer to that of man.

This reflection, however, is less vain than affecting; for my state is not the effect of choice, and could not be due to the merit of a being that did not before exist. Can I behold myself, nevertheless thus distinguished, without thinking myself happy in occupying so honorable a post; or without blessing the hand that placed me here? From the first view I thus took of myself, my heart began to glow with a sense of gratitude towards the author of our being; and hence arose my first idea of the worship due to a beneficent deity. I adore the supreme power, and melt into tenderness at his goodness. I have no need to be taught artificial forms of worship; the dictates of nature are sufficient. Is it not a natural consequence of self-love to honor those who protect us, and to love such as do us good?

But when I come afterwards to take a view of the particular rank and relation in which I stand, as an individual, among the fellow creatures of my species; to consider the different ranks of society and the persons by whom they are filled; what a scene is presented to me! Where is that order and regularity before observed? The scenes of nature present to my view the most perfect harmony and proportion: those of mankind nothing but confusion and disorder. The physical elements of things act in concert with each other; the moral world alone is a chaos of discord. Mere animals are happy; but man, their lord and sovereign, is miserable! Where, Supreme Wisdom! are thy laws? Is it thus, O Providence! thou governest the world? What is become of thy power, thou Supreme Beneficence, when I behold evil thus prevailing upon the earth?

Would you believe, my good friend, that from such gloomy reflections and apparent contradictions, I should form to myself more sublime ideas of the soul than ever resulted from my former researches? In meditating on the nature of man, I conceived that I discovered two distinct principles; the one raising him to the study of eternal truths, the love of justice and moral beauty—bearing him aloft to the regions of the intellectual world, the contemplation of which yields the truest delight to the philosopher—the other debasing him even below himself, subjecting him to the slavery of sense, the tyranny of the passions, and exciting these to counteract every noble and generous sentiment inspired by the former. When I perceived myself hurried away by two such contrary powers, I naturally concluded that man is not one simple and individual substance. I will, and I will not; I perceive myself at once free, and a slave; I see what is good, I admire it, and yet I do the evil: I am active when I listen to my reason, and passive when hurried away by my passions; while my greatest uneasiness is to find, when fallen under temptations, that I had the power of resisting them.

Attend, young man, with confidence to what I say; you will find I shall never deceive you. If conscience be the offspring of our prejudices, I am doubtless in the wrong, and moral virtue is not to be demonstrated; but if self-love, which makes us prefer ourselves to everything else, be natural to man, and if nevertheless an innate sense of justice be found in his heart, let those who imagine him to be a simple uncompounded being reconcile these contradictions, and I will give up my opinion and acknowledge him to be one substance.

You will please to observe that by the word substance I here mean, in general, a being possessed of some primitive quality, abstracted from all particular or secondary modifications. Now, if all known primitive qualities may be united in one and the same being, we have no need to admit of more than one substance; but if some of these qualities are incompatible with, and necessarily exclusive of each other, we must admit of the existence of as many different substances as there are such incompatible qualities. You will do well to reflect on this subject. For my part, notwithstanding what Mr. Locke hath said on this head, I need only to know that matter is extended and divisible, to be assured that it cannot think; and when a philosopher comes and tells me that trees and rocks have thought and perception, he may, perhaps, embarrass me with the subtlety of his arguments, but I cannot help regarding him as a disingenuous sophist, who had rather attribute sentiment to stocks and stones than acknowledge man to have a soul.

Let us suppose that a man, born deaf, should deny the reality of sounds, because his ears were never sensible of them. To convince him of his error, I place a violin before his eyes; and, by playing on another, concealed from him, give a vibration to the strings of the former. This motion, I tell him, is effected by sound.

"Not at all," says he, "the cause of the vibration of the string is in the string itself: it is a common quality in all bodies so to vibrate."

"Show me then," I reply, "the same vibration in other bodies; or, at least, the cause of it in this string."

"I cannot," the deaf man may reply, "but wherefore must I, because I do not conceive how this string vibrates, attribute the cause to your pretended sounds, of which I cannot entertain the least idea? This would be to attempt an explanation of one obscurity by another still greater. Either make your sounds perceptible to me, or I shall continue to doubt their existence."

The more I reflect on our capacity of thinking, and the nature of the human understanding, the greater is the resemblance I find between the arguments of our materialists and that of such a deaf man. They are, in effect, equally deaf to that internal voice which, nevertheless, calls to them so loud and emphatically. A mere machine is evidently incapable of thinking, it has neither motion nor figure productive of reflection: whereas in man there exists something perpetually prone to expand, and to burst the fetters by which it is confined. Space itself affords not bounds to the human mind: the whole universe is not extensive enough for man; his sentiments, his desires, his anxieties, and even his pride, take rise from a principle different from that body within which he perceives himself confined.

No material being can be self-active, and I perceive that I am so. It is in vain to dispute with me so clear a point. My own sentiment carries with it a stronger conviction than any reason which can ever be brought against it. I have a body on which other bodies act, and which acts reciprocally upon them. This reciprocal action is indubitable; but my will is independent of my senses. I can either consent to, or resist, their impressions. I am either vanquished or victor, and perceive clearly within myself when I act according to my will, and when I submit to be governed by my passions. I have always the power to will, though not the force to execute it. When I give myself up to any temptation, I act from the impulse of external objects. When I reproach myself for my weakness in so doing, I listen only to the dictates of my will. I am a slave in my vices, and free in my repentance. The sentiment of my liberty is effaced only by my depravation, and when I prevent the voice of the soul from being heard in opposition to the laws of the body. . . .

Enquire no longer then, who is the author of evil. Behold him in yourself. There exists no other evil in nature than what you either do or suffer, and you are equally the author of both. A general evil could exist only in disorder, but in the system of nature I see an established order, which is never disturbed. Particular evil exists only in the sentiment of the suffering being; and this sentiment is not given to man by nature, but is of his own acquisition. Pain and sorrow have but little hold on those who, unaccustomed to reflection, have neither memory nor foresight. Take away our fatal improvements, take away our errors and our vices, take away, in short, everything that is the work of man, and all that remains is good.

Where everything is good, nothing can be unjust, justice being inseparable from goodness. Now goodness is the necessary effect of infinite power and self-love essential to every being conscious of its existence. An omnipotent Being extends its existence also, if I may so express myself, with that of its creatures. Production and preservation follow from the constant exertion of its power: it does not act on non-existence. God is not the God of the dead, but of the living. He cannot be mischievous or wicked without hurting himself. A being capable of doing everything cannot *will* to do anything but what is good. He who is infinitely good, therefore, because he is infinitely powerful, must also be supremely just, otherwise he would be inconsistent with himself. For that love of order which produces it we call goodness, and that love of order which preserves it is called justice.

God, it is said, owes nothing to his creatures. For my part, I believe he owes them everything he promised them when he gave them being. Now what is less than to promise them a blessing, if he gives them an idea of it, and has so constituted them as to feel the want of it? The more I look into myself, the more plainly I read these words written in my soul: *Be just and thou wilt be happy.* I see not the truth of this, however, in the present state of things, wherein the wicked triumph and the just are trampled on and oppressed. What indignation, hence, arises within us to find that our hopes are frustrated! Conscience itself rises up and complains of its maker. It cries out to him, lamenting, *Thou hast deceived me!*

"I have deceived thee, rash man? Who hath told thee so? Is thy soul annihilated? Dost thou cease to exist? Oh, Brutus! stain not a life of glory in the end. Leave not thy honor and thy hopes with thy body in the fields of Philippi. Wherefore dost thou say, virtue is a shadow, when thou wilt yet enjoy the reward of thine own? Dost thou imagine thou art going to die? No! thou art going to live! and then will I make good every promise I have made to thee."

"NO NEED OF THEOLOGY . . . ONLY OF REASON . . ."

BARON D'HOLBACH

Paul Henri Thiry, baron d'Holbach (1723–1789), was a philosophical materialist who unabashedly preached atheism. The following selection is from his Common Sense, or Natural Ideas Opposed to Supernatural, *published in 1772.*

When we coolly examine the opinions of men, we are surprised to find, that in those, which they regard as the most essential, nothing is more uncommon than the use of common sense; or, in other words, a degree of judgment sufficient to discover the most simple truths, to reject the most striking absurdities, and to be shocked with palpable contradictions. We have an example of it in theology, a science revered in all times and countries, by the greatest number of men; an object they regard as the most important, the most useful, and the most indispensable to the happiness of societies. Indeed, with little examination of the principles, upon which this pretended science is founded, we are forced to acknowledge, that these principles, judged incontestable, are only hazardous suppositions, imagined by ignorance, propagated by enthusiasm or knavery, adopted by timid credulity, preserved by custom, which never reasons, and revered solely because not understood. *Some,* says Monta[i]gne, *make the world think, that they believe what they do not; others, in greater number, make themselves think, that they believe what they do not, not knowing what belief is.*

In a word, whoever will deign to consult common sense upon religious opinions, and bestow in this inquiry the attention that is commonly given to objects, we presume interesting, will easily perceive, that these opinions have no foundation; that all religion is an edifice in the air; that theology is only the ignorance of natural causes reduced to system; that it is a long tissue of chimeras and contradictions. That it represents, in every country, to the different nations of the earth, only romances void of probability, the hero of which is himself composed of qualities impossible to combine; that his name, exciting in all hearts respect and fear, is only a vague word, which men have continually in their mouths, without being able to affix to it ideas or qualities, which are not contradicted by facts, or evidently inconsistent with one another.

The idea of this being, of whom we have no idea, or rather, the word by which he is designated, would be an indifferent thing, did it not cause innumerable ravages in the world. Prepossessed with the opinion, that this phantom is an interesting reality, men, instead of concluding wisely from its incomprehensibility, that they are not bound to regard it; on the contrary infer, that they cannot sufficiently meditate upon it, that they must contemplate it without ceasing, reason upon it without end, and never lose sight of it. Their invincible ignorance, in this respect, far from discouraging them, irritates their curiosity; instead of putting them upon guard against their imagination, this ignorance renders them decisive, dogmatical, imperious, and even exasperates them against all, who oppose doubts to the reveries, which their brains have begotten.

What perplexity arises, when it is required to solve an insolvable problem! Restless meditations upon an object, impossible to understand, in which, however, he thinks himself much concerned, cannot but put man in a very ill humor, and produce in his head dangerous transports. Let interest, vanity and ambition, co-operate ever so little with these dispositions, and society must necessarily be disturbed. This is the reason that so many nations have often been the theaters of the extravagances of senseless dreamers, who, believing, or publishing their empty speculations as eternal truths, have kindled the enthusiasm of princes and people, and armed them for opinions, which they represented as essential to the glory of the Deity, and the happiness of empires. In all parts of our globe, intoxicated fanatics have been seen cutting each other's throats, lighting funeral piles, committing, without scruple and even as a duty, the greatest crimes, and shedding torrents of blood. For what? To strengthen, support, or propagate the impertinent conjectures of some enthusiasts, or to give validity to the cheats of some impostors, in the name and behalf of a being, who exists only in their imagination, and who has made himself known only by the ravages, disputes, and follies, he has caused upon the earth.

Fierce and uncultivated nations, perpetually at war, have in their origin, under divers names, adored some God, conformable to their ideas; that is to say, cruel, carnivorous, selfish, blood-thirsty. We find, in all religions of the earth, a *God of armies,* a *jealous God,* an *avenging God,* a *destroying God,* a *God,* who is pleased with carnage, and whom his worshippers, as a duty, serve to his taste. Lambs, bulls, children, men, heretics, infidels, kings, whole nations are sacrificed to him. Do not the zealous servants of this so barbarous God, even think it a duty to offer up themselves as a sacrifice to him? We every where see madmen, who, after dismal meditations upon their terrible God, imagine, that to please him, they must do themselves all possible injury, and inflict on themselves, for his honor, invented torments. In short, the gloomy ideas of the divinity, far from consoling men under the evils of life, have every where disquieted and confused their minds, and produced follies destructive to their happiness.

Infested with frightful phantoms, and guided by men, interested in perpetuating its ignorance and fears, how could the human mind have made any considerable progress? Man has been forced to vegetate in his primitive stupidity; nothing has been offered to his mind, but stories of invisible powers, upon whom his happiness was supposed to depend. Occupied solely by his fears, and unintelligible reveries, he has always been at the mercy of his priests, who have reserved to themselves the right of thinking for him, and directing his actions.

Thus man has been, and ever will remain, a child without experience, a slave without courage, a stupid animal, who has feared to reason, and who has never known how to extricate himself from the labyrinth, where his ancestors had strayed. He has believed himself forced to groan under the yoke of his gods, whom he has known only by the fabulous accounts of his ministers, who, after having bound him with the chords of opinion, have remained his masters; or rather have abandoned him, defenseless, to the absolute power of tyrants, no less terrible than the gods, whose representatives they have been upon earth.

Crushed under the double yoke of spiritual and temporal power, it was impossible for the people to know and pursue their happiness. As religion, politics, and morality became sanctuaries, into which the ungodly were not permitted to enter, men had no other morality, than what their legislators and priests brought down from the unknown regions of the Empyrean. The human mind, confused with its theological opinions, forgot itself, doubted its own powers, mistrusted experience, feared truth, disdained its reason, and abandoned her direction, blindly to follow authority. Man was a mere machine in the hands of his tyrants and priests, who alone had the right of directing his actions; always led like a slave, he ever had his vices and character. These are the true causes of the corruption of morals, to which religion ever opposes only ideal barriers, and that without effect. Ignorance and servitude are calculated to make men wicked and unhappy. Knowledge, reason, and liberty can alone reform them, and make them happier; but every thing conspires to blind them, and confirm their errors. Priests cheat them, tyrants corrupt, the better to enslave them. Tyranny ever was, and ever will be, the true cause of the corruption of morals, and the habitual calamities of men; who, almost always fascinated with religious notions, and metaphysical fictions, instead of turning their eyes to the natural and obvious causes of their misery, attribute their vices to the imperfection of their nature, and their unhappiness to the anger of the gods. They offer up to heaven vows, sacrifices, and presents, to obtain the end of their sufferings, which, in reality, are chargeable only to the negligence, ignorance, and perversity of their guides, the folly of their institutions, their silly customs, false opinions, irrational laws, and above all, to the want of knowledge. Let men's minds be filled with true ideas; let their reason be cultivated; let justice govern them; and there will be no need of opposing to the passions, such a feeble barrier, as a fear of gods. Men will be good, when they are well instructed, well governed, and when they are punished or despised for the evil, and justly rewarded for the good, they do to their fellow-creatures.

In vain should we attempt to cure men of their vices, unless we begin by curing them of their prejudices. It is only by shewing them the truth, that they will know their dearest interests, and the motives that ought to incline them to do good. Instructors have long enough fixed men's eyes upon heaven, let them now turn them upon earth. Fatigued with an inconceivable theology, ridiculous fables, impenetrable mysteries, puerile ceremonies, let the human mind apply itself to the study of nature, to intelligible objects, sensible truths, and useful knowledge. Let the vain chimeras of men be removed, and reasonable opinions will soon come of themselves, into those heads, which were thought to be forever destined to error.

Does it not suffice to annihilate or shake religious prejudices, to shew, that what is inconceivable to man, cannot be made for him? Does it then require any thing, but plain, common sense, to perceive, that a being incompatible with the most evident notions; that a cause continually opposed to the effects, which we attribute to it; that a being, of whom we can say nothing, without falling into contradiction; that a being, who, far from explaining the enigmas of the universe, only makes them more inexplicable; that a being, whom for so many ages men have so vainly addressed to obtain their happiness, and the end of their sufferings; does it require, I say, any thing but plain, common sense, to perceive, that the idea of such a being is an idea without model, and that it is evidently only a being of imagination? Is any thing necessary but common sense to perceive, at least, that it is madness and folly to hate and torment one another for unintelligible opinions upon a being of this kind? In short, does not every thing prove, that morality and virtue are totally incompatible with the notions of a God, whom his ministers and interpreters have described in every country, as the most capricious, unjust, and cruel of tyrants, whose pretended will, however, must serve as law and rule to the inhabitants of the earth?

To learn the true principles of morality, men have no need of theology, of revelation, or gods: They have need only of reason. They have only to enter into themselves, to reflect upon their own nature, consult their sensible interests, consider the object of society, and of the individuals, who compose it; and they will easily perceive, that virtue is the interest, and vice the unhappiness of beings of their kind. Let us persuade men to be just, beneficent, moderate, sociable; not because the gods demand it, but because they must please men. Let us advise them to abstain from vice and crimes; not because they will be punished in the other world, but because they will suffer for it in this.—*There are,* says a great man, *means to prevent crimes—these are punishments; there are those to reform manners—these are good examples.*

Truth is simple; error is complex, uncertain in its progress, and full of windings. The voice of nature is intelligible; that of falsehood is ambiguous, enigmatical, mysterious; the way of truth is straight; that of imposture is crooked and dark. Truth, forever necessary to man, must necessarily be felt by all upright minds; the lessons of reason are formed to be followed by all honest men. Men are unhappy only because they are ignorant; they are ignorant only because every thing conspires to prevent their being enlightened; they are so wicked only because their reason is not yet sufficiently unfolded.

By what fatality then, have the first founders of all sects given to their gods the most ferocious characters, at which nature recoils? Can we imagine a conduct more abominable, than that ascribed by Moses to his God, towards the Egyptians, where that assassin proceeds boldly to declare, in the name, and by the order of *his* God, that Egypt shall be afflicted with the greatest calamities, that can happen to man. Of all the different ideas, which they wish to give us of a supreme being, of a God, creator and preserver of men, there are none more horrible, than those of these impostors, who believed themselves inspired by a divine spirit.

Why, O theologians! do you presume to rummage in the impenetrable mysteries of a first being, whom you call inconceivable to the human mind. You are the first blasphemers, in attributing to a being, perfect according to you, so many horrors, committed towards creatures, whom he has made out of nothing. Confess, with us, your ignorance of a creating God; and forbear, in your turn, to meddle with mysteries, which man seems unworthy of knowing. . . .

Religion, especially with the moderns, has tried to identify itself with morality, the principles of which it has thereby totally obscured. It has rendered men unsociable by duty, and forced them to be inhuman to everyone who thought differently from themselves. Theological disputes, equally unintelligible to each of the enraged parties, have shaken empires, caused revolutions, been fatal to sovereigns and desolated all Europe. These contemptible quarrels have not been extinguished even in rivers of blood. Since the extinction of Paganism, the people have made it a religious principle to become outrageous, whenever any opinion is advanced which their priests think contrary to *sound doctrine*. The sectaries of a religion, which preaches, in appearance, nothing but charity, concord, and peace, have proved themselves more ferocious than cannibals or savages, whenever their divines excited them to destroy their brethren. There is no crime which men have not committed under the idea of pleasing the Divinity or appeasing his wrath. . . .

A morality, which contradicts the nature of man, is not made for man. "But," say you, "the nature of man is depraved." In what consists this pretended depravity? In having passions? But, are not passions essential to man? Is he not obliged to seek, desire, and love what is, or what he thinks is conducive to his happiness? Is he not forced to fear and avoid what he judges disagreeable or fatal? Kindle his passions for useful objects; connect his welfare with those objects; divert him, by sensible and known motives, from what may injure either him or others, and you will make him a reasonable and virtuous being. A man without passions would be equally indifferent to vice and to virtue. . . .

What is virtue according to theology? *It is,* we are told, *the conformity of the actions of men to the will of God.* But what is God? A being of whom nobody has the least conception, and whom everyone consequently modifies in his own way. What is the will of God? It is what men, who have seen God, or whom God has inspired, have declared to be the will of God. Who are those who have seen God? They are either fanatics or rogues, or ambitious men, whom we cannot readily believe upon their word.

To found morality upon a God, whom everyone paints to himself differently, composes in his way, and arranges according to his own temperament and interest, is evidently to found morality upon the caprice and imagination of men; it is to found it upon the whims of a sect, a faction, a party, who will believe they have the advantage to adore a true God to the exclusion of all others.

To establish morality of the duties of man upon the divine will, is to found it upon the will, the reveries and the interests of those who make God speak without ever fearing that he will contradict them. In every religion, priests alone have a right to decide what is pleasing or displeasing to their God; we are certain they will always decide that it is what pleases or displeases themselves. . . .

A morality, connected with religion, is necessarily subordinate to it. In the mind of a devout man, God must be regarded more than his creatures; it is better to obey him than men. The interests of the celestial monarch must prevail over those of weak mortals. But the interests of heaven are obviously those of its ministers; whence it evidently follows, that in every religion, priests, under pretext of the interests of heaven or the glory of God, can dispense with the duties of human morality, when they clash with the duties which God has a right to impose. Besides, must not he, who has power to pardon crimes, have a right to command the commission of crimes?

We are perpetually told, that, without a God there would be no *moral obligation;* that the people and even the sovereigns require a legislator powerful enough to constrain them. Moral constraint supposes a law; but this law arises from eternal and necessary relations of things with one another; relations, which have nothing common with the existence of a God. The rules of man's conduct are derived from his own nature which he is capable of knowing, and not from the divine nature of which he has no idea. These rules constrain or oblige us; that is, we render ourselves estimable or contemptible, amiable or detestable, worthy of reward or of punishment, happy or unhappy, according as we conform to, or deviate from these rules. The law, which obliges man not to hurt himself, is founded upon the nature of a sensible being, who, in whatever way he came into the world, or whatever may be his fate in a future one, is forced by his actual essence to seek good and shun evil, to love pleasure and fear pain. The law, which obliges man not to injure, and even to do good to others, is founded upon the nature of sensible beings, living in society, whose essence compels them to despise those who are useless, and to detest those who oppose their felicity.

Whether there exists a God or not, whether this God has spoken or not, the moral duties of men will be always the same, so long as they retain their peculiar nature, that is, as long as they are sensible beings. Have men then need of a God whom they know not, of an invisible legislator, of a mysterious religion and of chimerical fears, in order to learn that every excess evidently tends to destroy them, that to preserve health they must be temperate; that to gain the love of others it is necessary to do them good, that, to do them evil is the sure means to incur their vengeance and hatred?

"Before the law there was no sin." Nothing is more false than this maxim. It suffices that man is what he is, or that he is a sensible being, in order to distinguish what gives him pleasure or displeasure. It suffices that one man knows that another man is a sensible being like himself, to perceive what is useful or hurtful to him. It suffices that man needs his fellow creature, in order to know that he must fear to excite in him sentiments unfavorable to himself. Thus the feeling and thinking being has only to feel and think, in order to discover what he must do for himself and others. I feel, and another feels like me; this is the foundation of all morals. . . .

We can judge of the goodness of a system of morals, only by its conformity to the nature of man. By this comparison, we have a right to reject it, if contrary to the welfare of our species. Whoever has seriously meditated upon religion and its supernatural morality; whoever has carefully weighed their advantages and disadvantages, will be fully convinced, that both are injurious to the interests of man, or directly opposite to his nature. . . .

It is asserted, that the dogma of another life is of the utmost importance to the peace and happiness of societies; that without it, men would be destitute of motives to do good. What need is there of terrors and fables to make every rational man sensible how he ought to conduct himself upon earth? Does not everyone see, that he has the greatest interest in meriting the approbation, esteem, and benevolence of the beings who surround him, and in abstaining from everything, by which he may incur the censure, contempt, and resentment of society? However short an entertainment, a conversation, or visit, does not each desire to act his part decently, and agreeably to himself and others? If life is but a passage, let us strive to make it easy; which we cannot effect, if we fail in regard for those who travel with us.

Religion, occupied with its gloomy reveries, considers man merely as a pilgrim upon earth; and therefore supposes that, in order to travel the more securely, he must forsake company and deprive himself of the pleasures and amusements, which might console him for the tediousness and fatigue of the road. A stoical and morose philosopher sometimes gives us advice as irrational as that of religion. But a more rational philosophy invites us to spread flowers in the way of life, to dispel melancholy and panic terrors, to connect our interest with that of our fellow-travelers, and by gaiety and lawful pleasures, to divert our attention from the difficulties and cross accidents, to which we are often exposed; it teaches us, that, to travel agreeably, we should abstain from what might be injurious to ourselves, and carefully shun what might render us odious to our associates. . . .

It is asked, what motives an Atheist can have to do good? The motive to please himself and his fellow-creatures; to live happily and peaceably; to gain the affection and esteem of men, whose existence and dispositions are much more sure and known, than those of a being impossible to be known. "Can he who fears not the gods, fear anything?" He can fear men; he can fear contempt, dishonor, the punishment and vengeance of the laws; in short, he can fear himself, and the remorse felt by all those who are conscious of having incurred or merited the hatred of their fellow-creatures.

Conscience is the internal testimony, which we bear to ourselves, of having acted so as to merit the esteem or blame of the beings, with whom we live; and it is founded upon the clear knowledge we have of men, and of the sentiments which our actions must produce in them. The conscience of the religious man consists in imagining that he has pleased or displeased his God, of whom he has no idea, and whose obscure and doubtful intentions are explained to him only by men of doubtful veracity, who, like him, are utterly unacquainted with the essence of the Deity, and are little agreed upon what can please or displease him. In a word, the conscience of the credulous is directed by men, who have themselves an erroneous conscience, or whose interest stifles knowledge.

"Can an Atheist have a conscience? What are his motives to abstain from hidden vices and secret crimes, of which other men are ignorant, and which are beyond the reach of laws?" He may be assured by constant experience, that there is no vice, which by the nature of things, does not punish itself. Would he preserve this life? He will avoid every excess that may impair his health: he will not wish to lead a languishing life, which would render him a burden to himself and others. As for secret crimes, he will abstain from them, for fear he shall be forced to blush at himself, from whom he cannot fly. If he has any reason, he will know the value of the esteem which an honest man ought to have for himself. He will see that unforeseen circumstances may unveil the conduct which he feels interested in concealing from others. The other world furnishes the motives for doing good, to him who finds none here below. . . .

A man of reflection cannot be incapable of his duties, of discovering the relations subsisting between men, of mediating his own nature, of discerning his own wants, propensities, and desires, and of perceiving what he owes to beings, who are necessary to his happiness. These reflections naturally lead him to a knowledge of the morality most essential to social beings. Dangerous passions seldom fall to the lot of man who loves to commune with himself, to study, and to investigate the principles of things. The strongest passion of such a man will be to know truth, and his ambition to teach it to others. Philosophy is proper to cultivate both the mind and the heart. On the score of morals and honesty, has not he who reflects and reasons, evidently an advantage over him, who makes it a principle never to reason?

If ignorance is useful to priests, and to the oppressors of mankind, it is fatal to society. Man, void of knowledge, does not enjoy his reason; without reason and knowledge, he is a savage, every instant liable to be hurried into crimes. Morality, or the science of duties, is acquired only by the study of man, and of what is relative to man. He who does not reflect, is unacquainted with true morality, and walks with precarious steps in the path of virtue. The less men reason, the more wicked they are. Savages, princes, nobles, and the dregs of the people, are commonly the worst of men, because they reason the least. . . .

THE PROGRESS OF SUPERSTITION

EDWARD GIBBON

The greatest historian of the eighteenth century, Edward Gibbon (1737–1794) was a typical Enlightenment skeptic deeply suspicious of religious faith. He was convinced that Christianity had played a central role in undermining the glories of antiquity. His disdain for the Church is evident in this famous passage from his History of the Decline and Fall of the Roman Empire, *whose several volumes he published between 1776 and 1788.*

The miracles of the primitive church, after obtaining the sanction of ages, have been lately attacked in a very free and ingenious inquiry; which, though it has met with the most favorable reception from the Public, appears to have excited a general scandal among the divines of our own as well as of the other Protestant churches of Europe. Our different sentiments on this subject will be much less influenced by any particular arguments than by our habits of study and reflection; and, above all, by the degree of the evidence which we have accustomed ourselves to require for the proof of a miraculous event. The duty of an historian does not call upon him to interpose his private judgment in this nice and important controversy; but he ought not to dissemble the difficulty of adopting such a theory as may reconcile the interest of religion with that of reason, of making a proper application of that theory, and of defining with precision the limits of that happy period, exempt from error and from deceit, to which we might be disposed to extend the gift of supernatural powers. From the first of the fathers to the last of the popes, a succession of bishops, of saints, of martyrs, and of miracles is continued without interruption, and the progress of superstition was so gradual and almost imperceptible that we know not in what particular link we should break the chain of tradition. Every age bears testimony to the wonderful events by which it was distinguished, and its testimony appears no less weighty and respectable than that of the preceding generation, till we are insensibly led on to accuse our own inconsistency, if in the eighth or in the twelfth century we deny to the venerable Bede, or to the holy Bernard, the same degree of confidence which, in the second century, we had so liberally granted to Justin or to Irenæus. If the truth of any of those miracles is appreciated by their apparent use and propriety, every age had unbelievers to convince, heretics to confute, and idolatrous nations to convert; and sufficient motives might always be produced to justify the interposition of Heaven. And yet, since every friend to revelation is persuaded of the reality, and every reasonable man is convinced of the cessation, of miraculous powers, it is evident that there must have been *some period* in which they were either suddenly or gradually withdrawn from the Christian church. Whatever æra is chosen for that purpose, the death of the apostles, the conversion of the Roman empire, or the extinction of the Arian heresy, the insensibility of the Christians who lived at that time will equally afford a just matter of surprise. They still supported their pretensions after they had lost their power. Credulity performed the office of faith; fanaticism was permitted to assume the language of inspiration, and the effects of accident or contrivance were ascribed to supernatural causes. The recent experience of genuine miracles should have instructed the Christian world in the ways of Providence, and habituated their eye (if we may use a very inadequate expression) to the style of the divine artist. Should the most skillful painter of modern Italy presume to decorate his feeble imitations with the name of Raphael or of Correggio, the insolent fraud would be soon discovered and indignantly rejected.

Whatever opinion may be entertained of the miracles of the primitive church since the time of the apostles, this unresisting softness of temper, so conspicuous among the believers of the second and third centuries, proved of some accidental benefit to the cause of truth and religion. In modern times, a latent, and even involuntary, skepticism adheres to the most pious dispositions. Their admission of supernatural truths is much less an active consent than a cold and passive acquiescence. Accustomed long since to observe and to respect the invariable order of Nature, our reason, or at least our imagination, is not sufficiently prepared to sustain the visible action of the Deity. But, in the first ages of Christianity, the situation of mankind was extremely different. The most curious, or the most credulous, among the Pagans were often persuaded to enter into a society which asserted an actual claim of miraculous powers. The primitive Christians perpetually trod on mystic ground, and their minds were exercised by the habits of believing the most extraordinary events. They felt, or they fancied, that on every side they were incessantly assaulted by dæmons, comforted by visions, instructed by prophecy, and surprisingly delivered from danger, sickness, and from death itself, by the supplications of the church. The real or imaginary prodigies, of which they so frequently conceived themselves to be the objects, the instruments, or the spectators, very happily disposed them to adopt, with the same ease, but with far greater justice, the authentic wonders of the evangelic history; and thus miracles that exceeded not the measure of their own experience inspired them with the most lively assurance of mysteries which were acknowledged to surpass the limits of their understanding. It is this deep impression of supernatural truths which has been so much celebrated under the name of faith; a state of mind described as the surest pledge of the divine favor and of future felicity, and recommended as the first or perhaps the only merit of a Christian. According to the more rigid doctors, the moral virtues, which may be equally practiced by infidels, are destitute of any value or efficacy in the work of our justification.

But the primitive Christian demonstrated his faith by his virtues; and it was very justly supposed that the divine persuasion, which enlightened or subdued the understanding, must, at the same time, purify the heart, and direct the actions, of the believer. The first apologists of Christianity who justify the innocence of their brethren, and the writers of a later period who celebrate the sanctity of their ancestors, display, in the most lively colors, the reformation of manners which was introduced into the world by the preaching of the gospel. As it is my intention to remark only such human causes as were permitted to second the influence of revelation, I shall slightly mention two motives which might naturally render the lives of the primitive Christians much purer and more austere than those of their Pagan contemporaries, or their degenerate successors; repentance for their past sins, and the laudable desire of supporting the reputation of the society in which they were engaged.

The acquisition of knowledge, the exercise of our reason or fancy, and the cheerful flow of unguarded conversation, may employ the leisure of a liberal mind. Such amusements, however, were rejected with abhorrence, or admitted with the utmost caution, by the severity of the fathers, who despised all knowledge that was not useful to salvation, and who considered all levity of discourse as a criminal abuse of the gift of speech. In our present state of existence, the body is so inseparably connected with the soul that it seems to be our interest to taste, with innocence and moderation, the enjoyments of which that faithful companion is susceptible. Very different was the reasoning of our devout predecessors; vainly aspiring to imitate the perfection of angels, they disdained, or they affected to disdain, every earthly and corporeal delight. Some of our senses indeed are necessary for our preservation, others for our subsistence, and others again for our information, and thus far it was impossible to reject the use of them. The first sensation of pleasure was marked as the first moment of their abuse. The unfeeling candidate for Heaven was instructed, not only to resist the grosser allurements of the taste or smell, but even to shut his ears against the profane harmony of sounds, and to view with indifference the most finished productions of human art. Gay apparel, magnificent houses, and elegant furniture were supposed to unite the double guilt of pride and of sensuality: a simple and mortified appearance was more suitable to the Christian who was certain of his sins and doubtful of his salvation. In their censures of luxury, the fathers are extremely minute and circumstantial; and among the various articles which excite their pious indignation, we may enumerate false hair, garments of any color except white, instruments of music, vases of gold or silver, downy pillows (as Jacob reposed his head on a stone), white bread, foreign wines, public salutations, the use of warm baths, and the practice of shaving the beard, which, according to the expression of Tertullian, is a lie against our own faces, and an impious attempt to improve the works of the Creator. When Christianity was introduced among the rich and the polite, the observation of these singular laws was left, as it would be at present, to the few who were ambitious of superior sanctity. But it is always easy, as well as agreeable, for the inferior ranks of mankind to claim a merit from the contempt of that pomp and pleasure, which fortune has placed beyond their reach. The virtue of the primitive Christians, like that of the first Romans, was very frequently guarded by poverty and ignorance.

The chaste severity of the fathers, in whatever related to the commerce of the two sexes, flowed from the same principle; their abhorrence of every enjoyment which might gratify the sensual, and degrade the spiritual, nature of man. It was their favorite opinion that, if Adam had preserved his obedience to the Creator, he would have lived for ever in a state of virgin purity, and that some harmless mode of vegetation might have peopled paradise with a race of innocent and immortal beings. The use of marriage was permitted only to his fallen posterity, as a necessary expedient to continue the human species, and as a restraint, however imperfect, on the natural licentiousness of desire. The hesitation of the orthodox casuists on this interesting subject betrays the perplexity of men, unwilling to approve an institution which they were compelled to tolerate. The enumeration of the very whimsical laws, which they most circumstantially imposed on the marriage-bed, would force a smile from the young, and a blush from the fair. It was their unanimous sentiment that a first marriage was adequate to all the purposes of nature and of society. The sensual connexion was refined into a resemblance of the mystic union of Christ with his church, and was pronounced to be indissoluble either by divorce or by death. . . .

The decline of ancient prejudice exposed a very numerous portion of human kind to the danger of a painful and comfortless situation. A state of skepticism and suspense may amuse a few inquisitive minds. But the practice of superstition is so congenial to the multitude that, if they are forcibly awakened, they still regret the loss of their pleasing vision. Their love of the marvelous and supernatural, their curiosity with regard to future events, and their strong propensity to extend their hopes and fears beyond the limits of the visible world, were the principal causes which favored the establishment of Polytheism. So urgent on the vulgar is the necessity of believing that the fall of any system of mythology will most probably be succeeded by the introduction of some other mode of superstition. Some deities of a more recent and fashionable cast might soon have occupied the deserted temples of Jupiter and Apollo, if, in the decisive moment, the wisdom of Providence had not interposed a genuine revelation, fitted to inspire the most rational esteem and conviction, whilst, at the same time, it was adorned with all that could attract the curiosity, the wonder, and the veneration of the people. In their actual disposition, as many were almost disengaged from their artificial prejudices, but equally susceptible and desirous of a devout attachment; an object much less deserving would have been sufficient to fill the vacant place in their hearts, and to gratify the uncertain eagerness of their passions. Those who are inclined to pursue this reflection, instead of viewing with astonishment the rapid progress of Christianity, will perhaps be surprised that its success was not still more rapid and still more universal.

UNITARIANISM

JOSEPH PRIESTLEY

The scientist and Protestant minister Priestley was one of the founders of Unitarianism, which bears a striking intellectual kinship to deism. The creed, here called Socinian, would attract others like Jefferson. The selection is from Priestley's Letters to Dr. Horsley *of 1783.*

Having been educated in the strictest principles of Calvinism, and having from my early years had a serious turn of mind, promoted no doubt by a weak and sickly constitution, I was very sincere and zealous in my belief of the doctrine of the trinity; and this continued till I was about nineteen; and then I was as much shocked on hearing of any who denied the divinity of Christ (thinking it to be nothing less than impiety and blasphemy) as any of my opponents can be now. I therefore truly feel for them, and most sincerely excuse them.

About the age of twenty, being then in a regular course of theological studies, I saw reason to change my opinion, and became an Arian; and notwithstanding what appeared to me a fair and impartial study of the scriptures, and though I had no bias on my mind arising from subscribed creeds and confessions of faith, etc. I continued in that persuasion fifteen or sixteen years; and yet in that time I was well acquainted with Dr. Lardner, Dr. Fleming, and several other zealous Socinians, especially my friend Mr. Graham. The first theological tract of mine (which was on the doctrine of atonement) was published at the particular request, and under the direction of, Dr. Lardner; and he approving of the scheme which I had then formed of giving a short view (which was all that I had then thought of) of the progress of the corruptions of christianity, he gave me a few hints with respect to it. But still I continued till after his death indisposed to the Socinian hypothesis. After this, continuing my study of the scriptures, with the help of his *Letters on the Logos*, I at length changed my opinion, and became what is called a Socinian; and in this I see continually more reason to acquiesce, though it was a long time before the arguments in favor of it did more than barely preponderate in my mind.

I was greatly confirmed in this doctrine after I was fully satisfied that man is of an uniform composition, and wholly mortal; and that the doctrine of a separate immaterial soul, capable of sensation and action when the body is in the grave, is a notion borrowed from heathen philosophy, and unknown to the scriptures. Of this I had for a long time a mere suspicion; but having casually mentioned it as such, and a violent outcry being raised against me on that account, I was induced to give the greatest attention to the question, to examine it in every light, and to invite the fullest discussion of it. This terminated in as full a conviction with respect to this subject as I have with respect to any other whatever. The reasons on which that conviction is founded may be seen in my *Disquisitions on Matter and Spirit*. . . .

Being now fully persuaded that Christ was a man like ourselves, and consequently that his pre-existence, as well as that of other men, was a notion that had no foundation in reason or in the scriptures, and having been gradually led (in consequence of wishing to trace the principal corruptions of christianity) to give particular attention to ecclesiastical history, I could not help thinking but that (since the doctrine of the pre-existence of Christ was not the doctrine of the scriptures, and therefore could not have been taught by the apostles) there must be some traces of the rise and progress of the doctrine of the trinity, and some historical evidence that unitarianism was the general faith of christians in the apostolical age, independent of the evidence which arose from its being the doctrine of the scriptures.

In this state of mind, the reader will easily perceive that I naturally expected to find, what I was previously well persuaded was to be found; and in time I collected much more evidence than I at first expected, considering the early rise and the long and universal spread of what I deem to be a radical corruption of the genuine christian doctrine. This evidence I have fairly laid before the reader. He must judge of the weight of it, and also make whatever allowance he may think necessary for my particular situation and prejudices.

I am well aware that it is naturally impossible that the evidence I have produced should impress the minds of those who are Arians or Athanasians, as it will those of Socinians; nor are men to be convinced of the proper humanity of Christ, by arguments of this kind. They must begin, as I did, with the study of the scriptures; and whatever be the result of that study, it will be impossible for them, let them discipline their minds as they will, not to be influenced in the historical inquiry, as I was, by their previous persuasion concerning the subject of it. If, however, they should be so far impressed with the historical arguments, as to think it probable that the christian Church was, in a very early period, unitarian, it will, no doubt, lead them to expect that they shall find the doctrine of the scriptures, truly interpreted, to be so too.

With respect to myself, I do not know that I can do anything more. Being persuaded, as I am, from the study of the scriptures, that Christ is properly a man, I cannot cease to think so; nor can I possibly help the influence of that persuasion in my historical researches. Let other persons write as freely on their respective hypotheses as I have done on mine, and then indifferent persons, and especially younger persons, whose minds have not acquired the stiffness of ours, who are turned fifty, may derive benefit from it.

Firm as my persuasion now is concerning the proper humanity of Christ (a persuasion that has been the slow growth of years, and the result of much anxious and patient thinking) I do not know that, in the course of my enquiry, I have been under the influence of prejudice more than all other men naturally are. As to reputation, a man may distinguish himself just as much by the defense of old systems as by the erection of new ones; but I have neither formed any new systems, nor have I particularly distinguished myself in the defense of old ones. When I first became an Arian and afterwards a Socinian, I was only a convert, in company with many others, and was far from having any thoughts of troubling the world with publications on the subject. This I have been led to do by a series of events of which I had no foresight and of which I do not see the issue.

The conclusion that I have formed with respect to the subject of this work and my exertions in support of it, are, however, constantly ascribed by my opponents to a force of prejudice and prepossession so strong as to pervert my judgment in the plainest of all cases. Of this I may not be a proper judge; but analogy may be some guide to myself as well as to others in this case.

Now, what appears to have been my disposition in other similar cases? Have I been particularly attached to hypotheses in philosophy, even to my own, which always create a stronger attachment than those of other persons? On the contrary, I will venture to say that no person is generally thought to be less so; nor has it been imagined that my pursuits have been at all defeated or injured, by any prepossession in favor of particular theories; and yet theories are as apt to mislead in philosophical as in any other subjects. I have always shown the greatest readiness to abandon any hypothesis that I have advanced, and even defended, while I thought it defensible, the moment I have suspected it to be ill founded, whether the new facts that have refuted it were discovered by myself or others. My friends in general have blamed me for my extreme facility in this respect. And if I may judge of myself by my own feelings, after the closest examination that I can give myself, I am just the same with respect to theology.

In the course of my life I have held and defended opinions very different from those which I hold at present. Now, if my obstinacy in retaining and defending opinions had been so great as my opponents represent it, why did it not long ago put a stop to all my changes, and fix me a Trinitarian, or an Arian? Let those who have given stronger proofs of their minds being open to conviction than mine has been, throw the first stone at me.

I am well aware of the nature and force of that opposition and obloquy to which I am exposing myself in consequence of writing my *History of the Corruptions of Christianity*, the most valuable, I trust, of all my publications, and especially in consequence of the pains that have been taken to magnify and expose a few inaccuracies, to which all works of a similar nature have been and ever must be subject. But I have the fullest persuasion that the real oversights in it are of the smallest magnitude and do not at all affect any one position or argument in my work, as I hope to satisfy all candid judges; and as to mere cavil and reproach, I thank God I am well able to bear it.

The odium I brought upon myself by maintaining the doctrines of materialism and necessity, without attempting to cover or soften terms of so frightful a sound, and without palliating any of their consequences, was unspeakably greater than what this business can bring upon me. At the beginning of that controversy I had few, very few indeed, of my nearest friends who were with me in the argument. They, however, who knew me, knew my motives, and excused me; but the christian world in general regarded me with the greatest abhorrence. I was considered as an unprincipled infidel, either an atheist or in league with atheists. In this light I was repeatedly exhibited in all the public papers; and the *Monthly Review* and other Reviews, with all the similar publications of the day, joined in the popular cry. But a few years have seen the end of it. At least all that is left would not disturb the merest novice in these things. The consequence (which I now enjoy) is a great increase of materialists; not of atheistical ones, as some will still represent it, but of the most serious, the most rational and consistent christians.

A similar issue I firmly expect from the present controversy, unpromising as it may appear in the eyes of some, who are struck with what is speciously and confidently urged. For my own part, I truly rejoice in the present appearance of things; as I foresee that much good will arise from the attention that will by this means be drawn upon the subject, and as I hope I respect the hand of God in everything, I thank him for leading me into this business; as I hope to have occasion to thank him, some years hence, for leading me through it, and with as much advantage as I have been led through the other.

It is, indeed, my firm and it is my joyful persuasion, that there is a wise Providence over-ruling all inquiries as well as other events. The wisdom of God has appeared, as I have endeavored to point out, even in the corruptions of christianity, and the spread of error; and it is equally conspicuous in the discovery and propagation of truth.

I am far from thinking that that great Being who superintends all things, guides my pen, any more than he does that of my fiercest opponent; but I believe that by means of our joint labors and those of all who engage in theological controversy (which is eminently useful in rousing men to the utmost exertion of their faculties) he is promoting his own excellent purposes, and providing for the prevalence of truth in his own due time; and in this general prospect we ought all equally to rejoice.

It becomes us, however, to consider that they only will be entitled to praise who join in carrying on the designs of providence with right views of their own; who are actuated by a real love of truth, and also by that candor and benevolence, which a sense of our common difficulties in the investigation of truth most effectually inspires. A man who has never changed an opinion cannot have much feeling of this difficulty, and therefore cannot be expected to have much candor, unless his disposition be uncommonly excellent. I ought to have more candor than many others, because I have felt more than many can pretend to have done, the force of those obstacles which retard our progress in the search of truth.

''RELIGION . . . MY VIEWS OF IT . . .''

THOMAS JEFFERSON

America's third president, Jefferson (1743–1826) was a friend and correspondent of many of the leading writers and scientists in the English and French Enlightenment. In these two selections, Jefferson argues the case for toleration and describes his own religious beliefs. The first is from his one book, The Notes on Virginia *(1787); the second is a letter of 1803 to the Philadelphia scientist, physician, and political leader Benjamin Rush.*

The error seems not sufficiently eradicated, that the operations of the mind, as well as the acts of the body, are subject to the coercion of the laws. But our rulers can have authority over such natural rights only as we have submitted to them. The rights of conscience we never submitted, we could not submit. We are answerable for them to our God. The legitimate powers of government extend to such acts only as are injurious to others. But it does me no injury for my neighbor to say there are twenty gods, or no god. It neither picks my pocket nor breaks my leg. If it be said, his testimony in a court of justice cannot be relied on, reject it then, and be the stigma on him. Constraint may make him worse by making him a hypocrite, but it will never make him a truer man. It may fix him obstinately in his errors, but will not cure them. Reason and free enquiry are the only effectual agents against error. Give a loose to them, they will support the true religion, by bringing every false one to their tribunal, to the test of their investigation. They are the natural enemies of error, and of error only. Had not the Roman government permitted free enquiry, Christianity could never have been introduced. Had not free enquiry been indulged, at the æra of the reformation, the corruptions of Christianity could not have been purged away. If it be restrained now, the present corruptions will be protected, and new ones encouraged. Was the government to prescribe to us our medicine and diet, our bodies would be in such keeping as our souls are now. Thus in France the emetic was once forbidden as a medicine, and the potato as an article of food. Government is just as infallible too when it fixes systems in physics. Galileo was sent to the inquisition for affirming that the earth was a sphere: the government had declared it to be as flat as a trencher, and Galileo was obliged to adjure his error. This error however at length prevailed, the earth became a globe, and Descartes declared it was whirled round its axis by a vortex. The government in which he lived was wise enough to see that this was no question of civil jurisdiction, or we should all have been involved by authority in vortices. In fact, the vortices have been exploded, and the Newtonian principle of gravitation is now more firmly established, on the basis of reason, than it would be were the government to step in, and to make it an article of necessary faith. Reason and experiment have been indulged, and error has fled before them. It is error alone which needs the support of government. Truth can stand by itself. Subject opinion to coercion: whom will you make your inquisitors? Fallible men; men governed by bad passions, by private as well as public reasons. And why subject it to coercion? To produce uniformity. But is uniformity of opinion desirable? No more than of face and stature. Introduce the bed of Procrustes then, and as there is danger that the large men may beat the small, make us all of a size, by lopping the former and stretching the latter. Difference of opinion is advantageous in religion. The several sects perform the office of a Censor morum over each other. Is uniformity attainable? Millions of innocent men, women, and children, since the introduction of Christianity, have been burnt, tortured, fined, imprisoned; yet we have not advanced one inch towards uniformity. What has been the effect of coercion? To make one half the world fools, and the other half hypocrites. To support roguery and error all over the earth. Let us reflect that it is inhabited by a thousand millions of people. That these profess probably a thousand different systems of religion. That ours is but one of that thousand. That if there be but one right, and ours that one, we should wish to see the 999 wandering sects gathered into the fold of truth. But against such a majority we cannot effect this by force. Reason and persuasion are the only practicable instruments. To make way for these, free enquiry must be indulged; and how can we wish others to indulge it while we refuse it ourselves. But every state, says an inquisitor, has established some religion. No two, say I, have established the same. Is this a proof of the infallibility of establishments? Our sister states of Pennsylvania and New York, however, have long subsisted without any establishment at all. The experiment was new and doubtful when they made it. It has answered beyond conception. They flourish infinitely. Religion is well supported; of various kinds, indeed, but all good enough; all sufficient to preserve peace and order: or if a sect arises, whose tenets would subvert morals, good sense has fair play, and reasons and laughs it out of doors, without suffering the state to be troubled with it. They do not hang more malefactors than we do. They are not more disturbed with religious dissensions. On the contrary, their harmony is unparalleled, and can be ascribed to nothing but their unbounded tolerance, because there is no other circumstance in which they differ from every nation on earth. They have made the happy discovery, that the way to silence religious disputes, is to take no notice of them. Let us too give this experiment fair play, and get rid, while we may, of those tyrannical laws. It is true, we are as yet secured against them by the spirit of the times. I doubt whether the people of this country would suffer an execution for heresy, or a three years imprisonment for not comprehending the mysteries of the Trinity. But is the spirit of the people an infallible, a permanent reliance? Is it government? Is this the kind of protection we receive in return for the rights we give up? Besides, the spirit of the times may alter, will alter. Our rulers will become corrupt, our people careless. A single zealot may commence persecutor, and better men be his victims. It can never be too often repeated, that the time for fixing every essential right on a legal basis is while our rulers are honest, and ourselves united. From the conclusion of this war we shall be going down hill. It will not then be necessary to resort every moment to the people for support. They will be forgotten, therefore, and their rights disregarded. They will forget themselves, but in the sole faculty of making money, and will never think of uniting to effect a due respect for their rights. The shackles, therefore, which shall not be knocked off at the conclusion of this war, will remain on us long, will be made heavier and heavier, till our rights shall revive or expire in a convulsion.

. . .

Dear Sir,—

In some of the delightful conversations with you, in the evenings of 1798–99, and which serve as an anodyne to the afflictions of the crisis through which our country was then laboring, the Christian religion was sometimes our topic; and I then promised you, that one day or other, I would give you my views of it. They are the result of a life of inquiry and reflection, and very different from that anti-Christian system imputed to me by those who know nothing of my opinions. To the corruptions of Christianity I am, indeed, opposed; but not to the genuine precepts of Jesus himself. I am a Christian, in the only sense he wished any one to be; sincerely attached to his doctrines, in preference to all others; ascribing to himself every *human* excellence; and believing he never claimed any other. At the short interval since these conversations, when I could justifiably abstract my mind from public affairs, the subject has been under my contemplation. But the more I considered it, the more it expanded beyond the measure of either my time or information. In the moment of my late departure from Monticello, I received from Dr. Priestley, his little treatise of "Socrates and Jesus Compared." This being a section of the general view I had taken of the field, it became a subject of reflection while on the road, and unoccupied otherwise. The result was, to arrange in my mind a syllabus, or outline of such an estimate of the comparative merits of Christianity, as I wished to see executed by some one of more leisure and information for the task, than myself. This I now send you, as the only discharge of my promise I can probably ever execute. And in confiding it to you, I know it will not be exposed to the malignant perversions of those who make every word from me a text for new misrepresentations and calumnies. I am moreover averse to the communication of my religious tenets to the public; because it would countenance the presumption of those who have endeavored to draw them before that tribunal, and to seduce public opinion to erect itself into that inquisition over the rights of conscience, which the laws have so justly proscribed. It behooves every man who values liberty of conscience for himself, to resist invasions of it in the case of others; or their case may, by change of circumstances, become his own. It behooves him, too, in his own case, to give no example of concession, betraying the common right of independent opinion, by answering questions of faith, which the laws have left between God and himself. Accept my affectionate salutations.

Syllabus of an Estimate of the Merit of the Doctrines of Jesus, Compared with Those of Others.

In a comparative view of the Ethics of the enlightened nations of antiquity, of the Jews and of Jesus, no notice should be taken of the corruptions of reason among the ancients, to wit, the idolatry and superstition of the vulgar, nor of the corruptions of Christianity by the learned among its professors.

Let a just view be taken of the moral principles inculcated by the most esteemed of the sects of ancient philosophy, or of their individuals; particularly Pythagoras, Socrates, Epicurus, Cicero, Epictetus, Seneca, Antoninus.

I. Philosophers. 1. Their precepts related chiefly to ourselves, and the government of those passions which, unrestrained, would disturb our tranquility of mind. In this branch of philosophy they were really great.

2. In developing our duties to others, they were short and defective. They embraced, indeed, the circles of kindred and friends, and inculcated patriotism, or the love of our country in the aggregate, as a primary obligation; toward our neighbors and countrymen they taught justice, but scarcely viewed them as within the circle of benevolence. Still less have they inculcated peace, charity, and love to our fellow men, or embraced with benevolence the whole family of mankind.

II. Jews. 1. Their system was Deism; that is, the belief of one only God. But their ideas of him and of his attributes were degrading and injurious.

2. Their Ethics were not only imperfect, but often irreconcilable with the sound dictates of reason and morality, as they respect intercourse with those around us; and repulsive and anti-social, as respecting other nations. They needed reformation, therefore, in an eminent degree.

III. Jesus. In this state of things among the Jews, Jesus appeared. His parentage was obscure; his condition poor; his education null; his natural endowments great; his life correct and innocent; he was meek, benevolent, patient, firm, disinterested, and of the sublimest eloquence.

The disadvantages under which his doctrines appear are remarkable.

1. Like Socrates and Epictetus, he wrote nothing himself.

2. But he had not, like them, a Xenophon or an Arrian to write for him. I name not Plato, who only used the name of Socrates to cover the whimsies of his own brain. On the contrary, all the learned of his country, entrenched in its power and riches, were opposed to him, lest his labors should undermine their advantages; and the committing to writing his life and doctrines fell on unlettered and ignorant men; who wrote, too, from memory, and not till long after the transactions had passed.

3. According to the ordinary fate of those who attempt to enlighten and reform mankind, he fell an early victim to the jealousy and combination of the altar and the throne, at about thirty-three years of age, his reason having not yet attained the *maximum* of its energy, nor the course of his preaching, which was but of three years at most, presented occasions for developing a complete system of morals.

4. Hence the doctrines which he really delivered were defective as a whole, and fragments only of what he did deliver have come to us mutilated, misstated, and often unintelligible.

5. They have been still more disfigured by the corruptions of schismatizing followers, who have found an interest in sophisticating and perverting the simple doctrines he taught, by engrafting on them the mysticisms of a Grecian sophist, frittering them into subtleties, and obscuring them with jargon, until they have caused good men to reject the whole in disgust, and to view Jesus himself as an impostor.

Notwithstanding these disadvantages, a system of morals is presented to us, which, if filled up in the true style and spirit of the rich fragments he left us, would be the most perfect and sublime that has ever been taught by man.

The question of his being a member of the Godhead, or in direct communication with it, claimed for him by some of his followers, and denied by others, is foreign to the present view, which is merely an estimate of the intrinsic merit of his doctrines.

1. He corrected the Deism of the Jews, confirming them in their belief of one only God, and giving them juster notions of his attributes and government.

2. His moral doctrines, relating to kindred and friends, were more pure and perfect than those of the most correct of the philosophers, and greatly more so than those of the Jews; and they went far beyond both in inculcating universal philanthrophy, not only to kindred and friends,

to neighbors and countrymen, but to all mankind, gathering all into one family, under the bonds of love, charity, peace, common wants and common aids. A development of this head will evince the peculiar superiority of the system of Jesus over all others.

3. The precepts of philosophy, and of the Hebrew code, laid hold of actions only. He pushed his scrutinies into the heart of man; erected his tribunal in the region of his thoughts, and purified the waters at the fountain head.

4. He taught, emphatically, the doctrines of a future state, which was either doubted, or disbelieved by the Jews; and wielded it with efficacy, as an important incentive, supplementary to the other motives to moral conduct.

"SOMETHING OF MY RELIGION . . ."

BENJAMIN FRANKLIN

Franklin's personal creed seems quite close to Jefferson's as he outlines it in this letter of 1790 to Ezra Stiles, fellow member of the American Philosophical Society and president of Yale College.

REVEREND AND DEAR SIR,

You desire to know something of my Religion. It is the first time I have been questioned upon it. But I cannot take your curiosity amiss, and shall endeavor in a few words to gratify it. Here is my creed. I believe in one God, Creator of the universe. That he governs it by his Providence. That he ought to be worshipped. That the most acceptable service we render to him is doing good to his other children. That the soul of Man is immortal, and will be treated with justice in another life respecting its conduct in this. These I take to be the fundamental principles of all sound religion, and I regard them as you do in whatever sect I meet with them.

As to Jesus of Nazareth, my opinion of whom you particularly desire, I think the system of morals and his religion, as he left them to us, the best the world ever saw or is likely to see; but I apprehend it has received various corrupting changes, and I have, with most of the present dissenters in England, some doubts as to his divinity; tho' it is a question I do not dogmatize upon, having never studied it, and think it needless to busy myself with it now, when I expect soon an opportunity of knowing the truth with less trouble. I see no harm, however, in its being believed, if that belief has the good consequence, as probably it has, of making his doctrines more respected and better observed; especially as I do not perceive that the Supreme takes it amiss, by distinguishing the unbelievers in his government of the world with any peculiar marks of his displeasure.

I shall only add, respecting myself, that, having experienced the goodness of that Being in conducting me prosperously thro' a long life, I have no doubt of its continuance in the next, though without the smallest conceit of meriting such goodness. My sentiments on this head you will see in the copy of an old letter enclosed, which I wrote in answer to one from a zealous religionist, whom I had relieved in a paralytic case by electricity, and who, being afraid I should grow proud upon it, sent me his serious though rather impertinent caution. I send you also the copy of another letter, which will shew something of my disposition relating to religion. With great and sincere esteem and affection, I am, Your obliged old friend and most obedient humble servant

B. FRANKLIN

P.S. Had not your College some present of books from the King of France? Please to let me know if you had an expectation given you of more, and the nature of that expectation? I have a reason for the enquiry. I confide that you will not expose me to criticism and censure by publishing any part of this communication to you. I have ever let others enjoy their religious sentiments, without reflecting on them for those that appeared to me unsupportable and even absurd. All sects here, and we have a great variety, have experienced my good will in assisting them with subscriptions for building their new places of worship; and, as I have never opposed any of their doctrines, I hope to go out of the world in peace with them all.

THE TEMPLE OF REASON

In its more radical phase after 1792, the leaders of the French Revolution closed the churches and abolished the Christian calendar and sabbath. The Goddess of Reason was enshrined in Notre Dame, and Temples of Reason were established in many French cities. This selection is a contemporary description of a civic festival held in 1794 in Châlons-sur-Marne to inaugurate such a Temple.

The festival was announced in the whole Commune the evening before; for this purpose, retreat was sounded by all the drummers and by the trumpeters of the troops in barracks at Châlons, in all parts of the town.

The next day at daybreak, it was again announced by general quarters, which was likewise sounded in all parts; the artillery did not fire, in order to save the powder to destroy the despots' henchmen.

The former church of Notre Dame was, for lack of time and means, cleaned and prepared only provisionally for its new use, and in its former sanctuary there was erected a pedestal supporting the symbolic statue of Reason. It is of simple and free design, decorated only by an inset bearing this inscription:

"Do unto others as you would have them do unto you."

It was flanked by two columns surmounted by two antique bronze perfume boxes, which emitted incense smoke during the whole ceremony: in front, at the foot of three steps, was placed an altar of antique form, on which were to be placed the emblems that the various groups composing the procession would put there; on the four pillars at the corners of the sanctuary were four projecting brackets to receive the busts of Brutus, the father of Republics and the model of Republicans; of Marat, the faithful friend of the people; of Le Peletier, who died for the Republic; and of the immortal Chalier.

At precisely nine o'clock in the morning, the general assemblage formed on the gravel promenade, otherwise called the promenade of Liberty; the military detachments and other groups destined to form the procession had their places indicated there; commissioners from the Society arranged them in order. . . .

A detachment of cavalry, national constabulary, and hussars mingled together, to strengthen the bonds of fraternity, led the march, and on their pennant there were these words: "Reason guides us and enlightens us."

It was followed by the company of cannoneers of Châlons, preceded by a banner with this inscription: "Death to the Tyrants."

This company was followed by a cart loaded with broken chains, on which were six prisoners of war and a few wounded being cared for by a surgeon; this cart carried two banners, front and back, with these two inscriptions: "Humanity is a Republican virtue" [and] "They were very mistaken in fighting for tyrants."

This cart was accompanied by two detachments of national guardsmen and regular troops fully armed.

The drummers grouped together followed and in turn were followed by four *sans-culottes* carrying a superb fasces from which flew a tricolor banner on which were these words: "Let us be united like it, nothing can conquer us."

Forty women citizens dressed in white and decorated with tricolor ribbons surrounded the fasces, and each carried a large tricolor ribbon which was tied to her head.

A Liberty bonnet crowned this banner, and young national guardsmen accompanying the fasces carried various pennants on which were written different devices.

After them marched groups of national guardsmen and regular troops mingled together and fraternally and amicably united, arm in arm, singing hymns to Liberty and bearing with them two banners on which were written the following inscriptions: "Our Unity is our strength." "We will exterminate the last of the despots."

Then came the military band gathered from different barracks, playing alternately with the drummers who were in front during the procession. The band was followed by a chariot of antique type decorated with oak branches and bearing a sexagenarian couple, with a streamer on which were written these words: "Respect Old Age."

The Société Populaire marched next, preceded by its banner, on which was depicted a watchful eye, and underneath were these words: "We watch over the maintenance of Liberty and the public welfare."

In its train, groups of children of both sexes carried baskets of fruit and vases of flowers, accompanying a cart drawn by two white horses; in the cart was a young woman nursing an infant, beside her a group of children of different ages; it was preceded by a banner with this inscription: "They are the hope of the Patrie." From the cart flew a tricolor streamer with this inscription: "The virtuous mother will produce defenders for the Patrie."

Next marched a group of women citizens adorned with tricolor ribbons, bearing a standard with this inscription: "Austere Morals will strengthen the Republic." All who composed this group were dressed in white, as were the drivers of the cart, and all were bedecked with tricolor ribbons.

Then followed the surveillance committees of the sections of the Commune of Châlons, grouped together one after another; in front were four banners, each bearing the name of a section, and an emblem depicting a finger on the lips to indicate secrecy, and another banner with this inscription: "Our institution purges Society of a multitude of suspect people."

The Republic section went first; it accompanied a chariot pulled by two white horses and led by two men on foot dressed in Roman style; in it was a woman dressed in the same way, representing the Republic; on the front of this chariot appeared a tricolor ensign bearing these words: "Government of the Wise."

Next marched the Equality section, accompanying a plow pulled by two oxen and guided by a cultivator in work clothes; a couple seated on it carried a standard on which were written on one side, "Honor the Plow," and on the other side, "Respect conjugal love."

The principal inspector and all the employees in the military storehouses formed a group which followed the plow: two standards were carried by this group; the first had the words, "Military supplies," and the second, "Our activity produces abundance in our armies."

The Liberty section followed, accompanied by groups of citizens, artisans, and workmen of all kinds and types; each of them was carrying an instrument or a tool related to and representative of his art or occupation. This group was preceded by a tricolor standard, inscribed with a single word: "Sovereign."

Then marched the Fraternity section, consoling groups of convalescents, whose physicians were close by. In the middle of this section was an open cart from the Montagne hospital, containing men wounded in the defense of the Patrie, who appeared to have been cared for and bled by health officers who were binding their wounds. They were partly covered by their bloody bandages. The front of this cart carried a banner with this inscription: "Our blood will never cease to flow for the safety of the Patrie."

After the committees followed four women citizens dressed in white and adorned with tricolor belts decorated with the attributes of the four seasons they represented.

After the four seasons came the People's Representative in the midst of the constituted Authorities, civil and judicial, wearing their distinctive insignia. In their midst citizens carried litters draped in antique style and bearing the constitution and the busts of Brutus, Marat, Le Peletier, and Chalier. Each citizen held in his hand a wheat stalk, and on the banner which preceded the constituted Authorities was this inscription: "From the enforcement of the laws come prosperity and abundance."

The constituted Authorities were followed by various staff officers of the national guard of Châlons and by regular troops stationed in Châlons; they were preceded by a banner with this inscription: "Destroy the tyrants, or die."

Next, the natural children of the Patrie were led by a woman bearing a banner with this inscription: "The Patrie adopts us, we are eager to serve it."

Finally the old people, represented by veterans without weapons, formed a group preceded by two banners on which were these inscriptions: "The dawn of Reason and Liberty embellishes the end of our life" [and] "The French Republic honors loyalty, courage, old age, filial piety, misfortune; it places its constitution under the safekeeping of all the virtues."

After the group of veterans followed a cart drawn by four donkeys and containing remains of feudalism, such as armorial bearings, etc., as well as emblems of the superstition in which we were too long submerged. On the front was a man representing a pope adorned with tiara and pallium, having two cardinals for acolytes; on the front and rear of the cart were two billboards, the first of which bore the words "Prejudices pass away," and the second, "Reason is eternal."

The end of the procession was a detachment of cavalry, national guardsmen, and hussars mingled together, led by a trumpeter, and on their banner were these words: "The French government is revolutionary until the peace."

The whole being thus ordered, the procession left the promenade at exactly ten o'clock, crossed on the drawbridge, followed the avenue which is its continuation to reach the Rue de la Société Populaire, where there was a pause for the singing of . . . patriotic songs. . . . In the Place de la Liberté, there was another pause, for further singing. . . .

On the front steps of the city hall, there had been built and painted a mountain, at the top of which was placed a Hercules defending a fasces fourteen feet in height. A tricolor flag flew above it on which was written in large letters: "To the Mountain, the grateful French."

At the foot of the mountain, pure water flowed from a spring, falling by various cascades; twelve men dressed as mountaineers, armed with pikes and with civic crowns on their heads, were hidden in caverns in the mountain; as the procession arrived, singing the last couplet of the *Marseillaise*, the mountaineers quietly came out of their caverns without fully revealing themselves, and when "Aux armes, citoyens" was sung, they ran to get axes to defend their retreat, posted themselves on different sides of the mountain, but seeing the cart with feudalism and fanaticism drawn by asses with miters on their heads, they ran towards them, axe in hand, grabbed the miters, copes, and chasubles which adorned them as well as the pope and his acolytes, and chained them to the chariot of Liberty. During this, the band played a military charge; the carmagnole song was heard; but the mountaineers, seeing other carts arrive and feigning to believe that they were only the train following the one containing fanaticism, advanced in a column to meet the first one they saw, which was the chariot of Liberty; they lowered their axes as a sign of respect, and the band played a march; then a litter appeared, supporting a chair decorated with garlands; the Goddess descended from her cart, seated herself on the chair and was borne by eight mountaineers to the foot of the mountain; she was followed by two nymphs, one of whom was carrying a tricolor flag and the other the Declaration of the Rights of Man; they marched upon the trash remnants of nobility and superstition, which were then burned, to the great contentment of all the citizens, and climbing the mountain, with People's Representative Pfliéger, then present at this festival, and mountaineers who represented his colleagues, while the band played "Where can one better be than in the bosom of one's family," reached the summit. The Goddess was crowned by the graces, then a tricolor flag was displayed, and they sang "Our country's three colors," and still on the mountain they sang "When from the mountain peaks the sun," etc. The procession descended, the Goddess stopped at the spring, a vase was presented to her by the president of the Commune, she drank some water from the mountain, then presented some to the People's Representative, to all the constituted authorities, citizens and officers of the different corps present, who all drank to the health of the Republic, one and indivisible, and of the Mountain. The Goddess, again on her chair, was borne to her chariot by eight mountaineers, four others placed themselves at her sides, axes raised, to drive away the profane, the others took their places with the administrative bodies, to indicate that public dignities are consistent with virtue alone.

From there . . . they went . . . to . . . the Temple of Reason. . . .

All the musicians gathered behind the altar, with the singers; at the moment when the procession entered the Temple, the organ blared an overture, and the Société Populaire, the constituted Authorities, the surveillance committees, and the groups described above took places in rows facing the altar of Reason and a certain distance from it.

The military band played hymns to Reason, to Liberty, to hatred for tyrants, and to sacred love for the Patrie. After which the president of the Société Populaire delivered the inaugural speech, the Commune president, the Department president, the District president, the People's Representative, and General Debrun delivered speeches set forth hereafter.

After their harangues, various patriotic hymns were repeated and accompanied by the military band, after which, in front of the Temple entrance, the trumpeters announced that the inauguration festival and the ceremony were concluded.

In the evening fireworks were displayed on the mountain, a bouquet marked the gratitude of all the French to the mountaineers present, who were solemnly recognized to be the saviors of the Republic; then a ball was held, and so brotherhood was twice celebrated in a single day. Each citizen taking part in this fine day evidenced his civic spirit. All took the oath to live in freedom or to die.

THE AGE OF REASON

THOMAS PAINE

Few embodied the cosmopolitanism of the Enlightenment as did Thomas Paine (1737–1809). An Englishman who helped ignite the American Revolution, he would also sit in the French Revolutionary Assembly. His deistic plea for a rational Christianity, published in 1794, turned many Americans against Paine, the man they once regarded as a national hero.

To My Fellow-Citizens of the UNITED STATES OF AMERICA

I put the following work under your protection. It contains my opinion upon religion. You will do me the justice to remember that I have always strenuously supported the right of every man to his own opinion, however different that opinion might be to mine. He who denies to another this right makes a slave of himself to his present opinion, because he precludes himself the right of changing it.

The most formidable weapon against errors of every kind is reason. I have never used any other, and I trust I never shall.

It has been my intention for several years past to publish my thoughts upon Religion. I am well aware of the difficulties that attend the subject; and from that consideration had reserved it to a more advanced period of life. I intended it to be the last offering I should make to my fellow-citizens of all nations, and that at a time when the purity of the motive that induced me to it could not admit of a question, even by those who might disapprove the work.

The circumstance that has now taken place in France, of the total abolition of the whole national order of priesthood and of everything appertaining to compulsive systems of religion and compulsive articles of faith, has not only precipitated my intention, but rendered a work of this kind exceedingly necessary; lest, in the general wreck of superstition, of false systems of government, and false theology, we lose sight of morality, of humanity, and of the theology that is true.

As several of my colleagues, and others of my fellow-citizens of

France, have given me the example of making their voluntary and individual profession of faith, I also will make mine; and I do this with all that sincerity and frankness with which the mind of man communicates with itself.

I believe in one God, and no more; and I hope for happiness beyond this life.

I believe in the equality of man, and I believe that religious duties consist in doing justice, loving mercy, and endeavoring to make our fellow-creatures happy.

But lest it should be supposed that I believe many other things in addition to these, I shall, in the progress of this work, declare the things I do not believe and my reasons for not believing them.

I do not believe in the creed professed by the Jewish church, by the Roman church, by the Greek church, by the Turkish church, by the Protestant church, nor by any church that I know of. My own mind is my own church.

All national institutions of churches—whether Jewish, Christian, or Turkish—appear to me no other than human inventions set up to terrify and enslave mankind and monopolize power and profit.

I do not mean by this declaration to condemn those who believe otherwise. They have the same right to their belief as I have to mine. But it is necessary to the happiness of man that he be mentally faithful to himself. Infidelity does not consist in believing or in disbelieving; it consists in professing to believe what he does not believe.

It is impossible to calculate the moral mischief, if I may so express it, that mental lying has produced in society. When a man has so far corrupted and prostituted the chastity of his mind as to subscribe his professional belief to things he does not believe, he has prepared himself for the commission of every other crime. He takes up the trade of a priest for the sake of gain, and, in order to *qualify* himself for that trade, he begins with a perjury. Can we conceive anything more destructive to morality than this?

Soon after I had published the pamphlet, COMMON SENSE, in America, I saw the exceeding probability that a revolution in the system of government would be followed by a revolution in the system of religion. The adulterous connection of church and state, wherever it had taken place, whether Jewish, Christian, or Turkish, had so effectually prohibited, by pains and penalties, every discussion upon established creeds and upon first principles of religion, that until the system of government should be changed those subjects could not be brought fairly and openly before the world; but that whenever this should be done, a revolution in the system of religion would follow. Human inventions and priestcraft would be detected, and man would return to the pure, unmixed, and unadulterated belief of one God, and no more.

Every national church or religion has established itself by pretending some special mission from God, communicated to certain individuals. The Jews have their Moses; the Christians their Jesus Christ, their apostles and saints; and the Turks their Mahomet—as if the way to God was not open to every man alike.

Each of those churches show certain books which they call *revelation*, or the word of God. The Jews say that their word of God was given by God to Moses face to face; the Christians say that their word of God came by divine inspiration; and the Turks say that their word of God (the Koran) was brought by an angel from heaven. Each of those churches accuse the other of unbelief; and, for my own part, I disbelieve them all.

As it is necessary to affix right ideas to words, I will, before I proceed further into the subject, offer some observations on the word *revelation*. Revelation, when applied to religion, means something communicated *immediately* from God to man.

No one will deny or dispute the power of the Almighty to make such a communication, if he pleases. But admitting, for the sake of a case, that something has been revealed to a certain person, and not revealed to any other person, it is revelation to that person only. When he tells it to a second person, a second to a third, a third to a fourth, and so on, it ceases to be a revelation to all those persons. It is a revelation to the first person only, and *hearsay* to every other; and, consequently, they are not obliged to believe it.

It is a contradiction in terms and ideas to call anything a revelation that comes to us at second-hand, either verbally or in writing. Revelation is necessarily limited to the first communication. After this, it is only an account of something which that person says was a revelation made to him; and though he may find himself obliged to believe it, it cannot be incumbent upon me to believe it in the same manner, for it was not a revelation to *me*, and I have only his word for it that it was made to *him*.

When Moses told the children of Israel that he received the two tables of commandments from the hand of God, they were not obliged to believe him, because they had no other authority for it than his telling them so; and I have no other authority for it than some historian telling me so. The commandments carry no internal evidence of divinity with them. They contain some good moral precepts, such as any man qualified to be a lawgiver, or a legislator, could produce himself, without having recourse to supernatural intervention.

When I am told that the Koran was written in heaven, and brought to Mahomet by an angel, the account comes too near the same kind of hearsay evidence and secondhand authority as the former. I did not see the angel myself, and therefore I have a right not to believe it.

When also I am told that a woman, called the Virgin Mary, said, or gave out, that that she was with child without any cohabitation with a man, and that her betrothed husband, Joseph, said that an angel told him so, I have a right to believe them or not; such a circumstance required a much stronger evidence than their bare word for it; but we have not even this; for neither Joseph nor Mary wrote any such matter themselves. It is only reported by others that *they said so*. It is hearsay upon hearsay, and I do not choose to rest my belief upon such evidence.

It is, however, not difficult to account for the credit that was given to the story of Jesus Christ being the Son of God. He was born at a time when the heathen mythology had still some fashion and repute in the world, and that mythology had prepared the people for the belief of such a story. Almost all the extraordinary men that lived under the heathen mythology were reputed to be the sons of some of their gods. It was not a new thing, at that time, to believe a man to have been celestially begotten; the intercourse of gods with women was then a matter of familiar opinion. Their Jupiter, according to their accounts, had cohabited with hundreds; the story therefore had nothing in it either new, wonderful, or obscene; it was conformable to the opinions that then prevailed among the people called Gentiles, or mythologists, and it was those people only that believed it. The Jews, who had kept strictly to the belief of one God and no more, and who had always rejected the heathen mythology, never credited the story.

It is curious to observe how the theory of what is called the Christian church sprung out of the tail of the heathen mythology. A direct incorporation took place, in the first instance, by making the reputed founder to be celestially begotten. The trinity of gods that then followed was no other than a reduction of the former plurality, which was about twenty or thirty thousand. The statue of Mary succeeded the statue of

Diana of Ephesus. The deification of heroes changed into the canonization of saints. The mythologists had gods for everything; the Christian mythologists had saints for everything. The church became as crowded with the one as the pantheon had been with the other; and Rome was the place of both. The Christian theory is little else than the idolatry of the ancient mythologists, accommodated to the purposes of power and revenue; and it yet remains to reason and philosophy to abolish the amphibious fraud.

Nothing that is here said can apply, even with the most distant disrespect, to the real character of Jesus Christ. He was a virtuous and an amiable man. The morality that he preached and practiced was of the most benevolent kind; and though similar systems of morality had been preached by Confucius, and by some of the Greek philosophers, many years before, by the Quakers since, and by many good men in all ages, it has not been exceeded by any.

Jesus Christ wrote no account of himself, of his birth, parentage, or anything else. Not a line of what is called the New Testament is of his writing. The history of him is altogether the work of other people; and as to the account given of his resurrection and ascension, it was the necessary counterpart to the story of his birth. His historians, having brought him into the world in supernatural manner, were obliged to take him out again in the same manner, or the first part of the story must have fallen to the ground.

The wretched contrivance with which this latter part is told exceeds everything that went before it. . . . A small number of persons, not more than eight or nine, are introduced as proxies for the whole world, to say they *saw it*, and all the rest of the world are called upon to believe it. But it appears that Thomas did not believe the resurrection; and, as they say, would not believe without having ocular and manual demonstration himself. So *neither will I;* and the reason is equally as good for me, and for every other person, as for Thomas. . . .

But some perhaps will say: Are we to have no word of God—no revelation? I answer: Yes, there is a word of God; there is a revelation.

THE WORD OF GOD IS THE CREATION WE BEHOLD; and it is in *this* word, which no human invention can counterfeit or alter, that God speaketh universally to man.

Human language is local and changeable, and is therefore incapable of being used as the means of unchangeable and universal information. The idea that God sent Jesus Christ to publish, as they say, the glad tidings to all nations from one end of the earth unto the other, is consistent only with the ignorance of those who knew nothing of the extent of the world, and who believed, as those world-saviors believed and continued to believe for several centuries (and that in contradiction to the discoveries of philosophers and the experience of navigators), that the earth was flat like a trencher; and that a man might walk to the end of it. . . .

It is always necessary that the means that are to accomplish any end be equal to the accomplishment of that end, or the end cannot be accomplished. It is in this that the difference between finite and infinite power and wisdom discovers itself. Man frequently fails in accomplishing his ends from a natural inability of the power to the purpose; and frequently from the want of wisdom to apply power properly. But it is impossible for infinite power and wisdom to fail as man faileth. The means it useth are always equal to the end; but human language, more especially as there is not a universal language, is incapable of being used as a universal means of unchangeable and uniform information; and therefore it is not the means that God useth in manifesting himself universally to man.

It is only in the CREATION that all our ideas and conceptions of a *word of God* can unite! The creation speaketh a universal language, independently of human speech or human languages, multiplied and various as they be. It is an ever existing original which every man can read. It cannot be forged; it cannot be counterfeited; it cannot be lost; it cannot be altered; it cannot be suppressed. It does not depend upon the will of man whether it shall be published or not; it publishes itself from one end of the earth to the other. It preaches to all nations and to all worlds; and this *word of God* reveals to man all that is necessary for man to know of God.

Do we want to contemplate his power? We see it in the immensity of the creation. Do we want to contemplate his wisdom? We see it in the unchangeable order by which the incomprehensible whole is governed. Do we want to contemplate his munificence? We see it in the abundance with which he fills the earth. Do we want to contemplate his mercy? We see it in his not withholding that abundance even from the unthankful. In fine, do we want to know what God is? Search not the book called the Scripture, which any human hand might make, but the scripture called the Creation.

The only idea man can affix to the name of God is that of a *first cause*, the cause of all things. And incomprehensibly difficult as it is for man to conceive what a first cause is, he arrives at the belief of it from the tenfold greater difficulty of disbelieving it. It is difficult beyond description to conceive that space can have no end; but it is more difficult to conceive an end. It is difficult beyond the power of man to conceive an eternal duration of what we call time; but it is more impossible to conceive a time when there shall be no time. In like manner of reasoning, everything we behold carries in itself the internal evidence that it did not make itself. Every man is an evidence to himself that he did not make himself; neither could his father make himself, nor his grandfather, nor any of his race; neither could any tree, plant, or animal make itself; and it is the conviction arising from this evidence that carries us on, as it were, by necessity, to the belief of a first cause eternally existing, of a nature totally different to any material existence we know of, and by the power of which all things exist; and this first cause, man calls God.

It is only by the exercise of reason that man can discover God. Take away that reason and he would be incapable of understanding anything; and, in this case, it would be just as consistent to read even the book called the Bible to a horse as to a man. How then is it that those people pretend to reject reason?

PART IV

REASON AND HUMANITY

The Mind and Ideas

"I THINK, THEREFORE I AM . . ."

RENÉ DESCARTES

The French mathematician and philosopher Descartes (1596–1650) was one of the great precursors of the Enlightenment—indeed, one of the founders of modern rationalism. This famous selection is from his Discourse on Method, *published in Latin in 1637.*

Like a man who walks alone and in darkness, I resolved to go so slowly, and to use so much circumspection in everything, that if I did not advance speedily, at least I should keep from falling. I would not even have desired to begin by entirely rejecting any of the opinions which had formerly been able to slip into my belief without being introduced there by reason, had I not first spent much time in projecting the work which I was to undertake, and in seeking the true method of arriving at a knowledge of everything of which my understanding should be capable.

When I was younger, I had devoted a little study to logic, among philosophical matters, and to geometrical analysis and to algebra, among mathematical matters—three arts or sciences which, it seemed, ought to be able to contribute something to my design. But on examining them I noticed that the syllogisms of logic and the greater part of the rest of its teachings serve rather for explaining to other people the things we already know, or even, like the art of Lully, for speaking without judgment of things we know not, than for instructing us of them. And although they indeed contain many very true and very good precepts, there are always so many others mingled therewith that it is almost as difficult to separate them as to extract a Diana or a Minerva from a block of marble not yet rough hewn. Then, as to the analysis of the ancients and the algebra of the moderns, besides that they extend only to extremely abstract matters and appear to have no other use, the first is always so restricted to the consideration of figures that it cannot exercise the understanding without greatly fatiguing the imagination, and in the other one is so bound down to certain rules and ciphers that it has been made a confused and obscure art which embarrasses the mind, instead of a science which cultivates it. This made me think that some other method must be sought, which, while combining the advantages of these three, should be free from their defects. And as a multitude of laws often furnishes excuses for vice, so that a state is much better governed when it has but few, and those few strictly observed, so in place of the great number of precepts of which logic is composed, I believed that I should find the following four sufficient, provided that I made a firm and constant resolve not once to omit to observe them.

The first was, never to accept anything as true when I did not recognize it clearly to be so, that is to say, to carefully avoid precipitation and prejudice, and to include in my opinions nothing beyond that which should present itself so clearly and so distinctly to my mind that I might have no occasion to doubt it.

The second was, to divide each of the difficulties which I should examine into as many portions as were possible, and as should be required for its better solution.

The third was, to conduct my thoughts in order, by beginning with the simplest objects, and those most easy to know, so as to mount little by little, as if by steps, to the most complex knowledge, and even assuming an order among those which do not naturally precede one another.

And the last was, to make everywhere enumerations so complete, and surveys so wide, that I should be sure of omitting nothing.

The long chains of perfectly simple and easy reasons, which geometers are accustomed to employ in order to arrive at their most difficult demonstrations, had given me reason to believe that all things which can fall under the knowledge of man succeed each other in the same way, and that provided only we abstain from receiving as true any opinions which are not true, and always observe the necessary order in deducing one from the other, there can be none so remote that they may not be reached, or so hidden that they may not be discovered. And I was not put to much trouble to find out which it was necessary to begin with, for I knew already that it was with the simplest and most easily known; and considering that of all those who have heretofore sought truth in the sciences it is the mathematicians alone who have been able to find demonstrations, that is to say, clear and certain reasons, I did not doubt that I must start with the same things that they have considered, although I hoped for no other profit from them than that they would accustom my mind to feed on truths and not to content itself with false reasons. But I did not therefore design to try to learn all those particular sciences which bear the general name of mathematics: and seeing that although their objects were different they nevertheless all agree, in that they consider only the various relations or proportions found therein, I thought it would be better worth while if I merely examined these proportions in general, supposing them only in subjects which would serve to render the knowledge of them more easy to me, and even, also, without in any wise restricting them thereto, in order to be the better able to apply them subsequently to every other subject to which they should be suitable. Then, having remarked that in order to know them I should sometimes need to consider each separately, I had to suppose them in lines, because I found nothing more simple, or which I could more distinctly represent to my imagination and to my senses; but to retain them, or to comprehend many of them together, it was necessary that I should express them by certain ciphers as short as possible, and in this way I should borrow all the best in geometrical analysis, and in algebra, and correct all the faults of the one by means of the other.

I do not know whether I ought to discuss with you the earlier of my meditations, for they are so metaphysical and so out of the common that perhaps they would not be to everyone's taste; and yet, in order that it may be judged whether the bases I have taken are sufficiently firm, I am in some measure constrained to speak of them. I had remarked for long that, in conduct, it is sometimes necessary to follow opinions known to be very uncertain, just as if they were indubitable, as has been said above; but then, because I desired to devote myself only to the research of truth, I thought it necessary to do exactly the contrary, and reject as absolutely false all in which I could conceive the least doubt, in order to see if afterwards there did not remain in my belief something which was entirely indubitable. Thus, because our senses sometimes deceive us, I wanted to suppose that nothing is such as they make us imagine it; and because some men err in reasoning, even touching the simplest matters of geometry, and make paralogisms, and judging that I was as liable to fail as any other, I rejected as false all the reasons which I had formerly accepted as demonstrations; and finally, considering that all the thoughts which we have when awake can come to us also when we sleep, without any of them then being true, I resolved to feign that everything which had ever entered into my mind was no more true than the illusions of my dreams. But immediately afterwards I observed that while I thus desired everything to be false, I, who thought, must of necessity be something; and remarking that this truth, *I think, therefore I am*, was so firm and so assured that all the most extravagant suppositions of the skeptics were unable to shake it, I judged that I could unhesitatingly accept it as the first principle of the philosophy I was seeking.

Then, examining attentively what I was, and seeing that I could feign that I had no body, and that there was no world or any place where I was, but that nevertheless I could not feign that I did not exist, and that, on the contrary, from the fact that I thought to doubt of the truth of other things, it followed very evidently that I was; while if I had only ceased to think, although all else which I had previously imagined had been true I had no reason to believe that I might have been, therefore I knew that I was a substance whose essence or nature is only to think, and which, in order to be, has no need of any place, and depends on no material thing; so that this I, that is to say, the soul by which I am what I am, is entirely distinct from the body, and even easier to know than the body, and although the body were not, the soul would not cease to be all that it is.

After that I considered generally what is requisite to make a proposition true and certain; for since I had just found one which I knew to be so, I thought that I ought also to know in what this certainly consisted. And having remarked that there is nothing at all in this, *I think, therefore I am*, which assures me that I speak the truth, except that I see very clearly that in order to think it is necessary to exist, I judged that I might take it as a general rule that the things which we conceive very clearly and very distinctly are all true, and that there is difficulty only in seeing plainly which things they are that we conceive distinctly.

After this, and reflecting upon the fact that I doubted, and that in consequence my being was not quite perfect (for I saw clearly that to know was a greater perfection than to doubt), I bethought myself to find out from whence I had learned to think of something more perfect than I; and I knew for certain that it must be from some nature which was in reality more perfect. For as regards the thoughts I had of many other things outside myself, as of the sky, the earth, light, heat, and a thousand more, I was not so much at a loss to know whence they came, because, remarking nothing in them which seemed to make them superior to me, I could believe that if they were true they were dependencies of my nature, inasmuch as it had some perfection, and if they were not true that I derived them from nothing—that is to say, that they were in me because I had some defect. But it could not be the same with the idea of a Being more perfect than my own, for to derive it from nothing was manifestly impossible; and since it is no less repugnant to me that the more perfect should follow and depend on the less perfect than that out of nothing should proceed something, I could not derive it from myself; so that it remained that it had been put in me by a nature truly more perfect than I, which had in itself all perfections of which I could have any idea; that is, to explain myself in one word, God.

AN ESSAY CONCERNING HUMAN UNDERSTANDING

JOHN LOCKE

In his 1690 Essay on Human Understanding, *from which this selection comes, Locke set forth what would become the Enlightenment's dominant conception of the mind: a blank slate on which the sensations provided by sensory experience produce ideas.*

1. *Idea is the object of thinking.*—Every man being conscious to himself that he thinks, and that which his mind is applied about whilst thinking

being the ideas that are there, it is past doubt that men have in their minds several ideas, such as are those expressed by the words, "whiteness, hardness, sweetness, thinking, motion, man, elephant, army, drunkenness," and others. It is in the first place then to be enquired, How he comes by them? I know it is a received doctrine, that men have native ideas and original characters stamped upon their minds in their very first being. This opinion I have at large examined already; and, I suppose, what I have said in the foregoing Book will be much more easily admitted, when I have shown whence the understanding may get all the ideas it has, and by what ways and degrees they may come into the mind; for which I shall appeal to everyone's own observation and experience.

2. *All ideas come from sensation or reflection.*—Let us then suppose the mind to be, as we say, white paper, void of all characters, without any ideas; how comes it to be furnished? Whence comes it by that vast store, which the busy and boundless fancy of man has painted on it with an almost endless variety? Whence has it all the materials of reason and knowledge? To this I answer, in one word, from EXPERIENCE; in that all our knowledge is founded, and from that it ultimately derives itself. Our observation, employed either about external sensible objects, or about the internal operations of our minds, perceived and reflected on by ourselves, is that which supplies our understandings with all the materials of thinking. These two are the fountains of knowledge, from whence all the ideas we have, or can naturally have, do spring.

3. *The objects of sensation one source of ideas.*—First, our senses, conversant about particular sensible objects, do convey into the mind several distinct perceptions of things, according to those various ways wherein those objects do affect them; and thus we come by those *ideas* we have of yellow, white, heat, cold, soft, hard, bitter, sweet, and all those which we call sensible qualities; which when I say the senses convey into the mind, I mean, they from external objects convey into the mind what produces there those perceptions. This great source of most of the ideas we have, depending wholly upon our senses, and derived by them to the understanding, I call, SENSATION.

4. *The operations of our minds the other source of them.*—Secondly, the other fountain, from which experience furnisheth the understanding with ideas, is the perception of the operations of our own minds within us, as it is employed about the ideas it has got; which operations, when the soul comes to reflect on and consider, do furnish the understanding

with another set of ideas which could not be had from things without: and such are perception, thinking, doubting, believing, reasoning, knowing, willing, and all the different actings of our own minds; which we being conscious of, and observing in ourselves, do from these receive into our understanding as distinct ideas, as we do from bodies affecting our senses. This source of ideas every man has wholly in himself: and though it be not sense, as having nothing to do with external objects, yet it is very like it, and might properly enough be called internal sense. But as I call the other Sensation, so I call this REFLECTION, the ideas it affords being such only as the mind gets by reflecting on its own operations within itself. By Reflection, then, in the following part of this discourse, I would be understood to mean that notice which the mind takes of its own operations, and the manner of them, by reason whereof there come to be ideas of these operations in the understanding. These two, I say, viz., external material things as the objects of Sensation, and the operations of our own minds within as the objects of Reflection, are, to me, the only originals from whence all our ideas take their beginnings. The term *operations* here, I use in a large sense, as comprehending not barely the actions of the mind about its ideas, but some sort of passions arising sometimes from them, such as is the satisfaction or uneasiness arising from any thought.

5. *All our ideas are of the one or the other of these.*—The understanding seems to me not to have the least glimmering of any ideas which it doth not receive from one of these two. *External objects* furnish the mind with the ideas of sensible qualities, which are all those different perceptions they produce in us; and *the mind* furnishes the understanding with ideas of its own operations. These, when we have taken a full survey of them, and their several modes, combinations, and relations, we shall find to contain all our whole stock of ideas; and that we have nothing in our minds which did not come in one of these two ways. Let anyone examine his own thoughts, and thoroughly search into his understanding, and then let him tell me, whether all the original ideas he has there, are any other than of the objects of his senses, or of the operations of his mind considered as objects of his reflection; and how great a mass of knowledge soever he imagines to be lodged there, he will, upon taking a strict view, see that he has not any idea in his mind but what one of these two have imprinted, though perhaps with infinite variety compounded and enlarged by the understanding, as we shall see hereafter.

NEW ESSAYS ON HUMAN UNDERSTANDING

GOTTFRIED WILHELM LEIBNITZ

Locke was answered in 1696 by the German philosopher and mathematician Gottfried Wilhelm Leibnitz (1646–1716). There were innate ideas, Leibnitz insisted, and our senses were not the sole source of knowledge.

I find so many marks of unusual penetration in what Mr. Locke has given us on the Human Understanding and on Education, and I consider the matter so important, that I have thought I should not employ the time to no purpose which I should give to such profitable reading; so much the more as I have myself meditated deeply upon the subject of the foundations of our knowledge. This is my reason for putting upon this sheet some of the reflections which have occurred to me while reading his Essay on the Understanding.

Of all researches, there is none of greater importance, since it is the key to all others. The first book considers chiefly the principles said to be born with us. Mr. Locke does not admit them, any more than he admits innate ideas. He has doubtless had good reasons for opposing himself on this point to ordinary prejudices, for the name of ideas and principles is greatly abused. Common philosophers manufacture for themselves principles according to their fancy; and the Cartesians, who profess greater accuracy, do not cease to intrench themselves behind so-called ideas of extension, of matter, and of the soul, desiring to avoid thereby the necessity of proving what they advance, on the pretext that those who will meditate on these ideas will discover in them the same thing as they; that is to say, that those who will accustom themselves to their jargon and mode of thought will have the same prepossessions, which is very true.

My view, then, is that nothing should be taken as first principles but experiences and the axiom of identity or (what is the same thing) contradiction, which is primitive, since otherwise there would be no difference between truth and falsehood; and all investigation would cease at once, if to say yes or no were a matter of indifference. We cannot, then, prevent ourselves from assuming this principle as soon as we wish to reason. All other truths are demonstrable, and I value very highly the method of Euclid, who, without stopping at what would be supposed to be sufficiently proved by the so-called ideas, has demonstrated (for instance) that in a triangle one side is always less than the sum of the other two. Yet Euclid was right in taking some axioms for granted, not as if they were truly primitive and indemonstrable, but because he would have come to a standstill if he had wished to reach his conclusions only after an exact discussion of principles. Thus he judged it proper to content himself with having pushed the proofs up to this small number of propositions, so that it may be said that if they are true, all that he says is also true. He has left to others the task of demonstrating further these principles themselves, which besides are already justified by experience; but with this we are not satisfied in these matters. This is why Apollonius, Proclus, and others have taken the pains to demonstrate some of Euclid's axioms. Philosophers should imitate this method of procedure in order finally to attain some fixed principles, even though they be only provisional, after the way I have just mentioned.

As for ideas, I have given some explanation of them in a brief essay printed in the *Actes des Sçavans* of Leipzig for November, 1684, which is entitled "Meditationes de Cognitione, Veritate, et Ideis"; and I could have wished that Mr. Locke had seen and examined it; for I am one of the most docile of men, and nothing is better suited to advance our thought than the considerations and remarks of clever persons, when they are made with attention and sincerity. I shall only say here, that true or real ideas are those whose execution we are assured is possible; the others are doubtful, or (in case of proved impossibility) chimerical. Now the possibility of ideas is proved as much *a priori* by demonstrations, by making use of the possibility of other more simple ideas, as *a posteriori* by experience; for what exists cannot fail to be possible. But primitive ideas are those whose possibility is indemonstrable, and which are in truth nothing else than the attributes of God.

I do not find it absolutely essential for the beginning or for the practice of the art of thinking to decide the question whether there are ideas and truths born with us; whether they all come to us from without or from ourselves; we will reason correctly provided we observe what I have said above, and proceed in an orderly way and without prejudice.

The question of the origin of our ideas and of our maxims is not preliminary in Philosophy, and we must have made great progress in order to solve it successfully. I think, however, that I can say that our ideas, even those of sensible things, come from within our own soul, of which view you can the better judge by what I have published upon the nature and connection of substances and what is called the union of the soul with the body. For I have found that these things had not been well understood. I am nowise in favor of Aristotle's *tabula rasa;* and there is something substantial in what Plato called *reminiscence.* There is even something more; for we not only have a reminiscence of all our past thoughts, but also a presentiment of all our future thoughts. It is true that this is confused, and fails to distinguish them, in much the same way as when I hear the noise of the sea I hear that of all the particular waves which make up the noise as a whole, though without discerning one wave from another. Thus it is true in a certain sense, as I have explained, that not only our ideas, but also our sensations, spring from within our own soul, and that the soul is more independent than is thought, although it is always true that nothing takes place in it which is not determined, and nothing is found in creatures that God does not continually create.

ON MR. LOCKE

François-Marie Arouet de Voltaire

In this selection from his Letters Concerning the English Nation *(1733), Voltaire pays homage to Locke's seminal contribution to theories of the mind.*

Perhaps no man ever had a more judicious or more methodical mind, or was a more acute logician than Mr. Locke, and yet he was not a great mathematician. He could never subject himself to the tedious fatigue of calculations, nor to the dry pursuit of mathematical truths, which do not at first present any tangible objects to the mind; and no one has ever given better proofs than he, that it is possible for a man to have a geometrical head without the assistance of geometry. Before his time, several great philosophers had declared, in the most positive terms, what the soul of man is; but as these knew absolutely nothing about it, they might very well be allowed to differ entirely in opinion from one another.

In Greece, the cradle of arts and of errors, where the grandeur as well as the folly of the human mind went to such prodigious lengths, the people used to reason about the soul in the very same manner as we do.

The divine Anaxagoras, in whose honor an altar was erected for his having taught mankind that the sun was greater than Peloponnesus, that snow was black, and that the heavens were of stone, affirmed that the soul was an aërial spirit, but at the same time immortal. Diogenes (not he who was a cynical philosopher after having coined base money) declared that the soul was a portion of the substance of God: an idea which we must confess was very sublime. Epicurus maintained that it was composed of parts in the same manner as the body.

Aristotle, who has been explained in a thousand ways because he was unintelligible, was of the opinion, according to some of his disciples, that the understanding in all men is one and the same substance. The divine Plato, master of the divine Aristotle—and the divine Socrates, master of the divine Plato—used to say that the soul was corporeal and eternal. No doubt but the demon of Socrates had instructed him in the nature of it. Some people, indeed, pretended that a man who boasted his being attended by a familiar genius must infallibly be either a knave or a madman, but this kind of people are just too hard to please.

As for our Church Fathers, several in the primitive ages believed that the soul was human, and the angels and God corporeal. Men naturally improve upon every system. St. Bernard, as Father Mabillon confesses, taught that the soul after death did not behold God in the celestial regions, but conversed with Christ's human nature only. However, he was not believed this time on his bare word; the adventure of the crusade having a little discredited his oracles. Afterwards a thousand Schoolmen arose, such as the Irrefragable Doctor, the Subtile Doctor, the Angelic Doctor, the Seraphic Doctor, the Cherubic Doctor, who were all sure that they had a very clear and distinct idea of the soul, and yet wrote in such a manner that one would conclude they were resolved no one should understand a word in their writings. Our Descartes, born to discover the errors of antiquity, and at the same time to substitute his own, and carried away by that systematic spirit which throws a cloud over the minds of the greatest men, thought he had demonstrated that the soul is the same thing as thought, in the same manner that matter, in his opinion, is the same as extension. He asserted that man thinks eternally and that the soul, at its coming into the body, is informed with the whole series of metaphysical notions: knowing God, infinite space, possessing all abstract ideas—in a word, completely endued with the most sublime lights, which it unhappily forgets at its issuing from the womb.

Father Malebranche, the Oratorian, in his sublime illusions, not only admitted innate ideas, but did not doubt of our living wholly in God, and that God is, as it were, our soul.

Such a multitude of reasoners having written the romance of the soul, a sage at last arose, who gave very modestly its history. Mr. Locke has displayed the human soul in the same manner as an excellent anatomist explains the springs of the human body. He everywhere takes the light of physics for his guide. He sometimes presumes to speak affirmatively, but then he presumes also to doubt. Instead of concluding at once what we know not, he examines gradually what we want to know. He takes an infant at the instant of his birth; he traces step by step the progress of his understanding; examines what things he has in common with brutes, and what he possesses above them. Above all, he consults his own experience, the awareness of his own thought.

"I shall leave," says he, "to those who know more of this matter than I, the examining whether the soul exists before or after the organization of our bodies. But I confess that it is my lot to be animated with one of those heavy souls which do not always think; and I am even so unhappy as not to conceive how it is more necessary that the soul should think perpetually than that bodies should be forever in motion."

With regard to myself, I shall boast that I have the honor to be as stupid in this particular as Mr. Locke. No one shall ever make me believe that I always think: and I am as little inclined as he could be to fancy that some weeks after I was conceived I was a very learned soul; knowing at that time a thousand things which I forgot at my birth; and possessing when in the womb (though to no manner of purpose) knowledge which I lost the instant I had occasion for it; and which I have never since been able to recover perfectly.

Mr. Locke, after having destroyed innate ideas; after having fully renounced the vanity of believing that we always think; after having laid down, from the most solid principles, that ideas enter the mind through the senses; having examined our simple and complex ideas; having traced the human mind through its several operations; having shown that all the languages in the world are imperfect, and the great abuse that is made of words every moment, he at last comes to consider the extent or rather the narrow limits of human knowledge. It is in this chapter that he presumed to advance, but very modestly, the following words: "We shall perhaps never be capable of knowing whether a being, purely material, thinks or not." This sage assertion was, by more divines than one, looked upon as a scandalous declaration that the soul is material and mortal. Some Englishmen, devout after their way, sounded the alarm. The superstitious are the same in society as cowards in the army; they themselves are seized with a panic fear and communicate it to others. It was loudly exclaimed that Mr. Locke intended to destroy religion; nevertheless, religion had nothing to do with the business, it being a question purely philosophical, altogether independent of faith and revelation. Mr. Locke's opponents needed but to examine, calmly and impartially, whether the declaring that matter can think implies a contradiction; and whether God is able to communicate thought to matter. But divines are too apt to begin their declarations by saying that God is offended when people differ from them in opinion; in which they too much resemble the bad poets, who used to declare publicly that Boileau spoke irreverently of Louis XIV, because he ridiculed their stupid productions. Bishop Stillingfleet got the reputation of being a calm and unprejudiced divine because he did not expressly make use of injurious terms in his dispute with Mr. Locke. That divine entered the lists against him, but he was defeated; for he argued as a Schoolman, and Locke as a philosopher, who was perfectly acquainted with the strong as well as the weak side of the human mind and fought with weapons whose temper he knew.

If I might presume to give my opinion on so delicate a subject after Mr. Locke, I would say that men have long disputed on the nature and the immortality of the soul. With regard to its immortality, it is impossible to give a demonstration of it, since its nature is still the subject of controversy; which, however, must be thoroughly understood before a person can be able to determine whether it is immortal or not. Human reason is so little able by itself to demonstrate the immortality of the soul, that it was absolutely necessary for religion to reveal it to us. It is of advantage to society in general, that mankind should believe the soul to be immortal; faith commands us to do this; nothing more is required, and the matter is cleared up at once. But it is otherwise with respect to its nature; it is of little importance to religion, which only requires the soul to be virtuous, whatever substance it may be made of. It is a clock which is given us to regulate, but the artisan has not told us of what materials the spring of this clock is composed. . . .

Besides, we must not be apprehensive that any philosophical opinion will ever harm the religion of a country. Though our demonstrations clash directly with our mysteries, that is nothing to the purpose, for the latter are not less revered upon that account by our Christian philosophers, who know very well that the objects of reason and those of faith are of a very different nature. Philosophers will never form a religious sect, the reason of which is, their writings are not calculated for the common people, and they themselves are free from enthusiasm. If we divide mankind into twenty parts, it will be found that nineteen of these consist of persons employed in manual labor, who will never know that such a man as Mr. Locke existed. In the remaining twentieth part how few are readers? And among such as are so, twenty amuse themselves with romances to one who studies philosophy. The thinking part of mankind is confined to a very small number, and these will never disturb the peace and tranquillity of the world.

Neither Montaigne, Locke, Bayle, Spinoza, Hobbes, Lord Shaftesbury, Collins, nor Toland, lighted up the firebrand of discord in their countries; this has generally been the work of divines, who being at first puffed up with the ambition of becoming chiefs of a sect, grew very desirous of being the head of a party. But what do I say? All the works of the modern philosophers put together will never raise so much commotion as did the dispute among the Franciscans, over the form of their sleeves and cowls.

A TREATISE OF HUMAN NATURE

David Hume

In 1740 Hume published his magisterial Treatise of Human Nature, *the bible of skepticism, which insists that it is impossible to explain ultimate principles on anything other than the authority of experience. This selection, with its famous discussion of cause and effect with billiard balls, is from Hume's own summary of the argument of his* Treatise *in his* Abstract of a Book Lately Published: Entitled a Treatise of Human Nature.

This book seems to be wrote upon the same plan with several other works that have had a great vogue of late years in England. The philosophical spirit, which has been so much improved all over Europe within these last four score years, has been carried to as great length in this kingdom as in any other. Our writers seem even to have started a new kind of philosophy, which promises more both to the entertainment and advantage of mankind, than any other with which the world has been yet acquainted. Most of the philosophers of antiquity, who treated of human nature, have shown more of a delicacy of sentiment, a just sense of morals, or a greatness of soul, than a depth of reasoning and reflection. They content themselves with representing the common sense of mankind in the strongest lights, and with the best turn of thought and expression, without following out steadily a chain of propositions, or forming the several truths into a regular science. But 'tis at least worth while to try if the science of *man* will not admit of the same accuracy which several parts of natural philosophy are found susceptible of. There seems to be all the reason in the world to imagine that it may be carried to the greatest degree of exactness. If, in examining several phenomena, we find that they resolve themselves into one common principle, and can trace this principle into another, we shall at last arrive at those few simple principles, on which all the rest depend. And tho' we can never arrive at the ultimate principles, 'tis a satisfaction to go as far as our faculties will allow us.

This seems to have been the aim of our late philosophers, and, among the rest, of this author. He proposes to anatomize human nature in a regular manner, and promises to draw no conclusions but where he is authorized by experience. He talks with contempt of hypotheses; and insinuates, that such of our countrymen as have banished them from moral philosophy, have done a more signal service to the world, than *my Lord Bacon,* whom he considers as the father of experimental physics. He mentions, on this occasion, Mr. Locke, my Lord Shaftesbury, Dr. Mandeville, Mr. Hutcheson, Dr. Butler, who, tho' they differ in many points among themselves, seem all to agree in founding their accurate disquisitions of human nature entering upon experience.

Beside the satisfaction of being acquainted with what most nearly concerns us, it may be safely affirmed, that almost all the sciences are comprehended in the science of human nature, and are dependent on it. *The sole end of logic is to explain the principles and operations of our reasoning faculty, and the nature of our ideas;* morals and criticism *regard our tastes and sentiments; and* politics *consider men as united in society, and dependent on each other.* This treatise therefore of human nature seems intended for a system of the sciences. The author has finished what regards logic, and has laid the foundation of the other parts in his account of the passions. . . .

As his (the author's book) contains a great number of speculations very new and remarkable, it will be impossible to give the reader a just notion of the whole. We shall therefore chiefly confine ourselves to his explication of our reasoning from cause and effect. If we can make this intelligible to the reader, it may serve as a specimen of the whole.

Our author begins with some definitions. He calls a *perception* whatever can be present to the mind, whether we employ our senses, or are actuated with passion, or exercise our thought and reflection. He divides our perceptions into two kinds, viz. impressions and *ideas.* When we feel a passion or emotion of any kind, or have the images of external objects conveyed by our senses; the perception of the mind is what he calls an *impression,* which is a word that he employs in a new sense. When we reflect on a passion or an object which is not present, this perception is an *idea.* Impressions, therefore, are our lively and strong perceptions; *ideas* are the fainter and weaker. This distinction is evident; as evident as that betwixt feeling and thinking.

The first proposition he advances, is, that all our ideas, or weak perceptions, are derived from our impressions, or strong perceptions, and that we can never think of any thing which we have not seen without us, or felt in our own minds. This proposition seems to be equivalent to that which Mr. Locke has taken such pains to establish, *viz. that no ideas are innate.* Only it may be observed as an inaccuracy of that famous philosopher, that he comprehends all our perceptions under the term of idea, in which sense it is false, that we have no innate ideas. For it is evident our stronger perceptions or impressions are innate, and that natural affection, love of virtue, resentment, and all the other passions, arise immediately from nature. . . .

Our author thinks, "that no discovery could have been made more happily for deciding all controversies concerning ideas than this, that impressions always take the precedency of them, and that every idea with which the imagination is furnished, first makes its appearance in a correspondent impression. These latter perceptions are all so clear and evident, that they admit of no controversy; tho' many of our ideas are so obscure, that 'tis almost impossible even for the mind, which forms them, to tell exactly their nature and composition." Accordingly, wherever any idea is ambiguous, he has always recourse to the impression, which must render it clear and precise. And when he suspects that any philosophical term has no idea annexed to it (as is too common) he always asks *from what impression that idea is derived?* And if no impression can be produced, he concludes that the term is altogether insignificant. 'Tis after this manner he examines our idea of *substance* and *essence;* and it were to be wished, that this rigorous method were more practiced in all philosophical debates.

'Tis evident, that all reasonings concerning *matter of fact* are founded on the relation of cause and effect, and that we can never infer the existence of one object from another, unless they be connected together, either mediately or immediately. In order, therefore to understand these reasonings, we must be perfectly acquainted with the idea of a cause; and in order to that, must look about us to find something that is the cause of another.

Here is a billiard-ball lying on the table, and another ball moving towards it with rapidity. They strike; and the ball, which was formerly at rest, now acquires a motion. This is as perfect an instance of the relation of cause and effect as any which we know, either by sensation or reflection. Let us therefore examine it. 'Tis evident, that the two balls touched one another before the motion was communicated, and that there was no interval betwixt the shock and the motion. *Contiguity* in time and place is therefore a requisite circumstance to the operation of all causes. 'Tis evident likewise, that the motion, which was the cause, is prior to the motion, which was the effect. *Priority* in time, is therefore another requisite circumstance in every cause. But this is not all. Let us try any other balls of the same kind in a like situation, and we shall always find, that the impulse of the one produces motion in the other. Here therefore is a *third* circumstance, *viz.* that of a *constant conjunction* between the cause and effect. Every object like the cause, produces always some object like the effect. Beyond these three circumstances of contiguity, priority, and constant conjunction, I can discover nothing in this cause. The first ball is in motion; touches the second; immediately the second is in motion; and when I try the experiment with the same or like balls, in the same or like circumstances, I find, that upon the motion and touch of the one ball, motion always follows in the other. In whatever shape I turn this matter, and however I examine it, I can find nothing farther.

This is the case when both the cause and effect are present to the senses. Let us now see upon what our inference is founded, when we conclude from the one that the other has existed or will exist. Suppose I see a ball moving in a straight line towards another, I immediately conclude, that they will shock, and that the second will be in motion. This is the inference from cause to effect; and of this nature are all our reasonings in the conduct of life: on this is founded all our belief in history and from hence is derived all philosophy, excepting only geometry and arithmetic. If we can explain the inference from the shock of two balls, we shall be able to account for this operation of the mind in all instances.

Were a man, such as *Adam*, created in the full vigor of understanding, without experience, he would never be able to infer motion in the second ball from the motion and impulse of the first. It is not anything that reason sees in the cause, which make us *infer* the effect. Such an inference, were it possible, would amount to a demonstration, as being founded merely on the comparison of ideas. But no inference from cause to effect amounts to a demonstration, as being founded merely on the comparison of ideas. But no inference from cause to effect amounts to a demonstration. Of which there is this evident proof. The mind can always *conceive* any effect to follow from any cause, and indeed any event to follow upon another: whatever we *conceive* is possible, at least in a metaphysical sense: but wherever a demonstration takes place, the contrary is impossible, and implies a contradiction. There is no demonstration, therefore, for any conjunction of cause and effect. And this is a principle which is generally allowed by philosophers.

It would have been necessary, therefore, for *Adam* (if he was not inspired) to have had *experience* of the effect, which followed upon the impulse of these two balls. He must have seen, in several instances, that when the one ball struck upon the other, the second always acquired motion. If he had seen a sufficient number of instances of this kind, whenever he saw the one ball moving towards the other, he would always conclude without hesitation, that the second would acquire motion. His understanding would anticipate his sight, and form a conclusion suitable to his past experience.

It follows, then, that all reasonings concerning cause and effect, are founded on experience, and that all reasonings from experience are founded on the supposition, that the course of nature will continue uniformly the same. We conclude, that like causes, in like circumstances, will always produce like effects. It may now be worth while to consider, what determines us to form a conclusion of such infinite consequence.

'Tis evident, that *Adam* with all his science, would never have been able to *demonstrate*, that the course of nature must continue uniformly the same, and that the future must be conformable to the past. What is possible can never be demonstrated to be false; and 'tis possible the course of nature may change, since we can conceive such a change. Nay, I will go further, and assert, that he could not so much as prove by any *probable* arguments, that the future must be conformable to the past. All probable arguments are built on the supposition, that there is this conformity betwix the future and the past, and therefore can never prove it. This conformity is a *matter of fact*, and if it must be proved, will admit of no proof but from experience. But our experience in the past can be a proof of nothing for the future, but upon a supposition, that there is a resemblance betwixt them. This therefore is a point, which can admit of no proof at all, and which we take for granted without any proof.

We are determined by CUSTOM alone to suppose the future conformable to the past. When I see a billiard-ball moving towards another, my mind is immediately carried by habit to the usual effect, and anticipates my sight by conceiving the second ball in motion. There is nothing in these objects, abstractly considered, and independent of experience, which leads me to form any such conclusion: and even after I have had experience of many repeated effects of this kind, there is no argument, which determines me to suppose that the effect will be conformable to past experience. The powers, by which bodies operate, are entirely unknown. We perceive only their sensible qualities: and what *reason* have we to think, that the same powers will always be conjoined with the same sensible qualities?

'Tis not, therefore, reason, which is the guide of life, but custom. That alone determines the mind, in all instances, to suppose the future conformable to the past. However easy this step may seem, reason would never, to all eternity, be able to make it.

This is a very curious discovery, but leads us to others, that are still more curious. *When I see a billiard-ball moving towards another, my mind is immediately carried by habit to the usual effect, and anticipate my sight by conceiving the second ball in motion.* But is this all? Do I nothing but CONCEIVE the motion of the second ball? No surely. I also BELIEVE that it will move. What then is this *belief?* And how does it differ from the simple conception of any thing? Here is a new question unthought of by philosophers.

When a demonstration convinces me of any proposition, it not only makes me conceive the proposition, but also makes me sensible, that 'tis impossible to conceive any thing contrary. What is demonstratively false implies a contradiction; and what implies a contradiction cannot be conceived. But with regard to any matter of fact, however strong the proof may be from experience, I can always conceive the contrary, tho' I cannot always believe it. The belief, therefore, makes some difference betwix the conception to which we assent, and that to which we do not assent.

To account for this, there are only two hypotheses. It may be said, that belief joins some new idea to those which we may conceive without assenting to them. But this hypothesis is false. For *first* no such idea can be produced. When we simply conceive an object, we conceive it in all its parts. We conceive it as it might exist, tho' we do not believe it to exist. Our belief of it would discover no new qualities. We may paint out the entire object in imagination without believing it. We may set it, in a manner, before our eyes, with every circumstance of time and place. 'Tis the very object conceived as it might exist; and when we believe it, we can do no more.

Secondly, The mind has a faculty of joining all ideas together, which involve not a contradiction; and therefore if belief consisted in some idea, which we add to the simple conception, it would be in a man's power, by adding this idea to it, to believe any thing, which he can conceive.

SINCE therefore belief implies a conception, and yet is something more; and since it adds no new idea to the conception; it follows, that it is a different MANNER of conceiving an object; *something* that is distinguishable to the feeling, and depends not upon our will, as all our ideas do. My mind runs by habit from the visible object of one ball moving towards another, to the usual effect of motion in the second ball. It not only conceives that motion, but *feels* something different in the conception of it from a mere reverie of the imagination. The presence of this visible object, and the constant conjunction of that particular effect, render the idea different to the *feeling* from those loose ideas, which come into the mind without any introduction. This conclusion seems a little surprising; but we are led into it by a chain of propositions which admit of no doubt. To ease the reader's memory I shall briefly resume them. No matter of fact can be proved but from its cause or its effect. Nothing can be known to be the cause of another but by experience. We can give no reason for extending to the future our experience in the past; but are entirely determined by custom, when we conceive an effect to follow, from its usual cause. But we also believe an effect to follow as well as conceive it. This belief joins no new idea to the conception. It only varies the manner of conceiving, and makes a difference to the feeling or sentiment. Belief, therefore, in all matters of fact arises only from custom, and is an idea conceived in a peculiar *manner*.

Our author proceeds to explain the manner or feeling, which renders belief different from a loose conception. He seems sensible, that 'tis impossible by words to describe this feeling, which every one must be conscious of in his own breast. He calls it sometimes a *stronger* conception, sometimes a more *lively*, a more *vivid*, a *firmer*, or a more *intense* conception. And indeed, whatever name we may give to this feeling, which constitutes belief, our author thinks it evident, that it has a more forcible effect on the mind than fiction and mere conception. This he proves by its influence on the passions and on the imagination; which are only moved by truth or what is taken for such. . . .

By all that has been said the reader will easily perceive, that the philosophy contained in this book is very skeptical, and tends to give us a notion of the imperfections and narrow limits of human understanding. Almost all reasoning is there reduced to experience; and the belief, which attends experience, is explained to be nothing but a peculiar sentiment, or lively conception produced by habit. Nor is this all, when we believe anything of *external* existence, or suppose an object to exist a moment after it is no longer perceived, this belief is nothing but a sentiment of the same kind. Our author insists upon several other skeptical topics; and upon the whole concludes, that we assent to our faculties, and employ our reason only because we cannot help it. Philosophy would render us entirely *Pyrrhonian*, were not nature too strong for it.

MAN A MACHINE

Julien Offray de la Mettrie

The French physician and philosopher la Mettrie (1709–1751) developed a totally mechanistic and materialistic theory of the human mind and of the brain's functioning. The book from which this selection is taken, Man a Machine *(1747), shocked even some of the most irreligious of his fellow* philosophes.

A wise man should do more than study nature and truth; he should dare state the truth for the benefit of the few who are willing and able to think. As for the rest, who are the willing slaves of prejudice, they can no more attain truth than frogs can fly.

I reduce to two the systems of philosophers on the subject of man's soul. The first and older system is materialism; the second is spiritualism.

The metaphysicians who hinted that matter may well be endowed with the faculty of thought did not perhaps reason too badly. Why? Because they had the very real advantage in this case of not expressing their true meaning. For to ask whether matter can think, without considering it otherwise than in itself, is like asking whether matter can tell time. It may be foreseen that we shall avoid this reef on which Locke had the bad luck to founder.

The Leibnitzians with their monads set up an unintelligible hypothesis. They rather spiritualized matter than materialized the soul. How can we define a being whose nature is absolutely unknown to us?

Descartes and all the Cartesians, among whom the followers of Malebranche have long been numbered, made the same mistake. They recognized two distinct substances in man, as if they had seen them, and actually counted them. . . .

Experience and observation should here be our only guides. They are to be found throughout the records of physicians who were philosophers, and not in the works of philosophers who were not physicians. The former have traveled through and illuminated the labyrinth of man; they alone have exposed for us those vital elements hidden beneath the skin, which hides from us so many wonderful things. They alone, tranquilly contemplating our soul, have surprised it, a thousand times, both in its wretchedness and its glory, and have no more despised it in the first state, than admired it in the second. Once again we see that only physicians have the right to speak on this subject. What could the others, especially the theologians, have to tell us? Is it not ridiculous to hear them shamelessly dogmatize on a subject which lies completely out of their province and from which on the contrary they have been completely turned aside by obscure studies that have led them to a thousand prejudiced opinions, in a word, to fanaticism, which only increases their ignorance of the mechanism of the body?

But even though we have chosen the best guides, we shall still find many thorns and obstructions in our path.

Man is such a complicated machine that it is impossible to form a clear idea of it beforehand, and hence impossible to define it. For this reason, all the investigations which the greatest philosophers have conducted *a priori*, that is to say, by attempting in a way to use the wings of the spirit, have been fruitless. Thus it is only *a posteriori* or by seeking to discover the soul through the organs of the body, so to speak, that we can reach the highest probability concerning man's own nature, even though one can not discover with certainty what that nature is.

Let us lean then on the staff of experience and pay no attention to the history of all idle philosophical theories. To be blind and to think that we can do without this staff is the worst kind of blindness. How truly a modern writer has said that through vanity alone do we fail to draw from secondary causes the same conclusions as from primary causes! We even should admire all these fine geniuses in their most useless works, Descartes, Malebranche, Leibnitz, Wolff, and the rest, but what profit, I ask, has anyone gained from their profound meditations, and from all their works? Let us start afresh then and discover not what has been thought, but what must be thought for the sake of repose in life.

There are as many different minds, characters, and customs, as there are different temperaments. Even Galen knew this truth, which Descartes carried so far as to claim that medicine alone could change minds and morals, along with bodies. It is true that melancholy, bile, phlegm, blood, etc., and the nature, abundance and diverse combinations of these humors, make one man different from another.

In disease the soul is sometimes hidden, showing no sign of life; sometimes it is so inflamed by fury that it seems to be doubled; sometimes imbecility vanishes and convalescence turns a fool into a wit. Sometimes the greatest genius becomes imbecile and no longer recognizable. Farewell then to all that fine knowledge, acquired at so high a price, and with so much trouble! Here is a paralytic, who asks if his leg is in bed with him; there is a soldier, who thinks he still has the arm which has been cut off. The memory of his old sensations, and of the place to which they were referred by his soul, is the cause of his illusion and kind of delirium. The mere mention of the member which he has lost is enough to make him remember and feel all its motions; and this produces an indefinable and inexpressible kind of imaginary suffering.

This man cries like a child at death's approach, while this other jests. What was needed to change the bravery of Caius Julius, Seneca or Petronius into faintheartedness or cowardice? An obstruction in the spleen, in the liver, an impediment in the portal vein. Why? Because the imagination is obstructed along with the viscera, and this gives rise to all those strange phenomena of hysteria and hypochondria.

What could I add to what has been told of those who imagine themselves transformed into wolf-men, cocks or vampires, or those who think that the dead suck their blood? Why should I stop to speak of those who imagine that their noses or some other members are made of glass and who must be advised to sleep on straw to keep from breaking them, so that they may recover the use of their flesh-and-blood organs by setting the straw afire and scaring them—a fright that has sometimes cured paralysis? I must not tarry over facts that are common knowledge.

Nor shall I dwell at length on the effects of sleep. Take this tired soldier. He snores in a trench, to the sound of a hundred cannon. His soul hears nothing; his sleep is perfect apoplexy. A bomb is about to wipe him out. He will feel the shock less perhaps than an insect under his foot.

On the other hand, this man who is devoured by jealousy, hatred, avarice, or ambition, can never find any rest. The most peaceful spot, the coolest and most calming drinks, all have no effect on a man whose heart is a prey to the torment of passion.

The soul and the body fall asleep together. As the pulse gradually slows down, a sweet feeling of peace and quiet spreads throughout the whole machine. The soul feels itself gently sinking along with the eyelids and relaxing along with the fibers of the brain; thus little by little it becomes as if paralyzed along with all the muscles of the body. These can no longer sustain the weight of the head, and the soul can no longer bear the burden of thought; in sleep it is as if it did not exist.

Is the pulse too quick? the soul cannot sleep. Is the soul too agitated? the pulse cannot be quieted; the blood gallops through the veins with an audible murmur. Such are the two interacting causes of insomnia. A simple fright in our dreams makes the heart beat twice as fast and snatches us from needed or delightful repose, as a sharp pain or dire necessity would do. Lastly, just as the cessation of the functions of the soul induces sleep, the mind, even when we are awake (or in this case half awake), takes very frequent short naps, or day dreams, which show that the soul does not always wait for the body to sleep. For if the soul is not fast asleep, it surely is almost so, since it cannot point out a single object to which it has paid attention, among the countless confused ideas which, like so many clouds, so to speak, fill the atmosphere of our brains. . . .

The human body is a machine which winds itself up, the living image of perpetual motion. Food nourishes the movements which fever excites. Without food, the soul pines away, goes mad, and dies exhausted. It is a candle whose light flares up the moment before it goes out. But nourish the body, pour into its veins invigorating juices and strong liquors; then the soul, taking on their strength, arms itself with a proud courage, and the soldier whom water would have made flee, now made bold, runs joyously to death to the sound of drums. Thus a warming drink excites the blood which a cold drink would have calmed.

What power there is in a meal! Joy is born again in a sad heart; it infects the souls of table-companions, who burst into the friendly songs in which the French excel. The melancholy man alone is dejected, and the studious man is likewise out of place. . . .

In general, the form and structure of the brains of quadrupeds are almost the same as in man; the same shape, the same arrangement everywhere, but with this essential difference, that of all the animals man has the largest brain, and, in proportion to its mass, the brain with the most convolutions. Then comes the monkey, the beaver, the elephant, the dog, the fox, the cat, etc., animals which are the most like man; for among them, too, the same progressive analogy can be seen in relation to the *corpus callosum*, in which Lancisi established the seat of the soul—anticipating the late M. de la Peyronie, who illustrated the theory with a great many experiments.

After all the quadrupeds, birds have the most brains. Fish have large heads, but these are void of sense, like the heads of many men. Fish have no *corpus callosum*, and very little brain, while insects entirely lack brain. . . .

The imbecile may not lack brain, as commonly observed, but its consistency will be faulty, for instance, in being too soft. The same thing is true of the insane; the defects of their brains do not always escape our investigation; but if the causes of imbecility, insanity, etc., are not perceptible, how can we hope to discover the causes of the diversity of minds in general? They would escape the eyes of a lynx and an Argus. A mere nothing, a tiny fiber, something that the most delicate dissection cannot discover, would have made two idiots of Erasmus and Fontenelle, and Fontenelle himself makes this observation in one of his best dialogues. . . .

From animals to man, the transition is not violent, as good philosophers will admit. What was man before the invention of words and the knowledge of tongues? An animal of his species, who, with much less native instinct than the others, whose king he then considered himself to be, could not be distinguished from the ape and from the rest, except as the ape itself differs from the other animals; which means, by a face giving promise of more intelligence. Reduced to the bare "intuitive knowledge" of the Leibnitzians he saw only shapes and colors, without being able to distinguish between them; the same, old as young, child at all ages, he stammers out his feelings and needs, like a dog who asks for food when he is hungry or, tired of sleeping, wants to be let out.

Words, languages, laws, sciences, and the fine arts, have come, and by them our rough diamond of a mind has been polished. Man has been trained in the same way as animals; he has become an author, as they become beasts of burden. A geometrician has learned to perform the most difficult demonstrations and calculations, as a monkey has learned to take off or put on his little hat to mount his tame dog. All this has been done through signs, every species has learned what it could understand, and in this way men have acquired "symbolic knowledge," still so called by our German philosophers. . . .

All this knowledge, which blows up the balloon-like brains of our proud pedants, is therefore but a huge mass of words and figures, which form in the brain all the marks by which we distinguish and recall objects. All our ideas are awakened in the same way that a gardener who knows plants recalls, at the sight of them, all the stages of their growth. These words and the objects designated by them are so connected in the brain that it is comparatively rare to imagine a thing without the name or sign that is attached to it.

I always use the word "imagine," because I think that everything is imagined and that all the faculties of the soul can be correctly reduced to pure imagination, which gives form to them all. Thus judgment, reason and memory, are in no wise absolute parts of the soul, but real modifications of the kind of medullary screen upon which images of the objects painted in the eye are reflected as by a magic lantern.

But if such is the marvelous and incomprehensible result of the structure of the brain, if everything is perceived and explained by imagination, why should we divide the sensitive principle which thinks in man? Is not this clearly an inconsistency on the part of those who uphold the simplicity of the mind? For a thing that can be divided can no longer without absurdity be regarded as indivisible. This is where we come to through the abuse of language and those fine words "spirituality," "immateriality," etc., used haphazardly and not understood even by the most intelligent. . . .

We were not originally made to be learned; we have become so perhaps by a sort of abuse of our organic faculties, and at the expense of the State, which nourishes a host of loafers whom vanity has adorned with the name of "philosophers." Nature created us all solely to be happy—yes, all, from the crawling worm to the eagle that soars out of sight in the clouds. That is why she has given all animals some share of natural law, a share of greater or less delicacy according to the needs of each animal's organs when in good condition.

Now how shall we define natural law? It is a feeling which teaches us what we should not do, because we would not wish it to be done to us. Would I dare add to this common idea, that this feeling seems to me but a kind of fear or dread, as salutary to the race as to the individual? For perhaps we respect the purses and lives of others only to save our own possessions, our honor, and our own lives; like those "Ixions of Christianity" who love God and embrace so many fantastic virtues, merely because of their fear of hell.

You see that natural law is nothing but an intimate feeling which belongs also to the imagination like all other feelings, thought included. Consequently it evidently does not presuppose education, revelation or legislator, unless we confuse it with civil laws, in the ridiculous fashion of the theologians.

The arms of fanaticism may destroy those who maintain these truths, but they will never destroy the truths themselves.

Not that I call in question the existence of a supreme being; on the contrary it seems to me that the greatest degree of probability is in favor of this belief. But since the existence of this being does not prove that one form of worship is more necessary than any other, it is a theoretic truth with very little practical value. Therefore, since we may say, after such long experience, that religion does not imply exact honesty, we are authorized by the same reasons to think that atheism does not exclude it.

Furthermore, who knows whether the reason for man's existence is not simply the fact that he exists? Perhaps he was thrown by chance on some spot of the earth's surface, nobody knows how or why, but simply that he must live and die, like mushrooms that appear from one day to the next, or like the flowers which border ditches and cover walls. . . .

Let us conclude boldly then that man is a machine, and that in the whole universe there is but a single substance with various modifications. This is no hypothesis set up by dint of proposals and assumptions. It is not the work of prejudice, nor even of my reason alone; I would have disdained a guide which I believe so untrustworthy, had not my senses held the torch, so to speak, and induced me to follow reason by lighting the way. Experience has thus spoken to me in behalf of reason; and in this way I have combined the two.

But it must have been noticed that I have not allowed myself even the most forceful and immediately deduced reasoning, except as it followed a multitude of observations which no scholar will contest; and furthermore, I recognize only scientists as judges of the conclusions which I draw, and I hereby challenge every prejudiced man who is not an anatomist, or acquainted with the only philosophy which is to the purpose, that of the human body. Against such a strong and solid oak, what could the weak reeds of theology, metaphysics and scholasticism, avail; childish weapons, like our foils, which may well afford the pleasure of fencing, but can never wound an adversary. Need I say that I refer to the hollow and trivial notions, to the trite and pitiable arguments that will be urged, as long as the shadow of prejudice or superstition remains on earth, for the supposed incompatibility of two substances which meet and interact unceasingly? Such is my system, or rather the truth, unless I am very much mistaken. It is short and simple. Dispute it now who will.

OF IDEAS, THEIR GENERATION AND ASSOCIATIONS

DAVID HARTLEY

An English physician and theologian, Hartley (1705–1757) is associated with the doctrine of "associationism," which sought to explain how the ideas that Locke had suggested originate in sensory sensations become associated in a certain necessary order in the brain. This passage is from his 1749 book, Observations on Man.

I took notice in the Introduction, that those Ideas which resemble Sensations were called Ideas of Sensation; and also that they might be called *simple* Ideas, in respect of the intellectual ones which are formed from them, and of whose very Essence it is to be *complex*. But the Ideas of Sensation are not entirely simple, since they must consist of Parts both coexistent and successive, as the generating Sensations themselves do.

Now, that the simple Ideas of Sensation are thus generated, agreeably to the Proposition, appears, because the most vivid of these Ideas are those where the corresponding Sensations are most vigorously impressed, or most frequently renewed; whereas, if the Sensation be faint, or uncommon, the generated Idea is also faint in proportion, and, in extreme Cases, evanescent and imperceptible. The exact Observance of the Order of Place in visible Ideas, and of the Order of Time in audible ones, may likewise serve to show, that these Ideas are Copies and Offsprings of the Impressions made on the Eye and Ear, in which the same Orders were observed respectively. And though it happens, that Trains of visible and audible Ideas are presented in Sallies of the Fancy, and in Dreams, in which the Order of Time and Place is different from that of any former Impressions, yet the small component Parts of these Trains are Copies of former Impressions; and Reasons may be given for the Varieties of their Compositions.

It is also to be observed, that this Proposition bears a great Resemblance to the Third; and that, by this Resemblance, they somewhat confirm and illustrate one another. According to the Third Proposition, Sensations remain for a short time after the Impression is removed; and these remaining Sensations grow feebler and feebler, till they vanish. They are therefore, in some Part of their Declension, of about the same Strength with Ideas, and, in their first State, are intermediate between Sensations and Ideas. And it seems reasonable to expect, that, if a single Sensation can leave a perceptible Effect, Trace, or Vestige, for a short time, a sufficient Repetition of a Sensation may leave a perceptible Effect of the same kind, but of a more permanent Nature, *i.e.* an Idea, which shall recur occasionally, at long Distances of Time, from the Impression of the corresponding Sensation, & *vice versa.* As to the Occasions and Causes, which make Ideas recur, they will be considered in the next Proposition but one.

The Method of Reasoning used in the last Paragraph, is farther confirmed by the following Circumstance; *viz.* That both the diminutive declining Sensations, which remain for a short Space after the Impressions of the Objects cease, and the Ideas, which are the Copies of such Impressions, are far more distinct and vivid, in respect of visible and audible Impressions, than of any others. To which it may be added, that, after Traveling, hearing Music, & *c.* Trains of vivid Ideas are very apt to recur, which correspond very exactly to the late Impressions, and which are of an intermediate Nature between the remaining Sensations of the Third Proposition, in their greatest Vigor, and the Ideas mentioned in this.

The Sensations of Feeling, Taste, and Smell, can scarce be said to leave Ideas, unless very indistinct and obscure ones. However, as Analogy leads one to suppose, that these Sensations may leave Traces of the same kind, tho' not in the same degree, as those of Sight and Hearing; so the Readiness with which we reconnoiter Sensations of Feeling, Taste, and Smell, that have been often impressed, is an Evidence, that they do so; and these generated Traces or Dispositions of Mind may be called the Ideas of Feeling, Taste, and Smell. In Sleep, when all our Ideas are magnified, those of Feeling, Taste, and Smell, are often sufficiently vivid and distinct; and the same thing happens in some few Cases of Vigilance. . . .

This Correspondence of the diminutive Vibrations to the original sensory ones, consists in this, that they agree in Kind, Place, and Line of Direction; and differ only in being more feeble, *i.e.* in Degree.

This Proposition follows from the foregoing. For since Sensations, by being often repeated, beget Ideas, it cannot but be that those Vibrations, which accompany Sensations, should beget something which may accompany Ideas in like manner; and this can be nothing but feebler Vibrations, agreeing with the sensory generating Vibrations in Kind, Place, and Line of Direction.

Or thus: By the First Proposition it appears, that some Motion must be excited in the medullary Substance, during each Sensation; by the Fourth, this Motion is determined to be a vibratory one: Since therefore some Motion must also, by the Second, be excited in the medullary Substance during the Presence of each Idea, this Motion cannot be any other than a vibratory one: Else how should it proceed from the original Vibration attending the Sensation, in the same manner as the Idea does from the Sensation itself? It must also agree in Kind, Place, and Line of Direction, with the generating Vibration. A vibratory Motion, which recurs *t* times in a Second, cannot beget a diminutive one that recurs ½ *t,* or 2 *t* times; nor one originally impressed on the Region of the Brain corresponding to the auditory Nerves, beget diminutive Vibrations in the Region corresponding to the optic Nerves; and so of the rest. The Line of Direction must likewise be the same in the original and derivative Vibrations. It remains therefore, that each simple Idea of Sensation be attended by diminutive Vibrations of the same Kind, Place, and Line of Direction, with the original Vibrations attending the Sensation itself: Or, in the Words of the Proposition, that sensory Vibrations, by being frequently repeated, beget a Disposition to diminutive Vibrations corresponding to themselves respectively. We may add, that the vibratory Nature of the Motion which attends Ideas, may be inferred from the Continuance of some Ideas, visible ones for instance, in the Fancy for a few Moments.

This Proof of the present Proposition from the foregoing, appears to be incontestable, admitting the Fourth: However, it will much establish and illustrate the Doctrines of Vibrations and Association, to deduce it directly, if we can, from the Nature of vibratory Motions, and of an animal Body; and not only from the Relation between Sensations and Ideas. Let us see, therefore, what Progress we can make in such an Attempt.

First then, If we admit Vibrations of the medullary Particles at all, we must conceive, that some take place in the *Fœtus in Utero,* both on account of the Warmth in which it lies, and of the Pulsation of those considerable Arteries, which pass through the medullary Substance, and which consequently must compress and agitate it upon every Contraction of the Heart. And these Vibrations are probably either uniform in Kind and Degree, if we consider short Spaces of Time; or, if long ones, increase in a flow uniform manner, and that in Degree only, as the *Fœtus in Utero* increases in Bulk and Strength. They are also probably the same in all the different Regions of the medullary Substance. Let these Vibrations be called the *Natural Vibrations.*

Secondly, As soon as the Child is born, external Objects act upon it violently, and excite Vibrations in the medullary Substance, which differ from the natural ones, and from each other, in Degree, Kind, Place, and Line of Direction. We may also conceive, that each Region of the medullary Substance has such a Texture as to receive, with the greatest Facility, the several specific Vibrations, which the Objects corresponding respectively to these Regions, *i.e.*, to their Nerves, are most disposed to excite. Let these Vibrations be, for the present, called *preternatural* ones, in Contradistinction to those which we just now called *natural ones.*

Thirdly, Representing now the natural Vibrations by *N,* and the preternatural ones, from various Objects, by *A, B, C,* etc. let us suppose the first Object to impress the Vibrations *A,* and then to be removed. It is evident from the Nature of vibratory Motions, that the medullary Substance will not, immediately upon the Removal of this Object, return to its natural State *N,* but will remain, for a short Space of Time, in the preternatural State *A,* and pass gradually from *A* to *N.* Suppose the same Object to be impressed again and again, for a sufficient Number of Times, and it seems to follow, that the medullary Substance will be longer in passing from *A* to *N,* after the second Impression, than after the first, after the third Impression than second, & *c.* till, at last, it will not return to its natural original State of Vibrations *N* at all, but remain in the preternatural State *A,* after the Vibrations have fallen to a diminutive Pitch, their Kind and Place, or chief Seat, and their Line of Direction, continuing the same. This State may therefore be fitly denoted by *a,* and, being now in the Place of the natural State *N,* it will be kept up by the Heat of the medullary Substance, and the Pulsation of its Arteries. All this seems to follow from the above-mentioned Disposition of animal Bodies to accommodate themselves to, and continue in, almost any State that is often impressed; which is evident from innumerable both common and medical Observations, whatever be determined concerning the Manner of explaining and accounting for these Facts. For the Alterations which Habit, Custom, frequent Impression, & *c.* make in the small constituent Particles, can scarce be any thing besides Alterations of the Distances, and mutual Actions, of these Particles; and these last Alterations must alter the natural Tendency to vibrate. We must, however, here resume the Supposition made in the last Paragraph, *viz.* that the several Regions of the Brain have such a Texture as disposes them to those specific Vibrations, which are to be impressed by the proper Objects in the Events of Life. And this will much facilitate and accelerate the Transition of the State *N* into *a;* since we are to suppose a Predisposition to the State *A*, or *a*.

THE PHILOSOPHY OF COMMON SENSE

Thomas Reid

In the English-speaking world, the Scottish philosopher Thomas Reid (1710–1796) was the principal critic of Lockean sensationalist and Humean skeptical theories of the mind. He is the father of what has come to be called the "Scottish" or "Common Sense" school. This selection is taken from his Inquiry into the Human Mind *(1764) and* Essay on the Intellectual Powers of Man *(1785).*

Dedication, to the Right Honorable James, Earl of Findlater and Seafield. . . .

I acknowledge, my Lord, that I never thought of calling in question the principles commonly received with regard to the human understanding, until the "Treatise of Human Nature" was published in the year 1739. The ingenious author of that treatise upon the principles of Locke—who was no skeptic—hath built a system of skepticism, which leaves no ground to believe any one thing rather than its contrary. His reasoning appeared to me to be just; there was, therefore, a necessity to call in question the principles upon which it was founded, or to admit the conclusion.

But can any ingenuous mind admit this skeptical system without reluctance? I truly could not, my Lord; for I am persuaded that absolute skepticism is not more destructive of the faith of a Christian than of the science of a philosopher, and of the prudence of a man of common understanding. I am persuaded, that the unjust *live by faith* as well as the *just;* that, if all belief could be laid aside, piety, patriotism, friendship, parental affection, and private virtue, would appear as ridiculous as knight-errantry; and that the pursuits of pleasure, of ambition, and of avarice, must be grounded upon belief, as well as those that are honorable or virtuous.

The day-laborer toils at his work, in the belief that he shall receive his wages at night; and, if he had not this belief, he would not toil. We may venture to say, that even the author of this skeptical system wrote it in the belief that it should be read and regarded. I hope he wrote it in the belief also that it would be useful to mankind; and, perhaps, it may prove so at last. For I conceive the skeptical writers to be a set of men whose business it is to pick holes in the fabric of knowledge wherever it is weak and faulty; and, when these places are properly repaired, the whole building becomes more firm and solid than it was formerly.

For my own satisfaction, I entered into a serious examination of the principles upon which this skeptical system is built; and was not a little surprised to find, that it leans with its whole weight upon a hypothesis, which is ancient indeed, and hath been very generally received by philosophers, but of which I could find no solid proof. The hypothesis I mean, is, That nothing is perceived but what is in the mind which perceives it: That we do not really perceive things that are external, but only certain images and pictures of them impressed upon the mind, which are called *impressions and ideas*.

If this be true, supposing certain impressions and ideas to exist in my mind, I cannot, from their existence, infer the existence of anything else: my impressions and ideas are the only existences of which I can have any knowledge or conception; and they are such fleeting and transitory beings, that they can have no existence at all, any longer than I am conscious of them. So that, upon this hypothesis, the whole universe about me, bodies and spirits, sun, moon, stars, and earth, friends and relations, all things without exception, which I imagined to have a permanent existence, whether I thought of them or not, vanish at once;

> *And, like the baseless fabric of a vision,*
> *Leave not a rack behind.*

I thought it unreasonable, my Lord, upon the authority of philosophers to admit a hypothesis which, in my opinion, overturns all philosophy, all religion and virtue, and all common sense—and, finding that all the systems concerning the human understanding which I was acquainted with, were built upon this hypothesis, I resolved to inquire into this subject anew, without regard to any hypothesis. . . .

Upon the whole, it appears that our philosophers have imposed upon themselves and upon us, in pretending to deduce from sensation the first origin of our notions of external existences, of space, motion, and extension, and all the primary qualities of body—that is, the qualities whereof we have the most clear and distinct conception. These qualities do not at all tally with any system of the human faculties that hath been advanced. They have no resemblance to any sensation, or to any operation of our minds; and, therefore, they cannot be ideas either of sensation or of reflection. The very conception of them is irreconcilable to the principles of our philosophic systems of the understanding. The belief of them is no less so. . . .

It is beyond our power to say when, or in what order, we came by our notions of these qualities. When we trace the operations of our minds as far back as memory and reflection can carry us, we find them already in possession of our imagination and belief, and quite familiar to the mind: but how they came first into its acquaintance, or what has given them so strong a hold of our belief, and what regard they deserve, are, no doubt, very important questions in the philosophy of human nature. . . .

The wisdom of *philosophy* is set in opposition to the *common sense* of mankind. The first pretends to demonstrate, *a priori,* that there can be no such thing as a material world; that sun, moon, stars, and earth, vegetable and animal bodies, are, and can be nothing else, but sensations in the mind, or images of those sensations in the memory and imagination; that, like pain and joy, they can have no existence when they are not thought of. The last can conceive no otherwise of this opinion, than of a kind of metaphysical lunacy, and concludes that too much learning is apt to make men mad; and that the man who seriously entertains this belief, though in other respects he may be a very good man, as a man may be who believes that he is made of glass; yet, surely he hath a soft place in his understanding, and hath been hurt by much thinking. . . .

If this is wisdom, let me be deluded with the vulgar. I find something within me that recoils against it, and inspires more reverent sentiments of the human kind, and of the universal administration. Common Sense and Reason have both one author; that Almighty Author in all whose other works we observe a consistency, uniformity, and beauty which charm and delight the understanding: there must, therefore, be some order and consistency in the human faculties, as well as in other parts of his workmanship. A man that thinks reverently of his own kind, and esteems true wisdom and philosophy, will not be fond, nay, will be very suspicious, of such strange and paradoxical opinions. If they are false, they disgrace philosophy; and, if they are true, they degrade the human species, and make us justly ashamed of our frame.

To what purpose is it for philosophy to decide against common sense in this or any other matter? The belief of a material world is older, and of more authority, than any principles of philosophy. It declines the tribunal of reason, and laughs at all the artillery of the logician. It retains its sovereign authority in spite of all the edicts of philosophy, and reason itself must stoop to its orders. Even those philosophers who have disowned the authority of our notions of an external material world, confess that they find themselves under a necessity of submitting to their power. . . .

In order, therefore, to reconcile Reason to Common Sense in this matter, I beg leave to offer to the consideration of philosophers these two observations. First, that, in all this debate about the existence of a material world, it hath been taken for granted on both sides, that this same material world, if any such there be, must be the express image of our sensations; that we can have no conception of any material thing which is not like some sensation in our minds; and particularly that the sensations of touch are images of extension, hardness, figure, and motion. Every argument brought against the existence of a material world, either by the Bishop of Cloyne, or by the author of the "Treatise of Human Nature," supposeth this. If this is true, their arguments are conclusive and unanswerable; but, on the other hand, if it is not true, there is no shadow of argument left. Have those philosophers, then, given any solid proof of this hypothesis, upon which the whole weight of so strange a system rests? No. They have not so much as attempted to do it. But, because ancient and modern philosophers have agreed in this opinion, they have taken it for granted. But let us, as becomes philosophers, lay aside authority; we need not, surely, consult Aristotle or Locke, to know whether pain be like the point of a sword. I have as clear a conception of extension, hardness, and motion as I have of the point of a sword; and with some pains and practice, I can form as clear a notion of the other sensations of touch as I have of pain. When I do so, and compare them together, it appears to me clear as daylight, that the former are not of kin to the latter, nor resemble them in any one feature. They are as unlike, yea as certainly and manifestly unlike, as pain is to the point of a sword. It may be true, that those sensations first introduced the material world to our acquaintance; it may be true, that it seldom or never appears without their company; but, for all that, they are as unlike as the passion of anger is to those features of the countenance which attend it.

So that, in the sentence those philosophers have passed against the material world, there is an *error personae*. Their proof touches not matter, or any of its qualities; but strikes directly against an idol of their own imagination, a material world made of ideas and sensations, which never had, nor can have, an existence.

Secondly, The very existence of our conceptions of extension, figure and motion, since they are neither ideas of sensation nor reflection, overturns the whole ideal system by which the material world hath been tried and condemned; so that there hath been likewise in this sentence an *error juris*.

It is a very fine and a just observation of Locke, that as no human art can create a single particle of matter, and the whole extent of our power over the material world consists in compounding, combining, and disjoining the matter made to our hands; so, in the world of thought, the materials are all made by nature, and can only be variously combined and disjoined by us. So that it is impossible for reason or prejudice, true or false philosophy, to produce one simple notion or conception, which is not the work of nature, and the result of our constitution. The conception of extension, motion, and the other attributes of matter, cannot be the effect of error or prejudice; it must be the work of nature. And the power of faculty by which we acquire those conceptions, must be something different from any power of the human mind that hath been explained, since it is neither sensation or reflection.

• • •

When we see the sun or moon, we have no doubt that the very objects which we immediately see are very far distant from us, and from one another. We have not the least doubt that this is the sun and moon which God created some thousands of years ago, and which have continued to perform their revolutions in the heavens ever since. But how are we astonished when the philosopher informs us that we are mistaken in all this; that the sun and moon which we see are not, as we imagine, many miles distant from us, and from each other, but that they are in our own mind; that they had no existence before we saw them, and will have none when we cease to perceive and to think of them; because the objects we perceive are only ideas in our own minds, which can have no existence a moment longer than we think of them!

If a plain man, uninstructed in philosophy, has faith to receive these mysteries, how great must be his astonishment! He is brought into a new world, where everything he sees, tastes, or touches, is an idea—a fleeting kind of being which he can conjure into existence, or can annihilate in the twinkling of an eye.

After his mind is somewhat composed, it will be natural for him to ask his philosophical instructor: Pray, Sir, are there then no substantial and permanent beings called the sun and moon, which continue to exist whether we think of them or not? . . .

Almost all our perceptions have corresponding sensations which constantly accompany them, and, on that account, are very apt to be confounded with them. Neither ought we to expect that the sensation, and its corresponding perception, should be distinguished in common language, because the purposes of common life do not require it. Language is made to serve the purposes of ordinary conversation, and we have no reason to expect that it should make distinctions that are not of common use. Hence it happens that a quality perceived, and the sensation corresponding to that perception, often go under the same name.

This makes the names of most of our sensations ambiguous, and this ambiguity hath very much perplexed philosophers. It will be necessary to give some instances to illustrate the distinction between our sensations and the objects of perception.

When I smell a rose, there is in this operation both sensation and perception. The agreeable odor I feel, considered by itself without relation to any external object, is merely a sensation. It affects the mind in a certain way; and this affection of the mind may be conceived without a thought of the rose, or any other object. This sensation can be nothing else than it is felt to be. Its very essence consists in being felt, and, when it is not felt, it is not. There is no difference between the sensation and the feeling of it—they are one and the same thing. It is for this reason that we before observed that, in sensation, there is no object distinct from that act of the mind by which it is felt—and this holds true with regard to all sensations.

Let us next attend to the perception which we have in smelling a rose. Perception has always an external object; and the object of my perception, in this case, is that quality in the rose which I discern by the sense of smell. Observing that the agreeable sensation is raised when the rose is near, and ceases when it is removed, I am led, by my nature, to conclude some quality to be in the rose which is the cause of this sensation. This quality in the rose is the object perceived; and that act of my mind by which I have the conviction and belief of this quality is what in this case I call perception.

But it is here to be observed that the sensation I feel, and the quality in the rose which I perceive, are both called by the same name. The smell of a rose is the name given to both: so that this name hath two meanings; and the distinguishing its different meanings removes all perplexity and enables us to give clear and distinct answers to questions about which philosophers have held much dispute.

Thus, if it is asked whether the smell be in the rose, or in the mind that feels it, the answer is obvious: That there are two different things signified by the smell of a rose; one of which is in the mind, and can be in nothing but in a sentient being; the other is truly and properly in the rose. The sensation which I feel is in my mind. The mind is the sentient being; and, as the rose is insentient, there can be no sensation, nor anything resembling sensation, in it. But this sensation in my mind is occasioned by a certain quality in the rose, which is called by the same name with the sensation, not on account of any similitude, but because of their constant concomitancy.

All the names we have for smells, tastes, sounds, and for the various degrees of heat and cold, have a like ambiguity; and what has been said of the smell of a rose may be applied to them. They signify both a sensation and a quality perceived by means of that sensation. The first is the sign, the last the thing signified. As both are conjoined by nature, and as the purposes of common life do not require them to be disjoined in our thoughts, they are both expressed by the same name: and this ambiguity is to be found in all languages, because the reason of it extends to all.

TREATISE ON THE SENSATIONS

Ettienne Bonnot de Condillac

One of Locke's principal disciples was Condillac (1714–1780), a free-thinking French abbe, who popularized Locke's conviction that all processes of the mind could be broken down into original units of sensation. This extract is the conclusion of his 1784 book, Treatise on Sensations, *in which Condillac depicts a lifeless statue gradually acquiring the human "senses" of smell, taste, et cetera, one by one.*

It is impossible for me to apply all the suppositions I have made; but those I have instanced prove at least that all our cognitions come from the senses, and particularly from touch, because touch is the sense which instructs all the others. If in allowing my statue sensations alone it has acquired from them particular and general ideas, and has rendered itself capable of all the operations of the understanding; if it has formed desires and passions which it obeys or resists; finally, if pleasure and pain are the unique principle of the development of its faculties, it is reasonable to conclude that we too at first had only sensations, and that our cognitions and our passions are the effect of the pleasures and the pains which accompany the impressions of the senses.

In fact the more I reflect on it, the more convinced I am that this is the sole source of our enlightenment and of our feelings. Consider enlightenment, as soon as we receive it we enjoy a new life, quite different from that which our brute sensations procured for us, if I may so express it. Consider feeling, observe it especially when it is increased by all the judgments we confuse with sense impressions, these sensations, then, which at first only gave us few and coarse pleasures, cause in us the most delicate pleasures, and these follow one another with astonishing variety. So the farther we get from the original sensations the more our life expands and is varied. It will extend to so many things, that we shall with difficulty understand how all our faculties can have one common principle in sensation.

When we have regard only to sensations devoid of judgments the life of one man is hardly different from that of another. The difference will be only in the degree of the liveliness of their feeling. Experience and reflexion will be for them what the chisel is in the hands of the sculptor who discovers a perfect statue in the formless stone, for according to the way in which experience and reflexion are used new enlightenment and new pleasures will emerge from sensations. In some cases the material will remain rough and unpolished, in others it will become the finished work. Considering the difference between one man and another, we are surprised to see how with the same duration some men enjoy more life than others. For to live is to enjoy, and life is much longer for him who knows how to multiply the objects of his enjoyment.

We have seen that enjoyment may begin with the first pleasurable sensation. For example, the first time we endowed our statue with sight, it had enjoyment in the fact that its eyes were no longer sealed in darkness. We must not, however, judge its pleasures by our own. Many sensations may be indifferent or even disagreeable to us if we are tired of them or desire livelier ones. Quite different is the statue's situation. It may be enraptured with feelings which we do not deign to notice, or notice only with disgust.

Consider the sensation of light when touch first teaches the eyes to spread colors over the whole of nature. There are as many new feelings, and consequently as many new pleasures, as there are new enjoyments. We must reason in the same way with regard to all the other senses, and all the operations of the soul. For we not only enjoy by means of sight, hearing, taste, smell, touch, but also by means of memory, imagination, reflexion, passions, and hope; in a word by all our faculties. But these sources of our enjoyment are not equally active in all men.

We compare pleasures and pains, that is to say, needs which call forth our faculties. Consequently it is to pleasures and pains that we owe the happiness we enjoy. As many as are our needs so many are our different enjoyments, and as many as are the degrees in our needs, so many are the degrees in our enjoyment. In this lies the germ of all we are, the source of our happiness and of our unhappiness. In the observation of this principle we have therefore our sole means of studying ourselves.

The history of our statue's faculties make the progress of all these things clear. When it was limited to fundamental feeling, one uniform sensation comprised its whole existence, its whole knowledge, its whole pleasure. In giving it successively new modes of being, and new senses, we saw it form desires, learn from experience to regulate and satisfy them, and pass from needs to needs, from cognitions to cognitions, from pleasures to pleasures. The statue is therefore nothing but the sum of all it has acquired. May not this be the same with man?

EDUCATION AND CHILDHOOD

SOME THOUGHTS CONCERNING EDUCATION

JOHN LOCKE

While less well known today, Locke's essay on education, published in 1693, was widely read and deeply influential in the eighteenth century. Nowhere was this more the case than in Protestant America, where it became a principal guide on "how to breed" children.

I myself have been consulted of late by so many who profess themselves at a loss how to breed their children, and the early corruption of youth is now become so general a complaint that he cannot be thought wholly impertinent who brings the consideration of this matter on the stage, and offers something, if it be but to excite others, or afford matter of correction: for errors in education should be less indulged than any.

These, like faults in the first concoction, that are never mended in the second or third, carry their afterwards incorrigible taint with them through all the parts and stations of life. . . .

I have spoken so much of carrying a strict hand over children, that perhaps I shall be suspected of not considering enough what is due to their tender age and constitutions. But that opinion will vanish, when you have heard me a little farther. For I am very apt to think, that great severity of punishment does but very little good; nay, great harm in education: and I believe it will be found, that, cæteris paribus, those children who have been most chastised, seldom make the best men. All that I have hitherto contended for, is, that whatsoever rigor is necessary, it is more to be used, the younger children are; and, having by a due application wrought its effect, it is to be relaxed, and changed into a milder sort of government.

A compliance, and suppleness of their wills, being by a steady hand introduced by parents, before children have memories to retain the beginnings of it, will seem natural to them, and work afterwards in them, as if it were so; preventing all occasions of struggling, or repining. The only care is, that it be begun early, and inflexibly kept to, till awe and respect be grown familiar, and there appears not the least reluctancy in the submission and ready obedience of their minds. When this reverence is once thus established, (which it must be early, or else it will cost pains and blows to recover it, and the more, the longer it is deferred) it is by it, mixed still with as much indulgence as they made not an ill use of, and not by beating, chiding, or other servile punishments, they are for the future to be governed, as they grow up to more understanding.

That this is so, will be easily allowed, when it is but considered what is to be aimed at, in an ingenuous education; and upon what it turns.

1. He that has not a mastery over his inclinations, he that knows not how to resist the importunity of present pleasure or pain, for the sake of what reason tells him is fit to be done, wants the true principle of virtue and industry; and is in danger of never being good for any thing. This temper, therefore, so contrary to unguided nature, is to be got betimes; and this habit, as the true foundation of future ability and happiness, is to be wrought into the mind, as early as may be, even from the first dawnings of my knowledge or apprehension in children; and so to be confirmed in them, by all the care and ways imaginable, by those who have the oversight of their education.

2. On the other side, if the mind be curbed, and humbled too much in children; if their spirits be abased and broken much, by too strict an hand over them; they lose all their vigor and industry, and are in a worse state than the former. For extravagant young fellows, that have liveliness and spirit, come sometimes to be set right, and so make able and great men: but dejected minds, timorous and tame, and low spirits, are hardly ever to be raised, and very seldom attain to any thing. To avoid the danger that is on either hand is the great art: and he that has found a way how to keep up a child's spirit, easy, active, and free; and yet, at the same time, to restrain him from many things he has a mind to, and to draw him to things that are uneasy to him; he, I say, that knows how to reconcile these seeming contradictions, has, in my opinion, got the true secret of education.

The usual lazy and short way by chastisement, and the rod, which is the only instrument of government that tutors generally know, or ever think of, is the most unfit of any to be used in education; because it tends to both those mischiefs; which, as we have shown, are the Scylla and Charybdis, which, on the one hand or the other, ruin all that miscarry.

1. This kind of punishment contributes not at all to the mastery of our natural propensity to indulge corporal and present pleasure, and to avoid pain at any rate; but rather encourages it; and thereby strengthens that in us, which is the root, from whence spring all vicious actions and the irregularities of life. From what other motive, but of sensual pleasure, and pain, does a child act, who drudges at his book against his inclination, or abstains from eating unwholesome fruit, that he takes pleasure in, only out of fear of whipping? He in this only prefers the greater corporal pleasure, or avoids the greater corporal pain. And what is it to govern his actions, and direct his conduct, by such motives as these? what is it, I say, but to cherish that principle in him, which it is our business to root out and destroy? And therefore I cannot think any correction useful to a child, where the shame of suffering for having done amiss does not work more upon him than the pain.

2. This sort of correction naturally breeds an aversion to that which it is the tutor's business to create a liking to. How obvious is it to observe, that children come to hate things which were at first acceptable to them, when they find themselves whipped, and chid, and teased about them? And it is not to be wondered at in them; when grown men would not be able to be reconciled to any thing by such ways. Who is there

that would not be disgusted with any innocent recreation, in itself indifferent to him, if he should with blows, or ill language, be hauled to it, when he had no mind? or be constantly so treated, for some circumstances in his application to it? This is natural to be so. Offensive circumstances ordinarily infect innocent things, which they are joined with: and the very sight of a cup, wherein any one uses to take nauseous physic, turns his stomach; so that nothing will relish well out of it, though the cup be ever so clean, and well-shaped, and of the richest materials.

3. Such a sort of slavish discipline makes a slavish temper. The child submits, and dissembles obedience, whilst the fear of the rod hangs over him; but when that is removed, and, by being out of sight, he can promise himself impunity, he gives the greater scope to his natural inclination; which by this way is not at all altered, but on the contrary heightened and increased in him, and after such restraint, breaks out usually with the more violence. Or,

4. If severity carried to the highest pitch does prevail, and works a cure upon the present unruly distemper, it is often bringing in the room of it worse and more dangerous disease, by breaking the mind; and then, in the place of a disorderly young fellow, you have a low-spirited moped creature: who, however with his unnatural sobriety he may please silly people, who commend tame inactive children, because they make no noise, nor give them any trouble; yet, at last, will probably prove as uncomfortable a thing to his friends, as he will be, all his life, an useless thing to himself and others.

Beating then, and all other sorts of slavish and corporal punishments, are not the discipline fit to be used in the education of those who would have wise, good, and ingenuous men; and therefore very rarely to be applied, and that only on great occasions, and cases of extremity. On the other side, to flatter children by rewards of things that are pleasant to them, is as carefully to be avoided. He that will give to his son apples, or sugar-plums, or what else of this kind he is most delighted with, to make him learn his book, does but authorize his love of pleasure, and cocker up that dangerous propensity, which he ought by all means to subdue and stifle in him. You can never hope to teach him to master it, whilst you compound for the check you give his inclination in one place, by the satisfaction you propose to it in another. To make a good, a wise, and a virtuous man, it is fit he should learn to cross his appetite, and deny his inclination to riches, finery, or pleasing his palate, &c.

whenever his reason advises the contrary, and his duty requires it. But when you draw him to do any thing that is fit, by the offer of money; or reward the pains of learning his book, by the pleasure of a luscious morsel; when you promise him a lace-cravat, or a fine new suit, upon performance of some of his little tasks; what do you, by proposing these as rewards, but allow them to be the good things he should aim at, and thereby encourage his longing for them, and accustom him to place his happiness in them? Thus people, to prevail with children to be industrious about their grammar, dancing, or some other such matter, of no great moment to the happiness or usefulness of their lives, by misapplied rewards and punishments, sacrifice their virtue, invert the order of their education, and teach them luxury, pride, or covetousness, &c. For in this way, flattering those wrong inclinations, which they should restrain and suppress, they lay the foundations of those future vices, which cannot be avoided, but by curbing our desires, and accustoming them early to submit to reason. . . .

But if you take away the rod on one hand, and these little encouragements, which they are taken with, on the other; how then (will you say) shall children be governed? Remove hope and fear, and there is an end of all discipline. I grant, that good and evil, reward and punishment, are the only motives to a rational creature; these are the spur and reins, whereby all mankind are set on work and guided, and therefore they are to be made use of to children too. For I advise their parents and governors always to carry this in their minds, that children are to be treated as rational creatures.

The rewards and punishments then whereby we should keep children in order are quite of another kind; and of that force, that when we can get them once to work, the business, I think, is done, and the difficulty is over. Esteem and disgrace are, of all others, the most powerful incentives to the mind, when once it is brought to relish them. If you can once get into children a love of credit, and an apprehension of shame and disgrace, you have put into them the true principle, which will constantly work, and incline them to the right. . . .

When he can write well, and quick, I think it may be convenient, not only to continue the exercise of his hand in writing, but also to improve the use of it farther in drawing, a thing very useful to a gentleman on several occasions, but especially if he travel, as that which helps a man often to express, in a few lines well put together, what a whole sheet of paper in writing would not be able to represent and make intelligible. How many buildings may a man see, how many machines and habits meet with, the ideas whereof would be easily retained and communicated by a little skill in drawing; which, being committed to words, are in danger to be lost, or at best but ill retained in the most exact descriptions? I do not mean that I would have your son a perfect painter; to be that to any tolerable degree, will require more time than a young gentleman can spare from his other improvements of greater moment; but so much insight into perspective, and skill in drawing, as will enable him to represent tolerably on paper any thing he sees, except faces, may, I think, be got in a little time, especially if he have a genius to it: but where that is wanting, unless it be in the things absolutely necessary, it is better to let him pass them by quietly, than to vex him about them to no purpose: and therefore in this, as in all other things not absolutely necessary, the rule holds, "Nihil invita Minerva."

As soon as he can speak English, it is time for him to learn some other language: this nobody doubts of, when French is proposed. And the reason is, because people are accustomed to the right way of teaching that language, which is by talking it into children in constant conversation, and not by grammatical rules. The Latin tongue would easily be taught the same way, if his tutor, being constantly with him, would talk nothing else to him, and make him answer still in the same language. But because French is a living language, and to be used more in speaking, that should be first learned, that the yet pliant organs of speech might be accustomed to a due formation of those sounds, and he get the habit of pronouncing French well, which is the harder to be done the longer it is delayed.

When he can speak and read French well, which in this method is usually in a year or two, he should proceed to Latin, which it is a wonder parents, when they have had the experiment in French, should not think ought to be learned the same way, by talking and reading. Only care is to be taken, whilst he is learning these foreign languages, by speaking and reading nothing else with his tutor, that he do not forget to read English, which may be preserved by his mother, or somebody else, hearing him read some chosen parts of the scripture or other English book, every day.

Latin I look upon as absolutely necessary to a gentleman; and indeed custom, which prevails over every thing, has made it so much a part of education, that even those children are whipped to it, and made spend many hours of their precious time uneasily in Latin, who, after they are once gone from school, are never to have more to do with it, as long as they live. Can there be any thing more ridiculous, than that a father should waste his own money, and his son's time, in setting him to learn the Roman language, when, at the same time, he designs him for a trade, wherein he, having no use of Latin, fails not to forget that little which he brought from school, and which it is ten to one he abhors for the ill usage it procured him? Could it be believed, unless we had every where amongst us examples of it, that a child should be forced to learn the rudiments of a language, which he is never to use in the course of life that he is designed to, and neglect all the while the writing a good hand, and casting accounts, which are of great advantage in all conditions of life, and to most trades indispensably necessary? But though these qualifications, requisite to trade and commerce, and the business of the world, are seldom or never to be had at grammar-schools; yet thither not only gentlemen send their younger sons intended for trades, but even tradesmen and farmers fail not to send their children, though they have neither intention nor ability to make them scholars. If you ask them, why they do this? they think it as strange a question, as if you should ask them why they go to church? Custom serves for reason, and has, to those that take it for reason, so consecrated this method, that it is almost religiously observed by them; and they stick to it, as if their children had scarce an orthodox education, unless they learned Lilly's grammar.

But how necessary soever Latin be to some, and is thought to be to others, to whom it is of no manner of use or service, yet the ordinary way of learning it in a grammar-school, is that, which having had thoughts about, I cannot be forward to encourage. The reasons against it are so evident and cogent, that they have prevailed with some intelligent persons to quit the ordinary road, not without success, though the method made use of was not exactly that which I imagine the easiest, and in short is this: to trouble the child with no grammar at all, but to have Latin, as English has been, without the perplexity of rules, talked into him; for, if you will consider it, Latin is no more unknown to a child, when he comes into the world, than English: and yet he learns English without master, rule, or grammar: and so might he Latin too, as Tully did, if he had somebody always to talk to him in this language. And when we so often see a Frenchwoman teach an English girl to speak and read French perfectly, in a year or two, without any rule of grammar, or any thing else, but prattling to her; I cannot but wonder, how gentlemen have overseen this way for their sons, and thought them more dull or incapable than their daughters.

CHILDREN AND CIVIC EDUCATION

JEAN-JACQUES ROUSSEAU

Probably the most important text the Enlightenment produced on the education of children, Rousseau's Emile *(1762) is a landmark in the discovery of childhood as a special stage of life with its "own methods of seeing, thinking, and feeling." Rousseau was also one of the earliest advocates of state-sponsored public education. In the second selection, from his* Discourse on Political Economy *(1758), he insists that only when education is a civic responsibility will citizens be turned from love of self to public spirit.*

Reasoning should not begin too soon—Locke's great maxim was that we ought to reason with children, and just now this maxim is much in fashion. I think, however, that its success does not warrant its reputation, and I find nothing more stupid than children who have been so much reasoned with. Reason, apparently a compound of all other faculties, the one latest developed, and with most difficulty, is the one proposed as agent in unfolding the faculties earliest used! The noblest work of education is to make a reasoning man, and we expect to train a young child by making him reason! This is beginning at the end; this is making an instrument of a result. If children understood how to reason they would not need to be educated. But by addressing them from their tenderest years in a language they cannot understand, you accustom them to be satisfied with words, to find fault with whatever is said to them, to think themselves as wise as their teachers, to wrangle and rebel. And what we mean they shall do from reasonable motives we are forced to obtain from them by adding the motive of avarice, or of fear, or of vanity.

Nature intends that children shall be children before they are men. If we insist on reversing this order we shall have fruit early indeed, but unripe and tasteless, and liable to early decay; we shall have young savants and old children. Childhood has its own methods of seeing, thinking, and feeling. Nothing shows less sense than to try to substitute our own methods for these. I would rather require a child ten years old to be five feet tall than to be judicious. Indeed, what use would he have at that age for the power to reason? It is a check upon physical strength, and the child needs none.

In attempting to persuade your pupils to obedience you add to this alleged persuasion force and threats, or worse still, flattery and promises. Bought over in this way by interest, or constrained by force, they pretend to be convinced by reason. They see plainly that as soon as you discover obedience or disobedience in their conduct, the former is an advantage and the latter a disadvantage to them. But you ask of them only what is distasteful to them; it is always irksome to carry out the wishes of another, so by stealth they carry out their own. They are sure that if their disobedience is not known they are doing well; but they are ready, for fear of greater evils, to acknowledge, if found out, that they are doing wrong. As the reason for the duty required is beyond their capacity, no one can make them really understand it. But the fear of punishment, the hope of forgiveness, your importunity, their difficulty in answering you, extort from them the confession required of them. You think you have convinced them, when you have only wearied them out or intimidated them.

What results from this? First of all that, by imposing upon them a duty they do not feel as such, you set them against your tyranny, and dissuade them from loving you; you teach them to be dissemblers, deceitful, willfully untrue, for the sake of extorting rewards or of escaping punishments. Finally, by habituating them to cover a secret motive by an apparent motive, you give them the means of constantly misleading you, of concealing their true character from you, and of satisfying yourself and others with empty words when their occasion demands. You may say that the law, although binding on the conscience, uses constraint in dealing with grown men. I grant it; but what are these men but children spoiled by their education? This is precisely what ought to be prevented. With children use force, with men reason; such is the natural order of things. The wise man requires no laws. . . .

Nothing is more uncertain than the life span of individual man; very few men reach old age. The greatest risks are incurred at the beginning of life: the less we have lived the less we may expect to live. Of the children that are born half at most grow to adolescence; thus it is probable that your pupil will not attain the age of manhood.

What must we think then of the barbarous education which sacrifices the present for an uncertain future, which surrounds a child with all sorts of fetters and begins by making him wretched in order to prepare him for a hypothetical future happiness that he will probably never live to enjoy? Even if I supposed this educational objective to be reasonable, how could I behold without indignation poor unfortunates bowed beneath an insupportable yoke and condemned like galley-slaves to perpetual labor, with no assurance that all this attention will ever be of service to them? The age of gaiety is passed over amid tears, chastisement, threats and slavery. We torment the poor child for his own good and do not see that we are summoning death, which will seize him in the midst of this sad business. Who knows how many children perish the victims of a father's or tutor's extravagant wisdom? Happy to escape their cruelty, the only advantage children derive from the ills they have been made to suffer is to die without regretting life, of which they have tasted only the sorrows.

Men, be humane, that is your first duty: be so for all conditions, all ages, all that is germane to man. What does wisdom avail you except as it concerns humanity? Cherish childhood, look with favor on its games, its pleasures, its friendly instincts. Who of you has not at times longed for that age when laughter is always bursting forth and the soul is ever at peace? Why do you want to rob these young innocents of the pleasures of such brief and fleeting hours and of such precious gifts, which they are too young to misuse? Why wish to fill with bitterness and grief these early years that pass so quickly and will not return for them any more than for us? Fathers, do you know the moment that death awaits your child? Do not prepare for yourselves a life of sorrow by robbing them of the brief moment that nature gives them: as soon as they are able to sense the pleasure of existing, see to it that they enjoy themselves, see to it that at whatever hour God calls them, they do not die without having tasted of life. . . .

Let us not forget our human condition and pursue idle fancies. Humanity has its place in the general order; childhood, too, in the span of human life; we must look upon man in manhood and the child in childhood. To assign to each one his place and establish him in it, to order the human passions in accordance with man's constitution, that is all we can do for his well being. The rest depends on extraneous circumstances that are beyond our power to control. . . .

May I venture to state here that the greatest, most important, and most useful rule of all education is not to save time, but to lose it? Gentle reader, pardon my paradoxes: they follow necessarily upon reflection; and whatever you may say, I would rather be paradoxical than prejudiced. The most dangerous period of human life extends from birth to the age of twelve. That is the time when error and vice take root before there is any counteracting faculty; and when that faculty develops, the roots are so deep that it is too late to pull them up. If children jumped suddenly from the breast to the age of reason, the education that they now receive would suffice; but in the natural process of growth, they need an entirely different one. Their minds should be left uncultivated until all their faculties have developed; for until then it is impossible for them to see the light that you offer as a guide or to follow, in the immense realm of ideas, a path that reason traces ever so faintly even for the trained eye.

Early education should therefore be purely negative. It consists, not in teaching virtue or truth, but in protecting the heart from vice and the mind from error. If you could let your pupil alone and see that he is left alone; if you could bring him up sane and sound to the age of twelve, without his being able to tell his right hand from his left, then from his very first lessons, the eyes of his understanding would be open to reason; free from all prejudices and preconceptions, his mind would present no obstacle to the full effect of your teaching; and from a purely negative beginning, you would achieve an educational prodigy.

Proceed counter to customary practice and you will almost always be right. By trying to make a learned man out of a child, fathers and tutors begin all too soon tormenting, correcting, reprimanding, flattering, threatening, bribing, instructing, and reasoning. Rather than that, be reasonable and never reason with your pupil, especially when you want to make him change his dislikes; for by dragging reason into unpleasant matters you make it distasteful to him and discredit it early in a mind that is not ready to understand it. . . .

You put your trust in the present order of society without thinking that this order is subject to inevitable revolutions and that you cannot possibly foresee or provide against the society with which your children may have to deal. The great become small, the rich become poor, the monarch a subject; are these strokes of fortune so rare that you can count on immunity? We are approaching a crisis and the age of revolutions. Who can guarantee what will become of you then? Everything men have made, men can destroy: nature's characters alone are ineffaceable; and nature forms no princes, no rich men, or men of high degree.

• • •

There can be no patriotism without liberty, no liberty without virtue, no virtue without citizens; create citizens, and you have everything you need; without them, you will have nothing but debased slaves, from the rulers of the State downwards. To form citizens is not the work of a day; and in order to have men it is necessary to educate them when they are children. It will be said, perhaps, that whoever has men to govern, ought not to seek, beyond their nature, a perfection of which they are incapable; that he ought not to desire to destroy their passions; and that the execution of such an attempt is no more desirable than it is possible. I will agree, further, that a man without passions would certainly be a bad citizen; but it must be agreed also that, if men are not taught not to love some things, it is impossible to teach them to love one object more than another—to prefer that which is truly beautiful to that which is deformed. If, for example, they were early accustomed to regard their individuality only in its relation to the body of the State, and to be aware, so to speak, of their own existence merely as a part of that of the State, they might at length come to identify themselves in some degree with this greater whole, to feel themselves members of their country, and to love it with that exquisite feeling which no isolated person has save for himself; to lift up their spirits perpetually to this great object, and thus to transform into a sublime virtue that dangerous disposition which gives rise to all our vices. Not only does philosophy demonstrate the possibility of giving feeling these new directions; history furnishes us with a thousand striking examples. If they are so rare among us moderns, it is because nobody troubles himself whether citizens exist or not, and still less does anybody think of attending to the matter soon enough to make them. It is too late to change our natural inclinations, when they have taken their course, and egoism is confirmed by habit: it is too late to lead us out of ourselves when once the human Ego, concentrated in our hearts, has acquired that contemptible activity which absorbs all virtue and constitutes the life and being of little minds. How can patriotism germinate in the midst of so many other passions which smother it? And what can remain, for fellow-citizens, of a heart already divided between avarice, a mistress, and vanity?

From the first moment of life, men ought to begin learning to deserve to live; and, as at the instant of birth we partake of the rights of citizenship, that instant ought to be the beginning of the exercise of our duty. If there are laws for the age of maturity, there ought to be laws for infancy, teaching obedience to others: and as the reason of each man is not left to be the sole arbiter of his duties, government ought the less indiscriminately to abandon to the intelligence and prejudices of fathers the education of their children, as that education is of still greater importance to the State than to the fathers: for, according to the course of nature, the death of the father often deprives him of the final fruits of education; but his country sooner or later perceives its effects. Families dissolve, but the State remains.

Should the public authority, by taking the place of the father, and charging itself with that important function, acquire his rights by discharging his duties, he would have the less cause to complain, as he would only be changing his title, and would have in common, under the name of *citizen*, the same authority over his children, as he was exercising separately under the name of *father*, and would not be less obeyed when speaking in the name of the law, than when he spoke in that of nature. Public education, therefore, under regulations prescribed by the government, and under magistrates established by the Sovereign, is one of the fundamental rules of popular or legitimate government. If children are brought up in common in the bosom of equality; if they are imbued with the laws of the State and the precepts of the general will; if they are taught to respect these above all things; if they are surrounded by examples and objects which constantly remind them of the tender mother who nourishes them, of the love she bears them, of the inestimable benefits they receive from her, and of the return they owe her, we cannot doubt that they will learn to cherish one another mutually as brothers, to will nothing contrary to the will of society, to substitute the actions of men and citizens for the futile and vain babbling of sophists, and to become in time defenders and fathers of the country of which they will have been so long the children.

I shall say nothing of the Magistrates destined to preside over such an education, which is certainly the most important business of the State. It is easy to see that if such marks of public confidence were conferred on slight grounds, if this sublime function were not, for those who have worthily discharged all other offices, the reward of labor, the pleasant and honorable repose of old age, and the crown of all honors, the whole enterprise would be useless and the education void of success. For wherever the lesson is not supported by authority, and the precept by example, all instruction is fruitless; and virtue itself loses its credit in the mouth of one who does not practice it. But let illustrious warriors, bent under the weight of their laurels, preach courage: let upright Magistrates, grown white in the purple and on the bench, teach justice. Such teachers as these would thus get themselves virtuous successors, and transmit from age to age, to generations to come, the experience and talents of rulers, the courage and virtue of citizens, and common emulation in all to live and die for their country.

EDUCATION FOR CIVIL AND ACTIVE LIFE

JOSEPH PRIESTLEY

A schoolmaster at a Protestant Dissenting academy, Priestley was an educational innovator who introduced science, math, and commerce into the curriculum to better train students for an "active life" of business and citizenship. Ancient languages and the maxims of revered antiquity, he believed, would "not suit the world as it is at present." This selection is from Priestley's 1765 Essay on a Course of Liberal Education for Civil and Active Life.

It seems to be a defect in our present system of public education that a proper course of studies is not provided for gentlemen who are designed to fill the principal stations of active life, distinct from those which are adapted to the learned professions. We have hardly any medium between an education for the counting-house, consisting of writing, arithmetic and merchants' accounts and a method of institution in the abstract sciences: so that we have nothing liberal that is worth the attention of gentlemen, whose views neither of these two opposite plans may suit.

Formerly, none but the clergy were thought to have any occasion for learning. It was natural therefore that the whole plan of education from the grammar school to the finishing at the university, should be calculated for their use. If a few other persons who were not designed for holy orders, offered themselves for education, it could not be expected that a course of studies should be provided for them only. And indeed, as all those persons who superintended the business of education were of the clerical order and had themselves been taught nothing but the rhetoric, logic and school-divinity, or civil law, which comprised the whole compass of human learning for several centuries, it could not be expected that they should entertain larger or more liberal views of education; and still less that they should strike out a course of study for the use of men who were universally thought to have no need of study; and of whom few were so sensible of their own wants as to desire any such advantage. . . .

That the parents and friends of young gentlemen destined to act in any of these important spheres may not think a liberal education unnecessary to them and that the young gentlemen themselves may enter with spirit into the enlarged views of their friends and tutors, I would humbly propose some new articles of academical instruction, such as have a nearer and more evident connection with the business of active life, and which may therefore bid fairer to engage the attention and rouse the thinking powers of young gentlemen of an active genius. The subjects I would recommend are civil history and more especially the important objects of civil policy; such as the theory of laws, government, manufactures, commerce, naval force etc., with whatever may be demonstrated from history to have contributed to the flourishing state of nations, to rendering a people happy and populous at home, and formidable abroad; together with those articles of previous information without which it is impossible to understand the nature, connections, and mutual influences of those great objects.

To give a clearer idea of the subjects I would propose to the study of youth at places of public and liberal education, I have subjoined plans of three distinct courses of lectures, which, I apprehend, may be subservient to this design, divided into such portions as experience has taught me, may be conveniently discussed in familiar lectures of an hour each.

The first course is on the study of history in general and in its most extensive sense. It will be seen to consist of such articles as tend to enable a young gentleman to read history with understanding, and to reap the most valuable fruits of that engaging study. I shall not go over the particulars of the course in this place: let the syllabus speak for itself. Let it only be observed that my view was not merely to make history intelligible to persons who may choose to read it for their amusement, but principally to facilitate its subserviency to the highest uses to which it can be applied; to contribute to its forming the able statesman, and the intelligent and useful citizen. It is true that this is comprising a great deal more than the title of the course will suggest. But under the head of *Objects of attention to a reader of history*, it was found convenient to discuss the principle of those subjects which every gentleman of a liberal education is expected to understand, though they do not generally fall under any division of the sciences in a course of academical education: and yet, without a competent knowledge of these subjects, no person can be qualified to serve his country except in the lowest capacities.

This course of lectures, it is also presumed, will be found to contain a comprehensive system of that kind of knowledge which is peculiarly requisite to gentlemen who intend to travel. For, since the great objects of attention to a reader of history and to a gentleman upon his travels are evidently the same, it must be of equal service to them both, to have their importance and mutual influences pointed out to them.

It will likewise be evident to any person who inspects this syllabus, that the subject of commerce has by no means been overlooked. And it is hoped that when those gentlemen who are intended to serve themselves and their country in the respectable character of merchants have heard the great maxims of commerce discussed in a scientifical and connected manner, as they deserve, they will not easily be influenced by notions adopted in a random and hasty manner, and from superficial views of things, whereby they might otherwise be induced to enter into measures seemingly gainful at present but in the end prejudicial to their country, and to themselves and their posterity, as members of it.

The next course of lectures, the plan of which is briefly delineated, is upon the history of England, and is designed to be an exemplification of the manner of studying history recommended in the former course, in which the great uses of it are shown, and the actual progress of every important object of attention distinctly marked, from the earliest accounts of the island to the present time.

To make young gentlemen still more thoroughly acquainted with their own country, a third course of lectures (in connection with the two others) is subjoined, viz. on its present constitution and laws. But the particular uses of these two courses of lectures need not be pointed out here, as they are sufficiently explained in the introductory addresses prefixed to each of them.

That an acquaintance with the subjects of these lectures is calculated to form the statesman, the military commander, the lawyer, the merchant and the accomplished country gentleman, cannot be disputed. The principal objection that may be made to this scheme is the introduction of these subjects into academies, and submitting them to the examination of youth, of the age at which they are usually sent to such places of education. It will be said by some that these subjects are too deep and too intricate for their tender age and weak intellects; and that, after all, it can be no more than an outline of these great branches of knowledge that can be communicated to youth. . . .

I am aware of a different kind of objection from another quarter which it behooves me not to overlook. The advocates for the old plan of education and who dislike innovations in the number or the distribution of the sciences in which lectures are given, may object to the admission of these studies, as in danger of attracting the attention of those students who are designed for the learned professions and thereby interfering too much with that which has been found by the experience of generations, to be the best for scholars, the proper subjects of which are sufficient to fill up all their time, without these supernumerary articles. I answer that the subjects of these lectures are by no means necessary articles of a mere scholastic education, but that they are such as scholars ought to have some acquaintance with, and that without some acquaintance with them, they must on many occasions appear to great disadvantage in the present state of knowledge.

Time was when scholars might with a good grace disclaim all pretensions to any branch of knowledge, but what was taught in the universities. Perhaps they would be the more revered by the vulgar on account of such ignorance, as an argument of their being more abstracted from the world. Few books were written but by critics and antiquaries for the use of men like themselves. The literati of those days had comparatively little free intercourse but among themselves; the learned world and the common world being much more distinct from one another than they are now. Scholars by profession read, wrote, and conversed in no language but the Roman. They would have been ashamed to have expressed themselves in bad Latin, but not in the least of being guilty of any impropriety in the use of their mother tongue, which they considered as belonging only to the vulgar.

But those times of revived antiquity have had their use, and are now no more. We are obliged to the learned labors of our forefathers for searching into all the remains of antiquity, and illustrating valuable ancient authors; but their maxims of life will not suit the world as it is at present. The politeness of the times has brought the learned and the unlearned into more familiar intercourse than they had before. They find themselves obliged to converse upon the same topics. The subjects of modern history, policy, arts, manufactures, commerce etc. are the general topics of all sensible conversation. Everything is said in our own tongue, little is even written in a foreign or dead language; and every British author is studious of writing with propriety in his native English. Criticism, which was formerly the great business of a scholar's life, is now become the amusement of a leisure hour, and this but to a few; so that a hundredth part of the time which was formerly given to criticism and antiquities is enough in this age to gain a man the character of a profound scholar. The topics of sensible conversation are likewise the favorite subjects of all the capital writings of the present age which are read with equal avidity by gentlemen, merchants, lawyers, physicians, and divines.

Now, when the course of reading, thinking and conversation, even among scholars, is become so very different from what it was, is it not reasonable that the plan of even scholastic education should in some measure vary with it? The necessity of the thing has already in many instances forced a change, and the same increasing necessity will either force a greater and more general change, or we must not be surprised to find our schools, academies, and universities deserted as wholly unfit to qualify men to appear with advantage in the present age.

In many private schools and academies, we find several things taught now which were never made the subjects of systematical instruction in former times; and in those of our universities in which it is the interest of the tutors to make their lectures of real use to their pupils, and where lectures are not mere matters of form, the professors find the necessity of delivering themselves in English. And the evident propriety of the thing must necessarily make this practice more general, notwithstanding the most superstitious regard to established customs.

But let the professors conduct themselves by what maxims they please, the students will of course be influenced by the taste of the company they keep in the world at large, to which young gentlemen in this age have an earlier admission than they had formerly. How can it be expected that the present set of students for divinity should apply to the study of the dead languages with the assiduity of their fathers and grandfathers when they find so many of the uses of those languages no longer subsisting? What can they think it will avail them to make the purity of the Latin style their principal study for several years of the most improvable part of their life, when they are sensible that they shall have little more occasion for it than other gentlemen, or than persons in common life when they have left the university? And how can it be otherwise but that their private reading and studies should sometimes be different from the course of their public instructions, when the favorite authors of the public, the merits of whom they hear discussed in every company, even by their tutors themselves, write upon quite different subjects?

In such a state of things, the advantage of a regular systematical instruction in those subjects which are treated of in books that in fact engage the attention of all the world, the learned least of all excepted, and which enter into all conversations where it is worth a man's while to bear a part, or to make a figure, cannot be doubted. And I am of opinion that these studies may be conducted in such a manner as will interfere very little with a sufficiently close application to others. Students in medicine and divinity may be admitted to these studies later than those for whose real use in life they are principally intended; not till they be sufficiently grounded in the classics, have studied logic, oratory, and criticism, or anything else that may be deemed useful, previous to those studies which are peculiar to their respective professions; and even then these new studies may be made a matter of amusement, rather than an article of business. . . .

Some may object to the encouragement I would give the students to propose objections at the time of lecturing. This custom, they may say, will tend to interrupt the course of the lecture, and promote a spirit of impertinence and conceit in young persons. I answer that every inconvenience of this kind may be obviated by the manner in which a tutor delivers himself in lecturing. A proper mixture of dignity and freedom (which are so far from being incompatible that they mutually set off one another) will prevent, or repress, all impertinent and unseasonable remarks, at the same time that it will encourage those which are modest and pertinent.

But suppose a lecturer should not be able immediately to give a satisfactory answer to an objection that might be started by a sensible student. He must be conscious of his having made very ridiculous pretensions and having given himself improper airs, if it give him any pain to tell his class that he will reconsider a subject, or even to acknowledge himself mistaken. It depends wholly upon a tutor's general disposition, and his usual manner of address, whether he lose or gain ground in the esteem of his pupils by such a declaration. Every tutor ought to have considered the subjects on which he gives lectures with attention, but no man can be expected to be infallible. For my own part, I would not forgo the pleasure and advantage which accrue both to my pupils and to myself from this method, together with the opportunity it gives me of improving my lectures, by means of the many useful hints which are often started in this familiar way of discoursing upon a subject, for any inconvenience I have yet found to attend it or that I can imagine may possibly attend it. . . .

Some may perhaps object to these studies as giving too much encouragement to that turn for politics which they may think is already immoderate in the lower and middle ranks of men among us. But must not political knowledge be communicated to those to whom it may be of real use, because a fondness for the study may extend beyond its proper bounds and be caught by some persons who had better remain ignorant of it? Besides, it ought to be considered that how ridiculous soever some may make themselves by pretensions to politics, a true friend of liberty will be cautious how he discourages a fondness for that kind of knowledge which has ever been the favorite subject of writing and conversation in all free states. Only tyrants and the friends of arbitrary power have ever taken umbrage at a turn for political knowledge and political discourses among even the lowest of the people. Men will study and converse about what they are interested in especially if they have any influence; and though the ass in the fable was in no concern who was his master, since he could but carry his usual load, and though the subjects of a despotic monarch need not trouble themselves about political disputes and intrigues which never terminate in a change of measures, but only of men—yet, in a free country where even private persons have much at stake, every man is nearly interested in the conduct of his superiors, and cannot be an unconcerned spectator of what is transacted by them. With respect to influence, the sentiments of the lowest vulgar in England are not wholly insignificant, and a wise minister will ever pay some attention to them.

It is our wisdom, therefore, to provide that all persons who have any influence in political measures be well instructed in the great and leading principles of wise policy. This is certainly an object of the greatest importance. Inconveniences ever attend a general application to any kind of knowledge and no doubt will attend this. But they are inconveniences which a friend to liberty need be under no apprehensions about.

I may possibly promise myself too much from the general introduction of the studies I have recommended in this Essay into places of liberal education, but a little enthusiasm is always excusable in persons who propose and recommend useful innovations. I have endeavored to represent the state of education in this view as clearly and as fully as I have been able, and I desire my proposals for emendations to have no more weight than the fairest representation will give them in the minds of the cool and the unbiased.

MANNERS AND MORALS

THE FABLE OF THE BEES

BERNARD MANDEVILLE

A Dutchman who spent most of his life practicing medicine in England, Mandeville (1670–1733) wrote this poem, titled "The Grumbling Hives or Knaves Turn'd Honest," in 1705. Its shocking defense of the moral legitimacy of self-interest was reinforced in 1714 when he added an accompanying prose text and the new title, The Fable of the Bees, or Private Vices, Public Benefits.

A Spacious Hive well stock'd with Bees,
That lived in Luxury and Ease;
And yet as fam'd for Laws and Arms,
As yielding large and early Swarms;
Was counted the great Nursery
Of Sciences and Industry.

No Bees had better Government,
More Fickleness, or less Content.
They were not Slaves to Tyranny,
Nor ruled by wild Democracy;
But Kings, that could not wrong, because
Their Power was circumscrib'd by Laws.

These Insects lived like Men, and all
Our Actions they perform'd in small:
They did whatever's done in Town,
And what belongs to Sword, or Gown:
Tho' th' Artful Works, by nimble Slight
Of minute Limbs, 'scaped Human Sight;
Yet we've no Engines, Laborers,
Ships, Castles, Arms, Artificers,
Craft, Science, Shop, or Instrument;
But they had an Equivalent:
Which, since their Language is unknown,
Must be call'd, as we do our own.
As grant, that among other Things
They wanted Dice, yet they had Kings;
And those had Guards; from whence we may
Justly conclude, they had some Play;
Unless a Regiment be shewn
Of Soldiers, that make use of none.

Vast Numbers thronged the fruitful Hive;
Yet those vast Numbers made 'em thrive;
Millions endeavoring to supply
Each other's Lust and Vanity;
Whilst other Millions were employ'd,
To see their Handy-works destroy'd;
They furnish'd half the Universe;
Yet had more Work than Laborers.
Some with vast Stocks, and little Pains
Jump'd into Business of great Gains;
And some were damn'd to Sythes and Spades,
And all those hard laborious Trades;
Where willing Wretches daily sweat,

And wear out Strength and Limbs to eat:
Whilst others follow'd Mysteries,
To which few Folks bind 'Prentices;
That want no Stock, but that of Brass,
And may set up without a Cross;
As Sharpers, Parasites, Pimps, Players,
Pick-Pockets, Coiners, Quacks, Sooth-Sayers,
And all those, that, in Enmity
With down-right Working, cunningly
Convert to their own Use the Labor
Of their good-natur'd heedless Neighbor.
These were called Knaves; but, bar the Name,
The grave Industrious were the Same.
All Trades and Places knew some Cheat,
No Calling was without Deceit.

The Lawyers, of whose Art the Basis
Was raising Feuds and splitting Cases,
Opposed all Registers, that Cheats
Might make more Work with dipt Estates;
As were't unlawful, that one's own,
Without a Law-Suit, should be known.
They kept off Hearings willfully,
To finger the refreshing Fee;
And to defend a wicked Cause,
Examin'd and survey'd the Laws;
As Burglars Shops and Houses do;
To find out where they'd best break through.

Physicians valued Fame and Wealth
Above the drooping Patient's Health,
Or their own Skill: The greatest Part
Study'd, instead of Rules of Art,
Grave pensive Looks, and dull Behavior;
To gain th' Apothecary's Favor,
The Praise of Mid-wives, Priests and all,
That served at Birth, or Funeral;
To bear with th' ever-talking Tribe,
And hear my Lady's Aunt prescribe;

With formal Smile, and kind How d'ye,
To fawn on all the Family;
And, which of all the greatest Curse is,
T'endure th'Impertinence of Nurses.

Among the many Priests of *Jove,*
Hir'd to draw Blessings from Above,
Some few were learn'd and eloquent,
But Thousands hot and ignorant:
Yet all past Muster, that could hide
Their Sloth, Lust, Avarice and Pride;
For which they were as famed, as Taylors
For Cabbage; or for Brandy, Sailors:
Some meager look'd, and meanly clad
Would mystically pray for Bread,
Meaning by that an ample Store,
Yet lit'rally receiv'd no more;
And, whilst these holy Drudges starv'd,
The lazy Ones, for which they serv'd,
Indulg'd their Ease, with all the Graces
Of Health and Plenty in their Faces.

The Soldiers, that were forced to fight,
If they survived, got Honor by't;
Tho' some, that shunn'd the bloody Fray,
Had Limbs shot off, that ran away:
Some valiant Gen'rals fought the Foe;
Others took Bribes to let them go:
Some ventur'd always, where 'twas warm;
Lost now a Leg, and then an Arm;
Till quite disabled, and put by,
They lived on half their Salary;
Whilst others never came in Play,
And staid at Home for Double Pay.

Their Kings were serv'd; but Knavishly
Cheated by their own Ministry;
Many, that for their Welfare slaved,
Robbing the very Crown they saved:

Pensions were small, and they lived high,
Yet boasted of their Honesty.
Calling, whene'er they strain'd their Right,
The slipp'ry Trick a Perquisite;
And, when Folks understood their Cant,
They chang'd that for Emolument;
Unwilling to be short, or plain,
In any thing concerning Gain:
For there was not a Bee, but would
Get more, I won't say, than he should;
But than he dared to let them know,
That pay'd for't; as your Gamesters do,
That, tho' at fair Play, ne'er will own
Before the Losers what they've won.

But who can all their Frauds repeat!
The very Stuff, which in the Street
They sold for Dirt t'enrich the Ground,
Was often by the Buyers found
Sophisticated with a Quarter
Of Good-for-nothing, Stones and Mortar;
Tho' Flail had little Cause to mutter,
Who sold the other Salt for Butter.

Justice her self, famed for fair Dealing,
By Blindness had not lost her Feeling;
Her Left Hand, which the Scales should hold,
Had often dropt 'em, bribed with Gold;
And, tho' she seem'd impartial,
Where Punishment was corporal,
Pretended to a reg'lar Course,
In Murther, and all Crimes of Force;
Tho' some, first Pillory'd for Cheating,
Were hang'd in Hemp of their own beating;
Yet, it was thought, the Sword she bore
Check'd but the Desp'rate and the Poor;
That, urged by mere Necessity,
Were tied up to the wretched Tree
For Crimes, which not deserv'd that Fate,
But to secure the Rich, and Great.

Thus every Part was full of Vice,
Yet the whole Mass a Paradise;
Flatter'd in Peace, and fear'd in Wars
They were th' Esteem of Foreigners,
And lavish of their Wealth and Lives,
The Balance of all other Hives.
Such were the Blessings of that State;
Their Crimes conspired to make 'em Great;
And Virtue, who from Politicks
Had learn'd a Thousand cunning Tricks,
Was, by their happy Influence,
Made Friends with Vice: And ever since
The Worst of all the Multitude
Did something for the common Good.

This was the State's Craft, that maintain'd
The Whole, of which each Part complain'd:
This, as in Musick Harmony,
Made Jarrings in the Main agree;
Parties directly opposite
Assist each oth'r, as 'twere for Spite;
And Temp'rance with Sobriety
Serve Drunkenness and Gluttony.

The Root of evil Avarice,
That damn'd ill-natur'd baneful Vice,
Was Slave to Prodigality,
That Noble Sin; whilst Luxury
Employ'd a Million of the Poor,
And odious Pride a Million more.
Envy it self, and Vanity
Were Ministers of Industry;
Their darling Folly, Fickleness
In Diet, Furniture, and Dress,
That strange ridic'lous Vice, was made
The very Wheel, that turn'd the Trade.
Their Laws and Clothes were equally
Objects of Mutability;
For, what was well done for a Time,
In half a Year became a Crime;

Yet whilst they alter'd thus their Laws,
Still finding and correcting Flaws,
They mended by Inconstancy
Faults, which no Prudence could foresee.

Thus Vice nursed Ingenuity,
Which join'd with Time, and Industry
Had carry'd Life's Conveniencies,
It's real Pleasures, Comforts, Ease,
To such a Height, the very Poor
Lived better than the Rich before;
And nothing could be added more:

How vain is Mortal Happiness!
Had they but known the Bounds of Bliss;
And, that Perfection here below
Is more, than Gods can well bestow,
The grumbling Brutes had been content
With Ministers and Government.
But they, at every ill Success,
Like Creatures lost without Redress,
Cursed Politicians, Armies, Fleets,
Whilst every one cry'd, Damn the Cheats,
And would, tho' Conscious of his own,
In Others barb'rously bear none.

One, that had got a Princely Store,
By cheating Master, King, and Poor,
Dared cry aloud; The Land must sink
For all it's Fraud; And whom d'ye think
The Sermonizing Rascal chid?
A Glover that sold Lamb for Kid.

The least Thing was not done amiss,
Or cross'd the Public Business;
But all the Rogues cry'd brazenly,
Good Gods, had we but Honesty!
Merc'ry smiled at th' Impudence;
And Others call'd it want of Sence,

Always to rail at what they loved:
But *Jove,* with Indignation moved,
At last in Anger swore, he'd rid
The bawling Hive of Fraud, and did.
The very Moment it departs,
And Honesty fills all their Hearts;
There shews 'em, like th' Instructive Tree,
Those Crimes, which they're ashamed to see;
Which now in Silence they confess,
By Blushing at their Uglyness;
Like Children, that would hide their Faults,
And by their Color own their Thoughts;
Imag'ning, when they're look'd upon,
That Others see, what they have done.

But, Oh ye Gods! What Consternation,
How vast and sudden was th' Alteration!
In half an Hour, the Nation round,
Meat fell a Penny in the Pound.
The Mask Hypocrisie's flung down,
From the great Statesman to the Clown;
And some, in borrow'd Looks well known,
Appear'd like Strangers in their own.
The Bar was silent from that Day;
For now the willing Debtors pay,
Ev'n what's by Creditors forgot;
Who quitted them, that had it not.
Those, that were in the Wrong, stood mute,
And dropped the patch'd vexatious Suit.
On which, since nothing less can thrive,
Than Lawyers in an honest Hive,
All, except those, that got enough,
With Ink-horns by their Sides troop'd off.

Justice hang'd some, set others free;
And, after Goal delivery,
Her Presence be'ng no more requir'd,
With all her Train, and Pomp retir'd.
First march'd some Smiths, with Locks and Grates,

Fetters, and Doors with Iron-Plates;
Next Goalers, Turnkeys, and Assistants:
Before the Goddess, at some distance,
Her chief and faithful Minister
Squire Catch, the Laws great Finisher,
Bore not th' imaginary Sword,
But his own Tools, an Ax and Cord:
Then on a Cloud the Hood-wink'd fair
Justice her self was push'd by Air:
About her Chariot, and behind,
Were Sergeants, Bums of every kind,
Tip-staffs, and all those Officers,
That squeeze a Living out of Tears.

Tho' Physick lived, whilst Folks were ill,
None would prescribe, but Bees of Skill;
Which, through the Hive dispers'd so wide,
That none of 'em had need to ride,
Waved vain Disputes; and strove to free
The Patients of their Misery;
Left Drugs in cheating Countries grown,
And used the Product of their own,
Knowing the Gods sent no Disease
To Nations without Remedies.

Their Clergy rouz'd from Laziness,
Laid not their Charge on Journey-Bees,
But serv'd themselves, exempt from Vice,
The Gods with Pray'r and Sacrifice;
All those, that were unfit, or knew,
Their Service might be spared, withdrew:
Nor was there Business for so many,
(If th' Honest stand in need of any.)
Few only with the High-Priest staid,
To whom the rest Obedience paid:
Himself, employ'd in holy Cares,
Resign'd to others State-Affairs:
He chased no Starv'ling from his Door,
Nor pinch'd the Wages of the Poor;

But at his House the Hungry's fed,
The Hireling finds unmeasur'd Bread,
The needy Trav'ler Board and Bed.

Among the King's great Ministers,
And all th' inferior Officers
The Change was great; for frugally
They now lived on their Salary.
That a poor Bee should Ten times come,
To ask his Due, a trifling Sum,
And by some well-hir'd Clerk be made,
To give a Crown, or ne'er be paid;
Would now be call'd a down-right Cheat,
Tho' formerly a Perquisite.
All Places; managed first by Three,
Who watch'd each other's Knavery,
And often for a Fellow-feeling,
Promoted one another's Stealing;
Are happily supply'd by one;
By which some Thousands more are gone.

No Honor now could be content,
To live, and owe for what was spent.
Liv'ries in Brokers Shops are hung,
They part with Coaches for a Song;
Sell stately Horses by whole Sets;
And Country-Houses to pay Debts.

Vain Cost is shunn'd as much as Fraud;
They have no Forces kept Abroad;
Laugh at th' Esteem of Foreigners,
And empty Glory got by Wars;
They fight but for their Country's Sake,
When Right or Liberty's at Stake.

Now mind the glorious Hive, and see,
How Honesty and Trade agree:
The Shew is gone, it thins apace;
And looks with quite another Face,

For 'twas not only that they went,
By whom vast Sums were Yearly spent;
But Multitudes, that lived on them,
Were daily forc'd to do the Same.
In vain to other Trades they'd fly;
All were o'er-stock'd accordingly.

The Price of Land, and Houses falls;
Mirac'lous Palaces, whose Walls,
Like those of *Thebes,* were raised by Play,
Are to be let; whilst the once gay,
Well-seated Household Gods would be
More pleased t'expire in Flames, than see
The mean Inscription on the Door
Smile at the lofty Ones they bore.
The Building Trade is quite destroy'd,
Artificers are not employ'd;
No Limner for his Art is famed;
Stone-cutters, Carvers are not named.

Those, that remain'd, grown temp'rate, strive,
Not how to spend; but how to live;
And, when they paid their Tavern Score,
Resolv'd to enter it no more:
No Vintners Jilt in all the Hive
Could wear now Cloth of Gold and thrive;
Nor *Torcol* such vast Sums advance,
For *Burgundy* and *Ortelans;*
The Courtier's gone, that with his Miss
Supp'd at his House on *Christmass* Peas;
Spending as much in Two Hours stay,
As keeps a Troop of Horse a Day.

The haughty *Chloe,* to live Great,
Had made her Husband rob the State:
But now she sells her Furniture,
Which th' *Indies* had been ransack'd for;
Contracts th' expensive Bill of Fare,
And wears her strong Suit a whole Year:

The slight and fickle Age is past;
And Clothes, as well as Fashions last.
Weavers that join'd rich Silk with Plate,
And all the Trades subordinate,
Are gone. Still Peace and Plenty reign,
And every Thing is cheap, tho' plain:
Kind Nature, free from Gard'ners Force,
Allows all Fruits in her own Course;
But Rarities cannot be had,
Where Pains to get 'em are not paid.

As Pride and Luxury decrease,
So by degrees they leave the Seas.
Not Merchants now; but Companies
Remove whole Manufacturies.
All Arts and Crafts neglected lie;
Content the Bane of Industry,
Makes 'em admire their homely Store,
And neither seek, nor covet more.

So few in the vast Hive remain;
The Hundredth part they can't maintain
Against th' Insults of numerous Foes;
Whom yet they valiantly oppose:
Till some well-fenced Retreat is found;
And here they die, or stand their Ground.
No Hireling in their Armies known;
But bravely fighting for their own,
Their Courage and Integrity
At last were crown'd with Victory.
They triumph'd not without their Cost;
For many Thousand Bees were lost.
Hard'ned with Toils, and Exercise
They counted Ease it self a Vice;
Which so improved their Temperance;
That, to avoid Extravagance,
They flew into a hollow Tree,
Blest with Content and Honesty.

THE MORAL

Then leave Complaints: Fools only strive
To make a Great an honest Hive.
T' enjoy the World's Conveniencies,
Be famed in War, yet live in Ease
Without great Vices, is a vain
Eutopia seated in the Brain.
Fraud, Luxury, and Pride must live
Whilst we the Benefits receive.
Hunger's a dreadful Plague, no doubt,
Yet who digests or thrives without?
Do we not owe the Growth of Wine
To the dry shabby crooked Vine?
Which, whilst its Shutes neglected stood,
Choak'd other Plants, and ran to Wood;
But blest us with its Noble Fruit;
As soon as it was tied, and cut:
So Vice is beneficial found,
When it's by Justice lopt, and bound;
Nay, where the People would be great,
As necessary to the State
As Hunger is to make 'em eat.
Bare Virtue can't make Nations live
In Splendor; they, that would revive
A Golden Age, must be as free,
For Acorns, as for Honesty.

FINIS

AN ESSAY ON MAN

ALEXANDER POPE

One of the great poets of eighteenth-century England, Pope (1688–1744) offers in his poem "An Essay on Man," written in 1733, a characteristic Enlightenment vision of human nature. The following is an excerpt from Epistle II.

Know then thyself, presume not God to scan,
The proper study of mankind is Man.
Placed on this isthmus of a middle state,
A being darkly wise and rudely great:
With too much knowledge for the Sceptic side,
With too much weakness for the Stoic's pride,
He hangs between, in doubt to act or rest;
In doubt to deem himself a God or Beast;
In doubt his mind or body to prefer;
Born but to die, and reas'ning but to err;
Alike in ignorance, his reason such,
Whether he thinks too little or too much;
Chaos of thought and passion, all confused;
Still by himself abused or disabused;
Created half to rise, and half to fall;
Great lord of all things, yet a prey to all;
Sole judge of truth, in endless error hurl'd;
The glory, jest, and riddle of the world!

Go, wondrous creature! mount where Science guides;
Go, measure earth, weigh air, and state the tides;
Instruct the planets in what orbs to run,
Correct old Time, and regulate the sun;
Go, soar with Plato to th' empyreal sphere,
To the first good, first perfect, and first fair;
Or tread the mazy round his followers trod,

And quitting sense call imitating God;
As eastern priests in giddy circles run,
And turn their heads to imitate the sun.
Go, teach Eternal Wisdom how to rule—
Then drop into thyself, and be a fool!

Superior beings, when of late they saw
A mortal man unfold all Nature's law,
Admired such wisdom in an earthly shape,
And show'd a NEWTON as we show an ape.
Could he, whose rules the rapid comet bind,
Describe or fix one movement of his mind?
Who saw its fires here rise, and there descend,
Explain his own beginning or his end?
Alas! what wonder! Man's superior part
Uncheck'd may rise, and climb from art to art;
But when his own great work is but begun,
What Reason weaves, by Passion is undone.

Trace Science then, with modesty thy guide;
First strip off all her equipage of pride;
Deduct what is but vanity or dress,
Or learning's luxury, or idleness,
Or tricks to show the stretch of human brain,
Mere curious pleasure, or ingenious pain;
Expunge the whole, or lop th' excrescent parts
Of all, our vices have created arts;
Then see how little the remaining sum,
Which serv'd the past, and must the times to come!

MEMOIRS OF A WOMAN OF PLEASURE

JOHN CLELAND

Businessman, journalist, and writer, John Cleland (1710–1789) has the distinction of writing one of the enduring classics of erotic fiction. When his Fanny Hill, or Memoirs of a Woman of Pleasure, *was published in 1749, the bishop of London called it "an open insult upon religion and good manners." This excerpt from the novel is a vivid reminder of the Enlightenment's concern with the pursuit of pleasure.*

Mr. H—— had clapped a livery upon him; and his chief employ was, after being shown my lodgings, to bring and carry letters or messages between his master and me; and as the situation of all kept ladies is not the fittest to inspire respect even to the meanest of mankind, and perhaps less of it from the most ignorant, I could not help observing that this lad, who was, I suppose, acquainted with my relation to his master by his fellow servants, used to eye me in that bashful confused way, more expressive, more moving, and readier caught at by our sex than any other declarations whatever: my figure had, it seems, struck him, and modest and innocent as he was, he did not himself know that the pleasure he took in looking at me was love, or desire; but his eyes, naturally wanton, and now inflamed by passion, spoke a great deal more than he durst have imagined they did. Hitherto, indeed, I had only taken notice of the comeliness of the youth, but without the least design. My pride alone would have guarded me from a thought that way, had not Mr. H——'s condescension with my maid, where there was not half the temptation in point of person, set me a dangerous example; but now I began to look on this stripling as every way a delicious instrument of my designed retaliation upon Mr. H——, of an obligation for which I should have made a conscience to die in his debt.

In order then to pave the way for the accomplishment of my scheme, for two or three times that the young fellow came to me with messages, I managed so as without affectation to have him admitted to my bedside, or brought to me at my toilet, where I was dressing; and by carelessly showing or letting him see as if without meaning or design, sometimes my bosom rather more bare than it should be; sometimes my hair, of which I had a very fine head, in the natural flow of it while combing; sometimes a neat leg, that had unfortunately slipped its garter, which I made no scruple of tying before him, easily gave him the impressions favorable to my purpose, which I could perceive to sparkle in his eyes and glow in his cheeks. Then certain slight squeezes by the hand, as I took letters from him, did his business completely.

When I saw him thus moved and fired for my purpose, I inflamed him yet more by asking him several leading questions: such as had he a mistress?—was she prettier than me?—could he love such a one as I was?—and the like; to all which the blushing simpleton answered to my wish, in a strain of perfect nature, perfect undebauched innocence, but with all the awkwardness and simplicity of country breeding.

When I thought I had sufficiently ripened him for the laudable point I had in view, one day that I expected him at a particular hour, I took care to have the coast clear for the reception I designed him. And, as I had laid it, he came to the dining room door, tapped at it, and, on my bidding him come in, he did so and shut the door after him. I desired him then to bolt it on the inside, pretending it would not otherwise keep shut.

I was then lying at length on that very couch, the scene of Mr. H——'s polite joys, in an undress which was with all the art of negligence flowing loose, and in a most tempting disorder: no stays, no hoop—no encumbrance whatever; on the other hand, he stood at a little distance that gave me a full view of a fine featured, shapely, healthy, country lad, breathing the sweets of fresh blooming youth: his hair, which was of a perfect shining black, played to his face in natural side-curls and was set out with a smart tuck-up behind; new buckskin breeches that, clipping close, showed the shape of a plump well made thigh, white stockings, garter-laced livery, shoulder-knot, altogether composed a figure in which the beauties of pure flesh and blood appeared under no disgrace from the lowness of a dress, to which a certain spruce neatness seems peculiarly fitted.

I bid him come towards me and give me his letter, at the same time throwing down carelessly a book I had in my hands. He colored, and came within reach of delivering me the letter, which he held out awkwardly enough for me to take, with his eyes riveted on my bosom, which was, through the designed disorder of my handkerchief, sufficiently bare and rather shaded than hidden.

I, smiling in his face, took the letter, and immediately catching gently hold of his shirt-sleeve, drew him towards me, blushing and almost trembling; for surely his extreme bashfulness and utter inexperience called for at least all these advances to encourage him. His body was now conveniently inclined towards me, and just softly chucking his smooth beardless chin, I asked him, if he was afraid of a lady?—and with that taking and carrying his hand to my breasts, I pressed it tenderly to them. They were now finely furnished and raised in flesh, so that, panting with desire, they rose and fell, in quick heaves, under his touch: at this, the boy's eyes began to lighten with all the fires of inflamed nature, and his cheeks flushed with a deep scarlet; tongue-tied with joy, rapture, and bashfulness, he could not speak, but then his looks, his emotion, sufficiently satisfied me that my train had taken, and that I had no disappointment to fear.

My lips, which I threw in his way, so as that he could not escape kissing them, fixed, fired and emboldened him, and now, glancing my eyes towards that part of his dress which covered the essential object of enjoyment, I plainly discovered the swell and commotion there, and as I was now too far advanced to stop in so fair a way, and was indeed no longer able to contain myself or wait the slower progress of his maiden bashfulness (for such it seemed, and really was), I stole my hand upon his thighs, down one of which I could both see and feel a stiff hard body, confined by his breeches, that my fingers could discover no end to. Curious then, and eager to unfold so alarming a mystery, playing, as it were, with his buttons, which were bursting ripe from the active force within, those of his waistband and foreflap flew open at a touch, when out it started; and now, disengaged from the shirt, I saw with wonder and surprise, what? not the plaything of a boy, not the weapon of a man, but a maypole of so enormous a standard that, had proportions been observed, it must have belonged to a young giant; its prodigious size made me shrink again. Yet I could not, without pleasure, behold and even ventured to feel such a length! such a breadth of animated ivory, perfectly well turned and fashioned, the proud stiffness of which distended its skin, whose smooth polish and velvet softness might vie with that of the most delicate of our sex, and whose exquisite whiteness was not a little set off by a sprout of black curling hair round the root, through the jetty sprigs of which the fair skin showed as, in a fine evening, you may have remarked the clear light ether, through the branchwork of distant trees, overtopping the summit of a hill. Then the broad and bluish-casted incarnate of the head and blue serpentines of its veins altogether composed the most striking assemblage of figure and colors in nature; in short, it stood an object of terror and delight.

But what was yet more surprising, the owner of this natural curiosity (through the want of occasions in the strictness of his home breeding, and the little time he had been in town not having afforded him one) was hitherto an absolute stranger, in practice at least, to the use of all that manhood he was so nobly stocked with; and it now fell to my lot to stand his first trial of it, if I could resolve to run the risks of its disproportion to that tender part of me which such an over-sized machine was very fit to lay in ruins.

But it was now of the latest to deliberate; for by this time, the young fellow, overheated with the present objects, and too high-mettled to be longer curbed in by that modesty and awe which had hitherto restrained him, ventured, under the stronger impulse and instructive promptership of nature alone, to slip his hands, trembling with eager impetuous desires, under my petticoats, and seeing, I suppose, nothing extremely severe in my looks to stop, or dash him, he feels out and seizes gently the center-spot of his ardors. Oh then! the fiery touch of his fingers determines me, and my fears melting away before the growing intolerable heat, my thighs disclose of themselves and yield all liberty to his hand; and now, a favorable movement giving my petticoats a toss, the avenue lay too fair, too open to be missed; he is now upon me. I had placed myself with a jet under him, as commodious and open as possible to his attempts, which were untoward enough, for his machine, meeting with no inlet, bore and battered stiffly against me in random pushes, now above, now below, now beside its point, till, burning with impatience from its irritating touches, I guided gently with my hand this furious fescue to where my young novice was now to be taught his first lesson of pleasure. Thus he nicked at length the warm and insufficient orifice; but he was made to find no breach practicable, and mine, though so often entered, was still far from wide enough to take him easily in.

By my direction, however, the head of his unwieldy machine was so critically pointed that, feeling him foreright against the tender opening, a favorable motion from me met his timely thrust, by which the lips of it, strenuously dilated, gave way to his thus assisted impetuosity, so that we might both feel that he had gained a lodgment; pursuing then his point, he soon, by violent and, to me, most painful piercing thrusts, wedges himself at least so far in as to be now tolerably secure of his entrance: here he stuck; and I now felt such a mixture of pleasure and pain as there is no giving a definition of. I dreaded, alike, his splitting me farther up or his withdrawing: I could not bear either to keep or part with him; the sense of pain, however, prevailing, from his prodigious size and stiffness, acting upon me in those continued rapid thrusts with which he furiously pursued his penetration, made me cry out gently: "Oh, my dear, you hurt me!" This was enough to check the tender respectful boy, even in his mid-career; and he immediately drew out the sweet cause of my complaint, whilst his eyes eloquently expressed at once his grief for hurting me and his reluctance at dislodging from quarters of which the warmth and closeness had given him a gust of pleasure that he was now desire-mad to satisfy, and yet too much a novice not to be afraid of my withholding his relief, on account of the pain he had put me to.

But I was myself far from being pleased with his having too much regarded my tender exclaims, for now more and more fired with the object before me, as it still stood with the fiercest erection, unbonneted and displaying its broad vermillion head, I first gave the youth a reencouraging kiss, which he repaid me with a fervor that seemed at once to thank me and bribe my farther compliance, and I soon replaced myself in a posture to receive, at all risks, the renewed invasion, which he did not delay an instant; for, being presently remounted, I once more felt the smooth hard gristle forcing an entrance, which he achieved rather easier than before. Pained, however, as I was, with his efforts of gaining a complete admission, which he was so regardful as to manage by gentle degrees, I took care not to complain. In the meantime, the soft strait passage gradually loosens, yields, and, stretched to its utmost bearing by the stiff, thick, in-driven engine, sensible at once to the ravishing pleasure of the feel and the pain of the distension, let him in about half way, when all the most nervous activity he now exerted to further his penetration gained him not an inch of his purpose; for, whilst he hesitated there, the crisis of pleasure overtook him, and the close compressure of the warm surrounding fold drew from him the ecstatic gush, even before mine was ready to meet it, kept up by the pain I had endured in the course of the engagement, from the unsufferable size of his weapon, though it was not as yet in above half its length.

I expected then, but without wishing it, that he would draw, but was pleasingly disappointed; for he was not to be let off so. The well-breathed youth, hot-mettled, and flush with genial juices, was now fairly in for making me know my driver. As soon, then, as he had made a short pause, waking, as it were, out of the trance of pleasure (in which every sense seemed lost for a while, whilst, with his eyes shut and short quick breathings, he had yielded down his maiden tribute), he still kept his post, yet unsated with enjoyment, and solacing in these so new delights, till his stiffness, which had scarce perceptibly remitted, being thoroughly recovered to him, who had not once unsheathed, he proceeded afresh to cleave and open to himself an entire entry into me, which was not a little made easy to him by the balsamic injection with which he had just plentifully moistened the whole internals of the passage. Redoubling, then, the active energy of his thrusts, favored by the fervid appetency of my motions, the soft oiled wards can no longer stand so effectual a picklock, but yield and open him an entrance: and now, with conspiring nature and my industry, strong to aid him, he pierces, penetrates, and at length, winning his way inch by inch, gets entirely in, and finally, a home-made thrust, sheathes it up to the guard; on the information of which, from the close jointure of our bodies (insomuch that the hair on both sides perfectly interweaved and encurled together), the eyes of the transported youth sparkled with more joyous fires, and all his looks and motions acknowledged excess of pleasure, which I now began to share, for I felt him in my very vitals! I was quite sick with delight! stirred beyond bearing with its furious agitations within me, and gorged and crammed even to a surfeit: thus I lay gasping, panting, under him, till his broken breathings, faltering accents, eyes twinkling with humid fires, lunges more furious, and an increased stiffness gave me to hail the approaches of the second period:—it came—and the sweet youth, overpowered with ecstasy, died away in my arms, melting in a flood that shot in genial warmth into the innermost recesses of my body, every conduit of which, dedicated to that pleasure, was on flow to mix with it. Thus we continued for some instants, lost, breathless, senseless of everything and in every part but those favorite ones of nature, in which all that we enjoyed of life and sensation was now totally concentered.

When our mutual trance was a little over, and the young fellow had withdrawn that delicious stretcher with which he had most plentifully drowned all thoughts of revenge in the sense of actual pleasure, the widened wounded passage refunded a stream of pearly liquids, which flowed down my thighs, mixed with streaks of blood, the marks of the ravage of that monstrous machine of his, which had now triumphed over a kind of second maidenhead. I stole, however, my handkerchief to those parts and wiped them as dry as I could, whilst he was re-adjusting, and buttoning up.

I made him now sit down by me, and as he had gathered courage from such extreme intimacy, he gave me an aftercourse of pleasure, in a natural burst of tender gratitude and joy, at the new scenes of bliss I had opened to him; scenes positively so new that he had never before had the least acquaintance with that mysterious mark, the cloven stamp of female distinction, though nobody better qualified than he to penetrate into its deepest recesses or do it nobler justice. But when, by certain motions, certain unquietnesses of his hands, that wandered not without design, I found he languished for satisfying a curiosity natural enough, to view and handle those parts which attract and concenter the warmest force of imagination, charmed as I was to have any occasion of obliging and humoring his young desires, I suffered him to proceed as he pleased, without check or control, to the satisfaction of them.

Easily, then, reading in my eyes the full permission of myself to all his wishes, he scarce pleased himself more than me, when, having insinuated his hands under my petticoat and shift, he presently removed those bars to the sight by slily lifting them upwards, under favor of a thousand kisses, which he thought, perhaps, necessary to divert my attention to what he was about. All my drapery being now rolled up to my waist, I threw myself into such a posture upon the couch as gave up to him, in full view, the whole region of delight, and all the luxurious landscape round it. The transported youth devoured everything with his eyes and tried with his fingers to lay more open to his sight the secrets of that dark and delicious deep: he opens the folding lips, the softness of which, yielding entry to anything of a hard body, close round it, and oppose the sight; and feeling further, meets with, and wonders at, a soft fleshy excrescence, which, limber and relaxed after the late enjoyment, now grew, under the touch and examination of his fiery fingers, more and more stiff and considerable, till the titillating ardors of that so sensible part made me sigh as if he had hurt me. On which he withdrew his curious probing fingers, asking me pardon, as it were, in a kiss that rather increased the flame *there*.

Novelty ever makes the strongest impressions, and in pleasures especially: no wonder then that he was swallowed up in raptures of admiration of things so interesting by their nature, and now seen and handled for the first time. On my part, I was richly overpaid for the pleasure I gave him, in that of examining the power of those objects thus abandoned to him, naked and free to his loosest wish, over the artless, natural stripling: his eyes streaming fire, his cheeks glowing with a florid red, his fervid frequent sighs, whilst his hands convulsively squeezed, opened, pressed together again the lips and sides of that deep flesh-wound or gently twitched the over-growing moss; and all proclaimed the excess, the riot of joys, in having his wantonness thus humored. But he did not long abuse my patience, for the objects before him had now put him by all his, and coming out with that formidable machine of his, he lets the fury loose, and pointing it directly to the pouting-lipped mouth that bid him sweet defiance in dumb-show, squeezes in the head, and driving with refreshed rage, breaks in and plugs up the whole passage of that soft pleasure-conduit, where he makes all shake again, and put once more all within me into such an uproar as nothing could still but a fresh inundation from the very engine of those flames, as well as from all the springs with which nature floats that reservoir of joy, when risen to its floodmark.

I was now so bruised, so battered, so spent with this over-match that I could hardly stir or raise myself, but lay palpitating, till the ferment of my senses subsiding by degrees, and the hour striking at which I was obliged to dispatch my young man, I tenderly advised him of the necessity there was for parting, which I felt as much displeasure at as he could do, who seemed eagerly disposed to keep the field, and to enter on a fresh action; but the danger was too great, and after some hearty kisses of leave and recommendations of secrecy and discretion, I forced myself to force him away, not without assurances of seeing him again, to the same purpose, as soon as possible, and thrust a guinea into his hands: not more, lest, being too flush of money, a suspicion or discovery might arise from thence, having everything to fear from the dangerous indiscretion of that age in which young fellows would be too irresistible, too charming, if we had not that terrible fault to guard against.

ENJOYMENT AND TAHITI

Denis Diderot

In his Encylopédie *entry for "enjoyment"* (jouissance), *Diderot unabashedly praises the naturalness of sexual pleasure. This was a recurring theme in his writings, as we see in the second selection below, from his* Supplement to the Voyage of Bougainville *(1772).*

ENJOYMENT, f. n. *(Gram. and Moral.).* To enjoy means to know, to experience, to feel the advantages of possession. One often possesses without *enjoyment.* Who owns these magnificent palaces? Who has planted these immense gardens? The sovereign. But who enjoys them? I do.

Let us leave these magnificent palaces that the sovereign has constructed for other people than himself, these enchanting gardens in which he never walks, and stop to contemplate pleasure that perpetuates the chain of living beings and to which we have consecrated the word *enjoyment.*

Among the objects that nature everywhere offers to our desires, you who have a soul, tell me if there is anything more worthy of your pursuit, anything that can make us happier than the possession and enjoyment of a being who thinks and feels as you do, who has the same ideas, who experiences the same sensations, the same ecstasies, who brings her affectionate and sensitive arms toward yours, who embraces you, whose caresses will be followed with the existence of a new being who will resemble one of you, who will look for you in the first movements of life to hug you, whom you will bring up by your side and love together, who will protect you in old age, who will respect you at all times, and whose happy birth has already strengthened the tie that bound you together?

Crude, insensitive, and unmoved beings who are deprived of life's vital force and who surround us can be useful for our happiness, but without knowing or sharing it; and our sterile and destructive *enjoyment,* which affects all of these people, does not produce any real *enjoyment* in its turn.

If there is a perverse man who could take offense at the praise that I give to the most noble and universal of passions, I would evoke Nature before him, I would make it speak, and Nature would say to him: why do you blush to hear the word pleasure pronounced, when you do not blush to indulge in its temptations under the cover of night? Are you ignorant of its purpose and of what you owe it? Do you believe that your mother would have imperiled her life to give you yours if I had not attached an inexpressible charm to the embraces of her husband? Be quiet, unhappy man, and consider that pleasure pulled you out of nothingness.

The propagation of beings is the greatest object of nature. It imperiously solicits both sexes as soon as they have been granted their share of strength and beauty. A vague and brooding restlessness warns them of the moment; their condition is mixed with pain and pleasure. At that time they listen to their senses and turn their considered attention to themselves. But if an individual should be presented to another individual of the same species and of a different sex, then the feeling of all other needs is suspended: the heart palpitates; the limbs tremble; voluptuous images wander through the mind; a flood of spirits runs through the nerves, excites them, and proceeds to the seat of a new sense that reveals itself and torments the body. Sight is troubled, delirium is born; reason, the slave of instinct, limits itself to serving the latter, and nature is satisfied.

This is the way things took place at the beginning of the world, and the way they still take place in the back of the savage adult's cave.

But when woman began to discriminate, when she appeared to take care in choosing between several men upon whom passion cast her glances, there was one who stopped them, who could flatter himself that he was preferred, who believed that he brought to the heart he esteemed the very esteem that he had for himself, and who considered pleasure as the recompense for some merit; then, when the veils that modesty cast over the charms of a woman allowed an inflamed imagination the power to dispose of them at will, the most delicate illusions competed with the most exquisite of senses to exaggerate the happiness of the moment; the soul was possessed with an almost divine enthusiasm; two young hearts lost in love vowed themselves to each other forever, and heaven heard the first indiscreet oaths.

Yet how many happy moments existed before the one in which the entire soul sought to spring forth and lose itself in the soul of the person loved! *Enjoyment* began the moment that hope was born.

Nevertheless confidence, time, nature, and the freedom of caresses led to the forgetfulness of self; one swore after experiencing the final ecstasy that there was no other person who could be compared to her (or to him); and this was true in these circumstances each time people had sensitive and young organs, a tender heart and an innocent soul unacquainted with either mistrust or remorse.

• • •

In the sharing of Bougainville's crew among the Tahitians, the almoner was allotted to Orou; they were about the same age, thirty-five to thirty-six. Orou had then only his wife and three daughters, called Asto, Palli, and Thia. They undressed the almoner, bathed his face, hands, and feet, and served him a wholesome and frugal meal. When he was about to go to bed, Orou, who had been absent with his family, reappeared, and presenting to him his wife and three daughters, all naked, said: "You have eaten, you are young and in good health; if you sleep alone you will sleep badly, for man needs a companion beside him at night. There is my wife, there are my daughters; choose the one who pleases you best. But if you wish to oblige me you will give preference to the youngest of my daughters, who has not yet had any children." The mother added: "Alas! But it's no good complaining about it; poor Thia! it is not her fault."

The almoner answered that his religion, his office, good morals and decency would not allow him to accept these offers.

Orou replied: "I do not know what this thing is that you call 'religion'; but I can only think ill of it, since it prevents you from tasting an innocent pleasure to which nature, the sovereign mistress, invites us all; prevents you from giving existence to one of your own kind, from doing a service which a father, mother and children all ask of you, from doing something for a host who has received you well, and from enriching a nation, by giving it one more citizen. I do not know what this thing is which you call your 'office,' but your first duty is to be a man and to be grateful. I do not suggest that you should introduce into your country the ways of Orou, but Orou, your host and friend, begs you to lend yourself to the ways of Tahiti. Whether the ways of Tahiti are better or worse than yours is an easy question to decide. Has the land of your birth more people than it can feed? If so, your ways are neither worse nor better than ours. But can it feed more than it has? Our ways are better than yours. As to the sense of decency which you offer as objection, I understand you; I agree that I was wrong, and I ask your pardon. I do not want you to injure your health; if you are tired, you must have rest; but I hope that you will not continue to sadden us. See the care you have made appear on all these faces; they fear lest you should have found blemishes on them which merit your disdain. But when it is only the pleasure of doing honor to one of my daughters, amidst her companions and sisters, and of doing a good action, won't that suffice you? Be generous!"

The Almoner: It's not that: they are all equally beautiful; but my religion! my office!

Orou: They are mine and I offer them to you; they are their own and they give themselves to you. Whatever may be the purity of conscience which the thing "religion" and the thing "office" prescribe, you can accept them without scruple. I am not abusing my authority at all; be sure that I know and respect the rights of the individual.

Here the truthful almoner agrees that Providence had never exposed him to such violent temptation. He was young, he became agitated and tormented; he turned his eyes away from the lovely suppliants, and then regarded them again; he raised his hands and eyes to the sky. Thia, the youngest, clasped his knees and said: "Stranger, do not distress my father and mother, do not afflict me. Honor me in the hut, among my own people; raise me to the rank of my sisters, who mock me. Asto, the eldest, already has three children; the second, Palli, has two; but Thia has none at all. Stranger, honest stranger, do not repulse me; make me a mother, make me a child that I can one day lead by the hand, by my side, here in Tahiti; who may be seen held at my breast in nine months' time; one of whom I shall be so proud and who will be part of my dowry when I go from my parents' hut to another's. I shall perhaps be more lucky with you than with our young Tahitians. If you will grant me this favor I shall never forget you; I shall bless you all my life. I shall write your name on my arm and on your son's; we shall pronounce it always with joy. And when you leave these shores, my good wishes will go with you on the seas till you reach your own land."

The candid almoner said that she clasped his knees, and gazed into his eyes so expressively and so touchingly; that she wept; that her father, mother and sisters withdrew; that he remained alone with her, and that, still saying "my religion, my office," he found himself the next morning lying beside the young girl, who overwhelmed him with caresses, and who invited her parents and sisters, when they came to their bed in the morning, to join their gratitude to hers. Asto and Palli, who had withdrawn, returned bringing food, fruits and drink. They kissed their sister and made vows over her. They all ate together.

Then Orou, left alone with the almoner, said to him: "I see that my daughter is well satisfied with you and I thank you. But would you teach me what is meant by this word 'religion' which you have repeated so many times and so sorrowfully?"

The almoner, after having mused a moment, answered: "Who made your hut and the things which furnish it?"

OROU: I did.

THE ALMONER: Well then, we believe that this world and all that it contains is the work of a maker.

OROU: Has he feet, hands, and a head then?

THE ALMONER: No.

OROU: Where is his dwelling place?

THE ALMONER: Everywhere.

OROU: Here too?

THE ALMONER: Here.

OROU: We have never seen him.

THE ALMONER: One doesn't see him.

OROU: That's an indifferent father then! He must be old, for he will at least be as old as his work.

THE ALMONER: He does not age. He spoke to our ancestors, gave them laws, prescribed the manner in which he wished to be honored; he ordered a certain behavior as being good, and he forbade them certain other actions as being wicked.

OROU: I follow you; and one of the actions he forbade them, as wicked, was to lie with a woman or a girl? Why, then, did he make two sexes?

THE ALMONER: That they might unite; but with certain requisite conditions, after certain preliminary ceremonies in consequence of which the man belongs to the woman and only to her; and the woman belongs to the man, and only to him.

OROU: For their whole lives?

THE ALMONER: For the whole of their lives.

OROU: So that if it happened that a woman should lie with a man other than her husband, or a husband with another woman . . . but that couldn't happen. Since the maker is there and this displeases him, he will know how to prevent them doing it.

THE ALMONER: No; he lets them do it, and they sin against the law of God (for it is thus we call the great maker), against the law of the country; and they commit a crime.

OROU: I should be sorry to offend you by what I say, but if you would permit me, I would give you my opinion.

THE ALMONER: Speak.

OROU: I find these singular precepts opposed to nature and contrary to reason, made to multiply crimes and to plague at every moment this old maker, who has made everything, without help of hands, or head, or tools, who is everywhere and is not seen anywhere, who exists today and tomorrow and yet is not a day older, who commands and is not obeyed, who can prevent and yet does not do so. Contrary to nature because these precepts suppose that a free, thinking and sentient being can be the property of a being like himself. On what is this law founded? Don't you see that in your country they have confused the thing which has neither consciousness nor thought, nor desire, nor will; which one picks up, puts down, keeps or exchanges, without injury to it, or without its complaining, have confused this with the thing which cannot be exchanged or acquired, which has liberty, will, desire, which can give or refuse itself for a moment or forever, which laments and suffers, and which cannot become an article of commerce, without its character being forgotten and violence done to its nature, contrary to the general law of existence? In fact, nothing could appear to you more senseless than a precept which refuses to admit that change which is a part of us, which commands a constancy which cannot be found there, and which violates the liberty of the male and female by chaining them forever to each other; more senseless than a fidelity which limits the most capricious of enjoyments to one individual; than an oath of the immutability of two beings made of flesh; and all that in the face of a sky which never for a moment remains the same, in caverns which threaten destruction, below a rock which falls to powder, at the foot of a tree which cracks, on a stone which rocks? Believe me, you have made the condition of man worse than that of animals. I do not know what your great maker may be; but I rejoice that he has never spoken to our forefathers, and I wish that he may never speak to our children; for he might tell them the same foolishness, and they commit the folly of believing it. Yesterday, at supper, you mentioned "magistrates" and "priests," whose authority regulates your conduct; but, tell me, are they the masters of good and evil? Can they make what is just to be unjust, and unjust, just? Does it rest with them to attribute good to harmful actions, and evil to innocent or useful actions? You could not think it, for, at that rate, there would be neither true nor false, good nor bad, beautiful nor ugly; or at any rate only what pleased your great maker, your magistrates, and your priests to pronounce so. And from one moment to another you would be obliged to change your ideas and your conduct. One day someone would tell you, on behalf of one of your three masters, to kill, and you would be obliged by your conscience to kill; another day, "steal," and you would have to steal; or "do not eat this fruit," and you would not dare to eat it; "I forbid you this vegetable or animal," and you would take care not to touch them. There is no good thing that could not be forbidden you, and no wickedness that you could not be ordered to do. And what would you be reduced to, if your three masters, disagreeing among themselves, should at once permit, enjoin, and forbid you the same thing, as I believe must often happen. Then, to please the priest you must become embroiled with the magistrate; to satisfy the magistrate you must displease the great maker; and to make yourself agreeable to the great maker you must renounce nature. And do you know what will happen then? You will neglect all of them, and you will be neither man, nor citizen, nor pious; you will be nothing; you will be out of favor with all the kinds of authorities, at odds even with yourself, tormented by your heart, persecuted by your enraged masters; and wretched as I saw you yesterday evening when I offered my wife and daughters to you, and you cried out, "But my religion, my office!"

Do you want to know what is good and what is bad in all times and in all places? Hold fast to the nature of things and of actions; to your relations with your fellows; to the influence of your conduct on your individual usefulness and the general good. You are mad if you believe that there is anything, high or low in the universe, which can add to or subtract from the laws of nature. Her eternal will is that good should be preferred to evil, and the general good to the individual good. You may ordain the opposite but you will not be obeyed. You will multiply the number of malefactors and the wretched by fear, punishment, and remorse. You will deprave consciences; you will corrupt minds. They will not know what to do or what to avoid. Disturbed in their state of innocence, at ease with crime, they will have lost their guiding star. Answer me sincerely; in spite of the express orders of your three lawgivers, does a young man, in your country, never lie with a young girl without their permission?

THE ALMONER: I should deceive you if I asserted it.

OROU: Does a woman who has sworn to belong only to her husband never give herself to another man?

THE ALMONER: Nothing is more common.

OROU: Your lawgivers either punish or do not punish; if they punish they are ferocious beasts who fight against nature; if they do not punish, they are imbeciles who have exposed their authority to contempt by an empty prohibition.

THE ALMONER: The culprits who escape the severity of the law are punished by popular condemnation.

OROU: That is to say, justice is exercised through the lack of common sense of the whole nation, and the foolishness of opinion does duty for laws.

THE ALMONER: A girl who has been dishonored will not find a husband.

OROU: Dishonored! Why?

THE ALMONER: An unfaithful wife is more or less despised.

OROU: Despised! But why?

THE ALMONER: The young man is called a cowardly seducer.

OROU: A coward, a seducer! But why?

THE ALMONER: The father and mother and child are desolated. The unfaithful husband is a libertine; the betrayed husband shares his wife's shame.

OROU: What a monstrous tissue of extravagances you've just revealed to me! And yet you don't say everything; for as soon as one allows oneself to dispose at pleasure of the ideas of justice and ownership, to take away or to give an arbitrary character to things, to attribute or deny good or evil to certain actions, capriciously, then one can be censorious, vindictive, suspicious, tyrannical, envious, jealous, deceitful. There is spying, quarreling, cheating, and lying; daughters deceive their parents, wives their husbands. Girls, yes, I don't doubt it, will strangle their infants, suspicious fathers will hate and neglect theirs, mothers will leave them and abandon them to their fates. And crime and debauchery will show themselves in all their forms. I know all that as if I had lived among you. It is so, because it must be so; and your society, of which your leader boasts because of its good regulations, will only be a swarm of hypocrites who secretly trample all laws under foot; or of unfortunates who are themselves the instruments of their own suffering in submitting; or of imbeciles in whom prejudices have quite stifled the voice of nature; or of abnormal monsters in whom nature does not protest her rights.

THE ALMONER: So it would seem. But don't you marry then?

OROU: Yes, we marry.

THE ALMONER: But what does it consist in?

OROU: A mutual consent to live in the same hut and to lie in the same bed for as long as we find it good to do so.

THE ALMONER: And when you find it no longer good?

OROU: We separate.

THE ALMONER: What becomes of the children?

OROU: Oh, stranger! Your last question finally reveals to me the profound misery of your country. You must understand, my friend, that here the birth of a child is always a good fortune, and its death a subject for regret and tears. A child is precious because he ought to become a man; therefore we have a care for it, quite other than for our animals and plants. A child born causes both domestic and public joy. It is an increase of fortune for the hut and of strength for the nation. It means more hands and arms in Tahiti. We see in him a farmer, fisher, hunter, soldier, husband and father. When she returns from her husband's cabin to that of her parents, a woman takes with her the children which she had taken as dowry; those born during their companionship are shared; and as nearly as can be, males and females are divided, so that each one retains an equal number of boys and girls.

CONCERNING THE MORAL SENSE

FRANCIS HUTCHESON

A debate raged among Enlightenment thinkers on whether human beings were motivated principally by self-interest or by some feelings of empathy or benevolence to others. If Mandeville was firmly in the former camp, the Scottish minister and professor of moral philosophy Francis Hutcheson (1694–1746) was a leader of the latter. In this selection from his System of Moral Philosophy *(1755), he provides his school its name, "moral sense."*

There is therefore, as each one by close attention and reflection may convince himself, a natural and immediate determination to approve certain affections, and actions consequent upon them; or a natural sense of immediate excellence in them, not referred to any other quality perceivable by our other senses or by reasoning. When we call this determination a *sense* or *instinct*, we are not supposing it of that low kind dependent on bodily organs, such as even the brutes have. It may be a constant settled determination in the soul itself, as much as our powers of judging and reasoning. And 'tis pretty plain that *reason* is only a subservient power to our ultimate determinations either of perception or will. The ultimate end is settled by some sense, and some determination of will: by some sense we enjoy happiness, and self-love determines to it without reasoning. Reason can only direct to the means; or compare two ends previously constituted by some other immediate powers.

In other animal-kinds each one has instincts toward its proper action, and has the highest enjoyment in following them, even with toil and some pain. Can we suppose mankind void of such principles? as brutes seem not to reflect on their own temper and actions, or that of others, they may feel no more than present delight in following their impulses. But in men, who can make their own tempers and conduct the objects of reflection, the analogy of nature would make one expect a sense, a relish about them, as well as about other objects. To each of our powers we seem to have a corresponding taste or sense, recommending the proper use of it to the agent, and making him relish or value the like exercise of it by another. This we see as to the powers of voice, of imitation, designing, or machinery, motion, reasoning; there is a sense discerning and recommending the proper exercise of them. It would be anomalous in our structure if we had no relish or taste for powers and actions of yet greater importance; if a species of which each one is naturally capable of very contrary affections toward its fellows, and of consequent actions, each one also requiring a constant intercourse of actions with them, and dependent on them for his subsistence, had not an immediate relish for such affections and actions as the interest of the system requires. Shall an immediate sense recommend the proper use of the inferior powers, and yet shall we allow no natural relish for that of the superior?

As some others of our immediate perceptive powers are capable of culture and improvement, so is this moral sense, without presupposing any reference to a superior power of reason to which their perceptions are to be referred. We once had pleasure in the simple artless tunes of the vulgar. We indulge ourselves in music; we meet with finer and more complex compositions. In these we find a pleasure much higher, and begin to despise what formerly pleased us. A judge, from the motions of pity, gets many criminals acquitted: we approve this sweet tenderness of heart. But we find that violence and outrages abound; the sober, just, and industrious are plagued, and have no security. A more extensive view of a public interest shows some sorts of pity to occasion more extensive misery, than arises from a strict execution of justice. Pity of itself never appears deformed; but a more extensive affection, a love to society, a zeal to promote general happiness, is a more lovely principle, and the want of this renders a character deformed. This only shows, what we shall presently confirm, that among the several affections approved there are many degrees: some much more lovely than others. 'Tis thus alone we correct any apparent disorders in this *moral faculty*, even as we correct our reason itself. As we improve and correct a low taste for harmony by enuring the ear to finer compositions; a low taste for beauty, by presenting the finer works, which yield an higher pleasure; so we improve our *moral taste* by presenting larger systems to our mind, and more extensive affections toward them; and thus finer objects are exhibited to the moral faculty, which it will approve, even when these affections oppose the effect of some narrower affections, which considered by themselves would be truly lovely. No need here of reference to an higher power of perception, or to reason.

Is not our reason itself also often wrong, when we rashly conclude from imperfect or partial evidence? must there be an higher power too to correct our reason? no; presenting more fully all the evidence on both sides, by serious attention, or the best exercise of the reasoning power, corrects the hasty judgment. Just so in the moral perceptions.

This moral sense from its very nature appears to be designed for regulating and controlling all our powers. This dignity and commanding nature we are immediately conscious of, as we are conscious of the power itself. Nor can such matters of immediate feeling be otherways proved but by appeals to our hearts. It does not estimate the good it recommends as merely differing in degree, tho' of the same kind with other advantages recommended by other senses, so as to allow us to practice smaller moral evils acknowledged to remain such, in order to obtain some great advantages of other sorts; or to omit what we judge in the present case to be our duty or morally good, that we may decline great evils of another sort. But as we immediately perceive the difference in kind, and that the dignity of enjoyment from fine poetry, painting, or from knowledge is superior to the pleasures of the palate, were they never so delicate; so we immediately discern moral good to be superior in kind and dignity to all others which are perceived by the other perceptive powers.

In all other grateful perceptions, the less we shall relish our taste, the greater sacrifice we have made of inferior enjoyments to the superior; and our sense of the superior, after the first flutter of joy in our success is over, is not a whit increased by any sacrifice we have made to it: nay in the judgment of spectators, the superior enjoyment, or our state at least, is generally counted the worse on this account, and our conduct the less relished. Thus in sacrificing ease, or health, or pleasure, to wealth, power, or even to the ingenious arts; their pleasures gain no dignity by that means; and the conduct is not more alluring to others. But in moral good, the greater the necessary sacrifice was which was made to it, the moral excellence increases the more, and is the more approved by the agent, more admired by spectators, and the more they are roused to imitation. By this sense the heart can not only approve itself in sacrificing every other gratification to moral goodness, but have the highest self-enjoyment, and approbation of its own disposition in doing so: which plainly shows this moral sense to be naturally destined to command all the other powers.

To acknowledge the several generous ultimate affections of a limited kind to be natural, and yet maintain that we have no general controlling principle but self-love, which indulges or checks the generous affections as they conduce to, or oppose, our own noblest interest; sometimes allowing these kind affections their full exercise, because of that high enjoyment we expect to ourselves in gratifying them; at other times checking them, when their gratification does not over-balance the loss we may sustain by it; is a scheme which brings indeed all the powers of the mind into one direction by means of the reference made of them all to the calm desire of our own happiness, in our previous deliberations about our conduct: and it may be justly alleged that the Author of Nature has made a connection in the event at last between our gratifying our generous affections, and our own highest interest. But the feelings of our heart, reasons, and history, revolt against this account: which seems however to have been maintained by excellent authors and strenuous defenders of the cause of virtue.

This connection of our own highest interests with the gratifying our generous affections, in many cases is imperceptible to the mind; and the kind heart acts from its generous impulse, not thinking of its own interest. Nay all its own interests have sometimes appeared to it as opposite to, and inconsistent with the generous part, in which it persisted. Now were there no other calm original determination of soul but that toward one's own interest, that man must be approved entirely who steadily pursues his own happiness, in opposition to all kind affections and all public interest. That which is the sole calm determination, must justify every action in consequence of it, however opposite to particular kind affections. If it be said that " 'tis a mistake to imagine our interest opposite to them while there is a good providence": grant it to be a mistake; this is only a defect of reasoning; but that disposition of mind must upon this scheme be approved which coolly sacrifices the interest of the universe to its own interest. This is plainly contrary to the feelings of our hearts.

Can that be deemed the sole ultimate determination, the sole ultimate end, which the mind in the exercise of its noblest powers can calmly resolve, with inward approbation, deliberately to counteract? are there not instances of men who have voluntarily sacrificed their lives, without thinking of any other state of existence, for the sake of their friends or their country? does not every heart approve this temper and conduct, and admire it the more, the less presumption there is of the love of glory and posthumous fame, or of any sublimer private interest mixing itself with the generous affection? does not the admiration rise higher, the more deliberately such resolutions are formed and executed? all this is unquestionably true, and yet would be absurd and impossible if self-interest of any kind is the sole ultimate termination of all calm desire. There is therefore another ultimate determination which our souls are capable of, destined to be also an original spring of the calmest and most deliberate purposes of action; a desire of communicating happiness, an ultimate good-will, not referred to any private interest, and often operating without such reference.

In those cases where some inconsistency appears between these two determinations, the moral faculty at once points out and recommends the glorious, the amiable part; not by suggesting prospects of future interests of a sublime sort by pleasures of self-approbation, or of praise. It recommends the generous part by an immediate undefinable perception; it approves the kind ardor of the heart in the sacrificing even of life itself, and that even in those who have no hopes of surviving, or no attention to a future life in another world. And thus, where the moral sense is in its full vigor, it makes the generous determination to public happiness the supreme one in the soul, with that commanding power which it is naturally destined to exercise.

It must be obvious we are not speaking here of the ordinary condition of mankind, as if these calm determinations were generally exercised, and habitually controlled the particular passions; but of the condition our nature can be raised to by due culture; and of the principles which may and ought to operate, when by attention we present to our minds the objects or representations fit to excite them. Doubtless some good men have exercised in life only the particular kind affections, and found a constant approbation of them, without either the most extensive views of the whole system, or the most universal benevolence. Scarce any of the vicious have ever considered wherein it is that their highest private happiness consists, and in consequence of it exerted the calm rational self-love; but merely follow inconsiderately the selfish appetites and affections. Much less have all good men made actual references of all private or generous affections to the extensive benevolence, tho' the mind can make them; or bad men made references of all their affections to calm self-love.

But as the selfish principles are very strong, and by custom, by early and frequent indulgences, and other causes, are raised in the greatest part of men above their due proportion, while the generous principles are little cultivated, and the moral sense often asleep; our powers of reasoning and comparing the several enjoyments which our nature is capable of, that we may discover which of them are of greatest consequence to our happiness; our capacity, by reasoning, of arriving to the knowledge of a *Governing Mind* presiding in this world, and of a moral administration, are of the highest consequence and necessity to preserve our affections in a just order, and to corroborate our *moral faculty:* as by such reasoning and reflection we may discover a perfect consistency of all the generous motions of the soul with private interest, and find out a certain tenor of life and action the most effectually subservient to both these determinations.

THE IMPARTIAL SPECTATOR

Adam Smith

Known today primarily as an economic theorist, Adam Smith (1723–1790) was also an important Enlightenment writer on ethics. Professor of moral philosophy at Glasgow, he published in 1759 The Theory of Moral Sentiments, *which offers a very different picture of the place of self-interest than that found in his economic writings. His theory of sympathy and of the "impartial spectator" in these excerpts place him firmly in the Scottish "moral sense" school.*

The principle by which we naturally either approve or disapprove of our own conduct seems to be altogether the same with that by which we exercise the like judgments concerning the conduct of other people. We either approve or disapprove of the conduct of another man according as we feel that when we bring his case home to ourselves we either can or cannot entirely sympathize with the sentiments and motives which directed it. And in the same manner we either approve or disapprove of our own conduct according as we feel that when we place ourselves in the situation of another man and view it, as it were, with his eyes and from his station, we either can or cannot entirely enter into and sympathize with the sentiments and motives which influenced it. We can never survey our own sentiments and motives, we can never form any judgment concerning them unless we remove ourselves, as it were, from our own natural station and endeavor to view them as at a certain distance from us. But we can do this in no other way than by endeavoring to view them with the eyes of other people, or as other people are likely to view them. Whatever judgment we can form concerning them, accordingly, must always bear some secret reference either to what are or to what upon a certain condition would be, or to what, we imagine, ought to be the judgment of others. We endeavor to examine our own conduct as we imagine any other fair and impartial spectator would examine it. If, upon placing ourselves in his situation, we thoroughly enter into all the passions and motives which influenced it, we approve of it by sympathy with the approbation of this supposed equitable judge. If otherwise, we enter into his disapprobation and condemn it.

Were it possible that a human creature could grow up to manhood in some solitary place, without any communication with his own species, he could no more think of his own character, of the propriety or demerit of his own sentiments and conduct, of the beauty or deformity of his own mind, than of the beauty or deformity of his own face. All these are objects which he cannot easily see, which naturally he does not look at and with regard to which he is provided with no mirror which can present them to his view. Bring him into society, and he is immediately provided with the mirror which he wanted before. It is placed in the countenance and behavior of those he lives with which always mark when they enter into and when they disapprove of his sentiments; and it is here that he first views the propriety and impropriety of his own passions, the beauty and deformity of his own mind. To a man who from his birth was a stranger to society, the objects of his passions, the external bodies which either pleased or hurt him, would occupy his whole attention. The passions themselves, the desires or aversions, the joys or sorrows, which those objects excited, though of all things the most immediately present to him, could scarce ever be the objects of his thoughts. The idea of them could never interest him so much as to call upon his attentive consideration. The consideration of his joy could in him excite no new joy, nor that of his sorrow any new sorrow, though the consideration of the causes of those passions might often excite both. Bring him into society and all his own passions will immediately become the causes of new passions. He will observe that mankind approve of some of them and are disgusted by others. He will be elevated in the one case and cast down in the other; his desires and aversions, his joys and sorrows, will now often become the causes of new desires and new aversions, new joys, and new sorrows: they will now, therefore, interest him deeply and often call upon his most attentive consideration.

Our first ideas of personal beauty and deformity are drawn from the shape and appearance of others, not from our own. We soon become sensible, however, that others exercise the same criticism upon us. We are pleased when they approve of our figure and are disobliged when they seem to be disgusted. We become anxious to know how far our appearance deserves either their blame or approbation. We examine our persons limb by limb, and by placing ourselves before a looking-glass, or by some such expedient, endeavor, as much as possible, to view ourselves at the distance and with the eyes of other people. If after this examination we are satisfied with our own appearance, we can more easily support the most disadvantageous judgments of others. If, on the contrary, we are sensible that we are the natural objects of distaste, every appearance of their disapprobation mortifies us beyond all measure. A man who is tolerably handsome will allow you to laugh at any little irregularity in his person; but all such jokes are commonly unsupportable to one who is really deformed. It is evident, however, that we are anxious about our own beauty and deformity only upon account of its effect upon others. If we had no connection with society, we should be altogether indifferent about either.

In the same manner our first moral criticisms are exercised upon the characters and conduct of other people, and we are all very forward to observe how each of these affects us. But we soon learn that other people are equally frank with regard to our own. We become anxious to know how far we deserve their censure or applause, and whether to them we must necessarily appear those agreeable or disagreeable creatures which they represent us. We become anxious to know how far we deserve their censure or applause, and whether to them we must necessarily appear those agreeable or disagreeable creatures which they represent us. We begin, upon this account, to examine our own passions and conduct and to consider how these must appear to them by considering how they would appear to us if in their situation. We suppose ourselves the spectators of our own behavior and endeavor to imagine what effect it would, in this light, produce upon us. This is the only looking-glass by which we can, in some measure, with the eyes of other people, scrutinize the propriety of our own conduct. If in this view it pleases us, we are tolerably satisfied. We can be more indifferent about the applause, and, in some measure, despise the censure of the world; secure that, however misunderstood or misrepresented, we are the natural and proper objects of approbation. On the contrary, if we are doubtful about it, we are often, upon that very account, more anxious to gain their approbation and provided we have not already, as they say, shaken hands with infamy, we are altogether distracted at the thought of their censure which then strikes us with double severity.

When I endeavor to examine my own conduct, when I endeavor to pass sentence upon it, and either to approve or condemn it, it is evident that in all such cases I divide myself, as it were, into two persons, and that I, the examiner and judge, represent a different character from that other I, the person whose conduct is examined into and judged of. The first is the spectator, whose sentiments with regard to my own conduct I endeavor to enter into, by placing myself in his situation, and by considering how it would appear to me, when seen from that particular point of view. The second is the agent, the person whom I properly call myself, and of whose conduct, under the character of a spectator, I was endeavoring to form some opinion. The first is the judge; the second the person judged of. But that the judge should, in every respect, be the same with the person judged of is as impossible as that the cause should, in every respect, be the same with the effect.

To be amiable and to be meritorious, that is, to deserve love and to deserve reward, are the great characters of virtue; and to be odious and punishable, of vice. But all these characters have an immediate reference to the sentiments of others. Virtue is not said to be amiable, or to be meritorious because it is the object of its own love, or of its own gratitude, but because it excites those sentiments in other men. The consciousness that it is the object of such favorable regards is the source of that inward tranquility and self-satisfaction with which it is naturally attended, as the suspicion of the contrary gives occasion to the torments of vice. What so great happiness as to be beloved and to know that we deserve to be beloved? What so great misery as to be hated and to know that we deserve to be hated? . . .

As the love and admiration which we naturally conceive for some characters dispose us to wish to become ourselves the proper objects of such agreeable sentiments; so the hatred and contempt which we as naturally conceive for others dispose us, perhaps still more strongly, to dread the very thought of resembling them in any respect. Neither is it, in this case too, so much the thought of being hated and despised that we are afraid of as that of being hateful and despicable. We dread the thought of doing any thing which can render us the just and proper objects of the hatred and contempt of our fellow creatures; even though we had the most perfect security that those sentiments were never actually to be exerted against us. The man who has broken through all those measures of conduct which can alone render him agreeable to mankind, though he should have the most perfect assurance that what he had done was for ever to be concealed from every human eye, it is all to no purpose. When he looks back upon it and views it in the light in which the impartial spectator would view it, he finds that he can enter into none of the motives which influenced it. He is abashed and confounded at the thought of it and necessarily feels a very high degree of that shame which he would be exposed to, if his actions should ever come to be generally known. His imagination, in this case, too, anticipates the contempt and derision from which nothing saves him but the ignorance of those he lives with. He still feels that he is the natural object of these sentiments and still trembles at the thought of what he would suffer if they were ever actually exerted against him. But if what he had been guilty of was not merely one of those improprieties which are the objects of simple disapprobation, but one of those enormous crimes which excite detestation and resentment, he could never think of it as long as he had any sensibility left without feeling all the agony of horror and remorse; and though he could be assured that no man was ever to know it, and could even bring himself to believe that there was no God to revenge it, he would still feel enough of both these sentiments to embitter the whole of his life: he would still regard himself as the natural object of the hatred and indignation of all his fellow creatures; and if his heart was not grown callous by the habit of crimes, he could not think without terror and astonishment even of the manner in which mankind would look upon him, of what would be the expression of their countenance and of their eyes, if the dreadful truth should ever come to be known. These natural pangs of an affrighted conscience are the demons, the avenging furies, which, in this life, haunt the guilty, which allow them neither quiet nor repose, which often drive them to despair and distraction, from which no assurance of secrecy can protect them, from which no principle of irreligion can entirely deliver them, and from which nothing can free them but the vilest and most abject of all states, a complete insensibility to honor and infamy, to vice and virtue. Men of the most detestable characters, who in the execution of the most dreadful crimes had taken their measures so coolly as to avoid even the suspicion of guilt have sometimes been driven by the horror of their situation to discover of their own accord what no human sagacity could ever have investigated. By acknowledging their guilt, by submitting themselves to the resentment of their offended fellow citizens, and by thus satiating that vengeance of which they were sensible that they had become the proper objects they hoped by their death to reconcile themselves, at least in their own imagination, to the natural sentiments of mankind; to be able to consider themselves as less worthy of hatred and resentment; to atone in some measure for their crimes and by thus becoming the objects, rather of compassion than of horror, if possible to die in peace, and with the forgiveness of all their fellow creatures. Compared to what they felt before the discovery, even the thought of this, it seems, was happiness.

Let us suppose that the great empire of China, with all its myriads of inhabitants, was suddenly swallowed up by an earthquake, and let us consider how a man of humanity in Europe, who had no sort of connection with that part of the world, would be affected upon receiving intelligence of this dreadful calamity. He would, I imagine, first of all express very strongly his sorrow for the misfortune of that unhappy people, he would make many melancholy reflections upon the precariousness of human life and the vanity of all the labors of man, which could thus be annihilated in a moment. He would, too, perhaps, if he was a man of speculation, enter into many reasonings concerning the effects which this disaster might produce upon the commerce of Europe and the trade and business of the world in general. And when all this fine philosophy was over, when all these humane sentiments had been once fairly expressed, he would pursue his business or his pleasure, take his repose or his diversion with the same ease and tranquility as if no such accident had happened. The most frivolous disaster which could befall himself would occasion a more real disturbance. If he were to lose his little finger tomorrow, he would not sleep tonight; but, provided he never saw them, he will snore with the most profound security over the ruin of a hundred millions of his brethren and the destruction of that immense multitude seems plainly an object less interesting to him than this paltry misfortune of his own. To prevent, therefore, this paltry misfortune to himself, would a man of humanity be willing to sacrifice the lives of a hundred millions of his brethren provided he had never seen them? Human nature startles with horror at the thought, and the world, in its greatest depravity and corruption, never produced such a villain as could be capable of entertaining it. But what makes this difference? When our passive feelings are almost always so sordid and so selfish, how comes it that our active principles should often be so generous and so noble? When we are always so much more deeply affected by whatever concerns ourselves than by whatever concerns other men, what is it which prompts the generous upon all occasions, and the mean upon many, to sacrifice their own interests to the greater interests of others? It is not the soft power of humanity, it is not that feeble spark of benevolence which nature has lighted up in the human heart that is thus capable of counteracting the strongest impulses of self-love. It is a stronger power, a more forcible motive, which exerts itself upon such occasions. It is reason, principle, conscience, the inhabitant of the breast, the man within, the great judge, and arbiter of our conduct. It is he who whenever we are about to act so as to affect the happiness of others calls to us with a voice capable of astonishing the most presumptuous of our passions that we are but one of the multitude in no respect better than any other in it; and that when we prefer ourselves so shamefully and so blindly to others, we become the proper objects of resentment, abhorrence, and execration. It is from him only that we learn the real littleness of ourselves, and of whatever relates to ourselves, and the natural misrepresentations of self-love can be corrected only by the eye of this impartial spectator. It is he who shows us the propriety of generosity and the deformity of injustice, the propriety of resigning the greatest interests of our own for the yet greater interests of others, and the deformity of doing the smallest injury to another in order to obtain the greatest benefit to ourselves. It is not the love of our neighbor, it is not the love of mankind, which upon many occasions prompts us to the practice of those divine virtues. It is a stronger love, a more powerful affection, which generally takes place upon such occasions; the love of what is honorable and noble, of the grandeur and dignity and superiority of our own characters.

—

In solitude, we are apt to feel too strongly whatever relates to ourselves; we are apt to overrate the good offices we may have done and the injuries we may have suffered; we are apt to be too much elated by our own good and too much dejected by our own bad fortune. The conversation of a friend brings us to a better, that of a stranger to a still better temper. The man within the breast, the abstract and ideal spectator of our sentiments and conduct, requires often to be awakened and put in mind of his duty, by the presence of the real spectator; and it is always from that spectator, from whom we can expect the least sympathy and indulgence, that we are likely to learn the most complete lesson of self-command.

A TREATISE ON MAN

CLAUDE-ADRIEN HELVÉTIUS

Very much a proponent of the self-interest school was Helvétius (1715–1771), one of the most outspoken of the French philosophes. *His discussion of the centrality of pleasure and pain in his* A Treatise on Man: His Intellectual Faculties and His Education, *published the year after he died, would greatly influence Jeremy Bentham and the Utilitarian school in general.*

What is here said will be sufficient to convince the discerning reader, that every idea and every judgment may be reduced to a sensation. It would be therefore unnecessary, in order to explain the different operations of the mind, to admit a faculty of judging and comparing distinct from the faculty of sensation. But what, it may be asked, is the principle or motive that makes us compare objects with each other, and gives us the necessary attention to observe their relations? Interest, which is in like manner, as I am going to show, an effect of corporeal sensibility. . . .

All comparison of objects with each other supposes attention, all attention a trouble, and all trouble a motive for exerting it. If there could exist a man without desire, he would not compare any objects, or pronounce any judgment; but he might still judge of the immediate impressions of objects on himself, supposing their impressions to be strong. Their strength becoming a motive to attention, would carry with it a judgment. It would not be the same if the sensation were weak; he would then have no knowledge or remembrance of the judgment it had occasioned. A man surrounded by an infinity of objects, must necessarily be affected by an infinity of sensations, and consequently form an infinity of judgments; but he forms them unknown to himself. Why? Because these judgments are of the same nature with the sensations. If they make an impression that is effaced as soon as made, the judgments formed on these impressions are of the same sort; they leave no remembrance. There is in fact no man who does not, without perceiving it, make every day an infinity of reasonings, of which he is not conscious. I will take, for example, those that attend almost all the rapid motions of our bodies. . . .

It results from the contents of this chapter, that all judgments formed by comparing objects with each other, suppose an interest in us to compare them. Now that interest, necessarily founded on our love of happiness, cannot be anything else than the effect of bodily sensibility; because there all our pleasures, and all our pains have their source. This question being discussed, I conclude that corporeal pains and pleasures are the unknown principles of all human actions.

Action

It is to clothe himself and adorn his mistress, or his wife, to procure them amusements, to support himself and his family, in a word to enjoy the pleasures attached to the gratification of bodily desires that the artisan and the peasant thinks, contrives, and labors. Corporeal sensibility is therefore the sole mover of man, he is consequently susceptible, as I am going to prove, but of two sorts of pleasures and pains, the one are present bodily pains and pleasures, the other are the pains and pleasures of foresight or memory.

Pain

I know but two sorts of pain, that which we feel, and that which we foresee. I die of hunger; I feel a present pain. I foresee that I shall soon die of hunger. I feel a pain by foresight, the strength of whose impression is in proportion to the proximity and severity of the pain. The criminal who is going to the scaffold, feels yet no torment, but the foresight that constitutes his present punishment, is begun.

Remorse

Remorse is nothing more than a foresight of bodily pain, to which some crime has exposed us: and is consequently the effect of bodily sensibility. We tremble at the description of the flames, the wheels, the fiery scourges, which the heated imagination of the painter or the poet represents. Is a man without fear, and above the law? He feels no remorse from the commission of a wicked action; provided, however, that he have not previously contracted a virtuous habit; for then he will not pursue a contrary conduct, without feeling an uneasiness, a secret inquietude, to which is also given the name of remorse. Experience tells us, that every action which does not expose us to legal punishment, or to dishonor, is an action, performed in general without remorse. Solon and Plato loved women and even boys, and avowed it. Theft was not punished in Sparta: and the Lacedaemonians robbed without remorse. The princes of the East can, with impunity, load their subjects with taxes, and they do it effectually. The inquisitor can with impunity burn any person who does not think as he does, on certain metaphysical points, and it is without remorse that he gluts his vengeance by hideous torments, for the slight offense that is given to his vanity by the contradiction of a Jew or an Infidel. Remorse, therefore, owes its existence to the fear of punishment or of shame, which is always reducible, as I have already said to a bodily sensation.

Friendship

From bodily sensibility flow in like manner, the tears that bathe the urn of my friend. I lament the loss of the man whose conversation relieved me from disquietude, from that disagreeable sensation of the soul, which actually produces bodily pain: I deplore him who exposed his life and fortune to save me from sorrow and destruction; who was incessantly employed in promoting my felicity, and increasing it by every sort of pleasure. When a man enters into himself, when he examines the bottom of his soul, he perceives nothing in all these sentiments but the development of bodily pain and pleasure. What cannot this pain produce? It is by this medium that the magistrate enchains vice, and disarms the assassin.

Pleasure

There are two sorts of pleasures, as there are two sorts of pains: the one is the present bodily pleasure, the other is that of foresight. Does a man love fine slaves and beautiful paintings? If he discovers a treasure he is transported. He does not, however, yet feel any bodily pleasure, you will say. It is true; but he gains at that moment, the means of procuring the objects of his desires. Now this foresight of an approaching pleasure, is in fact an actual pleasure: for without the love of fine slaves and paintings, he would have been entirely unconcerned at the discovery of the treasure.

The pleasures of foresight, therefore, constantly suppose the existence of the pleasures of the senses. It is the hopes of enjoying my mistress to-morrow that makes me happy to-day. Foresight or memory converts into an actual enjoyment the acquisition of every means proper to procure pleasure. From what motive in fact, do I feel an agreeable sensation every time I obtain a new degree of esteem, of importance, riches, and above all, of power? It is because I esteem power as the most sure means of increasing my happiness.

Power

Men love themselves: they all desire to be happy, and think their happiness would be complete, if they were invested with a degree of power sufficient to procure them every sort of pleasure. The love of power therefore takes its source from the love of pleasure.

Suppose a man absolutely insensible. But, it will be said, he must then be without ideas, and consequently a mere statue. Be it so: but allow that he may exist, and even think. Of what consequence would the scepter of a monarch be to him? None. In fact, what could the most immense power add to the felicity of a man without feeling.

If power be so coveted by the ambitious, it is as the means of acquiring pleasure. Power is like gold, a money. The effect of power, and of a bill of exchange is the same. If I be in possession of such a bill, I receive at London or Paris a hundred thousand crowns, and consequently all the pleasures that sum can procure. Am I in possession of a letter of authority or command? I draw in like manner from my fellow-citizens, a like quantity of provisions or pleasures. The effects of riches and power are in a manner the same: for riches are power. . . .

The general conclusion of this chapter, is, that in man all is sensation: a truth of which I shall give a fresh proof, by showing that his sociability is nothing more than a consequence of the same sensations.

Of Sociability

Man is by nature a devourer of fruits and of flesh; but he is weak, unarmed, and consequently exposed to the voracity of animals stronger than himself. Man, therefore, to avoid the fury of the tiger and the lion, was forced to unite with man. The object of this union was to attack and kill other animals, either to feed on them, or to prevent their consuming the fruits and herbs that served him for nourishment. In the meantime mankind multiplied, and to support themselves, they were obliged to cultivate the earth; but to induce them to this, it became necessary to stipulate, that the harvest should belong to the husbandman. For this purpose the inhabitants made agreements or laws among themselves. These laws strengthened the bonds of a union, that, founded on their wants, was the immediate effect of corporeal sensibility. But cannot this sociability be regarded as an innate quality, a species of amiable morality? All that we learn from experience on this head, is, that in man, as in other animals, sociability is the effect of want. If the desire of defending themselves makes the grazing animals as horses, bulls, &c. assemble in herds; that of chasing, attacking, and conquering their prey, forms in like manner a society of carnivorous animals, such as foxes and wolves.

Interest and want are the principles of all sociability. It is, therefore, these principles alone (of which few writers have given clear ideas) that unite men among themselves: and the force of their union is always in proportion to that of habit and want. From the moment the young savage, or the young bear, is able to provide for his nourishment and his defense, the one quits the hut, and the other the den of his parents. The eagle, in like manner, drives away her young ones from the nest, the moment they have sufficient strength to dart upon their prey, and live without her aid.

The bond that attaches children to their parents, and parents to their children, is less strong than is commonly imagined. A too great strength in this bond would be even fatal to societies. The first regard of a citizen should be for the laws, and the public prosperity; I speak it with regret, filial affection should be in man subordinate to the love of patriotism. If this last affection do not take place of all others, where shall we find a measure of virtue and vice? It would then be no more, and all morality would be abolished.

For what reason, in fact, has justice and the love of God been recommended to men, above all things? On account of the danger to which a too great love of their parents would expose them. If the excess of this passion were sanctioned; if it were declared the principal attachment, a son would then have a right to rob his neighbor, or plunder the public treasury, to supply the wants, and promote the comforts of his father. Every family would form a little nation, and these nations having opposite interests, would be continually at war with each other.

Every writer, who to give us a good opinion of his own heart, founds the sociability of man on any other principle, than that of bodily and habitual wants, deceives weak minds, and gives them a false idea of morality.

Nature, no doubt, designed that gratitude and habit should form in man a sort of gravitation, by which they should be impelled to a love of their parents: but it has also designed that man should have, in the natural desire of independence, a repulsive power, which should diminish the too great force of that gravitation. Thus the daughter joyfully leaves the house of her mother to go to that of her husband; and the son quits with pleasure his native spot, for an employment in India, an office in a distant country, or merely for the pleasure of traveling.

Notwithstanding the pretended force of sentiment, friendship, and habit, mankind change at Paris, every day, the part of the town, their acquaintance and their friends. Do men seek to make dupes? They exaggerate the force of sentiment and friendship, they represent sociability as *an innate affection or principle.* Can they, in reality, forget that there is but one principle of this kind, which is corporeal sensibility? It is to this principle alone, that we owe our self-love, and the powerful love of independence: if men were, as it is said, drawn toward each other by a strong and mutual attraction, would the heavenly Legislator have commanded them to love each other, and to honor their parents? Would he not have left this point to nature, which, without the aid of any law, obliges men to eat and drink when they are hungry and thirsty, to open their eyes to the light, and keep their hands out of the fire.

Travelers do not inform us that the love which mankind bear to their fellows, is so common as pretended. The sailor, escaped from a wreck, and cast on an unknown coast, does not run with open arms to embrace the first man he meets. On the contrary, he hides himself in a thicket, where he observes the manners of the inhabitants, and then presents himself trembling before them.

But if a European vessel chance to approach an unknown island, do not the savages, it is said, run in crowds towards the ship? They are, without doubt, amazed at the sight, they are struck with the novelty of our dress, our arms and implements. The appearance excites their curiosity. But what desire succeeds to this first sensation? That of possessing the objects of their admiration. They become less gay and more thoughtful; are busied in contriving means to obtain, by force or fraud, the objects of their desires: for that purpose they watch the favorable opportunity to rob, plunder, and massacre the Europeans, who, in their conquests of Mexico and Peru, gave them early examples of similar injustice and cruelty.

The conclusion of this chapter is, that the principles of morality and politics, like those of all other sciences, ought to be established on a great number of facts and observations. Now, what is the result of the observations hitherto made on morality? That the love of men for their brethren is the effect of the necessity of mutual assistance, and of an affinity of wants, dependent on that corporeal sensibility, which I regard as the principle of our actions, our virtues, and our vices. . . .

Of the Goodness of Man in the Cradle

I love you, O my fellow citizens! and my chief desire is to be useful to you. I doubtless desire your approbation; but shall I owe your esteem and applause to a lie? A thousand others will deceive you; I shall not be their accomplice. Some will say you are good, and flatter the desire you have to think yourselves so: believe them not. Others will say you are wicked, and in like manner will say false. You are neither the one nor the other.

No individual is born good or bad. Men are the one or the other, according as a similar or opposite interest unites or divides them. Philosophers suppose men to be born in a state of war. A common desire to possess the same things arms them from the cradle, say they, against each other.

The state of war, without doubt, closely follows the instant of their birth. The peace between them is of short duration. They are not however both enemies. Goodness or badness is an incident to them; it is the consequence of their good or bad laws. What we call in man his goodness or moral sense, is his benevolence to others; and that benevolence is always proportionate to the utility they are of to him. I prefer my countrymen to strangers, and my friends to my countrymen. The prosperity of my friend is reflected on me. If he becomes more rich and powerful, I participate in his riches and power. Benevolence to others is therefore the effect of love for ourselves. Now if self-love, as I have proved in the fourth section, be the necessary effect of the faculty of sensation our love for others, whatever the Shaftesburians may say, is in like manner the effect of the same faculty.

What in fact is that original goodness or moral sense, so much boasted of by the English? What clear idea can we form of such a sense and on what fact do we found its existence? On the goodness of men? But there are also persons who are envious and liars, *omnis homo mendax*. Will they say in consequence, that those men have in them an immoral sense of envy, and a lying sense. Nothing is more absurd than this theological philosophy of Shaftesbury; and yet the greatest part of the English are as fond of it as the French were formerly of their music. It is not the same with other nations. No stranger can understand the one or bear the other. It is a web on the eye of the English. It must be taken away before they can see clearly.

According to their philosophy, the man indifferent and seated at his ease, desires the happiness of others: but as being indifferent, he does not, and cannot desire any thing. The states of desire and indifference are contradictory. Perhaps the state of perfect indifference is even impossible. Experience teaches us that man is born neither good nor bad: that his happiness is not necessarily connected with the misery of others:

that on the contrary, from a good education, the idea of my own happiness will be always more or less closely connected in my memory with that of my fellow-citizens; and that the desire of the one will produce in me the desire of the other: whence it follows, that the love of his neighbor is in every individual the effect of the love of himself. The most clamorous declaimers for original goodness have not moreover been always the greatest benefactors to humanity.

When the welfare of England was at stake, the idle Shaftesbury, that ardent apostle of the beauty of morality, would not, we are told, even go to the parliament-house to save it. It was not the sense of the beauty of morality, but the love of glory and of their country that formed Horatius Cocles, Brutus, and Scaevola. The English philosophers will in vain tell me that beauty of morality is a sense that is developed with the human fetus, and in a certain time, renders man compassionate to the misfortune of his brethren. I can form an idea of my five senses, and of the organs by which they are produced; but I confess I have no more idea of a moral sense, than of a moral castle and elephant.

How long will men continue to use words that are void of meaning, and that not conveying any clear and determinate idea, ought to be forever banished to the schools of theology. Do they mean by this moral sense that sentiment of compassion felt at the sight of an unhappy object? But to compassionate another man's miseries, we must first know what he suffers, and for that purpose must have felt pain. A compassion on report supposes also a knowledge of misery. Which are the evils moreover that in general we are most sensible of? Those which we suffer with the most impatience, and the remembrance of which is consequently the most habitually present to us. Compassion therefore is not an innate sentiment.

What do I feel at the presence of an unhappy person? A strong emotion. What produces it? The remembrance of pains to which men are subject, and to which I myself am exposed: such an idea troubles me, makes me uneasy, and as long as the unfortunate person is present I am afflicted. When I have assisted him, and see him no more, a calm takes place insensibly in my mind; for in proportion as he is distant from me, the remembrance of the miseries that his presence recalled, insensibly vanishes: when therefore I was afflicted at his presence, it was for myself I was afflicted. Which in fact are the evils I commiserate most. They are, as I have already said, not only those I have felt, but those I may still feel: those evils being most present to my memory, strike me most forcibly. My affliction for the miseries of an unhappy person, is always in proportion to the fear I have of being afflicted with the same miseries. I would, if it were possible, destroy in him the very root of his misfortune, and thereby free myself at the same time from the fear of suffering in the same manner. The love of others is therefore never anything else in man than an effect of the love of himself, and consequently of his corporeal sensibility. In vain does M. Rousseau repeat incessantly *that all men are good, and all the first movements of nature right.* The necessity of laws proves the contrary. What does this necessity imply? That the different interests of men render them good or bad; and that the only method to form virtuous citizens, is to unite the interest of the individual with that of the public. . . .

A proof that humanity is nothing more in man than the effect of the misfortunes he has known either by himself or by others is, that of all the ways to render him humane and compassionate, the most efficacious is to habituate him from his most tender age to put himself in the place of the miserable. Some have in consequence treated compassion as a weakness: let him call it so if they please; this weakness will always be in my eyes the first of virtues, because it always contributes the most to the happiness of humanity.

I have proved that compassion is not either a moral sense, or an innate sentiment, but the pure effect of self-love. What follows? That it is this same love, differently modified, according to the different education we receive, and the circumstances, and situations in which chance has placed us, which renders us humane or obdurate: that man is not born compassionate, but that all may and will become so when the laws, the form of government, and their education lead them to it.

O! you, to whom heaven has entrusted the legislative power, let your administration be gentle, your laws sagacious, and you will have subjects humane, valiant, and virtuous! But if you alter either those laws, or that wise administration, those virtuous citizens will expire without posterity, and you will be surrounded by wicked men only; for the laws will make them such. Man, by nature indifferent to evil, will not give himself up to it without a motive: the happy man is humane; he is the couching lion.

Unhappy is the prince who confides in the original goodness of characters; M. Rousseau supposes its existence; experience denies it: whoever consults that, will learn that the child kills flies, beats his dog, and strangles his sparrow; that the child, born without any humanity, has all the vices of the man.

The man in power is often unjust; the sturdy child is the same: when he is not restrained by the presence of his master, he appropriates by force, like the man in power, the sweetmeat or plaything of his companion. He does that for a coral or a doll which he would do at a mature age for a title or a scepter. The uniformity in the manner of acting at those two ages made M. de la Mothe say, *It is because the child is already a man, that the man is still a child.*

The original goodness of characters cannot be maintained by any argument. I will even add, that in man, goodness and humanity cannot be the work of nature, but of education only.

FUNDAMENTAL PRINCIPLES OF THE METAPHYSICS OF MORALS

IMMANUEL KANT

Kant, who lived most of his life in Königsberg, where he lectured at the university, wrote in 1785 what has endured as the grandest Enlightenment effort at setting a rational foundation for morality.

For as reason is not competent to guide the will with certainty in regard to its objects and the satisfaction of all our wants (which it to some extent even multiplies), this being an end to which an implanted instinct would have led with much greater certainty; and since, nevertheless, reason is imparted to us as a practical faculty, that is, as one which is to have influence on the *will*, therefore, admitting that nature generally in the distribution of her capacities has adapted the means to the end, its true destination must be to produce a *will*, not merely good as a *means* to something else, but *good in itself*, for which reason was absolutely necessary. This will then, though not indeed the sole and complete good, must be the supreme good and the condition of every other, even of the desire of happiness. Under these circumstances, there is nothing inconsistent with the wisdom of nature in the fact that the cultivation of the reason, which is requisite for the first and unconditional purpose, does in many ways interfere, at least in this life, with the attainment of the second, which is always conditional—namely, happiness. Nay, it may even reduce it to nothing, without nature thereby failing of her purpose. For reason recognizes the establishment of a good will as its highest practical destination, and in attaining this purpose is capable only of a satisfaction of its own proper kind, namely, that from the attainment of an end, which end again is determined by reason only, notwithstanding that this may involve many a disappointment to the ends of inclination.

We have then to develop the notion of a will which deserves to be highly esteemed for itself, and is good without a view to anything further, a notion which exists already in the sound natural understanding, requiring rather to be cleared up than to be taught, and which in estimating the value of our actions always takes the first place and constitutes the condition of all the rest. In order to do this, we will take the notion of duty, which includes that of a good will, although implying certain subjective restrictions and hindrances. These, however, far from concealing it or rendering it unrecognizable, rather bring it out by contrast and make it shine forth so much the brighter.

I omit here all actions which are already recognized as inconsistent with duty, although they may be useful for this or that purpose, for with these the question whether they are done *from duty* cannot arise at all, since they even conflict with it. I also set aside those actions which really conform to duty, but to which men have *no* direct *inclination*, performing them because they are impelled thereto by some other inclination. For in this case we can readily distinguish whether the action which agrees with duty is done *from duty* or from a selfish view. It is much harder to make this distinction when the action accords with duty, and the subject has besides a *direct* inclination to it. For example, it is always a matter of duty that a dealer should not overcharge an inexperienced purchaser; and wherever there is much commerce the prudent tradesman does not overcharge, but keeps a fixed price for everyone, so that a child buys of him as well as any other. Men are thus *honestly* served; but this is not enough to make us believe that the tradesman has so acted from duty and from principles of honesty; his own advantage required it; it is out of the question in this case to suppose that he might besides have a direct inclination in favor of the buyers, so that, as it were, from love he should give no advantage to one over another. Accordingly the action was done neither from duty nor from direct inclination, but merely with a selfish view.

On the other hand, it is a duty to maintain one's life; and, in addition, everyone has also a direct inclination to do so. But on this account the often anxious care which most men take for it has no intrinsic worth, and their maxim has no moral import. They preserve their life *as duty requires*, no doubt, but not *because duty requires*. On the other hand, if adversity and hopeless sorrow have completely taken away the relish for life, if the unfortunate one, strong in mind, indignant at his fate rather than desponding or dejected, wishes for death, and yet preserves his life without loving it—not from inclination or fear, but from duty—then his maxim has a moral worth.

The second proposition is: That an action done from duty derives its moral worth, *not from the purpose* which is to be attained by it, but from the maxim by which it is determined, and therefore does not depend on the realization of the object of the action, but merely on the *principle of volition* by which the action has taken place, without regard to any object of desire. It is clear from what precedes that the purposes which we may have in view in our actions, or their effects regarded as ends and springs of the will, cannot give to actions any unconditional or moral worth. In what, then, can their worth lie if it is not to consist in the will and in reference to its expected effect? It cannot lie anywhere but in the *principle of the will* without regard to the ends which can be attained by the action. For the will stands between its *a priori* principle, which is formal, and its *a posteriori* spring, which is material, as between two roads, and as it must be determined by something, it follows that it must be determined by the formal principle of volition when an action is done from duty, in which case every material principle has been withdrawn from it.

The third proposition, which is a consequence of the two preceding, I would express thus: *Duty is the necessity of acting from respect for the law.*

The pre-eminent good which we call moral can therefore consist in nothing else than *the conception of law* in itself, *which certainly is only possible in a rational being*, in so far as this conception, and not the expected effect, determines the will. This is a good which is already present in the person who acts accordingly, and we have not to wait for it to appear first in the result.

But what sort of law can that be the conception of which must determine the will, even without paying any regard to the effect expected from it, in order that this will may be called good absolutely and without qualification? As I have deprived the will of every impulse which could arise to it from obedience to any law, there remains nothing but the universal conformity of its actions to law in general, which alone is to serve the will as a principle, that is, I am never to act otherwise than so *that I could also will that my maxim should become a universal law.*

Without being an enemy of virtue, a cool observer, one that does not mistake the wish for good, however lively, for its reality, may sometimes doubt whether true virtue is actually found anywhere in the world, and this especially as years increase and the judgment is partly made wiser by experience, and partly also more acute in observation. This being so, nothing can secure us from falling away altogether from our ideas of duty, or maintain in the soul a well-grounded respect for its law, but the clear conviction that although there should never have been actions which really sprang from such pure sources, yet whether this or that takes place is not at all the question; but that reason of itself, independent on all experience, ordains what ought to take place, that accordingly actions of which perhaps the world has hitherto never given an example, the feasibility even of which might be very much doubted by one who founds everything on experience, are nevertheless inflexibly commanded by reason; that, for example, even though there might never yet have been a sincere friend, yet not a whit the less is pure sincerity in friendship required of every man, because, prior to all experience, this duty is involved as duty in the idea of a reason determining the will by *a priori* principles.

When we add further that, unless we deny that the notion of morality has any truth or reference to any possible object, we must admit that its law must be valid, not merely for men, but for all *rational creatures generally*, not merely under certain contingent conditions or with exceptions, but *with absolute necessity*, then it is clear that no experience could enable us to infer even the possibility of such apodictic laws.

Everything in nature works according to laws. Rational beings alone have the faculty of acting according *to the conception* of laws—that is, according to principles, that is, have a *will*. Since the deduction of actions from principles requires *reason*, the will is nothing but practical reason. If reason infallibly determines the will, then the actions of such a being which are recognized as objectively necessary are subjectively necessary also, that is, the will is a faculty to choose *that only* which reason independent on inclination recognizes as practically necessary, that is, as good. But if reason of itself does not sufficiently determine the will, if the latter is subject also to subjective conditions (particular impulses) which do not always coincide with the objective conditions, in a word, if the will does not *in itself* completely accord with reason (which is actually the case with men), then the actions which objectively are recognized as necessary are subjectively contingent, and the determination of such a will according to objective laws is *obligation*, that is to say, the relation of the objective laws to a will that is not thoroughly good is conceived as the determination of the will of a rational being by principles of reason, but which the will from its nature does not of necessity follow.

The conception of an objective principle, in so far as it is obligatory for a will, is called a command (of reason), and the formula of the command is called an Imperative.

There is therefore but one categorical imperative, namely, this: *Act only on that maxim whereby thou canst at the same time will that it should become a universal law.*

1. A man reduced to despair by a series of misfortunes feels wearied of life, but is still so far in possession of his reason that he can ask himself whether it would not be contrary to his duty to himself to take his own life. Now he inquires whether the maxim of his action could become a universal law of nature. His maxim is: From self-love I adopt it as a principle to shorten my life when its longer duration is likely to bring more evil than satisfaction. It is asked then simply whether this principle founded on self-love can become a universal law of nature. Now we see at once that a system of nature of which it should be a law to destroy life by means of the very feeling whose special nature it is to impel to the improvement of life would contradict itself, and therefore could not exist as a system of nature; hence that maxim cannot possibly exist as a universal law of nature, and consequently would be wholly inconsistent with the supreme principle of all duty.

2. Another finds himself forced by necessity to borrow money. He knows that he will not be able to repay it, but sees also that nothing will be lent to him unless he promises stoutly to repay it in a definite time. He desires to make this promise, but he has still so much conscience as to ask himself: Is it not unlawful and inconsistent with duty to get out of a difficulty in this way? Suppose, however, that he resolves to do so, then the maxim of his action would be expressed thus: When I think myself in want of money, I will borrow money and promise to repay it, although I know that I never can do so. Now this principle of self-love or of one's own advantage may perhaps be consistent with my whole future welfare; but the question now is, Is it right? I change then the suggestion of self-love into a universal law, and state the question thus: How would it be if my maxim were a universal law? Then I see at once that it could never hold as a universal law of nature, but would necessarily contradict itself. For supposing it to be a universal law that everyone when he thinks himself in a difficulty should be able to promise whatever he pleases, with the purpose of not keeping his promise, the promise itself would become impossible, as well as the end that one might have in view in it, since no one would consider that anything was promised to him, but would ridicule all such statements as vain pretenses.

3. A third finds in himself a talent which with the help of some culture might make him a useful man in many respects. But he finds himself in comfortable circumstances and prefers to indulge in pleasure rather than to take pains in enlarging and improving his happy natural capacities. He asks, however, whether his maxim of neglect of his natural gifts, besides agreeing with his inclination to indulgence, agrees also with what is called duty. He sees then that a system of nature could indeed subsist with such a universal law, although men (like the South Sea islanders) should let their talents rest and resolve to devote their lives merely to idleness, amusement, and propagation of their species—in a word, to enjoyment; but he cannot possibly *will* that this should be a universal law of nature, or be implanted in us as such by a natural instinct. For, as a rational being, he necessarily wills that his faculties be developed, since they serve him, and have been given him, for all sorts of possible purposes.

4. A fourth, who is in prosperity, while he sees that others have to contend with great wretchedness and that he could help them, thinks: What concern is it of mine? Let everyone be as happy as Heaven pleases,

or as he can make himself; I will take nothing from him nor even envy him, only I do not wish to contribute anything to his welfare or to his assistance in distress! Now no doubt, if such a mode of thinking were a universal law, the human race might very well subsist, and doubtless even better than in a state in which everyone talks of sympathy and good-will, or even takes care occasionally to put it into practice, but, on the other side, also cheats when he can, betrays the rights of men, or otherwise violates them. But although it is possible that a universal law of nature might exist in accordance with that maxim, it is impossible to *will* that such a principle should have the universal validity of a law of nature. For a will which resolved this would contradict itself, inasmuch as many cases might occur in which one would have need of the love and sympathy of others, and in which, by such a law of nature, sprung from his own will, he would deprive himself of all hope of the aid he desires.

These are a few of the many actual duties, or at least what we regard as such, which obviously fall into two classes on the one principle that we have laid down. We must be *able to will* that a maxim of our action should be a universal law. This is the canon of the moral appreciation of the action generally. Some actions are of such a character that their maxim cannot without contradiction be even *conceived* as a universal law of nature, far from it being possible that we should *will* that it *should* be so. In others, this intrinsic impossibility is not found, but still it is impossible to *will* that their maxim should be raised to the universality of a law of nature, since such a will would contradict itself. It is easily seen that the former violate strict or rigorous (inflexible) duty; the latter only laxer (meritorious) duty. Thus it has been completely shown by these examples how all duties depend as regards the nature of the obligation (not the object of the action) on the same principle.

If then there is a supreme practical principle or, in respect of the human will, a categorical imperative, it must be one which, being drawn from the conception of that which is necessarily an end for everyone because it is *an end in itself*, constitutes an *objective* principle of will, and can therefore serve as a universal practical law. The foundation of this principle is: *rational nature exists as an end in itself.* Man necessarily conceives his own existence as being so; so far then this is a *subjective* principle of human actions. But every other rational being regards its existence similarly, just on the same rational principle that holds for me; so that it is at the same time an objective principle from which as a supreme practical law all laws of the will must be capable of being deduced. Accordingly the practical imperative will be as follows: *So act as to treat humanity, whether in thine own person or in that of any other, in every case as an end withal, never as means only.*

This principle that humanity and generally every rational nature is *an end in itself* (which is the supreme limiting condition of every man's freedom of action), is not borrowed from experience, *first,* because it is universal, applying as it does to all rational beings whatever, and experience is not capable of determining anything about them; *secondly,* because it does not present humanity as an end to men (subjectively), that is, as an object which men do of themselves actually adopt as an end; but as an objective end which must as a law constitute the supreme limiting condition of all our subjective ends, let them be what we will; it must therefore spring from pure reason. In fact the objective principle of all practical legislation lies (according to the first principle) in *the rule* and its form of universality which makes it capable of being a law (say, for example, a law of nature); but the *subjective* principle is in the *end;* now by the second principle, the subject of all ends is each rational being inasmuch as it is an end in itself. Hence follows the third practical principle of the will, which is the ultimate condition of its harmony with the universal practical reason, viz., the idea of *the will of every rational being as a universally legislative will.*

On this principle all maxims are rejected which are inconsistent with the will being itself universal legislator. Thus the will is not subject to the law, but so subject that it must be regarded *as itself giving the law,* and on this ground only subject to the law (of which it can regard itself as the author).

Thus morality, and humanity as capable of it, is that which alone has dignity. Skill and diligence in labor have a market value; wit, lively imagination, and humor have fancy value; on the other hand, fidelity to promises, benevolence from principle (not from instinct), have an intrinsic worth. Neither nature nor art contains anything which in default of these it could put in their place, for their worth consists not in the effects which spring from them, not in the use and advantage which they secure, but in the disposition of mind, that is, the maxims of the will which are ready to manifest themselves in such actions, even though they should not have the desired effect. These actions also need no recommendation from any subjective taste or sentiment, that they may be looked on with immediate favor and satisfaction; they need no immediate propension or feeling for them; they exhibit the will that performs them as an object of an immediate respect, and nothing but reason is required to *impose* them on the will; not to *flatter* it into them, which, in the case of duties, would be a contradiction. This estimation therefore shows that the worth of such a disposition is dignity, and places it infinitely above all value, with which it cannot for a moment be brought into comparison or competition without as it were violating its sanctity.

What then is it which justifies virtue or the morally good disposition, in making such lofty claims? It is nothing less than the privilege it secures to the rational being of participating in the giving of universal laws, by which it qualifies him to be a member of a possible kingdom of ends, a privilege to which he was already destined by his own nature as being an end in himself, and on that account legislating in the kingdom of ends; free as regards all laws of physical nature, and obeying those only which he himself gives, and by which his maxims can belong to a system of universal law to which at the same time he submits himself. . . . *Autonomy* then is the basis of the dignity of human and of every rational nature.

The three modes of presenting the principle of morality that have been adduced are at bottom only so many formulae of the very same law, and each of itself involves the other two. There is, however, a difference in them, but it is rather subjectively than objectively practical, intended, namely, to bring an idea of the reason nearer to intuition (by means of a certain analogy), and thereby nearer to feeling. All maxims, in fact, have—

1. A *form*, consisting in universality; and in this view the formula of the moral imperative is expressed thus, that the maxims must be so chosen as if they were to serve as universal laws of nature.

2. A *matter*, namely, an end, and here the formula says that the rational being, as it is an end by its own nature and therefore an end in itself, must in every maxim serve as the condition limiting all merely relative and arbitrary ends.

3. A *complete characterization* of all maxims by means of that formula, namely, that all maxims ought, by their own legislation, to harmonize with a possible kingdom of ends as with a kingdom of nature. There is a progress here in the order of the categories of *unity* of the form of the will (its universality), *plurality* of the matter (the objects, that is, the ends), and *totality* of the system of these. In forming our moral *judgment* of

actions it is better to proceed always on the strict method, and start from the general formula of the categorical imperative: *Act according to a maxim which can at the same time make itself a universal law.*

THE PRINCIPLE OF UTILITY

JEREMY BENTHAM

Standing alongside Kant's writings as the great double legacy of Enlightenment ethics, and very much its foil, is Bentham's (1748–1833) Utilitarianism. The English philosopher, jurist, and reformer first published his speculations on pleasure and pain in his 1789 book, An Introduction to the Principles of Morals and Legislation, *from which this selection is excerpted.*

CHAPTER I: OF THE PRINCIPLE OF UTILITY

I. Nature has placed mankind under the governance of two sovereign masters, *pain* and *pleasure.* It is for them alone to point out what we ought to do, as well as to determine what we shall do. On the one hand the standard of right and wrong, on the other the chain of causes and effects, are fastened to their throne. They govern us in all we do, in all we say, in all we think: every effort we can make to throw off our subjection, will serve but to demonstrate and confirm it. In words a man may pretend to abjure their empire: but in reality he will remain subject to it all the while. The *principle of utility* recognizes this subjection, and assumes it for the foundation of that system, the object of which is to rear the fabric of felicity by the hands of reason and of law. Systems which attempt to question it, deal in sounds instead of sense, in caprice instead of reason, in darkness instead of light.

But enough of metaphor and declamation: it is not by such means that moral science is to be improved.

II. The principle of utility is the foundation of the present work: it will be proper therefore at the outset to give an explicit and determinate account of what is meant by it. By the principle of utility is meant that principle which approves or disapproves of every action whatsoever, according to the tendency which it appears to have to augment or diminish the happiness of the party whose interest is in question: or, what is the same thing in other words, to promote or to oppose that happiness. I say of every action whatsoever; and therefore not only of every action of a private individual, but of every measure of government.

III. By utility is meant that property in any object, whereby it tends to produce benefit, advantage, pleasure, good, or happiness (all this in the present case comes to the same thing) or (what comes again to the same thing) to prevent the happening of mischief, pain, evil, or unhappiness to the party whose interest is considered: if that party be the community in general, then the happiness of the community: if a particular individual, then the happiness of that individual.

IV. The interest of the community is one of the most general expressions that can occur in the phraseology of morals: no wonder that the meaning of it is often lost. When it has a meaning, it is this. The community is a fictitious *body*, composed of the individual persons who are considered as constituting as it were its *members*. The interest of the community then is, what?—the sum of the interests of the several members who compose it.

V. It is in vain to talk of the interest of the community, without understanding what is the interest of the individual. A thing is said to promote the interest, or to be *for* the interest, of an individual, when it tends to add to the sum total of his pleasures: or, what comes to the same thing, to diminish the sum total of his pains.

VI. An action then may be said to be conformable to the principle of utility, or, for shortness sake, to utility, (meaning with respect to the community at large) when the tendency it has to augment the happiness of the community is greater than any it has to diminish it.

VII. A measure of government (which is but a particular kind of action, performed by a particular person or persons) may be said to be conformable to or dictated by the principle of utility, when in like manner the tendency which it has to augment the happiness of the community is greater than any which it has to diminish it.

VIII. When an action, or in particular a measure of government, is supposed by a man to be conformable to the principle of utility, it may be convenient, for the purposes of discourse, to imagine a kind of law or dictate, called a law or dictate of utility: and to speak of the action in question, as being conformable to such law or dictate.

IX. A man may be said to be a partizan of the principle of utility, when the approbation or disapprobation he annexes to any action, or to any measure, is determined by and proportioned to the tendency which he conceives it to have to augment or to diminish the happiness of the community: or in other words, to its conformity or unconformity to the laws or dictates of utility.

X. Of an action that is conformable to the principle of utility one may always say either that it is one that ought to be done, or at least that it is not one that ought not to be done. One may say also, that it is right it should be done; at least that it is not wrong it should be done: that it is a right action; at least that it is not a wrong action. When thus interpreted, the words *ought*, and *right* and *wrong*, and others of that stamp, have a meaning: when otherwise, they have none.

XI. Has the rectitude of this principle been ever formally contested? It should seem that it had, by those who have not known what they have been meaning. Is it susceptible of any direct proof? it should seem not: for that which is used to prove every thing else, cannot itself be proved: a chain of proofs must have their commencement somewhere. To give such proof is as impossible as it is needless.

XII. Not that there is or ever has been that human creature breathing, however stupid or perverse, who has not on many, perhaps on most occasions of his life, deferred to it. By the natural constitution of the human frame, on most occasions of their lives men in general embrace this principle, without thinking of it: if not for the ordering of their own actions, yet for the trying of their own actions, as well as of those of other men. There have been, at the same time, not many, perhaps, even of the most intelligent, who have been disposed to embrace it purely and without reserve. There are even few who have not taken some occasion or other to quarrel with it, either on account of their not understanding always how to apply it, or on account of some prejudice or other which they were afraid to examine into, or could not bear to part with. For such is the stuff that man is made of: in principle and in practice, in a right track and in a wrong one, the rarest of all human qualities is consistency.

XIII. When a man attempts to combat the principle of utility, it is with reasons drawn, without his being aware of it, from that very principle itself. His arguments, if they prove any thing, prove not that the principle is *wrong*, but that, according to the applications he supposes to be made of it, it is *misapplied*. Is it possible for a man to move the earth? Yes; but he must first find out another earth to stand upon.

XIV. To disprove the propriety of it by arguments is impossible; but, from the causes that have been mentioned, or from some confused or partial view of it, a man may happen to be disposed not to relish it. Where this is the case, if he thinks the settling of his opinions on such a subject worth the trouble, let him take the following steps, and at length, perhaps, he may come to reconcile himself to it.

1. Let him settle with himself, whether he would wish to discard this principle altogether; if so, let him consider what it is that all his reasonings (in matters of politics especially) can amount to?

2. If he would, let him settle with himself, whether he would judge and act without any principle, or whether there is any other he would judge and act by?

3. If there be, let him examine and satisfy himself whether the principle he thinks he has found is really any separate intelligible principle; or whether it be not a mere principle in words, a kind of phrase, which at bottom expresses neither more nor less than the mere averment of his own unfounded sentiments; that is, what in another person he might be apt to call caprice?

4. If he is inclined to think that his own approbation or disapprobation, annexed to the idea of an act, without any regard to its consequences, is a sufficient foundation for him to judge and act upon, let him ask himself whether his sentiment is to be a standard of right and wrong, with respect to every other man, or whether every man's sentiment has the same privilege of being a standard to itself?

5. In the first case, let him ask himself whether his principle is not despotical, and hostile to all the rest of human race?

6. In the second case, whether it is not anarchial, and whether at this rate there are not as many different standards of right and wrong as there are men? and whether even to the same man, the same thing, which is right today, may not (without the least change in its nature) be wrong tomorrow? and whether the same thing is not right and wrong in the same place at the same time? and in either case, whether all argument is not at an end? and whether, when two men have said, "I like this," and "I don't like it," they can (upon such a principle) have any thing more to say?

7. If he should have said to himself, No: for that the sentiment which he proposes as a standard must be grounded on reflection, let him say on what particulars the reflection is to turn? if on particulars having relation to the utility of the act, then let him say whether this is not deserting his own principle, and borrowing assistance from that very one in opposition to which he sets it up: or if not on those particulars, on what other particulars?

8. If he should be for compounding the matter, and adopting his own principle in part, and the principle of utility in part, let him say how far he will adopt it?

9. When he has settled with himself where he will stop, then let him ask himself how he justifies to himself the adopting it so far? and why he will not adopt it any farther?

10. Admitting any other principle than the principle of utility to be a right principle, a principle that it is right for a man to pursue; admitting (what is not true) that the word *right* can have a meaning without reference to utility, let him say whether there is any such thing as a *motive* that a man can have to pursue the dictates of it: if there is, let him say what that motive is, and how it is to be distinguished from those which enforce the dictates of utility: if not, then lastly let him say what it is this other principle can be good for?

Chapter II: Of Principles Adverse to That of Utility

I. If the principle of utility be a right principle to be governed by, and that in all cases, it follows from what has been just observed, that whatever principle differs from it in any case must necessarily be a wrong one. To prove any other principle, therefore, to be a wrong one, there needs no more than just to show it to be what it is, a principle of which the dictates are in some point or other different from those of the principle of utility: to state it is to confute it.

II. A principle may be different from that of utility in two ways: 1. By being constantly opposed to it: this is the case with a principle which may be termed the principle of *asceticism*. 2. By being sometimes opposed to it, and sometimes not, as it may happen: this is the case with another, which may be termed the principle of *sympathy* and *antipathy*.

III. By the principle of asceticism I mean that principle, which, like the principle of utility, approves or disapproves of any action, according to the tendency which it appears to have to augment or diminish the happiness of the party whose interest is in question; but in an inverse manner: approving of actions in as far as they tend to diminish his happiness; disapproving of them in as far as they tend to augment it.

IV. It is evident that any one who reprobates any the least particle of pleasure, as such, from whatever source derived, is *pro tanto* a partizan of the principle of asceticism. It is only upon that principle, and not from the principle of utility, that the most abominable pleasure which the vilest of malefactors ever reaped from his crime would be to be reprobated, if it stood alone. The case is, that it never does stand alone; but is necessarily followed by such a quantity of pain (or, what comes to the same thing, such a chance for a certain quantity of pain) that the pleasure in comparison of it, is as nothing: and this is the true and sole, but perfectly sufficient, reason for making it a ground for punishment.

V. There are two classes of men of very different complexions, by whom the principle of asceticism appears to have been embraced; the one a set of moralists, the other a set of religionists. Different accordingly have been the motives which appear to have recommended it to the notice of these different parties. Hope, that is the prospect of pleasure, seems to have animated the former: hope, the aliment of philosophic pride: the hope of honor and reputation at the hands of men. Fear, that is the prospect of pain, the latter: fear, the offspring of superstitious fancy: the fear of future punishment at the hands of a splenetic and revengeful Deity. I say in this case fear: for of the invisible future, fear is more powerful than hope. These circumstances characterize the two different parties among the partizans of the principle of asceticism; the parties and their motives different, the principle the same.

VI. The religious party, however, appear to have carried it farther than the philosophical: they have acted more consistently and less wisely. The philosophical party have scarcely gone farther than to reprobate pleasure: the religious party have frequently gone so far as to make it a matter of merit and of duty to court pain. The philosophical party have hardly gone farther than the making pain a matter of indifference. It is no evil, they have said: they have not said, it is a good. They have not so much as reprobated all pleasure in the lump. They have discarded only what they have called the gross; that is, such as are organical, or of which the origin is easily traced up to such as are organical: they have even cherished and magnified the refined. Yet this, however, not under the name of pleasure: to cleanse itself from the sordes of its impure original, it was necessary it should change its name: the honorable, the glorious, the reputable, the becoming, the *honestum*, the *decorum*, it was to be called: in short, any thing but pleasure.

VII. From these two sources have flowed the doctrines from which the sentiments of the bulk of mankind have all along received a tincture of this principle; some from the philosophical, some from the religious, some from both. Men of education more frequently from the philosophical, as more suited to the elevation of their sentiments: the vulgar more frequently from the superstitious, as more suited to the narrowness of their intellect, undilated by knowledge: and to the abjectness of their condition, continually open to the attacks of fear. The tinctures, however, derived from the two sources, would naturally intermingle, insomuch that a man would not always know by which of them he was most influenced: and they would often serve to corroborate and enliven one another. It was this conformity that made a kind of alliance between parties of a complexion otherwise so dissimilar: and disposed them to unite upon various occasions against the common enemy, the partizan of the principle of utility, whom they joined in branding with the odious name of Epicurean.

VIII. The principle of asceticism, however, with whatever warmth it may have been embraced by its partizans as a rule of private conduct, seems not to have been carried to any considerable length, when applied to the business of government. In a few instances it has been carried a little way by the philosophical party: witness the Spartan regimen. Though then, perhaps, it may be considered as having been a measure of security: and an application, though a precipitate and perverse application, of the principle of utility. Scarcely in any instances, to any considerable length, by the religious: for the various monastic orders, and the societies of the Quakers, Dumplers, Moravians, and other religionists, have been free societies, whose regimen no man has been astricted to without the intervention of his own consent. Whatever merit a man may have thought there would be in making himself miserable, no such notion seems ever to have occurred to any of them, that it may be a merit, much less a duty, to make others miserable: although it should seem, that if a certain quantity of misery were a thing so desirable, it would not matter much whether it were brought by each man upon himself, or by one man upon another. It is true, that from the same source from whence, among the religionists, the attachment to the principle of asceticism took its rise, flowed other doctrines and practices, from which misery in abundance was produced in one man by the instrumentality of another: witness the holy wars, and the persecutions for religion. But the passion for producing misery in these cases proceeded upon some special ground: the exercise of it was confined to persons of particular descriptions: they were tormented, not as men, but as heretics and infidels. To have inflicted the same miseries on their fellow-believers and fellow-sectaries, would have been as blameable in the eyes even of these religionists, as in those of a partizan of the principle of utility. For a man to give himself a certain number of stripes was indeed meritorious: but to give the same number of stripes to another man, not consenting, would have been a sin. We read of saints, who for the good of their souls, and the mortification of their bodies, have voluntarily yielded themselves a prey to vermin: but though many persons of this class have wielded the reins of empire, we read of none who have set themselves to work, and made laws on purpose, with a view of stocking the body politic with the breed of highwaymen, housebreakers, or incendiaries. If at any time they have suffered the nation to be preyed upon by swarms of idle pensioners, or useless placemen, it has rather been from negligence and imbecility, than from any settled plan for oppressing and plundering of the people. If at any time they have sapped the sources of national wealth, by cramping commerce, and driving the inhabitants into emigration, it has been with other views, and in pursuit of other ends. If they have declaimed against the pursuit of pleasure, and the use of wealth, they have commonly stopped at declamation: they have not, like Lycurgus, made express ordinances for the purpose of banishing the precious metals. If they have established idleness by a law, it has been not because idleness, the mother of vice and misery, is itself a virtue, but because idleness (say they) is the road to holiness. If under the notion of fasting, they have joined in the plan of confining their subjects to a diet, thought by some to be of the most nourishing and prolific nature, it has been not for the sake of making them tributaries to the nations by whom that diet was to be supplied, but for the sake of manifesting their own power, and exercising the obedience of the people. If they have established, or suffered to be established, punishments for the breach of celibacy, they have done no more than comply with the petitions of those deluded rigorists, who, dupes to the ambitious and deep-laid policy of their rulers, first laid themselves under that idle obligation by a vow.

IX. The principle of asceticism seems originally to have been the reverie of certain hasty speculators, who having perceived, or fancied, that certain pleasures, when reaped in certain circumstances, have, at the long run, been attended with pains more than equivalent to them, took occasion to quarrel with every thing that offered itself under the name of pleasure. Having then got thus far, and having forgot the point which they set out from, they pushed on, and went so much further as to think it meritorious to fall in love with pain. Even this, we see, is at bottom but the principle of utility misapplied.

X. The principle of utility is capable of being consistently pursued; and it is but tautology to say, that the more consistently it is pursued, the better it must ever be for human kind. The principle of asceticism never was, nor ever can be, consistently pursued by any living creature. Let but one tenth part of the inhabitants of this earth pursue it consistently, and in a day's time they will have turned it into a hell.

Taste and Art

ON WIT

Joseph Addison

English essayist and Whig man of letters Joseph Addison (1672–1719) was editor of the widely read Spectator. *This philosophical discussion of wit is from Number 62 of the* Spectator, *which appeared on May 11, 1711.*

Mr. Locke has an admirable reflection upon the difference of wit and judgment, whereby he endeavors to show the reason why they are not always the talents of the same person. His words are as follow: "And hence, perhaps, may be given some reason of that common observation, that men who have a great deal of wit, and prompt memories, have not always the clearest judgment or deepest reason. For wit lying most in the assemblage of ideas, and putting those together with quickness and variety wherein can be found any resemblance or congruity, thereby to make up pleasant pictures, and agreeable visions in the fancy; judgment, on the contrary, lies quite on the other side, in separating carefully one from another ideas wherein can be found the least difference, thereby to avoid being misled by similitude, and by affinity to take one thing for another. This is a way of proceeding quite contrary to metaphor and allusion, wherein, for the most part, lies that entertainment and pleasantry of wit, which strikes so lively on the fancy, and is therefore so acceptable to all people."

This is, I think, the best and most philosophical account that I have ever met with of wit, which generally, though not always, consists in such a resemblance and congruity of ideas as this author mentions. I shall only add to it, by way of explanation, that every resemblance of ideas is not that which we call wit, unless it be such a one that gives delight and surprise to the reader. These two properties seem essential to wit, more particularly the last of them. In order, therefore, that the resemblance in the ideas be wit, it is necessary that the ideas should not lie too near one another in the nature of things; for where the likeness is obvious, it gives no surprise. To compare one man's singing to that of another, or to represent the whiteness of any object by that of milk and snow, or the variety of its colors by those of the rainbow, cannot be called wit, unless, besides this obvious resemblance, there be some further congruity discovered in the two ideas, that is capable of giving the reader some surprise. Thus when a poet tells us the bosom of his mistress is as white as snow, there is no wit in the comparison; but when he adds, with a sigh, it is as cold too, it then grows into wit. Every reader's memory may supply him with innumerable instances of the same nature. For this reason the similitudes in heroic poets, who endeavor rather to fill the mind with great conceptions than to divert it with such as are new and surprising, have seldom anything in them that can be called wit. Mr. Locke's account of wit, with this short explanation, comprehends most of the species of wit—as metaphors, similitudes, allegories, enigmas, mottos, parables, fables, dreams, visions, dramatic writings, burlesque, and all the methods of allusion. There are many other species of wit, how remote soever they may appear at first sight from the foregoing description, which upon examination will be found to agree with it.

As true wit generally consists in this resemblance and congruity of ideas, false wit chiefly consists in the resemblance and congruity, sometimes of single letters, as in anagrams, chronograms, lipograms, and acrostics; sometimes of syllables, as in echoes and doggerel rhymes; and sometimes of whole sentences or poems, cast into the figures of eggs, axes, or altars. Nay, some carry the notion of wit so far as to ascribe it even to external mimicry, and to look upon a man as an ingenious person that can resemble the tone, posture, or face of another.

As true wit consists in the resemblance of ideas, and false wit in the resemblance of words, according to the foregoing instances, there is another kind of wit which consists partly in the resemblance of ideas, and partly in the resemblance of words, which for distinction sake I shall call mixed wit. This kind of wit is that which abounds in Cowley, more than in any other author that ever wrote. Mr. Waller has likewise a great deal of it. Mr. Dryden is very sparing in it. Milton had a genius much above it. Spenser is in the same class with Milton. The Italians, even in their epic poetry, are full of it. Monsieur Boileau, who formed himself upon the ancient poets, has everywhere rejected it with scorn. . . .

Out of the innumerable branches of mixed wit, I shall choose one instance which may be met with in all the writers of this class. The passion of love in its nature has been thought to resemble fire, for which reason the words *fire* and *flame* are made use of to signify love. The witty poets therefore have taken an advantage from the double meaning of the word fire, to make an infinite number of witticisms. Cowley, observing the cold regard of his mistress's eyes, and at the same time their power of producing love in him, considers them as burning-glasses made of ice; and, finding himself able to live in the greatest extremities of love, concludes the torrid zone to be habitable. When his mistress has read his letter written in juice of lemon, by holding it to the fire, he desires her to read it over a second time by love's flame. When she weeps, he wishes it were inward heat that distilled those drops from the limbeck. When she is absent, he is beyond eighty—that is, thirty degrees nearer the Pole than when she is with him. His ambitious love is a fire that naturally mounts upwards; his happy love is the beams of heaven, and his unhappy love flames of hell. When it does not let him sleep, it is a flame that sends up no smoke; when it is opposed by counsel and advice, it is a fire that rages the more by the winds blowing upon it. Upon the dying of a tree in which he had cut his loves, he observed that his written flames had burnt up and withered the tree. When he resolves to give over his passion, he tells us that one burnt like him forever dreads the fire. His heart is an Ætna, that, instead of Vulcan's shop, encloses Cupid's forge in it. His endeavoring to drown his love in wine is throwing oil upon the fire. He would insinuate to his mistress that the fire of love, like that of the sun (which produces so many living creatures), should not only warm, but beget. Love, in another place, cooks pleasure at his fire. Sometimes the poet's heart is frozen in every breast, and sometimes scorched in every eye. Sometimes he is drowned in tears and burnt in love, like a ship set on fire in the middle of the sea.

The reader may observe in every one of these instances, that the poet mixes the qualities of fire with those of love; and, in the same sentence, speaking of it both as a passion and as real fire, surprises the reader with those seeming resemblances or contradictions that make up all the wit in this kind of writing. Mixed wit is therefore a composition of pun and true wit, and is more or less perfect as the resemblance lies in the ideas or in the words. Its foundations are laid partly in falsehood and partly in truth; reason puts in her claim for one half of it, and extravagance for the other. The only province, therefore, for this kind of wit is epigram, or those little occasional poems that in their own nature are nothing else but a tissue of epigrams. I cannot conclude this head of mixed wit without owning that the admirable poet out of whom I have taken the examples of it, had as much true wit as any author that ever writ, and indeed all other talents of an extraordinary genius. . . .

Bouhours, whom I look upon to be the most penetrating of all the French critics, has taken pains to show that it is impossible for any thought to be beautiful which is not just, and has not its foundation in the nature of things; that the basis of all wit is truth; and that no thought can be valuable of which good sense is not the ground work. Boileau has endeavored to inculcate the same notion in several parts of his writings, both in prose and verse. This is that natural way of writing, that beautiful simplicity, which we so much admire in the compositions of the ancients, and which nobody deviates from but those who want strength of genius to make a thought shine in its own natural beauties. Poets who want this strength of genius to give that majestic simplicity to nature which we so much admire in the works of the ancients, are forced to hunt after foreign ornaments, and not to let any piece of wit of what kind soever escape them. I look upon these writers as Goths in poetry, who, like those in architecture, not being able to come up to the simplicity of the old Greeks and Romans, have endeavored to supply its place with all the extravagancies of an irregular fancy. . . . Were I not supported by so great an authority as that of Mr. Dryden, I should not venture to observe that the taste of most of our English poets, as well as readers, is extremely Gothic.

IDEAS OF BEAUTY AND VIRTUE

FRANCIS HUTCHESON

Much like his claim that there is an innate moral sense, so Hutcheson here insists that our sense of beauty resides within us, stronger in some than in others. This selection is from his Inquiry into the Original of Our Ideas of Beauty and Virtue *(1726).*

Let it be observed, that in the following papers, the word *beauty* is taken for the idea raised in us, and a sense of beauty for our power of receiving this idea. Harmony also denotes our pleasant ideas arising from composition of sounds, and a good ear (as it is generally taken) a power of perceiving this pleasure. . . .

It is of no consequence whether we call these ideas of beauty and harmony perceptions of the external senses of seeing and hearing, or not. I should rather choose to call our power of perceiving these ideas, an internal sense, were it only for the convenience of distinguishing them from other sensations of seeing and hearing, which men may have without perception of beauty and harmony. It is plain from experience, that many men have in the common meaning, the senses of seeing, and hearing perfect enough; they perceive all the simple ideas separately, and have their pleasures; they distinguish them from each other, such as one color from another, either quite different, or the stronger or fainter of the same color, when they are placed beside each other, although they may often confound their names, when they occur apart from each other; as some do the names of green and blue: they can tell in separate notes, the higher, lower, sharper or flatter, when separately sounded; in figures they discern the length, breadth, wideness of each line, surface, angle; and may be as capable of hearing and seeing at great distances as any men whatsoever; and yet perhaps they shall find no pleasure in musical compositions, in painting, architecture, natural landscape; or but a very weak one in comparison of what others enjoy from the same objects. This greater capacity of receiving such pleasant ideas we commonly call a fine genius or taste: in music we seem universally to acknowledge something like a distinct sense from the external one of hearing, and call it a good ear; and the like distinction we should probably acknowledge in other objects, had we also got distinct names to denote these powers of perception by.

There will appear another reason perhaps afterwards, for calling this power of perceiving the ideas of beauty, an internal sense, from this, that in some other affairs, where our external senses are not much concerned, we discern a sort of beauty, very like, in many respects to that observed in sensible objects, and accompanied with like pleasure: such is that beauty perceived in theorems, or universal truths, in general causes, and in some extensive principles of action.

DISCOURSE ON STYLE

Comte de Buffon

In this selection from his 1753 essay, Discourse on Style, *Buffon offers a strikingly classical view of style.*

Style is nothing but the order and movement according to which a man arranges his thoughts. If he ties them closely together, if he tightens them up, the style becomes firm, lively, and concise; if he lets them pile themselves loosely one upon another, and unites them only by means of words, however elegant these may be, the style will be diffuse, loose, dragging. . . .

And yet, every subject is a whole; and, however great it may be, it can be covered in a single discourse. Breaks, rests, internal divisions, should be employed only in the treatment of diverse subjects or when, since it has to deal with vast, thorny, and disparate subjects, the march of the mind is interrupted by a multiplicity of obstacles and constrained by force of circumstances; otherwise, multiple divisions, far from making a work more solid, destroy it as a structural whole; the book may seem clear at a glance, but the author's plan remains obscure; he cannot make an impression on the mind of the reader, he cannot even make himself felt, save by the continuity of the thread of the work, by the harmonic interdependence of its ideas, by a successive development, a sustained gradation, a uniform movement which any interruption destroys or weakens.

Why are the works of nature so perfect? It is because each one of her works is a whole, and because she labors according to an immutable plan from which she never departs; she prepares in silence the seeds of her productions; she sketches by a unique act the original form of each living thing; she develops it, perfects it in a continuous movement within a prescribed time. The finished work astounds: but it is the divine imprint whose mark it carries that should impress us. The human mind can create nothing; it will produce only after having been made fecund by experience and reflection; the information it has amassed furnishes but the seeds of its end-products; but if the human mind will imitate nature in its movement and in its labor, if it will rise to the contemplation of the most sublime truths; if it will gather them together in due order, if it will make a whole of them, a system, by reflection, it will establish on unshakeable foundations immortal monuments.

It is for lack of a plan, for not having reflected sufficiently on his purpose, that an intelligent man finds himself embarrassed and unable to decide where to begin to write. He entertains a great number of ideas; and since he has neither compared them, nor subordinated them one to another, nothing determines him to prefer one over another; he remains in perplexity. But once he has made a plan, once he has assembled and put in order all the thoughts essential to his subject, he will be readily aware of the exact moment to take up his pen, he will recognize the point at which the mind is ready to produce, he will be anxious to hasten its work, he will indeed have no other pleasure than that of writing; ideas will follow one another easily and the style will be natural and unconstrained; warmth will be born of this pleasure, will spread throughout and give life to each expression; everything will grow livelier; the tone will be raised, objects will take on color; and emotion thus joined to penetration, will increase it, carry it further, make it pass from what is said to what is going to be said, and the style becomes interesting and luminous.

Nothing is more opposed to this warmth of style than the desire to put striking traits everywhere; nothing is more contrary to the penetrating light that ought to embody itself and spread itself evenly throughout a work than those sparks which are made only by force in the mutual shock of words, and which dazzle us for an instant only to leave us afterwards in the dark. These are the thoughts that shine only by artificial opposition; one aspect only of the object is shown, the others left in the shadow; and ordinarily the aspect chosen is a point, an angle, over which the mind may play with the more facility in that the great aspects on which good sense customarily dwells are pushed into the background. . . .

To write well, a man must, then, possess his subject fully; he must reflect upon it sufficiently to see clearly the order of his thoughts, and to make of them a sequence, a continuous chain, of which each point represents an idea; and when he has taken up his pen, he must guide it with due sequence along this chain, without letting it wander, or bear too heavily anywhere, or make any movement save that which will be determined by the ground it has to cover. It is in this that severity of style consists, and it is this also that will make unity of style, and regulate its flow; and this alone also will suffice to make the style precise and simple, even and clear, lively and consecutive. If to the observance of this first rule, dictated by the very nature of things, there is added delicacy of taste, scrupulous attention to the choice of words, care to name things only by the most general term possible, then the style will have nobility. If there is added further a distrust of first impulses, a scorn for what is no more than brilliant, and a steady repugnance for the equivocal and the jesting, the style will have graveness, even, indeed, majesty. Finally, if a man write as he thinks, if he believe what he seeks to get believed, this good faith with himself, which insures propriety in the eyes of others, and makes for the truth of a style, will give style all its effect, provided that this interior conviction is not marked by a too violent enthusiasm, and that everywhere there is displayed more candor than assurance, more reason than heat.

OF THE STANDARD OF TASTE

DAVID HUME

There are few areas of human speculation that did not elicit an essay from Hume. Here in an essay of 1757, Hume discusses whether "a certain degree of diversity in judgment is unavoidable" in matters of taste.

The great variety of Taste, as well as of opinion, which prevails in the world, is too obvious not to have fallen under everyone's observation. Men of the most confined knowledge are able to remark a difference of taste in the narrow circle of their acquaintance, even where the persons have been educated under the same government, and have early imbibed the same prejudices. But those, who can enlarge their view to contemplate distant nations and remote ages, are still more surprised at the great inconsistence and contrariety. We are apt to call *barbarous* whatever departs widely from our own taste and apprehension: But soon find the epithet of reproach retorted on us. And the highest arrogance and self-conceit is at last startled, on observing an equal assurance on all sides, and scruples, amidst such a contest of sentiment, to pronounce positively in its own favor.

As this variety of taste is obvious to the most careless enquirer; so will it be found, on examination, to be still greater in reality than in appearance. The sentiments of men often differ with regard to beauty and deformity of all kinds, even while their general discourse is the same. There are certain terms in every language, which import blame, and others praise; and all men, who use the same tongue, must agree in their application of them. Every voice is united in applauding elegance, propriety, simplicity, spirit in writing; and in blaming fustian, affectation, coldness, and a false brilliancy: But when critics come to particulars, this seeming unanimity vanishes; and it is found, that they had affixed a very different meaning to their expressions. In all matters of opinion and science, the case is opposite: The difference among men is there oftener found to lie in generals than in particulars; and to be less in reality than in appearance. An explanation of the terms commonly ends the controversy; and the disputants are surprised to find, that they had been quarreling, while at bottom they agreed in their judgment. . . .

It is natural for us to seek a *Standard of Taste;* a rule, by which the various sentiments of men may be reconciled; at least, a decision, afforded, confirming one sentiment, and condemning another. . . .

It appears then, that, amidst all the variety and caprice of taste, there are certain general principles of approbation or blame, whose influence a careful eye may trace in all operations of the mind. Some particular forms or qualities, from the original structure of the internal fabric, are calculated to please, and others to displease; and if they fail of their effect in any particular instance, it is from some apparent defect or imperfection in the organ. A man in a fever would not insist on his palate as able to decide concerning flavors; nor would one, affected with the jaundice, pretend to give a verdict with regard to colors. In each creature, there is a sound and a defective state; and the former alone can be supposed to afford us a true standard of taste and sentiment. If, in the sound state of the organ, there be an entire or a considerable uniformity of sentiment among men, we may thence derive an idea of the perfect beauty; in like manner as the appearance of objects in daylight, to the eye of a man in health, is denominated their true and real color, even while color is allowed to be merely a phantasm of the senses. . . .

One obvious cause, why many feel not the proper sentiment of beauty, is the want of that *delicacy* of imagination, which is requisite to convey a sensibility of those finer emotions. This delicacy every one pretends to: Every one talks of it; and would reduce every kind of taste or sentiment to its standard. . . .

But though there be naturally a wide difference in point of delicacy between one person and another, nothing tends further to increase and improve this talent, than *practice* in a particular art, and the frequent survey or contemplation of a particular species of beauty. When objects of any kind are first presented to the eye or imagination, the sentiment, which attends them, is obscure and confused; and the mind is, in a great measure, incapable of pronouncing concerning their merits or defects. The taste cannot perceive the several excellences of the performance; much less distinguish the particular character of each excellency, and ascertain its quality and degree. If it pronounce the whole in general to be beautiful or deformed, it is the utmost that can be expected; and even this judgment, a person, so unpracticed, will be apt to deliver with great hesitation and reserve. But allow him to acquire experience in those objects, his feeling becomes more exact and nice: He not only perceives the beauties and defects of each part, but marks the distinguishing species of each quality, and assigns it suitable praise or blame. A clear and distinct sentiment attends him through the whole survey of the objects; and he discerns that very degree and kind of approbation or displeasure, which each part is naturally fitted to produce. The mist dissipates, which seemed formerly to hang over the object: The organ acquires greater perfection in its operations; and can pronounce, without danger of mistake, concerning the merits of every performance. In a word, the same address and dexterity, which practice gives to the execution of any work, is also acquired by the same means, in the judging of it.

So advantageous is practice to the discernment of beauty, that, before we can give judgment on any work of importance, it will even be requisite, that that very individual performance be more than once perused by us, and be surveyed in different lights with attention and deliberation. There is a flutter or hurry of thought which attends the first perusal of any piece, and which confounds the genuine sentiment of beauty. The relation of the parts is not discerned: The true characters of style are little distinguished: The several perfections and defects seem wrapped up in a species of confusion, and present themselves indistinctly to the imagination. Not to mention, that there is a species of beauty, which, as it is florid and superficial, pleases at first; but being found incompatible with a just expression either of reason or passion, soon palls upon the taste, and is then rejected with disdain, at least rated at a much lower value.

It is impossible to continue in the practice of contemplating any order of beauty, without being frequently obliged to form *comparisons* between the several species and degrees of excellence, and estimating their proportion to each other. A man, who has had no opportunity of comparing the different kinds of beauty, is indeed totally unqualified to pronounce an opinion with regard to any object presented to him. By comparison alone we fix the epithets of praise or blame, and learn how to assign the due degree of each. The coarsest daubing contains a certain luster of colors and exactness of imitation, which are so far beauties, and would affect the mind of a peasant or Indian with the highest admiration. The most vulgar ballads are not entirely destitute of harmony or nature; and none but a person, familiarized to superior beauties, would pronounce their numbers harsh, or narration uninteresting. A great inferiority of beauty gives pain to a person conversant in the highest excellence of the kind, and is for that reason pronounced a deformity: As the most finished object, with which we are acquainted, is naturally supposed to have reached the pinnacle of perfection, and to be entitled to the highest applause. One accustomed to see, and examine, and weigh the several performances, admired in different ages and nations, can only rate the merits of a work exhibited to his view, and assign its proper rank among the productions of genius.

But to enable a critic the more fully to execute this undertaking, he must preserve his mind free from all *prejudice*, and allow nothing to enter into his consideration, but the very object which is submitted to his examination. We may observe, that every work of art, in order to produce its due effect on the mind, must be surveyed in a certain point of view, and cannot be fully relished by persons, whose situation, real or imaginary, is not conformable to that which is required by the performance. An orator addresses himself to a particular audience, and must have a regard to their particular genius, interests, opinions, passions, and prejudices; otherwise he hopes in vain to govern their resolutions, and inflame their affections. Should they even have entertained some prepossessions against him, however unreasonable, he must not overlook this disadvantage; but, before he enters upon the subject, must endeavor to conciliate their affection, and acquire their good graces. A critic of a different age or nation, who should peruse this discourse, must have all these circumstances in his eye, and must place himself in the same situation as the audience, in order to form a true judgment of the oration. In like manner, when any work is addressed to the public, though I should have a friendship or enmity with the author, I must depart from this situation; and considering myself as a man in general, forget, if possible, my individual being and my peculiar circumstances. A person influenced by prejudice, complies not with this condition; but obstinately maintains his natural position, without placing himself in that point of view, which the performance supposes. If the work be addressed to persons of a different age or nation, he makes no allowance for their peculiar views and prejudices; but, full of the manners of his own age and country, rashly condemns what seemed admirable in the eyes of those for whom alone the discourse was calculated. If the work be executed for the public, he never sufficiently enlarges his comprehension, or forgets his interest as a friend or enemy, as a rival or commentator. By this means, his sentiments are perverted; nor have the same beauties and blemishes the same influence upon him, as if he had imposed a proper violence on his imagination, and had forgotten himself for a moment. So far his taste evidently departs from the true standard; and of consequence loses all credit and authority.

It is well known, that in all questions, submitted to the understanding, prejudice is destructive of sound judgment, and perverts all operations of the intellectual faculties: It is no less contrary to good taste; nor has it less influence to corrupt our sentiment of beauty. It belongs to *good sense* to check its influence in both cases; and in this respect, as well as in many others, reason, if not an essential part of taste, is at least requisite to the operations of this latter faculty. In all the nobler productions of genius, there is a mutual relation and correspondence of parts; nor can either the beauties or blemishes be perceived by him, whose thought is not capacious enough to comprehend all those parts, and compare them with each other, in order to perceive the consistence and uniformity of the whole. Every work of art has also a certain end or purpose, for which it is calculated; and is to be deemed more or less perfect, as it is more or less fitted to attain this end. . . .

The same excellence of faculties which contributes to the improvement of reason, the same clearness of conception, the same exactness of distinction, the same vivacity of apprehension, are essential to the operations of true taste, and are its infallible concomitants. It seldom, or never happens, that a man of sense, who has experience in any art, cannot judge of its beauty; and it is no less rare to meet with a man who has a just taste without a sound understanding.

Thus, though the principles of taste be universal, and nearly, if not entirely, the same in all men; yet few are qualified to give judgment on any work of art, or establish their own sentiment as the standard of beauty. The organs of internal sensation are seldom so perfect as to allow the general principles their full play, and produce a feeling correspondent to those principles. They either labor under some defect, or are vitiated by some disorder; and by that means, excite a sentiment, which may be pronounced erroneous. When the critic has no delicacy, he judges without any distinction, and is only affected by the grosser and more palpable qualities of the object: The finer touches pass unnoticed and disregarded. Where he is not aided by practice, his verdict is attended with confusion and hesitation. Where no comparison has been employed, the most frivolous beauties, such as rather merit the name of defects, are the object of his admiration. Where he lies under the influence of prejudice, all his natural sentiments are perverted. Where good sense is wanting, he is not qualified to discern the beauties of design and reasoning, which are the highest and most excellent. Under some or other of these imperfections, the generality of men labor; and hence a true judge in the finer arts is observed, even during the most polished ages, to be so rare a character: Strong sense, united to delicate sentiment, improved by practice, perfected by comparison, and cleared of all prejudice, can alone entitle critics to this valuable character; and the joint verdict of such, wherever they are to be found, is the true standard of taste and beauty.

But where are such critics to be found? By what marks are they to be known? How distinguish them from pretenders? These questions are embarrassing; and seem to throw us back into the same uncertainty, from which, during the course of this essay, we have endeavored to extricate ourselves.

But if we consider the matter aright, these are questions of fact, not of sentiment. Whether any particular person be endowed with good sense and a delicate imagination, free from prejudice, may often be the subject of dispute, and be liable to great discussion and enquiry: But that such a character is valuable and estimable will be agreed in by all mankind. Where these doubts occur, men can do no more than in other disputable questions, which are submitted to the understanding: They must produce the best arguments, that their invention suggests to them; they must acknowledge a true and decisive standard to exist somewhere, to wit, real existence and matter of fact; and they must have indulgence to such as differ from them in their appeals to this standard. It is sufficient for our present purpose, if we have proved, that the taste of all individuals is not upon an equal footing, and that some men in general, however difficult to be particularly pitched upon, will be acknowledged by universal sentiment to have a preference above others.

But in reality the difficulty of finding, even in particulars, the standard of taste, is not so great as it is represented. Though in speculation, we may readily avow a certain criterion in science and deny it in sentiment, the matter is found in practice to be much more hard to ascertain in the former case than in the latter. Theories of abstract philosophy, systems of profound theology, have prevailed during one age: In a successive period, these have been universally exploded: Their absurdity has been detected: Other theories and systems have supplied their place, which again gave place to their successors: And nothing has been experienced more liable to the revolutions of chance and fashion than these pretended decisions of science. The case is not the same with the beauties of eloquence and poetry. Just expressions of passion and nature are sure, after a little time, to gain public applause, which they maintain forever. Aristotle, and Plato, and Epicurus, and Descartes, may successively yield to each other: But Terence and Virgil maintain an universal, undisputed empire over the minds of men. The abstract philosophy of Cicero has lost its credit: The vehemence of his oratory is still the object of our admiration.

Though men of delicate taste be rare, they are easily to be distinguished in society, by the soundness of their understanding and the superiority of their faculties above the rest of mankind. The ascendant, which they acquire, gives a prevalence to that lively approbation, with which they receive any productions of genius, and renders it generally predominant. Many men, when left to themselves, have but a faint and dubious perception of beauty, who yet are capable of relishing any fine stroke, which is pointed out to them. Every convert to the admiration of the real poet or orator is the cause of some new conversion. And though prejudices may prevail for a time, they never unite in celebrating any rival to the true genius, but yield at last to the force of nature and just sentiment. Thus, though a civilized nation may easily be mistaken in the choice of their admired philosopher, they never have been found long to err, in their affection for a favorite epic or tragic author.

But notwithstanding all our endeavors to fix a standard of taste, and reconcile the discordant apprehensions of men, there still remain two sources of variation, which are not sufficient indeed to confound all the boundaries of beauty and deformity, but will often serve to produce a difference in the degrees of our approbation or blame. The one is the different humors of particular men; the other, the particular manners and opinions of our age and country. The general principles of taste are uniform in human nature: Where men vary in their judgments, some defect or perversion in the faculties may commonly be remarked; proceeding either from prejudice, from want of practice, or want of delicacy; and there is just reason for approving one taste, and condemning another. But where there is such a diversity in the internal frame or external situation as is entirely blameless on both sides, and leaves no room to give one the preference above the other; in that case a certain degree of diversity in judgment is unavoidable, and we seek in vain for a standard, by which we can reconcile the contrary sentiments.

A young man, whose passions are warm, will be more sensibly

touched with amorous and tender images, than a man more advanced in years, who takes pleasure in wise, philosophical reflections concerning the conduct of life and moderation of the passions. At twenty, Ovid may be the favorite author; Horace at forty; and perhaps Tacitus at fifty. Vainly would we, in such cases, endeavor to enter into the sentiments of others, and divest ourselves of those propensities, which are natural to us. We choose our favorite author as we do our friend, from a conformity of humor and disposition. Mirth or passion, sentiment or reflection; whichever of these most predominates in our temper, it gives us a peculiar sympathy with the writer who resembles us.

THE SUBLIME

EDMUND BURKE

Before he entered on his political career and his writings on politics—in which he would prove to be the towering enemy of much that the Enlightenment stood for—Edmund Burke (1729–1797) wrote A Philosophical Enquiry into the Origin of Our Ideas of the Sublime and Beautiful *(1757). This selection is from that influential essay, which argues that crucial to our sense of the sublime is fear, even terror.*

The passion caused by the great and sublime in *nature*, when those causes operate most powerfully, is astonishment: and astonishment is that state of the soul in which all its motions are suspended, with some degree of horror. In this case the mind is so entirely filled with its object, that it cannot entertain any other, nor by consequence reason on that object which employs it. Hence arises the great power of the sublime, that, far from being produced by them, it anticipates our reasonings, and hurries us on by an irresistible force. Astonishment, as I have said, is the effect of the sublime in its highest degree; the inferior effects are admiration, reverence, and respect.

No passion so effectually robs the mind of all its powers of acting and reasoning as *fear*. For fear being an apprehension of pain or death, it operates in a manner that resembles actual pain. Whatever therefore is terrible, with regard to sight, is sublime too, whether this cause of terror be endued with greatness of dimensions or not; for it is impossible to look on anything as trifling, or contemptible, that may be dangerous. There are many animals, who, though far from being large, are yet capable of raising ideas of the sublime, because they are considered as objects of terror. As serpents and poisonous animals of almost all kinds. And to things of great dimensions, if we annex an adventitious idea of terror, they become without comparison greater. A level plain of a vast extent on land, is certainly no mean idea; the prospect of such a plain may be as extensive as a prospect of the ocean; but can it ever fill the mind with anything so great as the ocean itself? This is owing to several causes; but it is owing to none more than this, that the ocean is an object of no small terror. Indeed terror is in all cases whatsoever, either more openly or latently, the ruling principle of the sublime. Several languages bear a strong testimony to the affinity of these ideas. They frequently use the same word to signify indifferently the modes of astonishment or admiration and those of terror. . . .

The Romans used the verb *stupeo*, a term which strongly marks the state of an astonished mind, to express the effect either of simple fear, or of astonishment; the word *attonitus* (thunderstruck) is equally expressive of the alliance of these ideas; and do not the French *étonnement*, and the English *astonishment* and *amazement*, point out as clearly the kindred emotions which attend fear and wonder? They who have a more general knowledge of languages, could produce, I make no doubt, many other and equally striking examples.

To make anything very terrible, obscurity seems in general to be necessary. When we know the full extent of any danger, when we can accustom our eyes to it, a great deal of the apprehension vanishes. Every one will be sensible of this, who considers how greatly night adds to our dread, in all cases of danger, and how much the notions of ghosts and goblins, of which none can form clear ideas, affect minds which give credit to the popular tales concerning such sorts of beings. Those despotic governments which are founded on the passions of men, and principally upon the passion of fear, keep their chief as much as may be from the public eye. The policy has been the same in many cases of religion. Almost all the heathen temples were dark. Even in the barbarous temples of the Americans at this day, they keep their idol in a dark part of the hut, which is consecrated to his worship. For this purpose too the Druids performed all their ceremonies in the bosom of the darkest woods, and in the shade of the oldest and most spreading oaks. No person seems better to have understood the secret of heightening, or of setting terrible things, if I may use the expression, in their strongest light, by the force of a judicious obscurity than Milton. His description of death in the second book is admirably studied; it is astonishing with what a gloomy pomp, with what a significant and expressive uncertainty of strokes and coloring, he has finished the portrait of the king of terrors:

> The other shape,
> If shape it might be called that shape had none
> Distinguishable, in member, joint, or limb;
> Or substance might be called that shadow seemed;
> For each seemed either; black he stood as night;
> Fierce as ten furies; terrible as hell;
> And shook a deadly dart. What seemed his head
> The likeness of a kingly crown had on.
>
> *Paradise Lost, II, 666–73.*

In this description all is dark, uncertain, confused, terrible, and sublime to the last degree.

It is one thing to make an idea clear, and another to make it *affecting* to the imagination. If I make a drawing of a palace, or a temple, or a landscape, I present a very clear idea of those objects; but then (allowing for the effect of imitation which is something) my picture can at most affect only as the palace, temple, or landscape, would have affected in the reality. On the other hand, the most lively and spirited verbal description I can give raises a very obscure and imperfect *idea* of such objects; but then it is in my power to raise a stronger *emotion* by the description than I could do by the best painting. This experience constantly evinces. The proper manner of conveying the *affections* of the mind from one to another is by words; there is a great insufficiency in all other methods of communication; and so far is a clearness of imagery from being absolutely necessary to an influence upon the passions, that they may be considerably operated upon, without presenting any image at all, by certain sounds adapted to that purpose; of which we have a sufficient proof in the acknowledged and powerful effects of instrumental music. In reality, a great clearness helps but little towards affecting the passions, as it is in some sort an enemy to all enthusiasms whatsoever. . . .

I know several who admire and love painting, and yet who regard the objects of their admiration in that art with coolness enough in comparison of that warmth with which they are animated by affecting pieces of poetry or rhetoric. Among the common sort of people, I never could perceive that painting had much influence on their passions. It is true that the best sorts of painting, as well as the best sorts of poetry, are not much understood in that sphere. But it is most certain that their passions are very strongly roused by a fanatic preacher, or by the ballads of Chevy Chase, or the Children in the Wood, and by other little popular poems and tales that are current in that rank of life. I do not know of any paintings, bad or good, that produce the same effect. So that poetry, with all its obscurity, has a more general, as well as a more powerful dominion over the passions, than the other art. And I think there are reasons in nature, why the obscure idea, when properly conveyed, should be more affecting than the clear. It is our ignorance of things that causes all our admiration, and chiefly excites our passions. Knowledge and acquaintance make the most striking causes affect but little. It is thus with the vulgar; and all men are as the vulgar in what they do not understand. . . .

Besides those things which *directly* suggest the idea of danger, and those which produce a similar effect from a mechanical cause, I know of nothing sublime, which is not some modification of power. And this branch rises, as naturally as the other two branches, from terror, the common stock of everything that is sublime. The idea of power, at first view, seems of the class of those indifferent ones, which may equally belong to pain or to pleasure. But in reality, the affection arising from the idea of vast power is extremely remote from that neutral character. For first, we must remember that the idea of pain, in its highest degree, is much stronger than the highest degree of pleasure; and that it preserves the same superiority through all the subordinate gradations. From hence it is, that where the chances for equal degrees of suffering or enjoyment are in any sort equal, the idea of the suffering must always be prevalent. And indeed the ideas of pain, and, above all, of death, are so very affecting, that whilst we remain in the presence of whatever is supposed to have the power of inflicting either, it is impossible to be perfectly free from terror. Again, we know by experience, that, for the enjoyment of pleasure, no great efforts of power are at all necessary; nay, we know that such efforts would go a great way towards destroying our satisfaction: for pleasure must be stolen, and not forced upon us; pleasure follows the will; and therefore we are generally affected with it by many things of a force greatly inferior to our own. But pain is always inflicted by a power in some way superior, because we never submit to pain willingly. So that strength, violence, pain, and terror, are ideas that rush in upon the mind together. Look at a man, or any other animal of prodigious strength, and what is your idea before reflection? Is it that this strength will be subservient to you, to your ease, to your pleasure, to your interest in any sense? No; the emotion you feel is, lest this enormous strength should be employed to the purposes of rapine and destruction. That power derives all its sublimity from the terror with which it is generally accompanied, will appear evidently from its effect in the very few cases, in which it may be possible to strip a considerable degree of strength of its ability to hurt. When you do this, you spoil it of everything sublime, and it immediately becomes contemptible.

ON THEATER AND MORALS

Jean-Jacques Rousseau

D'Alembert wrote the entry for "Geneva" in the Encylopédie, *in which he criticized its prohibition of theater. Rousseau replied in 1758 in his* Epistle to Mr. d'Alembert, *arguing not only that theater encouraged idleness and inactivity but that it left people alone with only themselves. A republic required truly public entertainment, he concluded, which would promote civic spirit.*

The state of man hath its pleasures, which are derived from his nature, and arise from his occupations, his connections and his necessities; and as these pleasures are most agreeable to uncorrupted, innocent minds, they render all others in a manner useless. A father, a son, a husband, a citizen, lie under obligations of so pleasing and interesting a nature, that they can want no amusement more agreeable than the discharge of them. The proper employment of our time increases its value; while the better it is employed, the less have we still to spare. Thus we find that the habit of labor renders idleness tiresome, and that a good conscience deprives us of all taste for frivolous pleasures. But it is the being dissatisfied with ourselves; it is the weight of indolence; it is the loss of taste for simple and natural pleasures, that give occasion to the expediency of artificial entertainments. I do not like to see the heart set upon theatrical amusements, as if it was uneasy or unhappy within itself. The answer of the barbarian to a person who had been extolling the magnificence of the circus, and the games instituted at Rome, was dictated by nature itself. Have the Romans, said that honest creature, no wives nor children? The barbarian was in the right. People imagine themselves to be in company at the theater, but it is there that everybody is alone. We repair thither to forget our relations, our friends, our neighbors; to interest ourselves in fabulous representations, to mourn over the imaginary misfortunes of the dead, or to laugh at the expense of the living. But I should have perceived that this is not the language of the present age. Let us endeavor, therefore, to assume one that will be better understood.

To enquire whether public amusements are good or bad in themselves is a question too vague and indeterminate: it would be to examine into a relation before we had fixed the terms of it. They are made for the people, and it is only from their effects on the people, that we are to determine their real good or bad qualities. There may be an almost infinite variety of such entertainments; and there is a like variety in the manners, constitutions and characters of different people. I allow that man is every where the same; but when he is variously modified by religion, government, laws, customs, prepossessions, and climates, he becomes so different from himself that the question no longer is what is proper for mankind in general, but what is proper for him in such a particular age and country. Hence it is that the dramatic pieces of Menander, calculated for the Athenian stage, were ill-suited for that of Rome. Hence the combats of the gladiators, which, under the republican government, animated the people with courage, and a love of glory, only served, under the emperors, to render the populace brutal, bloodthirsty, and cruel. The very same objects, exhibited under different circumstances, taught the people at one time to despise their own lives, and at another to sport with the lives of others.

Let us not ascribe to the theater . . . the power of changing sentiments and manners, when it can only pursue and embellish them. A dramatic writer who should oppose the general taste of the public, would soon be left to write only for himself. When Molière corrected the comic drama, he attacked only ridiculous modes and characters; but in doing this, he indulged the public taste, as did also Corneille. It was the old French stage that began to displease this taste: because, while the nation improved in politeness, the stage still retained its primitive barbarism.

It is for the same reason that, as the general taste is so greatly altered since their times, the very best pieces of these two authors, if now first brought on the stage, would infallibly be damned. The connoisseurs may admire them as much as they please; the public admire them rather because they are ashamed to do otherwise, than from any real beauties they discover in them. It is said, indeed, that a good piece can never miscarry; truly I believe it; but this is because a really good piece is never disgusting to the manners of the times. There cannot be the least doubt that the very best tragedy of Sophocles would be totally damned in our theaters. It is impossible for us to put ourselves in the place of people, to whom we bear no sort of resemblance. . . .

What! Ought there to be no entertainments in a republic? On the contrary, there ought to be many. It is in republics that they were born, it is in their bosom that they are seen to flourish with a truly festive air. To what peoples is it more fitting to assemble often and form among themselves sweet bonds of pleasure and joy than to those who have so many reasons to like one another and remain forever united? We already have many of these public festivals; let us have even more; I will be only the more charmed for it. But let us not adopt these exclusive entertainments which close up a small number of people in melancholy fashion in a gloomy cavern, which keep them fearful and immobile in silence and inaction, which give them only prisons, lances, soldiers, and afflicting images of servitude and inequality to see. No, happy peoples, these are not your festivals. It is in the open air, under the sky, that you ought to gather and give yourselves to the sweet sentiment of your happiness. Let your pleasures not be effeminate or mercenary; let nothing that has an odor of constraint and selfishness poison them; let them be free and generous like you are, let the sun illuminate your innocent entertainments; you will constitute one yourselves, the worthiest it can illuminate.

But what then will be the objects of these entertainments? What will be shown in them? Nothing, if you please. With liberty, wherever abundance reigns, well-being also reigns. Plant a stake crowned with flowers in the middle of a square; gather the people together there, and you will have a festival. Do better yet; let the spectators become an entertainment to themselves; make them actors themselves; do it so that each sees and loves himself in the others so that all will be better united. I need not have recourse to the games of the ancient Greeks; there are modern ones which are still in existence, and I find them precisely in our city. Every year we have reviews, public prizes, kings of the harquebus, the cannon, and sailing. Institutions so useful and so agreeable cannot be too much multiplied; of such kings there cannot be too many. Why should we not do to make ourselves active and robust what we do to become skilled in the use of arms? Has the republic less need of workers than of soldiers? Why should we not found, on the model of the military prizes, other prizes for gymnastics, wrestling, runnings, discus, and the various bodily exercises? Why should we not animate our boatmen by contests on the lake? Could there be an entertainment in the world more brilliant than seeing, on this vast and superb body of water, hundreds of boats, elegantly equipped, starting together at the given signal to go and capture a flag planted at the finish, then serving as a cortege for the victor returning in triumph to receive his well-earned prize? All festivals of this sort are expensive only insofar as one wishes them to be, and the gathering alone renders them quite magnificent. Nevertheless, one must have been there with the Genevans to understand with what ardor they devote themselves to them. They are unrecognizable; they are no longer that steady people which never deviates from its economic rules; they are no longer those slow reasoners who weigh everything, including joking, in the scale of judgment. The people are lively, gay, and tender; their hearts are then in their eyes as they are always on their lips; they seek to communicate their joy and their pleasures. They invite, importune, and coerce the new arrivals and dispute over them. All the societies constitute but one, all become common to all. It is almost a matter of indifference at which table one seats oneself. It would be the image of Lacedaemon if a certain lavishness did not prevail here; but this very lavishness is at this time in its place, and the sight of the abundance makes that of the liberty which produces it more moving.

ON CUSTOM AND FASHION

ADAM SMITH

In his Theory of Moral Sentiments *(1759), Smith has some fascinating observations on the tyranny of fashion.*

Dress and furniture are allowed by all the world to be entirely under the dominion of custom and fashion. The influence of those principles, however, is by no means confined to so narrow a sphere, but extends itself to whatever is in any respect the object of taste, to music, to poetry, to architecture. The modes of dress and furniture are continually changing; and that fashion appearing ridiculous today which was admired five years ago, we are experimentally convinced that it owed its vogue chiefly or entirely to custom and fashion. Clothes and furniture are not made of very durable materials. A well-fancied coat is done in a twelve-month, and cannot continue longer to propagate, as the fashion, that form according to which it was made. The modes of furniture change less rapidly than those of dress; because furniture is commonly more durable. In five or six years, however, it generally undergoes an entire revolution, and every man in his own time sees the fashion in this respect change many different ways. The productions of the other arts are much more lasting, and, when happily imagined, may continue to propagate the fashion of their make for a much longer time. A well-contrived building may endure many centuries: a beautiful air may be delivered down, by a sort of tradition, through many successive generations: a well-written poem may last as long as the world: and all of them continue for ages together, to give the vogue to that particular style, to that particular taste or manner, according to which each of them was composed. Few men have an opportunity of seeing in their own times the fashion in any of these arts change very considerably. Few men have so much experience and acquaintance with the different modes which have obtained in remote ages and nations, as to be thoroughly reconciled to them, or to judge with impartiality between them, and what takes place in their own age and country. Few men therefore are willing to allow, that custom or fashion have much influence upon their judgments concerning what is beautiful, or otherwise, in the productions of any of those arts: but imagine, that all the rules, which they think ought to be observed in each of them, are founded upon reason and nature, not upon habit or prejudice. A very little attention, however, may convince them of the contrary, and satisfy them, that the influence of custom and fashion over dress and furniture is not more absolute than over architecture, poetry, and music.

Can any reason, for example, be assigned why the Doric capital should be appropriated to a pillar, whose height is equal to eight diameters; the Ionic volute to one of nine; and the Corinthian foliage to one of ten? The propriety of each of those appropriations can be founded upon nothing but habit and custom. The eye having been used to see a particular proportion, connected with a particular ornament, would be offended if they were not joined together. Each of the five orders has its peculiar ornament, which cannot be changed for any other, without giving offense to all those who know anything of the rules of architecture. According to some architects, indeed, such is the exquisite judgment with which the ancients have assigned to each order its proper ornaments, that no others can be found which are equally suitable. It seems, however, a little difficult to be conceived that these forms, though, no doubt, extremely agreeable, should be the only forms which can suit those proportions, or that there should not be five hundred others, which, antecedent to established custom, would have fitted them equally well. When custom, however, has established particular rules of building, provided they are not absolutely unreasonable, it is absurd to think of altering them for others which are only equally good, or even for others which, in point of elegance and beauty, have naturally some little advantage over them. A man would be ridiculous who should appear in public with a suit of clothes quite different from those which are commonly worn, though the new dress should in itself be ever so graceful or convenient. And there seems to be an absurdity of the same kind in ornamenting a house after a quite different manner from that which custom and fashion have prescribed; though the new ornaments should in themselves be somewhat superior to the common ones.

According to the ancient rhetoricians, a certain measure or verse was by nature appropriated to each particular species of writing, as being naturally expressive of that character, sentiment, or passion which ought to predominate in it. One verse, they said was fit for grave, and another for gay works, which could not, they thought, be interchanged without the greatest impropriety. The experience of modern times, however, seems to contradict this principle, though in itself it would appear to be extremely probable. What is the burlesque verse in English, is the heroic verse in French. The tragedies of Racine and the Henriad of Voltaire, are nearly in the same verse with,

Let me have your advice in a weighty affair.

The burlesque verse in French, on the contrary, is pretty much the same with the heroic verse of ten syllables in English. Custom has made the one nation associate the ideas of gravity, sublimity, and seriousness, to that measure which the other has connected with whatever is gay, flippant, and ludicrous. Nothing would appear more absurd in English, than a tragedy written in the alexandrine verses of the French; or in French, than a work of the same kind in verses of ten syllables.

THE BEAUTIFUL AND SUBLIME

Immanuel Kant

Kant speculated on aesthetic theory in his 1764 work, Observations on the Feeling of the Beautiful and Sublime. *His views are strikingly similar to Burke's.*

Finer feeling, which we now wish to consider, is chiefly of two kinds: the feeling of the *sublime* and that of the *beautiful.* The stirring of each is pleasant, but in different ways. The sight of a mountain whose snow-covered peak rises above the clouds, the description of a raging storm, or Milton's portrayal of the infernal kingdom, arouse enjoyment but with horror; on the other hand, the sight of flower-strewn meadows, valleys with winding brooks and covered with grazing flocks, the description of Elysium, or Homer's portrayal of the girdle of Venus, also occasion a pleasant sensation but one that is joyous and smiling. In order that the former impression could occur to us in due strength, we must have a *feeling of the sublime*, and, in order to enjoy the latter well, a *feeling of the beautiful*. Tall oaks and lonely shadows in a sacred grove are sublime; flower beds, low hedges and trees trimmed in figures are beautiful. Night is sublime, day is beautiful. Temperaments that possess a feeling for the sublime are drawn gradually, by the quiet stillness of a summer evening as the shimmering light of the stars breaks through the brown shadows of night and the lonely moon rises into view, into high feelings of friendship, of disdain for the world, of eternity. The shining day stimulates busy fervor and a feeling of gaiety. The sublime *moves*, the beautiful *charms*. The mien of a man who is undergoing the full feeling of the sublime is earnest, sometimes rigid and astonished. On the other hand the lively sensation of the beautiful proclaims itself through shining cheerfulness in the eyes, through smiling features, and often through audible mirth. The sublime is in turn of different kinds. Its feeling is sometimes accompanied with a certain dread, or melancholy; in some cases merely with quiet wonder; and in still others with a beauty completely pervading a sublime plan. The first I shall call the *terrifying sublime*, the second the *noble*, and the third the *splendid*. Deep loneliness is sublime, but in a way that stirs terror. Hence great far-reaching solitudes, like the colossal Komul Desert in Tartary, have always given us occasion for peopling them with fearsome spirits, goblins, and ghouls.

The sublime must always be great; the beautiful can also be small. The sublime must be simple; the beautiful can be adorned and ornamented. A great height is just as sublime as a great depth, except that the latter is accompanied with the sensation of shuddering, the former with one of wonder. Hence the latter feeling can be the terrifying sublime, and the former the noble. The sight of an Egyptian pyramid, as Hasselquist reports, moves one far more than one can imagine from all the descriptions; but its design is simple and noble. St. Peter's in Rome is splendid; because on its frame, which is large and simple, beauty is so distributed, for example, gold, mosaic work, and so on, that the feeling of the sublime still strikes through with the greatest effect; hence the object is called splendid. An arsenal must be noble and simple, a residence castle splendid, and a pleasure palace beautiful and ornamented.

A long duration is sublime. If it is of time past, then it is noble. If it is projected into an incalculable future, then it has something of the fearsome in it. A building of the remotest antiquity is venerable. Haller's description of the coming eternity stimulates a mild horror, and of the past, transfixed wonder. . . .

In human nature, praiseworthy qualities never are found without concurrent variations that must run through endless shadings to the utmost imperfection. The quality of the *terrifying sublime,* if it is quite unnatural, is adventurous. Unnatural things, so far as the sublime is supposed in them, although little or none at all may actually be found, are *grotesque.* Whoever loves and believes the fantastic is a *visionary;* the inclination toward whims makes the *crank.* On the other side, if the noble is completely lacking the feeling of the beautiful degenerates, and one calls it *trifling.* A male person of this quality, if he is young, is named a *fop;* if he is of middle age, he is a *dandy.* Since the sublime is most necessary to the elderly, an *old dandy* is the most contemptible creature in nature, just as a young crank is the most offensive and intolerable. Jests and liveliness pertain to the feeling of the beautiful. Nevertheless, much understanding can fittingly shine through, and to that extent they can be more or less related to the sublime. He in whose sprightliness this admixture is not detectable *chatters.* He who perpetually chatters is *silly.* One easily notices that even clever persons occasionally chatter, and that not a little intellect is needed to call the understanding away from its post for a short time without anything going wrong thereby. He whose words or deeds neither entertain nor move one is *boring.* The bore, if he is nevertheless zealous to do both, is *insipid.* The insipid one, if he is conceited, is a fool.

I shall make this curious sketch of human frailties somewhat more understandable by examples; for he to whom Hogarth's engraving stylus is wanting must compensate by description for what the drawing lacks in expression. Bold acceptance of danger for our own, our country's, or our friends' rights is sublime. The crusades and ancient knighthood were adventurous; duels, a wretched remnant of the latter arising from a perverted concept of chivalry, are grotesque. Melancholy separation from the bustle of the world due to a legitimate weariness is noble. Solitary devotion by the ancient hermits was adventurous. Monasteries and such tombs, to confine the living saints, are grotesque. Subduing one's passions through principles is sublime. Castigation, vows, and other such monks' virtues are grotesque. Holy bones, holy wood, and all similar rubbish, the holy stool of the High Lama of Tibet not excluded, are grotesque. Of the works of wit and fine feeling, the epic poems of Virgil and Klopstock fall into the noble, of Homer and Milton into the adventurous. The *Metamorphoses* of Ovid are grotesque; the fairy tales of French foolishness are the most miserable grotesqueries ever hatched. Anacreontic poems are generally very close to the trifling.

Works of understanding and ingenuity, so far as their objects also contain something for feeling, likewise take some part in the differences now being considered. Mathematical representation of the infinite magnitude of the universe, the meditations of metaphysics upon eternity, Providence, and the immortality of our souls contain a certain sublimity and dignity. On the other hand, philosophy is distorted by many empty subtleties, and the superficial appearance of profundity cannot prevent our regarding the four syllogistic figures as scholastic trifling.

DISCOURSE ON ART

JOSHUA REYNOLDS

One of eighteenth-century England's most famous painters, Joshua Reynolds (1723–1792) was the first president of the Royal Academy when it was established in 1768. Each year thereafter he delivered what became popular discourses on art, which were ultimately published. In this selection—from his seventh discourse, delivered in December 1776—Reynolds concludes that "taste is fixed and established in the nature of things."

GENTLEMEN,

Let me then, without further introduction, enter upon an examination, whether taste be so far beyond our reach, as to be unattainable by care; or be so very vague and capricious, that no care ought to be employed about it.

It has been the fate of arts to be enveloped in mysterious and incomprehensible language, as if it was thought necessary that even the terms should correspond to the idea entertained of the instability and uncertainty of the rules which they expressed.

To speak of genius and taste, as in any way connected with reason or common sense, would be, in the opinion of some towering talkers, to speak like a man who possessed neither; who had never felt that enthusiasm, or, to use their own inflated language, was never warmed by that Promethean fire, which animates the canvas and vivifies the marble.

If, in order to be intelligible, I appear to degrade art by bringing her down from the visionary situation in the clouds, it is only to give her a more solid mansion upon the earth. It is necessary that at some time or other we should see things as they really are, and not impose on ourselves by that false magnitude with which objects appear when viewed indistinctly as through a mist.

We will allow a poet to express his meaning, when his meaning is not well known to himself, with a certain degree of obscurity, as it is one sort of the sublime. But when, in plain prose, we gravely talk of courting the Muse in shady bowers; waiting the call and inspiration of Genius, finding out where he inhabits, and where he is to be invoked with the greatest success; of attending to times and seasons when the imagination shoots with the greatest vigor, whether at the summer solstice or the vernal equinox; sagaciously observing how much the wild freedom and liberty of imagination is cramped by attention to established rules; and how this same imagination begins to grow dim in advanced age, smothered and deadened by too much judgment; when we talk such language, or entertain such sentiments as these, we generally rest contented with mere words, or at best entertain notions not only groundless but pernicious.

If all this means, what it is very possible was originally intended only to be meant, that in order to cultivate an art, a man secludes himself from the commerce of the world, and retires into the country at particular seasons; or that at one time of the year his body is in better health, and consequently his mind fitter for the business of hard thinking than at another time; or that the mind may be fatigued and grow confused by long and unremitted application; this I can understand. I can likewise believe, that a man eminent when young for possessing poetical imagination, may, from having taken another road, so neglect its cultivation, as to show less of its powers in his latter life. But I am persuaded, that scarce a poet is to be found, from Homer down to Dryden, who preserved a sound mind in a sound body, and continued practicing his profession to the very last, whose latter works are not as replete with the fire of imagination, as those which were produced in his more youthful days.

To understand literally these metaphors, or ideas expressed in poetical language, seems to be equally absurd as to conclude, that because painters sometimes represent poets writing from the dictates of a little winged boy or genius, that this same genius did really inform him in a whisper what he was to write; and that he is himself but a mere machine, unconscious of the operations of his own mind. . . .

Genius and taste, in their common acceptation, appear to be very nearly related; the difference lies only in this, that genius has super-added to it a habit or power of execution; or we may say, that taste, when this power is added, changes its name, and is called genius. They both, in the popular opinion, pretend to an entire exemption from the restraint of rules. It is supposed that their powers are intuitive; that under the name of genius great works are produced, and under the name of taste an exact judgment is given, without our knowing why, and without our being under the least obligation to reason, precept, or experience.

One can scarce state these opinions without exposing their absurdity; yet they are constantly in the mouths of men, and particularly of artists. They who have thought seriously on this subject, do not carry the point so far; yet I am persuaded, that even among those few who may be called thinkers, the prevalent opinion allows less than it ought to the powers of reason; and considers the principles of taste, which give all their authority to the rules of art, as more fluctuating, and as having less solid foundations, than we shall find, upon examination, they really have.

The common saying, that *tastes are not to be disputed*, owes its influence, and its general reception, to the same error which leads us to imagine this faculty of too high an original to submit to the authority of an earthly tribunal. It likewise corresponds with the notions of those who consider it as a mere phantom of the imagination, so devoid of substance as to elude all criticism. . . .

We apply the term TASTE to that act of the mind by which we like or dislike, whatever be the subject. Our judgment upon an airy nothing, a fancy which has no foundation, is called by the same name which we give to our determination concerning those truths which refer to the most general and most unalterable principles of human nature; to the works which are only to be produced by the greatest efforts of the human understanding. However inconvenient this may be, we are obliged to take words as we find them; all we can do is to distinguish the THINGS to which they are applied.

We may let pass those things which are at once subjects of taste and sense, and which, having as much certainty as the senses themselves, give no occasion to inquiry or dispute. The natural appetite or taste of the human mind is for TRUTH; whether that truth results from the real agreement or equality of original ideas among themselves; from the agreement of the representation of any object with the thing represented; or from the correspondence of the several parts of any arrangement with each other. It is the very same taste which relishes a demonstration in geometry, that is pleased with the resemblance of a picture to an original and touched with the harmony of music.

All these have unalterable and fixed foundations in nature, and are therefore equally investigated by reason, and known by study; some with more, some with less clearness, but all exactly in the same way. A picture that is unlike, is false. Disproportionate ordonnance of parts is not right; because it cannot be true, until it ceases to be a contradiction to assert, that the parts have no relation to the whole. Coloring is true, when it is naturally adapted to the eye, from brightness, from softness, from harmony, from resemblance; because these agree with their object, NATURE, and therefore are true; as true as mathematical demonstration; but known to be true only to those who study these things.

But besides real, there is also apparent truth, or opinion, or prejudice. With regard to real truth, when it is known, the taste which conforms to it is, and must be, uniform. With regard to the second sort of truth, which may be called truth upon sufferance, or truth by courtesy, it is not fixed, but variable. However, whilst these opinions and prejudices, on which it is founded, continue, they operate as truth; and the art, whose office it is to please the mind, as well as instruct it, must direct itself according to opinion, or it will not attain its end.

In proportion as these prejudices are known to be generally diffused, or long received, the taste which conforms to them approaches nearer to certainty, and to a sort of resemblance to real science, even where opinions are found to be no better than prejudices. And since they deserve, on account of their duration and extent, to be considered as really true, they become capable of no small degree of stability and determination, by their permanent and uniform nature.

As these prejudices become more narrow, more local, more transitory, this secondary taste becomes more and more fantastical; recedes from real science; is less to be approved by reason, and less followed by practice: though in no case perhaps to be wholly neglected, where it does not stand, as it sometimes does, in direct defiance of the most respectable opinions received amongst mankind.

Having laid down these positions, I shall proceed with less method, because less will serve to explain and apply them.

We will take it for granted, that reason is something invariable, and fixed in the nature of things; and without endeavoring to go back to an account of first principles, which forever will elude our search, we will conclude, that whatever goes under the name of taste, which we can fairly bring under the dominion of reason, must be considered as equally exempt from change. If, therefore, in the course of this enquiry, we can show that there are rules for the conduct of the artist which are fixed and invariable, it follows of course, that the art of the connoisseur, or, in other words, taste, has likewise invariable principles.

Of the judgment which we make on the works of art, and the preference that we give to one class of art over another, if a reason be demanded, the question is perhaps evaded by answering, I judge from my taste; but it does not follow that a better answer cannot be given, though, for common gazers, this may be sufficient. Every man is not obliged to investigate the cause of his approbation or dislike.

The arts would lie open for ever to caprice and casualty, if those who are to judge of their excellencies had no settled principles by which they are to regulate their decisions, and the merit or defect of performances were to be determined by unguided fancy. And indeed we may venture to assert, that whatever speculative knowledge is necessary to the artist, is equally and indispensably necessary to the connoisseur.

The first idea that occurs in the consideration of what is fixed in art, or in taste, is that presiding principle of which I have so frequently spoken in former discourses,—the general idea of nature. The beginning, the middle, and the end of every thing that is valuable in taste, is comprised in the knowledge of what is truly nature; for whatever notions are not conformable to those of nature, or universal opinion, must be considered as more or less capricious.

My notion of nature comprehends not only the forms which nature produces, but also the nature and internal fabric and organization, as I may call it, of the human mind and imagination. The terms beauty, or nature, which are general ideas, are but different modes of expressing the same thing, whether we apply these terms to statues, poetry, or pictures. Deformity is not nature, but an accidental deviation from her accustomed practice. This general idea therefore ought to be called Nature; and nothing else, correctly speaking, has a right to that name. But we are sure so far from speaking, in common conversation, with any such accuracy, that, on the contrary, when we criticize Rembrandt and other Dutch painters, who introduced into their historical pictures exact representations of individual objects with all their imperfections, we say,—though it is not in a good taste, yet it is nature.

This misapplication of terms must be very often perplexing to the young student. Is not art, he may say, an imitation of nature? Must he not therefore who imitates her with the greatest fidelity be the best artist? By this mode of reasoning Rembrandt has a higher place than Raffaelle. But a very little reflection will serve to show us that these particularities cannot be nature; for how can that be the nature of man, in which no two individuals are the same?

It plainly appears, that as a work is conducted under the influence of general ideas, or partial, it is principally to be considered as the effect of a good or a bad taste.

As beauty therefore does not consist in taking what lies immediately before you, so neither, in our pursuit of taste, are those opinions which we first received and adopted, the best choice, or the most natural to the mind and imagination. In the infancy of our knowledge we seize with greediness the good that is within our reach; it is by after-consideration, and in consequence of discipline, that we refuse the present for a greater good at a distance. The nobility or elevation of all arts, like the excellency of virtue itself, consists in adopting this enlarged and comprehensive idea; and all criticism built upon the more confined view of what is natural, may properly be called *shallow* criticism, rather than false: its defect is, that the truth is not sufficiently extensive. . . .

I shall now say something on that part of *taste*, which as I have hinted to you before, does not belong so much to the external form of things, but is addressed to the mind, and depends on its original frame, or, to use the expression, the organization of the soul; I mean the imagination and the passions. The principles of these are as invariable as the former, and are to be known and reasoned upon in the same manner, by an appeal to common sense deciding upon the common feelings of mankind. This sense, and these feelings appear to me of equal authority, and equally conclusive. Now this appeal implies a general uniformity and agreement in the minds of men. It would be else an idle and vain endeavor to establish rules of art; it would be pursuing a phantom, to attempt to move affections with which we were entirely unacquainted. We have no reason to suspect there is a greater difference between our minds than between our forms; of which, though there are no two alike, yet there is a general similitude that goes through the whole race of mankind; and those who have cultivated their taste, can distinguish what is beautiful or deformed, or, in other words, what agrees with or deviates from the general idea of nature, in one case, as well as in the other.

The internal fabric of our minds, as well as the external form of our bodies, being nearly uniform; it seems then to follow of course, that as the imagination is incapable of producing anything originally of itself, and can only vary and combine those ideas with which it is furnished by means of the senses, there will be necessarily an agreement in the imaginations, as in the senses of men. There being this agreement, it follows, that in all cases, in our lightest amusements, as well as in our most serious actions and engagements of life, we must regulate our affections of every kind by that of others. The well-disciplined mind acknowledges this authority, and submits its own opinion to the public voice. It is from knowing what are the general feelings and passions of mankind, that we acquire a true idea of what imagination is; though it appears as if we had nothing to do but to consult our own particular sensations, and these were sufficient to ensure us from all error and mistake.

A knowledge of the disposition and character of the human mind can be acquired only by experience; a great deal will be learned, I admit, by a habit of examining what passes in our bosoms, what are our own motives of action, and of what kind of sentiments we are conscious on any occasion. We may suppose an uniformity, and conclude that the same effect will be produced by the same cause in the mind of others. This examination will contribute to suggest to us matters of inquiry; but we can never be sure that our own sentiments are true and right, till they are confirmed by more extensive observation. One man opposing another determines nothing; but a general union of minds, like a general combination of the forces of all mankind, makes a strength that is irresistible. In fact, as he who does not know himself, does not know others, so it may be said with equal truth, that he who does not know others, knows himself but very imperfectly.

A man who thinks he is guarding himself against prejudices by resisting the authority of others, leaves open every avenue to singularity, vanity, self-conceit, obstinacy, and many other vices, all tending to warp the judgment, and prevent the natural operation of his faculties. This submission to others is a deference which we owe, and indeed are forced involuntarily to pay. In fact, we never are satisfied with our opinions, whatever we may pretend, till they are ratified and confirmed by the suffrages of the rest of mankind. We dispute and wrangle forever; we endeavor to get men to come to us, when we do not go to them.

He therefore who is acquainted with the works which have pleased different ages and different countries, and has formed his opinion on them, has more materials, and more means of knowing what is analogous to the mind of man, than he who is conversant only with the works of his own age or country. What has pleased, and continues to please, is likely to please again: hence are derived the rules of art, and on this immovable foundation they must ever stand.

This search and study of the history of the mind, ought not to be confined to one art only. It is by the analogy that one art bears to another, that many things are ascertained, which either were but faintly seen, or, perhaps, would not have been discovered at all, if the inventor had not received the first hints from the practices of a sister art on a similar occasion. The frequent allusions which every man who treats of any art is obliged to make to others, in order to illustrate and confirm his principles, sufficiently show their near connection and inseparable relation.

All arts having the same general end, which is to please; and addressing themselves to the same faculties through the medium of the senses; it follows that their rules and principles must have as great affinity, as the different materials and the different organs or vehicles by which they pass to the mind, will permit them to retain.

We may therefore conclude, that the real substance, as it may be called, of what goes under the name of taste, is fixed and established in the nature of things; that there are certain and regular causes by which the imagination and passions of men are affected; and that the knowledge of these causes is acquired by a laborious and diligent investigation of nature, and by the same slow progress as wisdom or knowledge of every kind, however instantaneous its operations may appear when thus acquired.

PART V

REASON AND SOCIETY

Progress and History

THE NEW SCIENCE

GIAMBATTISTA VICO

One of the first to conceive of history as a progress through successive stages, the Italian lawyer and professor of Greek and Latin Giambattista Vico (1668–1744) published his monumental Principles of a New Science Concerning the Common Nature of the Nations *in 1725. This selection is from the introduction to the book, which Vico titled "Idea of the Work."*

This New Science studies the common nature of nations in the light of divine providence, discovers the origins of institutions, religious and secular, among the gentile nations, and thereby establishes a system of the natural law of the gentes, which proceeds with the greatest equality and constancy through the three ages which the Egyptians handed down to us as the three periods through which the world had passed up to their time. These are: (1) The age of gods, in which the gentiles believed they lived under divine governments and everything was commanded them by auspices and oracles, which are the oldest institutions in profane history. (2) The age of heroes, in which they reigned everywhere in aristocratic commonwealths, on account of a certain superiority of nature which they held themselves to have over the plebs. (3) The age of men, in which all men recognized themselves as equal in human nature, and therefore there were established first the popular commonwealths and then the monarchies, both of which are forms of human government.

In harmony with these three kinds of nature and government, three kinds of language were spoken which compose the vocabulary of this Science: (1) That of the time of the families, when gentile men were newly received into humanity. This was a mute language of signs and physical objects having natural relations to the ideas they wished to express. (2) That spoken by means of heroic emblems, or similitudes, comparisons, images, metaphors, and natural descriptions, which make up the great body of the heroic language which was spoken at the time the heroes reigned. (3) Human language using words agreed upon by the people, a language of which they are absolute lords, and which is proper to the popular commonwealths and monarchical states; a language whereby the people may fix the meaning of the laws by which the nobles as well as the plebs are bound. Hence, among all nations, once the laws had been put into the vulgar tongue, the science of laws passed from the control of the nobles. Hitherto, among all nations, the nobles, being also priests, had kept the laws in a secret language as a sacred thing. That is the natural reason for the secrecy of the laws among the Roman patricians until popular liberty arose.

Now these are the same three languages that the Egyptians claimed had been spoken before in their world, corresponding exactly both in number and in sequence to the three ages that had run their course before them. (1) The hieroglyphic or sacred or secret language, by means of mute acts. This is suited to the uses of religion, for which observance is more important than discussion. (2) The symbolic, by means of similitudes, such as we have just seen the heroic language to have been. (3) The epistolary or vulgar, which served the common uses of life. These three types of language are found among the Chaldeans, Scythians, Egyptians, Germans, and all the other ancient gentile nations; although hieroglyphic writing survived longest among the Egyptians, because for a longer time than the others they were closed to all foreign nations (as for the same reason it still survives among the Chinese), and hence we have a proof of the vanity of their imagined remote antiquity.

We here bring to light the beginnings not only of languages but also of letters, which philology has hitherto despaired of finding. . . . Philologists have believed that among the nations languages first came into being and then letters; whereas (to give here a brief indication of what will be fully proved in this volume) letters and languages were born twins and proceeded apace through all their three stages. Their beginnings are precisely exhibited in the causes of the Latin language. . . . By the reasoning out of these causes many discoveries have been made in ancient Roman history, government, and law, as you will observe a thousand times, O reader, in this volume. From this example, scholars of oriental languages, of Greek, and, among the modern languages, particularly of German, which is a mother language, will be enabled to make discoveries of antiquities far beyond their expectations and ours.

We find that the principle of these origins both of languages and of letters lies in the fact that the early gentile peoples, by a demonstrated necessity of nature, were poets who spoke in poetic characters. This discovery, which is the master key of this Science, has cost us the persistent research of almost all our literary life, because with our civilized natures we [moderns] cannot at all imagine and can understand only by great toil the poetic nature of these first men. The [poetic] characters of which we speak were certain imaginative genera (images for the most part of animated substances, of gods or heroes, formed by their imagination) to which they reduced all the species or all the particulars appertaining to each genus; exactly as the fables of human times, such as those of late comedy, are intelligible genera reasoned out by moral philosophy, from which the comic poets form imaginative genera (for the best ideas of the various human types are nothing but that) which are the persons of the comedies. These divine or heroic characters were true fables or myths, and their allegories are found to contain meanings not analogical but univocal, not philosophical but historical, of the peoples of Greece of those times.

Since these genera (for that is what the fables in essence are) were formed by most vigorous imaginations, as in men of the feeblest reasoning powers, we discover in them true poetic sentences, which must be sentiments clothed in the greatest passions and therefore full of sublimity and arousing wonder. Now the sources of all poetic locution are two: poverty of language and need to explain and be understood. From these comes the expressiveness of the heroic speech which followed immediately after the mute language of acts and objects that had natural relations to the ideas they were meant to signify, which was used in the divine times. Lastly, in the necessary natural course of human institutions, language among the Assyrians, Syrians, Phoenicians, Egyptians, Greeks, and Latins began with heroic verses, passed thence to iambics, and finally settled into prose. This gives certainty to the history of the ancient poets and explains why in the German language, particularly in Silesia, a province of peasants, there are many natural versifiers, and in the Spanish, French, and Italian languages the first authors wrote in verse.

From these three languages is formed the mental dictionary by which to interpret properly all the various articulated languages, and we make use of it here wherever it is needed. . . . Such a lexicon is necessary for learning the language spoken by the ideal eternal history traversed in time by the histories of all nations, and for scientifically adducing authorities to confirm what is treated of in the natural law of the gentes and hence in every particular jurisprudence.

Along with these three languages—proper to the three ages in which three forms of government prevailed, conforming to three types of civil natures, which succeed one another as the nations run their course—we find there went also in the same order a jurisprudence suited to each in its time.

Of these [three types of jurisprudence] the first was a mystic theology, which prevailed in the period when the gentiles were commanded by the gods. Its wise men were the theological poets (who are said to have founded gentile humanity), who interpreted the mysteries of the oracles, which among all nations gave their responses in verse. Thus we find that the mysteries of this vulgar wisdom were hidden in the fables. In this connection we enquire into the reasons why the philosophers later had such a desire to recover the wisdom of the ancients, as well as into the occasions the fables provided them for bestirring themselves to meditate lofty things in philosophy, and into the opportunities they had for reading their own hidden wisdom into the fables.

The second was the heroic jurisprudence, all verbal scrupulosity (in which Ulysses was manifestly expert). This jurisprudence looked to what the Roman jurisconsults called civil equity and we call reason of state. With their limited ideas, the heroes thought they had a natural right to precisely what, how much, and of what sort had been set forth in words; as even now we may observe in peasants and other crude men, who in conflicts between words and meanings obstinately say that their right stands for them in the words. And this by counsel of divine providence to the end that the gentiles, not yet being capable of universals, which good laws must be, might be led by this very particularity of their words to observe the laws universally. And if, as a consequence of this [civil] equity, the laws turned out in a given case to be not only harsh but actually cruel, they naturally bore it because they thought their law was naturally such. Furthermore, they were led to observe their laws by a sovereign private interest, which the heroes identified with that of their fatherlands, of which they were the sole citizens. Hence they did not hesitate, for the safety of their various fatherlands, to consecrate themselves and their families to the will of the laws, which by maintaining the common security of the fatherland kept secure for each of them a certain private monarchical reign over his family. Moreover, it was this great private interest, in conjunction with the supreme arrogance characteristic of barbarous times, which formed their heroic nature, whence came so many heroic actions in defense of their fatherlands. To these heroic deeds we must add the intolerable pride, profound avarice, and pitiless cruelty with which the ancient Roman patricians treated the unhappy plebeians, as is clearly seen in Roman history precisely during that period which Livy himself describes as having been the age of Roman virtue and of the most flourishing popular liberty yet dreamed of in Rome. It will then be evident that this public virtue was nothing but a good use which providence made of such grievous, ugly, and cruel private vices, in order that the cities might be preserved during a period when the minds of men, intent on particulars, could not naturally understand a common good. Thence are derived new principles by which to demonstrate the argument of St. Augustine's discussion of the virtue of the Romans; and the opinion hitherto held by the learned concerning the heroism of primitive peoples is put to rout. Civil equity of this sort we find naturally observed by the heroic nations in peace as well as in war (shining examples are adduced from the history of the first barbarian times as well as from that of the last); and it was practiced privately by the Romans as long as theirs was an aristocratic commonwealth, that is to say down to the times of the Publilian and Petelian laws, until which time everything was based on the Law of the Twelve Tables.

The last type of jurisprudence was that of natural equity, which reigns naturally in the free commonwealths, in which the people, each for his own particular good (without understanding that it is the same for all), are led to command universal laws. They naturally desire these laws to bend benignly to the least details of matters calling for equal utility. This is the *aequum bonum*, subject of the latest Roman jurisprudence, which from the times of Cicero had begun to be transformed by the edict of the Roman praetor. This type is also and perhaps even more connatural with the monarchies, in which the monarchs have accustomed their subjects to attend to their own private interests, while they themselves have taken charge of all public affairs and desire all nations subject to them to be made equal by the laws, in order that all may be equally interested in the state. Wherefore the emperor Hadrian reformed the entire heroic natural law of Rome with the aid of the human natural law of the provinces, and commanded that jurisprudence should be based on the Perpetual Edict which Salvius Julianus composed almost entirely from the provincial edicts.

THE UTILITY OF HISTORY

Henry St. John, Lord Bolingbroke

A Tory statesman and writer, a friend of Swift and Pope, Bolingbroke (1678–1751) stressed the moral value of studying the past more than most in the Enlightenment. History was, in his famous phrase, "philosophy teaching by examples." This selection is from his Letters on the Study and Use of History, *written in 1735.*

That the study of history, far from making us wiser, and more useful citizens, as well as better men, may be of no advantage whatsoever; that it may serve to render us mere antiquaries and scholars; or that it may help to make us forward coxcombs, and prating pedants, I have already allowed. But this is not the fault of history: and to convince us that it is not, we need only contrast the true use of history with the use that is made of it by such men as these. We ought always to keep in mind, that history is philosophy teaching by examples how to conduct ourselves in all the situations of private and public life; that therefore we must apply ourselves to it in a philosophical spirit and manner; that we must rise from particular to general knowledge, and that we must fit ourselves for the society and business of mankind by accustoming our minds to reflect and meditate on the characters we find described, and the course of events we find related there. . . .

Now, to improve by examples is to improve by imitation. We must catch the spirit, if we can, and conform ourselves to the reason of them; but we must not affect to translate servilely into our conduct, if your lordship will allow me the expression, the particular conduct of those good and great men, whose images history sets before us. Codrus and the Decii devoted themselves to death: one, because an oracle had foretold that the army whose general was killed would be victorious; the others in compliance with a superstition that bore great analogy to a ceremony practiced in the old Egyptian church, and added afterwards, as many others of the same origin were, to the ritual of the Israelites. These are examples of great magnanimity, to be sure, and of magnanimity employed in the most worthy cause. In the early days of the Athenian and Roman government, when the credit of oracles and all kinds of superstition prevailed, when heaven was piously thought to delight in blood, and even human blood was shed under wild notions of atonement, propitiation, purgation, expiation, and satisfaction; they who set such examples as these, acted an heroical and a rational part too. But if a general should act the same part now, and, in order to secure his victory, get killed as fast as he could, he might pass for a hero, but, I am sure, he would pass for a madman. Even these examples, however, are of use: they excite us at least to venture our lives freely in the service of our country, by proposing to our imitation men who devoted themselves to certain death in the service of theirs. They show us what a turn of imagination can operate, and how the greatest trifle, nay the greatest absurdity, dressed up in the solemn airs of religion, can carry ardor and confidence, or the contrary sentiments, into the breasts of thousands.

These are certain general principles, and rules of life and conduct, which always must be true, because they are conformable to the invariable nature of things. He who studies history as he would study philosophy, will soon distinguish and collect them, and by doing so will soon form to himself a general system of ethics and politics on the surest foundations, on the trial of these principles and rules in all ages, and on the confirmation of them by universal experience. I said he will distinguish them; for once more I must say, that as to particular modes of actions, and measures of conduct, which the customs of different countries, the manners of different ages, and the circumstances of different conjunctures, have appropriated, as it were; it is always ridiculous, or imprudent and dangerous to employ them. But this is not all. By contemplating the vast variety of particular characters and events; by examining the strange combination of causes, different, remote, and seemingly opposite, that often concur in producing one effect; and the surprising fertility of one single and uniform cause in the producing of a multitude of effects, as different, as remote, and seemingly as opposite;

by tracing carefully, as carefully as if the subject he considers were of personal and immediate concern to him, all the minute and sometimes scarce perceivable circumstances, either in the characters of actors, or in the course of actions, that history enables him to trace, and according to which the success of affairs, even the greatest, is mostly determined; by these, and such methods as these, for I might descend into a much greater detail, a man of parts may improve the study of history to its proper and principal use; he may sharpen the penetration, fix the attention of his mind, and strengthen his judgment; he may acquire the faculty and the habit of discerning quicker, and looking farther; and of exerting that flexibility, and steadiness, which are necessary to be joined in the conduct of all affairs that depend on the concurrence or opposition of other men.

Mr. Locke, I think, recommends the study of geometry even to those who have no design of being geometricians: and he gives a reason for it, that may be applied to the present case. Such persons may forget every problem that has been proposed, and every solution that they or others have given; but the habit of pursuing long trains of ideas will remain with them, and they will pierce through the mazes of sophism, and discover a latent truth, where persons who have not this habit will never find it.

In this manner the study of history will prepare us for action and observation. History is the ancient author: experience is the modern language. We form our taste on the first, we translate the sense and reason, we transfuse the spirit and force; but we imitate only the particular graces of the original; we imitate them according to the idiom of our own tongue, that is, we substitute often equivalents in the lieu of them, and are far from affecting to copy them servilely. To conclude, as experience is conversant about the present, and the present enables us to guess at the future; so history is conversant about the past, and by knowing the things that have been, we become better able to judge of the things that are.

HISTORY AS GUIDE

David Hume

Much the same philosophical appreciation of history—as a guide to present action—is found in Hume, who himself wrote a multivolume history of England. This selection is from his Enquiry Concerning Human Understanding, *published in 1748.*

It is universally acknowledged that there is a great uniformity among the actions of men, in all nations and ages, and that human nature remains still the same, in its principles and operations. The same motives always produce the same actions: The same events follow from the same causes. Ambition, avarice, self-love, vanity, friendship, generosity, public spirit: these passions, mixed in various degrees, and distributed through society, have been, from the beginning of the world, and still are, the source of all the actions and enterprises, which have ever been observed among mankind. Would you know the sentiments, inclinations, and course of life of the Greeks and Romans? Study well the temper and actions of the French and English: You cannot be much mistaken in transferring to the former *most* of the observations which you have made with regard to the latter. Mankind are so much the same, in all times and places that history informs us of nothing new or strange in this particular. Its chief use is only to discover the constant and universal principles of human nature, by showing men in all varieties of circumstances and situations, and furnishing us with materials from which we may form our observations and become acquainted with the regular springs of human action and behavior. These records or wars, intrigues, factions, and revolutions, are so many collections of experiments, by which the politician or moral philosopher fixes the principles of his science, in the same manner as the physician or natural philosopher becomes acquainted with the nature of plants, minerals, and other external objects, by the experiments which he forms concerning them. Nor are the earth, water, and other elements, examined by Aristotle, and Hippocrates, more like to those which at present lie under our observation than the men described by Polybius and Tacitus are to those who now govern the world.

Should a traveler, returning from a far country, bring us an account of men, wholly different from any with whom we were ever acquainted; men, who were entirely divested of avarice, ambition, or revenge; who knew no pleasure but friendship, generosity, and public spirit; we should immediately, from these circumstances, detect the falsehood, and prove him a liar, with the same certainty as if he had stuffed his narration with stories of centaurs and dragons, miracles and prodigies. And if we would explode any forgery in history, we cannot make use of a more convincing argument, than to prove, that the actions ascribed to any person are directly contrary to the course of nature, and that no human motives, in such circumstances, could ever induce him to such a conduct. The veracity of Quintus Curtius is as much to be suspected, when he describes the supernatural courage of Alexander, by which he was hurried on singly to attack multitudes, as when he describes his supernatural force and activity, by which he was able to resist them. So readily and universally do we acknowledge a uniformity in human motives and actions as well as in the operations of body.

Hence likewise the benefit of that experience, acquired by long life and a variety of business and company, in order to instruct us in the principles of human nature, and regulate our future conduct, as well as speculation. By means of this guide, we mount up to the knowledge of men's inclinations and motives, from their actions, expressions, and even gestures; and again descend to the interpretation of their actions from our knowledge of their motives and inclinations. The general observations treasured up by a course of experience, give us the clue of human nature, and teach us to unravel all its intricacies. Pretexts and appearances no longer deceive us. Public declarations pass for the specious coloring of a cause. And though virtue and honor be allowed their proper weight and authority, that perfect disinterestedness, so often pretended to, is never expected in multitudes and parties; seldom in their leaders; and scarcely even in individuals of any rank or station. But were there no uniformity in human actions, and were every experiment which we could form of this kind irregular and anomalous, it were impossible to collect any general observations concerning mankind; and no experience, however accurately digested by reflection, would ever serve to any purpose. Why is the aged husbandman more skillful in his calling than the young beginner but because there is a certain uniformity in the operation of the sun, rain, and earth towards the production of vegetables; and experience teaches the old practitioner the rules by which this operation is governed and directed.

ON PROGRESS

ANNE-ROBERT-JACQUES TURGOT

Like his fellow philosophes, *Anne-Robert-Jacques, baron de l'Aulne Turgot (1727–1781), a French statesman, economist, and political writer, was preoccupied with the progressive nature of historical development. This excerpt from his December 1750 discourse at the Sorbonne is titled "On the Successive Advances of the Human Mind."*

The phenomena of Nature, subjected to constant laws, are confined in a circle of ever the same revolutions. All perishes and all revives; in these successive generations, by which vegetables and animals reproduce themselves, time only gathers back in each case the image of what it had made disappear.

The succession of man, on the contrary, offers from age to age a spectacle ever varied. Reason, the passions, liberty, incessantly produce new events. All the ages are linked together by a sequence of causes and effects which connect the existing state of the world with all that has preceded it. The multiform signs of language and of writing, by giving to men the means of insuring the possession of their ideas and of communicating them to others, have made of all the individual funds of knowledge a common treasure, which one generation transmits to the next, along with an inheritance always increased by the discoveries of each age; thus the human race seen from its origin appears to the eye of a philosopher as one vast whole, which itself, like each individual composing it, has had its infancy and its development.

We see societies establishing themselves, nations forming themselves, which in turn dominate over other nations or become subject to them. Empires rise and fall; laws, forms of government, one succeeding another; the arts, the sciences, are discovered and are cultivated; sometimes retarded and sometimes accelerated in their progress, they pass from one region to another. Self-interest, ambition, vainglory, perpetually change the scene of the world, inundate the earth with blood. Yet in the midst of their ravages manners are gradually softened, the human mind takes enlightenment, separate nations draw nearer to each other, commerce and policy connect at last all parts of the globe, and the total mass of the human race, by the alternations of calm and agitation, of good conditions and of bad, marches always, although slowly, towards still higher perfection. . . .

An art suddenly rises by which are spread, in all directions, the thoughts and the glory of the great men of the past. Until now how slow, in every sense, progress has been! For two thousand years back medals have presented to all eyes characters impressed on bronze, and, after so many ages, it occurs for the first time to some obscure man that characters might be impressed on paper! As soon as the treasures of antiquity, drawn from the dust, pass into all hands, penetrate into all places, enlightenment is brought to the minds that were losing themselves in ignorance, and then genius is called forth from the depth of its retreat. The time has come.

Emerge, Europe, from the darkness that covered you! Immortal names of the Medicis, of Leo X, of Francis I, may you be consecrated forever, may the patrons of the arts share the glory of those who cultivated them! I salute you, Italy, happy land, for the second time the country of letters and of taste, the source whence their waters are shed to fertilize our regions. Our France, as yet, views your progress, but from a distance. Her language is still infected with some remnant of barbarism. . . .

And now that multiplicity of facts, of experiences, of instruments, of ingenious operations, which the practice of the arts had accumulated during so many ages, has been drawn from obscurity by the work of the printing press, the productions of the two worlds, brought together by an immense commerce, have become the foundation of a natural history and philosophy hitherto unknown, and freed at last from grotesque speculations. On all sides attentive eyes are fixed on Nature. Slight chances turned to profit bring forth discoveries. The son of an artisan in Zeeland, while amusing himself, brings together two convex glasses in a tube, and the limits of our senses are removed. In Italy the eyes of Galileo have discovered a new celestial world. Now Kepler, while seeking in the stars the numbers of Pythagoras, has found the two famous laws of the course of the planets which will become one day, in the hands of Newton, the key to the universe. Bacon had already traced for posterity the road she had to follow. . . . Great Descartes! if to find truth has not been always given to you, you have at least destroyed tyranny and error [that obscured it]. . . . At last all the clouds are dissipated. What a glorious light is cast on all sides! What a crowd of great men on all paths of knowledge! What perfection of human reason! One man, Newton, has submitted the infinite to the calculus; has unveiled the nature and properties of light, which, while revealing to us everything else, had concealed itself; he has placed in his balance the stars, the earth, and all the forces of Nature.

A CRITIQUE OF PROGRESS

JEAN-JACQUES ROUSSEAU

In 1751 Rousseau directly challenged the other philosophes *with his* Discourse on Arts and Sciences, *from which this selection is taken. No defense of science and learning here.*

"Has the re-establishment of arts and sciences contributed to purge or corrupt our manners?" This is the question in debate; which side shall I take, Gentlemen? That which becomes an honest man who knows nothing, and is not asham'd to own it.

I foresee the difficulty of appropriating what I have to say to the tribunal I appear before: How shall I dare to depreciate the sciences in the presence of one of the most learned Assemblies in *Europe?* Run out into the praises of ignorance in the midst of a celebrated Academy; or reconcile my disdain for study with the respect due to the truly learned?

I saw these difficulties, but was not deterr'd by them. 'Tis not the Sciences, said I to myself, that I attack; 'tis the Cause of Virtue that I support before virtuous judges; honor, honesty, and probity, are dearer to good men than erudition to even the learned—What then have I to dread? The penetration of the honorable assembly, before whom I speak, I own, is to be fear'd: but it is more for the construction of the oration, than for the sentiments of the orator; equitable sovereigns never hesitate to condemn themselves in all doubtful cases; and the happiest situation for a just cause is, to be admitted to a defense where its upright and learned adversary is judge.—If to this motive, which has encouraged me, another be wanting, let it be, that after having, to the best of my skill, defended the truth, whatever my success may be, there is a prize which cannot fail me, I shall find it at the bottom of my own heart.

It is a beautiful noble prospect to view man, as it were, rising again from nothing by his own efforts; dissipating, by the light of his reason, all the thick clouds in which nature had involv'd him; mounting above himself: soaring in thought even to the celestial regions; marching like the sun, with giant strides around the vast universe; and, what is still grander and more wonderful, re-entering into himself to study man, to dive into his nature, his duties, his end. All these wonders have been renew'd within these few last generations.

Europe was relapsed into the barbarity of the first ages; the inhabitants of that part of the world, which now makes so great a figure in knowledge, were plung'd, some centuries ago, into a state which was worse than utter ignorance. A certain school jargon, more despicable than ignorance itself, had usurp'd the name of knowledge, and opposed an almost invincible obstacle to its restoration, a revolution became necessary to lead people back into common sense: and it came at last from the corner of the world the least suspected; it was the stupid Mussulman, the sworn enemy to letters, that caus'd their revival among us. The fall of *Constantine's* throne brought the relics of ancient *Greece* into *Italy; France* in her turn was enrich'd by the precious spoils; the sciences soon follow'd letters, and the art of thinking was join'd to that of writing: this gradation seems strange, but it is perhaps but too natural; and men began to feel the principal advantage accruing from the love of the Muses, that of rendering mankind more sociable, by inspiring the thirst of pleasing each other by works worthy of mutual approbation.

There are necessaries for the mind, as well as for the body; these are the foundation of society, those its ornament. Whilst the government and laws provide for the safety and well-being of a people assembled;

the sciences, letters, and arts, less arbitrary, tho' perhaps more powerful, strow garlands of flowers on their iron fetters, smother those sentiments of original liberty, with which they would seem to have been born, make them in love with their slavery, and so form, what we call, a polish'd nation. Necessity rais'd thrones; and the arts and sciences support them.—Ye powers of the earth cherish all talents, and protect those who cultivate them: go on ye polish'd nations, improve, advance and enlarge them: to them, ye happy slaves, you owe that delicacy of taste you boast of, that sweetness of character, and that urbanity of manners, which renders your civil commerce so easy, so flowing, and so engaging: in a word, the appearance of every virtue without possessing one.

'Twas by these kind of accomplishments, which become much the more amiable for their affectation of not appearing, that *Athens* and *Rome* were formerly so renown'd in those boasted days of their magnificence and glory: and it is, no doubt, for the same reason that our days and our kingdom bear the sway from all ages and all nations;—An air of philosophy without pedantry, an address that is natural and yet engaging, equally distant from northern rusticity and *Italian* mimickry: those are the fruits produced by the arts and sciences which are ripened and brought to perfection by the commerce of the world.

What a happiness it would be to live amongst us, if our exterior appearance were always the true representation of our hearts; if our decency were virtue, if our maxims were the rules of our actions, if true philosophy were inseparably annex'd to the title of philosopher! But so many good qualities are not always found together, and virtue seldom appears in such pomp and state. Dress will set forth the man of fortune, and elegance the man of taste; but the wholesome robust man is known by other marks. The strength and vigor of body are found under the coarse homely coverings of the laboring peasant, not under the courtier's embroidery. So all ornaments are strangers to virtue, which is the strength and vigor of the soul: the honest man is a champion who wrestles stark naked; he disdains all those vile accoutrements which prove only incumbrances, that mar his natural force and activity, and were only first invented to hide some defect or deformity.

Before art had new molded our behaviors, and taught our passions to talk an affected language, our manners were indeed rustic, but sincere and natural; and the difference of our behaviors in an instant distinguished our characters.—'Tis true, that human nature was not then any wise better in the main than now: but man found a security in the ease with which he could dive into the thoughts of man; and this advantage, on which we seem to set no price, exempted them from many vices.

In these our days the art of pleasing is by subtle researches, and finery of taste, reduced to certain principles; insomuch that a vile deceitful uniformity runs thro' our whole system of manners: as if all our constitutions, all our minds had been cast in one and the same mold.—Politeness constantly requires, civility commands; we always follow customs, never our particular inclinations: no one, nowadays, dares to appear what he really is; and in this perpetual constraint, the individuals who compose the congregation called society, being put into the same circumstances, will one and all act in the same manner, unless some more powerful motive intervene. Shall we then never rightly know the man we converse with? Must we, in order to distinguish the sincere friend, wait for grand occasions, I mean till it be too late; for it is for grand occasions that it were of the highest consequence to know him beforehand.

What a train of vices attend this uncertainty? Friendships are insincere, esteem is not real, and confidence is ill founded; suspicions, jealousies, fears, coolnesses, reserve, hatred, and treasons, are hid under the uniform veil of perfidious politeness, under that boasted civility which we owe to the vast discoveries of our age. 'Tis true, no one will swear by the name of the Omnipotent Master of the universe, 'tis not polite; but he shall be blasphemed in speeches and writings, without offending our scrupulous ears. No one will boast of his own merit, but he will run down that of his neighbor. No one will outrageously insult his enemy, but he will slyly calumniate him; national hatreds will be quench'd, but it will be in the love of our country. The place of despised ignorance will be occupied by a more despicable Pyrrhonism. Some excesses indeed will be proscribed, some vices dishonored; but others will be adorn'd with the dress and name of virtues, which if we have not, we must affect to have. Let who will boast of the sobriety of the sages of our days; for my own part I can perceive nothing but a refinement of intemperance, as unworthy of my approbation as is their artificial simplicity.

Such is the purity which our manners have acquired. Thus we are become great and good. Let arts, letters, and sciences now claim what belongs to them in this noble and salutary work.—I shall only add one reflection; if the inhabitant of some far distant region would form an idea of our European manners on the condition in which the sciences are amongst us, on the perfection of our arts, on the decency of our public diversions, on the politeness of our behavior, on the affability of our conversations, on our perpetual demonstrations of goodwill to each other, and on that tumultuous concourse of men of all ages, of all conditions, who, from sunrise to sunset, seem eternally employ'd in obliging one another; would not this stranger conclude our manners to be the exact reverse of what they really are? Where we see no effect, 'tis in vain to seek for a cause; but here the effect is visible, the depravation palpable; our minds have been corrupted in proportion as our arts and sciences have made advances toward their perfection.—Shall we say that this is a misfortune particular to our times? No, gentlemen, the evils arising from our vain curiosity are as old as the world. The flow and ebb of the sea are not more regularly guided by the moon's course, than our manners and probity by that of the arts and sciences. We see virtue flying on one side, as their lights rise on the other of our horizon: and the same phenomenon has been observed in all times and in all places.

Let us view *Egypt*, the original school of the universe, that beautiful, fertile, and cloudless climate, that celebrated country, whence *Sesostris* formerly issued to conquer the world. *Egypt* becomes the mother of philosophy and arts, but soon after, the prey of *Cambyses*, and presently that of the *Greeks*, the *Romans*, the *Arabs*, and at last that of the *Turks*.

See *Greece*, formerly peopled by heroes who twice conquer'd *Asia*, once at *Troy*, and again at their own doors. Learning, in her infancy, had not yet corrupted the hearts of her inhabitants; but the progress of sciences, the dissolution of manners, and the *Macedonian* yoke, invaded her, as I may say, on the heels of one another: then poor *Greece*, still learned, still voluptuous, still a slave, knew no other revolutions but the frequent changes of her masters; nor could all the eloquence of *Demosthenes* revive a body, which luxury and the arts had totally enervated.

It was in the time of *Ennius*, in that of *Terence*, that *Rome*, which had been founded by a shepherd and made famous by Ploughmen, began to degenerate; but after, when the *Ovids*, the *Catullus's*, the *Martials*, and that crowd of obscene authors, whose names alone are enough to shock common modesty, when they appear'd, *Rome*, from being the temple of virtue, became the theater of wickedness, the aversion of nations, and the scoff of *Barbarians*. That great capital of the world falls herself under the same captivity which she so often impos'd on other nations; and the time of her fall was the eve of that day on which she bestow'd on one of her citizens the title of sole arbiter of *fine taste*. What shall I say of that metropolis of the eastern empire, which by its situation would seem to have had a right of command over the whole world? That refuge of arts and sciences, after they had been proscrib'd by the rest of *Europe* perhaps more through wisdom than barbarity? All that render corruption and debauchery shameful, that can blacken treasons, murders, and poisonings; all the concourse of the most atrocious crimes seem combin'd together to form the history of *Constantinople;* and yet that is the pure source whence have flow'd those floods of light and knowledge so boasted of in our days.

But what need we recur to those past ages for proofs of this truth whilst we have living evidences subsisting before our eyes? We have in *Asia* an immense track of land, where learning flourishes, and is the best qualification for filling the first and greatest places, employments, and dignities of the state. If the sciences really better'd manners, if they taught man to spill his blood for his country, if they heighten'd his courage; the inhabitants of *China* ought to be wise, free, and invincible.—But if they are tainted with every vice, familiar with every crime; if neither the skill of their magistrates, nor the pretended wisdom of their laws, nor the vast multitude of people inhabiting that great extent of empire, could protect or defend them from the yoke of an ignorant *Barbarian Tartar,* of what use was all their art, all their skill, all their learning? What was the benefit accruing from all the respect with which they were adorn'd and honor'd? unless that *China* is peopled with slaves and cheats.—Let us set, in opposition to these frightful pictures, that of those few countries, who, having the good fortune to have been preserv'd from the contagion of vain knowledge, have procur'd, by their virtue, happiness for themselves, and have prov'd the great examples of all other nations. Such were the first *Persians,* a very singular nation, who made virtue their study, as we do sciences; who subdued *Asia* with so much ease, and who alone had the glory of having the history of their institutions pass for a philosophical romance: such were the *Scythians,* of whom we have such magnificent elogiums: such the *Germans,* whom an able writer, wearied by describing the horrid crimes of an opulent voluptuous learned people, has taken delight to celebrate for their simplicity, their innocence, their virtues.—Such was even *Rome* herself in the times of her poverty and ignorance; and such, in short, appear'd, in our own days, that rude unpolish'd nation so renown'd for courage, which no adversity could abate, and for loyalty, which example could not corrupt.

It was not through stupidity that these preferred the bodily exercises to those of the mind; they knew well enough that idlers in other countries pass'd their whole lives in disputes about the *summum bonum,* about vice and virtue, and that proud reasoners, vainly bestowing praises on themselves, jumbled all other nations under the despicable denomination of *Barbarians:* but they have duly considered their lives and manners, and thence despised their doctrines.

Can we forget that in the very bosom of *Greece* herself there arose a city which became famous thro' a happy ignorance, and the wisdom of her laws? A commonwealth peopled rather by demi-gods than men, so far did their virtue outshine humanity. O *Sparta!* thou proof of the folly of vain learning! whilst all manner of vice, led by the arts and sciences were introduced into *Athens*, whilst a tyrant was busy in picking up the works of the prince of poets, thou wert chasing from thy walls all sciences, all learning, together with their professors.

The success of both was thus distinguished: *Athens* became the mansion of politeness and fine taste, the seat of eloquence and philosophy; the elegance of their buildings corresponded with that of their language. On all sides were seen the marble and animated canvas fresh from the hands of the greatest masters. 'Twas from *Athens* that all those surprising works, which will for ever be models for all corrupted ages, have sprung. The picture of *Lacedaemon* is not so brilliant. *There*, said all other nations, *there men are born virtuous, the very air of that country seems to inspire virtue.* Nothing remains of that people but the tradition of their heroic actions.

IN DEFENSE OF MODERNITY

François-Marie Arouet de Voltaire

In these two selections, Voltaire provides the more characteristic Enlightenment perspective on historical progress. The first, a selection from his 1754 Essay on the Manners and Spirits of Nations, *is noteworthy for its famous characterization of history as a "collection of crimes, follies, and misfortunes," as well as for its sympathetic reading of Asian cultures. The second selection is a letter Voltaire wrote in 1755 to Rousseau in response to his indictment of progress.*

I have now gone through the immense scene of revolutions that the world has experienced since the time of Charlemagne; and to what have they all tended? To desolation, and the loss of millions of lives! Every great event has been a capital misfortune. History has kept no account of times of peace and tranquillity; it relates only ravages and disasters.

We have beheld our Europe overspread with barbarians after the fall of the Roman Empire; and these barbarians, after becoming Christians, continually at war with the Mohammedans or else destroying each other.

We have seen Italy desolated by perpetual wars between city and city; the Guelphs and Ghibellines mutually destroying each other; whole ages of conspiracies, and successive eruptions of distant nations who have passed the Alps, and driven each other from their settlements by turns, till at length, in all this beautiful and extensive country, there remained only two states of any importance governed by their own natives—Venice and Rome. The others, namely, Naples, Sicily, Milan, Parma, Placentia, and Tuscany, are under the dominion of foreigners.

The other great states of Christendom have suffered equally by wars and internecine commotions; but none of them has been brought under subjection to a neighboring power. The result of these endless disturbances and perpetual jars has been only the separating of some small provinces from one state, to be transferred to another. Flanders, for example, formerly under the suzerainty of France, passed to the house of Burgundy from foreign hands, and from this house to that of Austria; and a small part of this Flanders came again into the hands of the French in the reign of Louis XIV. Several provinces of ancient Gaul were in former times dismembered. Alsace, which was a part of ancient Gaul, became a province of Germany, and is at this day a province of France. Upper Navarre, which should be a demesne of the elder branch of the house of Bourbon, belongs to the younger; and Roussillon, which formerly belonged to the Spaniards, now belongs to the crown of France.

During all these shocks, there have been formed since the time of Charlemagne only two absolutely independent republics—that of Switzerland and that of Holland.

No one great kingdom has been able to subdue another. France, notwithstanding the conquests of Edward III and Henry V; notwithstanding the victories and efforts of Charles V and Philip II, has still preserved its limits, and even extended them; Spain, Germany, Great Britain, Poland, and the northern states are nearly as they were formerly.

What then have been the fruits of the blood of so many millions of men shed in battle, and the sacking of so many cities? Nothing great or considerable. The Christian powers have lost a great deal to the Turks, within these five centuries, and have gained scarcely anything from each other.

All history, then, in short, is little else than a long succession of useless cruelties; and if there happens any great revolution, it will bury the remembrance of all past disputes, wars, and fraudulent treaties, which have produced so many transitory miseries.

In the number of these miseries we may with justice include the disturbances and civil wars on the score of religion. Of these Europe has experienced two kinds, and it is hard to say which of them has proved more fatal to her. The first, as we have already seen, was the dispute of the popes with the emperors and kings: this began in the time of Louis the Feeble, and was not entirely at an end, in Germany, till after the reign of Charles V, in England, till suppressed by the resolution of Queen Elizabeth, and in France, till the submission of Henry IV. The other source of so much bloodshed was the rage of dogmatizing. This has caused the subversion of more than one state, from the time of the massacre of the Albigenses to the thirteenth century, and from the small war of the Cévennois to the beginning of the eighteenth. The field and the scaffold ran with blood on account of theological arguments, sometimes in one century, sometimes in another, for almost five hundred years, without interruption; and the long continuance of this dreadful scourge was owing to the fact that morality was always neglected to indulge a spirit of dogmatizing.

It must once again be acknowledged that history in general is a collection of crimes, follies, and misfortunes, among which we have now and then met with a few virtues, and some happy times; as we sometimes see a few scattered huts in a barren desert.

In those times of darkness and ignorance, which we distinguish by the name of the Middle Ages, no one perhaps ever deserved so well of mankind as Pope Alexander VIII. It was he who abolished vassalage, in a council which he held in the twelfth century. It was he who triumphed in Venice by his prudence, over the brutal violence of Frederick Barbarossa, and who obliged Henry II of England to ask pardon of God and man for the murder of Thomas à Becket. He restored the rights of the people, and chastised the wickedness of crowned heads. We have had occasion to remark that before this time, all Europe, a very small number of cities excepted, was divided between two ranks of people—the lords or owners of lands, either ecclesiastical or secular, and the villeins, or slaves. The lawyers, who assisted the knights, bailiffs, and stewards of fiefs, in giving their sentences, were in fact, no other than bondmen, or villeins, themselves. And, if mankind at length enjoy their rights, it is to Pope Alexander VIII that they are chiefly indebted for this happy change. It is to him that so many cities owe their present splendor; nevertheless, we know that this liberty was not universally extended. It has never made its way into Poland; the husbandman there is still a slave, and confined to the glebe; it is the same in Bohemia, Swabia, and several other countries of Germany; and even in France, in some of the provinces the most remote from the capital, we still see remains of this slavery. There are some chapters and monks who claim a right to all the goods of the peasants.

In Asia, on the contrary, there are no slaves but those which are purchased with money, or taken prisoners in battle. In the Christian states of Europe they do not buy slaves, neither do they reduce their prisoners of war to a state of servitude. The Asiatics have only a domestic servitude; Christians only a civil one. The peasant in Poland is a bondman in the lands, but not in the house of his lord. We make household slaves only of the Negroes; we are severely reproached for this kind of traffic, but the people who make a trade of selling their children are certainly more blamable than those who purchase them, and this traffic is only a proof of our superiority. He who voluntarily subjects himself to a master is designed by nature for a slave.

We have seen that, from time immemorial, they have tolerated all religions in Asia, much as is at present done in England, Holland, and Germany. We have observed that this toleration was more general in Japan than in any other country whatever, till the fatal affair which rendered that government so inexorable.

We may have observed, in the course of so many revolutions, that several nations almost entirely savage have been formed both in Europe and Asia, in those very countries which were formerly the most civilized. Thus, some of the islands of the Archipelago, which were once so flourishing, are now little better than Indian habitations in America. The country where were formerly the cities of Artaxata, and Tigranocerta, have not now even half the value of some of our petty colonies. There are, in some of the islands, forests, and mountains in the very heart of Europe, a set of people who are in nothing superior to those of Canada, or the Negroes of Africa. The Turks are more civilized, but we hardly know of one city built by them; they have suffered the most noble and beautiful monuments of antiquity to fall to decay, and reign only over a pile of ruins.

They have nothing in Asia that in the least resembles our European nobility; nor is there to be found throughout the whole East any one order of citizens distinguished from the others by hereditary titles, or particular privileges and indulgences, annexed solely to birth. The Tartars seem to be the only people who have some faint shadow of this institution, in the race of their Mirzas. We meet with nothing, either in Turkey, Persia, the Indies, or China, that bears any similitude to that body of nobility which forms an essential part of every European monarchy. We must go as far as Malabar to meet with any likeness to this sort of constitution; and there again it is very different, and consists in a tribe wholly dedicated to bearing arms, and which never intermixes, by marriage or otherwise, with any of the other tribes or castes, and will not even condescend to hold any commerce with them.

The greatest differences between us and the Orientals is in the manner of treating our women. No female ever reigned in the East, unless that princess of Mingrelia, whom Sir John Chardin tells us of in his voyages, and whom he accuses of robbing him. In France, though the women cannot wear the crown, they may be regents of the kingdom, and have a right to every other throne but that of the empire and Poland.

Another difference in our manner of treating women is the custom of placing about their persons men deprived of their virility, a custom which has always prevailed in Asia and Africa, and has at times been introduced into Europe by the Roman emperors. At present there are not throughout all Christendom two hundred eunuchs employed, either in our churches or theaters, whereas all the Eastern seraglios swarm with them.

In short, we differ in every respect, in religion, policy, government, manners, food, clothing, and even in our manner of writing, expressing, and thinking. That in which we most resemble them is that propensity to war, slaughter, and destruction, which has always depopulated the face of the earth. It must be owned, however, that this rage has taken much less possession of the minds of the people of India and China than of ours. In particular, we have no instance of the Indians or Chinese having made war upon the inhabitants of the North. In this respect they are much better members of society than ourselves; but then, on the other hand, this very virtue, or rather meekness, of theirs has been their ruin; for they have been all enslaved.

In the midst of the ravages and desolations which we have observed during the space of nine hundred years, we perceive a love for order which secretly animates humankind, and has prevented its total ruin.

This is one of the springs of nature which always recovers its tone; it is this which has formed the code of all nations, and this inspires a veneration for the laws and the ministers of the laws at Tonkin, and in the island of Formosa, the same as at Rome. Children respect their parents in all countries, and in every country—let others say what they will—the son is his father's heir; for, though in Turkey the son of a Timariot does not inherit his father's dignity, nor, in India, the son of an Omra his lands, the reason is because neither the one nor the other belong to the father himself. A place for life is, in no country of the world, considered as an inheritance; but in Persia, in India, and throughout all Asia, every native, and even every stranger, of whatsoever religion, except in Japan, may purchase lands that are not part of the crown demesnes, and leave them to his family.

In Europe there are still some nations where the law will not suffer a stranger to purchase a field or a burying-place in their territories. The barbarous right of aubaine, by which a stranger beholds his father's estate go to the king's treasury, still exists in all the Christian states, unless where it is otherwise provided by private convention.

We likewise have a notion that in the Eastern countries the women are all slaves, because they are confined to the duties of domestic life. If they were really slaves, they must become beggars at the death of their husbands, which is not the case; the law everywhere provides a stated portion for them, and this portion they obtain in case of a divorce. In every part of the world, we find laws established for the support of families.

In all nations there is a proper curb to arbitrary power, either by law, custom, or manners. The Turkish sultan can neither touch the public treasure, break the janissaries, nor interfere with the inside of the seraglios of any of his subjects. The emperor of China cannot publish a single edict without the sanction of a tribunal. Every state is at times liable to violent oppressions; the grand viziers and the itimadoulets exercise rapine and murder, it is true, but they are no more authorized so to do by the laws than the wild Arabs or wandering Tartars are to plunder the caravans.

Religion teaches the same principles of morality to all nations, without exception; the ceremonies of the Asiatics are ridiculous, their belief absurd, but their precepts are just; the dervish, the fakir, the bonze, and the talapoin, are always crying out: "Be just and beneficent." The common people in China are accused of being great cheats in trade; they are perhaps encouraged to this vice by knowing that they can procure absolution for their crime of their bonzes for a trifling sum of money. The moral precepts taught them are good, the indulgence which is sold them is bad.

We are not to credit those travelers and missionaries, who have represented the Eastern priests to us as persons who preach up iniquity; this is traducing human nature; it is not possible that there should ever exist a religious society instituted for the encouragement or propagation of vice.

We should equally deceive ourselves, were we to believe that the Mohammedan religion owes its establishment wholly to the sword. The Mohammedans have had their missionaries in the Indies and in China; and the sects of Omar and Ali dispute with each other for proselytes, even on the coasts of Coromandel and Malabar.

From all that we have observed in this sketch of universal history, it follows that whatever concerns human nature is the same from one end of the universe to the other, and that what is dependent upon custom differs, or, if there is any resemblance, it is the effect of chance. The dominion of custom is much more extensive than that of nature, and influences all manners and all usages. It diffuses variety over the face of the universe. Nature establishes unity, and everywhere settles a few invariable principles; the soil is still the same, but culture produces various fruits.

As nature has placed in the heart of man interest, pride, and all the passions, it is no wonder that, during a period of about six centuries we meet with almost a continual succession of crimes and disasters. If we go back to earlier ages, we shall find them no better. Custom has ordered it so that evil has everywhere operated in a different manner.

• • •

TO JEAN-JACQUES ROUSSEAU

Les Délices, August 30, 1755.

I have received, sir, your new book against the human species, and I thank you for it. You will please people by your manner of telling them the truth about themselves, but you will not alter them. The horrors of that human society—from which in our feebleness and ignorance we expect so many consolations—have never been painted in more striking colors: no one has ever been so witty as you are in trying to turn us into brutes: to read your book makes one long to go on all fours. Since, however, it is now some sixty years since I gave up the practice, I feel that it is unfortunately impossible for me to resume it: I leave this natural habit to those more fit for it than are you and I. Nor can I set sail to discover the aborigines of Canada, in the first place because my ill health ties me to the side of the greatest doctor in Europe, and I should not find the same professional assistance among the Missouris: and secondly because war is going on in that country, and the example of the civilized nations has made the barbarians almost as wicked as we are ourselves. I must confine myself to being a peaceful savage in the retreat I have chosen—close to your country, where you yourself should be.

I agree with you that science and literature have sometimes done a great deal of harm. Tasso's enemies made his life a long series of misfortunes: Galileo's enemies kept him languishing in prison, at seventy years of age, for the crime of understanding the revolution of the earth: and, what is still more shameful, obliged him to forswear his discovery. Since your friends began the Encyclopedia, their rivals attack them as deists, atheists—even Jansenists.

If I might venture to include myself among those whose works have brought them persecution as their sole recompense, I could tell you of men set on ruining me from the day I produced my tragedy *Oedipe:* of a perfect library of absurd calumnies which have been written against me: of an ex-Jesuit priest whom I saved from utter disgrace rewarding me by defamatory libels: of a man yet more contemptible printing my *Century of Louis XIV* with *Notes* in which crass ignorance gave birth to the most abominable falsehoods: of yet another, who sold to a publisher some chapters of a *Universal History* supposed to be by me: of the publisher avaricious enough to print this shapeless mass of blunders, wrong dates, mutilated facts and names: and, finally, of men sufficiently base and craven to assign the production of this farago to me. I could show you all society poisoned by this class of person—a class unknown to the ancients—who, not being able to find any honest occupation—be it manual labor or service—and unluckily knowing how to read and write, become the brokers of literature, live on our works, steal our manuscripts, falsify them, and sell them. I could tell of some loose sheets of a gay trifle which I wrote thirty years ago (on the same subject that Chapelain was stupid enough to treat seriously) which are in circulation now through the breach of faith and the cupidity of those who added their own grossness to my *badinage* and filled in the gaps with a dullness only equalled by their malice; and who, finally, after twenty years, are selling everywhere a manuscript which, in very truth, is theirs and worthy of them only.

I may add, last of all, that someone has stolen part of the material I amassed in the public archives to use in my History of the War of 1741 when I was historiographer of France; that he sold that result of my labors to a bookseller in Paris; and is as set on getting hold of my property as if I were dead and he could turn it into money by putting it up to auction. I could show you ingratitude, imposture, and rapine pursuing me for forty years to the foot of the Alps and the brink of the grave. But what conclusion ought I to draw from all these misfortunes? This only: that I have no right to complain: Pope, Descartes, Bayle, Camoëns—a hundred others—have been subjected to the same, or greater, injustice: and my destiny is that of nearly everyone who has loved letters too well.

Confess, sir, that all these things are, after all, but little personal pinpricks, which society scarcely notices. What matter to humankind that a few drones steal the honey of a few bees? Literary men make a great fuss of their petty quarrels: the rest of the world ignores them, or laughs at them.

They are, perhaps, the least serious of all the ills attendant on human life. The thorns inseparable from literature and a modest degree of fame are flowers in comparison with the other evils which from all time have flooded the world. Neither Cicero, Varron, Lucretius, Virgil, or Horace had any part in the proscriptions of Marius, Scylla, that profligate Antony, or that fool Lepidus; while as for that cowardly tyrant, Octavius Caesar—servilely entitled Augustus—he only became an assassin when he was deprived of the society of men of letters.

Confess that Italy owed none of her troubles to Petrarch or to Boccaccio: that Marot's jests were not responsible for the massacre of St. Bartholomew: or that tragedy of the *Cid* for the wars of the Fronde. Great crimes are always committed by great ignoramuses. What makes, and will always make, this world a vale of tears is the insatiable greediness and the indomitable pride of men, from Thomas Koulikan, who did not know how to read, to a customhouse officer who can just count. Letters support, refine, and comfort the soul: they are serving you, sir, at the very moment you decry them: you are like Achilles declaiming against fame, and Father Malebranche using his brilliant imagination to belittle imagination.

If anyone has a right to complain of letters, I am that person, for in all times and in all places they have led to my being persecuted: still, we must needs love them in spite of the way they are abused—as we cling to society, though the wicked spoil its pleasantness: as we must love our country, though it treats us unjustly: and as we must love and serve the Supreme Being, despite the superstition and fanaticism which too often dishonor His service.

M. Chappus tells me your health is very unsatisfactory: you must come and recover here in your native place, enjoy its freedom, drink (with me) the milk of its cows, and browse on its grass.

I am yours most philosophically and with sincere esteem.

THE FOUR-STAGE THEORY OF DEVELOPMENT

ADAM SMITH

An important contribution to Enlightenment notions of progress came from Scottish sociological theories of social development. In Smith's Lectures on Jurisprudence *(1762), we find a conceptualization that would greatly influence subsequent writing on social theory.*

There are four distinct states which mankind passes through. 1st, the age of Hunters; 2nd, the age of Shepherds; 3rd, the age of Agriculture; 4th, the age of Commerce.

If one should suppose ten or twelve persons of different sexes settled in an uninhabited island, the first method they would fall upon for their sustenance would be to support themselves by the wild fruits and wild animals which the country afforded. Their sole business would be hunting the wild beasts or catching the fishes. The pulling of a wild fruit can hardly be called an employment. The only thing amongst them which deserved the appellation of a business would be the chase. This is the age of hunters. In process of time, as their numbers multiplied, they would find the chase too precarious for their support. They would be necessitated to contrive some other method whereby to support themselves. At first perhaps they would try to lay up at one time, when they had been successful, what would support them for a considerable time. But this would go no great length. The contrivance they would think of most naturally would be to tame some of those wild animals they caught, and by affording them better food than what they could get elsewhere, they would induce them to continue about their land themselves and multiply their kind.

Hence would arise the age of shepherds. They would more probably begin first by multiplying animals than vegetables, as less skill and observation would be required: nothing more than to know what food suited them. We find accordingly that in almost all countries the age of shepherds preceded that of agriculture. The Tartars and Arabians subsist almost entirely by their flocks and herds. The Arabs have a little agriculture, but the Tartars none at all. The whole of the savage nations which subsist by flocks have no notion of cultivating the ground. The only instance that has the appearance of an objection to this rule is the state of the North American Indians. They, though they have no conception of flocks and herds, have nevertheless some notion of agriculture. Their women plant a few stalks of Indian corn at the back of their huts: but this can hardly be called agriculture. This corn does not make any considerable part of their food: it serves only as a seasoning or something to give a relish to their common food, the flesh of those animals they have caught in the chase. Flocks and herds, therefore, are the first resource men would take themselves to when they found difficulty in subsisting by the chase.

But when a society becomes numerous they would find a difficulty in supporting themselves by herds and flocks. Then they would naturally turn themselves to the cultivation of land and the raising of such plants and trees as produced nourishment fit for them: they would observe that those weeds which fell on the dry, bare soil or on the rock, seldom came to anything, but that those which entered the soil generally produced a plant and bore seed similar to that which was sown. These observations they would extend to the different plants and trees they found produced agreeable and nourishing food. And by this means they would gradually advance into the age of Agriculture. As society was farther improved the several arts, which at first would be exercised by each individual as far as was necessary for his welfare, would be separated; some persons would cultivate one and others, as they severally inclined. They would exchange with one another what they produced more than was necessary for their support, and get in exchange for them the commodities they stood in need of and did not produce themselves. This exchange of commodities extends in time not only betwixt the individuals of the same society, but betwixt those of different nations. Thus we send to France our cloths, iron-work and other trinkets, and get in exchange their wines. To Spain and Portugal we send our superfluous corn, and bring from thence the Spanish and Portuguese wines. Thus at last the age of Commerce arises. When therefore a country is stored with all the flocks and herds it can support, the land cultivated so as to produce all the grain and other commodities necessary for our subsistence it can be brought to bear, or at least as much as supports the inhabitants when the superfluous products, whether of nature or art, are exported and other necessary ones brought in exchange, such as society has done all in its power towards its ease and convenience.

THE PROGRESSIVE CHARACTER OF HUMAN NATURE

ADAM FERGUSON

A leading figure in the Scottish Enlightenment, Adam Ferguson (1723–1816) was a professor of natural and moral philosophy at the University of Edinburgh. This selection is from his two-volume Principles of Moral and Political Science, *published in 1792.*

For our purpose, however, it is sufficient to observe, that the state of nature or the distinctive character of any progressive being is to be taken, not from its description at the outset, or at any subsequent stage of its progress: but from an accumulative view of its movement throughout. The oak is distinguishable from the pine, not merely by its seed leaf; but by every successive aspect of its form; by its foliage in every successive season; by its acorn; by its spreading top; by its lofty growth, and the length of its period. And the state of nature, relative to every tree in the wood, includes all the varieties of form or dimension through which it is known to pass in the course of its nature.

By parity of reason, the natural state of a living creature includes all its known variations, from the embryo and the fetus to the breathing animal, the adolescent and the adult, through which life in all its varieties is known to pass.

The state of nature, relative to man, is also a state of progression equally real, and of greater extent. The individual receives the first stamina of his frame in a growing state. His stature is waxing, his limbs and his organs gain strength, and he himself a growing faculty in the use of them. His faculties improve by exercise, and are in a continual state of exertion. . . .

The state of nature relative to the species is differently constituted, and of different extent. It consists in the continual succession of one generation to another; in progressive attainments made by different ages; communicated with additions from age to age; and in periods, the farthest advanced, not appearing to have arrived at any necessary limit. This progress indeed is subject to interruption, and may come to a close, or give way to vicissitudes at any of its stages; but not more necessarily at the period of highest attainment than at any other.

So long as the son continues to be taught what the father knew, or the pupil begins where the tutor has ended, and is equally bent on advancement; to every generation the state of art and accommodations already in use serves but as ground work for new inventions and successive improvement. As Newton did not acquiesce in what was observed by Kepler and Galileo; no more have successive astronomers restricted their view to what Newton has demonstrated. And with respect to the mechanic and commercial arts, even in the midst of the most labored accommodations, so long as there is any room for improvement, invention is busy as if nothing had yet been done to supply the necessities, or complete the conveniences of human life: But even here, and in all its steps of progression, this active nature, in respect to the advantages, whether of knowledge or art, derived from others, if there be not a certain effort to advance, is exposed to reverse and decline.

The generation, in which there is no desire to know more or practice better than its predecessors, will probably neither know so much nor practice so well. And the decline of successive generations, under this wane of intellectual ability, is not less certain than the progress made under the operation of a more active and forward disposition.

"HOW GLORIOUS, THEN, IS THE PROSPECT . . ."

JOSEPH PRIESTLEY

The American and French Revolutions evoked in Priestley a millenarian vision of social and intellectual progress culminating in utopian perfection. This paradise "foretold in many prophesies" is outlined in the concluding chapter—titled "Of the Prospect of the General Enlargement of Liberty, Civil and Religious, opened by the Revolution in France"—of his 1781 Letters to the Right Honorable Edmund Burke, *who, of course, profoundly disagreed with Priestley.*

I cannot conclude these Letters, without congratulating, not you, Sir [Burke], or the many admirers of your performance who have no feeling of joy on the occasion, but the French nation, and the world—I mean the liberal, the rational, and the virtuous part of the world—on the great revolution that has taken place in France, as well as on that which some time ago took place in America. Such events as these teach the doctrine of liberty, civil and religious, with infinitely greater clearness and force than a thousand treatises on the subject. They speak a language intelligible to all the world, and preach a doctrine congenial to every human heart.

These great events, in many respects unparalleled in all history, make a totally new, a most wonderful and important, era in the history of mankind. It is, to adopt your own rhetorical style, a change from darkness to light, from superstition to sound knowledge and from a most debasing servitude to a state of the most exalted freedom. It is a liberating of all the powers of man from that variety of fetters by which they have hitherto been held. So that, in comparison with what has been, now only can we expect to see what men really are, and what they can do.

The generality of governments have hitherto been little else than a combination of the few against the many; and to the mean passions and low cunning of these few, have the great interests of mankind been too long sacrificed. Whole nations have been deluged with blood, and every source of future prosperity has been drained, to gratify the caprices of some of the most despicable, or the most execrable, of the human species. For what else have been the generality of kings, their ministers of state, or their mistresses, to whose wills whole kingdoms have been subject? What can we say of those who have hitherto taken the lead in conducting the affairs of nations, but that they have commonly been either weak or wicked and sometimes both? Hence the common reproach of all histories that they exhibit little more than a view of the vices and miseries of mankind. From this time, therefore, we may expect that it will wear a different and more pleasing aspect.

Hitherto, also, infinite have been the mischiefs in which all nations have been involved on account of religion, with which, as it concerns only God and men's own consciences, civil government, as such, has nothing to do. Statesmen, misled by ignorant or interested priests, have taken upon them to prescribe what men should believe and practice in order to get to heaven, when they themselves have often neither believed, nor practiced, anything under that description. They have set up idols to which all men, under the severest penalties, have been compelled to bow; and the wealth and power of populous nations, which might have been employed in great and useful undertakings, have been diverted from their proper channels to enforce their unrighteous decrees. By this means have mankind been kept for ages in a state of bondage worse than Egyptian, the bondage of the mind.

How glorious, then, is the prospect, the reverse of all the past, which is now opening upon us, and upon the world. Government, we may now expect to see, not only in theory and in books but in actual practice, calculated for the general good, and taking no more upon it than the general good requires, leaving all men the enjoyment of as many of their natural rights as possible, and no more interfering with matters of religion, with men's notions concerning God, and a future state, than with philosophy, or medicine.

After the noble example of America, we may expect in due time to see the governing powers of all nations confining their attention to the civil concerns of them, and consulting their welfare in the present state only, in consequence of which they may all be flourishing and happy. Truth of all kinds and especially religious truth, meeting with no obstruction and standing in no need of heterogeneous supports, will then establish itself by its own evidence; and whatever is false and delusive, all the forms of superstition, every corruption of true religion, and all usurpation over the rights of conscience, which have been supported by power or prejudice, will be universally exploded, as they ought to be.

Together with the general prevalence of the true principles of civil government, we may expect to see the extinction of all national prejudice and enmity, and the establishment of universal peace and goodwill among all nations. When the affairs of the various societies of mankind shall be conducted by those who shall truly represent them, who shall feel as they feel and think as they think, who shall really understand and consult their interests, they will no more engage in those mutually offensive wars which the experience of many centuries has shown to be constantly expensive and ruinous. They will no longer covet what belongs to others, and which they have found to be of no real service to them, but will content themselves with making the most of their own. . . .

The causes of civil wars, the most distressing of all others, will likewise cease, as well as those of foreign ones. They are chiefly contentions for offices, on account of the power and emoluments annexed to them. But when the nature and uses of all civil offices shall be well understood, the power and emoluments annexed to them will not be an object sufficient to produce a war. Is it at all probable that there will ever be a civil war in America about the presidentship of the United States? And when the chief magistracies in other countries shall be reduced to their proper standard, they will be no more worth contending for than they are in America. If the actual business of a nation be done as well for the small emolument of that presidentship as the similar business of other nations, there will be no apparent reason why more should be given for doing it.

If there be a superfluity of public money it will not be employed to augment the profusion and increase the undue influence of individuals, but in works of great public utility—which are always wanted and which nothing but the enormous expenses of government and of wars, chiefly occasioned by the ambition of kings and courts, have prevented from being carried into execution. The expense of the late American war, only, would have converted all the waste grounds of this country into gardens. What canals, bridges, and noble roads, what public buildings, public libraries, and public laboratories, etc. etc. would it not have made for us? If the pride of nations must be gratified, let it be in such things as these, and not in the idle pageantry of a court, calculated only to corrupt and enslave a nation.

Another cause of civil wars has been an attachment to certain persons and families, as possessed of some inherent right to kingly power. Such were the bloody wars between the houses of York and Lancaster in this country. But when, besides the reduction of the power of crowns within their proper bounds (when it will be no greater than the public good requires) that kind of respect for princes which is founded on mere superstition (exactly similar to that which has been attached to priests in all countries) shall vanish, as all superstition certainly will before real knowledge, wise nations will not involve themselves in war for the sake of any particular persons, or families, who have never shown an equal regard for them. They will consider their own interest more and that of their magistrates, that is, their servants, less.

Other remaining causes of civil war are different opinions about modes of government, and differences of interests between provinces. But when mankind shall be a little more accustomed to reflection and consider the miseries of civil war, they will have recourse to any other method of deciding their differences in preference to that of the sword. It was taken for granted that the moment America had thrown off the yoke of Great Britain, the different states would go to war among themselves, on some of these accounts. But the event has not verified the prediction, nor is it at all probable that it ever will. The people of that country are wiser than such prophets in this.

If time be allowed for the discussion of differences, so great a majority will form one opinion, that the minority will see the necessity of giving way. Thus will reason be the umpire in all disputes and extinguish civil wars as well as foreign ones. The empire of reason will ever be the reign of peace.

This, Sir, will be the happy state of things, distinctly and repeatedly foretold in many prophecies, delivered more than two thousand years ago, when the common parent of mankind will cause wars to cease to the ends of the earth, when men shall beat their swords into plough shares, and their spears into pruning hooks, when nation shall no more rise up against nation, and when they shall learn war no more. This is a state of things which good sense, and the prevailing spirit of commerce, aided by christianity and true philosophy cannot fail to effect in time. But it can never take place while mankind are governed in the wretched manner in which they now are. For peace can never be established but upon the extinction of the causes of war which exist in all the present forms of government, and in the political maxims which will always be encouraged by them. I mention this topic in a letter to you, on the idea that you are a real believer in revelation, though your defense of all church establishments, as such, is no argument in favor of this opinion; the most zealous abettors of them, and the most determined enemies of all reformation having been unbelievers in all religion, which they have made use of merely as an engine of state.

In this new condition of the world, there may still be kings, but they will be no longer sovereigns or supreme lords, no human beings to whom will be ascribed such titles as those of most sacred or most excellent majesty. There will be no more such a profanation of epithets, belonging to God only by the application of them to mortals like ourselves. There will be magistrates appointed and paid for the conservation of order, but they will only be considered as the first servants of the people, and accountable to them. Standing armies, those instruments of tyranny, will be unknown, though the people may be trained to the use of arms for the purpose of repelling the invasion of Barbarians. For no other description of men will have recourse to war, or think of disturbing the repose of others; and till they become civilized, as in the natural progress of things they necessarily must, they will be sufficiently overawed by the superior power of nations that are so.

There will still be religion, and of course ministers of it, as there will be teachers of philosophy and practitioners in medicine; but it will no longer be the concern of the state. There will be no more Lord Bishops or Archbishops, with the titles and powers of temporal princes. Every man will provide religion for himself, and therefore it will be such as, after due enquiry, and examination, he shall think to be founded on truth and best calculated to make men good citizens, good friends, and good neighbors in this world, as well as to fit them for another.

Government being thus simple in its objects, will be unspeakably less expensive than it is at present as well as far more effectual in answering its proper purpose. There will then be little to provide for besides the administration of justice or the preservation of the peace, which it will be the interest of every man to attend to in aid of government.

THE PERFECTIBILITY OF MAN

MARQUIS DE CONDORCET

If Priestley's is the classic English-language expression of Enlightenment "perfectionism," than Condorcet's is the French. This selection is from the introduction to his Sketch for a Historical Picture of the Human Mind *(1794).*

Man is born with the faculty of receiving sensations. In *those* which he receives, he is capable of perceiving and of distinguishing the simple sensations of which they are composed. He can retain, recognize, and combine them. He can preserve or recall them to his memory; he can compare their different combinations; he can ascertain what they possess in common, and what characterizes each; lastly, he can affix signs to all these objects, the better to know them, and the more *easily* to form from them new combinations.

This faculty is developed in him by the action of external objects, that is, by the presence of certain complex sensations, the constancy of which, whether in their identical whole, or in the laws of their change, is independent of him. It is also exercised by communication with other similarly organized individuals, and by all the artificial means which, from the first development of this faculty, men have succeeded in inventing.

Sensations are accompanied with pleasure or pain, and man has the further faculty of converting these momentary impressions into durable sentiments of a corresponding nature, and of experiencing these sentiments either at the sight or recollection of the pleasure or pain of beings sensitive like himself. And from this faculty, united with that of forming and combining ideas, arise, between him and his fellow creatures, the ties of interest and duty, to which nature has affixed the most exquisite portion of our felicity, and the most poignant of our sufferings.

Were we to confine our observations to an enquiry into the general facts and unvarying laws which the development of these faculties presents to us, in what is common to the different individuals of the human species, our enquiry would bear the name of metaphysics.

But if we consider this development in its results, relative to the mass of individuals co-existing at the same time on a given space, and follow it from generation to generation, it then exhibits a picture of the progress of human intellect. This progress is subject to the same general laws, observable in the individual development of our faculties; being the result of that very development considered at once in a great number of individuals united in society. But the result which every instant presents, depends upon that of the preceding instants, and has an influence on the instants which follow.

This picture, therefore, is historical; since, subjected as it will be to perpetual variations, it is formed by the successive observation of human societies at the different eras through which they have passed. It will accordingly exhibit the order in which the changes have taken place, explain the influence of every past period upon that which follows it, and thus show, by the modifications which the human species has experienced, in its incessant renovation through the immensity of ages, the course which it has pursued, and the steps which it has advanced toward knowledge and happiness. From these observations on what man has heretofore been, and what he is at present, we shall be led to the means of securing and of accelerating the still further progress, of which, from his nature, we may indulge the hope.

Such is the object of the work I have undertaken; the result of which will be to show, from reasoning and from facts, that no bounds have been fixed to the improvement of the human faculties; that the perfectibility of man is absolutely indefinite; that the progress of this perfectibility, henceforth above the control of every power that would impede it, has no other limit than the duration of the globe upon which nature has placed us. The course of this progress may doubtless be more or less rapid, but it can never be retrograde; at least while the earth retains its situation in the system of the universe, and the laws of this system shall neither effect upon the globe a general overthrow, nor introduce such changes as would no longer permit the human race to preserve and exercise therein the same faculties, and find the same resources.

The first state of civilization observable in the human species, is that of a society of men, few in number, subsisting by means of hunting and fishing, unacquainted with every art but the imperfect one of fabricating in an uncouth manner their arms and some household utensils, and of constructing or digging for themselves a habitation; yet already in possession of a language for the communication of their wants, and a small number of moral ideas, from which are deduced their common rules of conduct, living in families, conforming themselves to general customs that serve instead of laws, and having even a rude form of government.

In this state it is apparent that the uncertainty and difficulty of procuring subsistence, and the unavoidable alternative of extreme fatigue or an absolute repose, leave not to man the leisure in which, by resigning himself to meditation, he might enrich his mind with new combinations. The means of satisfying his wants are even too dependent upon chance and the seasons, usefully to excite an industry, the progressive improvement of which might be transmitted to his progeny; and accordingly the attention of each is confined to the improvement of his individual skill and address.

For this reason, the progress of the human species must in this stage have been extremely slow; it could make no advance but at distant intervals, and when favored by extraordinary circumstances. Meanwhile, to the subsistence derived from hunting and fishing, or from the fruits which the earth spontaneously offered, succeeds the sustenance afforded by the animals which man has tamed, and which he knows how to preserve and multiply. To these means is afterwards added an imperfect agriculture; he is no longer content with the fruit or the plants which chance throws in his way; he learns to form a stock of them, to collect them around him, to sow or to plant them, to favor their reproduction by the labor of culture.

Property, which, in the first state, was confined to his household utensils, his arms, his nets, and the animals he killed, is now extended to his flock, and next to the land which he has cleared and cultivated. Upon the death of its head, this property naturally devolves to the family. Some individuals possess a superfluity capable of being preserved. If it be absolute, it gives rise to new wants. If confined to a single article, while the proprietor feels the want of other articles, this want suggests the idea of exchange. Hence moral relations multiply, and become complicated. A greater security, a more certain and more constant leisure, afford time for meditation, or at least for a continued series of observations. The custom is introduced, as to some individuals, of giving a part of their superfluity in exchange for labor, by which they might be exempt from labor themselves. There accordingly exists a class of men whose time is not engrossed by corporeal exertions, and whose desires extend beyond their simple wants. Industry awakes; the arts already known, expand and improve; the facts which chance presents to the observation of the most attentive and best cultivated minds, bring to light new arts; as the means of living become less dangerous and less precarious, population increases; agriculture, which can provide for a greater number of individuals upon the same space of ground, supplies the place of the other sources of subsistence; it favors the multiplication of the species, by which it is favored in its turn; in a society become more sedentary, more connected, more intimate, ideas that have been acquired communicate themselves more quickly, and are perpetuated with more certainty. And now the dawn of the sciences begins to appear; man exhibits an appearance distinct from the other classes of animals, and is no longer like them confined to an improvement purely individual.

The more extensive, more numerous and more complicated relations which men now form with each other, cause them to feel the necessity of having a mode of communicating their ideas to the absent, of preserving the remembrance of a fact with more precision than by oral tradition, of fixing the conditions of an agreement more securely than by the memory of witnesses, of stating, in a way less liable to change, those respected customs to which the members of any society agree to submit their conduct.

Accordingly the want of writing is felt, and the art invented. It appears at first to have been an absolute painting, to which succeeded a conventional painting, preserving such traits only as were characteristic of the objects. Afterwards, by a kind of metaphor analogous to that which was already introduced into their language, the image of a physical object became expressive of moral ideas. The origin of those signs, like the origin of words, was liable in time to be forgotten; and writing became the art of affixing signs of convention to every idea, every word, and of consequence to every combination of ideas and words.

There was now a language that was written, and a language that was spoken, which it was necessary equally to learn, between which there must be established a reciprocal correspondence.

Some men of genius, the eternal benefactors of the human race, but whose names and even country are forever buried in oblivion, observed that all the words of a language were only the combinations of a very limited number of primitive articulations; but that this number, small as it was, was sufficient to form a quantity almost infinite of different combinations. Hence they conceived the idea of representing by visible signs, not the ideas or the words that answered to them, but those simple elements of which the words are composed.

Alphabetical writing was then introduced. A small number of signs served to express everything in this mode, as a small number of sounds sufficed to express everything orally. The language written and the language spoken were the same; all that was necessary was to be able to know, and to form, the few given signs; and this last step secured forever the progress of the human race.

It would perhaps be desirable at the present day, to institute a written language, which, devoted to the sole use of the sciences, expressing only such combinations of simple ideas as are found to be exactly the same in every mind, employed only upon reasonings of logical strictness, upon operations of the mind precise and determinate, might be understood by men of every country, and be translated into all their idioms, without being, like those idioms, liable to corruption, by passing into common use.

Then, singular as it may appear, this kind of writing, the preservation of which would only have served to prolong ignorance, would become, in the hands of philosophy, a useful instrument for the speedy propagation of knowledge, and advancement of the sciences.

It is between this degree of civilization and that in which we still find the savage tribes, that we must place every people whose history has been handed down to us, and who, sometimes making new advancements, sometimes plunging themselves again into ignorance, sometimes floating between the two alternatives or stopping at a certain limit, sometimes totally disappearing from the earth under the sword of conquerors, mixing with those conquerors, or living in slavery; lastly, sometimes receiving knowledge from a more enlightened people, to transmit it to other nations—form an unbroken chain of connection between the earliest periods of history and the age in which we live, between the first people known to us, and the present nations of Europe.

In the picture then which I mean to sketch, three distinct parts are perceptible.

In the first, in which the relations of travelers exhibit to us the condition of mankind in the least civilized nations, we are obliged to guess by what steps man in an isolated state, or rather confined to the society necessary for the propagation of the species, was able to acquire those first degrees of improvement, the last term of which is the use of an articulate language: an acquisition that presents the most striking feature, and indeed the only one, a few more extensive moral ideas and a slight commencement of social order excepted, which distinguishes him from animals living like himself in regular and permanent society. In this part of our picture, then, we can have no other guide than an investigation of the development of our faculties.

To this first guide, in order to follow man to the point in which he exercises arts, in which the rays of science begin to enlighten him, in which nations are united by commercial intercourse; in which, in fine, alphabetical writing is invented, we may add the history of the several societies that have been observed in almost every intermediate state: though we can follow no individual one through all the space which separates these two grand epochs of the human race.

Here the picture begins to take its coloring in great measure from the series of facts transmitted to us by history: but it is necessary to select these facts from that of different nations, and at the same time compare and combine them, to form the supposed history of a single people, and delineate its progress.

From the period that alphabetical writing was known in Greece, history is connected by an uninterrupted series of facts and observations, with the period in which we live, with the present state of mankind in the most enlightened countries of Europe; and the picture of the progress and advancement of the human mind becomes strictly historical. Philosophy has no longer anything to guess, has no more hypothetical combinations to form; all it has to do is to collect and arrange facts, and exhibit the useful truths which arise from them as a whole, and from the different bearings of their several parts.

There remains only a third picture to form—that of our hopes, or the progress reserved for future generations, which the constancy of the laws of nature seems to secure to mankind. And here it will be necessary to show by what steps this progress, which at present may appear chimerical, is gradually to be rendered possible, and even easy; how truth, in spite of the transient success of prejudices, and the support they receive from the corruption of governments or of the people, must in the end obtain a durable triumph; by what ties nature has indissolubly united the advancement of knowledge with the progress of liberty, virtue, and respect for the natural rights of man; how these blessings, the only real ones, though so frequently seen apart as to be thought incompatible, must necessarily amalgamate and become inseparable, the moment knowledge shall have arrived at a certain pitch in a great number of nations at once, the moment it shall have penetrated the whole mass of a great people, whose language shall have become universal, and whose commercial intercourse shall embrace the whole extent of the globe. This union having once taken place in the whole enlightened class of men, this class will be considered as the friends of human kind, exerting themselves in concert to advance the improvement and happiness of the species.

We shall expose the origin and trace the history of general errors, which have more or less contributed to retard or suspend the advance of reason, and sometimes even, as much as political events, have been the cause of man's taking a retrograde course toward ignorance.

Those operations of the mind that lead to or retain us in error, from the subtle paralogism, by which the most penetrating mind may be deceived, to the mad reveries of enthusiasts, belong equally, with that just mode of reasoning that conducts us to truth, to the theory of the development of our individual faculties; and for the same reason, the manner in which general errors are introduced, propagated, transmitted, and rendered permanent among nations, forms a part of the picture of the progress of the human mind. Like truths which improve and enlighten it, they are the consequence of its activity, and of the disproportion that always exists between what it actually knows, what it has the desire to know, and what it conceives there is a necessity of acquiring.

It is even apparent that, from the general laws of the development of our faculties, certain prejudices must necessarily spring up in each stage of our progress, and extend their seductive influence beyond that stage; because men retain the errors of their infancy, their country, and the age in which they live, long after the truths necessary to the removal of those errors are acknowledged.

In short, there exist, at all times and in all countries, different prejudices, according to the degree of illumination of the different classes of men, and according to their professions. If the prejudices of philosophers be impediments to new acquisitions of truth, those of the less enlightened classes retard the propagation of truths already known, and those of esteemed and powerful professions oppose like obstacles. These are the three kinds of enemies which reason is continually obliged to encounter, and over which she frequently does not triumph till after a long and painful struggle. The history of these contests, together with that of the rise, triumph, and fall of prejudice, will occupy a considerable place in this work, and will by no means form the least important or least useful part of it.

If there be really such an art as that of foreseeing the future improvement of the human race, and of directing and hastening that improvement, the history of the progress it has already made must form the principal basis of this art. Philosophy, no doubt, ought to proscribe the superstitious idea, which supposes no rules of conduct are to be found but in the history of past ages, and no truths but in the study of the opinions of antiquity. But ought it not to include in the proscription the prejudice that would proudly reject the lessons of experience? Certainly it is meditation alone that can by happy combinations, conduct us to the general principles of the science of man. But if the study of individuals of the human species be of use to the metaphysician and moralist, why should that of societies be less useful to them? And why not of use to the political philosopher? If it be advantageous to observe the societies that exist at one and the same period, and to trace their connection and resemblance, why not to observe them in a succession of periods? Even supposing that such observation might be neglected in the investigation of speculative truths, ought it to be neglected when the question is to apply those truths to practice, and to deduce from science the art that should be the useful result? Do not our prejudices, and the evils that are the consequence of them, derive their source from the prejudices of our ancestors? And will it not be the surest way of undeceiving us respecting the one, and of preventing the other, to develop their origin and effects?

Are we not arrived at the point when there is no longer anything to fear, either from new errors, or the return of old ones; when no corrupt institution can be introduced by hypocrisy, and adopted by ignorance or enthusiasm, when no vicious combination can affect the infelicity of a great people? Accordingly would it not be of advantage to know how nations have been deceived, corrupted, and plunged in misery?

Everything tells us that we are approaching the era of one of the grand revolutions of the human race. What can better enlighten us as to what we may expect, what can be a surer guide to us, amidst its commotions, than the picture of the revolutions that have preceded and prepared the way for it? The present state of knowledge assures us that it will be happy. But is it not upon condition that we know how to assist it with all our strength? And, that the happiness it promises may be less dearly bought, that it may spread with more rapidity over a greater space, that it may be more complete in its effects, is it not requisite to study, in the history of the human mind, what obstacles remain to be feared, and by what means those obstacles are to be surmounted?

Politics and the State

THE SECOND TREATISE OF CIVIL GOVERNMENT

John Locke

For over two centuries it was assumed that this great statement of Enlightenment liberalism was written after 1688 to justify the Glorious Revolution. We now know that in fact it was an even more radical statement, written and circulated, though not published, in the early 1680s—when to proclaim these views was considered treasonable.

Chapter II: Of the State of Nature

4. To understand political power aright, and derive it from its original, we must consider what state all men are naturally in, and that is, a state of perfect freedom to order their actions and dispose of their possessions and persons as they think fit, within the bounds of the law of nature, without asking leave, or depending upon the will of any other man.

A state also of equality, wherein all the power and jurisdiction is reciprocal, no one having more than another; there being nothing more evident than that creatures of the same species and rank, promiscuously born to all the same advantages of nature, and the use of the same faculties, should also be equal one amongst another without subordination or subjection, unless the Lord and Master of them all should, by any manifest declaration of His will, set one above another, and confer on him by an evident and clear appointment an undoubted right to dominion and sovereignty. . . .

6. But though this be a state of liberty, yet it is not a state of license: though man in that state have an uncontrollable liberty to dispose of his person or possessions, yet he has not liberty to destroy himself, or so much as any creature in his possession, but where some nobler use than its bare preservation calls for it. The state of Nature has a law of Nature to govern it, which obliges everyone; and reason, which is that law, teaches all mankind who will but consult it, that, being all equal and independent, no one ought to harm another in his life, health, liberty, or possessions. For men being all the workmanship of one omnipotent and infinitely wise Maker—all the servants of one sovereign Master, sent into the world by His order, and about His business—they are His property, whose workmanship they are, made to last during His, not one another's pleasure; and being furnished with like faculties, sharing all in one community of Nature, there cannot be supposed any such subordination among us, that may authorize us to destroy one another, as if we were made for one another's uses, as the inferior ranks of creatures are for ours. Everyone, as he is bound to preserve himself, and not to quit his station willfully, so, by the like reason, when his own preservation comes not in competition, ought he, as much as he can, to preserve the rest of mankind, and not, unless it be to do justice on an offender, take away or impair the life, or what tends to the preservation of the life, the liberty, health, limb, or goods of another. . . .

Chapter IV: Of Slavery

22. The natural liberty of man is to be free from any superior power on earth, and not to be under the will or legislative authority of man, but to have only the law of nature for his rule. The liberty of man in society is to be under no other legislative power but that established by consent in the commonwealth; nor under the dominion of any will or restraint of any law, but what that legislative shall enact according to the trust

put in it. Freedom then is not what Sir R. R. tells us, O. A. 55, "a liberty for every one to do what he lists, to live as he pleases, and not to be tied by any laws." But freedom of men under government is to have a standing rule to live by, common to every one of that society, and made by the legislative power erected in it; a liberty to follow my own will in all things, where that rule prescribes not; and not to be subject to the inconstant, uncertain, unknown, arbitrary will of another man: as freedom of nature is to be under no other restraint but the law of nature. . . .

Chapter V: Of Property

. . . 27. Though the earth and all inferior creatures be common to all men, yet every man has a *property* in his own *person;* this nobody has any right to but himself. The *labor* of his body and the *work* of his hands we may say are properly his. Whatsoever, then, he removes out of the state that Nature hath provided and left it in, he hath mixed his labor with, and joined to it something that is his own, and thereby makes it his property. It being by him removed from the common state nature placed it in, it hath by this labor something annexed to it that excludes the common right of other men. For this *labor* being the unquestionable property of the laborer, no man but he can have a right to what that is once joined to, at least where there is enough, and as good left in common for others.

28. He that is nourished by the acorns he picked up under an oak, or the apples he gathered from the trees in the wood, has certainly appropriated them to himself. Nobody can deny but the nourishment is his. I ask, then, When did they begin to be his—when he digested, or when he ate, or when he boiled, or when he brought them home, or when he picked them up? And 'tis plain if the first gathering made them not his, nothing else could. That labor put a distinction between them and common; that added something to them more than Nature, the common mother of all, had done, and so they became his private right. And will anyone say he had no right to those acorns or apples he thus appropriated, because he had not the consent of all mankind to make them his? Was it a robbery thus to assume to himself what belonged to all in common? If such a consent as that was necessary, man had starved, notwithstanding the plenty God had given him. We see in commons

which remain so by compact that 'tis the taking any part of what is common and removing it out of the state Nature leaves it in, which begins the property; without which the common is of no use. And the taking of this or that part does not depend on the express consent of all the commoners. Thus the grass my horse has bit, the turfs my servant has cut, and the ore I have dug in any place where I have a right to them in common with others, become my property without the assignation or consent of anybody. The labor that was mine removing them out of that common state they were in, hath fixed my property in them. . . .

32. But the chief matter of property being now not the fruits of the earth, and the beasts that subsist on it, but the earth itself, as that which takes in and carries with it all the rest, I think it is plain that property in that, too, is acquired as the former. As much land as a man tills, plants, improves, cultivates, and can use the product of, so much is his property. He by his labor does as it were enclose it from the common. Nor will it invalidate his right to say, everybody else has an equal title to it; and therefore he cannot appropriate, he cannot enclose, without the consent of all his fellow-commoners, all mankind. God, when He gave the world in common to all mankind, commanded man also to labor, and the penury of his condition required it of him. God and his reason commanded him to subdue the earth, *i.e.,* improve it for the benefit of life, and therein lay out something upon it that was his own, his labor. He that, in obedience to this command of God, subdued, tilled, and sowed any part of it, thereby annexed to it something that was his property, which another had no title to, nor could without injury take from him.

33. Nor was this appropriation of any parcel of land, by improving it, any prejudice to any other man, since there was still enough and as good left; and more than the yet unprovided could use. So that in effect there was never the less left for others because of his enclosure for himself. For he that leaves as much as another can make use of, does as good as take nothing at all. Nobody could think himself injured by the drinking of another man, though he took a good draft, who had a whole river of the same water left him to quench his thirst; and the case of land and water, where there is enough of both, is perfectly the same.

34. God gave the world to men in common; but since He gave it them for their benefit, and the greatest conveniences of life they were capable to draw from it, it cannot be supposed He meant it should always

remain common and uncultivated. He gave it to the use of the industrious and rational (and labor was to be his title to it), not to the fancy or covetousness of the quarrelsome and contentious. He that had as good left for his improvement as was already taken up, needed not complain, ought not to meddle with what was already improved by another's labor; if he did, it is plain he desired the benefit of another's pains, which he had no right to, and not the ground which God had given him in common with others to labor on, and whereof there was as good left as that already possessed, and more than he knew what to do with, or his industry could reach to.

35. It is true, in land that is common in England, or any other country where there is plenty of people under Government, who have money and commerce, no one can enclose or appropriate any part without the consent of all his fellow-commoners: because this is left common by compact, *i.e.,* by the law of the land, which is not to be violated. And though it be common in respect of some men, it is not so to all mankind; but is the joint property of this country, or this parish. Besides, the remainder, after such enclosure, would not be as good to the rest of the commoners as the whole was, when they could all make use of the whole; whereas in the beginning and first peopling of the great common of the world it was quite otherwise. The law man was under was rather for appropriating. God commanded, and his wants forced him, to labor. That was his property, which could not be taken from him wherever he had fixed it. And hence subduing or cultivating the earth, and having dominion, we see are joined together. The one gave title to the other. So that God, by commanding to subdue, gave authority so far to appropriate. And the condition of human life, which requires labor and materials to work on, necessarily introduces private possessions. . . .

Chapter VII: Of Political or Civil Society

87. Man being born, as has been proved, with a title to perfect freedom, and an uncontrolled enjoyment of all the rights and privileges of the law of Nature equally with any other man or number of men in the world, hath by nature a power not only to preserve his property—that is, his life, liberty, and estate—against the injuries and attempts of other men, but to judge of and punish the breaches of that law in others as he is persuaded the offense deserves, even with death itself, in crimes where

the heinousness of the fact in his opinion requires it. But because no political society can be nor subsist without having in itself the power to preserve the property, and, in order thereunto, punish the offenses of all those of that society, there, and there only, is political society, where every one of the members hath quitted this natural power, resigned it up into the hands of the community in all cases that exclude him not from appealing for protection to the law established by it. And thus all private judgment of every particular member being excluded, the community comes to be umpire; and by understanding indifferent rules and men authorized by the community for their execution, decides all the differences that may happen between any members of that society concerning any matter of right, and punishes those offenses which any member hath committed against the society with such penalties as the law has established; whereby it is easy to discern who are and who are not in political society together. Those who are united into one body, and have a common established law and judicature to appeal to, with authority to decide controversies between them and punish offenders, are in civil society one with another; but those who have no such common appeal—I mean on earth—are still in the state of Nature, each being, where there is no other, judge for himself and executioner, which is, as I have before shown it, the perfect state of Nature.

88. And thus the commonwealth comes by a power to set down what punishment shall belong to the several transgressions which they think worthy of it committed amongst the members of that society, which is the power of making laws, as well as it has the power to punish any injury done unto any of its members by anyone that is not of it, which is the power of war and peace; and all this for the preservation of the property of all the members of that society as far as is possible. But though every man entered into civil society has quitted his power to punish offenses against the law of Nature in prosecution of his own private judgment, yet with the judgment of offenses, which he has given up to the legislative in all cases where he can appeal to the magistrate, he has given a right to the commonwealth to employ his force for the execution of the judgments of the commonwealth whenever he shall be called to it; which, indeed, are his own judgments, they being made by himself or his representative. And herein we have the original of the legislative and executive power of civil society, which is to judge by standing laws how far offenses are to be punished when committed within the commonwealth, and also by occasional judgments founded

on the present circumstances of the fact, how far injuries from without are to be vindicated; and in both these to employ all the force of all the members when there shall be need.

89. Wherever, therefore, any number of men so unite into one society, as to quit everyone his executive power of the law of Nature, and to resign it to the public, there, and there only, is a political or civil society. And this is done wherever any number of men, in the state of Nature, enter into society to make one people, one body politic, under one supreme government, or else when anyone joins himself to, and incorporates with, any government already made. For hereby he authorizes the society, or, which is all one, the legislative thereof, to make laws for him, as the public good of the society shall require, to the execution whereof his own assistance (as to his own decrees) is due. And this puts men out of a state of Nature into that of a commonwealth, by setting up a judge on earth with authority to determine all the controversies and redress the injuries that may happen to any member of the commonwealth; which judge is the legislative, or magistrates appointed by it. And wherever there are any number of men, however associated, that have no such decisive power to appeal to, there they are still in the state of Nature.

90. Hence it is evident that absolute monarchy, which by some men is counted the only government in the world, is indeed inconsistent with civil society, and so can be no form of civil government at all. . . .

Chapter VIII: Of the Beginning of Political Societies

95. Men being, as has been said, by nature all free, equal, and independent, no one can be put out of this estate, and subjected to the political power of another, without his own consent, which is done by agreeing with other men to join and unite into a community for their comfortable, safe, and peaceable living one amongst another, in a secure enjoyment of their properties, and a greater security against any that are not of it. This any number of men may do, because it injures not the freedom of the rest; they are left as they were in the liberty of the state of Nature. When any number of men have so consented to make one community or government, they are thereby presently incorporated, and make one body politic, wherein the majority have a right to act and conclude the rest.

96. For when any number of men have, by the consent of every individual, made a community, they have thereby made that community one body, with a power to act as one body, which is only by the will and determination of the majority. For that which acts any community being only the consent of the individuals of it, and it being one body must move one way, it is necessary the body should move that way whither the greater force carries it, which is the consent of the majority; or else it is impossible it should act or continue one body, one community which the consent of every individual that united into it agreed that it should; and so everyone is bound by that consent to be concluded by the majority. And therefore we see that in assemblies empowered to act by positive laws, where no number is set by that positive law which empowers them, the act of the majority passes for the act of the whole, and of course determines, as having by the law of nature and reason the power of the whole.

97. And thus every man, by consenting with others to make one body politic under one government, puts himself under an obligation to every one of that society, to submit to the determination of the majority, and to be concluded by it; or else this original compact, whereby he with others incorporates into one society, would signify nothing, and be no compact, if he be left free and under no other ties than he was in before in the state of nature. For what appearance would there be of any compact? . . .

Chapter IX: Of the Ends of Political Society and Government

123. If man in the state of Nature be so free, as has been said, if he be absolute lord of his own person and possessions, equal to the greatest, and subject to nobody, why will he part with his freedom, this empire, and subject himself to the dominion and control of any other power? To which, it is obvious to answer, that though in the state of Nature he hath such a right, yet the enjoyment of it is very uncertain, and constantly exposed to the invasions of others. For all being kings as much as he, every man his equal, and the greater part no strict observers of equity and justice, the enjoyment of the property he has in this state is very unsafe, very unsecure. This makes him willing to quit this condition, which, however free, is full of fears and continual dangers; and it

is not without reason that he seeks out and is willing to join in society with others, who are already united, or have a mind to unite, for the mutual preservation of their lives, liberties, and estates, which I call by the general name, property.

124. The great and chief end, therefore, of men's uniting into commonwealths, and putting themselves under government, is the preservation of their property; to which in the state of nature there are many things wanting.

First, There wants an established, settled, known law, received and allowed by common consent to be the standard of right and wrong, and the common measure to decide all controversies between them. For though the law of nature be plain and intelligible to all rational creatures; yet men, being biased by their interest, as well as ignorant for want of study of it, are not apt to allow of it as a law binding to them in the application of it to their particular cases.

125. Secondly, In the state of Nature there wants a known and indifferent judge, with authority to determine all differences according to the established law. For everyone in that state, being both judge and executioner of the law of nature, men being partial to themselves, passion and revenge is very apt to carry them too far, and with too much heat in their own cases, as well as negligence and unconcernedness, to make them too remiss in other men's. . . .

Chapter XI: Of the Extent of the Legislative Power

134. The great end of men's entering into society being the enjoyment of their properties in peace and safety, and the great instrument and means of that being the laws established in that society: the first and fundamental positive law of all commonwealths, is the establishing of the legislative power; as the first and fundamental natural law, which is to govern even the legislative itself, is the preservation of the society, and (as far as will consist with the public good) of every person in it. This legislative is not only the supreme power of the commonwealth, but sacred and unalterable in the hands where the community have once placed it; nor can any edict of anybody else, in what form so ever conceived, or by what power so ever backed, have the force and obligation of a law, which has not its sanction from that legislative which the public has chosen and appointed. For without this the law could not have that,

which is absolutely necessary to its being a law, the consent of the society over whom nobody can have a power to make laws; but by their own consent, and by authority received from them; and therefore all the obedience, which by the most solemn ties anyone can be obliged to pay, ultimately terminates in this supreme power, and is directed by those laws which it enacts; nor can any oaths to any foreign power whatsoever, or any domestic subordinate power discharge any member of the society from his obedience to the legislative, acting pursuant to their trust; nor oblige him to any obedience contrary to the laws so enacted, or farther than they do allow; it being ridiculous to imagine one can be tied ultimately to obey any power in the society which is not the supreme.

135. Though the legislative, whether placed in one or more, whether it be always in being, or only by intervals, though it be the supreme power in every commonwealth, yet,

First, It is not nor can possibly be absolutely arbitrary over the lives and fortunes of the people. For it being but the joint power of every member of the society given up to that person, or assembly, which is legislator; it can be no more than those persons had in a state of nature before they entered into society, and gave it up to the community. For nobody can transfer to another more power than he has in himself; and nobody has an absolute arbitrary power over himself, or over any other to destroy his own life, or take away the life or property of another. A man as has been proved cannot subject himself to the arbitrary power of another; and having in the state of Nature no arbitrary power over the life, liberty, or possession of another, but only so much as the law of Nature gave him for the preservation of himself, and the rest of mankind; this is all he doth, or can give up to the commonwealth, and by it to the legislative power, so that the legislative can have no more than this. Their power in the utmost bounds of it, is limited to the public good of the society. It is a power that hath no other end but preservation, and therefore can never have a right to destroy, enslave, or designedly to impoverish the subjects. The obligations of the law of nature cease not in society, but only in many cases are drawn closer, and have by human laws known penalties annexed to them to enforce their observation. Thus the law of nature stands as an eternal rule to all men, legislators as well as others. The rules that they make for other men's actions must, as well as their own, and other men's actions be conformable to the law of nature, i.e., to the will of God, of which that is a declaration, and the fundamental law of nature being the preservation of mankind, no human sanction can be good or valid against it.

THE SPIRIT OF THE LAWS

Baron de Montesquieu

A towering monument of Enlightenment political thought, Montesquieu's Spirit of the Laws, *published in 1748, would profoundly influence the American founding fathers with its ideal of the separation of powers and its claims about republican government.*

Preface

I have first of all considered mankind, and the result of my thoughts has been that amidst such an infinite diversity of laws and manners, they were not solely conducted by the caprice of fancy.

I have laid down the first principles, and have found that the particular cases follow naturally from them; that the histories of all nations are only consequences of them; and that every particular law is connected with another law, or depends on some other of a more general extent. . . .

I have not drawn my principles from my prejudices, but from the nature of things.

Here a great many truths will not appear till we have seen the chain which connects them with others. The more we enter into particulars, the more we shall perceive the certainty of the principles on which they are founded. I have not even given all these particulars, for who could mention them all without a most insupportable fatigue? . . .

Book III: Of the Principles of the Three Kinds of Government

I. Having examined the laws in relation to the nature of each government, we must investigate those which relate to its principle.

There is this difference between the nature and principle of government, that the former is that by which it is constituted, the latter that by which it is made to act. One is its particular structure, and the other the human passions which set it in motion.

Now, laws ought no less to relate to the principle than to the nature of each government. We must, therefore, enquire into this principle, which shall be the subject of this third book.

II. I have already observed that it is the nature of a republican government, that either the collective body of the people, or particular families, should be possessed of the supreme power; of a monarchy, that the prince should have this power, but in the execution of it should be directed by established laws; of a despotic government, that a single person should rule according to his own will and caprice. This enables me to discover their three principles, which are thence naturally derived. I shall begin with a republican government, and in particular with that of democracy.

III. There is no great share of probity necessary to support a monarchical or despotic government. The force of laws in one, and the prince's arm in the other, are sufficient to direct and maintain the whole. But in a popular state, one spring more is necessary—namely, virtue.

What I have here advanced is confirmed by the unanimous testimony of historians, and is extremely agreeable to the nature of things. For it is clear that in a monarchy, where he who commands the execution of the laws generally thinks himself above them, there is less need of virtue than in a popular government, where the person entrusted with the execution of the laws is sensible of his being subject to their direction.

Clear is it also that a monarch who, through bad advice or indolence, ceases to enforce the execution of the laws, may easily repair the evil; he has only to follow other advice, or to shake off his indolence. But when, in a popular government, there is a suspension of the laws, as this can proceed only from the corruption of the republic, the state is certainly undone.

A very droll spectacle it was in the last century to behold the impotent efforts of the English toward the establishment of democracy. As they who had a share in the direction of public affairs were void of virtue; as their ambition was inflamed by the success of the most daring of their members; as the prevailing parties were successively animated by the spirit of faction, the government was continually changing: the people, amazed at so many revolutions, in vain attempted to erect a commonwealth. At length, when the country had undergone the most violent shocks, they were obliged to have recourse to the very government which they had so wantonly proscribed. . . .

The politic Greeks, who lived under a popular government, knew no other support than virtue. The modern inhabitants of that country are entirely taken up with manufacture, commerce, finances, opulence, and luxury.

When virtue is banished, ambition invades the minds of those who are disposed to receive it, and avarice possesses the whole community. The objects of their desires are changed; what they were fond of before has become indifferent; they were free while under the restraint of laws, but they would fain now be free to act against law; and as each citizen is like a slave who has run away from his master, that which was a maxim of equity he calls rigor; that which was a rule of action he styles constraint; and to precaution he gives the name of fear. Frugality, and not the thirst of gain, now passes for avarice. Formerly the wealth of individuals constituted the public treasure; but now this has become the patrimony of private persons. The members of the commonwealth riot on the public spoils, and its strength is only the power of a few, and the license of many. . . .

IV. As virtue is necessary in a popular government, it is requisite also in an aristocracy. True it is that in the latter it is not so absolutely requisite.

The people, who in respect to the nobility are the same as the subjects with regard to a monarch, are restrained by their laws. They have, therefore, less occasion for virtue than the people in a democracy. But how are the nobility to be restrained? They who are to execute the laws against their colleagues will immediately perceive that they are acting against themselves. Virtue is therefore necessary in this body, from the very nature of the constitution.

An aristocratic government has an inherent vigor, unknown to democracy. The nobles form a body, who by their prerogative, and for their own particular interest, restrain the people; it is sufficient that there are laws in being to see them executed.

But easy as it may be for the body of the nobles to restrain the people, it is difficult to restrain themselves. Such is the nature of this constitution, that it seems to subject the very same persons to the power of the laws, and at the same time to exempt them.

Now, such a body as this can restrain itself only in two ways: either by a very eminent virtue, which puts the nobility in some measure on a level with the people, and may be the means of forming a great republic; or by an inferior virtue, which puts them at least upon a level with one another, and upon this their preservation depends.

Moderation is therefore the very soul of this government; a moderation, I mean, founded on virtue, not that which proceeds from indolence and pusillanimity.

V. In monarchies, policy effects great things with as little virtue as possible. Thus in the nicest machines, art has reduced the number of movements, springs, and wheels.

The state subsists independently of the love of our country, of the thirst of true glory, of self-denial, of the sacrifice of our dearest interests, and of all those heroic virtues which we admire in the ancients, and to us are known only by tradition.

The laws supply here the place of those virtues; they are by no means wanted, and the state dispenses with them: an action performed here in secret is in some measure of no consequence.

Though all crimes be in their own nature public, yet there is a distinction between crimes really public and those that are private, which are so called because they are more injurious to individuals than to the community.

Now, in republics private crimes are more public—that is, they attack the constitution more than they do individuals; and in monarchies, public crimes are more private—that is, they are more prejudicial to private people than to the constitution.

I beg that no one will be offended with what I have been saying; my observations are founded on the unanimous testimony of historians. I am not ignorant that virtuous princes are so very rare; but I venture to affirm, that in a monarchy it is extremely difficult for the people to be virtuous. . . .

VI. But it is high time for me to have done with this subject, lest I should be suspected of writing a satire against monarchical government. Far be it from me; if monarchy wants one spring, it is provided with another. Honor—that is, the prejudice of every person and rank—supplies the place of the political virtue of which I have been speaking, and is everywhere her representative: here it is capable of inspiring the most glorious actions, and, joined with the force of laws, may lead us to the end of government as well as virtue itself.

Hence, in well-regulated monarchies, they are almost all good subjects, and very few good men; for to be a good man, a good intention is necessary, and we should love our country, not so much on our own account, as out of regard to the community.

VII. A monarchical government supposes, as we have already observed, preeminences and ranks, as likewise a noble descent. Now, since it is the nature of honor to aspire to preferments and titles, it is properly placed in this government.

Ambition is pernicious in a republic. But in a monarchy it has some good effects; it gives life to the government, and is attended with this advantage, that it is in no way dangerous, because it may be continually checked.

It is with this kind of government as with the system of the universe, in which there is a power that constantly repels all bodies from the center, and a power of gravitation that attracts them to it. Honor sets all the parts of the body politic in motion, and by its very action connects them; thus each individual advances the public good, while he only thinks of promoting his own interest. . . .

VIII. Honor is far from being the principle of despotic government: mankind being here all upon a level, no one person can prefer himself to another; and as on the other hand they are all slaves, they can give themselves no sort of preference.

Besides, as honor has its laws and rules, as it knows not how to submit; as it depends in a great measure on a man's own caprice, and not on that of another person, it can be found only in countries in which the constitution is fixed, and where they are governed by settled laws.

How can despotism abide with honor? The one glories in the contempt of life, and the other is founded on the power of taking it away. How can honor, on the other hand, bear with despotism? The former has its fixed rules and peculiar caprices, but the latter is directed by no rule, and its own caprices are subversive of all others.

Honor, therefore, a thing unknown in arbitrary governments, some of which have not even a proper word to express it, is the prevailing principle in monarchies; here it gives life to the whole body politic, to the laws, and even to the virtues themselves.

IX. As virtue is necessary in a republic, and in a monarchy honor, so fear is necessary in a despotic government: with regard to virtue, there is no occasion for it, and honor would be extremely dangerous.

Here the immense power of the prince devolves entirely upon those whom he is pleased to entrust with the administration. Persons capable of setting a value upon themselves would be likely to create disturbances.

Fear must therefore depress their spirits, and extinguish even the least sense of ambition. . . .

X. In despotic states, the nature of government requires the most passive obedience; and when once the prince's will is made known, it ought infallibly to produce its effect.

Here they have no limitations or restrictions, no mediums, terms, equivalents, or remonstrances; no change to propose: man is a creature that blindly submits to the absolute will of the sovereign.

In a country like this they are no more allowed to represent their apprehensions of a future danger than to impute their miscarriage to the capriciousness of fortune. Man's portion here, like that of beasts, is instinct, compliance, and punishment.

Little does it then avail to plead the sentiments of Nature, filial respect, conjugal or parental tenderness, the laws of honor, or want of health; the order is given, and that is sufficient. . . .

Book IV: Of Education in a Republican Government

V. It is in a republican government that the whole power of education is required. The fear of despotic governments naturally arises of itself amidst threats and punishments; the honor of monarchies is favored by the passions, and favors them in its turn; but virtue is a self-renunciation, which is ever arduous and painful.

This virtue may be defined as the love of the laws and of our country. As such love requires a constant preference of public to private interest, it is the source of all private virtues; for they are nothing more than this very preference itself.

This love is peculiar to democracies. In these alone the government is entrusted to private citizens. Now, a government is like every thing else: to preserve it we must love it.

Has it ever been known that kings were not fond of monarchy, or that despotic princes hated arbitrary power?

Every thing, therefore, depends on establishing this love in a republic; and to inspire it ought to be the principal business of education: but the surest way of instilling it into children is for parents to set them an example.

People have it generally in their power to communicate their ideas to their children; but they are still better able to transfuse their passions. . . .

Book VIII: Of the Corruption of the Three Governments

XVI. It is natural for a republic to have only a small territory; otherwise it cannot long subsist. In an extensive republic there are men of large fortunes, and consequently of less moderation; there are trusts too considerable to be placed in any single subject; he has interests of his own; he soon begins to think that he may be happy and glorious by oppressing his fellow-citizens, and that he may raise himself to grandeur on the ruins of his country.

In an extensive republic the public good is sacrificed to a thousand private views; it is subordinate to exceptions, and depends on accidents. In a small one, the interest of the public is more obvious, better understood, and more within the reach of every citizen; abuses have less extent, and, of course, are less protected.

The long duration of the republic of Sparta was owing to her having continued in the same extent of territory after all her wars. The sole aim of Sparta was liberty; and the sole advantage of her liberty, glory.

It was the spirit of the Greek republics to be as contented with their territories as with their laws. Athens was first fired with ambition and gave it to Lacedæmon; but it was an ambition rather of commanding a free people than of governing slaves; rather of directing than of breaking the union. All was lost upon the starting up of monarchy—a government whose spirit is more turned to increase of dominion. . . .

Book XI: Of the Laws Which Establish Political Liberty with Regard to the Constitution

II. There is no word that admits of more various significations, and has made more varied impressions on the human mind, than that of "liberty." Some have taken it as a means of deposing a person on whom they had conferred a tyrannical authority; others for the power of choosing a superior whom they are obliged to obey; others for the right of bearing arms, and of being thereby enabled to use violence; others, in fine, for the privilege of being governed by a native of their own country, or by their own laws. A certain nation for a long time thought liberty consisted in the privilege of wearing a long beard. Some have annexed this name to one form of government exclusive of others: those who had a republican taste applied it to this species of polity; those who liked a monarchical state gave it to monarchy. Thus they have all applied the name of liberty to the government most suitable to their own customs and inclinations: and as in republics the people have not so constant and so present a view of the causes of their misery, and as the magistrates seem to act only in conformity to the laws, hence liberty is generally said to reside in republics, and to be banished from monarchies. In fine, as in democracies the people seem to act almost as they please, this sort of government has been deemed the most free, and the power of the people has been confounded with their liberty.

III. It is true that in democracies the people seem to act as they please; but political liberty does not consist in an unlimited freedom. In governments, that is, in societies directed by laws, liberty can consist only in the power of doing what we ought to will, and in not being constrained to do what we ought not to will.

We must continually present to our minds the difference between independence and liberty. Liberty is a right of doing whatever the laws permit, and if a citizen could do what they forbid, he would be no longer possessed of liberty, because all his fellow citizens would have the same power.

IV. Democratic and aristocratic states are not in their own nature free. Political liberty is to be found only in moderate governments; and even in these it is not always found. It is there only when there is no abuse of power. But constant experience shows us that every man invested with power is apt to abuse it, and to carry his authority as far as it will go. Is it not strange, though true, to say that virtue itself has need of limits?

To prevent this abuse, it is necessary from the very nature of things that power should be a check to power. A government may be so constituted as no man shall be compelled to do things to which the law does not oblige him, nor forced to abstain from things which the law permits. . . .

VI. In every government there are three sorts of power: the legislative; the executive in respect to things dependent on the law of nations; and the executive in regard to matters that depend on the civil law.

By virtue of the first, the prince or magistrate enacts temporary or perpetual laws, and amends or abrogates those that have been already enacted. By the second, he makes peace or war, sends or receives embassies, establishes the public security, and provides against invasions. By the third, he punishes criminals, or determines the disputes that arise between individuals. The latter we shall call the judiciary power, and the other simply the executive power of the state.

The political liberty of the subject is a tranquillity of mind arising from the opinion each person has of his safety. In order to have this liberty, it is requisite the government be so constituted as one man need not be afraid of another.

When the legislative and executive powers are united in the same person, or in the same body of magistrates, there can be no liberty, because apprehensions may arise lest the same monarch or senate should enact tyrannical laws, to execute them in a tyrannical manner.

Again, there is no liberty if the judiciary power be not separated from the legislative and executive. Were it joined with the legislative, the life and liberty of the subject would be exposed to arbitrary control; for the judge would be then the legislator. Were it joined to the executive power, the judge might behave with violence and oppression.

There would be an end of everything, were the same man or the same body, whether of the nobles or of the people, to exercise these three powers: that of enacting laws, that of executing the public resolutions, and of trying the causes of individuals. . . .

As in a country of liberty, every man who is supposed a free agent ought to be his own governor; the legislative power should reside in the whole body of the people. But since this is impossible in large states, and in small ones is subject to many inconveniences, it is fit that the people should transact by their representatives what they cannot transact by themselves.

The inhabitants of a particular town are much better acquainted with its wants and interests than with those of other places; and are better judges of the capacity of their neighbors than of that of the rest of their countrymen. The members, therefore, of the legislature should not be chosen from the general body of the nation; but it is proper that in every considerable place a representative should be elected by the inhabitants.

The great advantage of representatives is their capacity of discussing public affairs. For this the people collectively are extremely unfit, which is one of the chief inconveniences of a democracy. . . .

The executive power, pursuant of what has been already said, ought to have a share in the legislature by the power of rejecting, otherwise it would soon be stripped of its prerogative. But should the legislative power usurp a share of the executive, the latter would be equally undone.

If the prince were to have a part in the legislature by the power of resolving, liberty would be lost. But as it is necessary he should have a share in the legislature for the support of his own prerogative, this share must consist in the power of rejecting.

The change of government at Rome was owing to this, that neither the Senate, who had one part of the executive power, nor the magistrates, who were entrusted with the other, had the right of rejecting, which was entirely lodged in the people.

Here, then, is the fundamental constitution of the government we are treating of. The legislative body being composed of two parts, they check one another by the mutual privilege of rejecting. They are both restrained by the executive power, as the executive is by the legislative.

These three powers should naturally form a state of repose or inaction. But as there is a necessity for movement in the course of human affairs, they are forced to move, but still in concert.

As the executive power has no other part in the legislative than the privilege of rejecting, it can have no share in the public debates. It is not even necessary that it should propose, because as it may always disapprove of the resolutions that shall be taken, it may likewise reject the decisions on those proposals which were made against its will . . .

To prevent the executive power from being able to oppress, it is requisite that the armies with which it is entrusted should consist of the people, and have the same spirit as the people, as was the case at Rome till the time of Marius. To obtain this end, there are only two ways: either that the persons employed in the army should have sufficient property to answer for their conduct to their fellow subjects, and be enlisted only for a year, as was customary at Rome; or if there should be a standing army, composed chiefly of the most despicable part of the nation, the legislative power should have a right to disband them as soon as it pleased; the soldiers should live in common with the rest of the people; and no separate camp, barracks, or fortress should be suffered. . . .

Book XIV: Of Laws in Relation to the Nature of the Climate

I. If it be true that the temper of the mind and the passions of the heart are extremely different in different climates, the laws ought to be in relation both to the variety of these passions and to the variety of these tempers.

II. Cold air constringes the extremities of the external fibers of the body; this increases their elasticity, and favors the return of the blood from the extreme parts to the heart. It contracts those very fibers; consequently it increases also their force. On the contrary, warm air relaxes and lengthens the extremes of the fibers; of course, it diminishes their force and elasticity.

People are therefore more vigorous in cold climates. Here the action of the heart and the reaction of the extremities of the fibers are better performed, the temperature of the humors is greater, the blood moves more freely toward the heart, and reciprocally the heart has more power. This superiority of strength must produce various effects: for instance, a greater boldness—that is, more courage; a greater sense of superiority—that is, less desire of revenge; a greater opinion of security—that is, more frankness, less suspicion, policy, and cunning. In short, this must be productive of very different tempers. Put a man into a close, warm place, and for reasons above given he will feel a great faintness. If under this circumstance you propose a bold enterprise to him, I believe you will find him very little disposed toward it; his present weakness will throw him into despondency; he will be afraid of everything, being in a state of total incapacity. The inhabitants of warm countries are, like old men, timorous; the people in cold countries are, like young men, brave. If we reflect on the late wars, which are more recent in our memory, and in which we can better distinguish some particular effects that escape us at a greater distance of time, we shall find that the northern people transplanted into southern regions did not perform such exploits as their countrymen, who, fighting in their own climate, possessed their full vigor and courage.

POLITICAL ESSAYS

François-Marie Arouet de Voltaire

In these four short essays, which form part of Voltaire's Philosophical Dictionary *of 1750, one sees the wit, iconoclasm, and social realism of this great* philosophe.

Democracy

As a rule there is no comparison between the crimes of great men, who are always ambitious, and the crimes of the people, who always want, and can only want, liberty and equality. These two sentiments, Liberty and Equality, do not lead straight to calumny, rapine, assassination, poisoning, the devastation of one's neighbors' lands, etc. But ambitious might and the mania for power plunge men into all these crimes, whatever the time, whatever the place.

Popular government is in itself, therefore, less iniquitous, less abominable than despotic power.

The great vice of democracy is certainly not tyranny and cruelty. There have been mountain-dwelling republicans who were savage and ferocious; but it was not the republican spirit that made them so, it was nature.

The real vice of a civilized republic is expressed in the Turkish fable of the dragon with many heads and the dragon with many tails. The many heads injured one another, and the many tails obeyed a single head which sought to devour everything.

Democracy seems suitable only to a very little country, and one that is happily situated. However small it may be, it will make many mistakes, because it will be composed of men. Discord will reign there as in a monastery; but there will be no St. Bartholomew, no Irish massacres, no Sicilian vespers, no Inquisition, no condemnation to the galleys for having taken some water from the sea without paying for it—unless one assumes that this republic is composed of devils in a corner of hell.

Which is better—runs the endless question—a republic or a

monarchy? The dispute always resolves itself into an agreement that it is a very difficult business to govern men. The Jews had God Himself for their master, and see what has happened to them as a result: nearly always have they been oppressed and enslaved and even today they do not appear to cut a very pretty figure.

EQUALITY

It is clear that men, in the enjoyment of their natural faculties, are equal: they are equal when they perform animal functions, and when they exercise their understanding. The King of China, the Great Mogul, the Padisha of Turkey, cannot say to the least of men: "I forbid you to digest, to go to the privy, or to think." All the animals of each species are equal among themselves. Animals, by nature, have over us the advantage of independence. If a bull which is wooing a heifer is driven away with the blows of the horns by a stronger bull, it goes in search of another mistress in another field, and lives free. A cock, beaten by a cock, consoles itself in another poultry house. It is not so with us. A little vizier exiles a bostangi to Lemnos: the vizier Azem exiles the little vizier to Tenedos: the padisha exiles the vizier Azem to Rhodes: the Janissaries put the padisha in prison, and elect another who will exile good Mussulmans as he chooses; people will still be very obliged to him if he limits his sacred authority to this small exercise.

If this world were what it seems it should be, if man could find everywhere in it an easy subsistence, and a climate suitable to his nature, it is clear that it would be impossible for one man to enslave another. If this globe were covered with wholesome fruits; if the air, which should contribute to our life, gave us no diseases and no premature deaths; if man had no need of lodging and bed other than those of the buck and the deer; then the Gengis Khans and the Tamerlanes would have no servants other than their children, who would be decent enough to help them in their old age.

In the natural state enjoyed by all untamed quadrupeds, birds, and reptiles, man would be as happy as they. Domination would then be a chimera, an absurdity of which no one would think; for why seek servants when you have no need of their service?

If it came into the head of some individual of tyrannous mind and brawny arm to enslave a neighbor less strong than he, the thing would be impossible; the oppressed would be on the Danube before the oppressor had taken his measures on the Volga.

All men then would be necessarily equal, if they were without needs. It is the poverty connected with our species which subordinates one man to another. It is not the inequality which is the real misfortune, it is the dependence. It matters very little that So-and-so calls himself "His Highness," and So-and-so "His Holiness"; but to serve the one or the other is hard.

A big family has cultivated fruitful soil; two little families nearby have thankless and rebellious fields; the two poor families have to serve the opulent family, or slaughter it. There is no difficulty in that. But one of the two indigent families offers its arms to the rich family in exchange for bread, while the other attacks and is defeated. The subservient family is the origin of the servants and the workmen; the beaten family is the origin of the slaves.

In our unhappy world it is impossible for men living in society not to be divided into two classes, the one the rich who command, the other the poor who serve; and these two classes are subdivided into a thousand, and these thousand still have different gradations.

When the lots are drawn you come to us and say: "I am a man like you. I have two hands and two feet, as much pride as you, nay more, a mind as disordered, at least, as inconsequent, as contradictory as yours. I am a citizen of San Marino, or of Ragusa, or Vaugirard: give me my share of the land. In our known hemisphere there are about fifty thousand million arpents to cultivate, some passable, some sterile. We are only about a thousand million featherless bipeds in this continent; that makes fifty arpents apiece: be just; give me my fifty arpents."

"Go and take them in the land of the Kaffirs," we answer, "or the Hottentots, or the Samoyedes; come to an amicable arrangement with them; here all the shares are taken. If you want to eat, be clothed, lodged, and warmed among us, work for us as your father did; serve us or amuse us, and you will be paid; otherwise you will be obliged to ask charity, which would be too degrading to your sublime nature, and would stop your being really the equal of kings, and even of country parsons, according to the pretensions of your noble pride."

II. All the poor are not unhappy. The majority were born in that state, and continual work keeps them from feeling their position too keenly; but when they do feel it, then one sees wars, like that of the popular party against the senate party in Rome, like those of the peasants in Germany, England, and France. All these wars finish sooner or later with the subjection of the people, because the powerful have money, and money is master of everything in a state. I say in a state, for it is not the same between nations. The nation which makes the best use of the sword will always subjugate the nation which has more gold and less courage.

All men are born with a sufficiently violent liking for domination, wealth, and pleasure, and with a strong taste for idleness; consequently, all men covet the money, the wives, or the daughters of other men; they wish to be their master, to subject them to all their caprices, and to do nothing, or at least to do only very agreeable things. You see clearly that with these fine inclinations it is as impossible for men to be equal as it is impossible for two preachers or two professors of theology not to be jealous of each other.

The human race, such as it is, cannot subsist unless there is an infinity of useful men who possess nothing at all; for it is certain that a man who is well off will not leave his own land to come to till yours, and if you have need of a pair of shoes, it is not the Secretary to the Privy Council who will make them for you. Equality, therefore, is at once the most natural thing and the most fantastic.

As men go to excess in everything when they can, this inequality has been exaggerated. It has been maintained in many countries that it was not permissible for a citizen to leave the country where chance has caused him to be born. The sense of this law is obviously: "This land is so bad and so badly governed, that we forbid any individual to leave it, for fear that everyone will leave it." Do better: make all your subjects wish to live in your country, and foreigners wish to come to it.

All men have the right in the bottom of their hearts to think themselves entirely equal to other men. It does not follow from this that the cardinal's cook should order his master to prepare him his dinner, but the cook can say: "I am a man like my master; like him I was born crying; like me he will die with the same pangs and the same ceremonies. Both of us perform the same animal functions. If the Turks take possession of Rome, and if then I am cardinal and my master cook, I shall take him into my service." This discourse is reasonable and just, but while waiting for the Great Turk to take possession of Rome, the cook must do his duty, or else all human society is disordered.

As regards a man who is neither a cardinal's cook, nor endowed with any other employment in the state; as regards a private person who is connected with nothing, but who is vexed at being received everywhere with an air of being patronized or scorned, who sees quite clearly that many monseigneurs have no more knowledge, wit, or virtue than he, and who at times is bored at waiting in their antechambers, what should he decide to do? Why, to take himself off.

FATHERLAND

A young journeyman pastrycook who had been to college, and who still knew a few of Cicero's phrases, boasted one day of loving his fatherland. "What do you mean by your fatherland?" a neighbor asked him. "Is it your oven? Is it the village where you were born and which you have never seen since? Is it the street in which dwelt your father and mother, who have been ruined with the result that you are reduced to baking little pies for a living? Is it the town hall where you will never be the police superintendent's clerk? Is it the church of Our Lady where you have not been able to become a choirboy, while a stupid man is archbishop and duke with an income of twenty thousand golden louis?"

The journeyman pastrycook did not know what to answer. A philosopher, who was listening to this conversation, concluded that in a fatherland of any extent there must often be several million men who have no fatherland.

You, pleasure-loving Parisians, who have never traveled farther than Dieppe to eat fresh fish; who know nothing but your brilliant town house, your pretty country house, and your box at an Opera where the rest of Europe persists in being bored; who speak your own language well enough because you know no other—you love all these things, and you love the girls you keep, the champagne which comes to you from Reims, the dividends which the Hotel-de-Ville pays you every six months; and you say you love your fatherland!

Now, in all conscience, does a financier sincerely love his fatherland?

The officer and the soldier who pillage their winter quarters, if one lets them—have they a very warm love for the peasants they ruin?

Where was the fatherland of the scarred Duc de Guise, was it in Nancy, Paris, Madrid, Rome? What fatherland have you, Cardinals de La Balue, Duprat, Lorraine, Mazarin? Where was the fatherland of Attila, and of a hundred other heroes of his type? I would like someone to tell me which was Abraham's fatherland.

The first man to write that one's fatherland is wherever one feels comfortable was, I believe, Euripides in his *Phaeton*. But the first man who left his birthplace to seek his comfort elsewhere had said it before him.

What, then, is a fatherland? Is it not a good field, whose owner, lodged in a well-kept house, can say: "This field that I till, this house that I have built, are mine. I live here protected by laws which no tyrant can infringe. When those who own fields and houses, like myself, meet in their common interest, I have my voice in the assembly; I am a part of everything, a part of the community, a part of the dominion—there is my fatherland?"

Very well. But is it better for your fatherland to be a monarchy or a republic? For four thousand years has this question been debated. Ask the rich for an answer, they all prefer aristocracy; question the people, they want democracy: only kings prefer royalty. How then is it that nearly the whole world is governed by monarchs? Ask the rats who proposed to hang a bell round the cat's neck. But in truth, the real reason is, as has been said, that men are very rarely worthy of governing themselves.

It is sad that in order to be a good patriot one often has to be the enemy of the rest of mankind. Whenever old Cato, that excellent citizen, spoke before the Roman senate, he always used to say: "Such is my opinion, and Carthage must be destroyed." To be a good patriot is to wish that one's city may be enriched by trade, and be powerful by arms. It is clear that one country cannot gain without another's losing, and that one cannot conquer without bringing misery to another. Such then is the human state, that to wish greatness for one's country is to wish harm to one's neighbors. He who wished that his fatherland might never be greater, smaller, richer, or poorer, would be a citizen of the world.

Liberty of the Press

What harm can the prediction of Jean-Jacques do to Russia? None. He is free to explain it in a mystical, typical, allegorical sense, according to custom. The nations which will destroy the Russians will be bellesletters, mathematics, wit, and social graces, which degrade man and pervert nature.

From five to six thousand pamphlets have been printed in Holland against Louis XIV, none of which helped to make him lose the battles of Blenheim, Turin, and Ramillies.

In general, we have as natural a right to make use of our pens as of our tongue, at our peril, risk, and hazard. I know many books which have bored their readers, but I know of none which has done real evil. Theologians, or pretended politicians, cry: "Religion is destroyed, the government is lost, if you print certain truths or certain paradoxes. Never dare to think, till you have asked permission from a monk or a clerk. It is against the public welfare for a man to think for himself. Homer, Plato, Cicero, Virgil, Pliny, Horace, never published anything but with the approbation of the doctors of the Sorbonne and of the holy Inquisition.

"See into what horrible decadence the liberty of the press has brought England and Holland. It is true that they possess the commerce of the whole world, and that England is victorious on sea and land; but it is merely a false greatness, a false opulence: they are hastening to their ruin. An enlightened people cannot exist."

No one could reason more justly, my friends; but let us see, if you please, what state has been ruined by a book. The most dangerous, the most pernicious book of all, is that of Spinoza. Not only in the character of a Jew does he attack the New Testament, but in the character of a scholar he ruins the Old. His system of atheism is a thousand times better constructed and reasoned than those of Straton and of Epicurus. It requires the most profound sagacity to answer to the arguments by which he endeavors to prove that one substance cannot form another.

Like yourself, I detest this book, which I perhaps understand better than you, and to which you have replied very badly. But have you discovered that it has changed the face of the world? Has any preacher lost a florin of his income by the publication of the works of Spinoza? Is there a bishop whose rents have diminished? On the contrary, their revenues have doubled since his time: all the ill is limited to a small number of peaceable readers, who have examined Spinoza's arguments in their studies, and who have written for or against them in works that are little known.

For ourselves, you have hardly been consistent in having printed, *ad usum Delphini*, the atheism of Lucretius—as you have already been reproached with doing. No trouble, no scandal, has ensued from it; so Spinoza might be left to live in peace in Holland, as was Lucretius in Rome.

But if there appears among you any new book, the ideas of which shock your own—supposing you have any—or of which the author may be of a party contrary to yours—or what is worse, of which the author may not be of any party at all—then you cry out "Fire!" and all is noise, scandal, and uproar in your small corner of the earth. There is an abominable man who has declared in print that if we had no hands we would not be able to make shoes nor stockings. The devout cry out, furred doctors assemble, alarms multiply from college to college, from house to house, whole communities are disturbed. And why? For five or six pages, about which no one will give a fig at the end of three months. Does a book displease you? Refute it. Does it bore you? Don't read it.

Oh! you say to me, the books of Luther and Calvin have destroyed the Roman Catholic religion in one-half of Europe? Why not say also, that the books of the patriarch Photius have destroyed this Roman religion in Asia, Africa, Greece, and Russia?

You deceive yourself grossly, when you think that you have been ruined by books. The empire of Russia is two thousand leagues in extent, and there are not six men who are aware of the points disputed by the Greek and Latin Church. If the monk Luther, John Calvin, and the vicar Zwingli had been content with writing, Rome would still hold in subjugation all the states that it has lost; but these people and their adherents ran from town to town, from house to house, exciting the women, and they were supported by princes. The fury which tormented Amata and which, according to Virgil, whipped her like a top, was not more turbulent. Be assured that one enthusiastic, factious, ignorant, supple, vehement Capuchin—the emissary of some ambitious monks—who goes about preaching, confessing, communicating, and caballing, will much sooner overthrow a province than a hundred authors can enlighten it. It was not the Koran which made Mohammed succeed: it was Mohammed who caused the success of the Koran.

No! Rome has not been vanquished by books. It has been vanquished because it revolted Europe by its rapacity, by the public sale of indulgences, by insulting men and wishing to govern them like domestic animals, for having abused its power to such an extent that it is astonishing a single village remains to it. Henry VIII, Elizabeth, the duke of

Saxony, the landgrave of Hesse, the princes of Orange, the Condés and Colignys, have done all, and books nothing. Trumpets have never gained battles, nor caused any walls to fall except those of Jericho.

You fear books, as certain small cantons fear violins. Let men read, and let men dance—these two amusements will never do any harm to the world.

DISCOURSE ON THE ORIGIN OF INEQUALITY

JEAN-JACQUES ROUSSEAU

In his political thought, as well, Rousseau stood apart from his fellow thinkers of the Enlightenment. Individualism, he suggests here, produces a competitive civilization within which people seek only to surpass one another and to profit at the expense of others. The Discourse, *from which this selection is taken, was written in 1755 and dedicated to the Republic of Geneva.*

The cultivation of the earth necessarily brought about its distribution; and property, once recognized, gave rise to the first rules of justice; for, to secure each man his own, it had to be possible for each to have something. Besides, as men began to look forward to the future, and all had something to lose, every one had reason to apprehend that reprisals would follow any injury he might do to another. This origin is so much the more natural, as it is impossible to conceive how property can come from anything but manual labor: for what else can a man add to things which he does not originally create, so as to make them his own property? It is the husbandman's labor alone that, giving him a title to the produce of the ground he has tilled, gives him a claim also to the land itself, at least till harvest; and so, from year to year, a constant possession which is easily transformed into property. When the ancients, says Grotius, gave to Ceres the title of Legislatrix, and to a festival celebrated in her honor the name of Thesmophoria, they meant by that that the distribution of lands had produced a new kind of right: that is to say, the right of property, which is different from the right deducible from the law of nature.

In this state of affairs, equality might have been sustained, had the talents of individuals been equal, and had, for example, the use of iron and the consumption of commodities always exactly balanced each other; but, as there was nothing to preserve this balance, it was soon disturbed; the strongest did most work; the most skillful turned his labor to best account; the most ingenious devised methods of diminishing his labor: the husbandman wanted more iron, or the smith more corn, and, while both labored equally, the one gained a great deal by his work, while the other could hardly support himself. Thus natural inequality unfolds itself insensibly with that of combination, and the difference between men, developed by their different circumstances, becomes more sensible and permanent in its effects, and begins to have an influence, in the same proportion, over the lot of individuals.

Matters once at this pitch, it is easy to imagine the rest. I shall not detain the reader with a description of the successive invention of other arts, the development of language, the trial and utilization of talents, the inequality of fortunes, the use and abuse of riches, and all the details connected with them which the reader can easily supply for himself. I shall confine myself to a glance at mankind in this new situation.

Behold then all human faculties developed, memory and imagination in full play, egoism interested, reason active, and the mind almost at the highest point of its perfection. Behold all the natural qualities in action, the rank and condition of every man assigned him; not merely his share of property and his power to serve or injure others, but also his wit, beauty, strength or skill, merit or talents: and these being the only qualities capable of commanding respect, it soon became necessary to possess or to affect them.

It now became the interest of men to appear what they really were not. To be and to seem became two totally different things; and from this distinction sprang insolent pomp and cheating trickery, with all the numerous vices that go in their train. On the other hand, free and independent as men were before, they were now, in consequence of a multiplicity of new wants, brought into subjection, as it were, to all nature, and particularly to one another; and each became in some degree a slave even in becoming the master of other men: if rich, they stood in need of the services of others; if poor, of their assistance; and even a middle condition did not enable them to do without one another. Man must now, therefore, have been perpetually employed in getting others to interest themselves in his lot, and in making them, apparently at least, if not really, find their advantage in promoting his own. Thus he must have been sly and artful in his behavior to some, and imperious and cruel to others; being under a kind of necessity to ill-use all the persons of whom he stood in need, when he could not frighten them into compliance, and did not judge it his interest to be useful to them. Insatiable ambition, the thirst of raising their respective fortunes, not so much from real want as from the desire to surpass others, inspired all men with a vile propensity to injure one another, and with a secret jealousy, which is the more dangerous, as it puts on the mask of benevolence, to carry its point with greater security. In a word, there arose rivalry and competition on the one hand, and conflicting interests on the other, together with a secret desire on both of profiting at the expense of others. All these evils were the first effects of property, and the inseparable attendants of growing inequality.

Before the invention of signs to represent riches, wealth could hardly consist in anything but lands and cattle, the only real possessions men can have. But, when inheritances so increased in number and extent as to occupy the whole of the land, and to border on one another, one man could aggrandise himself only at the expense of another; at the same time the supernumeraries, who had been too weak or too indolent to make such acquisitions, and had grown poor without sustaining any loss, because, while they saw everything change around them, they remained still the same, were obliged to receive their subsistence, or steal it, from the rich; and this soon bred, according to their different characters, dominion and slavery, or violence and rapine. The wealthy, on their part, had no sooner begun to taste the pleasure of command, than they disdained all others, and, using their old slaves to acquire new, thought of nothing but subduing and enslaving their neighbors; like ravenous wolves, which, having once tasted human flesh, despise every other food and thenceforth seek only men to devour.

Thus, as the most powerful or the most miserable considered their might or misery as a kind of right to the possessions of others, equivalent, in their opinion, to that of property, the destruction of equality was attended by the most terrible disorders. Usurpations by the rich, robbery by the poor, and the unbridled passions of both, suppressed the cries of natural compassion and the still feeble voice of justice, and filled men with avarice, ambition and vice. Between the title of the strongest and that of the first occupier, there arose perpetual conflicts, which never ended but in battles and bloodshed. The new-born state of society thus gave rise to a horrible state of war; men thus harassed and depraved were no longer capable of retracing their steps or renouncing the fatal acquisitions they had made, but, laboring by the abuse of the faculties which do them honor, merely to their own confusion, brought themselves to the brink of ruin. . . .

It is impossible that men should not at length have reflected on so wretched a situation, and on the calamities that overwhelmed them. The rich, in particular, must have felt how much they suffered by a constant state of war, of which they bore all the expense; and in which, though all risked their lives, they alone risked their property. Besides, however speciously they might disguise their usurpations, they knew that they were founded on precarious and false titles; so that, if others took from them by force what they themselves had gained by force, they would have no reason to complain. Even those who had been enriched by their own industry, could hardly base their proprietorship on better claims. It was in vain to repeat, "I built this well; I gained this spot by my industry." Who gave you your standing, it might be answered, and what right have you to demand payment of us for doing what we never asked you to do? Do you not know that numbers of your fellow-creatures are starving, for want of what you have too much of? You ought to have had the express and universal consent of mankind, before appropriating more of the common subsistence than you needed for your own maintenance. Destitute of valid reasons to justify and sufficient strength to defend himself, able to crush individuals with ease, but easily crushed himself by a troop of bandits, one against all, and incapable, on account of mutual jealousy, of joining with his equals against numerous enemies united by the common hope of plunder, the rich man, thus urged by necessity, conceived at length the profoundest plan that ever entered the mind of man: this was to employ in his favor the forces of those who attacked him, to make allies of his adversaries, to inspire them with different maxims, and to give them other institutions as favorable to himself as the law of nature was unfavorable.

With this view, after having represented to his neighbors the horror of a situation which armed every man against the rest, and made their possessions as burdensome to them as their wants, and in which no safety could be expected either in riches or in poverty, he readily devised plausible arguments to make them close with his design. "Let us join," said he, "to guard the weak from oppression, to restrain the ambitious, and secure to every man the possession of what belongs to him: let us institute rules of justice and peace, to which all without exception may be obliged to conform; rules that may in some measure make amends for the caprices of fortune, by subjecting equally the powerful and the weak to the observance of reciprocal obligations. Let us, in a word, instead of turning our forces against ourselves, collect them in a supreme power which may govern us by wise laws, protect and defend all the members of the association, repulse their common enemies, and maintain eternal harmony among us."

Far fewer words to this purpose would have been enough to impose on men so barbarous and easily seduced; especially as they had too many disputes among themselves to do without arbitrators, and too much ambition and avarice to go long without masters. All ran headlong to their chains, in hopes of securing their liberty; for they had just wit enough to perceive the advantages of political institutions, without experience enough to enable them to foresee the dangers. The most capable of foreseeing the dangers were the very persons who expected to benefit by them; and even the most prudent judged it not inexpedient to sacrifice one part of their freedom to ensure the rest; as a wounded man has his arm cut off to save the rest of his body.

Such was, or may well have been, the origin of society and law, which bound new fetters on the poor, and gave new powers to the rich; which irretrievably destroyed natural liberty, eternally fixed the law of property and inequality, converted clever usurpation into unalterable right, and, for the advantage of a few ambitious individuals, subjected all mankind to perpetual labor, slavery and wretchedness. It is easy to see how the establishment of one community made that of all the rest necessary, and how, in order to make head against united forces, the rest of mankind had to unite in turn. Societies soon multiplied and spread over the face of the earth, till hardly a corner of the world was left in which a man could escape the yoke, and withdraw his head from beneath the sword which he saw perpetually hanging over him by a thread. Civil right having thus become the common rule among the members of each community, the law of nature maintained its place only between different communities, where, under the name of the right of nations, it was qualified by certain tacit conventions, in order to make commerce practicable, and serve as a substitute for natural compassion, which lost, when applied to societies, almost all the influence it had over individuals, and survived no longer except in some great cosmopolitan spirits, who, breaking down the imaginary barriers that separate different peoples, follow the example of our Sovereign Creator, and include the whole human race in their benevolence.

But bodies politic, remaining thus in a state of nature among themselves, presently experienced the inconveniences which had obliged individuals to forsake it; for this state became still more fatal to these great bodies than it had been to the individuals of whom they were composed. Hence arose national wars, battles, murders, and reprisals, which shock nature and outrage reason; together with all those horrible prejudices which class among the virtues the honor of shedding human blood. The most distinguished men hence learned to consider cutting each other's throats a duty; at length men massacred their fellow creatures by thousands without so much as knowing why, and committed more murders in a single day's fighting, and more violent outrages in the sack of a single town, than were committed in the state of nature during whole ages over the whole earth. Such were the first effects which we can see to have followed the division of mankind into different communities. But let us return to their institutions.

I know that some writers have given other explanations of the origin of political societies, such as the conquest of the powerful, or the association of the weak. It is, indeed, indifferent to my argument which of these causes we choose. That which I have just laid down, however, appears to me the most natural for the following reasons. First: because, in the first case, the right of conquest, being no right in itself, could not serve as a foundation on which to build any other; the victor and the vanquished people still remained with respect to each other in the state of war, unless the vanquished, restored to the full possession of their liberty, voluntarily made choice of the victor for their chief. For till then, whatever capitulation may have been made being founded on violence, and therefore *ipso facto* void, there could not have been on this hypothesis either a real society or body politic, or any law other than that of the strongest. Secondly: because the words *strong* and *weak* are, in the second case, ambiguous; for during the interval between the establishment of a right of property, or prior occupancy, and that of political government, the meaning of these words is better expressed by the terms *rich* and *poor:* because, in fact, before the institution of laws, men had no other way of reducing their equals to submission, than by attacking their goods, or making some of their own over to them. Thirdly: because, as the poor had nothing but their freedom to lose, it would have been in the highest degree absurd for them to resign voluntarily the only good they still enjoyed, without getting anything in exchange: whereas the rich having feelings, if I may so express myself, in every part of their possessions, it was much easier to harm them, and therefore more necessary for them to take precautions against it; and, in short, because it is more reasonable to suppose a thing to have been invented by those to whom it would be of service, than by those whom it must have harmed.

THE SOCIAL CONTRACT

Jean-Jacques Rousseau

In 1762 Rousseau published his most important political text, The Social Contract. *With its protean ideal of "the general will," it reveals him as a much more democratic theorist than his fellow* philosophes. *Critics have claimed, however, that its notion of the citizen being "forced to be free" opened the door to totalitarian dictatorship.*

[Book I] Chapter I: Subject of the First Book

Man is born free; and everywhere he is in chains. One thinks himself the master of others, and still remains a greater slave than they. How did this change come about? I do not know. What can make it legitimate? That question I think I can answer.

If I took into account only force, and the effects derived from it, I should say: "As long as a people is compelled to obey, and obeys, it does well; as soon as it can shake off the yoke, and shakes it off, it does still better; for, regaining its liberty by the same right as took it away, either it is justified in resuming it or there was no justification for those who took it away." But the social order is a sacred right which is the basis of all rights. Nevertheless, this right does not come from nature, and must therefore be founded on conventions. Before coming to that, I have to prove what I have just asserted. . . .

Chapter III: The Right of the Strongest

The strongest is never strong enough to be always the master, unless he transforms strength into right, and obedience into duty. Hence the right of the strongest, which, though to all seeming meant ironically, is really laid down as a fundamental principle. But are we never to have an explanation of this phrase? Force is a physical power, and I fail to see what moral effect it can have. To yield to force is an act of necessity, not of will—at the most, an act of prudence. In what sense can it be a duty?

Suppose for a moment that this so-called "right" exists. I maintain that the sole result is a mass of inexplicable nonsense. For, if force creates right, the effect changes with the cause: every force that is greater than the first succeeds to its right. As soon as it is possible to disobey with impunity, disobedience is legitimate; and, the strongest being always in the right, the only thing that matters is to act so as to become the strongest. But what kind of right is that which perishes when force fails? If we must obey perforce, there is no need to obey because we ought; and if we are not forced to obey, we are under no obligation to do so. Clearly, the word "right" adds nothing to force: in this connection, it means absolutely nothing.

Obey the powers that be. If this means yield to force, it is a good precept, but superfluous: I can answer for its never being violated. All power comes from God, I admit; but so does all sickness: does that mean that we are forbidden to call in the doctor? A brigand surprises me at the edge of a wood: must I not merely surrender my purse on compulsion, but, even if I could withhold it, am I in conscience bound to give it up? For certainly the pistol he holds is also a power.

Let us then admit that force does not create right, and that we are obliged to obey only legitimate powers. In that case, my original question recurs. . . .

Chapter VI: The Social Compact

I suppose men to have reached the point at which the obstacles in the way of their preservation in the state of nature show their power of resistance to be greater than the resources at the disposal of each individual for his maintenance in that state. That primitive condition can then subsist no longer; and the human race would perish unless it changed its manner of existence.

But, as men cannot engender new forces, but only unite and direct existing ones, they have no other means of preserving themselves than the formation, by aggregation, of a sum of forces great enough to overcome the resistance. These they have to bring into play by means of a single motive power, and cause to act in concert.

This sum of forces can arise only where several persons come together: but, as the force and liberty of each man are the chief instruments of his self-preservation, how can he pledge them without harming his own interests, and neglecting the care he owes to himself? This difficulty, in its bearing on my present subject, may be stated in the following terms:

"The problem is to find a form of association which will defend and protect with the whole common force the person and goods of each associate, and in which each, while uniting himself with all, may still obey himself alone, and remain as free as before." This is the fundamental problem of which the *social contract* provides the solution.

The clauses of this contract are so determined by the nature of the act that the slightest modification would make them vain and ineffective; so that, although they have perhaps never been formally set forth, they are everywhere the same and everywhere tacitly admitted and recognized, until, on the violation of the social compact, each regains his original rights and resumes his natural liberty, while losing the conventional liberty in favor of which he renounced it.

These clauses, properly understood, may be reduced to one—the total alienation of each associate, together with all his rights, to the whole community; for, in the first place, as each gives himself absolutely, the conditions are the same for all; and, this being so, no one has any interest in making them burdensome to others.

Moreover, the alienation being without reserve, the union is as perfect as it can be, and no associate has anything more to demand: for, if the individuals retained certain rights, as there would be no common superior to decide between them and the public, each, being on one point his own judge, would ask to be so on all; the state of nature would thus continue, and the association would necessarily become inoperative or tyrannical.

Finally, each man, in giving himself to all, gives himself to nobody; and as there is no associate over which he does not acquire the same right as he yields others over himself, he gains an equivalent for everything he loses, and an increase of force for the preservation of what he has.

If then we discard from the social compact what is not of its essence, we shall find that it reduces itself to the following terms:

"Each of us puts his person and all his power in common under the supreme direction of the general will, and, in our corporate capacity, we receive each member as an indivisible part of the whole."

At once, in place of the individual personality of each contracting party, this act of association creates a moral and collective body, composed of as many members as the assembly contains voters, and receiving from this act its unity, its common identity, its life, and its will. This public person, so formed by the union of all other persons, formerly took the name of *city*, and now takes that of *Republic* or *body politic;* it is called by its members *State* when passive, *Sovereign* when active, and *Power* when compared with others like itself. Those who are associated in it take collectively the name of *people*, and severally are called *citizens*, as sharing in the sovereign power, and *subjects*, as being under the laws of the State. But these terms are often confused and taken one for another: it is enough to know how to distinguish them when they are being used with precision.

Chapter VII: The Sovereign

This formula shows us that the act of association comprises a mutual undertaking between the public and the individuals, and that each individual, in making a contract, as we may say, with himself, is bound in a double capacity; as a member of the Sovereign he is bound to the individuals, and as a member of the State to the Sovereign. But the maxim of civil right, that no one is bound by undertakings made to himself, does not apply in this case; for there is a great difference between incurring an obligation to yourself and incurring one to a whole of which you form a part.

Attention must further be called to the fact that public deliberation, while competent to bind all the subjects to the Sovereign, because of the two different capacities in which each of them may be regarded, cannot, for the opposite reason, bind the Sovereign to itself; and that it is consequently against the nature of the body politic for the Sovereign to impose on itself a law which it cannot infringe. Being able to regard itself in only one capacity, it is in the position of an individual who makes a contract with himself; and this makes it clear that there neither is nor can be any kind of fundamental law binding on the body of the people—not even the social contract itself. This does not mean that the body politic cannot enter into undertakings with others, provided the contract is not infringed by them; for in relation to what is external to it, it becomes a simple being, an individual.

But the body politic or the Sovereign, drawing its being wholly from the sanctity of the contract, can never bind itself, even to an outsider, to do anything derogatory to the original act, for instance to alienate any part of itself, or to submit to another Sovereign. Violation of the act by which it exists would be self-annihilation; and that which is itself nothing can create nothing.

As soon as this multitude is so united in one body, it is impossible to offend against one of the members without attacking the body, and still more to offend against the body without the members resenting it. Duty and interest therefore equally oblige the two contracting parties to give each other help; and the same men should seek to combine, in their double capacity, all the advantages dependent upon that capacity.

Again, the Sovereign, being formed wholly of the individuals who compose it, neither has nor can have any interest contrary to theirs; and consequently the sovereign power need give no guarantee to its subjects, because it is impossible for the body to wish to hurt all its members. We shall also see later on that it cannot hurt any in particular. The Sovereign, merely by virtue of what it is, is always what it should be.

This, however, is not the case with the relation of the subjects to the Sovereign, which, despite the common interest, would have no security that they would fulfill their undertakings, unless it found means to assure itself of their fidelity.

In fact, each individual, as a man, may have a particular will contrary or dissimilar to the general will which he has as a citizen. His particular interest may speak to him quite differently from the common interest: his absolute and naturally independent existence may make him look upon what he owes to the common cause as a gratuitous contribution, the loss of which will do less harm to others than the payment of it is burdensome to himself; and, regarding the moral person which constitutes the State as a *persona ficta*, because not a man, he may wish to enjoy the rights of citizenship without being ready to fulfill the duties of a subject. The continuance of such an injustice could not but prove the undoing of the body politic.

In order then that the social compact may not be an empty formula, it tacitly includes the undertakings, which alone can give force to the rest, that whoever refuses to obey the general will shall be compelled to do so by the whole body. This means nothing less than that he will be forced to be free; for this is the condition which, by giving each citizen to his country, secures him against all personal dependence. In this lies the key to the working of the political machine; this alone legitimizes civil undertakings, which, without it, would be absurd, tyrannical, and liable to the most frightful abuses.

Chapter VIII: The Civil State

The passage from the state of nature to the civil state produces a very remarkable change in man, by substituting justice for instinct in his conduct, and giving his actions the morality they had formerly lacked. Then only, when the voice of duty takes the place of physical impulses and right of appetite, does man, who so far had considered only himself, find that he is forced to act on different principles, and to consult his reason before listening to his inclinations. Although, in this state, he deprives himself of some advantages which he got from nature, he gains in return others so great, his faculties are so stimulated and developed, his ideas so extended, his feelings so ennobled, and his whole soul so uplifted, that, did not the abuses of this new condition often degrade him below that which he left, he would be bound to bless continually the happy moment which took him from it forever, and, instead of a stupid and unimaginative animal, made him an intelligent being and a man.

Let us draw up the whole account in terms easily commensurable. What man loses by the social contract is his natural liberty and an unlimited right to everything he tries to get and succeeds in getting; what he gains is civil liberty and the proprietorship of all he possesses. If we are to avoid mistake in weighing one against the other, we must clearly distinguish natural liberty, which is bounded only by the strength of the individual, from civil liberty, which is limited by the general will; and possession, which is merely the effect of force or the right of the first occupier, from property, which can be founded only on a positive title.

We might, over and above all this, add, to what man acquires in the civil state, moral liberty, which alone makes him truly master of himself; for the mere impulse of appetite is slavery, while obedience to a law which we prescribe to ourselves is liberty. But I have already said too much on this head, and the philosophical meaning of the word "liberty" does not now concern us. . . .

[Book II] Chapter I: That Sovereignty Is Inalienable

The first and most important deduction from the principles we have so far laid down is that the general will alone can direct the State according to the object for which it was instituted, i.e. the common good: for if the clashing of particular interests made the establishment of societies necessary, the agreement of these very interests made it possible. The common element in these different interests is what forms the social tie; and, were there no point of agreement between them all, no society could exist. It is solely on the basis of this common interest that every society should be governed.

I hold, then, that Sovereignty, being nothing less than the exercise of the general will, can never be alienated, and that the Sovereign, who is no less than a collective being, cannot be represented except by himself: the power indeed may be transmitted, but not the will.

In reality, if it is not impossible for a particular will to agree on some point with the general will, it is at least impossible for the agreement to be lasting and constant; for the particular will tends, by its very nature, to partiality, while the general will tends to equality. It is even more impossible to have any guarantee of this agreement; for even if it should always exist, it would be the effect not of art, but of chance. The Sovereign may indeed say: "I now will actually what this man wills, or at least what he says he wills"; but it cannot say: "What he wills tomorrow, I too shall will," because it is absurd for the will to bind itself for the future, nor is it incumbent on any will to consent to anything that is not for the good of the being who wills. If then the people promises simply to obey, by that very act it dissolves itself and loses what makes it a people; the moment a master exists, there is no longer a Sovereign, and from that moment the body politic has ceased to exist. . . .

Chapter III: Whether the General Will Is Fallible

It follows from what has gone before that the general will is always right and tends to the public advantage; but it does not follow that the deliberations of the people are always equally correct. Our will is always for our own good, but we do not always see what that is; the people is never corrupted, but it is often deceived, and on such occasions only does it seem to will what is bad.

There is often a great deal of difference between the will of all and the general will; the latter considers only the common interest, while the former takes private interest into account, and is no more than a sum of particular wills: but take away from these same wills the pluses and minuses that cancel one another, and the general will remains as the sum of the differences.

If, when the people, being furnished with adequate information, held its deliberations, the citizens had no communication one with another, the grand total of the small differences would always give the general will, and the decision would always be good. But when factions arise, and partial associations are formed at the expense of the great association, the will of each of these associations becomes general in relation to its members, while it remains particular in relation to the State: it may then be said that there are no longer as many votes as there are men, but only as many as there are associations. The differences become less numerous and give a less general result. Lastly, when one of these associations is so great as to prevail over all the rest, the result is no longer a sum of small differences, but a single difference; in this case there is no longer a general will, and the opinion which prevails is purely particular.

It is therefore essential, if the general will is to be able to express itself, that there should be no partial society within the State, and that each citizen should think only his own thoughts; which was indeed the sublime and unique system established by the great Lycurgus. But if there are partial societies, it is best to have as many as possible and to prevent them from being unequal, as was done by Solon, Numa, and Servius. These precautions are the only ones that can guarantee that the general will shall be always enlightened, and that the people shall in no way deceive itself.

Chapter IV: The Limits of the Sovereign Power

If the State is a moral person whose life is in the union of its members, and if the most important of its cares is the care for its own preservation, it must have a universal and compelling force, in order to move and dispose each part as may be most advantageous to the whole. As nature gives each man absolute power over all his members, the social compact gives the body politic absolute power over all its members also; and it is this power which, under the direction of the general will, bears, as I have said, the name of Sovereignty.

But, besides the public person, we have to consider the private persons composing it, whose life and liberty are naturally independent of it. We are bound then to distinguish clearly between the respective rights of the citizens and the Sovereign, and between the duties the former have to fulfill as subjects and the natural rights they should enjoy as men.

Each man alienates, I admit, by the social compact, only such part of his powers, goods, and liberty as it is important for the community to control; but it must also be granted that the Sovereign is sole judge of what is important.

Every service a citizen can render the State he ought to render as soon as the Sovereign demands it; but the Sovereign, for its part, cannot impose upon its subjects any fetters that are useless to the community, nor can it even wish to do so; for no more by the law of reason than by the law of nature can anything occur without a cause.

The undertakings which bind us to the social body are obligatory only because they are mutual; and their nature is such that in fulfilling them we cannot work for others without working for ourselves. Why is it that the general will is always in the right, and that all continually will the happiness of each one, unless it is because there is not a man who does not think of "each" as meaning him, and consider himself in voting for all? This proves that equality of rights and the idea of justice which such equality creates originate in the preference each man gives to himself, and accordingly in the very nature of man. It proves that the general will, to be really such, must be general in its object as well as its essence; that it must both come from all and apply to all; and that it loses its natural rectitude when it is directed to some particular and determinate object, because in such a case we are judging of something foreign to us, and have no true principle of equity to guide us.

Indeed, as soon as a question of particular fact or right arises on a point not previously regulated by a general convention, the matter becomes contentious. It is a case in which the individuals concerned are one party, and the public the other, but in which I can see neither the law that ought to be followed nor the judge who ought to give the decision. In such a case, it would be absurd to propose to refer the question to an express decision of the general will, which can be only the conclusion reached by one of the parties and in consequence will be, for the other party, merely an external and particular will, inclined on this occasion to injustice and subject to error. Thus, just as a particular will cannot stand for the general will, the general will, in turn, changes its nature when its object is particular, and, as general, cannot pronounce on a man or a fact. When, for instance, the people of Athens nominated or displaced its rulers, decreed honors to one, and imposed penalties on another, and, by a multitude of particular decrees, exercised all the functions of government indiscriminately, it had in such cases no longer a general will in the strict sense; it was acting no longer as Sovereign, but as magistrate. This will seem contrary to current views; but I must be given time to expound my own.

It should be seen from the foregoing that what makes the will general is less the number of voters than the common interest uniting them; for, under this system, each necessarily submits to the conditions he imposes on others: and this admirable agreement between interest and justice gives to the common deliberations an equitable character which at once vanishes when any particular question is discussed, in the absence of a common interest to unite and identify the ruling of the judge with that of the party.

From whatever side we approach our principle, we reach the same conclusion, that the social compact sets up among the citizens an equality of such a kind that they all bind themselves to observe the same conditions and should therefore all enjoy the same rights. Thus, from the very nature of the compact, every act of Sovereignty, i.e. every authentic act of the general will, binds or favors all the citizens equally; so that the Sovereign recognizes only the body of the nation, and draws no distinctions between those of whom it is made up. What, then, strictly speaking, is an act of Sovereignty? It is not a convention between a superior and an inferior, but a convention between the body and each of its members. It is legitimate, because based on the social contract, and equitable, because common to all; useful, because it can have no other object than the general good, and stable, because guaranteed by the public force and the supreme power. So long as the subjects have to submit only to conventions of this sort, they obey no one but their own will; and to ask how far the respective rights of the Sovereign and the citizens extend is to ask up to what point the latter can enter into undertakings with themselves, each with all, and all with each.

We can see from this that the sovereign power, absolute, sacred, and inviolable as it is, does not and cannot exceed the limits of general conventions, and that every man may dispose at will of such goods and liberty as these conventions leave him; so that the Sovereign never has a right to lay more charges on one subject than on another, because, in that case, the question becomes particular, and ceases to be within its competency.

When these distinctions have once been admitted, it is seen to be so untrue that there is, in the social contract, any real renunciation on the part of the individuals, that the position in which they find themselves as a result of the contract is really preferable to that in which they were before. Instead of a renunciation, they have made an advantageous exchange; instead of an uncertain and precarious way of living they have got one that is better and more secure; instead of natural independence they have got liberty, instead of the power to harm others security for themselves, and instead of their strength, which others might overcome, a right which social union makes invincible. Their very life, which they have devoted to the State, is by it constantly protected; and when they risk it in the State's defense, what more are they doing than giving back what they have received from it? What are they doing that they would not do more often and with greater danger in the state of nature, in which they would inevitably have to fight battles at the peril of their lives in defense of that which is the means of their preservation? All have indeed to fight when their country needs them; but then no one has ever to fight for himself. Do we not gain something by running, on behalf of what gives us our security, only some of the risks we should have to run for ourselves, as soon as we lost it? . . .

Chapter XV: Deputies or Representatives

As soon as public service ceases to be the chief business of the citizens and they would rather serve with their money than with their persons, the State is not far from its fall. When it is necessary to march out to war, they pay troops and stay at home: when it is necessary to meet in council, they name deputies and stay at home. By reason of idleness and money, they end by having soldiers to enslave their country and representatives to sell it.

It is through the hustle of commerce and the arts, through the greedy self-interest of profit, and through softness and love of amenities that personal services are replaced by money payments. Men surrender a part of their profits in order to have time to increase them at leisure. Make gifts of money, and you will not be long without chains. The word "finance" is a slavish word, unknown in the city-state. In a country that is truly free, the citizens do everything with their own arms and nothing by means of money; so far from paying to be exempted from their duties, they would even pay for the privilege of fulfilling them themselves. I am far from taking the common view: I hold enforced labor to be less opposed to liberty than taxes.

The better the constitution of a State is, the more do public affairs encroach on private in the minds of the citizens. Private affairs are even of much less importance, because the aggregate of the common happiness furnishes a greater proportion of that of each individual, so that there is less for him to seek in particular cares. In a well-ordered city every man flies to the assemblies; under a bad government no one cares to stir a step to get to them, because no one is interested in what happens there, because it is foreseen that the general will will not prevail, and lastly because domestic cares are all-absorbing. Good laws lead to the making of better ones; bad ones bring about worse. As soon as any man says of the affairs of the State, "What does it matter to me?," the State may be given up for lost.

COMMON SENSE

THOMAS PAINE

Paine published his pamphlet Common Sense *early in 1776, shortly after he had arrived in America from his native Britain. It immediately became one of history's most influential pieces of political writing, convincing many Americans that they should choose independence. Its assault on monarchy and the aristocratic principle as well as its distinction between society and government reflect general Enlightenment liberal ideals.*

Some writers have so confounded society with government, as to leave little or no distinction between them; whereas they are not only different, but have different origins. Society is produced by our wants, and government by our wickedness; the former promotes our happiness *positively* by uniting our affections, the latter *negatively* by restraining our vices. The one encourages intercourse, the other creates distinctions. The first is a patron, the last a punisher.

Society in every state is a blessing, but Government, even in its best state, is but a necessary evil; in its worst state an intolerable one: for when we suffer, or are exposed to the same miseries *by a Government*, which we might expect in a country *without Government*, our calamity is heightened by reflecting that we furnish the means by which we suffer. Government, like dress, is the badge of lost innocence; the palaces of kings are built upon the ruins of the bowers of paradise. For were the impulses of conscience clear, uniform and irresistibly obeyed, man would need no other lawgiver; but that not being the case, he finds it necessary to surrender up a part of his property to furnish means for the protection of the rest; and this he is induced to do by the same prudence which in every other case advises him, out of two evils to choose the least. Wherefore, security being the true design and end of government, it unanswerably follows that whatever form thereof appears most likely to ensure it to us, with the least expense and greatest benefit, is preferable to all others.

In order to gain a clear and just idea of the design and end of government, let us suppose a small number of persons settled in some sequestered part of the earth, unconnected with the rest; they will then represent the first peopling of any country, or of the world. In this state of natural liberty, society will be their first thought. A thousand motives will excite them thereto; the strength of one man is so unequal to his wants, and his mind so unfitted for perpetual solitude, that he is soon obliged to seek assistance and relief of another, who in his turn requires the same. Four or five united would be able to raise a tolerable dwelling in the midst of a wilderness, but one man might labor out the common period of life without accomplishing any thing; when he had felled his timber he could not remove it, nor erect it after it was removed; hunger in the mean time would urge him to quit his work, and every different want would call him a different way. Disease, nay even misfortune, would be death; for though neither might be mortal, yet either would disable him from living, and reduce him to a state in which he might rather be said to perish than to die.

Thus necessity, like a gravitating power, would soon form our newly arrived emigrants into society, the reciprocal blessings of which would supercede, and render the obligations of law and government unnecessary while they remained perfectly just to each other; but as nothing but Heaven is impregnable to vice, it will unavoidably happen that in proportion as they surmount the first difficulties of emigration, which bound them together in a common cause, they will begin to relax in their duty and attachment to each other: and this remissness will point out the necessity of establishing some form of government to supply the defect of moral virtue.

Some convenient tree will afford them a State House, under the branches of which the whole Colony may assemble to deliberate on public matters. It is more than probable that their first laws will have the title only of Regulations and be enforced by no other penalty than public disesteem. In this first parliament every man by natural right will have a seat.

But as the Colony increases, the public concerns will increase likewise, and the distance at which the members may be separated, will render it too inconvenient for all of them to meet on every occasion as at first, when their number was small, their habitations near, and the public concerns few and trifling. This will point out the convenience of their consenting to leave the legislative part to be managed by a select number chosen from the whole body, who are supposed to have the same concerns at stake which those have who appointed them, and who will act in the same manner as the whole body would act were they present. If the colony continue increasing, it will become necessary to augment the number of representatives, and that the interest of every part of the colony may be attended to, it will be found best to divide the whole into convenient parts, each part sending its proper number: and that the *elected* might never form to themselves an interest separate from the *electors*, prudence will point out the propriety of having elections often: because as the *elected* might by that means return and mix again with the general body of the *electors* in a few months, their fidelity to the public will be secured by the prudent reflection of not making a rod for themselves. And as this frequent interchange will establish a common interest with every part of the community, they will mutually and naturally support each other, and on this, (not on the unmeaning name of king,) depends the *strength of government, and the happiness of the governed.*

Here then is the origin and rise of government; namely, a mode rendered necessary by the inability of moral virtue to govern the world; here too is the design and end of government, viz. Freedom and security. And however our eyes may be dazzled with show, or our ears deceived by sound; however prejudice may warp our wills, or interest darken our understanding, the simple voice of nature and reason will say, 'tis right.

I draw my idea of the form of government from a principle in nature which no art can overturn, viz. that the more simple any thing is, the less liable it is to be disordered, and the easier repaired when disordered; and with this maxim in view I offer a few remarks on the so much boasted constitution of England. That it was noble for the dark and slavish times in which it was erected, is granted. When the world was overrun with tyranny the least remove therefrom was a glorious rescue. But that it is imperfect, subject to convulsions, and incapable of producing what it seems to promise, is easily demonstrated.

Absolute governments, (tho' the disgrace of human nature) have this advantage with them, they are simple; if the people suffer, they know the head from which their suffering springs; know likewise the remedy; and are not bewildered by a variety of causes and cures. But the constitution of England is so exceedingly complex, that the nation may suffer for years together without being able to discover in which part the fault lies; some will say in one and some in another, and every political physician will advise a different medicine.

I know it is difficult to get over local or long standing prejudices, yet if we will suffer ourselves to examine the component parts of the English constitution, we shall find them to be the base remains of two ancient tyrannies, compounded with some new Republican materials.

First.—The remains of Monarchical tyranny in the person of the King.

Secondly.—The remains of Aristocratical tyranny in the persons of the Peers.

Thirdly.—The new Republican materials, in the persons of the Commons, on whose virtue depends the freedom of England.

The two first, by being hereditary, are independent of the People; wherefore in a *constitutional sense* they contribute nothing towards the freedom of the State.

To say that the constitution of England is an *union* of three powers, reciprocally *checking* each other, is farcical; either the words have no meaning, or they are flat contradictions.

To say that the Commons is a check upon the King, presupposes two things.

First.—That the King is not to be trusted without being looked after; or in other words, that a thirst for absolute power is the natural disease of monarchy.

Secondly.—That the Commons, by being appointed for that purpose, are either wiser or more worthy of confidence than the Crown.

But as the same constitution which gives the Commons a power to check the King by withholding the supplies, gives afterwards the King a power to check the Commons, by empowering him to reject their other bills; it again supposes that the King is wiser than those whom it has already supposed to be wiser than him. A mere absurdity!

There is something exceedingly ridiculous in the composition of Monarchy; it first excludes a man from the means of information, yet empowers him to act in cases where the highest judgment is required. The state of a king shuts him from the World, yet the business of a king requires him to know it thoroughly; wherefore the different parts, by unnaturally opposing and destroying each other, prove the whole character to be absurd and useless.

Some writers have explained the English constitution thus: the King, say they, is one, the people another; the Peers are a house in behalf of the King, the commons in behalf of the people; but this hath all the distinctions of a house divided against itself; and though the expressions be pleasantly arranged, yet when examined they appear idle and ambiguous; and it will always happen, that the nicest construction that words are capable of, when applied to the description of something which either cannot exist, or is too incomprehensible to be within the compass of description, will be words of sound only, and though they may amuse the ear, they cannot inform the mind: for this explanation includes a previous question, viz. *how came the king by a power which the people are afraid to trust, and always obliged to check?* Such a power could not be the gift of a wise people, neither can any power, *which needs checking*, be from God; yet the provision which the constitution makes supposes such a power to exist. . . .

To the evil of monarchy we have added that of hereditary succession; and as the first is a degradation and lessening of ourselves, so the second, claimed as a matter of right, is an insult and imposition on posterity. For all men being originally equals, no one by birth could have a right to set up his own family in perpetual preference to all others for ever, and tho' himself might deserve some decent degree of honors of his cotemporaries, yet his descendants might be far too unworthy to inherit them. One of the strongest natural proofs of the folly of hereditary right in Kings, is that nature disapproves it, otherwise she would not so frequently turn it into ridicule, by giving mankind an *Ass for a Lion.*

Secondly, as no man at first could possess any other public honors than were bestowed upon him, so the givers of those honors could have no power to give away the right of posterity, and though they might say "We choose you for our head," they could not without manifest injustice to their children say "that your children and your children's children shall reign over ours forever." Because such an unwise, unjust, unnatural compact might (perhaps) in the next succession put them under the government of a rogue or a fool. Most wise men in their private sentiments have ever treated hereditary right with contempt; yet it is one of those evils which when once established is not easily removed: many submit from fear, others from superstition, and the more powerful part shares with the king the plunder of the rest.

This is supposing the present race of kings in the world to have had an honorable origin: whereas it is more than probable, that, could we take off the dark covering of antiquity and trace them to their first rise, we should find the first of them nothing better than the principal ruffian of some restless gang, whose savage manners or pre-eminence in subtilty obtained him the title of chief among plunderers: and who by increasing in power and extending his depredations, overawed the quiet and defenseless to purchase their safety by frequent contributions. Yet his electors could have no idea of giving hereditary right to his descendants, because such a perpetual exclusion of themselves was incompatible with the free and unrestrained principles they professed to live by. Wherefore, hereditary succession in the early ages of monarchy could not take place as a matter of claim, but as something casual or complemental; but as few or no records were extant in those days, and traditionary history stuff'd with fables, it was very easy, after the lapse of a few generations, to trump up some superstitious tale conveniently timed, Mahomet-like, to cram hereditary right down the throats of the vulgar. Perhaps the disorders which threatened, or seemed to threaten, on the decease of a leader and the choice of a new one (for elections among ruffians could not be very orderly) induced many at first to favor hereditary pretensions; by which means it happened, as it hath happened since, that what at first was submitted to as a convenience was afterwards claimed as a right. . . .

But it is not so much the absurdity as the evil of hereditary succession which concerns mankind. Did it ensure a race of good and wise men it would have the seal of divine authority, but as it opens a door to the *foolish*, the *wicked*, and the *improper*, it hath in it the nature of oppression. Men who look upon themselves born to reign, and others to obey, soon grow insolent. Selected from the rest of mankind, their minds are early poisoned by importance; and the world they act in differs so materially from the world at large, that they have but little opportunity of knowing its true interests, and when they succeed to the government are frequently the most ignorant and unfit of any throughout the dominions. . . .

In England a King hath little more to do than to make war and give away places; which, in plain terms, is to empoverish the nation and set it together by the ears. A pretty business indeed for a man to be allowed eight hundred thousand sterling a year for, and worshipped into the bargain! Of more worth is one honest man to society, and in the sight of God, than all the crowned ruffians that ever lived. . . .

Volumes have been written on the subject of the struggle between England and America. Men of all ranks have embarked in the controversy, from different motives, and with various designs; but all have been ineffectual, and the period of debate is closed. Arms as the last resource decide the contest; the appeal was the choice of the King, and the Continent has accepted the challenge.

It hath been reported of the late Mr. Pelham (who tho' an able minister was not without his faults) that on his being attacked in the House of Commons on the score that his measures were only of a temporary kind, replied, *"they will last my time."* Should a thought so fatal and unmanly possess the Colonies in the present contest, the name of ancestors will be remembered by future generations with detestation.

The Sun never shined on a cause of greater worth. 'Tis not the affair of a City, a County, a Province, or a Kingdom; but of a Continent—of at least one eighth part of the habitable Globe. 'Tis not the concern of a day, a year, or an age; posterity are virtually involved in the contest, and will be more or less affected even to the end of time, by the proceedings now. Now is the seed-time of Continental union, faith and honor. The least fracture now will be like a name engraved with the point of a pin on the tender rind of a young oak; the wound would enlarge with the tree, and posterity read it in full grown characters.

By referring the matter from argument to arms, a new era for politics is struck—a new method of thinking hath arisen.

THE AMERICAN DECLARATION OF INDEPENDENCE

The document, passed by the Continental Congress on July 4, 1776, is in its first two paragraphs a veritable gloss and paraphrase of the Lockean principles at the heart of Enlightenment liberalism.

When in the Course of human Events, it becomes necessary for one People to dissolve the Political Bands which have connected them with another, and to assume among the Powers of the Earth, the separate and equal Station to which the Laws of Nature and of Nature's God entitle them, a decent Respect to the Opinions of Mankind requires that they should declare the causes which impel them to the Separation.

We hold these Truths to be self-evident, that all Men are created equal, that they are endowed by their Creator with certain unalienable Rights, that among these are Life, Liberty, and the Pursuit of Happiness—That to secure these Rights, Governments are instituted among Men, deriving their just Powers from the Consent of the Governed, that whenever any Form of Government becomes destructive of these Ends, it is the Right of the People to alter or to abolish it, and to institute new Government, laying its Foundation on such Principles, and organizing its Powers in such Form, as to them shall seem most likely to effect their Safety and Happiness. Prudence, indeed, will dictate that Governments long established should not be changed for light and transient Causes; and accordingly all Experience hath shewn, that Mankind are more disposed to suffer, while Evils are sufferable, than to right themselves by abolishing the Forms to which they are accustomed. But when a long Train of Abuses and Usurpations, pursuing invariably the same Object, evinces a Design to reduce them under absolute Despotism, it is their Right, it is their Duty, to throw off such Government, and to provide new Guards for their future Security. Such has been the patient Sufferance of these Colonies; and such is now the Necessity which constrains them to alter their former Systems of Government. The History of the present King of Great-Britain is a History of repeated Injuries and Usurpations, all having in direct Object the Establishment of an absolute Tyranny over these States. To prove this, let Facts be submitted to a candid World.

He has refused his Assent to Laws, the most wholesome and necessary for the public Good.

He has forbidden his Governors to pass Laws of immediate and pressing Importance, unless suspended in their Operation till his Assent should be obtained; and when so suspended, he has utterly neglected to attend to them.

He has refused to pass other Laws for the Accommodation of large Districts of People, unless those People would relinquish the Right of Representation in the Legislature, a Right inestimable to them, and formidable to Tyrants only.

He has called together Legislative Bodies at Places unusual, uncomfortable, and distant from the Depository of their public Records, for the sole Purpose of fatiguing them into Compliance with his Measures.

He has dissolved Representative Houses repeatedly, for opposing with manly Firmness his Invasions on the Rights of the People.

He has refused for a long Time, after such Dissolutions, to cause others to be elected; whereby the Legislative Powers, incapable of Annihilation, have returned to the People at large for their exercise; the State remaining in the mean time exposed to all the Dangers of Invasion from without, and Convulsions within.

He has endeavored to prevent the Population of these States; for that Purpose obstructing the Laws for Naturalization of Foreigners; refusing to pass others to encourage their Migrations hither, and raising the Conditions of new Appropriations of Lands.

He has obstructed the Administration of Justice, by refusing his Assent to Laws for establishing Judiciary Powers.

He has made Judges dependent on his Will alone, for the Tenure of their Offices, and the Amount and Payment of their Salaries.

He has erected a Multitude of new Offices, and sent hither Swarms of Officers to harass our People, and eat out their Substance.

He has kept among us, in Times of Peace, Standing Armies, without the consent of our Legislatures.

He has affected to render the Military independent of and superior to the Civil Power.

He has combined with others to subject us to a Jurisdiction foreign to our Constitution, and unacknowledged by our Laws; giving his Assent to their Acts of pretended Legislation:

For quartering large Bodies of Armed Troops among us:

For protecting them, by a mock Trial, from Punishment for any Murders which they should commit on the Inhabitants of these States:

For cutting off our Trade with all Parts of the World:

For imposing Taxes on us without our Consent:

For depriving us, in many Cases, of the Benefits of Trial by Jury:

For transporting us beyond Seas to be tried for pretended Offenses:

For abolishing the free System of English Laws in a neighboring Province, establishing therein an arbitrary Government, and enlarging its Boundaries, so as to render it at once an Example and fit Instrument for introducing the same absolute Rule into these Colonies:

For taking away our Charters, abolishing our most valuable Laws, and altering fundamentally the Forms of our Governments:

For suspending our own Legislatures, and declaring themselves invested with Power to legislate for us in all Cases whatsoever.

He has abdicated Government here, by declaring us out of his Protection and waging War against us.

He has plundered our Seas, ravaged our Coasts, burnt our Towns, and destroyed the Lives of our People.

He is, at this Time, transporting large Armies of foreign Mercenaries to complete the Works of Death, Desolation, and Tyranny, already begun with circumstances of Cruelty and Perfidy, scarcely paralleled in the most barbarous Ages, and totally unworthy the Head of a civilized Nation.

He has constrained our fellow Citizens taken Captive on the high Seas to bear Arms against their Country, to become the Executioners of their Friends and Brethren, or to fall themselves by their Hands.

He has excited domestic Insurrections amongst us, and has endeavored to bring on the Inhabitants of our Frontiers, the merciless Indian Savages, whose known Rule of Warfare, is an undistinguished Destruction, of all Ages, Sexes and Conditions.

In every stage of these Oppressions we have Petitioned for Redress in the most humble Terms: Our repeated Petitions have been answered only by repeated Injury. A Prince, whose Character is thus marked by every act which may define a Tyrant, is unfit to be the Ruler of a free People.

Nor have we been wanting in Attentions to our British Brethren. We have warned them from Time to Time of Attempts by their Legislature to extend an unwarrantable Jurisdiction over us. We have reminded them of the Circumstances of our Emigration and Settlement here. We have appealed to their native Justice and Magnanimity, and we have conjured them by the Ties of our common Kindred to disavow these Usurpations, which, would inevitably interrupt our Connections and Correspondence. They too have been deaf to the Voice of Justice and of Consanguinity. We must, therefore, acquiesce in the Necessity, which denounces our Separation, and hold them, as we hold the rest of Mankind, Enemies in War, in Peace, Friends.

We, therefore, the Representatives of the UNITED STATES OF AMERICA, in General Congress, Assembled, appealing to the Supreme Judge of the World for the Rectitude of our Intentions, do, in the Name, and by Authority of the good People of these Colonies, solemnly Publish and Declare, That these United Colonies are, and of Right ought to be, Free and Independent States; that they are absolved from all Allegiance to the British Crown, and that all political Connection between them and the State of Great-Britain, is and ought to be totally dissolved; and that as Free and Independent States, they have full Power to levy War, conclude Peace, contract Alliances, establish Commerce, and to do all other Acts and Things which Independent States may of right do. And for the support of this Declaration, with a firm Reliance on the

Protection of divine Providence, we mutually pledge to each other our Lives, our Fortunes, and our sacred Honor.

BENEVOLENT DESPOTISM

FREDERICK THE GREAT

Many in the eighteenth century believed that monarchs were not inherently the louts that Paine described. A reforming enlightened monarch was, indeed, the ideal of some of the philosophes, *like Voltaire. The particular model of such a ruler for him and others was Frederick, king of Prussia (1712–1786). In this selection from Frederick's 1777* Essay on Forms of Government, *the character of an enlightened despot is described.*

With respect to the true monarchical government, it is the best or the worst of all others, accordingly as it is administered.

We have remarked that men granted pre-eminence to one of their equals, in expectation that he should do them certain services. These services consisted in the maintenance of the laws; a strict execution of justice; an employment of his whole powers to prevent any corruption of manners; and defending the state against its enemies. It is the duty of this magistrate to pay attention to agriculture; it should be his care that provisions for the nation should be in abundance, and that commerce and industry should be encouraged. He is a perpetual sentinel, who must watch the acts and the conduct of the enemies of the state. His foresight and prudence should form timely alliances, which should be made with those who might most conduce to the interest of the association.

By this short abstract, the various branches of knowledge, which each article in particular requires, will be perceived. To this must be added a profound study of the local situation of the country, which it is the magistrate's duty to govern, and a perfect knowledge of the genius of the nation; for the sovereign who sins through ignorance is as culpable as he who sins through malice: the first is the guilt of idleness, the latter of a vicious heart; but the evil that results to society is the same.

Princes and monarchs, therefore, are not invested with supreme authority that they may, with impunity, riot in debauchery and voluptuousness. They are not raised by their fellow citizens in order that their pride may pompously display itself, and contemptuously insult simplicity of manners, poverty and wretchedness. Government is not entrusted to them that they may be surrounded by a crowd of useless people, whose idleness engenders every vice.

The ill administration of monarchical government originates in various causes, the source of which is in the character of the sovereign. Thus a prince addicted to women suffers himself to be governed by his mistresses, and his favorites, who abuse the ascendancy they have over his mind, commit injustice, protect the most vicious, sell places, and are guilty of other similar acts of infamy. If the prince, through debility, should abandon the helm of the state to mercenary hands, I mean to ministers, in that case, each having different views, no one proceeds on general plans: the new minister fritters away what he finds already established, however excellent that may be, to acquire the character of novelty, and execute his own schemes, generally to the detriment of the public good. His successors do the like; they destroy and overturn with equal want of understanding, that they may be supposed to possess originality. Hence that succession of change and variation which allows no project time to take root; hence confusion, disorder, and every vice of a bad administration. Prevaricators have a ready excuse; they shelter their turpitude under these perpetual changes.

Men attach themselves to that which appertains to them, and the state does not appertain to these ministers, for which reason they have not its real good at heart; business is carelessly executed, and with a kind of stoic indifference; and hence results the decay of justice, and the ill administration of the finances and the military. From a monarchy, as it was, the government degenerates into a true aristocracy, in which ministers and generals conduct affairs, according to their own fancies. There is no longer any comprehensive system; each pursues his own plans, and the central point, the point of unity, is lost. As all the wheels of a watch correspond to effect the same purpose, which is that of measuring time, so ought the springs of government to be regulated, that all the different branches of administration may equally concur to the greatest good of the state; an important object, of which we ought never to lose sight.

We may add, the personal interest of ministers and generals usually occasions them to counteract each other without ceasing, and sometimes to impede the execution of the best plans, because they had not been conceived by themselves. But the evil is at its utmost, when perverse minds are able to persuade the sovereign that his welfare and the public good are two things. The monarch then becomes the enemy of his people, without knowing why; is severe, rigorous, and inhuman, from mistake; for, the principle on which he acts being false, the consequences must necessarily be the same.

The sovereign is attached by indissoluble ties to the body of the state; hence it follows that he, by repercussion, is sensible of all the ills which afflict his subjects; and the people, in like manner, suffer from the misfortunes which affect their sovereign. There is but one general good, which is that of the state. If the monarch lose his provinces, he is no longer able as formerly to assist his subjects. If misfortune has obliged him to contract debts, they must be liquidated by the poor citizens; and, in return, if the people are not numerous, and if they are oppressed by poverty, the sovereign is destitute of all resource. These are truths so incontestable that there is no need to insist on them further.

I once more repeat, the sovereign represents the state; he and his people form but one body, which can only be happy as far as united by concord. The prince is to the nation he governs what the head is to the man; it is his duty to see, think, and act for the whole community, that he may procure it every advantage of which it is capable. If it be intended that a monarchical should excel a republican government, sentence is pronounced on the sovereign. He must be active, possess integrity, and collect his whole powers, that he may be able to run the career he has commenced. Here follow my ideas concerning his duties.

He ought to procure exact and circumstantial information of the strength and weakness of his country, as well relative to pecuniary resources as to population, finance, trade, laws, and the genius of the nation whom he is appointed to govern. If the laws are good they will be clear in their definitions; otherwise, chicanery will seek to elude their spirit to its advantage, and arbitrarily and irregularly determine the fortunes of individuals. Lawsuits ought to be as short as possible, to prevent the ruin of the appellants, who consume in useless expenses what is justly and duly their right. This branch of government cannot be too carefully watched, that every possible barrier may be opposed to the avidity of judges and counselors. Every person is kept within the limits of their duty, by occasional visits into the provinces. Whoever imagines himself to be injured will venture to make his complaints to the commission; and those who are found to be prevaricators ought to be severely punished. It is perhaps superfluous to add that the penalty ought never to exceed the crime; that violence never ought to supersede law; and that it were better the sovereign should be too merciful than too severe.

As every person who does not proceed on principle is inconsistent in his conduct, it is still more necessary that the magistrate who watches over the public good should act from a determinate system of politics, war, finance, commerce, and law. Thus, for example, a people of mild manners ought not to have severe laws, but such as are adapted to their character. The basis of such systems ought always to be correspondent to the greatest good society can receive. Their principles ought to be conformable to the situation of the country, to its ancient customs, if they are good, and to the genius of the nation. . . .

No government can exist without taxation, which is equally necessary to the republic and to the monarchy. The sovereign who labors in the public cause must be paid by the public; the judge the same, that he may have no need to prevaricate. The soldier must be supported that he may commit no violence, for want of having whereon to subsist. In like manner, it is necessary that those persons who are employed in collecting the finances should receive such salaries as may not lay them under any temptation to rob the public. These various expenses demand very considerable sums, and to these must still be added money that should only be laid apart to serve for extraordinary exigencies. This money must all be necessarily levied on the people; and the grand art consists in levying so as not to oppress. That taxes may be equally and not arbitrarily laid on, surveys and registers should be made, by which, if the people are properly classed, the money will be proportionate to the income of the persons paying. This is a thing so necessary that it would be an unpardonable fault, in finance, if ill-imposed taxes should disgust the husbandman with his labors. Having performed his duties, it is afterward necessary he and his family should live in a certain degree of ease. Far from oppressing the nursing fathers of the state, they ought to be encouraged in the cultivation of the lands; for in this cultivation the true riches of a country consists. . . .

Excise is another species of taxes, levied on cities, and this must be managed by able persons; otherwise, those provisions which are most necessary to life, such as bread, small beer, meat, &c, will be overloaded; and the weight will fall on the soldier, the laborer, and the artisan. The result will be, unhappily to the people, that the price of labor will be raised; consequently merchandise will become so dear as not to be salable in foreign markets. . . . To obviate such inconveniences, the sovereign ought frequently to remember the condition of the poor, to imagine himself in the place of the peasant or the manufacturer, and then to say, "Were I born one among the class of citizens whose labors constitute the wealth of the state, what should I require from the king?" The answer which, on such a supposition, good sense would suggest it is his duty to put in practice.

In most of the kingdoms of Europe there are provinces in which the peasants are attached to the glebe, or are serfs to their lords. This, of all conditions, is the most unhappy, and that at which humanity most revolts. No man certainly was born to be the slave of his equal. We reasonably detest such an abuse; and it is supposed that nothing more than will is wanting to abolish so barbarous a custom. But this is not true; it is held on ancient tenures, and contracts made between the landholders and the colonists. Tillage is regulated according to the service performed by the peasantry; and whoever should suddenly desire to abolish this abominable administration would entirely overthrow the mode of managing estates, and must be obliged, in part, to indemnify the nobility for the losses which their rents must suffer.

The state of manufactures and of trade, an article no less important, next presents itself. For the country to be preserved in prosperity, it is indubitably necessary that the balance of trade should be in its favor. If it pay more for importation than it gains by exportation, the result will be that it will be annually impoverished. Let us suppose a purse in which there are a hundred ducats, from which let us daily take one, and put none in, and everybody will allow that in a hundred days the purse will be empty. The means to avoid incurring any such loss are to work up all raw materials of which the country is in possession, and to manufacture foreign raw materials, that the price of labor may be gained, in order to procure a foreign market.

Three things are to be considered in respect to commerce: first the surplus of native products which are exported; next the products of foreign states, which enrich those by whom they are carried; and thirdly foreign merchandise, which home consumption obliges the state to import. The trade of any kingdom must be regulated according to these three articles, for of these only is it susceptible, according to the nature of things.

We shall now speak of another article, which perhaps is equally interesting. There are few countries in which the people are all of one religious opinion; they often totally differ. There are some who are called sectaries. The question then is started—Is it requisite that the people should all think alike, or may each one be allowed to think as he pleases? Gloomy politicians will tell us everybody ought to be of the same opinion, that there may be no division among the citizens. The priests will add whoever does not think like me is damned, and it is by no means proper that my king should be the king of the damned. The inevitable deduction is they must be destroyed in this world, that they may be the more prosperous in the next.

To this it is answered that all the members of one society never thought alike; that, among Christian nations, the majority are Anthropomorphites; that, among the Catholics, most of the people are idolaters, for I shall never be persuaded that a clown is capable of distinguishing between *Latria* and *Hyperdulia*. He simply and really adores the image he invokes. Therefore there are a number of heretics in all Christian sects. What is more, each man believes that which appears to him to be truth. A poor wretch may be constrained to pronounce a certain form of prayer, although he inwardly refuse his consent. His persecutor consequently has gained nothing. But, if we revert to the origin of all society, it will be found evident that the sovereign has no right to interfere in the belief of the subject. Would it not be madness to imagine men who have said to another man, their equal, "We raise you to be our superior, because we are in love with slavery; and we bestow on you the power of directing our thoughts, according to your will?" On the contrary, they have said, "We have need of you for the maintenance of those laws which we are willing to obey, and that we may be wisely governed and defended; but we also require that you should respect our freedom." This is the sentence pronounced, and it is without appeal. Nay, tolerance is itself so advantageous, to the people among whom it is established, that it constitutes the happiness of the state. As soon as there is that perfect freedom of opinion, the people are all at peace; whereas persecution has given birth to the most bloody civil wars, and such as have been the most inveterate and the most destructive. The least evil that results from persecution is to occasion the persecuted to emigrate. The population of France has suffered in certain provinces, and those provinces still are sensible to the revocation of the edict of Nantes.

Such are in general the duties imposed upon a prince, from which, in order that he may never depart, he ought often to recollect he himself is but a man, like the least of his subjects. If he be the first general, the first minister of the realm, it is not that he should remain the shadow of authority, but that he should fulfill the duties of such titles. He is only the first servant of the state, who is obliged to act with probity and prudence; and to remain as totally disinterested as if he were each moment liable to render an account of his administrations to his fellow citizens.

Thus he is culpable, if he be prodigal of the money of the people, dispersing the produce of the taxes in luxury, pomp, or licentiousness. It is for him to watch over morals, which are the guardians of the laws, and to improve the national education, and not pervert it by ill examples. One of the most important objects is the preservation of good morals, in all their purity; to which the sovereign may greatly contribute, by distinguishing and rewarding those citizens who have performed virtuous actions, and testifying his contempt for such as are so depraved as not to blush at their own disorders. The prince ought highly to disapprove of every dishonest act, and refuse distinctions to men who are incorrigible.

There is another interesting object which ought not to be lost sight of, and which, if neglected, would be of irreparable prejudice to good morality; which is that princes are liable too highly to notice persons who are possessed of no other merit than that of great wealth. Honors, so undeservedly bestowed, confirm the people in the vulgar prejudice that wealth, only, is necessary to gain respect. Interest and cupidity will then break forth from the curb by which they are restrained. Each will wish to accumulate riches; and, to acquire these, the most iniquitous means will be employed. Corruption increases, takes root, and becomes general. Men of abilities and virtue are despised, and the public honor none but the bastards of Midas, who dazzle by their excessive dissipation and their pomp. To prevent national manners from being perverted to an excess so horrible, the prince ought to be incessantly attentive to distinguish nothing but personal merit, and to show his contempt for that opulence which is destitute of morals and of virtue.

As the sovereign is properly the head of a family of citizens, the father of his people, he ought on all occasions to be the last refuge of the unfortunate; to be the parent of the orphan, and the husband of the widow; to have as much pity for the lowest wretch as for the greatest courtier; and to shed his benefactions over those who, deprived of all other aid, can only find succor in his benevolence.

Such, according to the principles which we established at the beginning of this Essay, is the most accurate conception we can form of the duties of a sovereign, and the only manner which can render monarchical government good and advantageous. Should the conduct of many princes be found different, it must be attributed to their having reflected but little on their institution, and its derivatory duties. They have borne a burden with the weight and importance of which they were unacquainted, and have been misled from the want of knowledge; for in our times ignorance commits more faults than vice. Such a sketch of sovereignty will perhaps appear to the censorious the archetype of the Stoics; an ideal sage, who never existed except in imagination, and to whom the nearest approach was Marcus Aurelius. We wish this feeble Essay were capable of forming men like Aurelius; it would be the highest reward we could possibly expect, at the same time that it would conduce to the good of mankind.

FEDERALIST NO. 10

JAMES MADISON

This is one of the series of Federalist Papers *written in 1787 and 1788 by Madison (1751–1836), Alexander Hamilton (1755–1804), and John Jay (1745–1829) to convince New Yorkers to ratify the Constitution drafted in the summer of 1787 in Philadelphia. Themes from Locke and Montesquieu are woven into Madison's own fears of direct democracy to produce perhaps the single most important statement of American political thought.*

Among the numerous advantages promised by a well-constructed Union, none deserves to be more accurately developed than its tendency to break and control the violence of faction. The friend of popular governments never finds himself so much alarmed for their character and fate, as when he contemplates their propensity to this dangerous vice. He will not fail, therefore, to set a due value on any plan which, without violating the principles to which he is attached, provides a proper cure for it. The instability, injustice, and confusion introduced into the public councils, have, in truth, been the mortal diseases under which popular governments have everywhere perished; as they continue to be the favorite and fruitful topics from which the adversaries to liberty derive their most specious declamations. The valuable improvements made by the American constitutions on the popular models, both ancient and modern, cannot certainly be too much admired; but it would be an unwarrantable partiality, to contend that they have as effectually obviated the danger on this side, as was wished and expected. Complaints are everywhere heard from our most considerate and virtuous citizens, equally the friends of public and private faith, and of public and personal liberty, that our governments are too unstable, that the public good is disregarded in the conflicts of rival parties, and that measures are too often decided, not according to the rules of justice and the rights of the minor party, but by the superior force of an interested and overbearing majority. However anxiously we may wish that these complaints had no foundation, the evidence of known facts will not permit us to deny that they are in some degree true. It will be found, indeed, on a candid review of our situation, that some of the distresses under which we labor have been erroneously charged on the operation of our governments; but it will be found, at the same time, that other causes will not alone account for many of our heaviest misfortunes; and, particularly, for that prevailing and increasing distrust of public engagements, and alarm for private rights, which are echoed from one end of the continent to the other. These must be chiefly, if not wholly, effects of the unsteadiness and injustice with which a factious spirit has tainted our public administrations.

By a faction, I understand a number of citizens, whether amounting to a majority or minority of the whole, who are united and actuated by some common impulse of passion, or of interest, adverse to the rights of other citizens, or to the permanent and aggregate interests of the community.

There are two methods of curing the mischiefs of faction: the one, by removing its causes; the other, by controlling its effects.

There are again two methods of removing the causes of faction: the one, by destroying the liberty which is essential to its existence; the other, by giving to every citizen the same opinions, the same passions, and the same interests.

It could never be more truly said than of the first remedy, that it was worse than the disease. Liberty is to faction what air is to fire, an aliment without which it instantly expires. But it could not be less folly to abolish liberty, which is essential to political life, because it nourishes faction, than it would be to wish the annihilation of air, which is essential to animal life, because it imparts to fire its destructive agency.

The second expedient is as impracticable as the first would be unwise. As long as the reason of man continues fallible, and he is at liberty to exercise it, different opinions will be formed. As long as the connection subsists between his reason and his self-love, his opinions and his passions will have a reciprocal influence on each other; and the former will be objects to which the latter will attach themselves. The diversity in the faculties of men, from which the rights of property originate, is not less an insuperable obstacle to a uniformity of interests. The protection of these faculties is the first object of government. From the protection of different and unequal faculties of acquiring property, the possession of different degrees and kinds of property immediately results; and from the influence of these on the sentiments and views of the respective proprietors, ensues a division of the society into different interests and parties.

The latent causes of faction are thus sown in the nature of man; and we see them everywhere brought into different degrees of activity, according to the different circumstances of civil society. A zeal for different opinions concerning religion, concerning government, and many other points, as well of speculation as of practice; an attachment to different leaders ambitiously contending for pre-eminence and power; or to persons of other descriptions whose fortunes have been interesting to the human passions, have, in turn, divided mankind into parties, inflamed them with mutual animosity, and rendered them much more disposed to vex and oppress each other than to cooperate for their common good. So strong is this propensity of mankind to fall into mutual animosities, that where no substantial occasion presents itself, the most frivolous and fanciful distinctions have been sufficient to kindle their unfriendly passions and excite their most violent conflicts. But the most common and durable source of factions has been the various and unequal distribution of property. Those who hold and those who are without property have ever formed distinct interests in society. Those who are creditors, and those who are debtors, fall under a like discrimination. A landed interest, a manufacturing interest, a mercantile interest, a moneyed interest, with many lesser interests, grow up of necessity in civilized nations, and divide them into different classes, actuated by different sentiments and views. The regulation of these various and interfering interests forms the principal task of modern legislation, and involves the spirit of party and faction in the necessary and ordinary operations of the government.

No man is allowed to be a judge in his own cause, because his interest would certainly bias his judgment, and, not improbably, corrupt his integrity. With equal, nay with greater reason, a body of men are unfit to be both judges and parties at the same time; yet what are many of the most important acts of legislation, but so many judicial determinations, not indeed concerning the rights of single persons, but concerning the rights of large bodies of citizens? And what are the different classes of legislators but advocates and parties to the causes which they determine? Is a law proposed concerning private debts? It is a question to which the creditors are parties on one side and the debtors on the other. Justice ought to hold the balance between them. Yet the parties are, and must be, themselves the judges; and the most numerous party, or, in other words, the most powerful faction must be expected to prevail. Shall domestic manufactures be encouraged, and in what degree, by restrictions on foreign manufactures? are questions which would be differently decided by the landed and the manufacturing classes, and probably by neither with a sole regard to justice and the public good. The apportionment of taxes on the various descriptions of property is an act which seems to require the most exact impartiality; yet there is, perhaps, no legislative act in which greater opportunity and temptation are given to a predominant party to trample on the rules of justice. Every shilling with which they overburden the inferior number, is a shilling saved to their own pockets.

It is in vain to say that enlightened statesmen will be able to adjust these clashing interests, and render them all subservient to the public good. Enlightened statesmen will not always be at the helm. Nor, in many cases, can such an adjustment be made at all without taking into view indirect and remote considerations, which will rarely prevail over the immediate interest which one party may find in disregarding the rights of another or the good of the whole.

The inference to which we are brought is, that the *causes* of faction cannot be removed, and that relief is only to be sought in the means of controlling its *effects.*

If a faction consists of less than a majority, relief is supplied by the republican principle, which enables the majority to defeat its sinister views by regular vote. It may clog the administration, it may convulse the society; but it will be unable to execute and mask its violence under the forms of the Constitution. When a majority is included in a faction, the form of popular government, on the other hand, enables it to sacrifice to its ruling passion or interest both the public good and the rights of other citizens. To secure the public good and private rights against the danger of such a faction, and at the same time to preserve the spirit and the form of popular government, is then the great object to which our enquiries are directed. Let me add that it is the great desideratum by which this form of government can be rescued from the opprobrium under which it has so long labored, and be recommended to the esteem and adoption of mankind.

By what means is this object attainable? Evidently by one of two only. Either the existence of the same passion or interest in a majority at the same time must be prevented, or the majority, having such coexistent passion or interest, must be rendered, by their number and local situation, unable to concert and carry into effect schemes of oppression. If the impulse and the opportunity be suffered to coincide, we well know that neither moral nor religious motives can be relied on as an adequate control. They are not found to be such on the injustice and violence of individuals, and lose their efficacy in proportion to the number combined together, that is, in proportion as their efficacy becomes needful.

From this view of the subject it may be concluded that a pure democracy, by which I mean a society consisting of a small number of citizens, who assemble and administer the government in person, can admit of no cure for the mischiefs of faction. A common passion or interest will, in almost every case, be felt by a majority of the whole; a communication and concert result from the form of government itself; and there is nothing to check the inducements to sacrifice the weaker party or an obnoxious individual. Hence it is that such democracies have ever been spectacles of turbulence and contention; have ever been found incompatible with personal security or the rights of property; and have in general been as short in their lives as they have been violent in their deaths. Theoretic politicians, who have patronized this species of government, have erroneously supposed that by reducing mankind to a perfect equality in their political rights, they would, at the same time, be perfectly equalized and assimilated in their possessions, their opinions, and their passions.

A republic, by which I mean a government in which the scheme of representation takes place, opens a different prospect, and promises the cure for which we are seeking. Let us examine the points in which it varies from pure democracy, and we shall comprehend both the nature of the cure and the efficacy which it must derive from the Union.

The two great points of difference between a democracy and a republic are: first, the delegation of the government, in the latter, to a small number of citizens elected by the rest; secondly, the greater number of citizens, and greater sphere of country, over which the latter may be extended.

The effect of the first difference is, on the one hand, to refine and enlarge the public views, by passing them through the medium of a chosen body of citizens, whose wisdom may best discern the true interest of their country, and whose patriotism and love of justice will be least likely to sacrifice it to temporary or partial considerations. Under such a regulation, it may well happen that the public voice, pronounced by the representatives of the people, will be more consonant to the public good than if pronounced by the people themselves, convened for the purpose. On the other hand, the effect may be inverted. Men of factious tempers, of local prejudices, or of sinister designs, may, by intrigue, by corruption, or by other means, first obtain the suffrages, and then betray the interests, of the people. The question resulting is, whether small or extensive republics are more favorable to the election of proper guardians of the public weal; and it is clearly decided in favor of the latter by two obvious considerations:

In the first place, it is to be remarked that, however small the republic may be, the representatives must be raised to a certain number, in order to guard against the cabals of a few; and that, however large it may be, they must be limited to a certain number, in order to guard against the confusion of a multitude. Hence, the number of representatives in the two cases not being in proportion to that of the two constituents, and being proportionally greater in the small republic, it follows that, if the proportion of fit characters be not less in the large than in the small republic, the former will present a greater option, and consequently a greater probability of a fit choice.

In the next place, as each representative will be chosen by a greater number of citizens in the large than in the small republic, it will be more difficult for unworthy candidates to practice with success the vicious arts by which elections are too often carried; and the suffrages of the people being more free, will be more likely to center in men who possess the most attractive merit and the most diffusive and established characters.

It must be confessed that in this, as in most other cases, there is a mean, on both sides of which inconveniences will be found to lie. By enlarging too much the number of electors, you render the representatives too little acquainted with all their local circumstances and lesser interests; as by reducing it too much, you render him unduly attached to these, and too little fit to comprehend and pursue great and national objects. The federal Constitution forms a happy combination in this respect; the great and aggregate interests being referred to the national, the local and particular to the State legislatures.

The other point of difference is, the greater number of citizens and extent of territory which may be brought within the compass of republican than of democratic government; and it is this circumstance principally which renders factious combinations less to be dreaded in the former than in the latter. The smaller the society, the fewer probably will be the distinct parties and interests composing it; the fewer the distinct parties and interests, the more frequently will a majority be found of the same party; and the smaller the number of individuals composing a majority, and the smaller the compass within which they are placed, the more easily will they concert and execute their plans of oppression. Extend the sphere, and you take in a greater variety of parties and interests; you make it less probable that a majority of the whole will have a common motive to invade the rights of other citizens; or if such a common motive exists, it will be more difficult for all who feel it to discover their own strength, and to act in unison with each other. Besides other impediments, it may be remarked that, where there is a consciousness of unjust or dishonorable purposes, communication is always checked by distrust in proportion to the number whose concurrence is necessary.

Hence, it clearly appears, that the same advantage which a republic has over a democracy, in controlling the effects of faction, is enjoyed by a large over a small republic—is enjoyed by the Union over the States composing it. Does the advantage consist in the substitution of representatives whose enlightened views and virtuous sentiments render them superior to local prejudices and to schemes of injustice? It will not be denied that the representation of the Union will be most likely to possess these requisite endowments. Does it consist in the greater security afforded by a greater variety of parties, against the event of any one party being able to outnumber and oppress the rest? In an equal degree does the increased variety of parties comprised within the Union, increase this security. Does it, in fine, consist in the greater obstacles opposed to the concert and accomplishment of the secret wishes of an unjust and interested majority? Here, again, the extent of the Union gives it the most palpable advantage.

The influence of factious leaders may kindle a flame within their particular States, but will be unable to spread a general conflagration through the other States. A religious sect may degenerate into a political faction in a part of the Confederacy; but the variety of sects dispersed over the entire face of it must secure the national councils against any danger from that source. A rage for paper money, for an abolition of debts, for an equal division of property, or for any other improper or wicked project, will be less apt to pervade the whole body of the Union than a particular member of it; in the same proportion as such a malady is more likely to taint a particular country or district, than an entire State.

In the extent and proper structure of the Union therefore, we behold a republican remedy for the diseases most incident to republican government. And according to the degree of pleasure and pride we feel in being republicans, ought to be our zeal in cherishing the spirit and supporting the character of Federalists.

THE DECLARATION OF THE RIGHTS OF MAN AND THE CITIZEN

Enduring as a monumental summary of Enlightenment political thought, this declaration was approved by the French National Assembly on August 27, 1789.

The representatives of the French people, organized in National Assembly, considering that ignorance, forgetfulness, or contempt of the rights of man are the sole causes of public misfortunes and of the corruption of governments, have resolved to set forth in a solemn declaration the natural, inalienable, and sacred rights of man, in order that such declaration, continually before all members of the social body, may be a perpetual reminder of their rights and duties; in order that the acts of the legislative power and those of the executive power may constantly be compared with the aim of every political institution and may accordingly be more respected; in order that the demands of the citizens, founded henceforth upon simple and incontestable principles, may always be directed towards the maintenance of the Constitution and the welfare of all.

Accordingly, the National Assembly recognizes and proclaims, in the presence and under the auspices of the Supreme Being, the following rights of man and citizen.

1. Men are born and remain free and equal in rights; social distinctions may be based only upon general usefulness.

2. The aim of every political association is the preservation of the natural and inalienable rights of man; these rights are liberty, property, security, and resistance to oppression.

3. The source of all sovereignty resides essentially in the nation; no group, no individual, may exercise authority not emanating expressly therefrom.

4. Liberty consists of the power to do whatever is not injurious to others; thus the enjoyment of the natural rights of every man has for its limits only those that assure other members of society the enjoyment of those same rights; such limits may be determined only by law.

5. The law has the right to forbid only actions that are injurious to society. Whatever is not forbidden by law may not be prevented, and no one may be constrained to do what it does not prescribe.

6. Law is the expression of the general will; all citizens have the right to concur personally, or through their representatives, in its formation; it must be the same for all, whether it protects or punishes. All citizens, being equal before it, are equally admissible to all public offices, positions, and employments, according to their capacity, and without other distinction than that of virtues and talents.

7. No man may be accused, arrested, or detained except in the cases determined by law, and according to the forms prescribed thereby. Whoever solicit, expedite, or execute arbitrary orders, or have them executed, must be punished; but every citizen summoned or appre-

hended in pursuance of the law must obey immediately; he renders himself culpable by resistance.

8. The law is to establish only penalties that are absolutely and obviously necessary; and no one may be punished except by virtue of a law established and promulgated prior to the offense and legally applied.

9. Since every man is presumed innocent until declared guilty, if arrest be deemed indispensable, all unnecessary severity for securing the person of the accused must be severely repressed by law.

10. No one is to be disquieted because of his opinions, even religious, provided their manifestation does not disturb the public order established by law.

11. Free communication of ideas and opinions is one of the most precious of the rights of man. Consequently, every citizen may speak, write, and print freely, subject to responsibility for the abuse of such liberty in the cases determined by law.

12. The guarantee of the rights of man and citizen necessitates a public force; such a force, therefore, is instituted for the advantage of all and not for the particular benefit of those to whom it is entrusted.

13. For the maintenance of the public force and for the expenses of administration a common tax is indispensable; it must be assessed equally on all citizens in proportion to their means.

14. Citizens have the right to ascertain, by themselves or through their representatives, the necessity of the public tax, to consent to it freely, to supervise its use, and to determine its quota, assessment, payment, and duration.

15. Society has the right to require of every public agent an accounting of his administration.

16. Every society in which the guarantee of rights is not assured or the separation of powers not determined has no constitution at all.

17. Since property is a sacred and inviolable right, no one may be deprived thereof unless a legally established public necessity obviously requires it, and upon condition of a just and previous indemnity.

THE RIGHTS OF MAN

THOMAS PAINE

Written to defend the French Revolution and liberal principles in general from the devastating attack of Edmund Burke's Reflections on the Revolution in France, *Paine's* Rights of Man *(1791–1792) reflects the Enlightenment consensus that America embodied best its progressive ideals.*

From the revolutions of America and France, and the symptoms that have appeared in other countries, it is evident that the opinion of the world is changed with respect to systems of government, and that revolutions are not within the compass of political calculations. The progress of time and circumstances, which men assign to the accomplishment of great changes, is too mechanical to measure the force of the mind, and the rapidity of reflection, by which revolutions are generated: All the old governments have received a shock from those that already appear, and which were once more improbable, and are a greater subject of wonder, than a general revolution in Europe would be now.

When we survey the wretched condition of man under the monarchical and hereditary systems of government, dragged from his home by one power, or driven by another, and impoverished by taxes more than by enemies, it becomes evident that those systems are bad, and that a general revolution in the principle and construction of governments is necessary.

What is government more than the management of the affairs of a Nation? It is not, and from its nature cannot be, the property of any particular man or family, but of the whole community, at whose expense it is supported; and though by force or contrivance it has been usurped into an inheritance, the usurpation cannot alter the right of things. Sovereignty, as a matter of right, appertains to the Nation only, and not to any individual; and a Nation has at all times an inherent indefeasible right to abolish any form of government it finds inconvenient, and establish such as accords with its interest, disposition, and happiness. The romantic and barbarous distinction of men into Kings and subjects, though it may suit the condition of courtiers, cannot that of citizens; and is exploded by the principle upon which governments are now founded. Every citizen is a member of the Sovereignty, and, as such, can acknowledge no personal subjection; and his obedience can be only to the laws.

When men think of what government is, they must necessarily suppose it to possess a knowledge of all the objects and matters upon which its authority is to be exercised. In this view of government, the republican system, as established by America and France, operates to embrace the whole of a Nation; and the knowledge necessary to the interest of all the parts, is to be found in the center, which the parts by representation form: But the old governments are on a construction that excludes knowledge as well as happiness; government by monks, who know nothing of the world beyond the walls of a convent, is as consistent as government by Kings.

What were formerly called revolutions, were little more than a change of persons, or an alteration of local circumstances. They rose and fell like things of course, and had nothing in their existence or their fate that could influence beyond the spot that produced them. But what we now see in the world, from the revolutions of America and France, are a renovation of the natural order of things, a system of principles as universal as truth and the existence of man, and combining moral with political happiness and national prosperity.

"*I. Men are born and always continue free, and equal in respect of their rights. Civil distinctions, therefore, can be founded only on public utility.*

"*II. The end of all political associations is the preservation of the natural and imprescriptible rights of man; and these rights are liberty, property, security, and resistance of oppression.*

"*III. The Nation is essentially the source of all Sovereignty; nor can any* INDIVIDUAL, *or* ANY BODY OF MEN, *be entitled to any authority which is not expressly derived from it.*"

In these principles, there is nothing to throw a Nation into confusion by inflaming ambition. They are calculated to call forth wisdom and abilities, and to exercise them for the public good, and not for the emolument or aggrandizement of particular descriptions of men or families. Monarchical sovereignty, the enemy of mankind, and the source of misery, is abolished; and sovereignty itself is restored to its natural and original place, the Nation. Were this the case through Europe, the cause of wars would be taken away. . . .

What Archimedes said of the mechanical powers, may be applied to Reason and Liberty: *"Had we,"* said he, *"a place to stand upon, we might raise the world."*

The revolution of America presented in politics what was only theory in mechanics. So deeply rooted were all the governments of the old world, and so effectually had the tyranny and the antiquity of habit established itself over the mind, that no beginning could be made in Asia, Africa, or Europe, to reform the political condition of man. Freedom had been hunted round the globe; reason was considered as rebellion; and the slavery of fear had made men afraid to think.

But such is the irresistible nature of truth, that all it asks, and all it wants, is the liberty of appearing. The sun needs no inscription to distinguish him from darkness; and no sooner did the American governments display themselves to the world, than despotism felt a shock, and man began to contemplate redress.

The independence of America, considered merely as a separation from England, would have been a matter but of little importance, had it not been accompanied by a revolution in the principles and practice of governments. She made a stand, not for herself only, but for the world, and looked beyond the advantages herself could receive. Even the Hessian, though hired to fight against her, may live to bless his defeat; and England, condemning the viciousness of its government, rejoice in its miscarriage.

As America was the only spot in the political world, where the principles of universal reformation could begin, so also was it the best in the natural world. An assemblage of circumstances conspired, not only to give birth, but to add gigantic maturity to its principles. The scene which that country presents to the eye of a spectator, has something in it which generates and encourages great ideas. Nature appears to him in magnitude. The mighty objects he beholds, act upon his mind by enlarging it, and he partakes of the greatness he contemplates.—Its first settlers were emigrants from different European nations, and of diversified professions of religion, retiring from the governmental persecutions of the old world, and meeting in the new, not as enemies, but as brothers. The wants which necessarily accompany the cultivation of a wilderness produced among them a state of society, which countries, long harassed by the quarrels and intrigues of governments, had neglected to cherish. In such a situation man becomes what he ought. He sees his species, not with the inhuman idea of a natural enemy, but as kindred; and the example shows to the artificial world, that man must go back to Nature for information. . . .

If systems of government can be introduced, less expensive, and more productive of general happiness, than those which have existed, all attempts to oppose their progress will in the end be fruitless. Reason, like time, will make its own way, and prejudice will fall in a combat with interest. If universal peace, civilization, and commerce, are ever to be the happy lot of man, it cannot be accomplished but by a revolution in the system of governments. All the monarchical governments are military. War is their trade, plunder and revenue their objects. While such governments continue, peace has not the absolute security of a day. What is the history of all monarchical governments, but a disgustful picture of human wretchedness, and the accidental respite of a few years' repose? Wearied with war, and tired with human butchery, they sat down to rest, and called it peace. This certainly is not the condition that Heaven intended for man; and if *this be monarchy*, well might monarchy be reckoned among the sins of the Jews.

The revolutions which formerly took place in the world, had nothing in them that interested the bulk of mankind. They extended only to a change of persons and measures, but not of principles, and rose or fell among the common transactions of the moment. What we now behold, may not improperly be called a *"counter-revolution."* Conquest and tyranny, at some early period, dispossessed man of his rights, and he is now recovering them. And as the tide of all human affairs has its ebb and flow in directions contrary to each other, so also is it in this. Government founded on a *moral theory, on a system of universal peace, on the indefeasible hereditary Rights of Man*, is now revolving from west to east, by a stronger impulse than the government of the sword revolved from east to west. It interests not particular individuals, but nations, in its progress, and promises a new era to the human race.

ENQUIRY CONCERNING POLITICAL JUSTICE

William Godwin

One of the most thoroughgoing radical thinkers found in the English Enlightenment, Godwin (1756–1836) was so passionately an individualist and rationalist that he advocated anarchy—or, as he describes it here, "the dissolution of political government." He disapproved of marriage as well, though he would nevertheless marry the feminist writer Mary Wollstonecraft. This is a selection from his three-volume Enquiry Concerning Political Justice, *published in 1793.*

If we would arrive at truth, each man must be taught to enquire and think for himself. If a hundred men spontaneously engage the whole energy of their faculties upon the solution of a given question, the chance of success will be greater, than if only ten men are so employed. By the same reason, the chance will also be increased, in proportion as the intellectual operations of these men are individual, and their conclusions are suggested by the reason of the thing, uninfluenced by the force either of compulsion or sympathy. But, in political associations, the object of each man, is to identify his creed with that of his neighbor. We learn the Shibboleth of a party. We dare not leave our minds at large in the field of enquiry, lest we should arrive at some tenet disrelished by our party. We have no temptation to enquire. Party has a more powerful tendency, than perhaps any other circumstance in human affairs, to render the mind quiescent and stationary. Instead of making each man an individual, which the interest of the whole requires, it resolves all understandings into one common mass, and subtracts from each the varieties, that could alone distinguish him from a brute machine. Having learned the creed of our party, we have no longer any employment for those faculties, which might lead us to detect its errors. We have arrived, in our own opinion, at the last page of the volume of truth; and all that remains, is by some means to effect the adoption of our sentiments, as the standard of right to the whole race of mankind. . . . In fine, from these considerations it appears, that associations, instead of promoting the growth and diffusion of truth, tend only to check its accumulation, and render its operation, as far as possible, unnatural and mischievous.

There is another circumstance to be mentioned, strongly calculated to confirm this position. A necessary attendant upon political associations, is harangue and declamation. A majority of the members of any numerous popular society, will look to these harangues, as the school in which they are to study, in order to become the reservoirs of practical truth to the rest of mankind. But harangues and declamation, lead to passion, and not to knowledge. The memory of the hearer is crowded with pompous nothings, with images and not arguments. He is never permitted to be sober enough, to weigh things with an unshaken hand. It would be inconsistent with the art of eloquence, to strip the subject of every meretricious ornament. Instead of informing the understanding of the hearer by a slow and regular progression, the orator must beware of detail, must render every thing rapid, and from time to time work up the passions of his hearers to a tempest of applause. Truth can scarcely be acquired in crowded halls and amidst noisy debates. Where hope and fear, triumph and resentment, are perpetually afloat, the severer faculties of investigation are compelled to quit the field. Truth dwells with contemplation. We can seldom make much progress in the business of disentangling error and delusion, but in sequestered privacy, or in the tranquil interchange of sentiments that takes place between two persons. . . .

All the arguments that have been employed to prove the insufficiency of democracy, grow out of this one root, the supposed necessity of deception and prejudice for restraining the turbulence of human passions. Without the assumption of this principle the argument could not be sustained for a moment. The direct and decisive answer would be, "Are kings and lords intrinsically wiser and better than their humbler neighbors? Can there be any solid ground of distinction, except what is founded in personal merit? Are not men, really and strictly considered, equal, except so far as what is personal and inalienable, establishes a difference?" To these questions there can be but one reply, "Such is the order of reason and absolute truth, but artificial distinctions are necessary for the happiness of mankind. Without deception and prejudice the turbulence of human passions cannot be restrained." Let us then examine the merits of this theory. . .

How many arts, and how noxious to those towards whom we employ them, are necessary, if we would successfully deceive? We must not only leave their reason in indolence at first, but endeavor to supersede its exertion in any future instance. If men be, for the present, kept right by prejudice, what will become of them hereafter, if, by any future penetration, or any accidental discovery, this prejudice shall be annihilated? Detection is not always the fruit of systematical improvement, but may be effected by some solitary exertion of the faculty, or some luminous and irresistible argument, while every thing else remains as it was. If we would first deceive, and then maintain our deception unimpaired, we shall need penal statutes, and licensers of the press, and hired ministers of falsehold and imposture. Admirable modes these for the propagation of the wisdom and virtue!

There is another case . . . upon which much stress has been laid by political writers. "Obedience," say they, "must either be courted or compelled. We must either make a judicious use of the prejudices and the ignorance of mankind, or be contented to have no hold upon them but their fears, and to maintain social order entirely by the severity of punishment. To dispense us from this painful necessity, authority ought carefully to be invested with a sort of magic persuasion. Citizens should serve their country, not with a frigid submission that scrupulously weighs its duties, but with an enthusiasm that places its honor in its loyalty. For this reason, our governors and superiors must not be spoken of with levity. They must be considered, independently of their individual character, as deriving a sacredness from their office. They must be accompanied with splendor and veneration. . . .

This is still the same argument under another form. It takes for granted, that a true observation of things, is inadequate to teach us our duty; and, of consequence, recommends an equivocal engine, which may, with equal case, be employed in the service of justice and injustice, but would surely appear somewhat more in its place in the service of the latter. It is injustice that stands most in need of superstition and mystery, and will most frequently be a gainer by the imposition. This hypothesis proceeds upon an assumption, which young men sometimes impute to their parents and preceptors. It says, "Mankind must be kept in ignorance: if they know vice, they will love it too well; if they perceive the charms of error, they will never return to the simplicity of truth." And, strange as it may appear, this bare-faced and unplausible argument, has been the foundation of a very popular and generally received hypothesis. It has taught politicians to believe, that a people, once sunk into decrepitude, as it has been termed, could never afterwards be endued with purity and vigor. . . .

The system of political imposture divides men into two classes, one of which is to think and reason for the whole, and the other to take the conclusions of their superiors on trust. This distinction is not founded in the nature of things; there is no such inherent difference between man and man, as it thinks proper to suppose. Nor is it less injurious, than it is unfounded. The two classes which it creates, must be more and less than man. It is too much to expect of the former, while we consign to them an unnatural monopoly, that they should rigidly consult for the good of the whole. It is an iniquitous requisition upon the latter, that they should never employ their understandings, or penetrate into the essences of things, but always rest in a deceitful appearance. It is iniquitous, to deprive them of that chance for additional wisdom, which would result, from a greater number of minds being employed in the enquiry, and from the disinterested and impartial spirit that might be expected to accompany it. . . .

With respect to the multitude, in this system, they are placed in the middle between two fearful calamities, suspicion on one side, and infatuation on the other. . . . Sometimes they suppose their governors to be the messengers and favorites of heaven, a supernatural order of beings; and sometimes they suspect them to be a combination of usurpers to rob and oppress them. For they dare not indulge themselves in solving the dilemma, because they are held in awe by oppression and the gallows.

Is this the genuine state of man? Is this a condition so desirable, that we should be anxious to entail it upon posterity for ever? Is it high treason to enquire whether it may be meliorated? Are we sure, that every change from such a situation of things, is severely to be deprecated? Is it not worth while, to suffer that experiment, which shall consist in a gradual, and almost insensible, abolition of such mischievous institutions?

It may not be uninstructive to consider what sort of discourse must be held, or book written, by him who should make himself the champion of political imposture. He cannot avoid secretly wishing that the occasion had never existed. What he undertakes is to lengthen the reign of "salutary prejudices." For this end, he must propose to himself the two opposite purposes, of prolonging the deception, and proving that it is necessary to deceive. By whom is it that he intends his book should be read? Chiefly by the governed; the governors need little inducement to continue the system. But, at the same time that he tells us, we should cherish the mistake as mistake, and the prejudice as prejudice, he is himself lifting the veil, and destroying his own system. While the affair of our superiors and the enlightened, is simply, to impose upon us, the talk is plain and intelligible. But, the moment they begin to write books, to persuade us that we ought to be willing to be deceived, it may well be suspected that their system is upon the decline. It is not to be wondered at, if the greatest genius, and the sincerest and most benevolent champion, should fail in producing a perspicuous or very persuasive treatise, when he undertakes so hopeless a task. . . .

In proportion as the spirit of party was extirpated, as the restlessness of public commotion subsided, and as the political machine became simple, the voice of reason would be secure to be heard. . . .

At first, we will suppose, that some degree of authority and violence would be necessary. But this necessity does not appear to arise out of the nature of man, but out of the institutions by which he has been corrupted. Man is not originally vicious. He would not refuse to listen to, or to be convinced by, the expostulations that are addressed to him, had he not been accustomed to regard them as hypocritical, and to conceive that, while his neighbor, his parent, and his political governor, pretended to be actuated by a pure regard to his interest or pleasure, they were, in reality, at the expense of his, promoting their own. Such are the fatal effects of mysteriousness and complexity. Simplify the social system, in the manner which every motive, but those of usurpation and ambition, powerfully recommends; render the plain dictates of justice level to every capacity; remove the necessity of implicit faith; and we may expect the whole species to become reasonable and virtuous. It might then be sufficient for juries to recommend a certain mode of adjusting controversies, without assuming the prerogative of dictating that adjustment. It might then be sufficient for them to invite offenders to forsake their errors. . . .

The reader has probably anticipated the ultimate conclusion from these remarks. If juries might at length cease to decide, and be contented to invite, if force might gradually be withdrawn and reason trusted alone, shall we not one day find, that juries themselves, and every other species of public institution, may be laid aside as unnecessary? Will not the reasonings of one wise man, be as effectual as those of twelve? Will not the competence of one individual to instruct his neighbors, be a matter of sufficient notoriety, without the formality of an election? Will there be many vices to correct, and much obstinacy to conquer? This is one of the most memorable stages of human improvement. With what delight must every well informed friend of mankind look forward, to the auspicious period, the dissolution of political government, of that brute engine, which has been the only perennial cause of the vices of mankind, and which, as has abundantly appeared in the progress of the present work, has mischiefs of various sorts incorporated with its substance, and no otherwise removable than by its utter annihilation! . . .

Individuality is of the very essence of intellectual excellence. . . . The truly venerable, and the truly happy, must have the fortitude to maintain his individuality. . . .

From these principles it appears, that every thing that is usually understood by the term cooperation, is, in some degree, an evil. . . . In society he will find pleasure; the temper of his mind will prepare him for friendship and for love. But he will resort with a scarcely inferior eagerness to solitude; and will find in it the highest complacence and the purest delight.

Another article which belongs to the subject of cooperation, is cohabitation. The evils attendant on this practice, are obvious. In order to the human understanding's being successfully cultivated, it is necessary, that the intellectual operations of men should be independent of each other. We should avoid such practices as are calculated to melt our opinions into a common mold. Cohabitation is also hostile to that fortitude, which should accustom a man, in his actions, as well as in his opinions, to judge for himself, and feel competent to the discharge of his own duties. Add to this, that it is absurd to expect the inclinations and wishes of two human beings to coincide, through any long period of time. To oblige them to act and to live together, is to subject them to some inevitable portion of thwarting, bickering and unhappiness. . . .

The subject of cohabitation is particularly interesting, as it includes in it the subject of marriage. It will therefore be proper to pursue the enquiry in greater detail. The evil of marriage, as it is practiced in the European countries, extends further than we have yet described. The method is, for a thoughtless and romantic youth of each sex, to come together, to see each other, for a few times, and under circumstances full of delusion, and then to vow eternal attachment. What is the consequence of this? In almost every instance they find themselves deceived. They are reduced to make the best of an irretrievable mistake. They are led to conceive it their wisest policy, to shut their eyes upon realities, happy, if, by any perversion of intellect, they can persuade themselves that they were right in their first crude opinion of each other. Thus the institution of marriage is made a system of fraud; and men who carefully mislead their judgments in the daily affair of their life, must be expected to have a crippled judgment in every other concern.

Add to this, that marriage, as now understood, is a monopoly, and the worst of monopolies. So long as two human beings are forbidden, by positive institution, to follow the dictates of their own mind, prejudice will be alive and vigorous. So long as I seek, by despotic and artificial means, to maintain my possession of a woman, I am guilty of the most odious selfishness. . . .

The abolition of the present system of marriage, appears to involve no evils. We are apt to represent that abolition to ourselves, as the harbinger of brutal lust and depravity. But it really happens, in this, as in other cases, that the positive laws which are made to restrain our vices, irritate and multiply them. Not to say, that the same sentiments of justice and happiness, which, in a state of equality, would destroy our relish for expensive gratifications, might be expected to decrease our inordinate appetites of every kind, and to lead us universally to prefer the pleasures of intellect to the pleasures of sense.

It is a question of some moment, whether the intercourse of the sexes, in a reasonable state of society, would be promiscuous, or whether each man would select for himself a partner, to whom he will adhere, as long as that adherence shall continue to be the choice of both parties. Probability seems to be greatly in favor of the latter. Perhaps this side of the alternative is most favorable to population. . . . It is the nature of the human mind, to persist, for a certain length of time, in its opinion or choice. The parties therefore, having acted upon selection, are not likely to forget this selection when the interview is over. Friendship, if by friendship we understand that affection for an individual which is measured singly by what we know of his worth, is one of the most exquisite gratifications, perhaps one of the most improving exercises, of a rational mind. Friendship therefore may be expected to come in aid of the sexual intercourse, to refine its grossness, and increase its delight. All these arguments are calculated to determine our judgment in favor of marriage as a salutary and respectable institution, but not of that species of marriage, in which there is no room for repentance, and to which liberty and hope are equally strangers.

Admitting these principles therefore as the basis of the sexual commerce, what opinion ought we to form respecting infidelity to this attachment? Certainly no ties ought to be imposed upon either party, preventing them from quitting the attachment, whenever their judgment directs them to quit it.

The Economy and Markets

THE ROYAL EXCHANGE

Joseph Addison

Like Voltaire, Addison saw England's greatness and commercial progress as signs of an enlightened age, and he too saw it best symbolized by the Royal Exchange. Merchants, trade, and luxury are praised in this article, which appeared as The Spectator *No. 69 on May 19, 1711.*

There is no place in the town which I so much love to frequent as the Royal Exchange. It gives me a secret satisfaction, and, in some measure, gratifies my vanity, as I am an Englishman, to see so rich an assembly of countrymen and foreigners consulting together upon the private business of mankind, and making this metropolis a kind of emporium for the whole earth. I must confess I look upon high-change to be a great council, in which all considerable nations have their representatives. Factors in the trading world are what ambassadors are in the politic world; they negotiate affairs, conclude treaties, and maintain a good correspondence between those wealthy societies of men that are divided from one another by seas and oceans, or live on the different extremities of a continent. I have often been pleased to hear disputes adjusted between an inhabitant of Japan and an alderman of London, or to see a subject of the Great Mogul entering into a league with one of the Czar of Muscovy. I am infinitely delighted in mixing with these several ministers of commerce, as they are distinguished by their different walks and different languages: sometimes I am justled among a body of Armenians; sometimes I am lost in a crowd of Jews; and sometimes make one in a group of Dutchmen. I am a Dane, Swede, or Frenchman at different times; or rather fancy myself like the old philosopher, who upon being asked what countryman he was, replied that he was a citizen of the world.

Though I very frequently visit this busy multitude of people, I am known to nobody there but my friend Sir Andrew, who often smiles upon me as he sees me bustling in the crowd, but at the same time connives at my presence without taking any further notice of me. There is indeed a merchant of Egypt, who just knows me by sight, having formerly remitted me some money to Grand Cairo; but as I am not versed in the modern Coptic, our conferences go no further than a bow and a grimace.

This grand scene of business gives me an infinite variety of solid and substantial entertainments. As I am a great lover of mankind, my heart naturally overflows with pleasure at the sight of a prosperous and happy multitude, insomuch that at many public solemnities I cannot forbear expressing my joy with tears that have stolen down my cheeks. For this reason I am wonderfully delighted to see such a body of men thriving in their own private fortunes, and at the same time promoting the public stock; or, in other words, raising estates for their own families, by bringing into their country whatever is wanting, and carrying out of it whatever is superfluous.

Nature seems to have taken a peculiar care to disseminate the blessings among the different regions of the world, with an eye to this mutual intercourse and traffic among mankind, that the natives of the several parts of the globe might have a kind of dependence upon one another, and be united together by this common interest. Almost every degree produces something peculiar to it. The food often grows in one country, and the sauce in another. The fruits of Portugal are corrected by the products of Barbadoes; the infusion of a China plant sweetened with the pith of an Indian cane. The Philippic Islands give a flavor to our European bowls. The single dress of a woman of quality is often the product of an hundred climates. The muff and the fan come together from the different ends of the earth. The scarf is sent from the torrid zone, and the tippet from beneath the pole. The brocade petticoat rises out of the mines of Peru, and the diamond necklace out of the bowels of Indostan.

If we consider our own country in its natural prospect, without any of the benefits and advantages of commerce, what a barren, uncomfortable spot of earth falls to our share! Natural historians tell us that no fruit grows originally among us besides hips and haws, acorns and pig-nuts, with other delicacies of the like nature; that our climate of itself, and without the assistances of art, can make no further advances towards a plum than to a sloe, and carries an apple to no greater a perfection than a crab: that our melons, our peaches, our figs, our apricots, and cherries are strangers among us, imported in different ages, and naturalized in our English gardens; and that they would all degenerate and fall away into the trash of our own country, if they were wholly neglected by the planter, and left to the mercy of our sun and soil. Nor has traffic more enriched our vegetable world, than it has improved the whole face of nature among us. Our ships are laden with the harvest of every climate: our tables are stored with spices, and oils, and wines; our rooms are filled with pyramids of China, and adorned with the workmanship of Japan: our morning's draught comes to us from the remotest corners of the earth; we repair our bodies by the drugs of America, and repose ourselves under Indian canopies. My friend Sir Andrew calls the vineyards of France our gardens; the spice-islands our hot-beds; the Persians our silk-weavers, and the Chinese our potters. Nature indeed furnishes us with the bare necessaries of life, but traffic gives us a great variety of what is useful, and at the same time supplies us with everything that is convenient and ornamental. Nor is it the least part of this our happiness that, while we enjoy the remotest products of the north and south, we are free from those extremities of weather which give them birth; that our eyes are refreshed with the green fields of Britain at the same time that our palates are feasted with fruits that rise between the tropics.

For these reasons, there are not more useful members in a commonwealth than merchants. They knit mankind together in a mutual intercourse of good offices, distribute the gifts of nature, find work for the poor, and wealth to the rich, and magnificence to the great. Our English merchant converts the tin of his own country into gold, and exchanges his wool for rubies. The Mahometans are clothed in our British manufacture, and the inhabitants of the frozen zone warmed with the fleeces of our sheep.

When I have been upon the Change, I have often fancied one of our old kings standing in person where he is represented in effigy, and looking down upon the wealthy concourse of people with which that place is every day filled. In this case, how would he be surprised to hear all the languages of Europe spoken in this little spot of his former dominions, and to see so many private men, who in his time would have been the vassals of some powerful baron, negotiating like princes for greater sums of money than were formerly to be met with in the Royal Treasury! Trade, without enlarging the British territories, has given us a kind of additional empire: it has multiplied the number of the rich, made our landed estates infinitely more valuable than they were formerly, and added to them an accession of other estates as valuable as the lands themselves.

INDUSTRY AND THE WAY TO WEALTH

BENJAMIN FRANKLIN

Franklin is the epitome of the self-made man, an Enlightenment ideal that was as much a moral ideal as economic. In these two selections, the first from his Autobiography *(1771–1784) and the second his preface to* Poor Richard's Almanack *(1732–1757), Franklin spells out the regimen and the virtues essential for success in market society.*

Reading was the only amusement I allowed myself. I spent no time in taverns, games, or frolics of any kind; and my industry in my business continued as indefatigable as it was necessary. I was indebted for my printing-house; I had a young family coming on to be educated, and I had to contend with, for business, two printers who were established in the place before me. My circumstances, however, grew daily easier. My original habits of frugality continuing, and my father having, among his instructions to me when a boy, frequently repeated a proverb of Solomon, "Seest thou a man diligent in his calling, he shall stand before kings, he shall not stand before mean men," I from thence considered industry as a means of obtaining wealth and distinction, which encouraged me, though I did not think that I should ever literally *stand before kings*, which, however, has since happened; for I have stood before *five*, and even had the honor of sitting down with one—the King of Denmark—to dinner. . . .

It was about this time I conceived the bold and arduous project of arriving at moral perfection. I wished to live without committing any fault any time; I would conquer all that either natural inclination, custom, or company might lead me into. As I knew, or thought I knew, what was right and wrong, I did not see why I might not always do the one and avoid the other. But I soon found I had undertaken a task of more difficulty than I had imagined. While my care was employed in guarding against one fault, I was often surprised by another; habit took the advantage of inattention; inclination was sometimes too strong for reason. I concluded at length, that the mere speculative conviction that it was our interest to be completely virtuous was not sufficient to prevent our slipping; and that the contrary habits must be broken, and good ones acquired and established, before we can have any dependence on a steady, uniform rectitude of conduct. For this purpose I therefore contrived the following method.

In the various enumerations of the moral virtues I had met with in my reading, I found the catalogue more or less numerous, as different writers included more or fewer ideas under the same name. Temperance, for example, was by some confined to eating and drinking, while by others it was extended to mean the moderating every other pleasure, appetite, inclination, or passion, bodily or mental, even to our avarice and ambition. I proposed to myself, for the sake of clearness, to use rather more names, with fewer ideas annexed to each, than a few names with more ideas; and I included under thirteen names of virtues all that at that time occurred to me as necessary or desirable, and annexed to each a short precept, which fully expressed the extent I gave to its meaning.

These names of virtues, with their precepts, were:

1. TEMPERANCE. Eat not to dullness; drink not to elevation.
2. SILENCE. Speak not but what may benefit others or yourself; avoid trifling conversation.
3. ORDER. Let all your things have their places; let each part of your business have its time.

4. RESOLUTION. Resolve to perform what you ought; perform without fail what you resolve.
5. FRUGALITY. Make no expense but to do good to others or yourself; *i.e.,* waste nothing.
6. INDUSTRY. Lose no time; be always employed in something useful; cut off all unnecessary actions.
7. SINCERITY. Use no hurtful deceit; think innocently and justly, and, if you speak, speak accordingly.
8. JUSTICE. Wrong none by doing injuries, or omitting the benefits that are your duty.
9. MODERATION. Avoid extremes; forbear resenting injuries so much as you think they deserve.
10. CLEANLINESS. Tolerate no uncleanliness in body, clothes, or habitation.
11. TRANQUILITY. Be not disturbed at trifles, or at accidents common or unavoidable.
12. CHASTITY. Rarely use venery but for health or offspring, never to dullness, weakness, or the injury of your own or another's peace or reputation.
13. HUMILITY. Imitate Jesus and Socrates.

My intention being to acquire the *habitude* of all these virtues, I judged it would be well not to distract my attention by attempting the whole at once, but to fix it on one of them at a time; and, when I should be master of that, then to proceed to another, and so on, till I should have gone through the thirteen; and, as the previous acquisition of some might facilitate the acquisiton of certain others, I arranged them with that view, as they stand above. *Temperance* first, as it tends to procure that coolness and clearness of head, which is so necessary where constant vigilance was to be kept up, and guard maintained against the unremitting attraction of ancient habits, and the force of perpetual temptations. This being acquired and established, *Silence* would be more easy; and my desire being to gain knowledge at the same time that I improved in virtue, and considering that in conversation it was obtained rather by the use of the ears than of the tongue, and therefore wishing to break a habit I was getting into of prattling, punning, and joking, which only made me acceptable to trifling company, I gave *Silence* the second place. This and the next, *Order,* I expected would allow me more time for attending to my project and my studies. *Resolution,* once become habitual, would keep me firm in my endeavors to obtain all the subsequent virtues; *Frugality* and *Industry* freeing me from my remaining debt, and producing affluence and independence, would make more easy the practice of *Sincerity and Justice*, etc., etc. Conceiving then, that, agreeably to the advice of Pythagoras in his Golden Verses, daily examination would be necessary, I contrived the following method for conducting that examination. . . .

The precept of *Order* requiring that *every part of my business should have its allotted time*, one page in my little book contained the following scheme of employment for the twenty-four hours of a natural day.

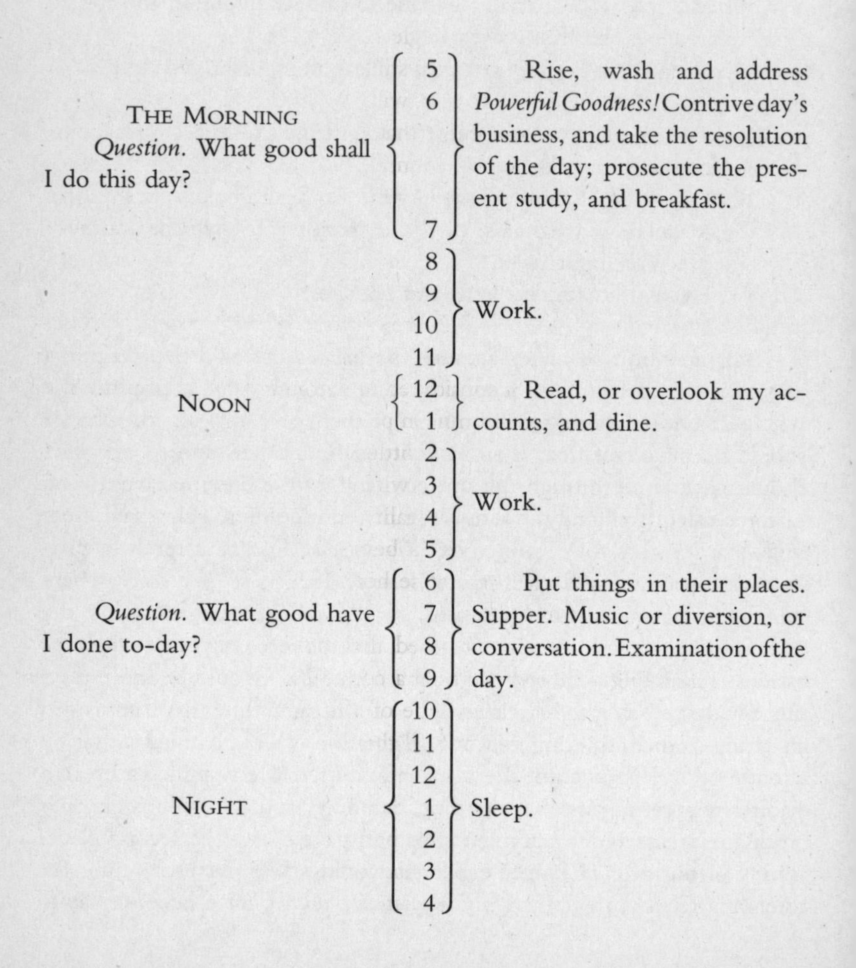

	Hours	
THE MORNING *Question.* What good shall I do this day?	5 6 7	Rise, wash and address *Powerful Goodness!* Contrive day's business, and take the resolution of the day; prosecute the present study, and breakfast.
	8 9 10 11	Work.
NOON	12 1	Read, or overlook my accounts, and dine.
	2 3 4 5	Work.
Question. What good have I done to-day?	6 7 8 9	Put things in their places. Supper. Music or diversion, or conversation. Examination of the day.
NIGHT	10 11 12 1 2 3 4	Sleep.

My list of virtues contained at first but twelve; but a Quaker friend having kindly informed me that I was generally thought proud; that my pride showed itself frequently in conversation; that I was not content with being in the right when discussing any point, but was overbearing, and rather insolent, of which he convinced me by mentioning several instances; I determined endeavoring to cure myself, if I could, of this vice or folly among the rest, and I added *Humility* to my list, giving an extensive meaning to the word.

I cannot boast of much success in acquiring the *reality* of this virtue, but I had a good deal with regard to the *appearance* of it. . . .

In reality, there is, perhaps, no one of our natural passions so hard to subdue as *pride*. Disguise it, struggle with it, beat it down, stifle it, mortify it as much as one pleases, it is still alive, and will every now and then peep out and show itself; you will see it, perhaps, often in the history; for, even if I could conceive that I had completely overcome it, I should probably be proud of my humility. . . .

In 1732 I first published my almanac, under the name of *Richard Saunders;* it was continued by me about twenty-five years, commonly called *Poor Richard's Almanack.* I endeavored to make it both entertaining and useful, and it accordingly came to be in such demand that I reaped considerable profit from it, vending annually near ten thousand. And observing that it was generally read, scarce any neighborhood in the province being without it, I considered it as a proper vehicle for conveying instruction among the common people, who bought scarcely any other books; I therefore filled all the little spaces that occurred between the remarkable days in the calendar with proverbial sentences, chiefly such as inculcated industry and frugality, as the means of procuring wealth, and thereby securing virtue; it being more difficult for a man in want, to act always honesty, as, to use here one of those proverbs, *it is hard for an empty sack to stand upright.*

These proverbs, which contained the wisdom of many ages and nations, I assembled and formed into a connected discourse prefixed to the Almanac of 1757, as the harangue of a wise old man to the people attending an auction. The bringing all these scattered counsels thus into a focus enabled them to make greater impression. The piece, being universally approved, was copied in all the newspapers of the continent; reprinted in Britain on a broadside, to be stuck up in houses; two translations were made of it in French, and great numbers bought by the clergy and gentry, to distribute gratis among their poor parishioners and tenants. In Pennsylvania, as it discouraged useless expense in foreign superfluities, some thought it had its share of influence in producing that growing plenty of money which was observable for several years after its publication.

• • •

COURTEOUS READER,

I have heard that nothing gives an Author so great Pleasure, as to find his Works respectfully quoted by other learned Authors. This Pleasure I have seldom enjoyed; for tho' I have been, if I may say it without Vanity, an *eminent Author* of Almanacks annually now a full Quarter of a Century, my Brother Authors in the same Way, for what Reason I know not, have ever been very sparing in their Applauses; and no other Author has taken the least Notice of me, so that did not my Writings produce me some *solid Pudding*, the great Deficiency of *Praise* would have quite discouraged me.

I concluded at length, that the People were the best Judges of my Merit; for they buy my Works; and besides, in my Rambles, where I am not personally known, I have frequently heard one or other of my Adages repeated, with, *as poor Richard says*, at the End on't; this gave me some Satisfaction, as it showed not only that my Instructions were regarded, but discovered likewise some Respect for my Authority; and I own, that to encourage the Practice of remembering and repeating those wise Sentences, I have sometimes *quoted* myself with great Gravity.

Judge then how much I must have been gratified by an Incident I am going to relate to you. I stopt my Horse lately where a great Number of People were collected at a Vendue of Merchant Goods. The Hour of Sale not being come, they were conversing on the Badness of the Times, and one of the Company call'd to a plain clean old Man, with white Locks, *Pray, Father* Abraham, *what think you of the Times? Won't these heavy Taxes quite ruin the Country? How shall we ever be able to pay them? What would you advise us to?*—Father *Abraham* stood up, and reply'd, If you'd have my Advice, I'll give it you in short, for a *Word to the Wise is enough*, and *many Words won't fill a Bushel*, as *Poor Richard* says. They join'd in desiring him to speak his Mind, and gathering round him, he proceeded as follows;

Friends, says he, and Neighbors, the Taxes are indeed very heavy, and if those laid on by the Government were the only Ones we had to pay, we might more easily discharge them; but we have many others, and much more grievous to some of us. We are taxed twice as much by our *Idleness*, three times as much by our *Pride*, and four times as much by our *Folly*, and from these Taxes the Commissioners cannot ease or deliver us by allowing an Abatement. However let us hearken to good Advice, and something may be done for us; *God helps them that help themselves*, as *Poor Richard* says, in his Almanack of 1733.

It would be thought a hard Government that should tax its People one tenth Part of their *Time*, to be employed in its Service. But *Idleness* taxes many of us much more, if we reckon all that is spent in absolute *Sloth*, or doing of nothing, with that which is spent in idle Employments or Amusements, that amount to nothing. *Sloth*, by bringing on Diseases, absolutely shortens Life. *Sloth, like Rust, consumes faster than Labor wears, while the used Key is always bright*, as *Poor Richard* says. But *dost thou love Life, then do not squander Time, for that's the Stuff Life is made of*, as *Poor Richard* says.—How much more than is necessary do we spend in Sleep! forgetting that *The sleeping Fox catches no Poultry*, and that *there will be sleeping enough in the Grave*, as *Poor Richard* says. If Time be of all Things the most precious, *wasting Time* must be, as *Poor Richard* says, *the greatest Prodigality*, since, as he elsewhere tells us, *Lost Time is never found again;* and what we call *Time-enough, always proves little enough:* Let us then up and be doing, and doing to the Purpose; so by Diligence shall we do more with less Perplexity. *Sloth makes all Things difficult, but Industry all easy*, as *Poor Richard* says; and *He that riseth late, must trot all Day, and shall scarce overtake his Business at Night*. While *Laziness travels so slowly, that Poverty soon overtakes him*, as we read in *Poor Richard*, who adds, *Drive thy Business, let not that drive thee;* and *Early to Bed, and early to rise, makes a Man healthy, wealthy and wise*.

So what signifies *wishing* and *hoping* for better Times. We may make these Times better if we bestir ourselves. *Industry need not wish*, as *Poor Richard* says, and *He that lives upon Hope will die fasting. There are no Gains, without Pains;* then *Help Hands, for I have no Lands*, or if I have, they are smartly taxed. And, as *Poor Richard* likewise observes, *He that hath a Trade hath an Estate*, and *He that hath a Calling, hath an Office of Profit and Honor;* but then the *Trade* must be worked at, and the *Calling* well followed, or neither the *Estate*, nor the *Office*, will enable us to pay our Taxes.—If we are industrious we shall never starve; for, as *Poor Richard* says, *At the working Man's House* Hunger *looks in, but dares not enter*. Nor will the Bailiff or the Constable enter, for *Industry pays Debts, while Despair encreaseth them*, says *Poor Richard*.—What though you have found no Treasure, nor has any rich Relation left you a Legacy, *Diligence is the Mother of Good luck*, as *Poor Richard* says, *and God gives all Things to Industry*. Then *plough deep, while Sluggards sleep, and you shall have Corn to sell and to keep*, says *Poor Dick*. Work while it is called To-day, for you know not how much you may be hindered To-morrow, which makes *Poor Richard* say, *One To-day is worth two To-morrows;* and farther, *Have you somewhat to do To-morrow, do it To-day*. If you were a Servant, would you not be ashamed that a good Master should catch you idle? Are you then your own Master, *be ashamed to catch yourself idle*, as *Poor Dick* says. When there is so much to be done for yourself, your Family, your Country, and your gracious King, be up by Peep of Day; *Let not the Sun look down and say, Inglorious here he lies*. Handle your Tools without Mittens; remember that *the Cat in Gloves catches no Mice*, as *Poor Richard* says. 'Tis true there is much to be done, and perhaps you are weak handed, but stick to it steadily, and you will see great Effects, for *constant Dropping wears away Stones*, and by *Diligence and Patience the Mouse ate in two the Cable;* and *little Strokes fell great Oaks*, as *Poor Richard* says in his Almanack, the Year I cannot just now remember.

Methinks I hear some of you say, *Must a Man afford himself no Leisure?*—I will tell thee, my Friend, what *Poor Richard* says *Employ thy Time well if thou meanest to gain Leisure;* and *since thou art not sure of a Minute, throw not away an Hour*. Leisure, is Time for doing something useful; this Leisure the diligent Man will obtain, but the lazy Man never; so that, as *Poor Richard* says, a *Life of Leisure and a Life of Laziness are two Things*. Do you imagine that Sloth will afford you more Comfort than Labor? No, for as *Poor Richard* says, *Trouble springs from Idleness, and grievous Toil from needless Ease. Many without Labor, would live by their* WITS *only, but they break for want of Stock*. Whereas Industry gives Comfort, and Plenty, and Respect: *Fly Pleasures, and they'll follow you. The diligent Spinner has a large Shift;* and *now I have a Sheep and a Cow, every Body bids me Good morrow;* all which is well said by *Poor Richard*.

OF LUXURY

DAVID HUME

In this essay, written in 1742, Hume captures the general Enlightenment celebration of commercial civilization, which he labels "refinement in the arts."

Another advantage of industry and of refinements in the mechanical arts is that they commonly produce some refinements in the liberal [arts]; nor can one be carried to perfection without being accompanied, in some degree, with the other. The same age which produces great philosophers and politicians, renowned generals and poets, usually abounds with skillful weavers and ship carpenters. We cannot reasonably expect that a piece of woolen cloth will be wrought to perfection in a nation which is ignorant of astronomy or where ethics are neglected. The spirit of the age affects all the arts, and the minds of men being once roused from their lethargy and put into a fermentation turn themselves on all sides and carry improvements into every art and science. Profound ignorance is totally banished, and men enjoy the privilege of rational creatures to think as well as to act, to cultivate the pleasures of the mind as well as those of the body.

The more these refined arts advance, the more sociable men become; nor is it possible that, when enriched with science and possessed of a fund of conversation, they should be contented to remain in solitude or live with their fellow citizens in that distant manner which is peculiar to ignorant and barbarous nations. They flock into cities; love to receive and communicate knowledge, to show their wit or their breeding, their taste in conversation or living, in clothes or furniture. Curiosity allures the wise, vanity the foolish, and pleasure both. Particular clubs and societies are everywhere formed; both sexes meet in an easy and sociable manner; and the tempers of men, as well as their behavior, refine apace. So that, beside the improvements which they receive from knowledge and the liberal arts, it is impossible but they must feel an increase of humanity from the very habit of conversing together and contributing to each other's pleasure and entertainment. Thus *industry, knowledge,* and *humanity* are linked together by an indissoluble chain, and are found, from experience as well as reason, to be peculiar to the more polished and what are commonly denominated the more luxurious ages.

Nor are these advantages attended with disadvantages that bear any proportion to them. The more men refine upon pleasure, the less will they indulge in excesses of any kind, because nothing is more destructive to true pleasure than such excesses. One may safely affirm that the Tartars are oftener guilty of beastly gluttony when they feast on their dead horses than European courtiers with all their refinement of cookery. And if libertine love, or even infidelity to the marriage bed, be more frequent in polite ages, when it is often regarded only as a piece of gallantry, drunkenness, on the other hand, is much less common—a vice more odious and more pernicious, both to mind and body. And in this matter I would appeal, not only to an Ovid or a Petronius, but to a Seneca or a Cato. We know that Caesar, during Catiline's conspiracy, being necessitated to put into Cato's hands a *billet-doux* which discovered an intrigue with Servilla, Cato's own sister, that stern philosopher threw it back to him with indignation and, in the bitterness of his wrath, gave him the appellation of drunkard, as a term more opprobrious than that with which he could more justly have reproached him.

But industry, knowledge, and humanity are not advantageous in private life alone; they diffuse their beneficial influence on the *public,* and render the government as great and flourishing as they make individuals happy and prosperous. The increase and consumption of all the commodities which serve to the ornament and pleasure of life are advantages to society, because at the same time that they multiply those innocent gratifications to individuals they are a kind of *storehouse* of labor, which, in the exigencies of state, may be turned to the public service. In a nation where there is no demand for such superfluities men sink into indolence, lose all enjoyment of life, and are useless to the public, which cannot maintain or support its fleets and armies from the industry of such slothful members.

The bounds of all the European kingdoms are at present nearly the same they were two hundred years ago. But what a difference is there in the power and grandeur of those kingdoms which can be ascribed to nothing but the increase of art and industry? When Charles VIII of France invaded Italy, he carried with him about 20,000 men; yet this armament so exhausted the nation, as we learn from Guicciardin, that for some years it was not able to make so great an effort. The late King of France, in time of war, kept in pay above 400,000 men, though from Mazarin's death to his own he was engaged in a course of wars that lasted near thirty years.

This industry is much promoted by the knowledge inseparable from ages of art and refinement; as, on the other hand, this knowledge enables the public to make the best advantage of the industry of its subjects. Laws, order, police, discipline—these can never be carried to any degree of perfection before human reason has refined itself by exercise and by an application to the more vulgar arts, at least of commerce and manufacture. Can we expect that a government will be well modeled by a people who know not how to make a spinning wheel or to employ a loom to advantage? Not to mention that all ignorant ages are infested with superstition, which throws the government off its bias and disturbs men in the pursuit of their interest and happiness. Knowledge in the arts of government begets mildness and moderation by instructing men in the advantages of human maxims above rigor and severity, which drive subjects into rebellion and make the return to submission impracticable, by cutting off all hopes of pardon. When the tempers of men are softened, as well as their knowledge improved, this humanity appears still more conspicuous and is the chief characteristic which distinguishes a civilized age from times of barbarity and ignorance. Factions are then less inveterate, revolutions less tragical, authority less severe, and seditions less frequent. Even foreign wars abate of their cruelty; and after the field of battle, where honor and interest steel men against compassion as well as fear, the combatants divest themselves of the brute and resume the man.

Nor need we fear that men, by losing their ferocity, will lose their martial spirit or become less undaunted and vigorous in defense of their country or their liberty. The arts have no such effect in enervating either the mind or body. On the contrary, industry, their inseparable attendant, adds new force to both. And if anger, which is said to be the whetstone of courage, loses somewhat of its asperity by politeness and refinement, a sense of honor, which is a stronger, more constant, and more governable principle, acquires fresh vigor by that elevation of genius which arises from knowledge and a good education. Add to this that courage can neither have any duration nor be of any use when not accompanied with discipline and martial skill, which are seldom found among a barbarous people. The ancients remarked that Datames was the only barbarian that ever knew the art of war. And Pyrrhus, seeing the Romans marshal their army with some art and skill, said with surprise, "These barbarians have nothing barbarous in their discipline!" It is observable that as the old Romans, by applying themselves solely to war, were almost the only uncivilized people that ever possessed military discipline, so the modern Italians are the only civilized people, among Europeans, that ever wanted courage and a martial spirit. Those who would ascribe this effeminacy of the Italians to their luxury or politeness or application to the arts need but consider the French and English, whose bravery is as incontestable as their love for the arts and their assiduity in commerce. The Italian historians give us a more satisfactory reason for the degeneracy of their countrymen. They show us how the sword was dropped at once by all the Italian sovereigns; while the Venetian aristocracy was jealous of its subjects, the Florentine democracy applied itself entirely to commerce; Rome was governed by priests, and Naples by women. War then became the business of soldiers of fortune, who spared one another and, to the astonishment of the world, could engage a whole day in what they called a battle and return at night to their camp without the least bloodshed.

What has chiefly induced severe moralists to declaim against refinement in the arts is the example of ancient Rome, which, joining to its poverty and rusticity virtue and public spirit, rose to such a surprising height of grandeur and liberty; but having learned from its conquered provinces the Asiatic luxury fell into every kind of corruption, whence arose sedition and civil wars, attended at last with the total loss of liberty. All the Latin classics, whom we peruse in our infancy, are full of these sentiments and universally ascribe the ruin of their state to the arts and riches imported from the East, insomuch that Sallust represents a taste for painting as a vice no less than lewdness and drinking. And so popular were these sentiments during the latter ages of the republic that this author abounds in praises of the old rigid Roman virtue, though himself the most egregious instance of modern luxury and corruption; speaks contemptuously of the Grecian eloquence, though the most elegant writer in the world; nay, employs preposterous digressions and declamations to this purpose, though a model of taste and correctness.

But it would be easy to prove that these writers mistook the cause of the disorders in the Roman state and ascribed to luxury and the arts what really proceeded from an ill-modeled government and the unlimited extent of conquests. Refinement on the pleasures and conveniences of life has no natural tendency to beget venality and corruption. The value which all men put upon any particular pleasure depends on comparison and experience; nor is a porter less greedy of money which he spends on bacon and brandy than a courtier who purchases champagne and ortolans. Riches are valuable at all times and to all men because they always purchase pleasures such as men are accustomed to and desire; nor can anything restrain or regulate the love of money but a sense of honor and virtue, which, if it be not nearly equal at all times, will naturally abound most in ages of knowledge and refinement.

Of all European kingdoms Poland seems the most defective in the arts of war as well as peace, mechanical as well as liberal; yet it is there that venality and corruption do most prevail. The nobles seem to have preserved their crown elective for no other purpose than regularly to sell it to the highest bidder. This is almost the only species of commerce with which that people are acquainted.

The liberties of England, so far from decaying since the improvements in the arts, have never flourished so much as during that period. And though corruption may seem to increase of late years, this is chiefly to be ascribed to our established liberty, when our princes have found the impossibility of governing without parliaments or of terrifying parliaments by the phantom of prerogative. Not to mention that this corruption or venality prevails much more among the electors than the elected, and therefore cannot justly be ascribed to any refinements in luxury.

If we consider the matter in a proper light, we shall find that a progress in the arts is rather favorable to liberty and has a natural tendency to preserve, if not produce, a free government. In rude, unpolished nations, where the arts are neglected, all labor is bestowed on the cultivation of the ground, and the whole society is divided into two classes, proprietors of land and their vassals or tenants. The latter are necessarily dependent and fitted for slavery and subjection, especially where they possess no riches and are not valued for their knowledge in agriculture, as must always be the case where the arts are neglected. The former naturally erect themselves into petty tyrants and must either submit to an absolute master for the sake of peace and order; or, if they will preserve their independence like the ancient barons, they must fall into feuds and contests among themselves and throw the whole society into such confusion as is perhaps worse than the most despotic government. But where luxury nourishes commerce and industry, the peasants, by a proper cultivation of the land, become rich and independent; while the tradesmen and merchants acquire a share of the property and draw authority and consideration to that middling rank of men who are the best and firmest basis of public liberty. These submit not to slavery, like the peasants, from poverty and meanness of spirit; and having no hopes of tyrannizing over others, like the barons, they are not tempted for the sake of that gratification to submit to the tyranny of their sovereign. They covet equal laws, which may secure their property and preserve them from monarchical as well as aristocratical tyranny.

The lower house is the support of our popular government, and all the world acknowledges that it owed its chief influence and consideration to the increase of commerce, which threw such a balance of property into the hands of the Commons. How inconsistent, then, is it to blame so violently a refinement in the arts, and to represent it as the bane of liberty and public spirit!

THE PHYSIOCRATIC FORMULA

François Quesnay

The physician and economist Quesnay (1684–1774) was a leader of the physiocratic school, which before Smith preached the principles of economic laissez-faire: *free trade and governmental nonintervention in the marketplace. This selection is from his* General Rules for the Economic Government of an Agricultural Kingdom, *written in 1758.*

1. Sovereign authority should be exercised by one; it should be superior to all members of society and above the unjust aspirations of private interests, for the object of rulership and of obedience is the security and the protection of the legitimate interests of all. The principle of the separation of power through a system of checks and balances is a sinister idea which can only lead to discord among the great and to the op-

pression of the small. The division of society into different groups of citizens in such a way that one group exercises sovereign authority over the others is in opposition to the national interest, and tends to give rise to conflicts between the private interests of different classes of citizens: such division would invert the system of government of an agricultural kingdom which has to unite all interests in a supreme end—namely, the prosperity of agriculture, which is the source of all wealth of the nation as well as that of all citizens.

II. The nation should be instructed in the general laws of the natural order, which for obvious reasons constitutes the most perfect order. The study of human jurisprudence is not at all sufficient to produce capable statesmen; those who devote themselves to public administration must be instructed also in the principles of the natural order, which is most advantageous to men organized in society. Moreover, it is necessary that the sum total of the practical and enlightened knowledge which the nation acquires through experience and reflection be added to the general science of government, so that sovereign authority, always guided by evidence, may decree the best possible laws and see to it that they are observed in the interest of the security of all and in order to achieve the greatest possible prosperity of society.

III. Let the sovereign and the nation never forget that the land is the only source of wealth and that it is agriculture which multiplies it. For the increase of wealth assures the increase of population. Men and wealth make agriculture prosperous, expand trade, stimulate industry, and increase and perpetuate riches. Upon this rich source depends the success of all parts of the administration of the kingdom.

IV. The property rights in land and personal wealth should be guaranteed to their legitimate owners; for the safety of property is the real basis of the economic order of society. Without this safety of property, the land would remain uncultivated. There would be neither proprietors nor peasants to make the necessary investments required in agriculture if they had not the guarantee that their land and the products thereof belonged to them. It is this feeling of security and the guarantee of permanent ownership which gives people the incentive to work and to employ their wealth in the improvement and cultivation of the land as well as in trade and industry. Only the sovereign power is capable of guaranteeing the safety of property of the subjects who have an original right (*droit primitif*) to the division of the fruits of the land, which is the sole source of wealth.

V. Taxes should not be destructive or out of proportion to the sum total of the national revenue. Any increase of taxes should be dependent upon the increase of this revenue. Moreover, taxes should be levied directly and without delay on the net product of land and not on wages or on the price of foodstuffs, in which case they would not only be expensive to administer but would also be detrimental to trade and would destroy annually part of the national revenues. Nor should taxes be levied on the cultivators of the soil, for the advances in agriculture should be considered as a capital fund which must be preserved in the most careful manner in order to provide the money required for the government as well as the income and the subsistence for all classes of citizens: otherwise, taxes degenerate into a system of spoliation causing a general decline which must promptly ruin the state.

VI. The advances of the cultivators of the soil must be adequate to make possible, with the aid of annual expenses, the greatest possible product; for if the advances are not adequate, annual expenditures will increase in proportion and will yield a smaller net product.

VII. The entire annual revenue ought to find its way back into the circulation of wealth and should pass through this process to the fullest extent; there should not be created pecuniary fortunes, or at least the magnitude of such fortunes should not exceed the amount of pecuniary fortunes re-entering into circulation. For, otherwise these fortunes are bound to interfere with the distribution of one part of the annual national revenue; the owners of these fortunes would intercept for their own use part of the national capital—thereby interfering with the return into circulation of the advances in agriculture, the wages of artisans, and the expenses on consumption which have to be made by the various classes of persons engaged in remunerative professions. This interception of national capital would have the effect of diminishing the reproduction of the national revenue and of the fund available for taxes.

VIII. The economic government should concern itself only with the encouragement of productive outlays and trade in raw produce, and should not intervene at all in matters pertaining to the sterile expenditures.

IX. A nation with a substantial area of agricultural land and capable of carrying on an extensive trade in raw produce should not encourage too much the use of money and the employment of men in the manufacturing and trade of luxuries at the expense of work and outlays in agriculture. For, above all, the kingdom ought to be well populated with well-to-do cultivators of the soil.

X. Never should a part of the annual revenue leave the country without compensation in money or in merchandise.

XI. Emigration of inhabitants who take their wealth with them should be avoided.

XII. The children of rich, independent peasants should stay in the rural areas in order to perpetuate the labor force. For if some discontent causes them to leave rural areas and to move to the cities, they will carry with them the riches of their fathers which were used in the cultivation of the soil. It is not so much human beings but riches which ought to be attracted into the rural areas; for the greater the amount of capital employed in the cultivation of the soil, the fewer the number of men required in agriculture and the greater its prosperity and its revenue. This is true, for example, with reference to the large-scale and efficient production of grain (*grande culture*) by well-to-do peasant farmers, in contrast to the small-scale production (*petite culture*) of poor and dependent peasants (*metayers*) who work with oxen or cows.

XIII. Everybody ought to be free to raise on his land such products as his interests, his abilities, and the nature of the soil seem to suggest as the most profitable crops. Monopoly should not be encouraged in agriculture, since it is likely to reduce the net social revenue. The prejudice which tends to promote an abundance of necessities in preference to other products and to the detriment of the price of both is based upon a short-run point of view which fails to take into account the effects of foreign trade . . . which determines the price of the foodstuffs that each nation is able to raise with the greatest advantage. Apart from the funds designed for the cultivation of the soil, it is primarily the revenue and the tax fund which are riches of the greatest importance, in view of the fact that they permit the protection of the subjects against famine and foreign enemies, as well as the maintenance of the glory and the power of the monarch and the prosperity of the nation.

XIV. The increase of livestock should be encouraged, for it is these animals which provide the manure which renders possible rich harvests.

XV. The lands used for the production of grains should be combined, as far as possible, into large holdings administered by well-to-do farmers; for costs of maintenance and repair of structures are smaller in the case of large farm enterprises, which operate with proportionately lower costs and yield a much higher net product than small farms. The existence of a great number of small peasants is not in harmony with the national interest. The most independent part of the population, which is also most easily available for the various occupations and the different kinds of work which separate men into different classes, is the part maintained by the net product. Each economically worth-while measure of economy in the performance of work which can be carried out with the aid of animals, machines, water power, etc., is advantageous for the nation and the state, because a greater net product secures a higher income available for other services and other works.

XVI. International trade in raw produce should not be prohibited, for the rate of reproduction is determined by the extent of the market.

XVII. It is important to create outlets for, and to facilitate the shipment of, agricultural and manufactured products by keeping roads in good condition and by improving ocean shipping and navigation on inland waterways. For the greater the reduction of the costs of trade, the greater the addition to the national revenue.

XVIII. The price of foodstuffs and finished articles in the kingdom should not be reduced; for the mutual exchange of commodities with foreign countries becomes disadvantageous for a nation under these circumstances. Upon the price depends the return. Abundance with cheapness is not wealth; scarcity and dearness are misery; abundance and dearness are opulence.

XIX. It should not be assumed that cheapness of foodstuffs is beneficial for the common people. The low price of foodstuffs tends to reduce the wages of the common men, lowers their standard of living, leaves them with fewer work and employment opportunities, and diminishes the national revenue.

XX. The standard of living of the poorer classes of citizens should not be lowered, for these classes would then be unable to contribute their share to the consumption of consumers' goods which can be consumed only within the country. Such a reduction of consumption would have the effect of curtailing the reproduction of wealth, and thus lower the national revenue.

XXI. The proprietors and members of the professional groups should not engage in hoarding (*épargnes stériles*), which would have the effect of withdrawing from circulation and distribution part of their revenues or gains.

XXII. Luxury of a purely decorative kind (*luxe de décoration*) should under no circumstances be encouraged at the expense of outlays which might otherwise be devoted to agriculture, to its improvement, or to the consumption of essential commodities. Such expenditures tend to maintain the low price and sale abroad of raw produce and guarantee the reproduction of national wealth.

XXIII. The nation should not suffer any loss in its reciprocal foreign trade even if such trade were profitable for merchants who would gain by the sale of goods abroad at the expense of their compatriots. For the increase of the fortunes of these merchants would cause a contraction in the circulation of wealth, which would have negative effects on the process of distribution and the reproduction of the national revenue.

XXIV. One should not be deceived by an apparent advantage resulting from international trade by simply taking into account the balance of monetary payments without considering the greater or smaller profit yielded by the goods sold and bought. For frequently the nation which receives a surplus of money is the loser, and this loss affects negatively the distribution and reproduction of national revenue.

XXV. Complete liberty of trade should be maintained. For complete freedom of competition is the safest, the most exacting, and, from the point of view of the nation and the state, the most profitable method of control of domestic and external trade.

XXVI. It is less important to increase population than to increase revenue. For a higher standard of living rendered possible by greater revenue is to be preferred to an urgent need of necessities which would result from an excess of population over revenues; moreover, a higher standard of living makes available more funds for the requirements of the state as well as additional means to make agriculture prosper.

XXVII. The government should be less concerned with economies than with measures necessary for the prosperity of the kingdom. For very great expenditures may cease to be excessive if they lead to an increase of wealth. However, simple expenditures must not be confused with abuses. For abuses could completely absorb the wealth of the nation as well as that of the sovereign.

XXVIII. The administration of government finances either with respect to public revenues or public expenditures should not give rise to pecuniary fortunes which withdraw one part of the revenues from circulation, distribution, and reproduction.

XXIX. The means required to finance extraordinary public expenditures should be obtained from funds available in times of prosperity and should not be borrowed from financiers. For financial fortunes are secret wealth which knows neither king nor fatherland.

XXX. The state should avoid loans giving rise to financial incomes (*rentes financières*); such loans burden the state with debts which are not only all-consuming, but also, through the intermediary of negotiable papers, give rise to financial transactions where discounts add more and more to sterile pecuniary fortunes. These fortunes tend to separate finance from agriculture and deprive the rural areas of funds required for the improvement and cultivation of the land.

ECONOMIC LIBERTY

Anne-Robert-Jacques Turgot

The philosophe *Turgot was also a physiocratic exponent of* laissez-faire. *This selection is from a letter of 1773 to the Abbe Terray about "protection to native manufacturers."*

I have the honor to report to you on the state of the ironworks and manufactures in the Generality of Limoges. . . .

As to the observations you seem to desire on the means of giving more activity to this branch of industry (or of restoring to it what it is said to have lost), I have few to offer. I know of no means of stimulating any trade or industry whatever but that of giving to it the greatest liberty, and of freeing it from all those burdens which the ill-understood interest of the revenue has multiplied to excess upon all kinds of merchandise, and particularly upon the manufactures in iron.

I must not conceal from you that one of the chief causes of the delay in my responding to your inquiries has been the rumor spread that they had for their object the establishment of new burdens or the extension of old ones. The opinion, founded on too much experience, that the investigations of Government have for their sole object the finding of means to extract more money from the people, has given rise to a general mistrust, and the most of those to whom inquiries have been addressed either have not replied, or have sought to mislead the Government by replies sometimes incomplete, sometimes false. I cannot believe that your intention is to impose new charges upon a commerce which, on the contrary, you announce your desire to favor. If I thought so, I confess I should congratulate myself on the involuntary delay in my furnishing you with the information you have requested, and I should regret my not being able to prolong the delay still further.

If, after complete liberty has been obtained by the relief from all taxes on the fabrication, the transport, the sale, and the consumption of commodities, there remains to the Government any means of favoring a branch of trade, that can only be by the means of instruction; that is to say, by encouraging those researches of scientific men and artists which tend to perfect art, and, above all, by extending the knowledge of practical processes which it is the interest of cupidity to keep as so many secrets. It would be advisable for the Government to incur some expense by sending young men to foreign countries in order to instruct themselves in processes of manufacture unknown in France, and for the Government to publish the result of these researches. These means are good; but liberty of movement and freedom from taxes are much more efficacious and much more necessary.

You appear, in the letters with which you have honored me on this subject, to believe that certain obstacles which might be placed to the import of foreign irons would act as an encouragement to our national trade. You intimate even that you have received from different provinces several representations to the effect that the demand which these foreign irons obtain acts to the prejudice of commerce in manufacture of the native iron. I believe, indeed, that iron-masters, who think only of their own iron, imagine that they would gain more if they had fewer competitors. It is not the merchant only who wishes to be the sole seller of his commodity. There is no department in commerce in which those who exercise it do not seek to escape from competition, and who do not find sophisms to make the State believe that it is interested, at least, to exclude the rivalry of foreigners, whom they easily represent to be the enemies of national commerce. If we listen to them, and we have listened to them too often, all branches of commerce would be infected by this spirit of monopoly. These foolish men do not see that this same monopoly is not, as they would have it believed, to the advantage of the State, against foreigners, but is directed against their own fellow-subjects, consumers of the commodity, and is retaliated upon themselves by these fellow-subjects—sellers in their turn—in all the other branches of trade. They do not see that all associations of men engaged in a particular trade need only to arm themselves with the same pretexts in order to obtain from the misled Government the same exclusion of foreigners; they do not see that in this balancing of vexation and injustice between all kinds of industry, in which the artisans and the merchants of each kind oppress as sellers, and are oppressed as buyers, there is no advantage to any party; but that there is a real loss on the total of the national commerce, or rather a loss to the State, which, buying less from the foreigner, must consequently sell him less. This forced increase of price for all buyers necessarily diminishes the sum of enjoyments, the sum of disposable revenues, the wealth of the proprietors and of the sovereign, and the sum of the wages to be distributed among the people.

Again, this loss is doubled, because in this war of reciprocal oppression, in which the Government lends its strength to all against all, the only one left outside excepted is the small cultivator of the soil, whom all oppress in concert by their monopolies, and who, far from being able to oppress anyone, cannot even enjoy the natural right to sell his commodity, either to foreigners or to those of his fellow-subjects who would buy it; so that he remains the only one who suffers from monopoly as buyer, and at the same time as seller. There is only he who cannot buy freely from foreigners the things of which he has need; there is only he who cannot sell to foreigners the commodity he produces, while the cloth-merchant or any other buys as much wheat as he wants from the foreigner and sells to him as much as he can of his cloth.

Whatever sophisms the self-interests of some commercial classes may heap up, the truth is that *all* branches of commerce ought to be free, equally free, *entirely* free; that the system of some modern politicians who imagine they favor national commerce by prohibiting the import of foreign merchandise is a pure illusion; that this system results only in rendering all branches of commerce enemies one to another, in nourishing among nations a germ of hatred and of wars, even the most feeble effects of which are a thousand times more costly to the people, more destructive of its wealth, of population and of happiness, than all those paltry mercantile profits imaginable *to individuals* can be advantageous to their nations. The truth is, that in wishing to hurt others we hurt only ourselves, not only because the reprisal for these prohibitions is so easy that other nations do not fail in their turn to make it, but still more because we deprive our own nation of the incalculable advantages of a free commerce—advantages such, that if a great state like France would but make experience of them, the rapid advancement of her commerce would soon compel other nations to imitate her in order not to be impoverished by the loss of their own.

THE WEALTH OF NATIONS

Adam Smith

Smith's Wealth of Nations *(1776) is the* classicus locus *for liberal economics. Individual self-interest, not the "benevolence of the butcher, the brewer, or the baker," is the energy that drives market society. Smith's brilliant analysis of human nature in a commercial age emphasizes "ambition," the "desire of bettering our condition," which "comes with us from the womb, and never leaves us till we go into the grave." These selections from* Wealth of Nations, *including the famous "invisible hand" passage, is followed by a particularly insightful discussion of ambition from Smith's* Theory of Moral Sentiments *(1759).*

To take an example, therefore, from a very trifling manufacture, but one in which the division of labor has been very often taken notice of, the trade of the pinmaker; a workman not educated to this business (which the division of labor has rendered a distinct trade), nor acquainted with the use of the machinery employed in it (to the invention of which the same division of labor has probably given occasion), could scarce, perhaps, with his utmost industry, make one pin in a day, and certainly could not make twenty. But in the way in which this business is now carried on, not only the whole work is a peculiar trade, but it is divided into a number of branches, of which the greater part are likewise peculiar trades. One man draws out the wire, another straights it, a third cuts it, a fourth points it, a fifth grinds it at the top for receiving the head; to make the head requires two or three distinct operations; to put it on is a peculiar business, to whiten the pins is another; it is even a trade by itself to put them into the paper; and the important business of making a pin is, in this manner, divided into about eighteen distinct operations, which in some manufactories are all performed by distinct hands, though in others the same man will sometimes perform two or three of them. I have seen a small manufactory of this kind where ten men only were employed, and where some of them consequently performed two or three distinct operations. But though they were very poor, and therefore but indifferently accommodated with the necessary machinery, they could when they exerted themselves make among them about twelve pounds of pins in a day. There are in a pound upwards of four thousand pins of a middling size. Those ten persons, therefore, could make among them upwards of forty-eight thousand pins in a day. Each person, therefore, making a tenth part of forty-eight thousand pins, might be considered as making four thousand eight hundred pins in a day. But if they had all wrought separately and independently, and without any of them having been educated to this peculiar business, they certainly could not each of them have made twenty, perhaps not one in a day; that is, certainly, not the two hundred and fortieth, perhaps not the four thousand eight hundredth part of what they are at present capable of performing, in consequence of a proper division and combination of their different operations. . . .

This division of labor, from which so many advantages are derived, is not originally the effect of any human wisdom, which foresees and intends that general opulence to which it gives occasion. It is the necessary, though very slow and gradual, consequence of a certain propensity in human nature which has in view no such extensive utility; the propensity to truck, barter, and exchange one thing for another.

Whether this propensity be one of those original principles in human nature, of which no further account can be given; or whether, as seems more probable, it be the necessary consequence of the faculties of reason and speech, it belongs not to our present subject to enquire. It is common to all men, and to be found in no other race of animals, which seem to know neither this nor any other species of contracts. Two greyhounds, in running down the same hare, have sometimes the appearance of acting in some sort of concert. Each turns her towards his companion, or endeavors to intercept her when his companion turns her towards himself. This, however, is not the effect of any contract, but of the accidental concurrence of their passions in the same object at that particular time. Nobody ever saw a dog make a fair and deliberate exchange of one bone for another with another dog. Nobody ever saw one animal by its gestures and natural cries signify to another, this is mine, that yours; I am willing to give this for that. When an animal wants to obtain something either of a man or of another animal, it has no other means of persuasion but to gain the favor of those whose service it requires. A puppy fawns upon its dam, and a spaniel endeavors by a thousand attractions to engage the attention of its master who is at dinner, when it wants to be fed by him. Man sometimes uses the same arts with his brethren, and when he has no other means of engaging them to act according to his inclinations, endeavors by every servile and fawning attention to obtain their good will. He has not time, however, to do this upon every occasion. In civilized society he stands at all times in need of the co-operation and assistance of great multitudes, while his whole life is scarce sufficient to gain the friendship of a few persons. In almost every other race of animals each individual, when it is grown up to maturity, is entirely independent, and in its natural state has occasion for the assistance of no other living creature. But man has almost constant occasion for the help of his brethren, and it is in vain for him to expect it from their benevolence only. He will be more likely to prevail if he can interest their self-love in his favor, and shew them that it is for their own advantage to do for him what he requires of them. Whoever offers to another a bargain of any kind, proposes to do this. Give me that which I want, and you shall have this which you want, is the meaning of every such offer; and it is in this manner that we obtain from one another the far greater part of those good offices which we stand in need of. It is not from the benevolence of the butcher, the brewer, or the baker, that we expect our dinner, but from their regard to their own interest. We address ourselves, not to their humanity but to their self-love, and never talk to them of our own necessities but of their advantages. Nobody but beggar chooses to depend chiefly upon the benevolence of his fellow citizens. Even a beggar does not depend upon it entirely. The charity of well-disposed people, indeed, supplies him with the whole fund of his subsistence. But though this principle ultimately provides him with all the necessaries of life which he has occasion for, neither does nor can provide him with them as he has occasion for them. The greater part of his occasional wants are supplied in the same manner as those of other people, by treaty, by barter, and purchase. With the money which one man gives him he purchased food. The old clothes which another bestows upon him he exchanged for other old clothes which suit him better, or for lodging, or for food or for money, with which he can buy either food, clothes, or lodging as he has occasion. . . .

Capitals are increased by parsimony, and diminished by prodigality and misconduct.

Whatever a person saves from his revenue he adds to his capital, and either employs it himself in maintaining an additional number of productive hands, or enables some other person to do so, by lending it to him for an interest, that is, for a share of the profits. As the capital of an individual can be increased only by what he saves from his annual revenue or his annual gains, so the capital of a society, which is the same with that of all the individuals who compose it, can be increased only in the same manner.

Parsimony, and not industry, is the immediate cause of the increase of capital. Industry, indeed, provides the subject which parsimony accumulates. But whatever industry might acquire, if parsimony did not save and store up, the capital would never be the greater. . . .

Whatever, therefore, we may imagine the real wealth and revenue of a country to consist in, whether in the value of the annual produce of its land and labor, as plain reason seems to dictate; or in the quantity of the precious metals which circulate within it, as vulgar prejudices suppose; in either view of the matter, every prodigal appears to be a public enemy, and every frugal man a public benefactor.

The effects of misconduct are often the same as those of prodigality. Every injudicious and unsuccessful project in agriculture, mines, fisheries, trade, or manufactures, tends in the same manner to diminish the funds destined for the maintenance of productive labor. In every such project, though the capital is consumed by productive hands only, yet, as by the injudicious manner in which they are employed, they do not reproduce the full value of their consumption, there must always be some diminution in what would otherwise have been the productive funds of the society.

It can seldom happen, indeed, that the circumstances of a great nation can be much affected either by the prodigality or misconduct of individuals; the profusion or imprudence of some, being always more than compensated by the frugality and good conduct of others.

With regard to profusion, the principle which prompts to expense, is the passion for present enjoyment; which, though sometimes violent and very difficult to be restrained, is in general only momentary and occasional. But the principle which prompts to save, is the desire of bettering our condition, a desire which, though generally calm and dispassionate, comes with us from the womb, and never leaves us till we go into the grave. In the whole interval which separates those two moments, there is scarce perhaps a single instant in which any man is so perfectly and completely satisfied with his situation, as to be without any wish of alteration or improvement of any kind. An augmentation of fortune is the means by which the greater part of men propose and wish to better their condition. It is the means the most vulgar and the most obvious; and the most likely way of augmenting their fortune, is to save and accumulate some part of what they acquire, either regularly and annually, or upon some extraordinary occasions. Though the principle of expense, therefore, prevails in almost all men upon some occasions, and in some men upon almost all occasions, yet in the greater part of men, taking the whole course of their life at an average, the principle of frugality seems not only to predominate, but to predominate very greatly. . . .

Every individual who employs his capital in the support of domestic industry, necessarily endeavors so to direct that industry, that its produce may be of the greatest possible value.

The produce of industry is what it adds to the subject or materials upon which it is employed. In proportion as the value of this produce is great or small, so will likewise be the profits of the employer. But it is only for the sake of profit that any man employs a capital in the support of industry; and he will always, therefore, endeavor to employ it in the support of that industry of which the produce is likely to be of the greatest value, or to exchange for the greatest quantity either of money or of other goods.

But the annual revenue of every society is always precisely equal to the exchangeable value of the whole annual produce of its industry, or rather is precisely the same thing with that exchangeable value. As every individual, therefore, endeavors as much as he can both to employ his capital in the support of domestic industry, and so to direct that industry that its produce may be of the greatest value; every individual necessarily labors to render the annual revenue of the society as great as he can. He generally, indeed, neither intends to promote the public interest, nor knows how much he is promoting it. By preferring the support of domestic to that of foreign industry, he intends only his own security; and by directing that industry in such a manner as its produce may be of the greatest value, he intends only his own gain, and he is in this, as in many other cases, led by an invisible hand to promote an end which was no part of his intention. Nor is it always the worse for the society that it was no part of it. By pursuing his own interest he frequently promotes that of the society more effectually than when he really intends to promote it. I have never known much good done by those who affected to trade for the public good. It is an affectation, indeed, not very common among merchants, and very few words need be employed in dissuading them from it.

What is the species of domestic industry which his capital can employ, and of which the produce is likely to be of the greatest value, every individual, it is evident, can, in his local situation, judge much better than any statesman or lawgiver can do for him. The statesman, who should attempt to direct private people in what manner they ought to employ their capitals, would not only load himself with a most unnecessary attention, but assume an authority which could safely be trusted, not only to no single person, but to no council or senate whatever, and which would no-where be so dangerous as in the hands of a man who had folly and presumption enough to fancy himself fit to exercise it. . . .

That system of laws, therefore, which is connected with the establishment of the bounty, seems to deserve no part of the praise which has been bestowed upon it. The improvement and prosperity of Great Britain, which has been so often ascribed to those laws, may very easily be accounted for by other causes. That security which the laws in Great Britain give to every man that he shall enjoy the fruits of his own labor, is alone sufficient to make any country flourish, notwithstanding these and twenty other absurd regulations of commerce; and this security was perfected by the revolution, much about the same time that the bounty was established. The natural effort of every individual to better his own condition, when suffered to exert itself with freedom and security, is so powerful a principle, that it is alone, and without any assistance, not only capable of carrying on the society to wealth and prosperity, but of surmounting a hundred impertinent obstructions with which the folly of human laws too often encumbers its operations; though the effect of these obstructions is always more or less either to encroach upon its freedom, or to diminish its security. In Great Britain industry is perfectly secure; and though it is far from being perfectly free, it is as free or freer than in any other part of Europe. . . .

It is thus that the private interests and passions of individuals naturally dispose them to turn their stock towards the employments which in ordinary cases are most advantageous to the society. But if from this natural preference they should turn too much of it towards those employments, the fall of profit in them and the rise of it in all others immediately dispose them to alter this faulty distribution. Without any intervention of law, therefore, the private interests and passions of men naturally lead them to divide and distribute the stock of every society, among all the different employments carried on in it, as nearly as possible in the proportion which is most agreeable to the interest of the whole society.

All the different regulations of the mercantile system, necessarily derange more or less this natural and most advantageous distribution of stock. But those which concern the trade to America and the East Indies derange it perhaps more than any other; because the trade to those two great continents absorbs a greater quantity of stock than any two other branches of trade. The regulations, however, by which this derangement is effected in those two different branches of trade are not altogether the same. Monopoly is the great engine of both; but it is a different sort of monopoly. Monopoly of one kind or another, indeed, seems to be the sole engine of the mercantile system. . . .

It is thus that every system which endeavors, either, by extraordinary encouragements, to draw towards a particular species of industry a greater share of the capital of the society than what would naturally go to it; or, by extraordinary restraints, to force from a particular species of industry some share of the capital which would otherwise be employed in it; is in reality subversive of the great purpose which it means to promote. It retards, instead of accelerating, the progress of the society towards real wealth and greatness; and diminishes, instead of increasing, the real value of the annual produce of its land and labor.

All systems either of preference or of restraint, therefore, being thus completely taken away, the obvious and simple system of natural liberty establishes itself of its own accord. Every man, as long as he does not violate the laws of justice, is left perfectly free to pursue his own interest his own way, and to bring both his industry and capital into competition with those of any other man, or order of men. The sovereign is completely discharged from a duty, in the attempting to perform which he must always be exposed to innumerable delusions, and for the proper performance of which no human wisdom or knowledge could ever be sufficient; the duty of superintending the industry of private people, and of directing it towards the employments most suitable to the interest of the society. According to the system of natural liberty, the sovereign has only three duties to attend to; three duties of great importance, indeed, but plain and intelligible to common understandings: first, the duty of protecting the society from the violence and invasion of other independent societies; secondly, the duty of protecting, as far as possible, every member of the society from the injustice or oppression of every other member of it, or the duty of establishing an exact administration of justice; and, thirdly, the duty of erecting and maintaining certain public works and certain public institutions, which it can never be for the interest of any individual, or small number of individuals, to erect and maintain; because the profit could never repay the expense to any individual or small number of individuals, though it may frequently do much more than repay it to a great society.

• • •

It is because mankind are disposed to sympathize more entirely with our joy than with our sorrow that we make parade of our riches and conceal our poverty. Nothing is so mortifying as to be obliged to expose our distress to the view of the public and to feel that though our situation is open to the eyes of all mankind no mortal conceives for us the half of what we suffer. Nay, it is chiefly from this regard to the sentiments of mankind that we pursue riches and avoid poverty. For to what purpose is all the toil and bustle of this world? What is the end of avarice and ambition, of the pursuit of wealth, of power, and preeminence? Is it to supply the necessities of nature? The wages of the meanest laborer can supply them. We see that they afford him food and clothing, the comfort of a house, and of a family. If we examine his economy with rigor, we should find that he spends a great part of them upon conveniences, which may be regarded as superfluities, and that upon extraordinary occasions he can give something even to vanity and distinction. What then is the cause of our aversion to his situation, and why should those who have been educated in the higher ranks of life regard it as worse than death to be reduced to live, even without labor, upon the same simple fare with him, to dwell under the same lowly roof, and to be clothed in the same humble attire? Do they imagine that their stomach is better, or their sleep sounder, in a palace than in a cottage? The contrary has been so often observed and indeed is so very obvious, though it had never been observed, that there is nobody ignorant of it. From whence then arises that emulation which runs through all the different ranks of men and what are the advantages which we propose by that great purpose of human life which we call bettering our condition? To be observed, to be attended to, to be taken notice of with sympathy, complacency, and approbation, are all the advantages which we can propose to derive from it. It is the vanity, not the ease or the pleasure, which interests us. But vanity is always founded upon the belief of our being the object of attention and approbation. The rich man glories in his riches because he feels that they naturally draw upon him the attention of the world and that mankind are disposed to go along with him in all those agreeable emotions with which the advantages of his situation so readily inspire him. At the thought of this his heart seems to swell and dilate itself within him, and he is fonder of his wealth, upon this account, than for all the other advantages it procures him. The poor man, on the contrary, is ashamed of his poverty. He feels that it either places him out of the sight of mankind, or that if they take any notice of him they have, however, scarce any fellow-feeling with the misery and distress which he suffers. He is mortified upon both accounts; for though to be overlooked and to be disapproved of are things entirely different, yet as obscurity covers us from the daylight of honor and approbation, to feel that we are taken no notice of necessarily damps the most agreeable hope and disappoints the most ardent desire of human nature. The poor man goes out and comes in unheeded, and when in the midst of a crowd is in the same obscurity as if shut up in his own hovel. Those humble cares and painful attentions which occupy those in his situation afford no amusement to the dissipated and the gay. They turn away their eyes from him, or if the extremity of his distress forces them to look at him, it is only to spurn so disagreeable an object from among them. The fortunate and the proud wonder at the insolence of human wretchedness, that it should dare to present itself before them, and with the loathsome aspect of its misery presume to disturb the serenity of their happiness. The man of rank and distinction, on the contrary, is observed by all the world. Everybody is eager to look at him and to conceive, at least by sympathy, that joy and exultation with which his circumstances naturally inspire him. His actions are the objects of the public care. Scarce a word, scarce a gesture, can fall from him that is altogether neglected. In a great assembly he is the person upon whom all direct their eyes; it is upon him that their passions seem all to wait with expectation, in order to receive that movement and direction which he shall impress upon them; and if his behavior is not altogether absurd, he has every moment an opportunity of interesting mankind and of rendering himself the object of the observation and fellow-feeling of everybody about him. It is this, which, notwithstanding the restraint it imposes, notwithstanding the loss of liberty with which it is attended, renders greatness the object of envy, and compensates, in the opinion of mankind, all that toil, all that anxiety, all those mortifications, which must be undergone in the pursuit of it; and what is of yet more consequence, all that leisure, all that ease, that careless security, which are forfeited forever by the acquisition.

When we consider the condition of the great, in those delusive colors in which the imagination is apt to paint it, it seems to be almost the abstract idea of a perfect and happy state. It is the very state which, in all our waking dreams and idle reveries, we had sketched out to ourselves as the final object of all our desires. We feel, therefore, a peculiar sympathy with the satisfaction of those who are in it. We favor all their inclinations and forward all their wishes. What pity, we think, that any thing should spoil and corrupt so agreeable a situation! . . .

Upon this disposition of mankind to go along with all the passions of the rich and the powerful, is founded the distinction of ranks and the order of society. Our obsequiousness to our superiors more frequently arises from our admiration for the advantages of their situation than from any private expectations of benefit from their goodwill. . . .

"Love," says my Lord Rochefoucauld, "is commonly succeeded by ambition, but ambition is hardly ever succeeded by love." That passion, when once it has got entire possession of the breast, will admit neither a rival nor a successor. To those who have been accustomed to the possession, or even to the hope, of public admiration, all other pleasures sicken and decay. Of all the discarded statesmen who, for their own ease, have studied to get the better of ambition, and to despise those honors which they could no longer arrive at, how few have been able to succeed? The greater part have spent their time in the most listless and insipid indolence, chagrined at the thought of their own insignificancy, incapable of being interested in the occupations of private life, without enjoyment, except when they talked of their former greatness, and without satisfaction, except when they were employed in some vain project to recover it. Are you in earnest resolved never to barter your liberty for the lordly servitude of a court, but to live free, fearless, and independent? There seems to be one way to continue in that virtuous resolution; and perhaps but one. Never enter the place from whence so few have been able to return; never come within the circle of ambition; nor ever bring yourself into comparison with those masters of the earth who have already engrossed the attention of half mankind before you.

Of such mighty importance does it appear to be, in the imaginations of men, to stand in that situation which sets them most in the view of general sympathy and attention. And thus, place, that great object which divides the wives of aldermen, is the end of half the labors of human life; and is the cause of all the tumult and bustle, all the rapine and injustice, which avarice and ambition have introduced into this world.

People of sense, it is said, indeed despise place, that is, they despise sitting at the head of the table and are indifferent who it is that is pointed out to the company by that frivolous circumstance, which the smallest advantage is capable of overbalancing. But rank, distinction, pre-eminince, no man despises, unless he is either raised very much above, or sunk very much below, the ordinary standard of human nature; unless he is either so confirmed in wisdom and real philosophy as to be satisfied that, while the propriety of his conduct renders him the just object of approbation, it is of little consequence though he be neither attended to nor approved of; or so habituated to the idea of his own meanness, so sunk in slothful and sottish indifference, as entirely to have forgot the desire, and almost the very wish, for superiority.

CRIME AND PUNISHMENT

THE SEVERITY OF CRIMINAL LAWS

BARON DE MONTESQUIEU

In his Spirit of the Laws *(1748) Montesquieu, like so many of the* philosophes, *attacks the severity and inhumanity with which criminals were treated. He offers the principle that punishment fit the crime, "the particular nature of the crime."*

BOOK VI: CONSEQUENCES OF THE PRINCIPLES OF DIFFERENT GOVERNMENTS

12. . . . Mankind must not be governed with too much severity; we ought to make a prudent use of the means which nature has given us to conduct them. If we inquire into the cause of all human corruptions,

we shall find that they proceed from the impunity of criminals, and not from the moderation of punishments.

Let us follow nature, who has given shame to man for his scourge; and let the heaviest part of the punishment be the infamy attending it.

But if there be some countries where shame is not a consequence of punishment, this must be owing to tyranny, which has inflicted the same penalties on villains and honest men.

And if there are others where men are deterred only by cruel punishments, we may be sure that this must, in a great measure, arise from the violence of the government which has used such penalties for slight transgressions.

It often happens that a legislator, desirous of remedying an abuse, thinks of nothing else; his eyes are open only to this object, and shut to its inconveniences. When the abuse is redressed, you see only the severity of the legislator; yet there remains an evil in the state that has sprung from this severity; the minds of the people are corrupted, and become habituated to despotism. . . .

There are two sorts of corruptions—one when the people do not observe the laws; the other when they are corrupted by the laws: an incurable evil, because it is in the very remedy itself. . . .

17. The wickedness of mankind makes it necessary for the law to suppose them better than they really are. Hence the deposition of two witnesses is sufficient in the punishment of all crimes. The law believes them, as if they spoke by the mouth of truth. Thus we judge that every child conceived in wedlock is legitimate; the law having a confidence in the mother, as if she were chastity itself. But the use of the rack against criminals cannot be defended on a like plea of necessity.

We have before us the example of a nation blessed with an excellent civil government [England], where without any inconvenience the practice of racking criminals is rejected. It is not, therefore, in its own nature necessary.

So many men of learning and genius have written against the custom of torturing criminals, that after them I dare not presume to meddle with the subject. I was going to say that it might suit despotic states, where whatever inspires fear is the fittest spring of government. I was going to say that the slaves among the Greeks and Romans—but nature cries out aloud, and asserts her rights.

Book XII: Of the Laws that Establish Political Liberty, in Relation to the Subject

3. Liberty is in perfection when criminal laws derive each punishment from the particular nature of the crime. There are then no arbitrary decisions; the punishment does not flow from the capriciousness of the legislator, but from the very nature of the thing; and man uses no violence to man.

There are four sorts of crimes. Those of the first species are prejudicial to religion, the second to morals, the third to the public tranquillity, and the fourth to the security of the subject. The punishments inflicted for these crimes ought to proceed from the nature of each of these species.

In the class of crimes that concern religion, I rank only those which attack it directly, such as all simple sacrileges. For as to crimes that disturb the exercise of it, they are of the nature of those which prejudice the tranquillity or security of the subject, and ought to be referred to those classes.

In order to derive the punishment of simple sacrileges from the nature of the thing, it should consist in depriving people of the advantages conferred by religion in expelling them out of the temples, in a temporary or perpetual exclusion from the society of the faithful, in shunning their presence, in execrations, comminations, and conjurations.

In things that prejudice the tranquillity or security of the state, secret actions are subject to human jurisdiction. But in those which offend the Deity, where there is no public act, there can be no criminal matter; the whole passes between man and God, who knows the measure and time of his vengeance. Now, if magistrates confounding things should inquire also into hidden sacrileges, this inquisition would be directed to a kind of action that does not at all require it; the liberty of the subject would be subverted by arming the zeal of timorous as well as of presumptuous consciences against him.

The mischief arises from a notion which some people have entertained of revenging the cause of the Deity. But we must honor the Deity and leave him to avenge his own cause. And, indeed, were we to be directed by such a notion, where would be the end of punishments? If human laws are to avenge the cause of an infinite Being, they will be directed by his infinity, and not by the weakness, ignorance, and caprice of man.

A historian of Provence relates a fact which furnishes us with an excellent description of the consequences that may arise in weak capacities from the notion of avenging the Deity's cause. A Jew was accused of having blasphemed against the Virgin Mary, and upon conviction was condemned to be flayed alive. A strange spectacle was then exhibited: gentlemen masked, with knives in their hands, mounted the scaffold, and drove away the executioner, in order to be the avengers themselves of the honor of the blessed Virgin. I do not here choose to anticipate the reflections of the reader.

The second class consists of those crimes which are prejudicial to morals. Such is the violation of public or private continence—that is, of the police directing the manner in which the pleasure annexed to the conjunction of the sexes is to be enjoyed. The punishment of those crimes ought to be also derived from the nature of the thing; the privation of such advantages as society has attached to the purity of morals, fines, shame, necessity of concealment, public infamy, expulsion from home and society, and, in fine, all such punishments as belong to a corrective jurisdiction, are sufficient to repress the temerity of the two sexes. In effect these things are less founded on malice than on carelessness and self-neglect.

We speak here of none but crimes which relate merely to morals, for as to those that are also prejudicial to the public security, such as rapes, they belong to the fourth species.

The crimes of the third class are those which disturb the public tranquillity. The punishments ought therefore to be derived from the nature of the thing, and to be in relation to this tranquillity: such as imprisonment, exile, and other like chastisements, proper for reclaiming turbulent spirits, and obliging them to conform to the established order.

I confine those crimes that injure the public tranquillity to things which imply a bare offense against the police; for as to those which by disturbing the public peace attack at the same time the security of the subject, they ought to be ranked in the fourth class.

The punishments inflicted upon the latter crimes are such as are properly distinguished by that name. They are a kind of retaliation, by which the society refuses security to a member who has actually or intentionally deprived another of his security. These punishments are derived from the nature of the thing, founded on reason, and drawn from the very source of good and evil. A man deserves death when he has violated the security of the subject so far as to deprive, or attempt to deprive, another man of his life. This punishment of death is the remedy, as it were, of a sick society. When there is a breach of security with regard to property, there may be some reasons for inflicting a capital punishment; but it would be much better, and perhaps more natural, that crimes committed against the security of property should be punished with the loss of property; and this ought, indeed, to be the case if men's fortunes were common or equal. But as those who have no property of their own are generally the readiest to attack that of others, it has been found necessary, instead of a pecuniary, to substitute a corporal, punishment.

All that I have here advanced is founded in Nature, and extremely favorable to the liberty of the subject.

IV. It is an important maxim that we ought to be very circumspect in the prosecution of witchcraft and heresy. The accusation of these two crimes may be vastly injurious to liberty, and productive of infinite oppression, if the legislator knows not how to set bounds to it. For as it does not directly point at a person's actions, but at his character, it grows dangerous in proportion to the ignorance of the people; and then a man is sure to be always in danger, because the most exceptional conduct, the purest morals, and the constant practice of every duty in life are not a sufficient security against the suspicion of his being guilty of the like crimes.

Under Manuel Comnenus, the Protestator was accused of having conspired against the emperor, and of having employed for that purpose some secrets that render men invisible. It is mentioned in the life of this emperor that Aaron was detected as he was poring over a book of Solomon's, the reading of which was sufficient to conjure up whole legions of devils. Now, by supposing a power in witchcraft to rouse the infernal spirits to arms, people look upon a man whom they call a sorcerer as the person in the world most likely to disturb and subvert society, and of course they are disposed to punish him with the utmost severity.

But their indignation increases when witchcraft is supposed to have the power of subverting religion. The history of Constantinople informs us that in consequence of a revelation made to a bishop of a miracle having ceased because of the magic practices of a certain person, both that person and his son were put to death. On how many surprising things did not this single crime depend!—that revelations should not be uncommon, that the bishop should be favored with one, that it was real, that there had been a miracle in the case, that this miracle had ceased, that there was an art magic, that magic could subvert religion, that this particular person was a magician, and, in fine, that he had committed that magic act.

The Emperor Theodorus Lascarus attributed his illness to witchcraft. Those who were accused of this crime had no other resource left than to handle a red-hot iron without being hurt. Thus among the Greeks a person ought to have been a sorcerer to be able to clear himself of the imputation of witchcraft. Such was the excess of their stupidity that to the most dubious crime in the world they joined the most dubious proofs of innocence.

Under the reign of Philip the Long, the Jews were expelled from France, being accused of having poisoned the springs with their lepers. So absurd an accusation ought to make us doubt all those that are founded on public hatred.

I have not here asserted that heresy ought not to be punished; I said only that we ought to be extremely circumspect in punishing it.

V. God forbid that I should have the least inclination to diminish the public horror against a crime which religion, morality, and civil government equally condemn. It ought to be proscribed, were it only for its communicating to one sex the weaknesses of the other, and for leading people by a scandalous prostitution of their youth to an ignominious old age. What I shall say concerning it will in no way diminish its infamy, being leveled only against the tyranny that may abuse the very horror we ought to have against the vice.

As a natural circumstance of this crime is secrecy, there are frequent instances of its having been punished by legislators upon the deposition of a child. This was opening a very wide door to calumny. "Justinian," says Procopius, "published a law against this crime; he ordered an inquiry to be made not only against those who were guilty of it, after the enacting of that law, but even before. The deposition of a single witness, sometimes of a child, sometimes of a slave, was sufficient, especially against such as were rich, and against those of the green faction."

It is very odd that these three crimes—witchcraft, heresy, and that against Nature, of which the first might easily be proved not to exist, the second to be susceptible of an infinite number of distinctions, interpretations, and limitations, the third to be often obscure and uncertain—it is very odd, I say, that these three crimes should among us be punished with fire.

I may venture to affirm that the crime against Nature will never make any great progress in society, unless people are prompted to it by some particular custom, as among the Greeks, where the youths of that country performed all their exercises naked; as among us, where domestic education is disused; as among the Asiatics, where particular persons have a great number of women whom they despise, while others can have none at all. Let there be no customs preparatory to this crime; let it, like every other violation of morals, be severely proscribed by the civil magistrate; and Nature will soon defend or resume her rights. Nature, that fond, that indulgent parent, has strewed her pleasures with a bounteous hand, and while she fills us with delights she prepares us, by means of our issue, in whom we see ourselves, as it were, reproduced—she prepares us, I say, for future satisfactions of a more exquisite kind than those very delights.

VI. It is determined by the laws of China that whosoever shows any disrespect to the emperor is to be punished with death. As they do not mention in what this disrespect consists, everything may furnish a pretext to take away a man's life, and to exterminate any family whatsoever.

Two persons of that country who were employed to write the court gazette, having inserted some circumstances relating to a certain fact that was not true, it was pretended that to tell a lie in the court gazette was a disrespect shown to the court, in consequence of which they were put to death. A prince of the blood having inadvertently made some mark on a memorial signed with the red pencil by the emperor, it was determined that he had behaved disrespectfully to the sovereign, which occasioned one of the most terrible persecutions against that family that ever was recorded in history. . . .

IX. Nothing renders the crime of high treason more arbitrary than declaring people guilty of it for indiscreet speeches. Speech is so subject to interpretation; there is so great a difference between indiscretion and malice; and frequently so little is there of the latter in the freedom of expression, that the law can hardly subject people to a capital punishment for words unless it expressly declares what words they are.

Words do not constitute an overt act; they remain only in idea. When considered by themselves, they have generally no determinate signification, for this depends on the tone in which they are uttered. It often happens that in repeating the same words they have not the same meaning; this depends on their connection with other things, and sometimes more is signified by silence than by any expression whatever. Since there can be nothing so equivocal and ambiguous as all this, how is it possible to convert it into a crime of high treason? Wherever this law is established, there is an end not only of liberty, but even of its very shadow.

In the manifesto of the late Czarina [Anna Ivanovna] against the family of the Dolgorukis, one of these princes is condemned to death for having uttered some indecent words concerning her person; another, for having maliciously interpreted her imperial laws, and for having offended her sacred person by disrespectful expressions.

Not that I pretend to diminish the just indignation of the public against those who presume to stain the glory of their sovereign; what I mean is, that if despotic princes are willing to moderate their power, a milder chastisement would be more proper on those occasions than the charge of high treason—a thing always terrible even to innocence itself.

Overt acts do not happen every day; they are exposed to the eye of the public, and a false charge with regard to matters of fact may be easily detected. Words carried into action assume the nature of that action. Thus a man who goes into a public marketplace to incite the subject to revolt incurs the guilt of high treason, because the words are joined to the action, and partake of its nature. It is not the words that are punished, but an action in which words are employed. They do not become criminal but when they are annexed to a criminal action; everything is confounded if words are construed into a capital crime, instead of considering them only as a mark of that crime.

The Emperors Theodosius, Arcadius, and Honorius wrote thus to Rufinus, who was *praefectus praetorio:* "Though a man should happen to speak amiss of our person or government, we do not intend to punish him. If he has spoken through levity, we must despise him; if through folly, we must pity him; and if he wrongs us, we must forgive him. Therefore, leaving things as they are, you are to inform us accordingly, that we may be able to judge of words by persons, and that we may duly consider whether we ought to punish or overlook them."

X. In writings there is something more permanent than in words, but when they are in no way preparative to high treason they cannot amount to that charge. . . .

Book XXV: Of Laws in Relation to Religion

13. A Jewess of eighteen years of age, who was burned at Lisbon at the last *auto-da-fé,* gave occasion to the following little piece, the most idle, I believe, that ever was written. When we attempt to prove things so evident, we are sure never to convince.

The author declares, that though a Jew he has a respect for the Christian religion; and that he should be glad to take away from the princes who are not Christians a plausible pretense for persecuting this religion.

"You complain," says he to the Inquisitors, "that the Emperor of Japan caused all the Christians in his dominions to be burned by a slow fire. But he will answer, we treat you who do not believe like us, as you yourselves treat those who do not believe like you; you can only complain of your weakness, which has hindered you from exterminating us, and which has enabled us to exterminate you.

"But it must be confessed, that you are much more cruel than this emperor. You put us to death who belive only what you believe, because we do not believe all that you believe. We follow a religion which you yourselves know to have been formerly dear to God. We think that God loves it still, and you think that he loves it no more: and because you judge thus, you make those suffer by sword and fire who hold an error so pardonable as to believe that God still loves what he once loved.

"If you are cruel to us, you are much more so to our children; you cause them to be burned because they follow the inspirations given them by those whom the law of nature and the laws of all nations teach them to regard as gods.

"You deprive yourselves of the advantage you have over the Mahommedans, with respect to the manner in which their religion was established. When they boast of the number of their believers, you tell them that they have obtained them by violence, and that they have extended their religion by the sword; why then do you establish yours by fire?

"When you would bring us over to you, we object to a source from which you glory to have descended. You reply to us that though your religion is new, it is divine; and you prove it from its growing amidst the persecutions of pagans, and when watered by the blood of your martyrs; but at present you play the part of the Diocletians, and make us take yours.

"We conjure you, not by the mighty God whom both you and we serve, but by that Christ, who, you tell us, took upon him a human form, to propose himself as an example for you to follow; we conjure you to behave to us as he himself would behave were he upon earth. You would have us become Christians, and you will not be so yourselves.

"But if you will not be Christians, be at least men; treat us as you would, if having only the weak light of justice which nature bestows, you had not a religion to conduct, and a revelation to enlighten you.

"If Heaven has had so great a love for you as to make you see the truth, you have received a singular favor; but is it for children who have received the inheritance of their father, to hate those who have not?

"If you have this truth, hide it not from us by the manner in which you propose it. The characteristic of truth is its triumph over hearts and minds, and not that impotency which you confess when you would force us to receive it by tortures.

"If you were wise, you would not put us to death for no other reason than because we are unwilling to deceive you. If your Christ is the son of God, we hope he will reward us for being so unwilling to profane his mysteries; and we believe that the God whom both you and we serve will not punish us for having suffered death for a religion which he formerly gave us, only because we believe that he still continues to give it.

"You live in an age in which the light of nature shines more brightly than it has ever done; in which philosophy has enlightened human understandings; in which the morality of your gospel has been better known; in which the respective rights of mankind with regard to each other and the empire which one conscience has over another are best understood. If you do not, therefore, shake off your ancient prejudices, which, whilst unregarded, mingle with your passions, it must be confessed that you are incorrigible, incapable of any degree of light or instruction; and a nation must be very unhappy that gives authority to such men.

"Would you have us frankly tell you our thoughts? You consider us rather as your enemies than as the enemies of your religion; for if you loved your religion you would not suffer it to be corrupted by such gross ignorance.

"It is necessary that we should warn you of one thing, that is, if any one in times to come shall dare to assert that in the age in which we live the people of Europe were civilized, you will be cited to prove that they were barbarians; and the idea they will have of you will be such as will dishonor your age, and spread hatred over all your contemporaries."

AN ESSAY ON CRIMES AND PUNISHMENTS

CESARE BECCARIA

By far the most important Enlightenment statement advocating reform of criminal justice was the Essay on Crimes and Justice, *published in 1764 by the Italian economist Cesare Bonesana, marchese di Beccaria (1735–1794). It was translated immediately into English and French. Voltaire described Beccaria's criticism of capital punishment and torture a plea "in behalf of reason and humanity."*

The knowledge of the true relations between a sovereign and his subjects, and of those between different nations; the revival of commerce by the light of philosophical truths, diffused by printing; and the silent international war of industry, the most humane and the most worthy of rational men—these are the fruits which we owe to the enlightenment of this century. But how few have examined and combated the cruelty of punishments, and the irregularities of criminal procedures, a part of legislation so elementary and yet so neglected in almost the whole of Europe; and how few have sought, by a return to first principles, to dissipate the mistakes accumulated by many centuries, or to mitigate, with at least that force which belongs only to ascertained truths, the excessive caprice of ill-directed power, which has presented up to this time but one long example of lawful and cold-blooded atrocity! And yet the groans of the weak, sacrificed to the cruelty of the ignorant or to the indolence of the rich; the barbarous tortures, multiplied with a severity as useless as it is prodigal, for crimes either not proved or quite chimerical; the disgusting horrors of a prison, enhanced by that which is the cruelest executioner of the miserable—namely, uncertainty—these ought to startle those rulers whose function it is to guide the opinion of men's minds.

The immortal President, Montesquieu, has treated cursorily of this matter; and truth, which is indivisible, has forced me to follow the luminous footsteps of this great man; but thinking men, for whom I write, will be able to distinguish my steps from his. Happy shall I esteem myself if, like him, I shall succeed in obtaining the secret gratitude of the unknown and peaceable followers of reason, and if I shall inspire them with that pleasing thrill of emotion with which sensitive minds respond to the advocate of the interests of humanity.

To examine and distinguish all the different sorts of crimes and the manner of punishing them would now be our natural task, were it not that their nature, which varies with the different circumstances of times and places, would compel us to enter upon too vast and wearisome a mass of detail. But it will suffice to indicate the most general principles and the most pernicious and common errors, in order to undeceive no less those who, from a mistaken love of liberty, would introduce anarchy, than those who would be glad to reduce their fellow men to the uniform regularity of a convent.

What will be the penalty suitable for such and such crimes?

Is death a penalty really *useful and necessary* for the security and good order of society?

Are torture and torments *just*, and do they attain the *end* which the law aims at?

What is the best way of preventing crimes?

Are the same penalties equally useful in all times?

What influence have they on customs?

These problems deserve to be solved with such geometrical precision as shall suffice to prevail over the clouds of sophistication, over seductive eloquence, or timid doubt. Had I no other merit than that of having been the first to make clearer to Italy that which other nations have dared to write and are beginning to practice, I should deem myself fortunate; but if, in maintaining the rights of men and of invincible truth, I should contribute to rescue from the spasms and agonies of death any unfortunate victim of tyranny or ignorance, both so equally fatal, the blessings and tears of a single innocent man in the transports of his joy would console me for the contempt of mankind. . . .

It is not only the common interest of mankind, that crimes should not be committed, but that crimes of every kind should be less frequent, in proportion to the evil they produce to society. Therefore, the means made use of by the legislature to prevent crimes, should be more powerful, in proportion as they are destructive of the public safety and happiness, and as the inducements to commit them are stronger. Therefore there ought to be a fixed proportion between crimes and punishments.

It is impossible to prevent entirely all the disorders which the passions of mankind cause in society. These disorders increase in proportion to the number of people, and the opposition of private interests. If we consult history, we shall find them increasing, in every state, with the extent of dominion. In political arithmetic, it is necessary to substitute a calculation of probabilities, to mathematical exactness. That force, which continually impels us to our own private interest, like gravity, acts incessantly, unless it meets with an obstacle to oppose it. The effects of this force are the confused series of human actions. Punishments, which I would call political obstacles, prevent the fatal effects of private interest, without destroying the impelling cause, which is that sensibility inseparable from man. The legislator acts, in this case, like a skillful architect, who endeavors to counteract the force of gravity by combining the circumstances which may contribute to the strength of his edifice.

The necessity of uniting in society being granted, together with the conventions, which the opposite interests of individuals must necessarily require, a scale of crimes may be formed, of which the first degree should consist of those, which immediately tend to the dissolution of society, and the last, of the smallest possible injustice done to a private member of that society. Between these extremes will be comprehended, all actions contrary to the public good, which are called criminal, and which descend by insensible degrees, decreasing from the highest to the lowest. If mathematical calculation could be applied to the obscure and infinite combinations of human actions, there might be a corresponding scale of punishments, descending from the greatest to the least: but it will be sufficient that the wise legislator mark the principal divisions, without disturbing the order, lest to crimes of the *first* degree, be assigned punishments of the *last.* If there were an exact and universal scale of crimes and punishments, we should there have a common measure of the degree of liberty and slavery, humanity and cruelty of different nations.

Any action, which is not comprehended in the above-mentioned scale, will not be called a crime, or punished as such, except by those who have an interest in the denomination. The uncertainty of the extreme points of this scale, hath produced a system of morality which contradicts the laws; a multitude of laws that contradict each other; and many, which expose the best men to the severest punishments, rendering the ideas of *vice* and *virtue* vague, and fluctuating, and even their existence doubtful. Hence that fatal lethargy of political bodies, which terminates in their destruction.

Whoever reads, with a philosophic eye, the history of nations, and their laws, will generally find, that the ideas of virtue and vice, of a good or a bad citizen, change with the revolution of ages; not in proportion to the alteration of circumstances, and consequently conformable to the common good; but in proportion to the passions and errors by which the different law-givers were successively influenced. He will frequently observe, that the passions and vices of one age, are the foundation of the morality of the following; that violent passion, the offspring of fanaticism and enthusiasm, being weakened by time, which reduces all the phenomena of the natural and moral world to an equality, become, by degrees, the prudence of the age, and an useful instrument in the hands of the powerful, or artful politician. Hence the uncertainty of our notions of honor and virtue; an uncertainty which will ever remain, because they change with the revolutions of time, and names survive the things they originally signified; they change with the boundaries of states, which are often the same both in physical and moral geography.

Pleasure and pain are the only springs of action in beings endowed with sensibility. Even amongst the motives which incite men to acts of religion, the invisible legislator has ordained rewards and punishments. From a partial distribution of these, will arise that contradiction, so little observed, because so common; I mean, that of punishing by the laws, the crimes which the laws have occasioned. If an equal punishment be ordained for two crimes that injure society in different degrees, there is nothing to deter men from committing the greater, as often as it is attended with greater advantage. . . .

The foregoing reflections authorize me to assert, that crimes are only to be measured by the injury done to society.

They err, therefore, who imagine that a crime is greater, or less, according to the intention of the person by whom it is committed; for this will depend on the actual impression of objects on the senses, and on the previous disposition of the mind; both which will vary in different persons, and even in the same person at different times, according to the succession of ideas, passions, and circumstances. Upon that system, it would be necessary to form, not only a particular code for every individual, but a new penal law for every crime. Men, often with the best intention, do the greatest injury to society, and with the worst, do it the most essential services.

Others have estimated crimes rather by the dignity of the person offended, than by their consequences to society. If this were the true standard, the smallest irreverence to the divine Being ought to be punished with infinitely more severity, than the assassination of a monarch.

In short, others have imagined, that the greatness of the sin should aggravate the crime. But the fallacy of this opinion will appear on the slightest consideration of the relations between man and man, and between God and man. The relations between man and man, are relations of equality. Necessity alone hath produced, from the opposition of private passions and interests, the idea of public utility, which is the foundation of human justice. The other are relations of dependence, between an imperfect creature and his creator, the most perfect of beings, who has reserved to himself the sole right of being both lawgiver, and judge; for he alone can, without injustice, be, at the same time, both one and the other. If he hath decreed eternal punishments for those who disobey his will, shall an insect dare to put himself in the place of divine justice, or pretend to punish for the Almighty, who is himself all-sufficient; who cannot receive impressions of pleasure, or pain, and who alone, of all other beings, acts without being acted upon? The degree of sin depends on the malignity of the heart, which is impenetrable to finite beings. How then can the degree of sin serve as a standard to determine the degree of crimes? if that were admitted, men may punish when God pardons, and pardon when God condemns; and thus act in opposition to the supreme Being. . . .

We have proved, then, that crimes are to be estimated by *the injury done to society*. This is one of those palpable truths, which, though evident to the meanest capacity, yet, by a combination of circumstances, are only known to a few thinking men in every nation, and in every age. But opinions, worthy only of the despotism of Asia, and passions, armed with power and authority, have, generally by insensible and sometimes by violent impressions on the timid credulity of men, effaced those simple ideas, which perhaps constituted the first philosophy of infant society. Happily the philosophy of the present enlightened age seems again to conduct us to the same principles, and with that degree of certainty, which is obtained by a rational examination, and repeated experience. . . .

A cruelty consecrated among most nations by custom is the torture of the accused during his trial, on the pretext of compelling him to confess his crime, of clearing up contradictions in his statements, of discovering his accomplices, of purging him in some metaphysical and incomprehensible way from infamy, or finally of finding out other crimes of which he may possibly be guilty, but of which he is not accused.

A man cannot be called *guilty* before sentence has been passed on him by a judge, nor can society deprive him of its protection till it has been decided that he has broken the condition on which it was granted. What, then, is that right but one of mere might by which a judge is empowered to inflict a punishment on a citizen whilst his guilt or innocence are still undetermined? The following dilemma is no new one: either the crime is certain or uncertain; if certain, no other punishment is suitable for it than that affixed to it by law; and torture is useless, for the same reason that the criminal's confession is useless. If it is uncertain, it is wrong to torture an innocent person, such as the law adjudges him to be, whose crimes are not yet proved.

What is the political object of punishments? The intimidation of other men. But what shall we say of the secret and private tortures which the tyranny of custom exercises alike upon the guilty and the innocent? It is important, indeed, that no open crime shall pass unpunished; but the public exposure of a criminal whose crime was hidden in darkness is utterly useless. An evil that has been done and cannot be undone can only be punished by civil society insofar as it may affect others with the hope of impunity. If it be true that there are a greater number of men who either from fear or virtue respect the laws than of those who transgress them, the risk of torturing an innocent man should be estimated according to the probability that any man will have been more likely, other things being equal, to have respected than to have despised the laws.

But I say in addition: it is to seek to confound all the relations of things to require a man to be at the same time accuser and accused, to make pain the crucible of truth, as if the test of it lay in the muscles and sinews of an unfortunate wretch. The law which ordains the use of torture is a law which says to men: "Resist pain; and if Nature has created in you an inextinguishable self-love, if she has given you an inalienable right of self-defense, I create in you a totally contrary affection, namely, an heroic self-hatred, and I command you to accuse yourselves, and to speak the truth between the laceration of your muscles and the dislocation of your bones."

This infamous crucible of truth is a still-existing monument of that primitive and savage legal system which called trials by fire and boiling water, or the accidental decisions of combat, *judgments of God*, as if the rings of the eternal chain in the control of the First Cause must at every moment be disarranged and put out for the petty institutions of mankind. The only difference between torture and the trial by fire and water is, that the result of the former seems to depend on the will of the accused, and that of the other two on a fact which is purely physical and extrinsic to the sufferer; but the difference is only apparent, not real. The avowal of truth under tortures and agonies is as little free as was in those times the prevention without fraud of the usual effects of fire and boiling water. Every act of our will is ever proportioned to the force of the sensible impression which causes it, and the sensibility of every man is limited. Hence the impression produced by pain may be so intense as to occupy a man's entire sensibility and leave him no other liberty than the choice of the shortest way of escape, for the present moment, from his penalty. Under such circumstances the answer of the accused is as inevitable as the impressions produced by fire and water; and the innocent man who is sensitive will declare himself guilty, when by so doing he hopes to bring his agonies to an end. All the difference between guilt and innocence is lost by virtue of the very means which they profess to employ for its discovery.

Torture is a certain method for the acquittal of robust villains and for the condemnation of innocent but feeble men. See the fatal drawbacks of this pretended test of truth—a test, indeed, that is worthy of cannibals; a test which the Romans, barbarous as they too were in many respects, reserved for slaves alone, the victims of their fierce and too highly lauded virtue. Of two men, equally innocent or equally guilty, the robust and courageous will be acquitted, the weak and the timid will be condemned, by virtue of the following exact train of reasoning on the part of the judge: "I as judge had to find you guilty of such and such a crime; you, A B, have by your physical strength been able to resist pain, and therefore I acquit you; you, C D, in your weakness have yielded to it; therefore I condemn you. I feel that a confession extorted amid torments can have no force, but I will torture you afresh unless you corroborate what you have now confessed."

The result, then, of torture is a matter of temperament, of calculation, which varies with each man according to his strength and sensibility; so that by this method a mathematician might solve better than a judge this problem: "Given the muscular force and the nervous sensibility of an innocent man, to find the degree of pain which will cause him to plead guilty to a given crime."

ON TORTURE AND CAPITAL PUNISHMENT

François-Marie Arouet de Voltaire

In his Philosophical Dictionary *(1764), Voltaire included the following article on "torture," and two years later, in his* Commentary on the Book of Crimes and Punishments *(Beccaria's), he made his attack on "capital punishment."*

Although there are few articles of jurisprudence in these honest alphabetical reflections, a word must be said concerning torture, otherwise called the *question.* It is a strange manner of questioning men. It was not invented, however, out of idle curiosity; there is every likelihood that this part of our legislation owes its origin to a highway robber. Most of these gentlemen still are accustomed to squeeze thumbs, burn feet and question by other torments those who refuse to tell them where they have put their money.

When conquerors had succeeded these thieves, they found the invention very useful to their interests: they put it to use when they suspected that anyone opposed them with certain evil designs, such, for instance, as the desire to be free; that was a crime of high treason against God and man. They wanted to know the accomplices; and to accomplish this, they subjected to the suffering of a thousand deaths those whom they suspected, because according to the jurisprudence of these early heroes, whoever was suspected merely of entertaining against them any slightly disrespectful thought was worthy of death. The moment that anyone has thus merited death, it matters little that terrible torments are added for several days, and even for several weeks, a practice which smacks somewhat of the Divinity. Providence sometimes puts us to the torture by means of stone, gravel, gout, scurvy, leprosy, pox of both varieties, excruciating bowel pains, nervous convulsions, and other executioners of providential vengeance.

Now as the early despots were, by the admission of all their courtiers, images of the Divinity, they imitated it as much as they could. . . .

The grave magistrate who has bought for a little money the right to perform experiments on his neighbor tells his wife at dinner what took place during the morning. The first time, madam was revolted by it; the second time she got a taste for it, because after all women are curious; and now the first thing she says to him when he comes home in his gown is: "My dear, didn't you have anyone put to the question today?"

The French who are considered, I do not know why, a very humane people, are astonished that the English, who had the inhumanity to take all Canada from us, have given up the pleasure of putting the question.

When the Chevalier de la Barrè, grandson of a lieutenant-general in the king's service, a young man of great intelligence and much promise, but possessing all the thoughtlessness of unbridled youth, was convicted of having sung impious songs and even of having passed in front of a procession of Capuchins without taking off his hat, the judges of Abbeville, men comparable to the Roman Senators, ordered not only that his tongue should be torn out, his hand cut off and his body burned by slow fire; but they applied torture to him to find out how many songs he had sung and how many processions he had seen pass with his hat on his head.

It was not in the thirteenth nor the fourteenth century that this adventure took place; it was in the eighteenth. Foreign nations judge France by its plays, novels and pretty poetry; by its opera girls, who are very gentle of manner; by its opera dancers, who are graceful; by Mlle. Clairon, who recites her lines in a ravishing manner. They do not know that there is no nation more fundamentally cruel than the French.

The Russians were considered barbarians in 1700, and it is now only 1769; an Empress has just given to that vast state laws which would honor Minos, Numa and Solon, if they had been intelligent enough to invent them. The most remarkable is universal tolerance, the next is the abolition of torture. Justice and humanity guided her pen: she has reformed everything. Woe unto the nation which, though long civilized, is still led by ancient atrocious customs! "Why should we change our jurisprudence?" we say. "Europe uses our cooks, our tailors and our wig makers; therefore our laws are good."

• • •

It is an old saying that a man after he is hanged is good for nothing, and that the punishments invented for the welfare of society should be useful to that society. It is clear that twenty vigorous thieves, condemned to hard labor at public works for the rest of their life, serve the state by their punishment; and their death would serve only the executioner, who is paid for killing men in public. Only rarely are thieves punished by death in England; they are transported overseas to the colonies. The same is true in the vast Russian empire. Not a single criminal was executed during the reign of the autocratic Elizabeth. Catherine II who succeeded her, endowed with a very superior mind, followed the same policy. Crimes have not increased as a result of this humanity, and almost always, criminals banished to Siberia become good men. The same thing has been noticed in the English colonies. This happy change astonishes us, but nothing is more natural. These condemned men are forced to work constantly in order to live. Opportunities for vice are lacking; they marry and have children. Force men to work and you make them honest. It is well known that great crimes are not committed in the country, except, perhaps, when too many holidays bring on idleness and lead to debauchery.

A Roman citizen was condemned to death only for crimes affecting the welfare of the state. Our teachers, our first legislators, respected the blood of their fellow citizens; we lavish that of ours.

This dark and delicate question has been long discussed: whether judges may punish by death when the law does not expressly require this punishment. This question was solemnly debated before Emperor Henri IV. He judged, and decided that no magistrate could have this power.

There are some criminal cases that are so unusual or so complicated, or are accompanied by such strange circumstances, that the law itself has been forced in more than one country to leave these singular cases to the discretion of the judges. If there really should be one instance in which the law permits a criminal to be put to death who has not committed a capital offense, there will be a thousand instances in which humanity, which is stronger than the law, should spare the life of those whom the law has sentenced to death.

The sword of justice is in our hands; but we ought to blunt it more often than sharpen it. It is carried in its sheath before kings, to warn us that it should be rarely drawn.

There have been judges who loved to make blood flow; such was Jeffreys in England; such in France was a man who was called *coupe-tête.* Men like these were not born to be judges; nature made them to be executioners.

THE STATE OF PRISONS

John Howard

The most important prison reformer in the Enlightenment was the English Quaker John Howard (1726–1790). In 1777 he published The State of the Prisons in England and Wales, *from which this selection is taken. Along with his indictment of the "distress in prisons," he offers proposals for humane reform. Noteworthy is his suggestion, informed by his Quaker belief in the silent working of the inner light, that prisoners sleep alone in their own rooms.*

There are prisons, into which whoever looks will, at first sight of the people confined, be convinced, that there is some great error in the management of them: their sallow meager countenances declare, without words, that they are very miserable. Many who went in healthy, are in a few months changed to emaciated dejected objects. Some are seen pining under diseases, "sick, and in prison"; expiring on the floors, in loathsome cells, of pestilential fevers, and the confluent smallpox; victims, I must not say to the cruelty, but I will say to the inattention, of sheriffs, and gentlemen in the commission of the peace.

The cause of this distress is, that many prisons are scantily supplied, and some almost totally destitute of the necessaries of life.

There are several bridewells (to begin with them) in which prisoners have no allowance of food at all. In some, the keeper farms what little is allowed them: and where he engages to supply each prisoner with one or two pennyworth of bread a day, I have known this shrunk to half, sometimes less than half the quantity, cut or broken from his own loaf.

It will perhaps be asked, does not their work maintain them? for every one knows that those offenders are committed to hard labor. The answer to that question, though true, will hardly be believed. There are few bridewells in which any work is done, or can be done. The prisoners have neither tools, nor materials of any kind: but spend their time in sloth, profaneness and debauchery, to a degree which, in some of those houses that I have seen, is extremely shocking.

Some keepers of these houses, who have represented to the magistrates the wants of their prisoners, and desired for them necessary food, have been silenced with these inconsiderate words, Let them work or starve. When those gentlemen know the former is impossible, do they not by that thoughtless sentence, inevitably doom poor creatures to the latter?

I have asked some keepers, since the late act for preserving the health of prisoners, why no care is taken of their sick: and have been answered, that the magistrates tell them the act does not extend to bridewells.

In consequence of this, at the quarter sessions you see prisoners covered (hardly covered) with rags; almost famished; and sick of diseases, which the discharged spread where they go; and with which those who are sent to the county gaols infect these prisons.

The same complaint, want of food, is to be found in many county gaols. In above half these, debtors have no bread; although it is granted to the highwayman, the house-breaker, and the murderer: and medical assistance, which is provided for the latter, is withheld from the former. In many of these gaols, debtors who would work are not permitted to have any tools, lest they should furnish felons with them for escape or other mischief. I have often seen these prisoners eating their water-soup (bread boiled in mere water) and heard them say, "We are locked up and almost starved to death. . . ."

Many prisons have no water. This defect is frequent in bridewells, and town gaols. In the felons' courts of some county gaols there is no water: in some places where there is water, prisoners are always locked up within doors, and have no more than the keeper or his servants think fit to bring them: in one place they were limited to three pints a day each: a scanty provision for drink and cleanliness!

And as to air, which is no less necessary than either of the two preceding articles, and given us by Providence quite gratis, without any care or labor of our own; yet, as if the bounteous goodness of Heaven excited our envy, methods are contrived to rob prisoners of this genuine cordial of life, as Dr. Hales very properly calls it: I mean by preventing that circulation and change of the salutiferous fluid, without which animals cannot live and thrive. It is well known that air which has performed its office in the lungs, is feculent and noxious. Writers upon the subject show, that a hogshead of air will last a man only an hour: but those who do not choose to consult philosophers; may judge from a notorious fact. In 1756, at Calcutta in Bengal, out of a hundred and seventy persons who were confined in a hole there one night, a hundred and fifty-four were taken out dead. The few survivors ascribed the mortality to their want of fresh air, and called the place Hell in miniature.

Air which has been breathed, is made poisonous to a more intense degree, by the effluvia from the sick, and what else in prisons is offensive. My reader will judge of its malignity, when I assure him, that my clothes were in my first journeys so offensive, that in a post-chaise I could not bear the windows drawn up; and was therefore obliged to travel commonly on horseback. The leaves of my memorandum book were often so tainted, that I could not use it till after spreading it an hour or two before the fire: and even my antidote, a vial of vinegar, has, after using it in a few prisons, become intolerably disagreeable. I did not wonder that in those journeys many gaolers made excuses; and did not go with me into the felons' wards. . . .

The evils mentioned hitherto affect the health and life of prisoners. I have now to complain of what is pernicious to their morals; and that is, the confining all sorts of prisoners together: debtors and felons, men and women, the young beginner and the old offender; and with all these, in some counties, such as are guilty of misdemeanors only; who should have been committed to bridewell to be corrected, by diligence and labor; but for want of food, and the means of procuring it in those prisons, are in pity sent to such county gaols as afford these offenders prison-allowance.

Few prisons separate men and women in the daytime. In some

counties the gaol is also the bridewell: in others those prisons are contiguous, and the courtyard common. There the petty offender is committed for instruction to the most profligate. In some gaols you see (and who can see it without sorrow) boys of twelve or fourteen eagerly listening to the stories told by practiced and experienced criminals, of their adventures, successes, stratagems, and escapes.

I must here add, that in some few gaols are confined idiots and lunatics. These serve for sport to idle visitants at assizes, and other times of general resort. Many of the bridewells are crowded and offensive, because the rooms which were designed for prisoners are occupied by the insane. Where these are not kept separate, they disturb and terrify other prisoners. No care is taken of them, although it is probable that by medicines, and proper regimen, some of them might be restored to their senses, and to usefulness in life. . . .

In order to redress these various evils, the first thing to be taken into consideration is the prison itself. Many county gaols and other prisons are so decayed and ruinous, or, for other reasons, so totally unfit for the purpose, that new ones must be built in their stead. Others are very incommodious, but may be improved upon the ground about them, which is occupied by the keeper, or not used at all. Some need little more than a thorough repair. In order to give what little assistance I can to those who must build a new county gaol, I will take the liberty to suggest what hath occurred to me upon this head, in hopes that some more skillful hand will undertake the generous and benevolent task of carrying to perfection a scheme, of which I can only draw the outlines. . . .

A county gaol, and indeed every prison, should be built on a spot that is airy, and if possible near a river, or brook. I have commonly found prisons situated near a river, the cleanest and most healthy. They generally have not (they could not well have) subterraneous dungeons, which have been so fatal to thousands: and by their nearness to running water, another evil, almost as noxious, is prevented, that is the stench of sewers.

I said a gaol should be near a stream; but I must annex this caution, that it be not so near as that either the house or yard shall be within the reach of floods. This circumstance was so little thought of at Appleby in Westmorland, when their new gaol was first building, that I saw the walls marked from nine inches to three feet high by floods.

If it be not practicable to build near a stream; then an eminence should be chosen: for as the walls round a prison must be so high as greatly to obstruct a free circulation of air, this inconvenience should be lessened by a rising ground. And the prison should not be surrounded by other buildings; nor built in the middle of a town or city.

That part of the building which is detached from the walls, and contains the men-felons' ward, may be square, or rectangular, raised on arcades, that it may be more airy, and leave under it a dry walk in wet weather. These wards over arcades are also best for safety, for I have found that escapes have been most commonly effected by undermining cells and dungeons. When I went into Horsham gaol with the keeper, we saw a heap of stones and rubbish. The felons had been for two or three days undermining the foundation of their room; and a general escape was intended that night. We were but just in time to prevent it; for it was almost night when we went in. Our lives were at their mercy: but (thank God) they did not attempt to murder us, and rush out. If felons should find any other means to break out of this raised ward, they will still be stopped by the wall of the court, which is the principal security; and the walls of the wards need not then be of that great thickness they are generally built, whereby the access of light and air is impeded. Every room should be vaulted; for I have known many poor creatures burnt to death, as at Halstead, etc., who would have been saved if such a precaution had been used. The staircases of all prisons should be stone.

I wish to have so many small rooms or cabins that each criminal may sleep alone. These rooms to be ten feet high to the crown of the arch, and have double doors, one of them iron-latticed, for the circulation of air. If it be difficult to prevent their being together in the daytime, they should by all means be separated at night. Solitude and silence are favorable to reflection, and may possibly lead them to repentance. Privacy and hours of thoughtfulness are necessary for those who must soon leave the world (yet how contrary to this is our practice! Keepers have assured me, that they have made £5 a day after the condemnation of their prisoners). In the Old Newgate there were fifteen cells for persons in this situation, which are still left standing, and are annexed to the new building. The like provision for such as return to society cannot be less needful. Bishop Butler, one of the writers cited in the note, affirms that it is much more so, "since it must be acknowledged, of greater consequence in a religious, as well as civil respect, how persons live than how they die."

The separation I am pleading for, especially at night, would prevent escapes, or make them very difficult: for that is the time in which they are generally planned, and effected. This also would prevent their robbing one another in the night. Another reason for separation is, that it would free gaolers from a difficulty of which I have heard them complain: they hardly know where to keep criminals admitted to be evidence for the king: these would be murdered by their accomplices if put among them; and in more than one prison, I have seen them, for that reason, put in the women's ward.

Where there are opposite windows they should have shutters; but these should be open all day. In the men-felons' ward the windows should be six feet from the floor; there should be no glass; nor should the prisoners be allowed to stop them with straw, etc.

The women-felons' ward should be quite distinct from that of the men; and the young criminals from old and hardened offenders. Each of these three classes should also have their day-room or kitchen with a fireplace; and their court and offices all separate.

Every court should be paved with flags or flat stones for the more convenient washing it; and have a good pump, or water laid on; both if possible: and the pump and pipes should be repaired as soon as they need it; otherwise the gaols will soon be offensive and unwholesome: as I have always found them to be in such cases. A small stream constantly running in the court is very desirable. In a room or shed near the pump or pipe, there should be a commodious bath, with steps (as there is in some county hospitals) to wash prisoners that come in dirty, and to induce them afterwards to the frequent use of it.

"CASES UNMEET FOR PUNISHMENT . . ."

JEREMY BENTHAM

In chapter 25 of his Introduction to the Principles of Morals and Legislation, *published in 1789, Bentham analyzes punishment from the perspective of his ruling principle of Utility.*

§ I. GENERAL VIEW OF CASES UNMEET FOR PUNISHMENT.

I. The general object which all laws have, or ought to have, in common, is to augment the total happiness of the community; and therefore, in the first place, to exclude, as far as may be, every thing that tends to subtract from that happiness: in other words, to exclude mischief.

II. But all punishment is mischief: all punishment in itself is evil. Upon the principle of utility, if it ought at all to be admitted, it ought only to be admitted in as far as it promises to exclude some greater evil.

III. It is plain, therefore, that in the following cases punishment ought not to be inflicted.

1. Where it is *groundless:* where there is no mischief for it to prevent; the act not being mischievous upon the whole.

2. Where it must be *inefficacious:* where it cannot act so as to prevent the mischief.

3. Where it is *unprofitable*, or too *expensive:* where the mischief it would produce would be greater than what it prevented.

4. Where it is *needless:* where the mischief may be prevented, or cease of itself, without it: that is, at a cheaper rate.

§ 2. CASES IN WHICH PUNISHMENT IS GROUNDLESS.

These are,

IV. 1. Where there has never been any mischief: where no mischief has been produced to any body by the act in question. Of this number are those in which the act was such as might, on some occasions, be mischievous or disagreeable, but the person whose interest it concerns gave his *consent* to the performance of it. This consent, provided it be free, and fairly obtained, is the best proof that can be produced, that, to the person who gives it, no mischief, at least no immediate mischief, upon the whole, is done. For no man can be so good a judge as the man himself, what it is gives him pleasure or displeasure.

V. 2. Where the mischief was *outweighed:* although a mischief was produced by that act, yet the same act was necessary to the production of a benefit which was of greater value than the mischief. This may be the case with any thing that is done in the way of precaution against instant calamity, as also with any thing that is done in the exercise of the several sorts of powers necessary to be established in every community, to wit, domestic, judicial, military, and supreme.

VI. 3. Where there is a certainty of an adequate compensation: and that in all cases where the offense can be committed. This supposes two things: 1. That the offense is such as admits of an adequate compensation: 2. That such a compensation is sure to be forthcoming. Of these suppositions, the latter will be found to be a merely ideal one: a supposition that cannot, in the universality here given to it, be verified by fact. It cannot, therefore, in practice, be numbered amongst the grounds of absolute impunity. It may, however, be admitted as a ground for an abatement of that punishment, which other considerations, standing by themselves, would seem to dictate.

§ 3. Cases in which punishment must be inefficacious.

These are,

VII. 1. Where the penal provision is *not established* until after the act is done. Such are the cases, 1. Of an *ex-post-facto* law; where the legislator himself appoints not a punishment till after the act is done. 2. Of a sentence beyond the law; where the judge, of his own authority, appoints a punishment which the legislator had not appointed.

VIII. 2. Where the penal provision, though established, is *not conveyed* to the notice of the person on whom it seems intended that it should operate. Such is the case where the law has omitted to employ any of the expedients which are necessary, to make sure that every person whatsoever, who is within the reach of the law, be apprised of all the cases whatsoever, in which (being in the station of life he is in) he can be subjected to the penalties of the law.

IX. 3. Where the penal provision, though it were conveyed to a man's notice, *could produce no effect* on him, with respect to the preventing him from engaging in any act of the *sort* in question. Such is the case, 1. In extreme *infancy;* where a man has not yet attained that state or disposition of mind in which the prospect of evils so distant as those which are held forth by the law, has the effect of influencing his conduct. 2. In *insanity;* where the person, if he has attained to that disposition, has since been deprived of it through the influence of some permanent though unseen cause. 3. In *intoxication;* where he has been deprived of it by the transient influence of a visible cause: such as the use of wine, or opium, or other drugs, that act in this manner on the nervous system: which condition is indeed neither more nor less than a temporary insanity produced by an assignable cause.

X. 4. Where the penal provision (although, being conveyed to the party's notice, it might very well prevent his engaging in acts of the sort in question, provided he knew that it related to those acts) could not have this effect, with regard to the *individual* act he is about to engage in: to wit, because he knows not that it is of the number of those to which the penal provision relates. This may happen, 1. In the case of *unintentionality;* where he intends not to engage, and thereby knows not that he is about to engage, in the *act* in which eventually he is about to engage. 2. In the case of *unconsciousness;* where, although he may know that he is about to engage in the *act* itself, yet, from not knowing all the material *circumstances* attending it, he knows not of the *tendency* it has to produce that mischief, in contemplation of which it has been made penal in most instances. 3. In the case of *missupposal;* where, although he may know of the tendency the act has to produce that degree of mischief, he supposes it, though mistakenly, to be attended with some circumstance, or set of circumstances, which, if it had been attended with, it would either not have been productive of that mischief, or have been productive of such a greater degree of good, as has determined the legislator in such a case not to make it penal.

XI. 5. Where, though the penal clause might exercise a full and prevailing influence, were it to act alone, yet by the *predominant* influence of some opposite cause upon the will, it must necessarily be ineffectual; because the evil which he sets himself about to undergo, in the case of his *not* engaging in the act, is so great, that the evil denounced by the penal clause, in case of his engaging in it, cannot appear greater. This may happen, 1. In the case of *physical danger;* where the evil is such as appears likely to be brought about by the unassisted powers of *nature.* 2. In the case of a *threatened mischief;* where it is such as appears likely to be brought about through the intentional and conscious agency of *man.*

XII. 6. Where (though the penal clause may exert a full and prevailing influence over the *will* of the party) yet his *physical faculties* (owing to the predominant influence of some physical cause) are not in a condition to follow the determination of the will: insomuch that the act is absolutely *involuntary.* Such is the case of physical *compulsion* or *restraint,* by whatever means brought about; where the man's hand, for instance, is pushed against some object which his will disposes him *not* to touch; or tied down from touching some object which his will disposes him to touch.

§ 4. Cases where punishment is unprofitable.

These are,

XIII. 1. Where, on the one hand, the nature of the offense, on the other hand, that of the punishment, are, *in the ordinary state of things,* such, that when compared together, the evil of the latter will turn out to be greater than that of the former.

XIV. Now the evil of the punishment divides itself into four branches, by which so many different sets of persons are affected.

1. The evil of *coercion* or *restraint:* or the pain which it gives a man not to be able to do the act, whatever it be, which by the apprehension of the punishment he is deterred from doing. This is felt by those by whom the law is *observed.* 2. The evil of *apprehension:* or the pain which a man, who has exposed himself to punishment, feels at the thoughts of undergoing it. This is felt by those by whom the law has been *broken,* and who feel themselves in *danger* of its being executed upon them. 3. The evil of *sufferance:* or the pain which a man feels, in virtue of the punishment itself, from the time when he begins to undergo it. This is felt by those by whom the law is broken, and upon whom it comes actually to be executed. 4. The pain of sympathy, and the other *derivative* evils resulting to the persons who are in *connection* with the several classes of original sufferers just mentioned. Now of these four lots of evil, the first will be greater or less, according to the nature of the act from which

the party is restrained: the second and third according to the nature of the punishment which stands annexed to that offense.

XV. On the other hand, as to the evil of the offense, this will also, of course, be greater or less, according to the nature of each offense. The proportion between the one evil and the other will therefore be different in the case of each particular offense. The cases, therefore, where punishment is unprofitable on this ground, can by no other means be discovered, than by an examination of each particular offense; which is what will be the business of the body of the work.

XVI. 2. Where, although in the *ordinary state* of things, the evil resulting from the punishment is not greater than the benefit which is likely to result from the force with which it operates, during the same space of time, towards the excluding the evil of the offenses, yet it may have been rendered so by the influence of some *occasional circumstances.* In the number of these circumstances may be, 1. The multitude of delinquents at a particular juncture; being such as would increase, beyond the ordinary measure, the *quantum* of the second and third lots, and thereby also of a part of the fourth lot, in the evil of the punishment. 2. The extraordinary value of the services of some one delinquent; in the case where the effect of the punishment would be to deprive the community of the benefit of those services. 3. The displeasure of the *people;* that is, of an indefinite number of the members of the *same* community, in cases where (owing to the influence of some occasional incident) they happen to conceive, that the offense or the offender ought not to be punished at all, or at least ought not to be punished in the way in question. 4. The displeasure of *foreign powers;* that is, of the governing body, or a considerable number of the members of some *foreign* community or communities, with which the community in question is connected.

§ 5. Cases where punishment is needless.

These are,

XVII. 1. Where the purpose of putting an end to the practice may be attained as effectually at a cheaper rate: by instruction, for instance, as well as by terror: by informing the understanding, as well as by exercising an immediate influence on the will. This seems to be the case with respect to all those offenses which consist in the disseminating pernicious principles in matters of *duty;* of whatever kind the duty be; whether political, or moral, or religious. And this, whether such principles be disseminated *under,* or even *without,* a sincere persuasion of their being bicial. I say, even *without:* for though in such a case it is not instrution that can prevent the writer from endeavoring to inculcate his principles, yet it may the readers from adopting them: without which, his endeavoring to inculcate them will do no harm. In such a case, the sovereign will commonly have little need to take an active part: if it be the interest of *one* individual to inculcate principles that are pernicious, it will as surely be the interest of *other* individuals to expose them. But if the sovereign must needs take a part in the controversy, the pen is the proper weapon to combat error with, not the sword.

War and Peace

SPLENDID ARMIES

François-Marie Arouet de Voltaire

With his characteristic wit, Voltaire mocks militarism and war in this selection, which forms chapters 3 and 4 of his Candide, *published in 1759 and probably his best-known work.*

Nothing could be smarter, more splendid, more brilliant, better drawn up than the two armies. Trumpets, fifes, hautboys, drums, cannons, formed a harmony such as has never been heard even in hell. The cannons first of all laid flat about six thousand men on each side; then the musketry removed from the best of worlds some nine or ten thousand blackguards who infested its surface. The bayonet also was the sufficient reason for the death of some thousands of men. The whole might amount to thirty thousand souls. Candide, who trembled like a philosopher, hid himself as well as he could during this heroic butchery. At last, while the two Kings each commanded a Te Deum in his camp, Candide decided to go elsewhere to reason about effects and causes. He clambered over heaps of dead and dying men and reached a neighboring village, which was in ashes; it was an Abare village which the Bulgarians had burned in accordance with international law. Here, old men dazed with blows watched the dying agonies of their murdered wives who clutched their children to their bleeding breasts; there, disemboweled girls who had been made to satisfy the natural appetites of heroes gasped their last sighs; others, half-burned, begged to be put to death. Brains were scattered on the ground among dismembered arms and legs. Candide fled to another village as fast as he could; it belonged to the Bulgarians, and Abarian heroes had treated it in the same way. Candide, stumbling over quivering limbs or across ruins, at last escaped from the theater of war, carrying a little food in his knapsack, and never forgetting Mademoiselle Cunegonde. His provisions were all gone when he reached Holland; but, having heard that everyone in that country was rich and a Christian, he had no doubt at all but that he would be as well treated as he had been in the Baron's castle before he had been expelled on account of Mademoiselle Cunegonde's pretty eyes. He asked an alms of several grave persons, who all replied that if he continued in that way he would be shut up in a house of correction to teach him how to live. He then addressed himself to a man who had been discoursing on charity in a large assembly for an hour on end. This orator, glancing at him askance, said: "What are you doing here? Are you for a good cause?" "There is no effect without a cause," said Candide modestly. "Everything is necessarily linked up and arranged for the best. It was necessary that I should be expelled from the company of Mademoiselle Cunegonde, that I ran the gauntlet, and that I beg my bread until I can earn it; all this could not have happened differently." "My friend," said the orator, "do you believe that the Pope is Anti-Christ?" "I had never heard so before," said Candide, "but whether he is or isn't, I am starving." "You don't deserve to eat," said the other. "Hence, rascal; hence, you wretch; and never come near me again." The orator's wife thrust her head out of the window and seeing a man who did not believe that the Pope was Anti-Christ, she poured on his head a full . . . O Heavens! To what excess religious zeal is carried by ladies! A man who had not been baptized, an honest Anabaptist named Jacques, saw the cruel and ignominious treatment of one of his brothers, a featherless two-legged creature with a soul; he took him home, cleaned him up, gave him bread and beer, presented him with two florins, and even offered to teach him to work at the manufacture of Persian stuffs which are made in Holland. Candide threw himself at the man's feet, exclaiming: "Doctor Pangloss was right in telling me that all is for the best in this world, for I am vastly more touched by your extreme generosity than by the harshness of the gentleman in the black cloak and his good lady." The next day when he walked out he met a beggar covered with sores, dull-eyed, with the end of his nose fallen away, his mouth awry, his teeth black, who talked huskily, was tormented with a violent cough and spat out a tooth at every cough.

Candide, moved even more by compassion than by horror, gave this horrible beggar the two florins he had received from the honest Anabaptist, Jacques. The phantom gazed fixedly at him, shed tears and threw its arms round his neck. Candide recoiled in terror. "Alas!" said the wretch to the other wretch, "don't you recognize your dear Pangloss?" "What do I hear? You, my dear master! You, in this horrible state! What misfortune has happened to you? Why are you no longer in the noblest of castles? What has become of Mademoiselle Cunegonde, the pearl of young ladies, the masterpiece of Nature?" "I am exhausted," said Pangloss. Candide immediately took him to the Anabaptist's stable where he gave him a little bread to eat; and when Pangloss had recovered: "Well!" said he, "Cunegonde?" "Dead," replied the other. At this word Candide swooned; his friend restored him to his senses with a little bad vinegar which happened to be in the stable. Candide opened his eyes. "Cunegonde dead! Ah! best of worlds, where are you? But what illness did she die of? Was it because she saw me kicked out of her father's noble castle?" "No," said Pangloss. "She was disemboweled by Bulgarian soldiers, after having been raped to the limit of possibility; they broke the Baron's head when he tried to defend her; the Baroness was cut to pieces; my poor pupil was treated exactly like his sister; and as to the castle, there is not one stone standing on another, not a barn, not a sheep, not a duck, not a tree; but we were well avenged, for the Abares did exactly the same to a neighboring barony which belonged to a Bulgarian Lord." At this, Candide swooned again; but, having recovered and having said all that he ought to say, he inquired the cause and effect, the sufficient reason which had reduced Pangloss to so piteous a state. "Alas!" said Pangloss, " 'tis love; love, the consoler of the human race, the preserver of the universe, the soul of all tender creatures, gentle love." "Alas!" said Candide, "I am acquainted with this love, this sovereign of hearts, this soul of our soul; it has never brought me anything but one kiss and twenty kicks in the backside. How could this beautiful cause produce in you so abominable an effect?" Pangloss replied as follows: "My dear Candide! You remember Paquette, the maid-servant of our august Baroness; in her arms I enjoyed the delights of Paradise which have produced the tortures of Hell by which you see I am devoured; she was infected and perhaps is dead. Paquette received this present from a most learned monk, who had it from the source; for he received it from an old countess, who had it from a cavalry captain, who owed it to a marchioness, who derived it from a page, who had received it from a Jesuit, who, when a novice, had it in a direct line from one of the companions of Christopher Columbus. For my part, I shall not give it to anyone, for I am dying." "O Pangloss!" exclaimed Candide, "this is a strange genealogy! Wasn't the devil at the root of it?" "Not at all," replied that great man. "It was something indispensable in this best of worlds, a necessary ingredient; for, if Columbus in an island of America had not caught this disease, which poisons the source of generation, and often indeed prevents generation, we should not have chocolate and cochineal; it must also be noticed that hitherto in our continent this disease is peculiar to us, like theological disputes. The Turks, the Indians, the Persians, the Chinese, the Siamese and the Japanese are not yet familiar with it; but there is a sufficient reason why they in their turn should become familiar with it in a few centuries. Meanwhile, it has made marvelous progress among us, and especially in those large armies composed of honest, well-bred stipendiaries who decide the destiny of States; it may be asserted that when thirty thousand men fight a pitched battle against an equal number of troops, there are about twenty thousand with the pox on either side." "Admirable!" said Candide. "But you must get cured." "How can I?" said Pangloss. "I haven't a sou, my friend, and in the whole extent of this globe, you cannot be bled or receive an enema without paying or without someone paying for you." This last speech determined Candide; he went and threw himself at the feet of his charitable Anabaptist, Jacques, and drew so touching a picture of the state to which his friend was reduced that the good easy man did not hesitate to succor Pangloss; he had him cured at his own expense. In this cure Pangloss only lost one eye and one ear. He could write well and knew arithmetic perfectly. The Anabaptist made him his bookkeeper. At the end of two months he was compelled to go to Lisbon on business and took his two philosophers on the boat with him. Pangloss explained to him how everything was for the best. Jacques was not of this opinion. "Men," said he, "must have corrupted nature a little, for they were not born wolves, and they have become wolves. God did not give them twenty-four-pounder cannons or bayonets, and they have made bayonets and cannons to destroy each other. I might bring bankruptcies into the account and Justice which seizes the goods of bankrupts in order to deprive the creditors of them." "It was all indispensable," replied the one-eyed doctor, "and private misfortunes make the public good, so that the more private misfortunes there are, the more everything is well." While he was reasoning, the air grew dark, the winds blew from the four quarters of the globe and the ship was attacked by the most horrible tempest in sight of the port of Lisbon.

"THERE NEVER WAS A GOOD WAR . . ."

BENJAMIN FRANKLIN

In this letter written from France to Sir Joseph Banks, president of the Royal Society of London, of which Franklin had been elected a fellow in 1756, the American statesman and scientist rejoices in the end of hostilities between Britain and America. One should note, as well, his linkage of science and progress, epitomized by his postscript, a reference to the first successful balloon ascent, in June of that year, by the Montgolfier brothers near Lyons, France.

PASSY, July 27, 1783.

DEAR SIR,

I received your very kind letter by Dr. Blagden, and esteem myself much honored by your friendly remembrance. I have been too much and too closely engaged in public affairs, since his being here, to enjoy all the benefit of his conversation you were so good as to intend me. I hope soon to have more leisure, and to spend a part of it in those studies, that are much more agreeable to me than political operations.

I join with you most cordially in rejoicing at the return of peace. I hope it will be lasting, and that mankind will at length, as they call themselves reasonable creatures, have reason and sense enough to settle their differences without cutting throats; for, in my opinion, *there never was a good war, or a bad peace.* What vast additions to the conveniences and comforts of living might mankind have acquired, if the money spent in wars had been employed in works of public utility! What an extension of agriculture, even to the tops of our mountains; what rivers rendered navigable, or joined by canals: what bridges, aqueducts, new roads, and other public works, edifices, and improvements, rendering England a complete paradise, might have been obtained by spending those millions in doing good, which in the last war have been spent in doing mischief; in bringing misery into thousands of families, and destroying the lives of so many thousands of working people, who might have performed the useful labor!

I am pleased with the late astronomical discoveries made by our society. Furnished as all Europe now is with academies of science, with nice instruments and the spirit of experiment, the progress of human knowledge will be rapid, and discoveries made, of which we have at present no conception. I begin to be almost sorry I was born so soon, since I cannot have the happiness of knowing what will be known 100 years hence.

I wish continued success to the labors of the royal society, and that you may long adorn their chair; being, with the highest esteem, dear Sir, &c.,

B. FRANKLIN.

P.S. Dr. Blagden will acquaint you with the experiment of a vast globe sent up into the air, much talked of here, and which, if prosecuted, may furnish means of new knowledge.

PERPETUAL PEACE

IMMANUEL KANT

Several times in the course of his writings Kant linked his faith in moral progress and ethical perfection to a vision of peace among nations. The first selection is from his Idea of a Universal History on a Cosmopolitan Plan, *published in 1784, and the second is from his* Project for a Perpetual Peace *(1795).*

PROPOSITION: *The problem of the establishment of a perfect constitution of society depends upon the problem of a system of international relations adjusted to law; and, apart from this latter problem, cannot be solved.*

To what purpose is labor bestowed upon a civil constitution adjusted to law for individual men, i.e., upon the creation of a commonwealth? The same antisocial impulses, which first drove men to such a creation, is again the cause, that every commonwealth in its external relations, i.e., as a state in reference to other states, occupies the same ground of lawless and uncontrolled liberty; consequently each must anticipate from the other the very same evils which compelled individuals to enter the social state. Nature accordingly avails herself of the spirit of enmity in man, as existing even in the great national corporations of that animal, for the purpose of attaining through the inevitable antagonism of this spirit a state of rest and security; i.e., by wars, by the immoderate exhaustion of incessant preparations for war, and by the pressure of evil consequences which war at last entails upon any nation even through the midst of peace—she drives nations to all sorts of experiments and expedients; and finally, after infinite devastations, ruin, and universal exhaustion of energy, to one which reason should have suggested without the cost of so sad an experience; viz., to quit the barbarous condition of lawless power, and to enter into a federal league of nations, in which even the weakest member looks for its rights and for protection—not to its own power, or its own adjudication, but to this great confederation (*Fœdus Amphictyonum*), to the united power, and the adjudication of the collective will. Visionary as this idea may seem, and as such laughed at the Abbé de Saint-Pierre and in Rousseau (possibly because they deemed it too near to its accomplishment)—it is notwithstanding the inevitable resource and mode of escape under that pressure of evil which nations reciprocally inflict; and, hard as it may be to realize such an idea, states must of necessity be driven at last to the very same resolution to which the savage man of nature was driven with equal reluctance—viz., to sacrifice brutal liberty, and to seek peace and security in a civil constitution founded upon law. All wars therefore are so many tentative essays (not in the intention of man, but in the intention of nature) to bring about new relations of states, and by revolutions and dismemberments to form new political bodies: these again, either from internal defects or external attacks, cannot support themselves, but must undergo similar revolutions; until at last, partly by the best possible arrangement of civil government within, and partly by common concert and legal compact without, a condition is attained which, like a well-ordered commonwealth, can maintain itself in the way of an automaton.

Now, whether (in the first place) it is to be anticipated from an epicurean concourse of efficient causes that states, like atoms, by accidental shocking together, should go through all sorts of new combinations to be again dissolved by the fortuitous impulse of fresh shocks, until at length by pure accident some combination emerges capable of supporting itself (a case of luck that could hardly be looked for); or whether (in the second place) we should rather assume that nature is in this instance pursuing her regular course of raising our species gradually from the lower steps of animal existence to the very highest of a human existence, and *that* not by any direct interposition in our favor, but through man's own spontaneous and artificial efforts (spontaneous, but yet extorted from him by his situation), and in this apparently wild arrangement of things is developing with perfect regularity the original tendencies she has implanted: or whether (in the third place) it is more reasonable to believe that out of all this action and reaction of the human species upon itself nothing in the shape of a wise result will ever issue; that it will continue to be as it has been; and therefore that it cannot be known beforehand, but that the discord, which is so natural to our species, will finally prepare for us a hell of evils under the most moral condition of society, such as may swallow up this very moral condition itself and all previous advance in culture by a reflux of the original barbaric spirit of desolation (a fate, by the way, against which it is impossible to be secured under the government of blind chance, with which liberty uncontrolled by law is identical, unless by underlaying this chance with a secret nexus of wisdom)—to all this the answer turns upon the following question; whether it be reasonable to assume a final purpose of all natural processes and arrangements in the parts, and yet a want of purpose in the whole? What therefore the objectless condition of savage life effected in the end, viz., that it checked the development of the natural tendencies in the human species, but then, by the very evils it thus caused, drove man into a state where those tendencies could unfold and mature themselves, namely, the state of civilization; that same service is performed for states by the barbaric freedom in which they are now existing, viz., that, by causing the dedication of all national energies and resources to war, by the desolations of war and still more by causing the necessity of standing continually in a state of preparation for war, it checks the full development of the natural tendencies in its progress; but on the other hand, by these very evils and their consequences, it compels our species at last to discover some law of counterbalance to the principle of antagonism between nations, and in order to give effect to this law to introduce a federation of states and consequently a cosmopolitical condition of security (or police)—corresponding to that municipal security which arises out of internal police. This federation will itself not be exempt from danger, else the powers of the human race would go to sleep; it will be sufficient that it contain a principle for restoring the equilibrium between its own action and reaction, and thus checking the two functions from destroying each other. Before this last step is taken, human nature—then about halfway advanced in its progress—is in the deepest abyss of evils under the deceitful semblance of external prosperity; and Rousseau was not so much in the wrong when he preferred the condition of the savage to that of the civilized man at the point where he has reached, but is hesitating to take the final step of his ascent. We are at this time in a high degree of *culture* as to arts and sciences. We are *civilized* to superfluity in what regards the graces and decorums of life. But to entitle us to consider ourselves *moralized* much is still wanting. Yet the idea of morality belongs even to that of *culture;* but the use of this idea, as it comes forward in mere *civilization*, is restrained to its influence on manners, as seen in the principle of honor, in respectability of deportment, etc. Nothing indeed of a true moral influence can be expected so long as states direct all their energies to idle plans of aggrandizement by force, and thus incessantly check the slow motions by which the intellect of the species is unfolding and forming itself, to say nothing of their shrinking from all *positive* aid to those motions. But all good, that is not engrafted upon moral good, is mere show and hollow speciousness—the dust and ashes of mortality. And in this delusive condition will the human race linger, until it shall have toiled upwards in the way I have mentioned from its present chaotic abyss of political relations.

• • •

The public right ought to be founded upon a federation of free states.

Nations, as states, like individuals, if they live in a state of nature and without laws, by their vicinity alone commit an act of lesion. One may, in order to secure its own safety, require of another to establish within it a constitution which should guarantee to all their rights. This would be a federation of nations, without the people however forming one and the same state, the idea of a state supposing the relation of a sovereign to the people, of a superior to his inferior. Now several nations, united into one state, would no longer form but one; which contradicts the supposition, the question here being of the reciprocal rights of nations, inasmuch as they compose a multitude of different states, which ought not to be incorporated into one and the same state.

But when we see savages in their anarchy, prefer the perpetual combats of licentious liberty to a reasonable liberty, founded upon constitutional order, can we refrain to look down with the most profound contempt on this animal degradation of humanity? Must we not blush at the contempt to which the want of civilization reduces men? And would one not rather be led to think that civilized nations, each of which form a constituted state, would hasten to extricate themselves from an order of things so ignominious? But what, on the contrary, do we behold? Every state placing its majesty (for it is absurd to talk of the majesty of the people) precisely in this independence of every constraint of any external legislation whatever.

The sovereign places his glory in the power of disposing at his pleasure (without much exposing himself) of many millions of men, ever ready to sacrifice themselves for an object that does not concern them. The only difference between the savages of America and those of Europe, is, that the former have eaten up many a hostile tribe, whereas the latter have known how to make a better use of their enemies; they preserve them to augment the number of their subjects, that is to say, of instruments destined to more extensive conquests. When we consider the perverseness of human nature, which shows itself unveiled and unrestrained in the relations of nations with each other, where it is not checked, as in a state of civilization, by the coercive power of the law, one may well be astonished that the word right has not yet been totally abolished from war-politics as a pedantic word, and that a state has not yet been found bold enough openly to profess this doctrine. For hitherto Grotius, Puffendorf, Vattel, and other useless and impotent defenders of the rights of nations, have been constantly cited in justification of war; though their code, purely philosophic or diplomatic, has never had the force of law, and cannot obtain it; states not being as yet subjected to any coercive power. There is no instance where their reasonings, supported by such respectable authorities, have induced a state to desist from its pretentions. However this homage which all states render to the principle of right, if even consisting only in words, is a proof of a moral disposition, which, though still slumbering, tends nevertheless vigorously to subdue in man that evil principle, of which he cannot entirely divest himself. For otherwise states would never pronounce the word right, when going to war with each other; it were then ironically, as a Gallic prince interpreted it. "It is," said he, "the prerogative nature has given to the stronger, to make himself obeyed by the weaker."

However, the field of battle is the only tribunal before which states plead their cause; but victory, by gaining the suit, does not decide in favor of their cause. Though the treaty of peace puts an end to the present war, it does not abolish a state of war (a state where continually new pretences for war are found); which one cannot affirm to be unjust, since being their own judges, they have no other means of terminating their differences. The law of nations cannot even force them, as the law of nature obliges individuals to get free from this state of war, since having already a legal constitution, as states, they are secure against every foreign compulsion, which might tend to establish among them a more extended constitutional order.

Since, however, from her highest tribunal of moral legislation, reason without exception condemns war as a mean of right, and makes a state of peace an absolute duty; and since this peace cannot be effected or be guaranteed without a compact among nations, they must form an alliance of a peculiar kind, which might be called a pacific alliance different from a treaty of peace inasmuch as it would for ever terminate all wars, whereas the latter only finishes one. This alliance does not tend to any dominion over a state, but solely to the certain maintenance of the liberty of each particular state, partaking of this association, without being therefore obliged to submit, like men in a state of nature, to the legal constraint of public force. It can be proved, that the idea of a federation, which should insensibly extend to all states, and thus lead them to a perpetual peace, may be realized. For if fortune should so direct, that a people as powerful as enlightened, should constitute itself into a republic (a government which in its nature inclines to a perpetual peace) from that time there would be a center for this federative association; other states might adhere thereto, in order to guarantee their liberty according to the principles of public right; and this alliance might insensibly be extended.

That a people should say, "There shall not be war among us: we will form ourselves into a state; that is to say, we will ourselves establish a legislative, executive, and judiciary power, to decide our differences,"—can be conceived.

But if this state should say, "There shall not be war between us and other states, although we do not acknowledge a supreme power, that guarantees our reciprocal rights;" upon what then can this confidence in one's rights be founded, except it is upon this free federation, this supplement of the social compact, which reason necessarily associates with the idea of public right.

The expression of public right, taken in a sense of right of war, presents properly no idea to the mind; since thereby is understood a power of deciding right, not according to universal laws, which restrain within the same limits all individuals, but according to partial maxims, namely, by force. Except one would wish to insinuate by this expression, that it is right, that men who admit such principles should destroy each other, and thus find perpetual peace only in the vast grave that swallows them and their iniquities.

At the tribunal of reason, there is but one means of extricating states from this turbulent situation, in which they are constantly menaced with war; namely, to renounce, like individuals, the anarchic liberty of savages, in order to submit themselves to coercive laws, and thus form a society of nations (*civitas gentium*) which would insensibly embrace all the nations of the earth. But as the ideas which they have of public right, absolutely prevent the realization of this plan, and make them reject in practice what is true in theory, there can only be substituted, to the positive idea of an universal republic (if all is not to be lost) the negative supplement of a permanent alliance, which prevents war, insensibly spreads, and stops the torrent of those unjust and inhuman passions, which always threaten to break down this fence.

The cosmopolitical right shall be limited to conditions of universal hospitality.

In this article, as well as in the preceding ones, it is a question of right, not of philanthropy. Hospitality there signifies solely the right every stranger has of not being treated as an enemy in the country in which he arrives. One may refuse to receive him, if it can be done without endangering his existence; but dares not act hostily towards him, so long as he does not offend any one. The question is not about the right of being received and admitted into the house of an individual: this benevolent custom demanding particular conventions. One speaks here only of the right all men have, of demanding of others to be admitted into their society; a right founded upon that of the common possession of the surface of the earth, whose spherical form obliges them to suffer others to subsist contiguous to them, because they cannot disperse themselves to an indefinite distance, and because originally one has not a greater right to a country than another. The sea and uninhabitable deserts divide the surface of the globe; but the ship and the camel, that vessel of the desert, re-establish the communication and facilitate the right which the human species all possess, of profiting in common by its surface. The inhospitality of the inhabitants of the coasts (for instance of the coast of Barbary) their custom of taking the vessels in the neighboring seas, or that of reducing to slavery the unhappy wretches shipwrecked on their shores; the barbarous practice which in their sandy deserts the Bedouin Arabs exercise of pillaging all those who approach their wandering tribes; all these customs then are contrary to the right of nature, which, nevertheless, in ordaining hospitality, was contented with fixing the conditions on which one may endeavor to form connections with the inhabitants of a country. In this manner distant regions may contract amicable relations with each other, sanctioned in the end by public laws, and thus insensibly mankind may approach towards a cosmopolitical constitution.

At how great a distance from this perfection are the civilized nations, and especially the commercial nations of Europe? At what an excess of injustice do we not behold them arrived, when they discover strange countries and nations? (which with them is the same thing as to conquer). America, the countries inhabited by the negroes, the Spice

Islands, the Cape, &c. were to them countries without proprietors, for the inhabitants they counted as nothing. Under pretext of establishing factories in Hindostan, they carried thither foreign troops, and by their means oppressed the natives, excited wars among the different states of that vast country; spread famine, rebellion, perfidy, and the whole deluge of evils that afflict mankind, among them.

The Chinese and Japanese, whom experience has taught to know the Europeans, wisely refuse their entry into the country, though the former permit their approach, which the latter grant to one European nation only, the Dutch; still, however, excluding them like captives from every communication with the inhabitants. The worst, or to speak with the moralist, the best of the matter is, that all these outrages are to no purpose; that all the commercial companies, guilty of them, touch upon the instant of their ruin; that the sugar islands, that den of slavery the most refined and cruel, produce no real revenue, and are profitable only indirectly, serving views not very laudable, namely, to form sailors for the navies, consequently to carry on war in Europe; which service they render to powers who boast the most of piety, and who, whilst they drink iniquity like water, pretend to equal the elect in point of orthodoxy.

The connections, more or less near, which have taken place among the nations of the earth, having been carried to that point, that a violation of rights, committed in one place, is felt throughout the whole, the idea of a cosmopolitical right can no longer pass for a fantastic exaggeration of right; but is the last step of perfection necessary to the tacit code of civil and public right; these systems at length conducting towards a public right of men in general, and towards a perpetual peace, but to which one cannot hope continually to advance, except by means of the conditions here indicated.

Gender and Race

SOME REFLECTIONS UPON MARRIAGE

Mary Astell

One of the earliest feminist writers was Mary Astell (1666–1731), the daughter of a Newcastle, England, coal merchant, who, after being educated by a clergyman uncle, spent most of her writing career in London. The selection here is from an essay of the name that she wrote in 1700 and makes, perhaps for the first time, the argument that if absolutist rule is illegitimate in the state, it ought to be so in the family.

The Reflector, who hopes Reflector is not bad English, (now Governor is happily of the Feminine Gender) guarded against Curiosity in vain: For a certain ingenuous Gentleman, as she is inform'd, had the Good-nature to own these Reflections, so far, as to affirm that he had the Original MS. in his Closet, a Proof she is not able to produce; and so to make himself responsible for all their Faults, for which, she returns him all due Acknowledgement. However, the Generality being of Opinion, that a Man would have had more Prudence and Manners than to have Publish'd such unseasonable Truths, or to have betray'd the *Arcana Imperii* of his Sex; she humbly confesses, that the Contrivance and Execution of this Design, which is unfortunately accus'd of being so destructive to the Government, (of the Men, I mean) is entirely her own. She neither advis'd with Friends, nor turn'd over ancient or modern Authors, nor prudently submitted to the Correction of such as are, or such as *think* they are good Judges, but with an *English* Spirit and Genius, set out upon the Forlorn Hope, meaning no Hurt to any body, nor designing any thing but the public Good, and to retrieve, if possible, the Native Liberty, the Rights and Privileges of the Subject.

FAR be it from her to stir up Sedition of any sort: none can abhor it more; and she heartily wishes, that our Masters would pay their Civil and Ecclesiastical Governors the same Submission, which they themselves exact from their Domestic Subjects. Nor can she imagine how she any way undermines the Masculine Empire, or blows the Trumpet of Rebellion to the Moiety of Mankind. Is it by exhorting Women, not to expect to have their own Will in any thing, but to be entirely Submissive, when once they have made Choice of a Lord and Master, though he happen not to be so wise, so kind, or even so just a Governor as was expected? She did not, indeed, advise them to think his Folly Wisdom, nor his Brutality, that Love and Worship he promised in his Matrimonial Oath; for this required a Flight of Wit and Sense much above her poor Ability, and proper only to Masculine Understandings. However, she did not in any manner prompt them to Resist, or to Abdicate the Perjur'd spouse, though the Laws of GOD, and the Land, make special Provision for it, in a Case, wherein, as is to be fear'd, few Men can truly plead Not Guilty.

'Tis true, through want of Learning, and that of Superior Genius which Men, as Men, lay claim to, she was ignorant of the Natural Inferiority of our Sex, which our Masters lay down as a Self-evident and Fundamental Truth. She saw nothing in the Reason of Things, to make this either a Principle or a Conclusion, but much to the contrary; it being Sedition at least, if not Treason, to assert it in this Reign. For if by the Natural Superiority of their Sex, they mean, that every Man is by Nature superior to every Woman, which is the obvious Meaning, and that which must be stuck to if they would speak Sense, it would be a Sin in any Woman, to have Dominion over any Man, and the greatest Queen ought not to command, but to obey, her Footman: because no Municipal Laws can supersede or change the Law of Nature: So that if the Dominion of the Men be such, the Salique Law, as unjust as English Men have ever thought it, ought to take Place over all the Earth, and the most glorious Reigns in the English, Danish, Castilian, and other Annals, were wicked Violations of the Law of Nature!

If they mean that some Men are superior to some Women, this is no great Discovery; had they turn'd the Tables, they might have seen that some Women are superior to some Men. Or had they been pleased to remember their Oaths of Allegiance and Supremacy, they might have known, that One Woman is superior to All the Men in these Nations, or else they have sworn to very little Purpose. And it must not be suppos'd, that their Reason and Religion would suffer them to take Oaths, contrary to the Law of Nature and Reason of Things. . . .

BUT what says the Holy Scripture? It speaks of Women as in a State of Subjection, and so it does of the Jews and Christians, when under the Dominion of the Chaldeans and Romans, requiring of the one as well as of the other, a quiet Submission to them under whose Power they liv'd. But will any one say, that these had a Natural Superiority and Right to Dominion? that they had a superior Understanding, or any Preeminence, except what their greater Strength acquir'd? Or, that the other were subjected to their Adversaries for any other Reason but the Punishment of their Sins, and, in order to their Reformation? Or for the Exercise of their Virtue, and because the Order of the World and the Good of Society requir'd it?

If Mankind had never Sinn'd, Reason would always have been obeyed, there would have been no Struggle for Dominion, and Brutal Power would not have prevail'd. But in the lapsed State of Mankind, and now, that Men will not be guided by their Reason but by their Appetites, and do not what they ought but what they can, the Reason, or that which stands for it, the Will and Pleasure of the Governor, is to be the Reason of those who will not be guided by their own, and must take Place for Order's sake, although it should not be conformable to right Reason. Nor can there be any Society great or little, from Empires down to private Families, without a last Resort, to determine the Affairs of that Society by an irresistible Sentence. Now unless this Supremacy be fix'd somewhere, there will be a perpetual Contention about it, such is the Love of Dominion, and let the Reason of Things be what it may, those who have least Force or Cunning to supply it, will have the Disadvantage. So that since Women are acknowledged to have least Bodily Strength, their being commanded to Obey is in pure Kindness to them, and for their Quiet and Security, as well as for the Exercise of their Virtue. But does it follow, that Domestic Governors have more Sense than their Subjects, any more than other Governors have? We do not find that any Man thinks the worse of his own Understanding, because another has superior Power; or concludes himself less capable of a Post of Honor and Authority, because he is not prefer'd to it. How much Time would lie on Mens Hands, how empty would the Places of Concourse be, and how silent most Companies, did Men forbear to censure their Governors, that is, in effect, to think themselves wiser. Indeed, Government would be much more desirable than it is, did it invest the Possessor with a superior Understanding as well as Power. And if mere Power gives a Right to Rule, there can be no such Thing as Usurpation; but a Highway-Man, so long as he has Strength to force, has also a Right to require our Obedience.

AGAIN, if absolute Sovereignty be not necessary in a State, how comes it to be so in a Family? Or if in a Family why not in a State; since no Reason can be alleged for the one that will not hold more strongly for the other? If the Authority of the Husband, so far as it extends, is sacred and inalienable, why not that of the Prince? The Domestic Sovereign is without Dispute elected; and the Stipulations and Contract are mutual; is it not then partial in Men to the last Degree, to contend for, and practice that Arbitrary Dominion in their Families, which they abhor and exclaim against in the State? For if Arbitrary Power is evil in it self, and an improper Method of Governing Rational and Free Agents, it ought not to be practis'd any where; nor is it less, but rather more mischievous in Families than in Kingdoms, by how much 100,000 Tyrants are worse than one. What though a Husband can't deprive a Wife of Life without being responsible to the Law, he may, however, do what is much more grievous to a generous Mind, render Life miserable, for which she has no Redress, scarce Pity, which is afforded to every other Complainant, it being thought a Wife's Duty to suffer every thing without Complaint. If all Men are born Free, how is it that all Women are born Slaves? As they must be, if the being subjected to the inconstant, uncertain, unknown, arbitrary Will of Men be the perfect Condition of Slavery? And, if the Essence of Freedom consists, as our Masters say it does, in having a standing Rule to live by? And why is Slavery so much condemn'd and strove against in one Case, and so highly applauded, and held so necessary and so sacred in another.

'TIS true, that GOD told Eve after the Fall, that her Husband should Rule over her: And so it is, that he told Esau by the Mouth of Isaac his Father, that he should serve his younger Brother, and should in Time, and when he was strong enough to do it, break the Yoke from off his Neck. Now, why one Text should be a Command any more than the other, and not both of them be Predictions only; or why the former should prove Adam's Natural Right to Rule, and much less every Man's, and any more than the latter is a Proof of Jacob's Right to Rule, and of Esau's to Rebel, one is yet to learn? The Text in both Cases foretelling what would be; but neither of them determining what ought to be.

BUT the Scripture commands Wives to submit themselves to their own Husbands. True; for which St. Paul gives a Mystical Reason (Eph.

v. 22, &c.) and St. Peter, a Prudential and Charitable one, (I Pet. iii.) but neither of them derive that Subjection from the Law of Nature. Nay, St. Paul, as if he foresaw and meant to prevent this Plea, giving Directions for their Conduct to Women in general, I Tim. ii. when he comes to speak of Subjection, he changes his Phrase from Women, which denotes the whole Sex, to Woman, which in the New Testament is appropriated to a Wife.

As for his not suffering Women to speak in the Church, no sober Person that I know of pretends to it. That learned Paraphrast, indeed, who lays so much Stress on the Natural Subjection, provided this Prerogative be secur'd, is willing to give up the other. For he endeavors to prove, that Inspir'd Women, as well as Men, us'd to speak in the Church, and that St. Paul does not forbid it, but only takes Care that the Women should signify their Subjection by wearing a Veil. But the Apostle is his own best Expositor, let us therefore compare his Precepts with his Practice, for he was all of a Piece, and did not contradict himself. Now by this Comparison we find, that though he forbids Women to teach in the Church, and this for several Prudential Reasons, like those he introduces with an "I give my Opinion, and now speak I, not the Lord," and not because of any Law of Nature, or positive Divine Precept, for that the Words they are commanded (I Cor. xiv. 24.) are not in the Original, appears from the Italic Character, yet he did not found this Prohibition or any suppos'd Want of Understanding in Woman, or of Ability to teach; neither does he confine them at all Times to learn in Silence. For the eloquent Apollos, who was himself a Teacher, was instructed by Priscilla, as well as by her Husband Aquila, and was improv'd by them both in the Christian Faith. Nor does St. Paul blame her for this, or suppose that she usurp'd Authority over that great Man; so far from this, that as she is always honorably mention'd in Holy Scripture, so our Apostle, in his Salutations, Rom. xvi. places her in the Front, even before her Husband, giving to her, as well as to him, the Noble Title of, his Helper in Christ Jesus, and of one to whom all the Churches of the Gentiles had great Obligations. . . .

SOME Men will have it, that the Reason of our LORD's appearing first to the Women, was, their being least able to keep a Secret; a witty and masculine Remark, and wonderfully Reverent! But not to dispute whether those Women were Blabs or no, there are many Instances in Holy Scripture, of Women who did not betray the Confidence repos'd in them. Thus Rahab, though formerly an ill Woman, being converted by the Report of those Miracles, which, though the Israelites saw, yet they believed not in GOD, nor put their Trust in his Word. She acknowledges the GOD in Heaven, and, as a Reward of her faithful Service, in concealing Joshua's Spies, is, with her Family, exempted from the Ruin of her Country, and also, has the Honor of being named in the Messiah's Genealogy. Michal, to save David's Life, exposes her self to the Fury of a Jealous and Tyrannical Prince. A Girl was trusted by David's grave Counselors to convey him Intelligence in his Son's Rebellion; and when a Lad had found it out, and blab'd it to Absalom, the King's Friends confiding in the Prudence and Fidelity of a Woman, were secur'd by her. When our LORD escaped from the Jews, he trusted Himself in the Hands of Martha and Mary. So does St. Peter with another Mary, when the Angel deliver'd him from Herod, the Damsel Rhoda too, was acquainted with the Secret. More might be said, but one would think here is enough to show, that whatever other great and wise Reasons Men may have for despising Women, and keeping them in Ignorance and Slavery, it can't be from their having learnt to do so in Holy Scripture. The Bible is for, and not against us, and cannot without great Violence done to it, be urg'd to our Prejudice.

HOWEVER, there are strong and prevalent Reasons which demonstrate the Superiority and Pre-eminence of the Men. For in the first Place, Boys have much Time and Pains, Care and Cost bestow'd on their Education, Girls have little or none. The former are early initiated in the Sciences, are made acquainted with ancient and modern Discoveries, they study Books and Men, have all imaginable Encouragement; not only Fame, a dry Reward now a-days, but also Title, Authority, Power, and Riches themselves, which purchase all Things, are the Reward of their Improvement. The latter are restrain'd, frown'd upon, and beat, nor for, but from the Muses; Laughter and Ridicule, that never-failing Scare-Crow, is set up to drive them from the Tree of Knowledge. But if, in spite of all Difficulties Nature prevails, and they can't be kept so ignorant as their Masters would have them, they are star'd upon as Monsters, censur'd, envied, and every way discouraged, or, at the best, they have the Fate the Proverb assigns them, Virtue is prais'd and starv'd. And therefore, since the coarsest Materials need the most Curing, as every Workman can inform you, and the worst Ground the most elaborate Culture, it undeniably follows, that Mens Understandings are superior to Womens, for, after many Years Study and Experience, they become wise and learned, and Women are not born so!

AGAIN, Men are possessed of all Places of Power, Trust and Profit, they make Laws and exercise the Magistracy, not only the sharpest Sword, but even all the Swords and Blunderbusses are theirs; which by the strongest Logic in the World, gives them the best Title to every Thing they please to claim as their Prerogative: Who shall contend with them? Immemorial Prescription is on their Side in these Parts of the World, ancient Tradition and modern Usage! Our Fathers, have all along, both taught and practiced Superiority over the weaker Sex, and consequently Women are by Nature inferior to Men, as was to be demonstrated. An Argument which must be acknowledged unanswerable; for, as well as I love my Sex, I will not pretend a Reply to such Demonstration!

ONLY let me beg to be inform'd, to whom we poor Fatherless Maids, and Widows who have lost their Masters, owe Subjection? It can't be to all Men in general, unless all Men were agreed to give the same Commands; Do we then fall as Strays, to the first who finds us? by the Maxims of some Men, and the Conduct of some Women one would think so. But whoever he be that thus happens to become our Master, if he allows us to be reasonable Creatures, and does not merely Compliment us with that Title, since no Man denies our Readiness to use our Tongues, it would tend, I should think, to our Master's Advantage, and therefore he may please to be advis'd to teach us to improve our Reason. But if Reason is only allow'd us by way of Raillery, and the secret Maxim is, that we have none, or little more than Brutes, 'tis the best way to confine us with Chain and Block to the Chimney-Corner, which, probably, might save the Estates of some Families and the Honor of others.

I do not propose this to prevent a Rebellion, for Women are not so well united as to form an Insurrection. They are for the most part wise enough to love their Chains, and to discern how very becomingly they fit. They think as humbly of themselves as their Masters can wish, with respect to the other Sex, but in regard to their own, they have a Spice of Masculine Ambition; every one would Lead, and none would Follow. Both Sexes being too apt to Envy, and too backward in Emulating, and take more Delight in Detracting from their Neighbor's Virtue, than in Improving their own. And therefore, as to those Women who find themselves born for Slavery, and are so sensible of their own Meanness, as to conclude it impossible to attain to any thing excellent, since they are, or ought to be best acquainted with their own Strength and Genius, She's a Fool who would attempt their Deliverance or Improvement. No, let them enjoy the great Honor and Felicity of their tame, submissive and depending Temper! Let the Men applaud, and let them glory in this wonderful Humility! Let them receive the Flatteries and Grimaces of the other Sex, live unenvied by their own, and be as much belov'd as one such Woman can afford to love another! Let them enjoy the Glory of treading in the Footsteps of their Predecessors, and of having the Prudence to avoid that audacious Attempt of soaring beyond their Sphere! Let them Huswife or Play, Dress, and be pretty entertaining Company! Or, which is better, relieve the Poor to ease their own Compassions, read pious Books, say their Prayers, and go to Church, because they have been taught and us'd to do so, without being able to give a better Reason for their Faith and Practice! Let them not by any Means aspire at being Women of Understanding, because no Man can endure a Woman of Superior Sense, or would treat a reasonable Woman civilly, but that he thinks he stands on higher Ground, and, that she is so wise as to make Exceptions in his Favor, and to take her Measures by his Directions; they may pretend to Sense, indeed, since mere Pretenses only render one the more ridiculous! Let them, in short, be what is call'd very Women, for this is most acceptable to all sorts of Men; or let them aim at the Title of good devout Women, since some Men can bear with this; but let them not judge of the Sex by their own Scantling: For the great Author of Nature and Fountain of all Perfection, never design'd that the Mean and Imperfect, but that the most Complete and Excellent of His Creatures of every Kind, should be the Standard to the rest.

TO conclude; If that GREAT QUEEN who has subdued the Proud, and made the pretended Invincible more than once fly before her; who has Rescued an Empire, Reduced a Kingdom, Conquer'd Provinces in as little Time almost as one can Travel them, and seems to have chain'd Victory to her Standard; who disposes of Crowns, gives Laws and Liberty to Europe, and is the chief Instrument in the Hand of the Almighty, to pull down and to set up the great Men of the Earth; who conquers every where for others, and no where for her self but in the Hearts of the Conquer'd, who are of the Number of those who reap the Benefit of her Triumphs; whilst she only reaps for her self the Laurels of disinterested Glory, and the Royal Pleasure of doing Heroically; if this Glory of her own Sex, and Envy of the other, will not think we need, or does not hold us worthy of, the Protection of her ever victorious Arms, and Men have not the Gratitude, for her sake at least, to do Justice to her Sex, who has been such a universal Benefactress to theirs: Adieu to the Liberties, not of this or that Nation or Reign only, but of the Moiety of Mankind! To all the great Things that Women might perform, inspir'd by her Example, encouraged by her Smiles, and supported by her Power! To their Discovery of new Worlds for the Exercise of her Goodness, new Sciences to publish her Fame, and reducing Nature it self to a Subjection to her Empire! To their destroying those worst of Tyrants Impiety and Immorality, which dare to stalk about even in her own Dominions, and to devour Souls almost within View of her Throne, leaving a Stench behind them scarce to be corrected even by the Incense of her Devotions! To the Women's tracing a new Path to Honor, in which none shall walk but such as scorn to Cringe in order to Rise, and who are Proof both against giving and receiving Flattery! In a Word, to those Halcyon, or, if you will, Millennium Days, in which the Wolf and the Lamb shall feed together, and a Tyrannous Domination, which Nature never meant, shall no longer render useless, if not hurtful, the Industry and Understandings of half Mankind!

DUTIES OF WOMEN

Jean-Jacques Rousseau

The most egalitarian of all the philosophes, *Rousseau was also the most outspoken about what he considered to be women's naturally subordinate role and their duty to please and delight men. While this theme is found in all his writings, its most developed statement is in his 1762 novel,* Emile.

Taste, good or bad, takes its shape especially in the intercourse between the two sexes; the cultivation of taste is a necessary consequence of this form of society. But when enjoyment is easily obtained, and the desire to please becomes lukewarm, taste must degenerate; and this is, in my opinion, one of the best reasons why good taste implies good morals.

Consult the women's opinions in bodily matters, in all that concerns the senses; consult the men in matters of morality and all that concerns the understanding. When women are what they ought to be, they will keep to what they can understand, and their judgment will be right; but since they have set themselves up as judges of literature, since they have begun to criticize books and to make them with might and main, they are altogether astray. Authors who take the advice of blue-stockings will always be ill-advised; gallants who consult them about their clothes will always be absurdly dressed. I shall presently have an opportunity of speaking of the real talents of the female sex, the way to cultivate these talents, and the matters in regard to which their decisions should receive attention. . . .

In the union of the sexes each alike contributes to the common end, but in different ways. From this diversity springs the first difference which may be observed between man and woman in their moral relations. The man should be strong and active; the woman should be weak and passive; the one must have both the power and the will; it is enough that the other should offer little resistance.

When this principle is admitted, it follows that woman is specially made for man's delight. If man in his turn ought to be pleasing in her eyes, the necessity is less urgent, his virtue is in his strength, he pleases because he is strong. I grant you this is not the law of love, but it is the law of nature, which is older than love itself.

If woman is made to please and to be in subjection to man, she ought to make herself pleasing in his eyes and not provoke him to anger; her strength is in her charms, by their means she should compel him to discover and use his strength. The surest way of arousing this strength is to make it necessary by resistance. Thus pride comes to the help of desire and each exults in the other's victory. This is the origin of attack and defense, of the boldness of one sex and the timidity of the other, and even of the shame and modesty with which nature has armed the weak for the conquest of the strong.

Who can possibly suppose that nature has prescribed the same advances to the one sex as to the other, or that the first to feel desire should be the first to show it? What strange depravity of judgment! The consequences of the act being so different for the two sexes, is it natural that they should enter upon it with equal boldness? How can any one fail to see that when the share of each is so unequal, if the one were not controlled by modesty as the other is controlled by nature, the result would be the destruction of both, and the human race would perish through the very means ordained for its continuance?

Women so easily stir a man's senses and fan the ashes of a dying passion, that if philosophy ever succeeded in introducing this custom into any unlucky country, especially if it were a warm country where more women are born than men, the men, tyrannized over by the women, would at last become their victims, and would be dragged to their death without the least chance of escape.

Female animals are without this sense of shame, but what of that? Are their desires as boundless as those of women, which are curbed by this shame? The desires of the animals are the result of necessity, and when the need is satisfied, the desire ceases; they no longer make a feint of repulsing the male, they do it in earnest. Their seasons of complaisance are short and soon over. Impulse and restraint are alike the work of nature. But what would take the place of this negative instinct in women if you rob them of their modesty?

The Most High has deigned to do honor to mankind; he has endowed man with boundless passions, together with a law to guide them, so that man may be alike free and self-controlled; though swayed by these passions man is endowed with reason by which to control them. Woman is also endowed with boundless passions; God has given her modesty to restrain them. Moreover, he has given to both a present reward for the right use of their powers, in the delight which springs from that right use of them, *i.e.,* the taste for right conduct established as the law of our behavior. To my mind this is far higher than the instinct of the beasts.

Whether the woman shares the man's passion or not, whether she is willing or unwilling to satisfy it, she always repulses him and defends herself, though not always with the same vigor, and therefore not always with the same success. If the siege is to be successful, the besieged must permit or direct the attack. How skillfully can she stimulate the efforts of the aggressor. The freest and most delightful of activities does not permit of any real violence; reason and nature are alike against it; nature, in that she has given the weaker party strength enough to resist if she chooses; reason, in that actual violence is not only most brutal in itself, but it defeats its own ends, not only because the man thus declares war against his companion and thus gives her a right to defend her person and her liberty even at the cost of the enemy's life, but also because the woman alone is the judge of her condition, and a child would have no father if any man might usurp a father's rights.

Thus the different constitution of the two sexes leads us to a third conclusion, that the stronger party seems to be master, but is as a matter of fact dependent on the weaker, and that, not by any foolish custom of gallantry, nor yet by the magnanimity of the protector, but by an inexorable law of nature. For nature has endowed woman with a power of stimulating man's passions in excess of man's power of satisfying those passions, and has thus made him dependent on her goodwill, and compelled him in his turn to endeavor to please her, so that she may be willing to yield to his superior strength. Is it weakness which yields to force, or is it voluntary self-surrender? This uncertainty constitutes the chief charm of the man's victory, and the woman is usually cunning enough to leave him in doubt. In this respect the woman's mind exactly resembles her body; far from being ashamed of her weakness, she is proud of it; her soft muscles offer no resistance, she professes that she cannot lift the lightest weight; she would be ashamed to be strong. And why? Not only to gain an appearance of refinement; she is too clever for that; she is providing herself beforehand with excuses, with the right to be weak if she chooses.

The consequences of sex are wholly unlike for man and woman. The male is only a male now and again, the female is always a female, or at least all her youth; everything reminds her of her sex; the performance of her functions requires a special constitution. She needs care during pregnancy and freedom from work when her child is born; she must have a quiet, easy life while she nurses her children; their education calls for patience and gentleness, for a zeal and love which nothing can dismay; she forms a bond between father and child, she alone can win the father's love for his children and convince him that they are indeed his own. What loving care is required to preserve a united family! And there should be no question of virtue in all this, it must be a labor of love, without which the human race would be doomed to extinction.

The mutual duties of the two sexes are not, and cannot be, equally binding on both. Women do wrong to complain of the inequality of man-made laws; this inequality is not of man's making, or at any rate it is not the result of mere prejudice, but of reason. She to whom nature has entrusted the care of the children must hold herself responsible for them to their father. No doubt every breach of faith is wrong, and every faithless husband, who robs his wife of the sole reward of the stern duties of her sex, is cruel and unjust; but the faithless wife is worse; she destroys the family and breaks the bonds of nature; when she gives her husband children who are not his own, she is false both to him and them, her crime is not infidelity but treason. To my mind, it is the source of dissension and of crime of every kind. Can any position be more wretched than that of the unhappy father who, when he clasps his child to his breast, is haunted by the suspicion that this is the child of another, the badge of his own dishonor, a thief who is robbing his own children of their inheritance. Under such circumstances the family is little more than a group of secret enemies, armed against each other by a guilty woman, who compels them to pretend to love one another.

Thus it is not enough that a wife should be faithful; her husband, along with his friends and neighbors, must believe in her fidelity; she must be modest, devoted, retiring; she should have the witness not only of a good conscience, but of a good reputation. In a word, if a father must love his children, he must be able to respect their mother. For these reasons it is not enough that the woman should be chaste, she must preserve her reputation and her good name. From these principles there arises not only a moral difference between the sexes, but also a fresh motive for duty and propriety, which prescribes to women in particular the most scrupulous attention to their conduct, their manners, their behavior. Vague assertions as to the equality of the sexes and the similarity of their duties are only empty words; they are no answer to my argument.

It is a poor sort of logic to quote isolated exceptions against laws so firmly established. Women, you say, are not always bearing children. Granted; yet that is their proper business. Because there are a hundred or so of large towns in the world where women live licentiously and have few children, will you maintain that it is their business to have few children? And what would become of your towns if the remote country districts, with their simpler and purer women, did not make up for the barrenness of your fine ladies? There are plenty of country places where women with only four or five children are reckoned unfruitful. In conclusion, although here and there a woman may have few children, what difference does it make? Is it any the less a woman's business to be a mother? And do not the general laws of nature and morality make provision for this state of things?

Even if there were these long intervals, which you assume, between the periods of pregnancy, can a woman suddenly change her way of life without danger? Can she be a nursing mother today and a soldier tomorrow? Will she change her tastes and her feelings as a chameleon changes his color? Will she pass at once from the privacy of household duties and indoor occupations to the buffeting of the winds, the toils, the labors, the perils of war? Will she be now timid, now brave, now fragile, now robust? If the young men of Paris find a soldier's life too hard for them, how would a woman put up with it, a woman who has hardly ventured out of doors without a parasol and who has scarcely put a foot to the ground? Will she make a good soldier at an age when even men are retiring from this arduous business?

There are countries, I grant you, where women bear and rear children with little or no difficulty, but in those lands the men go half-naked in all weathers, they strike down the wild beasts, they carry a canoe as easily as a knapsack, they pursue the chase for 700 or 800 leagues, they sleep in the open on the bare ground, they bear incredible fatigues and go many days without food. When women become strong, men become still stronger; when men become soft, women become softer; change both the terms and the ratio remains unaltered.

I am quite aware that Plato, in the *Republic*, assigns the same gymnastics to women and men. Having got rid of the family there is no place for women in his system of government, so he is forced to turn them into men. That great genius has worked out his plans in detail and has provided for every contingency; he has even provided against a difficulty which in all likelihood no one would ever have raised; but he has not succeeded in meeting the real difficulty. I am not speaking of the alleged community of wives which has often been laid to his charge; this assertion only shows that his detractors have never read his works. I refer to that political promiscuity under which the same occupations are assigned to both sexes alike, a scheme which could only lead to intolerable evils; I refer to that subversion of all the tenderest of our natural feelings, which he sacrificed to an artificial sentiment which can only exist by their aid. Will the bonds of convention hold firm without some foundation in nature? Can devotion to the state exist apart from the love of those near and dear to us? Can patriotism thrive except in the soil of that miniature fatherland, the home? Is it not the good son, the good husband, the good father, who makes the good citizen?

When once it is proved that men and women are and ought to be unlike in constitution and in temperament, it follows that their education must be different. Nature teaches us that they should work together, but that each has its own share of the work; the end is the same, but the means are different, as are also the feelings which direct them. We have attempted to paint a natural man, let us try to paint a helpmeet for him.

You must follow nature's guidance if you would walk aright. The native characters of sex should be respected as nature's handiwork. You are always saying, "Women have such and such faults, from which we are free." You are misled by your vanity; what would be faults in you are virtues in them; and things would go worse, if they were without these so-called faults. Take care that they do not degenerate into evil, but beware of destroying them.

On the other hand, women are always exclaiming that we educate them for nothing but vanity and coquetry, that we keep them amused with trifles that we may be their masters; we are responsible, so they say, for the faults we attribute to them. How silly! What have men to do with the education of girls? What is there to hinder their mothers educating them as they please? There are no colleges for girls; so much the better for them! Would God there were none for the boys, their education would be more sensible and more wholesome. Who is it that compels a girl to waste her time on foolish trifles? Are they forced, against their will, to spend half their time over their toilet, following the example set them by you? Who prevents you teaching them, or having them taught, whatever seems good in your eyes? Is it our fault that we are charmed by their beauty and delighted by their airs and graces, if we are attracted and flattered by the arts they learn from you, if we love to see them prettily dressed, if we let them display at leisure the weapons by which we are subjugated? Well then, educate them like men. The more women are like men, the less influence they will have over men, and then men will be masters indeed.

All the faculties common to both sexes are not equally shared between them, but taken as a whole they are fairly divided. Woman is worth more as a woman and less as a man; when she makes a good use of her own rights, she has the best of it; when she tries to usurp our rights, she is our inferior. It is impossible to controvert this, except by quoting exceptions after the usual fashion of the partisans of the fair sex.

To cultivate the masculine virtues in women and to neglect their own is evidently to do them an injury. Women are too clear-sighted to be thus deceived; when they try to usurp our privileges they do not abandon their own; with this result: they are unable to make use of two incompatible things, so they fall below their own level as women, instead of rising to the level of men. If you are a sensible mother you will take my advice. Do not try to make your daughter a good man in defiance of nature. Make her a good woman, and be sure it will be better both for her and us.

Does this mean that she must be brought up in ignorance and kept to housework only? Is she to be man's handmaid or his helpmeet? Will he dispense with her greatest charm, her companionship? To keep her a slave will he prevent her knowing and feeling? Will he make an automaton of her? No, indeed, that is not the teaching of nature, who has given women such a pleasant easy wit. On the contrary, nature means them to think, to will, to love, to cultivate their minds as well as their persons; she puts these weapons in their hands to make up for their lack of strength and to enable them to direct the strength of men. They should learn many things, but only such things as are suitable.

When I consider the special purpose of woman, when I observe her inclinations or reckon up her duties, everything combines to indicate the mode of education she requires. Men and women are made for each other, but their mutual dependence differs in degree; man is dependent on woman through his desires; woman is dependent on man through her desires and also through her needs; he could do without her better than she can do without him. She cannot fulfill her purpose in life without his aid, without his goodwill, without his respect; she is dependent on our feelings, on the price we put upon her virtue, and the opinion we have of her charms and her deserts. Nature herself has decreed that woman, both for herself and her children, should be at the mercy of man's judgment.

Worth alone will not suffice, a woman must be thought worthy; nor beauty, she must be admired; nor virtue, she must be respected. A woman's honor does not depend on her conduct alone, but on her reputation, and no woman who permits herself to be considered vile is really virtuous. A man has no one but himself to consider, and so long as he does right he may defy public opinion; but when a woman does right her task is only half finished, and what people think of her matters as much as what she really is. Hence her education must, in this respect, be different from man's education. "What will people think" is the grave of a man's virtue and the throne of a woman's.

The children's health depends in the first place on the mother's, and the early education of man is also in a woman's hands; his morals, his passions, his tastes, his pleasures, his happiness itself, depend on her. A woman's education must therefore be planned in relation to man. To be pleasing in his sight, to win his respect and love, to train him in childhood, to tend him in manhood, to counsel and console, to make his life pleasant and happy, these are the duties of woman for all time, and this is what she should be taught while she is young. The further we depart from this principle, the further we shall be from our goal, and all our precepts will fail to secure her happiness or our own.

Every woman desires to be pleasing in men's eyes, and this is right; but there is a great difference between wishing to please a man of worth, a really lovable man, and seeking to please those foppish manikins who are a disgrace to their own sex and to the sex which they imitate. Neither nature nor reason can induce a woman to love an effeminate person, nor will she win love by imitating such a person.

If a woman discards the quiet modest bearing of her sex, and adopts the airs of such foolish creatures, she is not following her vocation, she is forsaking it; she is robbing herself of the rights to which she lays claim. "If we were different," she says, "the men would not like us." She is mistaken. Only a fool likes folly; to wish to attract such men only shows her own foolishness. If there were no frivolous men, women would soon make them, and women are more responsible for men's follies than men are for theirs. The woman who loves true manhood and seeks to find favor in its sight will adopt means adapted to her ends. Woman is a coquette by profession, but her coquetry varies with her aims; let these aims be in accordance with those of nature, and a woman will receive a fitting education.

Even the tiniest little girls love finery; they are not content to be pretty, they must be admired; their little airs and graces show that their heads are full of this idea, and as soon as they can understand they are controlled by "What will people think of you?" If you are foolish enough to try this way with little boys, it will not have the same effect; give them their freedom and their sports, and they care very little what people think; it is a work of time to bring them under the control of this law.

However acquired, this early education of little girls is an excellent thing in itself. As the birth of the body must precede the birth of the mind, so the training of the body must precede the cultivation of the mind. This is true of both sexes; but the aim of physical training for boys and girls is not the same; in the one case it is the development of strength, in the other of grace; not that these qualities should be peculiar to either sex, but that their relative values should be different. Women should be strong enough to do anything gracefully; men should be skillful enough to do anything easily.

The exaggeration of feminine delicacy leads to effeminacy in men. Women should not be strong like men but for them, so that their sons may be strong. Convents and boarding-schools, with their plain food and ample opportunities for amusements, races, and games in the open air and in the garden, are better in this respect than the home, where the little girl is fed on delicacies, continually encouraged or reproved, where she is kept sitting in a stuffy room, always under her mother's eye, afraid to stand or walk or speak or breathe, without a moment's freedom to play or jump or run or shout, or to be her natural, lively, little self; there is either harmful indulgence or misguided severity, and no trace of reason. In this fashion heart and body are alike destroyed. . . .

Boys and girls have many games in common, and this is as it should be; do they not play together when they are grown up? They have also special tastes of their own. Boys want movement and noise, drums, tops, toy-carts; girls prefer things which appeal to the eye, and can be used for dressing-up—mirrors, jewelry, finery, and specially dolls. The doll is the girl's special plaything; this shows her instinctive bent towards her life's work. The art of pleasing finds its physical basis in personal adornment, and this physical side of the art is the only one which the child can cultivate.

Here is a little girl busy all day with her doll; she is always changing its clothes, dressing and undressing it, trying new combinations of trimmings well or ill matched; her fingers are clumsy, her taste is crude, but there is no mistaking her bent; in this endless occupation time flies unheeded, the hours slip away unnoticed, even meals are forgotten. She is more eager for adornment than for food. "But she is dressing her doll, not herself," you will say. Just so; she sees her doll, she cannot see herself; she cannot do anything for herself, she has neither the training, nor the talent, nor the strength; as yet she herself is nothing, she is engrossed in her doll and all her coquetry is devoted to it. This will not always be so; in due time she will be her own doll.

We have here a very early and clearly marked bent; you have only to follow it and train it. What the little girl most clearly desires is to dress her doll, to make its bows, its tippets, its sashes, and its tuckers; she is dependent on other people's kindness in all this, and it would be much pleasanter to be able to do it herself. Here is a motive for her earliest lessons, they are not tasks prescribed, but favors bestowed. Little girls always dislike learning to read and write, but they are always ready to learn to sew. They think they are grown up, and in imagination they are using their knowledge for their own adornment. . . .

Show the sense of the tasks you set your little girls, but keep them busy. Idleness and insubordination are two very dangerous faults, and very hard to cure when once established. Girls should be attentive and industrious, but this is not enough by itself; they should early be accustomed to restraint. This misfortune, if such it be, is inherent in their sex, and they will never escape from it, unless to endure more cruel sufferings. All their life long, they will have to submit to the strictest and most enduring restraints, those of propriety. They must be trained to bear the yoke from the first, so that they may not feel it, to master their own caprices and to submit themselves to the will of others. If they were always eager to be at work, they should sometimes be compelled to do nothing. Their childish faults, unchecked and unheeded, may easily lead to dissipation, frivolity, and inconstancy. To guard against this, teach them above all things self-control. Under our senseless conditions, the life of a good woman is a perpetual struggle against self; it is only fair that woman should bear her share of the ills she has brought upon man. . . .

Just because they have, or ought to have, little freedom, they are apt to indulge themselves too fully with regard to such freedom as they have; they carry everything to extremes, and they devote themselves to their games with an enthusiasm even greater than that of boys. This is the second difficulty to which I referred. This enthusiasm must be kept in check, for it is the source of several vices commonly found among women, caprice and that extravagant admiration which leads a woman to regard a thing with rapture today and to be quite indifferent to it tomorrow. This fickleness of taste is as dangerous as exaggeration; and both spring from the same cause. Do not deprive them of mirth, laughter, noise, and romping games, but do not let them tire of one game and go off to another; do not leave them for a moment without restraint. Train them to break off their games and return to their other occupations without a murmur. Habit is all that is needed, as you have nature on your side.

This habitual restraint produces a docility which woman requires all her life long, for she will always be in subjection to a man, or to man's judgment, and she will never be free to set her own opinion above his. What is most wanted in a woman is gentleness; formed to obey a creature so imperfect as man, a creature often vicious and always faulty, she should early learn to submit to injustice and to suffer the wrongs inflicted on her by her husband without complaint; she must be gentle for her own sake, not his. Bitterness and obstinacy only multiply the sufferings of the wife and the misdeeds of the husband; the man feels that these are not the weapons to be used against him. Heaven did not make women attractive and persuasive that they might degenerate into bitterness, or meek that they should desire the mastery; their soft voice was not meant for hard words, nor their delicate features for the frowns of anger. When they lose their temper they forget themselves; often enough they have just cause of complaint; but when they scold they always put themselves in the wrong. We should each adopt the tone which befits our sex; a soft-hearted husband may make an overbearing wife, but a man, unless he is a perfect monster, will sooner or later yield to his wife's gentleness, and the victory will be hers.

Daughters must always be obedient, but mothers need not always be harsh. To make a girl docile you need not make her miserable; to make her modest you need not terrify her; on the contrary, I should not be sorry to see her allowed occasionally to exercise a little ingenuity, not to escape punishment for her disobedience, but to evade the necessity for obedience. Her dependence need not be made unpleasant, it is enough that she should realize that she is dependent. Cunning is a natural gift of woman, and so convinced am I that all our natural inclinations are right, that I would cultivate this among others, only guarding against its abuse.

THE FAIR SEX

IMMANUEL KANT

Two years after Rousseau, Kant provided a similar, albeit more philosophically sophisticated, set of gender stereotypes. His gendered juxtaposition of beauty and sublimity reflects the theme of his Observations on the Feeling of the Beautiful and Sublime *(1764), from which the selection is taken.*

He who first conceived of woman under the name of the *fair sex* probably wanted to say something flattering, but he has hit upon it better than even he himself might have believed. For without taking into consideration that her figure in general is finer, her features more delicate and gentler, and her mien more engaging and more expressive of friendliness, pleasantry, and kindness than in the male sex, and not forgetting what one must reckon as a secret magic with which she makes our passion inclined to judgments favorable to her—even so, certain specific traits lie especially in the personality of this sex which distinguish it clearly from ours and chiefly result in making her known by the mark of the beautiful. On the other side, we could make a claim on the title of the *noble sex*, if it were not required of a noble disposition to decline honorific titles and rather to bestow than to receive them. It is not to be understood by this that woman lacks noble qualities, or that the male sex must do without beauty completely. On the contrary, one expects that a person of either sex brings both together, in such a way that all the other merits of a woman should unite solely to enhance the character of the beautiful, which is the proper reference point; and on the other hand, among the masculine qualities the sublime clearly stands out as the criterion of his kind. All judgments of the two sexes must refer to these criteria, those that praise as well as those that blame; all education and instruction must have these before its eyes, and all efforts to advance the moral perfection of the one or the other—unless one wants to disguise the charming distinction that nature has chosen to make between the two sorts of human being. For here it is not enough to keep in mind that we are dealing with human beings; we must also remember that they are not all alike.

Women have a strong inborn feeling for all that is beautiful, elegant, and decorated. Even in childhood they like to be dressed up, and take pleasure when they are adorned. They are cleanly and very delicate in respect to all that provokes disgust. They love pleasantry and can be entertained by trivialities if only these are merry and laughing. Very early they have a modest manner about themselves, know how to give themselves a fine demeanor and be self-possessed—and this at an age when our well-bred male youth is still unruly, clumsy, and confused. They have many sympathetic sensations, goodheartedness, and compassion, prefer the beautiful to the useful, and gladly turn abundance of circumstance into parsimony, in order to support expenditure on adornment and glitter. They have very delicate feelings in regard to the least offense, and are exceedingly precise to notice the most trifling lack of attention and respect toward them. In short, they contain the chief cause in human nature for the contrast of the beautiful qualities with the noble, and they refine even the masculine sex.

I hope the reader will spare me the reckoning of the manly qualities, so far as they are parallel to the feminine, and be content only to consider both in comparison with each other. The fair sex has just as much understanding as the male, but it is a *beautiful understanding*, whereas ours should be a *deep understanding*, an expression that signifies identity with the sublime.

To the beauty of all actions belongs above all the mark that they display facility, and appear to be accomplished without painful toil. On the other hand, strivings and surmounted difficulties arouse admiration and belong to the sublime. Deep meditation and a long-sustained reflection are noble but difficult, and do not well befit a person in whom unconstrained charms should show nothing else than a beautiful nature. Laborious learning or painful pondering, even if a woman should greatly succeed in it, destroy the merits that are proper to her sex, and because of their rarity they can make of her an object of cold admiration; but at the same time they will weaken the charms with which she exercises her great power over the other sex. A woman who has a head full of Greek, like Mme Dacier, or carries on fundamental controversies about mechanics, like the Marquise de Châtelet, might as well even have a beard; for perhaps that would express more obviously the mien of profundity for which she strives. The beautiful understanding selects for its objects everything closely related to the finer feeling, and relinquishes to the diligent, fundamental, and deep understanding abstract speculations or branches of knowledge useful but dry. A woman therefore will learn no geometry; of the principle of sufficient reason or the monads she will know only so much as is needed to perceive the salt in a satire which the insipid grubs of our sex have censured. The fair can leave Descartes his vortices to whirl forever without troubling themselves about them, even though the suave Fontenelle wished to afford them company among the planets; and the attraction of their charms loses none of its strength even if they know nothing of what Algarotti has taken the trouble to sketch out for their benefit about the gravitational attraction of matter according to Newton. In history they will not fill their heads with battles, nor in geography with fortresses, for it becomes them just as little to reek of gunpowder as it does the males to reek of musk.

It appears to be a malicious stratagem of men that they have wanted to influence the fair sex to this perverted taste. For, well aware of their weakness before her natural charms and of the fact that a single sly glance sets them more in confusion than the most difficult problem of science, so soon as woman enters upon this taste they see themselves in a decided superiority and are at an advantage that otherwise they hardly would have, being able to succor their vanity in its weakness by a generous indulgence toward her. The content of woman's great science, rather, is humankind, and among humanity, men. Her philosophy is not to reason, but to sense. In the opportunity that one wants to give to women to cultivate their beautiful nature, one must always keep this relation before his eyes. One will seek to broaden their total moral feeling and not their memory, and that of course not by universal rules but by some judgment upon the conduct that they see about them. The examples one borrows from other times in order to examine the influence the fair sex has had in culture, the various relations to the masculine in which it has stood in other ages or in foreign lands, the character of both so far as it can be illustrated by these, and the changing taste in amusements—these comprise her whole history and geography. For the ladies, it is well to make it a pleasant diversion to see a map setting forth the entire globe or the principal parts of the world. This is brought about by showing it only with the intention of portraying the different characters of peoples that dwell there, and the differences of their taste and moral feeling, especially in respect to the effect these have upon the relations of the sexes—together with a few easy illustrations taken from the differences of their climates, or their freedom or slavery. It is of little consequence whether or not the women know the particular subdivisions of these lands, their industry, power, and sovereigns. Similarly, they will need to know nothing more of the cosmos than is necessary to make the appearance of the heavens on a beautiful evening a stimulating sight to them, if they can conceive to some extent that yet more worlds, and in them yet more beautiful creatures, are to be found. Feeling for expressive painting and for music, not so far as it manifests artistry but sensitivity—all this refines or elevates the taste of this sex, and always has some connection with moral impulses. Never a cold and speculative instruction but always feelings, and those indeed which remain as close as possible to the situation of her sex. Such instruction is very rare because it demands talents, experience, and a heart full of feeling; and a woman can do very well without any other, as in fact without this she usually develops very well by her own efforts.

The virtue of a woman is a *beautiful virtue*. That of the male sex should be a *noble virtue*. Women will avoid the wicked not because it is unright, but because it is ugly; and virtuous actions mean to them such as are morally beautiful. Nothing of duty, nothing of compulsion, nothing of obligation! Woman is intolerant of all commands and all morose constraint. They do something only because it pleases them, and the art consists in making only that please them which is good. I hardly believe that the fair sex is capable of principles, and I hope by that not to offend, for these are also extremely rare in the male. But in place of it Providence has put in their breast kind and benevolent sensations, a fine feeling for propriety, and a complaisant soul. One should not at all demand sacrifices and generous self-restraint. A man must never tell his wife if he risks a part of his fortune on behalf of a friend. Why should he fetter her merry talkativeness by burdening her mind with a weighty secret whose keeping lies solely upon him? Even many of her weaknesses are, so to speak, *beautiful faults*. Offense or misfortune moves her tender soul to sadness. A man must never weep other than magnanimous tears. Those he sheds in pain or over circumstances of fortune make him contemptible. *Vanity*, for which one reproaches the fair sex so frequently, so far as it is a fault in that sex, yet is only a beautiful fault. For—not to mention that the men who so gladly flatter a woman would be left in a strait if she were not inclined to take it well—by that they actually enliven their charms. This inclination is an impulsion to exhibit pleasantness and good demeanor, to let her merry wit play, to radiate through the changing devices of dress, and to heighten her beauty. Now in this there is not at all any offensiveness toward others, but rather so much courtesy, if it is done with good taste, that to scold against it with peevish rebukes is very ill-bred. A woman who is too inconstant and deceitful is called a coquette; which expression yet has not so harsh a meaning as what, with a changed syllable, is applied to man, so that if we understand each other, it can sometimes indicate a familiar flattery. If vanity is a fault that in a woman much merits excuse, a *haughty bearing* is not only as reproachable in her as in people in general, but completely disfigures the character of her sex. For this quality is exceedingly stupid and ugly, and is set completely in opposition to her captivating, modest charms. Then such a person is in a slippery position. She will suffer herself to be judged sharply and without any pity; for whoever presumes an esteem invites all around him to rebuke. Each disclosure of even the least fault gives everyone a true joy, and the word *coquette* here loses its mitigated meaning. One must always distinguish between vanity and conceit. The first seeks approbation and to some extent honors those on whose account it gives itself the trouble. The second believes itself already in full possession of approbation, and because it never strives to gain any, it wins none.

If a few ingredients of vanity do not deform a woman in the eyes of the male sex, still, the more apparent they are, the more they serve to divide the fair sex among themselves. Then they judge one another very severely, because the one seems to obscure the charms of the other, and in fact, those who make strong presumptions of conquest actually are seldom friends of one another in a true sense. . . .

The noble qualities of this sex, which still, as we have already noted, must never disguise the feeling of the beautiful, proclaim themselves by nothing more clearly and surely than by *modesty*, a sort of noble simplicity and innocence in great excellences. Out of it shines a quiet benevolence and respect toward others, linked at the same time with a certain *noble trust* in oneself, and a reasonable self-esteem that is always to be found in a sublime disposition. Since this fine mixture at once captivates by charms and moves by respect, it puts all the remaining shining qualities in security against the mischief of censure and mockery. Persons of this temperament also have a heart for friendship, which in a woman can never be valued highly enough, because it is so rare and moreover must be so exceedingly charming. . . .

In order to keep close to my text, I want to undertake a few reflections on the influence one sex can have upon the other, to beautify or ennoble its feeling. Woman has a superior feeling for the beautiful, so far as it pertains to herself; but for the noble, so far as it is encountered in the male sex. Man on the other hand has a decided feeling for the noble, which belongs to his qualities, but for the beautiful, so far as it is to be found in woman. From this it must follow that the purposes of nature are directed still more to ennoble man, by the sexual inclination, and likewise still more to beautify woman. A woman is embarrassed little that she does not possess certain high insights, that she is timid, and not fit for serious employments, and so forth; she is beautiful and captivates, and that is enough. On the other hand, she demands all these qualities in a man, and the sublimity of her soul shows itself only in that she knows to treasure these noble qualities so far as they are found in him. How else indeed would it be possible that so many grotesque male faces, whatever merits they may possess, could gain such well-bred and fine wives! Man on the other hand is much more delicate in respect to the beautiful charms of woman. By their fine figure, merry naïveté, and charming friendliness he is sufficiently repaid for the lack of book learning and for other deficiencies that he must supply by his own talents. Vanity and fashion can give these natural drives a false direction and make out of many a male a *sweet gentleman*, but out of a woman either a prude or an Amazon; but still nature always seeks to reassert her own order. One can thereby judge what powerful influences the sexual inclination could have especially upon the male sex, to ennoble it, if instead of many dry instructions the moral feeling of woman were seasonably developed to sense properly what belongs to the dignity and the sublime qualities of the other sex, and were thus prepared to look upon the trifling fops with disdain and to yield to no other qualities than the merits. It is also certain that the power of her charms on the whole would gain through that; for it is apparent that their fascination for the most part works only upon nobler souls; the others are not fine enough to sense them. Just as the poet Simonides said, when someone advised him to let the Thessalians hear his beautiful songs: "These fellows are too stupid to be beguiled by such a man as I am." It has been regarded moreover as an effect of association with the fair sex that men's customs have become gentler, their conduct more polite and refined, and their bearing more elegant; but the advantage of this is only incidental. The principal object is that the man should become more perfect as a man, and the woman as a wife; that is, that the motives of the sexual inclination work according to the hint of nature, still more to ennoble the one and to beautify the qualities of the other. If all comes to the extreme, the man, confident in his merits, will be able to say: "Even if you do not love me, I will constrain you to esteem me," and the woman, secure in the might of her charms, will answer: "Even if you do not inwardly admire me, I will still constrain you to love me." In default of such principles one sees men take on femininity in order to please, and woman occasionally (although much more seldom) affect a masculine demeanor in order to stimulate esteem; but whatever one does contrary to nature's will, one always does very poorly.

WOMEN, ADORED AND OPPRESSED

THOMAS PAINE (ATTR.)

This stirring and sympathetic essay on women appeared anonymously in the Pennsylvania Magazine *in August 1775 under the title "An Occasional Letter on the Female Sex." Paine was by then a writer for the magazine, and this piece was included in early editions of his published works. Uncertainty, however, still surrounds its authorship.*

If we take a survey of ages and of countries, we shall find the women, almost—without exception—at all times and in all places, adored and oppressed. Man, who has never neglected an opportunity of exerting his power, in paying homage to their beauty, has always availed himself of their weakness. He has been at once their tyrant and their slave.

Nature herself, in forming beings so susceptible and tender, appears to have been more attentive to their charms than to their happiness. Continually surrounded with griefs and fears, the women more than share all our miseries, and are besides subjected to ills which are peculiarly their own. They cannot be the means of life without exposing themselves to the loss of it; every revolution which they undergo, alters their health, and threatens their existence. Cruel distempers attack their beauty—and the hour, which confirms their release from those, is perhaps the most melancholy of their lives. It robs them of the most essential characteristic of their sex. They can then only hope for protection from the humiliating claims of pity, or the feeble voice of gratitude.

Society, instead of alleviating their condition, is to them the source of new miseries. More than one half of the globe is covered with savages; and among all these people women are completely wretched. Man, in a state of barbarity, equally cruel and indolent, active by necessity, but naturally inclined to repose, is acquainted with little more than the physical effects of love; and, having none of those moral ideas which only can soften the empire of force, he is led to consider it as his supreme law, subjecting to his despotism those whom reason had made his equal, but whose imbecility betrayed them to his strength. "Nothing" (says Professor Miller, speaking of the women of barbarous nations) "can exceed the dependence and subjection in which they are kept, or the toil and drudgery which they are obliged to undergo. The husband, when he is not engaged in some warlike exercise, indulges himself in idleness, and devolves upon his wife the whole burden of his domestic affairs. He disdains to assist her in any of those servile employments. She sleeps in a different bed, and is seldom permitted to have any conversation or correspondence with him."

The women among the Indians of America are what the Helots were among the Spartans, a vanquished people, obliged to toil for their conquerors. Hence on the banks of the Oroonoko, we have seen mothers slaying their daughters out of compassion, and smothering them in the hour of their birth. They consider this barbarous pity as a virtue.

"The men" (says Commodore Byron, in his account of the inhabitants of South America) "exercise a most despotic authority over their wives, whom they consider in the same view they do any other part of their property, and dispose of them accordingly: Even their common treatment of them is cruel; for though the toil and hazard of procuring food lies entirely on the women, yet they are not suffered to touch any part of it till the husband is satisfied; and then he assigns them their portion, which is generally very scanty, and such as he has not a stomach for himself."

Among the nations of the East we find another kind of despotism and dominion prevail—the Seraglio, and the domestic servitude of woman, authorized by the manners and established by the laws. In Turkey, in Persia, in India, in Japan, and over the vast empire of China, one half of the human species is oppressed by the other.

The excess of oppression in those countries springs from the excess of love.

All Asia is covered with prisons, where beauty in bondage waits the caprices of a master. The multitude of women there assembled have no will, no inclinations but his: Their triumphs are only for a moment; and their rivalry, their hate, and their animosities, continue till death. There the lovely sex are obliged to repay even their servitude with the most tender affections; or, what is still more mortifying, with the counterfeit of an affection, which they do not feel: There the most gloomy tyranny has subjected them to creatures, who, being of neither sex, are a dishonor to both: There, in short, their education tends only to debase them; their virtues are forced; their very pleasures are involuntary and joyless; and after an existence of a few years—till the bloom of youth is over—their period of neglect commences, which is long and dreadful. In the temperate latitude where the climates, giving less ardor to passion, leave more confidence in virtue, the women have not been deprived of their liberty, but a severe legislation has, at all times, kept them in a state of dependence. One while, they were confined to their own apartments, and debarred at once from business and amusement; at other times, a tedious guardianship defrauded their hearts, and insulted their understandings. Affronted in one country by polygamy, which gives them their rivals for their inseparable companions; inslaved in another by indissoluble ties, which often join the gentle to the rude, and sensibility to brutality: Even in countries where they may be esteemed most happy, constrained in their desires in the disposal of their goods, robbed of freedom of will by the laws, the slaves of opinion, which rules them with absolute sway, and construes the slightest appearances into guilt; surrounded on all sides by judges, who are at once tyrants and their seducers, and who, after having prepared their faults, punish every lapse with dishonor—nay, usurp the right of degrading them on suspicion! Who does not feel for the tender sex? Yet such, I am sorry to say, is the lot of woman over the whole earth. Man with regard to them, in all climates, and in all ages, has been either an insensible husband or an oppressor; but they have sometimes experienced the cold and deliberate oppression of pride, and sometimes the violent and terrible tyranny of jealousy. When they are not beloved they are nothing; and, when they are, they are tormented. They have almost equal cause to be afraid of indifference and of love. Over three quarters of the globe nature has placed them between contempt and misery.

"The melting desires, or the fiery passions," says Professor Ferguson, "which in one climate take place between the sexes, are, in another, changed into a sober consideration, or a patience of mutual disgust. This change is remarked in crossing the Mediterranean, in following the course of the Mississippi, in ascending the mountains of Caucasus, and in passing from the Alps and the Pyrenees to the shores of the Baltic.

"The burning ardors and torturing jealousies of the Seraglio and Harem, which have reigned so long in Asia and Africa, and which, in the southern parts of Europe, have scarcely given way to the differences of religion and civil establishments, are found, however, with an abatement of heat in the climate, to be more easily changed, in one latitude, into a temporary passion, which engrosses the mind without infeebling it, and which excites to romantic achievements. By a farther progress to the north it is changed into a spirit of gallantry, which employs the wit and fancy more than the heart, which prefers intrigue to enjoyment, and substitutes affection and vanity where sentiment and desire have failed. As it departs from the sun, the same passion is farther composed into a habit of domestic connection, or frozen into a state of insensibility, under which the sexes at freedom scarcely choose to unite their society."

Even among people where beauty received the highest homage, we find men who would deprive the sex of every kind of reputation: "The most virtuous woman," says a celebrated Greek, "is she who is least talked of." That morose man, while he imposes duties upon women, would deprive them of the sweets of public esteem, and in exacting virtues from them, would make it a crime to aspire at honor.

If a woman were to defend the cause of her sex, she might address him in the following manner:

"How great is your injustice? If we have an equal right with you to virtue, why should we not have an equal right to praise? The public esteem ought to wait upon merit. Our duties are different from yours, but they are not therefore less difficult to fulfill, or of less consequence to society: They are the fountains of your felicity, and the sweetness of life. We are wives and mothers. 'T is we who form the union and the cordiality of families: 'T is we who soften that savage rudeness which considers everything as due to force, and which would involve man with man in eternal war. We cultivate in you that humanity which makes you feel for the misfortunes of others, and our tears forewarn you of your own danger. Nay, you cannot be ignorant that we have need of courage not less than you: More feeble in ourselves, we have perhaps more trials to encounter. Nature assails us with sorrow, law and custom press us with constraint, and sensibility and virtue alarm us with their continual conflict. Sometimes also the name of citizen demands from us the tribute of fortitude. When you offer your blood to the State think that it is ours. In giving it our sons and our husbands we give more than ourselves. You can only die on the field of battle, but we have the misfortune to survive those whom we love most. Alas! while your ambitious vanity is unceasingly laboring to cover the earth with statues, with monuments, and with inscriptions to eternize, if possible, your names, and give yourselves an existence, when this body is no more, why must we be condemned to live and to die unknown? Would that the grave and eternal forgetfulness should be our lot. Be not our tyrants in all: Permit our names to be sometimes pronounced beyond the narrow circle in which we live: Permit friendship, or at least love, to inscribe its emblems on the tomb where our ashes repose; and deny us not that public esteem which, after the esteem of one's self, is the sweetest reward of well doing."

All men, however, it must be owned, have not been equally unjust to their fair companions. In some countries public honors have been paid to women. Art has erected them monuments. Eloquence has celebrated their virtues, and History has collected whatever could adorn their character.

"A WOMAN . . . GOSSIPS MUCH . . ."

WOLFGANG AMADEUS MOZART

Mozart and his librettist, Schikaneder, fill The Magic Flute *with misogynist comments; indeed, the Queen of the Night is its principal villain, the representation of darkness, the foil of enlightenment.*

SPEAKER: Has a woman so deceived you? A woman does little, gossips much; you, youth, believe in wagging tongues?

SARASTRO: She is an arrogant woman! A man must guide your heart, for without that, every woman tends to overstep her natural sphere.

TWO PRIESTS: Guard yourself from women's tricks: this is the first duty of our order! Many a wise man has been deceived, has failed and never seen his error; he found himself finally abandoned, his faithfulness paid back with scorn! In vain were all his struggles, for death and despair were his reward.

WOMEN'S EDUCATION

CATHERINE SAWBRIDGE MACAULAY GRAHAM

An important radical pamphleteer and eminent historian, Macaulay (1731–1791) was a friend of Washington, Adams, and Franklin. In her Letters on Education *(1790), addressed to a friend, Hortensia, she replies directly to Rousseau.*

The great difference that is observable in the characters of the sexes, Hortensia, as they display themselves in the scenes of social life, has given rise to much false speculation on the natural qualities of the female mind.—For though the doctrine of innate ideas, and innate affections, are in a great measure exploded by the learned, yet few persons reason so closely and so accurately on abstract subjects as, through a long chain of deductions, to bring forth a conclusion which in no respect militates with their premises.

It is a long time before the crowd give up opinions they have been taught to look upon with respect; and I know many persons who will follow you willingly through the course of your argument, till they perceive it tends to the overthrow of some fond prejudice; and then they will either sound a retreat, or begin a contest in which the contender for truth, though he cannot be overcome, is effectually silenced, from the mere weariness of answering positive assertions, reiterated without end. It is from such causes that the notion of a sexual difference in the human character has, with a very few exceptions, universally prevailed from the earliest times, and the pride of one sex, and the ignorance and vanity of the other, have helped to support an opinion which a close observation of Nature, and a more accurate way of reasoning, would disprove.

It must be confessed, that the virtues of the males among the human species, though mixed and blended with a variety of vices and errors, have displayed a bolder and a more consistent picture of excellence than female nature has hitherto done. It is on these reasons that, when we compliment the appearance of a more than ordinary energy in the female mind, we call it masculine; and hence it is, that Pope has elegantly said a perfect woman's but a softer man. And if we take in the consideration, that there can be but one rule of moral excellence for beings made of the same materials, organized after the same manner, and subjected to similar laws of Nature, we must either agree with Mr. Pope, or we must reverse the proposition, and say, that a perfect man is a woman formed after a coarser mold. The difference that actually does subsist between the sexes, is too flattering for men to be willingly imputed to accident; for what accident occasions, wisdom might correct; and it is better, says Pride, to give up the advantages we might derive from the perfection of our fellow associates, than to own that Nature has been just in the equal distribution of her favors. These are the sentiments of the men; but mark how readily they are yielded to by the women; not from humility I assure you, but merely to preserve with character those fond vanities on which they set their hearts. No; suffer them to idolize their persons, to throw away their life in the pursuit of trifles, and to indulge in the gratification of the meaner passions, and they will heartily join in the sentence of their degradation.

Among the most strenuous asserters of a sexual difference in character, Rousseau is the most conspicuous, both on account of that warmth of sentiment which distinguishes all his writings, and the eloquence of his compositions: but never did enthusiasm and the love of paradox, those enemies to philosophical disquisition, appear in more strong opposition to plain sense than in Rousseau's definition of this difference. He sets out with a supposition, that Nature intended the subjection of the one sex to the other; that consequently there must be an inferiority of intellect in the subjected party; but as man is a very imperfect being, and apt to play the capricious tyrant, Nature, to bring things nearer to an equality, bestowed on the woman such attractive graces, and such an insinuating address, as to turn the balance on the other scale. Thus Nature, in a giddy mood, recedes from her purposes, and subjects prerogative to an influence which must produce confusion and disorder in the system of human affairs. Rousseau saw this objection; and in order to obviate it, he has made up a moral person of the union of the two sexes, which, for contradiction and absurdity, outdoes every metaphysical riddle that was ever formed in the schools. In short, it is not reason, it is not wit; it is pride and sensuality that speak in Rousseau, and, in this instance, has lowered the man of genius to the licentious pedant.

But whatever might be the wise purpose intended by Providence in such a disposition of things, certain it is, that some degree of inferiority, in point of corporal strength, seems always to have existed between the two sexes; and this advantage, in the barbarous ages of mankind, was abused to such a degree, as to destroy all the natural rights of the female species, and reduce them to a state of abject slavery. What accidents have contributed in Europe to better their condition, would not be to my purpose to relate; for I do not intend to give you a history of women; I mean only to trace the sources of their peculiar foibles and vices; and these I firmly believe to originate in situation and education only: for so little did a wise and just Providence intend to make the condition of slavery an unalterable law of female nature, that in the same proportion as the male sex have consulted the interest of their own happiness, they have relaxed in their tyranny over women; and such is their use in the system of mundane creation, and such their natural influence over the male mind, that were these advantages properly exerted, they might carry every point of any importance to their honor and happiness. However, till that period arrives in which women will act wisely, we will amuse ourselves in talking of their follies.

The situation and education of women, Hortensia, is precisely that which must necessarily tend to corrupt and debilitate both the powers of mind and body. From a false notion of beauty and delicacy, their system of nerves is depraved before they come out of their nursery; and this kind of depravity has more influence over the mind, and consequently over morals, than is commonly apprehended. But it would be well if such causes only acted towards the debasement of the sex; their moral education is, if possible, more absurd than their physical. The principles and nature of virtue, which is never properly explained to boys, is kept quite a mystery to girls. They are told indeed, that they must abstain from those vices which are contrary to their personal happiness, or they will be regarded as criminals, both by God and man; but all the higher parts of rectitude, every thing that ennobles our being, and that renders us both innoxious and useful, is either not taught, or is taught in such a manner as to leave no proper impression on the mind. This is so obvious a truth, that the defects of female education have ever been a fruitful topic of declamation for the moralist; but not one of this class of writers have laid down any judicious rules for amendment. Whilst we still retain the absurd notion of a sexual excellence, it will militate against the perfecting a plan of education for either sex. The judicious Addison animadverts on the absurdity of bringing a young lady up with no higher idea of the end of education than to make her agreeable to a husband, and confining the necessary excellence for this happy acquisition to the mere graces of person.

Every parent and tutor may not express himself in the same manner as is marked out by Addison: yet certain it is, that the admiration of the other sex is held out to women as the highest honor they can attain; and whilst this is considered as their *summum bonum*, and the beauty of their persons the chief *desideratum* of men, Vanity, and its companion Envy, must taint, in their characters, every native and every acquired excellence. Nor can you, Hortensia, deny, that these qualities, when united to ignorance, are fully equal to the engendering and riveting all those vices and foibles which are peculiar to the female sex; vices and foibles which have caused them to be considered, in ancient times, as beneath cultivation, and in modern days have subjected them to the censure and ridicule of writers of all descriptions, from the deep thinking philosopher to the man of ton and gallantry, who, by the bye, sometimes distinguishes himself by qualities which are not greatly superior to those he despises in women. Nor can I better illustrate the truth of this observation than by the following picture, to be found in the polite and gallant Chesterfield. "Women," says his Lordship, "are only children of a larger growth. They have an entertaining tattle, sometimes wit; but for solid reasoning, and good sense, I never in my life knew one that had it, or who acted or reasoned in consequence of it for four and twenty hours together. A man of sense only trifles with them, plays with them, humors and flatters them, as he does an engaging child; but he neither consults them, nor trusts them in serious matters."

Though the situation of women in modern Europe, Hortensia, when compared with that condition of abject slavery in which they have always been held in the east, may be considered as brilliant; yet if we withhold comparison, and take the matter in a positive sense, we shall have no great reason to boast of our privileges, or of the candor and indulgence of the men towards us. For with a total and absolute exclusion of every political right to the sex in general, married women, whose situation demand a particular indulgence, have hardly a civil right to save them from the grossest injuries; and though the gallantry of some of the European societies have necessarily produced indulgence, yet in others the faults of women are treated with a severity and rancor which militates against every principle of religion and common sense. Faults, my friend, I hear you say; you take the matter in too general a sense; you know there is but one fault which a woman of honor may not commit with impunity; let her only take care that she is not caught in a love intrigue, and she may lie, she may deceive, she may defame, she may ruin her own family with gaming, and the peace of twenty others with her coquettry, and yet preserve both her reputation and her peace. These are glorious privileges indeed, Hortensia; but whilst plays and novels are the favorite study of the fair, whilst the admiration of men continues to be set forth as the chief honor of woman, whilst power is only acquired by personal charms, whilst continual dissipation banishes the hour of reflection, Nature and flattery will too often prevail; and when this is the case, self preservation will suggest to conscious weakness those methods which are the most likely to conceal the ruinous trespass, however safe and criminal they may be in their nature. The crimes that women have committed, both to conceal and to indulge their natural failings, shock the feelings of moral sense; but indeed every love intrigue, though it does not terminate in such horrid catastrophes, must naturally tend to debase the female mind, from its violence to educational impressions, from the secrecy with which it must be conducted, and the debasing dependency to which the intriguer, if she is a woman of reputation, is subjected. Lying, flattery, hypocrisy, bribery, and a long catalogue of the meanest of the human vices, must all be employed to preserve necessary appearances. Hence delicacy of sentiment gradually decreases; the warnings of virtue are no longer felt; the mind becomes corrupted, and lies open to every solicitation which appetite or passion presents. This must be the natural course of things in every being formed after the human plan; but it gives rise to the trite and foolish observation, that the first fault against chastity in woman has a radical power to deprave the character. But no such frail beings come out of the hands of Nature. The human mind is built of nobler materials than to be so easily corrupted; and with all the disadvantages of situation and education, women seldom become entirely abandoned till they are thrown into a state of desperation by the venomous rancor of their own sex.

The superiority of address peculiar to the female sex, says Rousseau, is a very equitable indemnification for their inferiority in point of strength. Without this, woman would not be the companion of man, but his slave; it is by her superior art and ingenuity that she preserves her equality, and governs him, whilst she affects to obey. Woman has every thing against her; as well our faults, as her own timidity and weakness. She has nothing in her favor but her subtlety and her beauty; is it not very reasonable therefore that she should cultivate both?

I am persuaded that Rousseau's understanding was too good to have led him into this error, had he not been blinded by his pride and his sensuality. The first was soothed by the opinion of superiority, lulled into acquiescence by cajolement; and the second was attracted by the idea of women playing off all the arts of coquettry to raise the passions of the sex. Indeed the author fully avows his sentiments, by acknowledging that he would have a young French woman cultivate her agreeable talents, in order to please her future husband, with as much care and assiduity as a young Circassian cultivates her's to fit her for the harem of an eastern bashaw.

These agreeable talents, as the author expresses it, are played off to great advantage by women in all the courts of Europe; who, for the arts of female allurement, do not give place to the Circassian. But it is the practice of these very arts, directed to enthrall the man, which act in a peculiar manner to corrupting the female mind. Envy, malice, jealousy, a cruel delight in inspiring sentiments which at first perhaps were never intended to be reciprocal, are leading features in the character of the coquet, whose aim is to subject the whole world to her own humor; but in this vain attempt she commonly sacrifices both her decency and her virtue.

By the intrigues of women, and their rage for personal power and importance, the whole world has been filled with violence and injury; and their levity and influence have proved so hostile to the existence or permanence of rational manners, that it fully justifies the keenness of Mr. Pope's satire on the sex.

But I hear my Hortensia say, whither will this fit of moral anger carry you? I expected an apology, instead of a libel, on women; according to your description of the sex, the philosopher has more reason to regret the indulgence, than what you have sometimes termed the injustice of the men; and to look with greater complacency on the surly manners of the ancient Greeks, and the selfishness of Asiatic luxury, than on the gallantry of modern Europe.

Though you have often heard me express myself with warmth in the vindication of female nature, Hortensia, yet I never was an apologist for the conduct of women. But I cannot think the surliness of the Greek manners, or the selfishness of Asiatic luxury, a proper remedy to apply to the evil. If we could inspect narrowly into the domestic concerns of ancient and modern Asia, I dare say we should perceive that the first springs of the vast machine of society were set a going by women; and as to the Greeks, though it might be supposed that the peculiarity of their manners would have rendered them indifferent to the sex, yet they were avowedly governed by them. They only transferred that confidence which they ought to have given their wives, to their courtesans, in the same manner as our English husbands do their tenderness and their complaisance. They will sacrifice a wife of fortune and family to resentment, or the love of change, provided she give them opportunity, and bear with much Christian patience to be supplanted by their footman in the person of their mistress.

No; as Rousseau observes, it was ordained by Providence that women should govern some way or another; and all that reformation can do, is to take power out of the hands of vice and folly, and place it where it will not be liable to be abused.

To do the sex justice, it must be confessed that history does not set forth more instances of positive power abused by women, than by men; and when the sex have been taught wisdom by education, they will be glad to give up indirect influence for rational privileges; and the precarious sovereignty of an hour enjoyed with the meanest and most infamous of the species, for those established rights which, independent of accidental circumstances, may afford protection to the whole sex. . . .

After all that has been advanced, Hortensia, the happiness and perfection of the two sexes are so reciprocally dependent on one another that, till both are reformed, there is no expecting excellence in either. The candid Addison has confessed, that in order to embellish the mistress, you must give a new education to the lover, and teach the men not to be any longer dazzled by false charms and unreal beauty. Till this is the case, we must endeavor to palliate the evil we cannot remedy; and, in the education of our females, raise as many barriers to the corruptions of the world, as our understanding and sense of things will permit.

As I give no credit to the opinion of a sexual excellence, I have made no variation in the fundamental principles of the education of the two sexes; but it will be necessary to admit of such a difference in the plan as shall in some degree form the female mind to the particularity of its situation.

The fruits of true philosophy are modesty and humility; for as we advance in knowledge, our deficiencies become more conspicuous; and by learning to [form?] a just estimate on what we possess, we find little gratification for the passion of pride. This is so just an observation, that we may venture to pronounce, without any exception to the rule, that a vain or proud man is, in a positive sense, an ignorant man. However if it should be our lot to have one of the fair sex, distinguished for any eminent degree of personal charms, committed to our care, we must not attempt by a premature cultivation to gather the fruits of philosophy before their season, nor expect to find the qualities of true modesty and humility make their appearance till the blaze of beauty has in some measure been subdued by time. For should we exhaust all the powers of oratory, and all the strength of sound argument, in the endeavor to convince our pupil that beauty is of small weight in the scale of real excellence, the enflamed praises she will continually hear bestowed on this quality will fix her in the opinion, that we mean to keep her in ignorance of her true worth. She will think herself deceived, and she will resent the injury by giving little credit to our precepts, and placing her confidence in those who tickle her ears with lavish panegyric on the captivating graces of her person.

Thus vanity steals on the mind, and thus a daughter, kept under by the ill exerted power of parental authority, gives a full ear to the flattery of a coxcomb. Happy would it be for the sex did the mischief end here; but the soothings of flattery never fail to operate on the affections of the heart; and when love creeps into the bosom, the empire of reason is at an end. To prevent our fair pupils therefore from becoming the prey of coxcombs, and serving either to swell their triumph, or repair their ruined fortunes, it will be necessary to give them a full idea of the magnitude of their beauty, and the power this quality has over the frail mind of man. Nor have we in this case so much to fear from the intimations of a judicious friend, as from the insidious adulation of a designing admirer. The haughty beauty is too proud to regard the admiration of fops and triflers; she will never condescend to the base, the treacherous, the dangerous arts of coquettry; and by keeping her heart free from the snares of love, she will have time to cultivate that philosophy which, if well understood, is a never failing remedy to human pride.

But the most difficult part of female education, is to give girls such an idea of chastity, as shall arm their reason and their sentiments on the side of this useful virtue. For I believe there are more women of understanding led into acts of imprudence by the ignorance, the prejudices, and the false craft of those by whom they are educated, than from any other cause founded either in nature or in chance. You may train up a docile idiot to any mode of thinking or acting, as may best suit the intended purpose; but a reasoning being will scan over your propositions, and if they find them grounded in falsehood, they will reject them with disdain. When you tell a girl of spirit and reflection that chastity is a sexual virtue, and the want of it a sexual vice, she will be apt to examine into the principles of religion, morals, and the reason of things, in order to satisfy herself on the truth of your proposition. And when, after the strictest enquiries, she finds nothing that will warrant the confining the propositions to a particular sense, she will entertain doubts either of your wisdom or your sincerity; and regarding you either as a deceiver or a fool, she will transfer her confidence to the companion of the easy vacant hour, whose compliance with her opinions can flatter her vanity. Thus left to Nature, with an unfortunate bias on her mind, she will fall a victim to the first plausible being who has formed a design on her person.

Rousseau is so sensible of this truth, that he quarrels with human reason, and would put her out of the question in all considerations of duty. But this is being as great a fanatic in morals, as some are in religion; and I should much doubt the reality of that duty which would not stand the test of fair inquiry; beside, as I intend to breed my pupils up to act a rational part in the world, and not to fill up a niche in the seraglio of a sultan, I shall certainly give them leave to use their reason in all matters which concern their duty and happiness, and shall spare no pains in the cultivation of this only sure guide to virtue. I shall inform them of the great utility of chastity and continence; that the one preserves the body in health and vigor, and the other, the purity and independence of the mind, without which it is impossible to possess virtue or happiness. I shall intimate, that the great difference now beheld in the external consequences which follow the deviations from chastity in the two sexes, did in all probability arise from women having been considered as the mere property of the men; and, on this account had no right to dispose of their own persons: that policy adopted this difference, when the plea of property had been given up; and it was still preserved in society from the unruly licentiousness of the men, who, finding no obstacles in the delicacy of the other sex, continue to set at defiance both divine and moral law, and by mutual support and general opinion to use their natural freedom with impunity. I shall observe, that this state of things renders the situation of females, in their individual capacity very precarious; for the strength which Nature has given to the passion of love, in order to serve her purposes, has made it the most ungovernal propensity of any which attends us. The snares therefore, that are continually laid for women, by persons who run no risk in compassing their seduction, exposes them to continual danger; whilst the implacability of their own sex, who fear to give up any advantages which a superior prudence, or even its appearances, give them, renders one false step an irretrievable misfortune. That, for these reasons, coquettry in women is as dangerous as it is dishonorable. That a coquet commonly finds her own perdition, in the very flames which she raises to consume others; and that if any thing can excuse the baseness of female seduction, it is the baits which are flung out by women to entangle the affections, and excite the passions of men.

I know not what you may think of my method, Hortensia, which I must acknowledge to carry the stamp of singularity; but for my part, I am sanguine enough to expect to turn out of my hands a careless, modest beauty, grave, manly, noble, full of strength and majesty; and carrying about her an aegis sufficiently powerful to defend her against the sharpest arrow that ever was shot from Cupid's bow. A woman, whose virtue will not be of the kind to wrankle into an inveterate malignity against her own sex for faults which she even encourages in the men, but who, understanding the principles of true religion and morality, will regard chastity and truth as indispensable qualities in virtuous characters of either sex; whose justice will incline her to extend her benevolence to the frailties of the fair as circumstances invite, and to manifest her resentment against the underminers of female happiness; in short, a woman who will not take a male rake either for a husband or a friend. And let me tell you, Hortensia, if women had as much regard for the virtue of chastity as in some cases they pretend to have, a reformation would long since have taken place in the world; but whilst they continue to cherish immodesty in the men, their bitter persecution of their own sex will not save them from the imputation of those concealed propensities with which they are accused by Pope, and other severe satirists on the sex.

ON THE EQUALITY OF THE SEXES

CONSTANTIA

Like the French and English Enlightenment, the American produced a woman in the 1790s who proclaimed women's equal capacities based on "some arguments from nature, reason, and experience." Judith Sargent Stevens Murray, of Gloucester, Massachusetts, wrote under the pen name "Constantia" and published this piece in the Massachusetts Magazine *in 1790.*

May not the intellectual powers be ranged under these four heads—imagination, reason, memory, and judgment. The province of imagination hath long since been surrendered up to us, and we have been crowned undoubted sovereigns of the regions of fancy. Invention is perhaps the most arduous effort of the mind; this branch of imagination hath been particularly ceded to us, and we have been time out of mind invested with that creative faculty. Observe the variety of fashions (here I bar the contemptuous smile) which distinguish and adorn the female world; how continually they are changing, insomuch that they almost render the wise man's assertion problematical, and we are ready to say, *there is something new under the sun.* Now what a playfulness, what an exuberance of fancy, what strength of inventive imagination, doth this continual variation discover? Again, it hath been observed, that if the turpitude of the conduct of our sex, hath been ever so enormous, so extremely ready are we, that the very first thought presents with an apology, so plausible, as to produce our actions even in an amiable light. Another instance of our creative powers, is our talent for slander; how ingenious are we at inventive scandal? what a formidable story can we in a moment fabricate merely from the force of a prolific imagination? how many reputations, in the fertile brain of a female, have been utterly despoiled? how industrious are we at improving a hint? suspicion how easily do we convert into conviction, and conviction, embellished by the power of eloquence, stalks abroad to the surprise and confusion of unsuspecting innocence. Perhaps it will be asked if I furnish these facts as instances of excellency in our sex. Certainly not; but as proofs of a creative faculty, of a lively imagination. Assuredly great activity of mind is thereby discovered, and was this activity properly directed, what beneficial effects would follow. Is the needle and kitchen sufficient to employ the operations of a soul thus organized? I should conceive not. Nay, it is a truth that those very departments leave the intelligent principle vacant, and at liberty for speculation. Are we deficient in reason? we can only reason from what we know, and if an opportunity of acquiring knowledge hath been denied us, the inferiority of our sex cannot fairly be deduced from thence. Memory, I believe, will be allowed us in common, since every one's experience must testify, that a loquacious old woman is as frequently met with, as a communicative old man; their subjects are alike drawn from the fund of other times, and the transactions of their youth, or of maturer life, entertain, or perhaps fatigue you, in the evening of their lives. "But our judgment is not so strong—we do not distinguish so well."—Yet it may be questioned, from what doth this superiority, in this determining faculty of the soul, proceed. May we not trace its source in the difference of education, and continued advantages? Will it be said that the judgment of a male of two years old, is more sage than that of a female of the same age? I believe the reverse is generally observed to be true. But from that period what partiality! how is the one exalted, and the other depressed, by the contrary modes of education which are adopted! the one is taught to aspire, and the other is early confined and limited. As their years increase, the sister must be wholly domesticated, while the brother is led by the hand through all the flowery paths of science. Grant that their minds are by nature equal, yet who shall wonder at the *apparent* superiority, if indeed custom becomes *second nature;* nay if it taketh the place of nature, and that it doth the experience of each day will evince. At length arrived at womanhood, the uncultivated fair one feels a void, which the employments allotted her are by no means capable of filling. What can she do? to books she may not apply; or if she doth, *to those only of the novel kind*, lest she merit the appellation of a *learned lady;* and what ideas have been affixed to this term, the observation of many can testify. Fashion, scandal, and sometimes what is still more reprehensible, are then called in to her relief; and who can say to what lengths the liberties she takes may proceed. Meantime she herself is most unhappy; she feels the want of a cultivated mind. Is she single, she in vain seeks to fill up time from sexual employments or amusements. Is she united to a person whose soul nature made equal to her own, education hath set him so far above her, that in those entertainments which are productive of such rational felicity, she is not qualified to accompany him. She experiences a mortifying consciousness of inferiority, which embitters every enjoyment. Doth the person to whom her adverse fate hath consigned her, possess a mind incapable of improvement, she is equally wretched, in being so closely connected with an individual whom she cannot but despise. Now, was she permitted the same instructors as her brother (with an eye however to their particular departments) for the employment of a rational mind an ample field would be opened. In astronomy she might catch a glimpse of the immensity of the Deity, and thence she would form amazing conceptions of the august and supreme Intelligence. In geography she would admire Jehovah in the midst of his benevolence; thus adapting this globe to the various wants and amusements of its inhabitants. In natural philosophy she would adore the infinite majesty of heaven, clothed in condescension; and as she traversed the reptile world, she would hail the goodness of a creating God. A mind, thus filled, would have little room for the trifles with which our sex are, with too much justice, accused of amusing themselves, and they would thus be rendered fit companions for those, who should one day wear them as their crown. Fashions, in their variety, would then give place to conjectures, which might perhaps conduce to the improvement of the literary world; and there would be no leisure for slander or detraction. Reputation would not then be blasted, but serious speculations would occupy the lively imaginations of the sex. Unnecessary visits would be precluded, and that custom would only be indulged by way of relaxation, or to answer the demands of consanguinity and friendship. Females would become discreet, their judgments would be invigorated, and their partners for life being circumspectly chosen, an unhappy Hymen would then be as rare, as is now the reverse.

Will it be urged that those acquirements would supersede our domestic duties. I answer that every requisite in female economy is easily attained; and, with truth I can add, that when once attained, they require no further *mental attention*. Nay, while we are pursuing the needle, or the superintendency of the family, I repeat, that our minds are at full liberty for reflection; that imagination may exert itself in full vigor; and that if a just foundation is early laid, our ideas will then be worthy of rational beings. If we were industrious we might easily find time to arrange them upon paper, or should avocations press too hard for such an indulgence, the hours allotted for conversation would at least become more refined and rational. Should it still be vociferated, "Your domestic employments are sufficient"—I would calmly ask, is it reasonable, that a candidate for immortality, for the joys of heaven, an intelligent being, who is to spend an eternity in contemplating the works of Deity, should at present be so degraded, as to be allowed no other ideas, than those which are suggested by the mechanism of a pudding, or the sewing the seams of a garment? Pity that all such censurers of female improvement do not go one step further, and deny their future existence; to be consistent they surely ought.

Yes, ye lordly, ye haughty sex, our souls are by nature *equal* to yours; the same breath of God animates, enlivens, and invigorates us; and that we are not fallen lower than yourselves, let those witness who have greatly towered above the various discouragements by which they have been so heavily oppressed; and though I am unacquainted with the list of celebrated characters on either side, yet from the observations I have made in the contracted circle in which I have moved, I dare confidently believe, that from the commencement of time to the present day, there hath been as many females, as males, who, by the *mere force of natural powers*, have merited the crown of applause; who, *thus unassisted*, have seized the wreath of fame. I know there are those who assert, that as the animal powers of the one sex are superior, of course their mental faculties also must be stronger; thus attributing strength of mind to the transient organization of this earth born tenement. But if this reasoning is just, man must be content to yield the palm to many of the brute creation, since by not a few of his brethren of the field, he is far surpassed in bodily strength. Moreover, was this argument admitted, it would prove too much, for occular demonstration evinceth, that there are many robust masculine ladies, and effeminate gentlemen. Yet I fancy that Mr. Pope, though clogged with an enervated body, and distinguished by a diminutive stature, could nevertheless lay claim to greatness of soul; and perhaps there are many other instances which might be adduced to combat so unphilosophical an opinion. Do we not often see, that when the clay built tabernacle is well nigh dissolved, when it is just ready to mingle with the parent soil, the immortal inhabitant aspires to, and even attaineth heights the most sublime, and which were before wholly unexplored. Besides, were we to grant that animal strength proved any thing, taking into consideration the accustomed impartiality of nature, we should be induced to imagine, that she had invested the female mind with superior strength as an equivalent for the bodily powers of man. But wa[i]ving this however palpable advantage, for *equality only*, we wish to contend.

I am aware that there are many passages in the sacred oracles which seem to give the advantage to the other sex; but I consider all these as wholly metaphorical. Thus David was a man after God's own heart, yet see him enervated by his licentious passions! behold him following Uriah to the death, and shew me wherein could consist the immaculate Being's complacency. Listen to the curses which Job bestoweth upon the day of his nativity, and tell me where is his perfection, where his patience—*literally* it existed not. David and Job were types of him who was to come; and the superiority of man, as exhibited in scripture, being also emblematical, all arguments deduced from thence, of course fall to the ground. The exquisite delicacy of the female mind proclaimeth the exactness of its texture, while its nice sense of honor announceth its innate, its native grandeur. And indeed, in one respect, the preeminence seems to be tacitly allowed us, for after an education which limits and confines, and employments and recreations which naturally tend to enervate the body, and debilitate the mind; after we have from early youth been adorned with ribbons, and other gewgaws, dressed out like the ancient victims previous to a sacrifice, being taught by the care of our parents in collecting the most showy materials that the ornamenting our exterior ought to be the principal object of our attention; after, I say, fifteen years thus spent, we are introduced into the world, amid the united adulation of every beholder. Praise is sweet to the soul; we are immediately intoxicated by large draughts of flattery, which being plentifully administered, is to the pride of our hearts the most acceptable incense. It is expected that with the other sex we should commence immediate war, and that we should triumph over the machinations of the most artful. We must be constantly upon our guard; prudence and discretion must be our characteristics; and we must rise superior to, and obtain a complete victory over those who have been long adding to the native strength of their minds, by an unremitted study of men and books, and who have, moreover, conceived from the loose characters which they have seen portrayed in the extensive variety of their reading, a most contemptible opinion of the sex. Thus unequal, we are, notwithstanding forced to the combat, and the infamy which is consequent upon the smallest deviation in our conduct, proclaims the high idea which was formed of our native strength; and thus, indirectly at least, is the preference acknowledged to be our due. And if we are allowed an equality of acquirements, let serious studies equally employ our minds, and we will bid our souls arise to equal strength. We will meet upon even ground, the despot man; we will rush with alacrity to the combat, and, crowned by success, we shall then answer the exalted expectations which are formed. Though sensibility, soft compassion, and gentle commiseration, are inmates in the female bosom, yet against every deep laid art, altogether fearless of the event, we will set them in array; for assuredly the wreath of victory will encircle the spotless brow. If we meet an equal, a sensible friend, we will reward him with the hand of amity, and through life we will be assiduous to promote his happiness; but from every deep laid scheme for our rule, retiring into ourselves, amid the flowery paths of science, we will indulge in all the refined and sentimental pleasures of contemplation. And should it still be urged, that the studies thus insisted upon would interfere with our more peculiar department, I must further reply, that *early hours*, and close application, will do wonders; and to her who is from the first dawn of reason taught to fill up time rationally, both the requisites will be easy. I grant that niggard fortune is too generally unfriendly to the mind, and that much of that valuable treasure, time, is necessarily expended upon the wants of the body; but it should be remembered, that in embarrassed circumstances our companions have as little leisure for literary improvement, as is afforded to us; for most certainly their provident care is at least as requisite as our exertions. Nay, we have even more leisure for sedentary pleasures, as our avocations are more retired, much less laborious, and, as hath been observed, by no means require that avidity of attention which is proper to the employments of the other sex. In high life, or, in other words, where the parties are in possession of affluence, the objection respecting time is wholly obviated, and of course falls to the ground; and it may also be repeated, that many of those hours which are at present swallowed up in fashion and scandal, might be redeemed, were we habituated to useful reflections. But in one respect, O ye arbiters of our fate! we confess that the superiority is indubitably yours; you are by nature formed for our protectors; we pretend not to vie with you in bodily strength; upon this point we will never contend for victory. Shield us then, we beseech you, from external evils, and in return *we* will transact *your* domestic affairs. Yes, *your*, for are you not equally interested in those matters with ourselves? Is not the elegancy of neatness as agreeable to your sight as to ours; is not the well favored viand equally delightful to your taste; and doth not your sense of hearing suffer as much, from the discordant sounds prevalent in an ill regulated family, produced by the voices of children and many *et ceteras?*

CONSTANTIA.

By way of Supplement to the foregoing pages, I subjoin the following extract from a letter, wrote to a friend in the December of 1780.

. . . The superiority of your sex hath, I grant, been time out of mind esteemed a truth incontrovertible; in consequence of which persuasion, every plan of education hath been calculated to establish this favorite tenet. Not long since, weak and presuming as I was, I amused myself with selecting some arguments from nature, reason, and experience, against this so generally received idea. I confess that to sacred testimonies I had not recourse. I held them to be merely metaphorical, and thus regarding them, I could not persuade myself that there was any propriety in bringing them to decide in this *very important debate.* However, as you, sir, confine yourself entirely to the sacred oracles, I mean to bend the whole of my artillery against those supposed proofs, which you have from thence provided, and from which you have formed an intrenchment *apparently* so invulnerable. And first, to begin with our great progenitors; but here, suffer me to premise, that it is for mental strength I mean to contend, for with respect to animal powers, I yield them undisputed to that sex, which enjoys them in common with the lion, the tiger, and many other beasts of prey; therefore your observations respecting the *rib, under the arm, at a distance from the head*, &c. &c. in no sort militate against my view. Well, but the woman was first in the transgression. Strange how blind *self love* renders you men; were you not wholly absorbed in a partial admiration of your own abilities, you would long since have acknowledged the force of what I am now going to say. It is true some ignoramuses have absurdly enough informed us, that the beauteous fair of paradise, was seduced from her obedience, by a malignant demon, *in the guise of a baleful serpent;* but we, who are better informed, know that the fallen spirit presented himself to her view, *a shining angel still;* for thus, saith the critics in the Hebrew tongue, ought the word to be rendered. Let us examine her motive—Hark! the seraph declares that she shall attain a perfection of knowledge; for is there aught which is not comprehended under one or other of the terms *good* and *evil.* It doth not appear that she was governed by any sensual appetite; but merely by a desire of adorning her mind; a laudable ambition fired her soul, and a thirst for knowledge impelled the predilection so fatal in its consequences. Adam could not plead the same deception; assuredly he was not deceived; nor ought we to admire his superior strength, or wonder at his sagacity, when we so often confess that example is much more influential than precept. His gentle partner stood before him, a melancholy instance of the direful effects of disobedience; he saw her not possessed of that wisdom which she had fondly hoped to obtain, but he beheld the once blooming female, disrobed of that innocence, which had heretofore rendered her so lovely. To him then deception became impossible, as he had proof positive of the fallacy of the argument, which the deceiver had suggested. What then could be his inducement to burst the barriers, and to fly directly in the face of that command, which *immediately* from the mouth of deity *he* had received, since, I say, he could not plead that fascinating stimulous, the accumulation of knowledge, as indisputable conviction was so visibly portrayed before him. What mighty cause impelled him to sacrifice myriads of beings yet unborn, and by one impious act, which *he saw* would be productive of such fatal effects, entail undistinguished ruin upon a race of beings, which he was yet to produce. Blush, ye vaunters of fortitude; ye boasters of resolution; ye haughty lords of the creation; blush when ye remember, that he was influenced by no other motive than a bare pusillanimous attachment to a woman! by sentiments so exquisitely soft, that all his sons have, from that period, when they have designed to degrade them, described as highly feminine. Thus it should seem, that all the arts of the grand deceiver (since means adequate to the purpose are, I conceive, invariably pursued) were requisite to mislead our general mother, while the father of mankind forfeited his own, and relinquished the happiness of posterity, merely in compliance with the blandishments of a female.

THE RIGHTS OF WOMAN

OLYMPE DE GOUGES

In 1791, two years after the fall of the Bastille, Olympe de Gouges (1748–1793), a butcher's daughter, playwright, and pamphleteer, criticized the Declaration of the Rights of Man for its exclusion of women. Her essay, "The Rights of Woman," was addressed to the Queen, hoping to convert her to the feminist cause.

To the Queen: Madame,

Little suited to the language one holds to with kings, I will not use the adulation of courtiers to pay you homage with this singular production. My purpose, Madame, is to speak frankly to you; I have not awaited the epoch of liberty to thus explain myself; I bestirred myself as energetically in a time when the blindness of despots punished such noble audacity.

When the whole empire accused you and held you responsible for its calamities, I alone in a time of trouble and storm, I alone had the strength to take up your defense. I could never convince myself that a princess, raised in the midst of grandeur, had all the vices of baseness.

Yes, Madame, when I saw the sword raised against you, I threw my observations between that sword and you, but today when I see who is observed near the crowd of useless hirelings, and [when I see] that she is restrained by fear of the laws, I will tell you, Madame, what I did not say then.

If the foreigner bears arms into France, you are no longer in my eyes this falsely accused Queen, this attractive Queen, but an implacable enemy of the French. Oh, Madame, bear in mind that you are mother and wife; employ all your credit for the return of the Princes. This credit, if wisely applied, strengthens the father's crown, saves it for the son, and reconciles you to the love of the French. This worthy negotiation is the true duty of a queen. Intrigue, cabals, bloody projects will precipitate your fall, if it is possible to suspect that you are capable of such plots.

Madame, may a nobler function characterize you, excite your ambition, and fix your attentions. Only one whom chance has elevated to an eminent position can assume the task of lending weight to the progress of the Rights of Woman and of hastening its success. If you were less well informed, Madame, I might fear that your individual interests would outweigh those of your sex. You love glory; think, Madame, the greatest crimes immortalize one as much as the greatest virtues, but what a different fame in the annals of history! The one is ceaselessly taken as an example, and the other is eternally the execration of the human race.

It will never be a crime for you to work for the restoration of customs, to give your sex all the firmness of which it is capable. This is not the work of one day, unfortunately for the new regime. This revolution will happen only when all women are aware of their deplorable fate, and of the rights they have lost in society. Madame, support such a beautiful cause; defend this unfortunate sex, and soon you will have half the realm on your side, and at least one-third of the other half.

Those, Madame, are the feats by which you should show and use your credit. Believe me, Madame, our life is a pretty small thing, especially for a Queen, when it is not embellished by people's affection and by the eternal delights of good deeds.

If it is true that the French arm all the powers against their own Fatherland, why? For frivolous prerogatives, for chimeras. Believe, Madame, if I judge by what I feel—the monarchical party will be destroyed by itself, it will abandon all tyrants, and all hearts will rally around the fatherland to defend it.

There are my principles, Madame. In speaking to you of my fatherland, I lose sight of the purpose of this dedication. Thus, any good citizen sacrifices his glory and his interests when he has none other than those of his country.

I am with the most profound respect, Madame,

Your most humble and most obedient servant,

de Gouges

The Rights of Woman

Man, are you capable of being just? It is a woman who poses the question; you will not deprive her of that right at least. Tell me, what gives you sovereign empire to oppress my sex? Your strength? Your talents? Observe the Creator in his wisdom; survey in all her grandeur that nature with whom you seem to want to be in harmony, and give me, if you dare, an example of this tyrannical empire. Go back to animals, consult the elements, study plants, finally glance at all the modifications of organic matter, and surrender to the evidence when I offer you the means; search, probe, and distinguish, if you can, the sexes in the administration of nature. Everywhere you will find them mingled; everywhere they cooperate in harmonious togetherness in this immortal masterpiece.

Man alone has raised his exceptional circumstances to a principle. Bizarre, blind, bloated with science and degenerated—in a century of enlightenment and wisdom—into the crassest ignorance, he wants to command as a despot a sex which is in full possession of its intellectual faculties; he pretends to enjoy the Revolution and to claim his rights to equality in order to say nothing more about it.

Declaration of the Rights of Woman and the Female Citizen

For the National Assembly to decree in its last sessions, or in those of the next legislature:

Preamble. Mothers, daughters, sisters [and] representatives of the nation demand to be constituted into a national assembly. Believing that ignorance, omission, or scorn for the rights of woman are the only causes of public misfortunes and of the corruption of governments, [the women] have resolved to set forth in a solemn declaration the natural, inalienable, and sacred rights of woman in order that this declaration, constantly exposed before all the members of the society, will ceaselessly remind them of their rights and duties; in order that the authoritative acts of women and the authoritative acts of men may be at any moment compared with and respectful of the purpose of all political institutions; and in order that citizens' demands, henceforth based on simple and incontestable principles, will always support the constitution, good morals, and the happiness of all.

Consequently, the sex that is as superior in beauty as it is in courage during the sufferings of maternity recognizes and declares in the presence and under the auspices of the Supreme Being, the following Rights of Woman and of Female Citizens.

Article I. Woman is born free and lives equal to man in her rights. Social distinctions can be based only on the common utility.

Article II. The purpose of any political association is the conservation of the natural and imprescriptible rights of woman and man; these rights are liberty, property, security, and especially resistance to oppression.

Article III. The principle of all sovereignty rests essentially with the nation, which is nothing but the union of woman and man; no body and no individual can exercise any authority which does not come expressly from it [the nation].

Article IV. Liberty and justice consist of restoring all that belongs to others; thus, the only limits on the exercise of the natural rights of woman are perpetual male tyranny; these limits are to be reformed by the laws of nature and reason.

Article V. Laws of nature and reason proscribe all acts harmful to society; everything which is not prohibited by these wise and divine laws cannot be prevented, and no one can be constrained to do what they do not command.

Article VI. The law must be the expression of the general will; all female and male citizens must contribute either personally or through their representatives to its formation; it must be the same for all: male and female citizens, being equal in the eyes of the law, must be equally admitted to all honors, positions, and public employment according to their capacity and without other distinctions besides those of their virtues and talents.

Article VII. No woman is an exception; she is accused, arrested, and detained in cases determined by law. Women, like men, obey this rigorous law.

Article VIII. The law must establish only those penalties that are strictly and obviously necessary, and no one can be punished except by virtue of a law established and promulgated prior to the crime and legally applicable to women.

Article IX. Once any woman is declared guilty, complete rigor is [to be] exercised by the law.

Article X. No one is to be disquieted for his very basic opinions; woman has the right to mount the scaffold; she must equally have the right to mount the rostrum, provided that her demonstrations do not disturb the legally established public order.

Article XI. The free communication of thoughts and opinions is one of the most precious rights of woman, since that liberty assures the recognition of children by their fathers. Any female citizen thus may say freely, I am the mother of a child which belongs to you, without being forced by a barbarous prejudice to hide the truth; [an exception may be made] to respond to the abuse of this liberty in cases determined by the law.

Article XII. The guarantee of the rights of woman and the female citizen implies a major benefit; this guarantee must be instituted for the advantage of all, and not for the particular benefit of those to whom it is entrusted.

Article XIII. For the support of the public force and the expenses of administration, the contributions of woman and man are equal; she shares all the duties [*corvées*] and all the painful tasks; therefore, she must have the same share in the distribution of positions, employment, offices, honors, and jobs [*industrie*].

Article XIV. Female and male citizens have the right to verify, either by themselves or through their representatives, the necessity of the public contribution. This can only apply to women if they are granted an equal share, not only of wealth, but also of public administration, and in the determination of the proportion, the base, the collection, and the duration of the tax.

Article XV. The collectivity of women, joined for tax purposes to the aggregate of men, has the right to demand an accounting of his administration from any public agent.

Article XVI. No society has a constitution without the guarantee of rights and the separation of powers; the constitution is null if the majority of individuals comprising the nation have not cooperated in drafting it.

Article XVII. Property belongs to both sexes whether united or separate; for each it is an inviolable and sacred right; no one can be deprived of it, since it is the true patrimony of nature, unless the legally determined public need obviously dictates it, and then only with a just and prior indemnity.

Postscript. Woman, wake up; the tocsin of reason is being heard throughout the whole universe; discover your rights. The powerful empire of nature is no longer surrounded by prejudice, fanaticism, superstition, and lies. The flame of truth has dispersed all the clouds of folly and usurpation. Enslaved man has multiplied his strength and needs recourse to yours to break his chains. Having become free, he has become unjust to his companion. Oh, women, women! When will you cease to be blind? What advantage have you received from the Revolution? A more pronounced scorn, a more marked disdain. In the centuries of corruption you ruled only over the weakness of men. The reclamation of your patrimony, based on the wise decrees of nature—what have you to dread from such a fine undertaking? The *bon mot* of the legislator of the marriage of Cana? Do you fear that our French legislators, correctors of that morality, long ensnared by political practices now out of date, will only say again to you: women, what is there in common between you and us? Everything, you will have to answer. If they persist in their weakness in putting this non sequitur in contradiction to their principles, courageously oppose the force of reason to the empty pretentions of superiority; unite yourselves beneath the standards of philosophy; deploy all the energy of your character, and you will soon see these haughty men, not groveling at your feet as servile adorers, but proud to share with you the treasures of the Supreme Being. Regardless of what barriers confront you, it is in your power to free yourselves; you have only to want to. Let us pass now to the shocking tableau of what you have been in society; and since national education is in question at this moment, let us see whether our wise legislators will think judiciously about the education of women.

Women have done more harm than good. Constraint and dissimulation have been their lot. What force had robbed them of, ruse returned to them; they had recourse to all the resources of their charms, and the most irreproachable person did not resist them. Poison and the sword were both subject to them; they commanded in crime as in fortune. The French government, especially, depended throughout the centuries on the nocturnal administration of women; the cabinet kept no secret from their indiscretion; ambassadorial post, command, ministry, presidency, pontificate, college of cardinals; finally, anything which characterizes the folly of men, profane and sacred, all have been subject to the cupidity and ambition of this sex, formerly contemptible and respected, and since the revolution, respectable and scorned.

In this sort of contradictory situation, what remarks could I not make! I have but a moment to make them, but this moment will fix the attention of the remotest posterity. Under the Old Regime, all was vicious, all was guilty; but could not the amelioration of conditions be perceived even in the substance of vices? A woman only had to be beautiful or amiable; when she possessed these two advantages, she saw a hundred fortunes at her feet. If she did not profit from them, she had a bizarre character or a rare philosophy which made her scorn wealth; then she was deemed to be like a crazy woman; the most indecent made herself respected with gold; commerce in women was a kind of industry in the first class [of society], which, henceforth, will have no more credit. If it still had it, the revolution would be lost, and under the new relationships we would always be corrupted; however, reason can always be deceived [into believing] that any other road to fortune is closed to the woman whom a man buys, like the slave on the African coasts. The difference is great; that is known. The slave is commanded by the master; but if the master gives her liberty without recompense, and at an age when the slave has lost all her charms, what will become of this unfortunate woman? The victim of scorn, even the doors of charity are closed to her; she is poor and old, they say; why did she not know how to make her fortune? Reason finds other examples that are even more touching. A young, inexperienced woman, seduced by a man whom she loves, will abandon her parents to follow him; the ingrate will leave her after a few years, and the older she has become with him, the more inhuman is his inconstancy; if she has children, he will likewise abandon them. If he is rich, he will consider himself excused from sharing his fortune with his noble victims. If some involvement binds him to his duties, he will deny them, trusting that the laws will support him. If he is married, any other obligation loses its rights. Then what laws remain to extirpate vice all the way to its root? The law of dividing wealth and public administration between men and women. It can easily be seen that one who is born into a rich family gains very much from such equal sharing. But the one born into a poor family with merit and virtue—what is her lot? Poverty and opprobrium. If she does not precisely excel in music or painting, she cannot be admitted to any public function when she has all the capacity for it. I do not want to give only a sketch of things; I will go more deeply into this in the new edition of all my political writings, with notes, which I propose to give to the public in a few days.

I take up my text again on the subject of morals. Marriage is the tomb of trust and love. The married woman can with impunity give bastards to her husband, and also give them the wealth which does not belong to them. The woman who is unmarried has only one feeble right; ancient and inhuman laws refuse to her for her children the right to the name and the wealth of their father; no new laws have been made in this matter. If it is considered a paradox and an impossibility on my part to try to give my sex an honorable and just consistency, I leave it to men to attain glory for dealing with this matter; but while we wait, the way can be prepared through national education, the restoration of morals, and conjugal conventions.

Form for a Social Contract Between Man and Woman

We, __________ and __________, moved by our own will, unite ourselves for the duration of our lives, and for the duration of our mutual inclinations, under the following conditions: We intend and wish to make our wealth communal, meanwhile reserving to ourselves the right to divide it in favor of our children and of those toward whom we might have a particular inclination, mutually recognizing that our property belongs directly to our children, from whatever bed they come, and that all of them without distinction have the right to bear the name of the fathers and mothers who have acknowledged them, and we are charged to subscribe to the law which punishes the renunciation of one's own blood. We likewise obligate ourselves, in case of separation, to divide our wealth and to set aside in advance the portion the law indicates for our children, and in the event of a perfect union, the one who dies will divest himself of half his property in his children's favor, and if one dies childless, the survivor will inherit by right, unless the dying person has disposed of half the common property in favor of one whom he judged deserving.

That is approximately the formula for the marriage act I propose for execution. Upon reading this strange document, I see rising up against me the hypocrites, the prudes, the clergy, and the whole infernal sequence. But how it [my proposal] offers to the wise the moral means of achieving the perfection of a happy government! I am going to give in a few words the physical proof of it. The rich, childless Epicurean finds it very good to go to his poor neighbor to augment his family. When there is a law authorizing a poor man's wife to have a rich one adopt their children, the bonds of society will be strengthened and morals will be purer. This law will perhaps save the community's wealth and hold back the disorder which drives so many victims to the almshouses of shame, to a low station, and into degenerate human principles where nature has groaned for so long. May the detractors of wise philosophy then cease to cry out against primitive morals, or may they lose their point in the source of their citations.

Moreover, I would like a law which would assist widows and young girls deceived by the false promises of a man to whom they were attached; I would like, I say, this law to force an inconstant man to hold to his obligations or at least [to pay] an indemnity equal to his wealth. Again, I would like this law to be rigorous against women, at least those who have the effrontery to have recourse to a law which they themselves had violated by their misconduct, if proof of that were given. At the same time, as I showed in *Le Bonheur primitif de l'homme*, in 1788, that prostitutes should be placed in designated quarters. It is not prostitutes who contribute the most to the depravity of morals, it is the women of society. In regenerating the latter, the former are changed. This link of fraternal union will first bring disorder, but in consequence it will produce at the end a perfect harmony.

I offer a foolproof way to elevate the soul of women; it is to join them to all the activities of man; if man persists in finding this way impractical, let him share his fortune with woman, not at his caprice, but by the wisdom of laws. Prejudice falls, morals are purified, and nature regains all her rights. Add to this the marriage of priests and the strengthening of the king on his throne, and the French government cannot fail.

It would be very necessary to say a few words on the troubles which are said to be caused by the decree in favor of colored men in our islands. There is where nature shudders with horror; there is where reason and humanity have still not touched callous souls; there, especially, is where division and discord stir up their inhabitants. It is not difficult to divine the instigators of these incendiary fermentations; they are even in the midst of the National Assembly; they ignite the fire in Europe which must inflame America. Colonists make a claim to reign as despots over the men whose fathers and brothers they are; and, disowning the rights of nature, they trace the source of [their rule] to the scantiest tint of their blood. These inhuman colonists say: our blood flows in their veins, but we will shed it all if necessary to glut our greed or our blind ambition. It is in these places nearest to nature where the father scorns the son; deaf to the cries of blood, they stifle all its attraction; what can be hoped from the resistance opposed to them? To constrain [blood] violently is to render it terrible; to leave [blood] still enchained is to direct all calamities towards America. A divine hand seems to spread liberty abroad throughout the realms of man; only the law has the right to curb this liberty if it degenerates into license, but it must be equal for all; liberty must hold the National Assembly to its decree dictated by prudence and justice. May it act the same way for the state of France and render her as attentive to new abuses as she was to the ancient ones which each day become more dreadful. My opinion would be to reconcile the executive and legislative power, for it seems to me that the one is everything and the other is nothing—whence comes, unfortunately perhaps, the loss of the French Empire. I think that these two powers, like man and woman, should be united but equal in force and virtue to make a good household.

VINDICATION OF THE RIGHTS OF WOMAN

MARY WOLLSTONECRAFT

Mary Wollstonecraft (1759–1797), whose Vindication, *published in 1792, has become the manifesto of feminism, had been a teacher, a tutor, and a governess before she became an independent writer on politics and novelist. The section here is Chapter IX, titled "Of the Pernicious Effects Which Arise from the Unnatural Distinctions Established in Society," of her* Vindication. *Wollstonecraft married the anarchist philosopher Godwin, and shortly after giving birth to their child she died. Their daughter, Mary, married the poet Shelley and eventually wrote the novel* Frankenstein, *itself an enduring legacy of the Enlightenment.*

From the respect paid to property flow, as from a poisoned fountain, most of the evils and vices which render this world such a dreary scene to the contemplative mind. For it is in the most polished society that noisesome reptiles and venomous serpents lurk under the rank herbage; and there is voluptuousness pampered by the still sultry air, which relaxes every good disposition before it ripens into virtue.

One class presses on another; for all are aiming to procure respect on account of their property: and property, once gained, will procure the respect due only to talents and virtue. Men neglect the duties incumbent on man, yet are treated like demi-gods; religion is also separated from morality by a ceremonial veil, yet men wonder that the world is almost, literally speaking, a den of sharpers or oppressors.

There is a homely proverb, which speaks a shrewd truth, that whoever the devil finds idle he will employ. And what but habitual idleness can hereditary wealth and titles produce? For man is so constituted that he can only attain a proper use of his faculties by exercising them, and will not exercise them unless necessity of some kind first set the wheels in motion. Virtue likewise can only be acquired by the discharge of relative duties; but the importance of these sacred duties will scarcely be felt by the being who is cajoled out of his humanity by the flattery of sycophants. There must be more equality established in society, or morality will never gain ground, and this virtuous equality will not rest firmly even when founded on a rock, if one half of mankind be chained to its bottom by fate, for they will be continually undermining it through ignorance or pride.

It is vain to expect virtue from women till they are in some degree, independent of men; nay, it is vain to expect that strength of natural affection which would make them good wives and mothers. Whilst they are absolutely dependent on their husbands they will be cunning, mean, and selfish, and the men who can be gratified by the fawning fondness of spaniel-like affection have not much delicacy, for love is not to be bought, in any sense of the words, its silken wings are instantly shriveled up when anything beside a return in kind is sought. Yet whilst wealth enervates men, and women live, as it were, by their personal charms, how can we expect them to discharge those ennobling duties which equally require exertion and self-denial? Hereditary property sophisticates the mind, and the unfortunate victims to it, if I may so express myself, swathed from their birth, seldom exert the locomotive faculty of body or mind; and, thus viewing everything through one medium, and that a false one, they are unable to discern in what true merit and happiness consist. False, indeed, must be the light when the drapery of situation hides the man, and makes him stalk in masquerade, dragging from one scene of dissipation to another the nerveless limbs that hang with stupid listlessness, and rolling round the vacant eye which plainly tells us that there is no mind at home.

I mean, therefore, to infer that the society is not properly organized which does not compel men and women to discharge their respective duties, by making it the only way to acquire that countenance from their fellow-creatures which every human being wishes some way to attain. The respect, consequently, which is paid to wealth and mere personal charms, is a true north-east blast that blights the tender blossoms of affection and virtue. Nature has wisely attached affections to duties to sweeten toil, and to give that vigor to the exertions of reason which only the heart can give. But the affection which is put on merely because it is the appropriated insignia of a certain character, when its duties are not fulfilled, is one of the empty compliments which vice and folly are obliged to pay to virtue and the real nature of things.

To illustrate my opinion, I need only observe that when a woman is admired for her beauty, and suffers herself to be so far intoxicated by the admiration she receives as to neglect to discharge the indispensable duty of a mother, she sins against herself by neglecting to cultivate an affection that would equally tend to make her useful and happy. True happiness, I mean all the contentment and virtuous satisfaction that can be snatched in this imperfect state, must arise from well-regulated affections; and an affection includes a duty. Men are not aware of the misery they cause and the vicious weakness they cherish by only inciting women to render themselves pleasing; they do not consider that they thus make natural and artificial duties clash by sacrificing the comfort and respectability of a woman's life to voluptuous notions of beauty when in nature they all harmonize.

Cold would be the heart of a husband, were he not rendered unnatural by early debauchery, who did not feel more delight at seeing his child suckled by its mother, than the most artful wanton tricks could ever raise; yet this natural way of cementing the matrimonial tie and twisting esteem with fonder recollections, wealth leads women to spurn. To preserve their beauty and wear the flowery crown of the day, which gives them a kind of right to reign for a short time over the sex, they neglect to stamp impressions on their husbands' hearts that would be remembered with more tenderness when the snow on the head began to chill the bosom than even their virgin charms. The maternal solicitude of a reasonable affectionate woman is very interesting, and the chastened dignity with which a mother returns the caresses that she and her child receive from a father who has been fulfilling the serious duties of his station, is not only a respectable but a beautiful sight. So singular indeed are my feelings, and I have endeavored not to catch factitious ones, that after having been fatigued with the sight of insipid grandeur and the slavish ceremonies that with cumbrous pomp supplied the place of domestic affections, I have turned to some other scene to relieve my eye by resting it on the refreshing green everywhere scattered by nature. I have then viewed with pleasure a woman nursing her children, and discharging the duties of her station with, perhaps, merely a servant maid to take off her hands the servile part of the household business. I have seen her prepare herself and children, with only the luxury of cleanliness, to receive her husband, who returning weary home in the evening found smiling babes and a clean hearth. My heart has loitered in the midst of the group, and has even throbbed with sympathetic emotion, when the scraping of the well known foot has raised a pleasing tumult.

Whilst my benevolence has been gratified by contemplating this artless picture, I have thought that a couple of this description, equally necessary and independent of each other, because each fulfilled the respective duties of their station, possessed all that life could give.—Raised sufficiently above abject poverty not to be obliged to weigh the consequence of every farthing they spend, and having sufficient to prevent their attending to a frigid system of economy, which narrows both heart and mind. I declare, so vulgar are my conceptions, that I know not what is wanted to render this the happiest as well as the most respectable situation in the world, but a taste for literature, to throw a little variety and interest into social converse, and some superfluous money to give to the needy and to buy books. For it is not pleasant when the heart is opened by compassion and the head active in arranging plans of usefulness, to have a prim urchin continually twitching back the elbow to prevent the hand from drawing out an almost empty purse, whispering at the same time some prudential maxim about the priority of justice.

Destructive, however, as riches and inherited honors are to the human character, women are more debased and cramped, if possible, by them than men, because men may still, in some degree, unfold their faculties by becoming soldiers and statesmen.

As soldiers, I grant, they can now only gather, for the most part, vain glorious laurels, whilst they adjust to a hair the European balance, taking especial care that no bleak northern nook or sound incline the beam. But the days of true heroism are over, when a citizen fought for his country like a Fabricius or a Washington, and then returned to his farm to let his virtuous fervor run in a more placid, but not a less salutary, stream. No, our British heroes are oftener sent from the gaming table than from the plough, and their passions have been rather inflamed by hanging with dumb suspense on the turn of a die, than sublimated by panting after the adventurous march of virtue in the historic page.

The statesman, it is true, might with more propriety quit the faro bank, or card-table, to guide the helm, for he has still but to shuffle and trick. The whole system of British politics, if system it may courteously be called, consisting in multiplying dependents and contriving taxes which grind the poor to pamper the rich; thus a war, or any wild goose chase, is, as the vulgar use the phrase, a lucky turn-up of patronage for the minister, whose chief merit is the art of keeping himself in place. It is not necessary then that he should have bowels for the poor, so he can secure for his family the odd trick. Or should some show of respect, for what is termed with ignorant ostentation an Englishman's birthright, be expedient to bubble the gruff mastiff that he has to lead by the nose, he can make an empty show very safely by giving his single voice and suffering his light squadron to file off to the other side. And when a question of humanity is agitated he may dip a sop in the milk of human kindness to silence Cerberus, and talk of the interest which his heart takes in an attempt to make the earth no longer cry for vengeance as it sucks in its children's blood, though his cold hand may at the very moment rivet their chains by sanctioning the abominable traffic. A minister is no longer a minister than while he can carry a point which he is determined to carry. Yet it is not necessary that a minister should feel like a man, when a bold push might shake his seat.

But, to have done with these episodical observations, let me return to the more specious slavery which chains the very soul of woman, keeping her for ever under the bondage of ignorance.

The preposterous distinctions of rank, which render civilization a curse by dividing the world between voluptuous tyrants, and cunning envious dependents, corrupt, almost equally, every class of people, because respectability is not attached to the discharge of the relative duties of life, but to the station, and when the duties are not fulfilled the affections cannot gain sufficient strength to fortify the virtue of which they are the natural reward. Still there are some loopholes out of which a man may creep, and dare to think and act for himself; but for a woman it is a herculean task, because she has difficulties peculiar to her sex to overcome which require almost superhuman powers.

A truly benevolent legislator always endeavors to make it the interest of each individual to be virtuous; and thus private virtue becoming the cement of public happiness, an orderly whole is consolidated by the tendency of all the parts towards a common center. But, the private or public virtue of woman is very problematical; for Rousseau, and a numerous list of male writers, insist that she should all her life be subjected to a severe restraint, that of propriety. Why subject her to propriety—blind propriety, if she be capable of acting from a nobler spring, if she be an heir of immortality? Is sugar always to be produced by vital blood? Is one half of the human species, like the poor African slaves, to be subject to prejudices that brutalize them, when principles would be a surer guard, only to sweeten the cup of man? Is not this indirectly to deny woman reason? for a gift is a mockery, if it be unfit for use.

Women are, in common with men, rendered weak and luxurious by the relaxing pleasures which wealth procures; but added to this they are made slaves to their persons, and must render them alluring that man may lend them his reason to guide their tottering steps aright. Or should they be ambitious, they must govern their tyrants by sinister tricks, for without rights there cannot be any incumbent duties. The laws respecting woman, which I mean to discuss in a future part, make an absurd unit of a man and his wife, and then, by the easy transition of only considering him as responsible, she is reduced to a mere cypher.

The being who discharges the duties of its station is independent; and, speaking of women at large, their first duty is to themselves as rational creatures, and the next in point of importance, as citizens, is that which includes so many, of a mother. The rank in life which dispenses with their fulfilling this duty necessarily degrades them by making them mere dolls. Or, should they turn to something more important than merely fitting drapery upon a smooth block, their minds are only occupied by some soft platonic attachment; or, the actual management of an intrigue may keep their thoughts in motion; for when they neglect domestic duties, they have it not in their own power to take the field and march and counter-march like soldiers, or wrangle in the senate to keep their faculties from rusting.

I know that, as a proof of the inferiority of the sex, Rousseau has exultingly exclaimed, How can they leave the nursery for the camp! And the camp has by some moralists been termed the school of the most heroic virtues; though, I think, it would puzzle a keen casuist to prove the reasonableness of the greater number of wars that have dubbed heroes. I do not mean to consider this question critically; because, having frequently viewed these freaks of ambition as the first natural mode of civilization, when the ground must be torn up, and the woods cleared by fire and sword, I do not choose to call them pests; but surely the present system of war has little connection with virtue of any denomination, being rather the school of *finesse* and effeminacy, than of fortitude.

Yet, if defensive war, the only justifiable war, in the present advanced state of society, where virtue can show its face and ripen amidst the rigors which purify the air on the mountain's top, were alone to be adopted as just and glorious, the true heroism of antiquity might again animate female bosoms. But fair and softly, gentle reader, male or female, do not alarm thyself, for though I have compared the character of a modern soldier with that of a civilized woman, I am not going to advise them to turn their distaff into a musket, though I sincerely wish to see the bayonet converted into a pruning-hook. I only recreated an imagination, fatigued by contemplating the vices and follies which all proceed from a feculent stream of wealth that has muddied the pure rills of natural affection, by supposing that society will some time or other be so constituted, that man must necessarily fulfill the duties of a citizen or be despised, and that while he was employed in any of the departments of civil life, his wife, also an active citizen, should be equally intent to manage her family, educate her children, and assist her neighbors.

But, to render her really virtuous and useful, she must not, if she discharge her civil duties, want, individually, the protection of civil laws; she must not be dependent on her husband's bounty for her subsistence during his life or support after his death—for how can a being be generous who has nothing of its own? or virtuous, who is not free? The wife, in the present state of things, who is faithful to her husband, and neither suckles nor educates her children, scarcely deserves the name of a wife, and has no right to that of a citizen. But take away natural rights, and duties become null.

Women then must be considered as only the wanton solace of men, when they become so weak in mind and body that they cannot exert themselves unless to pursue some frothy pleasure, or to invent some frivolous fashion. What can be a more melancholy sight to a thinking mind, than to look into the numerous carriages that drive helter-skelter about this metropolis in a morning full of pale-faced creatures who are flying from themselves! I have often wished, with Dr. Johnson, to place some of them in a little shop with half a dozen children looking up to their languid countenances for support. I am much mistaken, if some latent vigor would not soon give health and spirit to their eyes, and some lines drawn by the exercise of reason on the blank cheeks, which before were only undulated by dimples, might restore lost dignity to the character, or rather enable it to attain the true dignity of its nature. Virtue is not to be acquired even by speculation, much less by the negative supineness that wealth naturally generates.

Besides, when poverty is more disgraceful than even vice, is not morality cut to the quick? Still to avoid misconstruction, though I consider that women in the common walks of life are called to fulfill the duties of wives and mothers, by religion and reason, I cannot help lamenting that women of a superior cast have not a road open by which they can pursue more extensive plans of usefulness and independence. I may excite laughter, by dropping a hint, which I mean to pursue, some future time, for I really think that women ought to have representatives, instead of being arbitrarily governed without having any direct share allowed them in the deliberations of government.

But, as the whole system of representation is now, in this country, only a convenient handle for despotism, they need not complain, for they are as well represented as a numerous class of hard-working mechanics, who pay for the support of royalty when they can scarcely stop their children's mouths with bread. How are they represented whose very sweat supports the splendid stud of an heir-apparent, or varnishes the chariot of some female favorite who looks down on shame? Taxes on the very necessaries of life, enable an endless tribe of idle princes and princesses to pass with stupid pomp before a gaping crowd, who almost worship the very parade which costs them so dear. This is mere gothic grandeur, something like the barbarous useless parade of having sentinels on horseback at Whitehall, which I could never view without a mixture of contempt and indignation.

How strangely must the mind be sophisticated when this sort of state impresses it! But, till these monuments of folly are leveled by virtue, similar follies will leaven the whole mass. For the same character, in some degree, will prevail in the aggregate of society; and the refinements of luxury, or the vicious repinings of envious poverty, will equally banish virtue from society, considered as the characteristic of that society, or only allow it to appear as one of the stripes of the harlequin coat, worn by the civilized man.

In the superior ranks of life, every duty is done by deputies, as if duties could ever be waived, and the vain pleasures which consequent idleness forces the rich to pursue, appear so enticing to the next rank, that the numerous scramblers for wealth sacrifice everything to tread on their heels. The most sacred trusts are then considered as sinecures, because they were procured by interest, and only sought to enable a man to keep *good company*. Women, in particular, all want to be ladies. Which is simply to have nothing to do, but listlessly to go they scarcely care where, for they cannot tell what.

But what have women to do in society? I may be asked, but to loiter with easy grace; surely you would not condemn them all to suckle fools and chronicle small beer! No. Women might certainly study the art of healing and be physicians as well as nurses. And midwifery, decency seems to allot to them though I am afraid the word midwife, in our dictionaries, will soon give place to *accoucheur*, and one proof of the former delicacy of the sex can be effaced from the language.

They might also study politics, and settle their benevolence on the broadest basis; for the reading of history will scarcely be more useful than the perusal of romances, if read as mere biography; if the character of the times, the political improvements, arts, etc., be not observed. In short, if it be not considered as the history of man; and not of particular men, who filled a niche in the temple of fame, and dropped into the black rolling stream of time, that silently sweeps all before it into the shapeless void called—eternity.—For shape, can it be called, "that shape hath none?"

Business of various kinds, they might likewise pursue, if they were educated in a more orderly manner, which might save many from common and legal prostitution. Women would not then marry for a support, as men accept of places under Government, and neglect the implied duties; nor would an attempt to earn their own subsistence, a most laudable one! sink them almost to the level of those poor abandoned creatures who live by prostitution. For are not milliners and mantua-makers reckoned the next class? The few employments open to women, so far, from being liberal, are menial; and when a superior education enables them to take charge of the education of children as governesses, they are not treated like the tutors of sons, though even clerical tutors are not always treated in a manner calculated to render them respectable in the eyes of their pupils, to say nothing of the private comfort of the individual. But as women educated like gentlewomen are never designed for the humiliating situation which necessity sometimes forces them to fill, these situations are considered in the light of a degradation; and they know little of the human heart, who need to be told, that nothing so painfully sharpens sensibility as such a fall in life.

Some of these women might be restrained from marrying by a proper spirit or delicacy, and others may not have had it in their power to escape in this pitiful way from servitude; is not that government then very defective, and very unmindful of the happiness of one half of its members, that does not provide for honest, independent women, by encouraging them to fill respectable stations? But in order to render their private virtue a public benefit, they must have a civil existence in the state, married or single; else we shall continually see some worthy woman, whose sensibility has been rendered painfully acute by undeserved contempt, droop like "the lily broken down by a plow-share."

It is a melancholy truth—yet such is the blessed effect of civilization!—the most respectable women are the most oppressed; and, unless they have understandings far superior to the common run of understandings, taking in both sexes, they must, from being treated like contemptible beings, become contemptible. How many women thus waste life away the prey of discontent, who might have practiced as physicians, regulated a farm, managed a shop, and stood erect, supported by their own industry, instead of hanging their heads surcharged with the dew of sensibility, that consumes the beauty to which it at first gave luster; nay, I doubt whether pity and love are so near akin as poets feign, for I have seldom seen much compassion excited by the helplessness of females, unless they were fair; then, perhaps, pity was the soft handmaid of love, or the harbinger of lust.

How much more respectable is the woman who earns her own bread by fulfilling any duty, than the most accomplished beauty!—beauty did I say?—so sensible am I of the beauty of moral loveliness, or the harmonious propriety that attunes the passions of a well-regulated mind, that I blush at making the comparison; yet I sigh to think how few women aim at attaining this respectability by withdrawing from the giddy whirl of pleasure, or the indolent calm that stupefies the good sort of women it sucks in.

Proud of their weakness, however, they must always be protected, guarded from care, and all the rough toils that dignify the mind. If this be the fiat of fate, if they will make themselves insignificant and contemptible, sweetly to waste "life away," let them not expect to be valued when their beauty fades, for it is the fate of the fairest flowers to be admired and pulled to pieces by the careless hand that plucked them. In how many ways do I wish, from the purest benevolence, to impress this truth on my sex; yet I fear that they will not listen to a truth that dear-bought experience has brought home to many an agitated bosom, nor willingly resign the privileges of rank and sex for the privileges of humanity, to which those have no claim who do not discharge its duties.

Those writers are particularly useful, in my opinion, who make man feel for man, independent of the station he fills, or the drapery of factitious sentiments. I then would fain convince reasonable men of the importance of some of my remarks; and prevail on them to weigh dispassionately the whole tenor of my observations. I appeal to their understandings; and, as a fellow-creature, claim, in the name of my sex, some interest in their hearts. I entreat them to assist to emancipate their companion, to make her a *help meet* for them!

Would men but generously snap our chains, and be content with rational fellowship instead of slavish obedience, they would find us more observant daughters, more affectionate sisters, more faithful wives, more reasonable mothers—in a word, better citizens. We should then love them with true affection, because we should learn to respect ourselves; and the peace of mind of a worthy man would not be interrupted by the idle vanity of his wife, nor the babes sent to nestle in a strange bosom, having never found a home in their mother's.

"NEGROES . . . NATURALLY INFERIOR TO THE WHITES . . ."

DAVID HUME

In the second edition of his Essays, Moral and Political *(1742), David Hume added the following racist note to his essay "Of National Characters." To the philosopher of the Enlightenment "ingenious manufactures," "arts," and "sciences" were the sole criteria of civilization.*

I am apt to suspect the negroes and in general all the other species of men (for there are four or five different kinds) to be naturally inferior to the whites. There never was a civilized nation of any other complexion than white, nor even any individual eminent either in action or speculation. No ingenious manufactures amongst them, no arts, no sciences. On the other hand, the most rude and barbarous of the whites, such as the ancient GERMANS, the present TARTARS, have still something eminent about them, in their valor, form of government, or some other particular. Such a uniform and constant difference could not happen in so many countries and ages, if nature had not made an original distinction betwixt these breeds of men. Not to mention our colonies, there are NEGRO slaves dispersed all over EUROPE, of which none ever discovered any symptoms of ingenuity, tho' low people, without education, will start up amongst us, and distinguish themselves in every profession. In JAMAICA indeed they talk of one negro as a man of parts and learning; but 'tis likely he is admired for very slender accomplishments like a parrot, who speaks a few words plainly.

CONSIDERATIONS ON THE KEEPING OF NEGROES

JOHN WOOLMAN

Voices were nevertheless heard in the Enlightenment insisting on the equality of the races. The Quaker John Woolman (1720–1772), a tailor and shopkeeper by trade, was a zealous critic of American slavery. This selection is from a 1762 Philadelphia tract, Some Considerations on the Keeping of Negroes.

Some who keep slaves, have doubted as to the equity of the practice; but as they knew men, noted for their piety, who were in it, this, they say, has made their minds easy.

To lean on the example of men in doubtful cases, is difficult: for only admit, that those men were not faithful and upright to the highest degree, but that in some particular case they erred, and it may follow that this one case was the same, about which we are in doubt; and to quiet our minds by their example, may be dangerous to ourselves; and continuing in it, prove a stumbling block to tender-minded people who succeed us, in like manner as their examples are to us.

But supposing charity was their only motive, and they not foreseeing the tendency of paying robbers for their booty, were not justly under the imputation of being partners with a thief, Prov. xxix. 24. but were really innocent in what they did, are we assured that we keep them with the same views they kept them? If we keep them from no other motive than a real sense of duty, and true charity governs us in all our proceedings toward them, we are so far safe: but if another spirit, which inclines our minds to the ways of this world, prevail upon us, and we are concerned for our own outward gain more than for their real happiness, it will avail us nothing that some good men have had the care and management of Negroes.

Since mankind spread upon the earth, many have been the revolutions attending the several families, and their customs and ways of life different from each other. This diversity of manners, though some are preferable to others, operates not in favor of any, so far as to justify them to do violence to innocent men; to bring them from their own to another way of life. The mind, when moved by a principle of true love, may feel a warmth of gratitude to the universal father, and a lively sympathy with those nations, where divine Light has been less manifest.

This desire for their real good may beget a willingness to undergo hardships for their sakes, that the true knowledge of God may be spread amongst them: but to take them from their own land, with views of profit to ourselves, by means inconsistent with pure justice, is foreign to that principle which seeks the happiness of the whole creation. Forced subjection, of innocent persons of full age, is inconsistent with right reason; on one side, the human mind is not naturally fortified with that firmness in wisdom and goodness, necessary to an independent ruler; on the other side, to be subject to the uncontrollable will of a man, liable to err, is most painful and afflicting to a conscientious creature.

It is our happiness faithfully to serve the divine Being, who made us: his perfection makes our service reasonable; but so long as men are biased by narrow self-love, so long an absolute power over other men is unfit for them.

Men, taking on them the government of others, may intend to govern reasonably, and make their subjects more happy than they would be otherwise; but, as absolute command belongs only to him who is perfect, where frail men, in their own wills, assume such command, it hath a direct tendency to vitiate their minds, and make them more unfit for government.

Placing on men the ignominious title SLAVE, dressing them in uncomely garments, keeping them to servile labor, in which they are often dirty, tends gradually to fix a notion in the mind, that they are a sort of people below us in nature, and leads us to consider them as such in all our conclusions about them. And, moreover, a person which in our esteem is mean and contemptible, if their language or behavior toward us is unseemly or disrespectful, it excites wrath more powerfully than the like conduct in one we accounted our equal or superior; and where this happens to be the case, it disqualifies for candid judgment; for it is unfit for a person to sit as judge in a case where his own personal resentments are stirred up; and, as members of society in a well framed government, we are mutually dependent. Present interest incites to duty, and makes each man attentive to the convenience of others; but he whose will is a law to others, and can enforce obedience by punishment;

he whose wants are supplied without feeling any obligation to make equal returns to his benefactor, his irregular appetites find an open field for motion, and he is in danger of growing hard, and inattentive to their convenience who labor for his support; and so loses that disposition, in which alone men are fit to govern.

The English government hath been commended by candid foreigners for the disuse of racks and tortures, so much practiced in some states; but this multiplying slaves now leads to it; for where people exact hard labor of others, without a suitable reward, and are resolved to continue in that way, severity to such who oppose them becomes the consequence; and several Negro criminals, among the English in America, have been executed in a lingering, painful way, very terrifying to others.

It is a happy case to set out right, and persevere in the same way: a wrong beginning leads into many difficulties; for to support one evil, another becomes customary; two produces more; and the further men proceed in this way, the greater their dangers, their doubts and fears; and the more painful and perplexing are their circumstances; so that such who are true friends to the real and lasting interest of our country, and candidly consider the tendency of things, cannot but feel some concern on this account.

There is that superiority in men over the brute creatures, and some of them so manifestly dependent on men for a living, that for them to serve us in moderation, so far as relates to the right use of things, looks consonant to the design of our Creator.

There is nothing in their frame, nothing relative to the propagating their species, which argues the contrary; but in men there is. The frame of men's bodies, and the disposition of their minds are different; some, who are tough and strong, and their minds active, choose ways of life requiring much labor to support them; others are soon weary; and though use makes labor more tolerable, yet some are less apt for toil than others, and their minds less sprightly. These latter laboring for their subsistence, commonly choose a life easy to support, being content with a little. When they are weary they may rest, take the most advantageous part of the day for labor; and in all cases proportion one thing to another, that their bodies be not oppressed.

Now, while each is at liberty, the latter may be as happy, and live as comfortably as the former; but where men of the first sort have the latter under absolute command, not considering the odds in strength and firmness, do, sometimes, in their eager pursuit, lay on burthens grievous to be borne; by degrees grow rigorous, and, aspiring to greatness, they increase oppression, and the true order of kind Providence is subverted.

There are weaknesses sometimes attending us, which make little or no alteration in our countenances, nor much lessen our appetite for food, and yet so affect us, as to make labor very uneasy. In such case masters, intent on putting forward business, and jealous of the sincerity of their slaves, may disbelieve what they say, and grievously afflict them.

Action is necessary for all men, and our exhausting frame requires a support, which is the fruit of action. The earth must be labored to keep us alive: labor is a proper part of our life; to make one answer the other in some useful motion, looks agreeable to the design of our Creator. Motion, rightly managed, tends to our satisfaction, health and support.

Those who quit all useful business, and live wholly on the labor of others, have their exercise to seek; some such use less than their health requires; others choose that which, by the circumstances attending it, proves utterly reverse to true happiness. Thus, while some are divers ways distressed for want of an open channel of useful action, those who support them sigh, and are exhausted in a stream too powerful for nature, spending their days with too little cessation from labor.

Seed sown with the tears of a confined oppressed people, harvest cut down by an overborne discontented reaper, makes bread less sweet to the taste of an honest man, than that which is the produce, or just reward of such voluntary action, which is one proper part of the business of human creatures.

Again, the weak state of the human species, in bearing and bringing forth their young, and the helpless condition of their young beyond that of other creatures, clearly shew that Perfect Goodness designs a tender care and regard should be exercised toward them; and that no imperfect, arbitrary power should prevent the cordial effects of that sympathy, which is, in the minds of well-met pairs, to each other, and toward their offspring.

In our species the mutual ties of affection are more rational and durable than in others below us; the care and labor of raising our offspring much greater. The satisfaction arising to us in their innocent company, and in their advances from one rational improvement to another, is considerable, when two are thus joined, and their affections sincere. It however happens among slaves, that they are often situate in different places; and their seeing each other depends on the will of men, liable to human passions, and a bias in judgment; who, with views of self-interest, may keep them apart more than is right. Being absent from each other, and often with other company, there is a danger of their affections being alienated, jealousies arising, the happiness otherwise resulting from their offspring frustrated, and the comforts of marriage destroyed.—These things being considered closely, as happening to a near friend, will appear to be hard and painful.

He who reverently observes that goodness manifested by our gracious Creator toward the various species of beings in this world, will see, that in our frame and constitution is clearly shown that innocent men, capable to manage for themselves, were not intended to be slaves. . . .

Through the force of long custom, it appears needful to speak in relation to color.—Suppose a white child, born of parents of the meanest sort, who died and left him an infant, falls into the hands of a person, who endeavors to keep him a slave, some men would account him an unjust man in doing so, who yet appear easy while many black people, of honest lives, and good abilities, are enslaved, in a manner more shocking than the case here supposed. This is owing chiefly to the idea of slavery being connected with the black color, and liberty with the white:—and where false ideas are twisted into our minds, it is with difficulty we get fairly disentangled.

A traveler, in cloudy weather, misseth his way, makes many turns while he is lost; still forms in his mind, the bearing and situation of places, and though the ideas are wrong, they fix as fast as if they were right. Finding how things are, we see our mistake; yet the force of reason, with repeated observations on places and things, do not soon remove those false notions, so fastened upon us, but it will seem in the imagination as if the annual course of the sun was altered; and though, by recollection, we are assured it is not, yet those ideas do not suddenly leave us.

Selfishness being indulged, clouds the understanding; and where selfish men, for a long time, proceed on their way, without opposition, the deceivableness of unrighteousness gets so rooted in their intellects, that a candid examination of things relating to self-interest is prevented; and in this circumstance, some who would not agree to make a slave of a person whose color is like their own, appear easy in making slaves of others of a different color, though their understandings and morals are equal to the generality of men of their own color.

The color of a man avails nothing, in matters of right and equity. Consider color in relation to treaties; by such, disputes betwixt nations are sometimes settled. And should the father of us all so dispose things, that treaties with black men should sometimes be necessary, how then would it appear amongst the princes and ambassadors, to insist on the prerogative of the white color?

Whence is it that men, who believe in a righteous omnipotent Being, to whom all nations stand equally related, and are equally accountable, remain so easy in it; but for that the ideas of Negroes and slaves are so interwoven in the mind, that they do not discuss this matter with that candor and freedom of thought, which the case justly calls for?

To come at a right feeling of their condition, requires humble serious thinking; for, in their present situation, they have but little to engage our natural affection in their favor.

Had we a son or a daughter involved in the same case, in which many of them are, it would alarm us, and make us feel their condition without seeking for it. The adversity of an intimate friend will incite our compassion, while others, equally good, in the like trouble, will but little affect us.

Again, the man in worldly honor, whom we consider as our superior, treating us with kindness and generosity, begets a return of gratitude and friendship toward him. We may receive as great benefits from men a degree lower than ourselves, in the common way of reckoning, and feel ourselves less engaged in favor of them. Such is our condition by nature; and these things being narrowly watched and examined, will be found to center in self-love.

The blacks seem far from being our kinsfolks, and did we find an agreeable disposition and sound understanding in some of them, which appeared as a good foundation for a true friendship between us, the disgrace arising from an open friendship with a person of so vile a stock, in the common esteem, would naturally tend to hinder it.—They have neither honors, riches, outward magnificence nor power; their dress coarse, and often ragged; their employ drudgery, and much in the dirt: they have little or nothing at command; but must wait upon and work for others, to obtain the necessaries of life; so that, in their present situation, there is not much to engage the friendship, or move the affection of selfish men: but such who live in the spirit of true charity, to sympathize with the afflicted in the lowest stations of life, is a thing familiar to them.

Such is the kindness of our Creator, that people, applying their minds to sound wisdom, may, in general, with moderate exercise, live comfortably, where no misapplied power hinders it.—We in these parts have cause gratefully to acknowledge it. But men leaving the true use of things, their lives are less calm, and have less of real happiness in them.

Many are desirous of purchasing and keeping slaves, that they may live in some measure conformable to those customs of the times, which have in them a tincture of luxury; for when we, in the least degree, depart from that use of the creatures, for which the Creator of all things intended them, there luxury begins.

And if we consider this way of life seriously, we shall see there is nothing in it sufficient to induce a wise man to choose it, before a plain, simple way of living. If we examine stately buildings and equipage, delicious food, superfine cloths, silks and linens; if we consider the splendor of choice metal fastened upon raiment, and the most showy inventions of men; it will yet appear that the humble-minded man, who is contented with the true use of houses, food and garments, and cheerfully exerciseth himself agreeable to his station in civil society, to earn them, acts more reasonably, and discovers more soundness of understanding in his conduct, than such who lay heavy burdens on others, to support themselves in a luxurious way of living. . . .

In true gospel simplicity, free from all wrong use of things, a spirit which breathes peace and good will is cherished; but when we aspire after imaginary grandeur, and apply to selfish means to attain our end, this desire, in its original, is the same with the Picts in cutting figures on their bodies; but the evil consequences attending our proceedings are the greatest.

A covetous mind, which seeks opportunity to exalt itself, is a great enemy to true harmony in a country: envy and grudging usually accompany this disposition, and it tends to stir up its likeness in others. And where this disposition ariseth so high, as to embolden us to look upon honest industrious men as our own property during life, and to keep them to hard labor, to support us in those customs which have not their foundation in right reason; or to use any means of oppression; a haughty spirit is cherished on one side, and the desire of revenge frequently on the other, till the inhabitants of the land are ripe for great commotion and trouble; and thus luxury and oppression have the seeds of war and desolation in them.

THE DIFFERENCE BETWEEN THE RACES

IMMANUEL KANT

Even Kant, the Enlightenment's great moral philosopher, was not immune to racial stereotyping that decreed Negroes to be "stupid" and "the lowest rabble." This selection, in which he cites approvingly Hume's verdict on the races, is from his 1764 essay Observations on the Feeling of the Beautiful and Sublime.

If we cast a fleeting glance over the other parts of the world, we find the Arab the noblest man in the Orient, yet of a feeling that degenerates very much into the adventurous. He is hospitable, generous, and truthful; yet his narrative and history and on the whole his feeling are always interwoven with some wonderful thing. His inflamed imagination presents things to him in unnatural and distorted images, and even the propagation of his religion was a great adventure. If the Arabs are, so to speak, the Spaniards of the Orient, similarly the Persians are the French of Asia. They are good poets, courteous and of fairly fine taste. They are not such strict followers of Islam, and they permit to their pleasure-prone disposition a tolerably mild interpretation of the Koran. The Japanese could in a way be regarded as the Englishmen of this part of the world, but hardly in any other quality than their resoluteness—which degenerates into the utmost stubbornness—their valor, and disdain of death. For the rest, they display few signs of a finer feeling. The Indians have a dominating taste of the grotesque, of the sort that falls into the adventurous. Their religion consists of grotesqueries. Idols of monstrous form, the priceless tooth of the mighty monkey Hanuman, the unnatural atonements of the fakirs (heathen mendicant friars) and so forth are in this taste. The despotic sacrifice of wives in the very same funeral pyre that consumes the corpse of the husband is a hideous excess. What trifling grotesqueries do the verbose and studied compliments of the Chinese contain! Even their paintings are grotesque and portray strange and unnatural figures such as are encountered nowhere in the world. They also have venerable grotesqueries because they are of very ancient custom, and no nation in the world has more of these than this one.

The Negroes of Africa have by nature no feeling that rises above the trifling. Mr. Hume challenges anyone to cite a single example in which a Negro has shown talents, and asserts that among the hundreds of thousands of blacks who are transported elsewhere from their countries, although many of them have even been set free, still not a single one was ever found who presented anything great in art or science or any other praiseworthy quality, even though among the whites some continually rise aloft from the lowest rabble, and through superior gifts earn respect in the world. So fundamental is the difference between these two races of man, and it appears to be as great in regard to mental capacities as in color. The religion of fetishes so widespread among them is perhaps a sort of idolatry that sinks as deeply into the trifling as appears to be possible to human nature. A bird feather, a cow's horn, a conch shell, or any other common object, as soon as it becomes consecrated by a few words, is an object of veneration and of invocation in swearing oaths. The blacks are very vain but in the Negro's way, and so talkative that they must be driven apart from each other with thrashings.

Among all savages there is no nation that displays so sublime a mental character as those of North America. They have a strong feeling for honor, and as in quest of it they seek wild adventures hundreds of miles abroad, they are still extremely careful to avert the least injury to it when their equally harsh enemy, upon capturing them, seeks by cruel pain to extort cowardly groans from them. The Canadian savage, moreover, is truthful and honest. The friendship he establishes is just as adventurous and enthusiastic as anything of that kind reported from the most ancient and fabled times. He is extremely proud, feels the whole worth of freedom, and even in his education suffers no encounter that would let him feel a low subservience. Lycurgus probably gave statutes to just such savages; and if a lawgiver arose among the Six Nations, one would see a Spartan republic rise in the New World; for the undertaking of the Argonauts is little different from the war parties of these Indians, and Jason excels Attakakullakulla in nothing but the honor of a Greek name. All these savages have little feeling for the beautiful in moral understanding, and the generous forgiveness of an injury, which is at once noble and beautiful, is completely unknown as a virtue among the savages, but rather is disdained as a miserable cowardice. Valor is the greatest merit of the savage and revenge his sweetest bliss. The remaining natives of this part of the world show few traces of a mental character disposed to the finer feelings, and an extraordinary apathy constitutes the mark of this type of race.

If we examine the relation of the sexes in these parts of the world, we find that the European alone has found the secret of decorating with so many flowers the sensual charm of a mighty inclination and of interlacing it with so much morality that he has not only extremely elevated its agreeableness but has also made it very decorous. The inhabitant of the Orient is of a very false taste in this respect. Since he has no concept of the morally beautiful which can be united with this impulse, he loses even the worth of the sensuous enjoyment, and his harem is a constant source of unrest. He thrives on all sorts of amorous grotesqueries, among which the imaginary jewel is only the foremost, which he seeks to safeguard above all else, whose whole worth consists only in smashing it, and of which one in our part of the world generally entertains much malicious doubt—and yet to whose preservation he makes use of very unjust and often loathsome means. Hence there a woman is always in a prison, whether she may be a maid, or have a barbaric, good-for-nothing and always suspicious husband. In the lands of the black, what better can one expect than what is found prevailing, namely the feminine sex in the deepest slavery? A despairing man is always a strict master over anyone weaker, just as with us that man is always a tyrant in the kitchen who outside his own house hardly dares to look anyone in the face. Of course, Father Labat reports that a Negro carpenter, whom he reproached for haughty treatment toward his wives, answered: "You whites are indeed fools, for first you make great concessions to your wives, and afterward you complain when they drive you mad." And it might be that there were something in this which perhaps deserved to be considered; but in short, this fellow was quite black from head to foot, a clear proof that what he said was stupid.

"WHO ARE YOU, THEN, TO MAKE SLAVES . . ."

DENIS DIDEROT

In this selection from his Supplement to Bougainville's Voyage *(1772), Diderot bitterly indicts slavery, colonialism, and general European convictions about cultural supremacy.*

He was the father of a large family. At the arrival of the Europeans, he looked disdainfully at them, showing neither astonishment, fear nor curiosity. They accosted him. He turned his back on them, and withdrew into his hut. His silence and his anxiety revealed his thoughts only too well: he lamented within himself for the great days of his country, now eclipsed. At the departure of Bougainville, when the inhabitants ran in a crowd to the shore, clinging to his garments, embracing his companions and weeping, the old man came forward with a stern air and said:

"Weep, poor folk of Tahiti, weep! Would that this were the arrival and not the departure of these ambitious and wicked men. One day you will know them better. One day they will return, in one hand the piece of wood you now see attached to the belt of this one, and the other grasping the blade you now see hanging from the belt of another. And with these they will enslave you, murder you or subject you to their extravagances and vices. One day you will serve under them, as corrupted, as vile, as loathsome as themselves.

"But I console myself; I am reaching the end of my journey; I shall not live to see the calamity I foretell. Oh people of Tahiti! Oh my friends! You have a means to escape this tragic future; but I would rather die than counsel it. Let them go their ways, let them live."

Then, addressing himself to Bougainville, he continued:

"And you, chief of these brigands who obey you, quickly take your vessel from our shores. We are innocent, we are happy; and you can only spoil our happiness. We follow the pure instincts of nature; and you have tried to wipe its impress from our souls. Here everything belongs to everybody. You have preached to us I know not what distinctions between 'mine' and 'thine.' Our daughters and our wives are common to us all. You have shared this privilege with us; and you have lighted passions in them before unknown. They have become maddened in your arms; you have become ferocious in theirs. They have begun to hate each other; you have slain each other for them, and they have returned to us stained with your blood.

"We are a free people; and now you have planted in our country the title deeds of our future slavery. You are neither god nor demon; who are you, then, to make slaves? Orou! You understand the language of these men, tell us all, as you have told me, what they have written on this sheet of metal: 'This country is ours.' This country yours? And why? Because you have walked thereon? If a Tahitian landed one day on your shores, and scratched on one of your rocks or on the bark of your trees: 'This country belongs to the people of Tahiti'—what would you think?

"You are the strongest! And what of that? When someone took one of the contemptible trifles with which your vessel is filled, you cried out and you were revenged. Yet at the same time in the depths of your heart you plotted the theft of a whole country! You are not a slave; you would suffer death rather than be one; yet you want to enslave us. Do you think the Tahitian does not know how to defend his liberty and to die? The Tahitian you want to seize like a wild animal is your brother. You are both children of nature; what right have you over him that he has not over you? When you came, did we rush upon you, did we pillage your ship? Did we seize you and expose you to the arrows of our enemies? Did we yoke you with the animals for toil in our fields? No. We respected our own likeness in you. Leave us to our ways; they are wiser and more honest than yours. We do not want to barter what you call our ignorance for your useless civilization. Everything that is necessary and good for us we possess. Do we deserve contempt, because we have not known how to develop superfluous wants? When we hunger, we have enough to eat; when we are cold we have wherewith to clothe us. You have been in our huts; what is lacking there, in your opinion? You may pursue as far as you like what you call the comforts of life; but allow sensible people to stop, when they would only have obtained imaginary good from the continuation of their painful efforts. If you persuade us to exceed the narrow limits of our wants, when shall we ever finish toiling? When shall we enjoy ourselves? We have reduced the sum of our annual and daily labors to the least possible, because nothing seems to us preferable to repose. Go to your own country to agitate and torment yourself as much as you like; leave us in peace. Do not worry us with your artificial needs nor with your imaginary virtues. Look on these men; see how upright, healthy and robust they are. Look on these women; see how upright, healthy, fresh and beautiful they are. Take this bow; it is my own. Call one, two, three or four of your friends to help you and try to bend it. I can bend it myself, alone. I till the soil. I climb mountains. I pierce the forest. I can run a league on the plains in less than an hour. Your young companions would be hard put to follow me, yet I am more than ninety years old.

"Woe unto this island! Woe to these people of Tahiti and to all who will come after them, woe from the day you first visited us! We should know only one disease; that to which all men, animals and plants are subject—old age; but you have brought us another; you have infected our blood.

"It will perhaps be necessary to exterminate our daughters, wives, children, with our own hands; all those who have approached your women; those who have approached your men.

"Our fields shall be soaked with the foul blood which has passed from your veins into ours; or else our children, condemned to nourish and perpetuate the evil which you have given to the fathers and mothers, will transmit it for ever to their descendants. Villains! You will be the guilty ones; guilty either of the ravages of disease that will follow the fatal embraces of your people, or of the murders which we shall commit to stop the spread of the poison.

"You speak of crimes! Do you know any more enormous than your own? What is your punishment for him who kills his neighbor?—death by the sword; what is your punishment for the coward who poisons?—death by fire. Compare your crime to his; tell us then, poisoner of whole peoples, what should be the torment you deserve? But a short while ago, the young Tahitian girl yielded herself to the transports and embraces of the Tahitian youth; waited impatiently until her mother, authorized by her having reached the age of marriage, should remove her veil and make naked her breast. She was proud to excite the desire and to attract the amorous glances of unknown men, of relatives, of her brother. Without dread and without shame, in our presence, in the midst of a circle of innocent Tahitians, to the sound of flutes, between the dances, she accepted the caresses of the one to whom her young heart and the secret voice of her senses urged her. The idea of crime and the peril of disease came with you. Our enjoyments, once so sweet, are now accompanied by remorse and terror. That man in black who stands near you listening to me, has spoken to our lads. I do not know what he has said to our girls. But our lads are hesitant; our girls blush. Plunge if you will into the dark depths of the forest with the perverse companion of your pleasure; but let the good and simple Tahitians reproduce themselves without shame, under the open sky, in the full light of day. What finer and more noble feeling could you put in place of that with which we have inspired them, and which animates them now? They think that the moment to enrich the nation and the family with a new citizen is come, and they glory in it. They eat to live and to grow; they grow in order to multiply and they find in it nothing vicious nor shameful.

"Listen to the continuation of your crimes. You had hardly come among our people than they became thieves. You had scarcely landed on our soil, than it reeked with blood. That Tahitian who ran to meet you, to receive you crying 'Taio! friend, friend,' you slew. And why did you slay him? . . . because he had been taken by the glitter of your little serpents' eggs. He gave you of his fruits; he offered you his wife and daughter, he ceded you his hut; yet you killed him for a handful of beads which he had taken without having asked. And the people? At the noise of your murderous shot, terror seized them, and they fled to the mountains. But be assured that they would not have waited long to descend again. Then you would all have perished, but for me. Ah! why did I pacify them, why did I hold them back, why do I still restrain them, even now? I do not know; for you deserve no pity; for you have a ferocious soul which will never feel it. You have wandered, you and yours, everywhere in our island. You have been respected; you have enjoyed all things; you have found neither barrier nor refusal in your ways; you have been invited within, you have sat, and all the abundance of our country has been spread before you. When you desired young girls, only excepting those who had not yet the privilege of unveiling their faces and breasts, their mothers have presented to you all the others, quite naked. You have possessed the tender victim of the duties of hospitality; flowers and leaves were heaped up for you and her; musicians sounded their instruments; nothing has spoiled the sweetness, nor hindered the freedom of your caresses nor of hers. They have sung the anthem exhorting you to be a man, and our child to be a woman, yielding and voluptuous. They danced around your couch. And it was when you came from the arms of this woman, after experiencing on her breast the sweetest of all intoxications, that you slew her brother, friend or father.

"You have done still worse. Look over there, see that enclosure bristling with weapons. These arms which have menaced only your enemies are now turned against our own children. See these unhappy companions of our pleasures. See their sadness, the grief of their fathers and the despair of their mothers. They are those condemned to die, either by our hands or by the diseases you have given them.

"Away now, unless your cruel eyes revel in the spectacle of death. Go now, go; and may the guilty seas which spared you on your voyage hither, absolve themselves and avenge us, by engulfing you before you return.

"And you, oh people of Tahiti! Go into your huts, go, all of you; and let these strangers as they leave hear only the roar of the tide and see only the foam of its fury whitening a deserted shore."

He had scarcely finished before the crowd of people had disappeared. A vast silence reigned over the whole island, and only the keen whistling of the wind and the dull sound of the breakers along the shore could be heard. One might have said that the air and the sea, conscious of the voice of the aged man, were moved to obey him.

''BESTIAL MANNERS, STUPIDITY, AND VICES . . .''

JAMES LONG

One of the most influential descriptions of Negroes in eighteenth-century England is found in Edward Long's (1734–1813) 1774 book, The History of Jamaica. *Writing of American Negroes in general, he repeats Hume's claims about the lack of ''mechanic arts, or manufacture.''*

We find them marked with the same bestial manners, stupidity, and vices, which debase their brethren on the continent, who seem to be distinguished from the rest of mankind, not in person only, but in possessing, in abstract, every species of inherent turpitude, that is to be found dispersed at large among the rest of of the human creation, with scarce a single virtue to extenuate this shade of character, differing in this particular from all other men; for, in other countries, the most abandoned villain we ever heard of has rarely, if ever, been known unportioned with some good quality at least in his composition. It is astonishing, that although they have been acquainted with Europeans, and their manufactures, for so many hundred years, they have, in all this series of time, manifested so little taste for arts, or a genius either inventive or imitative. Among so great a number of provinces on this extensive continent, and among so many millions of people, we have heard but of one or two insignificant tribes, who comprehend any thing of mechanic arts, or manufacture; and even these, for the most part, are said to perform their work in a very bungling and slovenly manner, perhaps not better than an *oranoutang* might, with little pains, be brought to do.

AFRICAN SLAVERY IN AMERICA

THOMAS PAINE

This passionate attack on slavery appeared in the Philadelphia Magazine *in 1775, shortly after Paine arrived from London. In contrast to the uncertainty surrounding the essay on women, this piece is assumed to be Paine's.*

TO AMERICANS.

That some desperate wretches should be willing to steal and enslave men by violence and murder for gain, is rather lamentable than strange. But that many civilized, nay, christianized people should approve, and be concerned in the savage practice, is surprising; and still persist, though it has been so often proved contrary to the light of nature, to every principle of Justice and Humanity, and even good policy, by a succession of eminent men, and several late publications.

Our Traders in MEN (*an unnatural commodity!*) must know the wickedness of that SLAVE-TRADE, if they attend to reasoning, or the dictates of their own hearts; and such as shun and stiffle all these, willfully sacrifice Conscience, and the character of integrity to that golden Idol.

The Managers of that Trade themselves, and others, testify, that many of these African nations inhabit fertile countries, are industrious farmers, enjoy plenty, and lived quietly, averse to war, before the Europeans debauched them with liquors, and bribing them against one another; and that these inoffensive people are brought into slavery, by stealing them, tempting Kings to sell subjects, which they can have no right to do, and hiring one tribe to war against another, in order to catch prisoners. By such wicked and inhuman ways the English are said to enslave towards one hundred thousand yearly; of which thirty thousand are supposed to die by barbarous treatment in the first year; besides all that are slain in the unnatural wars excited to take them. So much innocent blood have the Managers and Supporters of this inhuman Trade to answer for to the common Lord of all!

Many of these were not prisoners of war, and redeemed from savage conquerors, as some plead; and they who were such prisoners, the English, who promote the war for that very end, are the guilty authors of their being so; and if they were redeemed, as is alleged, they would owe nothing to the redeemer but what he paid for them.

They show as little Reason as Conscience who put the matter by with saying—"Men, in some cases, are lawfully made Slaves, and why may not these?" So men, in some cases, are lawfully put to death, deprived of their goods, without their consent; may any man, therefore, be treated so, without any conviction of desert? Nor is this plea mended by adding—"They are set forth to us as slaves, and we buy them without farther inquiry, let the sellers see to it." Such men may as well join with a known band of robbers, buy their ill-got goods, and help on the trade; ignorance is no more pleadable in one case than the other; the sellers plainly own how they obtain them. But none can lawfully buy without evidence that they are not concurring with Men-Stealers; and as the true owner has a right to reclaim his goods that were stolen, and sold; so the slave, who is proper owner of his freedom, has a right to reclaim it, however often sold.

Most shocking of all is alledging the Sacred Scriptures to favor this wicked practice. One would have thought none but infidel cavilers would endeavor to make them appear contrary to the plain dictates of natural light, and Conscience, in a matter of common Justice and Humanity; which they cannot be. Such worthy men, as referred to before, judged otherways; MR. BAXTER declared, *the Slave-Traders should be called Devils, rather than Christians; and that it is a heinous crime to buy them.* But some say, "the practice was permitted to the Jews." To which may be replied,

1. The example of the Jews, in many things, may not be imitated by us; they had not only orders to cut off several nations altogether, but if they were obliged to war with others, and conquered them, to cut off every male; they were suffered to use polygamy and divorces, and other things utterly unlawful to us under clearer light.

2. The plea is, in a great measure, false; they had no permission to catch and enslave people who never injured them.

3. Such arguments ill become us, *since the time of reformation came,* under Gospel light. All distinctions of nations and privileges of one above others, are ceased; Christians are taught to *account all men their neighbors; and love their neighbors as themselves; and do to all men as they would be done by; to do good to all men; and Man-stealing is ranked with enormous crimes.* Is the barbarous enslaving our inoffensive neighbors, and treating them like wild beasts subdued by force, reconcilable with all these *Divine precepts?* Is this doing to them as we would desire they should do to us? If they could carry off and enslave some thousands of us, would we think it just?—One would almost wish they could for once; it might convince more than Reason, or the Bible.

As much in vain, perhaps, will they search ancient history for examples of the modern Slave-Trade. Too many nations enslaved the prisoners they took in war. But to go to nations with whom there is no war, who have no way provoked, without farther design of conquest, purely to catch inoffensive people, like wild beasts, for slaves, is an height of outrage against Humanity and Justice, that seems left by Heathen nations to be practiced by pretended Christians. How shameful are all attempts to color and excuse it!

As these people are not convicted of forfeiting freedom, they have still a natural, perfect right to it; and the Governments whenever they come should, in justice set them free, and punish those who hold them in slavery.

So monstrous is the making and keeping them slaves at all, abstracted from the barbarous usage they suffer, and the many evils attending the practice; as selling husbands away from wives, children from parents, and from each other, in violation of sacred and natural ties; and opening the way for adulteries, incests, and many shocking consequences, for all of which the guilty Masters must answer to the final Judge.

If the slavery of the parents be unjust, much more is their children's; if the parents were justly slaves, yet the children are born free; this is the natural, perfect right of all mankind; they are nothing but a just recompense to those who bring them up: And as much less is commonly spent on them than others, they have a right, in justice, to be proportionably sooner free.

Certainly one may, with as much reason and decency, plead for murder, robbery, lewdness, and barbarity, as for this practice: They are not more contrary to the natural dictates of Conscience, and feelings of Humanity; nay, they are all comprehended in it.

But the chief design of this paper is not to disprove it, which many have sufficiently done; but to entreat Americans to consider.

1. With what consistency, or decency they complain so loudly of attempts to enslave them, while they hold so many hundred thousands in slavery; and annually enslave many thousands more, without any pretense of authority, or claim upon them?

2. How just, how suitable to our crime is the punishment with which Providence threatens us? We have enslaved multitudes, and shed much innocent blood in doing it: and now are threatened with the same. And while other evils are confessed, and bewailed, why not this especially, and publicly; than which no other vice, if all others, has brought so much guilt on the land?

3. Whether, then, all ought not immediately to discontinue and renounce it, with grief and abhorrence? Should not every society bear testimony against it, and account obstinate persisters in it bad men, enemies to their country, and exclude them from fellowship; as they often do for much lesser faults?

4. The great Question may be—What should be done with those who are enslaved already? To turn the old and infirm free, would be injustice and cruelty; they who enjoyed the labors of their better days should keep, and treat them humanely. As to the rest, let prudent men, with the assistance of legislatures, determine what is practicable for masters, and best for them. Perhaps some could give them lands upon reasonable rent, some, employing them in their labor still, might give them some reasonable allowances for it; so as all may have some property, and fruits of their labors at their own disposal, and be encouraged to industry;

the family may live together, and enjoy the natural satisfaction of exercising relative affections and duties, with civil protection, and other advantages, like fellow men. Perhaps they might sometime form useful barrier settlements on the frontiers. Thus they may become interested in the public welfare, and assist in promoting it; instead of being dangerous, as now they are, should any enemy promise them a better condition.

5. The past treatment of Africans must naturally fill them with abhorrence of Christians; lead them to think our religion would make them more inhuman savages, if they embraced it; thus the gain of that trade has been pursued in opposition to the Redeemer's cause, and the happiness of men: Are we not, therefore, bound in duty to him and to them to repair these injuries, as far as possible, by taking some proper measures to instruct, not only the slaves here, but the Africans in their own countries? Primitive Christians labored always to spread their *Divine Religion;* and this is equally our duty while there is an Heathen nation: But what singular obligations are we under to these injured people!

These are the sentiments of

JUSTICE AND HUMANITY.

OF EMPIRES AND SAVAGES

EDWARD GIBBON

In this selection from his Decline and Fall of the Roman Empire *(1776–1788), Gibbon draws the lesson of his vast study for late eighteenth-century Europe. Western history is a tale of recurring moral strife between the forces of civilization and barbarism. Rome fell to Christian fanaticism and voracious, turbulent tribalism. "Savage nations" of the world were in his day the enemies of enlightened "civilized society."*

The Greeks, after their country had been reduced into a province, imputed the triumphs of Rome not to the merit but to the *Fortune* of the republic. The inconstant goddess, who so blindly distributes and resumes her favors, had *now* consented (such was the language of envious flattery) to resign her wings, to descend from her globe, and to fix her firm and immutable throne on the banks of the Tiber. A wiser Greek [Polybius], who has composed with a philosophic spirit the memorable history of his own times, deprived his countrymen of this vain and delusive comfort by opening to their view the deep foundations of the greatness of Rome. The fidelity of the citizens to each other and to the state was confirmed by the habits of education and the prejudices of religion. Honor, as well as virtue, was the principle of the republic; the ambitious citizens labored to deserve the solemn glories of a triumph; and the ardor of the Roman youth was kindled into active emulation as often as they beheld the domestic images of their ancestors. The temperate struggles of the patricians and plebeians had finally established the firm and equal balance of the constitution, which united the freedom of popular assemblies with the authority and wisdom of a senate and the executive powers of a regal magistrate. When the consul displayed the standard of the republic, each citizen bound himself, by the obligation of an oath, to draw his sword in the cause of his country till he had discharged the sacred duty by a military service of ten years. This wise institution continually poured into the field the rising generations of freemen and soldiers; and their numbers were reinforced by the warlike and populous states of Italy, who after a brave resistance had yielded to the valor and embraced the alliance of the Romans.

The sage historian, who excited the virtue of the younger Scipio and beheld the ruin of Carthage, has accurately described their military system, their levies, arms, exercises, subordination, marches, encampments, and the invincible legion, superior in active strength to the Macedonian phalanx of Philip and Alexander. From these institutions of peace and war Polybius has deduced the spirit and success of a people incapable of fear and impatient of repose. The ambitious design of conquest, which might have been defeated by the seasonable conspiracy of mankind, was attempted and achieved; and the perpetual violation of justice was maintained by the political virtues of prudence and courage. The arms of the republic, sometimes vanquished in battle, always victorious in war, advanced with rapid steps to the Euphrates, the Danube, the Rhine, and the ocean; and the images of gold, or silver, or brass that might serve to represent the nations and their kings were successively broken by the *iron* monarchy of Rome.

The rise of a city which swelled into an empire may deserve, as a singular prodigy, the reflection of a philosophic mind. But the decline of Rome was the natural and inevitable effect of immoderate greatness. Prosperity ripened the principle of decay; the causes of destruction multiplied with the extent of conquest; and as soon as time or accident had removed the artificial supports, the stupendous fabric yielded to the pressure of its own weight. The story of its ruin is simple and obvious; and instead of inquiring *why* the Roman empire was destroyed, we should rather be surprised that it had subsisted so long. The victorious legions, who in distant wars acquired the vices of strangers and mercenaries, first oppressed the freedom of the republic and afterwards violated the majesty of the purple. The emperors, anxious for their personal safety and the public peace, were reduced to the base expedient of corrupting the discipline which rendered them alike formidable to their sovereign and to the enemy; the vigor of the military government was relaxed and finally dissolved by the partial institutions of Constantine; and the Roman world was overwhelmed by a deluge of barbarians.

The decay of Rome has been frequently ascribed to the translation of the seat of empire; but this history has already shown that the powers of government were *divided* rather than *removed*. The throne of Constantinople was erected in the East; while the West was still possessed by a series of emperors who held their residence in Italy and claimed their equal inheritance of the legions and provinces. This dangerous novelty impaired the strength and fomented the vices of a double reign; the instruments of an oppressive and arbitrary system were multiplied; and a vain emulation of luxury, not of merit, was introduced and supported between the degenerate successors of Theodosius. Extreme distress, which unites the virtue of a free people, embitters the factions of a declining monarchy. The hostile favorites of Arcadius and Honorius betrayed the republic to its common enemies; and the Byzantine court beheld with indifference, perhaps with pleasure, the disgrace of Rome, the misfortunes of Italy, and the loss of the West. Under the succeeding reigns the alliance of the two empires was restored; but the aid of the Oriental Romans was tardy, doubtful, and ineffectual; and the national schism of the Greeks and Latins was enlarged by the perpetual difference of language and manners, of interests, and even of religion. Yet the salutary event approved in some measure the judgment of Constantine. During a long period of decay his impregnable city repelled the victorious armies of barbarians, protected the wealth of Asia, and commanded, both in peace and war, the important straits which connect the Euxine and Mediterranean Seas. The foundation of Constantinople more essentially contributed to the preservation of the East than to the ruin of the West.

As the happiness of a *future* life is the great object of religion, we may hear without surprise or scandal that the introduction, or at least the abuse, of Christianity had some influence on the decline and fall of the Roman empire. The clergy successfully preached the doctrines of patience and pusillanimity; the active virtues of society were discouraged; and the last remains of military spirit were buried in the cloister. A large portion of public and private wealth was consecrated to the specious demands of charity and devotion, and the soldiers' pay was lavished on the useless multitudes of both sexes who could only plead the merits of abstinence and chastity. Faith, zeal, curiosity, and more earthly passions of malice and ambition kindled the flame of theological discord; the church and even the state were distracted by religious factions, whose conflicts were sometimes bloody and always implacable; the attention of the emperors was diverted from camps to synods; the Roman world was oppressed by a new species of tyranny, and the persecuted sects became the secret enemies of their country.

Yet party spirit, however pernicious or absurd, is a principle of union as well as of dissension. The bishops, from eighteen hundred pulpits, inculcated the duty of passive obedience to a lawful and orthodox sovereign; their frequent assemblies and perpetual correspondence maintained the communion of distant churches; and the benevolent temper of the Gospel was strengthened, though confined, by the spiritual alliance of the catholics. The sacred indolence of the monks was devoutly embraced by a servile and effeminate age; but if superstition had not afforded a decent retreat, the same vices would have tempted the unworthy Romans to desert, from baser motives, the standard of the republic. Religious precepts are easily obeyed which indulge and sanctify the natural inclinations of their votaries; but the pure and genuine influence of Christianity may be traced in its beneficial though imperfect effects on the barbarian proselytes of the North. If the decline of the Roman empire was hastened by the conversion of Constantine, his victorious religion broke the violence of the fall and mollified the ferocious temper of the conquerors.

This awful revolution may be usefully applied to the instruction of the present age. It is the duty of a patriot to prefer and promote the exclusive interest and glory of his native country; but a philosopher may be permitted to enlarge his views and to consider Europe as one great republic whose various inhabitants have attained almost the same level of politeness and cultivation. The balance of power will continue to fluctuate, and the prosperity of our own or the neighboring kingdoms may be alternately exalted or depressed; but these partial events cannot essentially injure our general state of happiness, the system of arts and laws and manners which so advantageously distinguish, above the rest of mankind, the Europeans and their colonies. The savage nations of the globe are the common enemies of civilized society; and we may inquire, with anxious curiosity, whether Europe is still threatened with a repetition of those calamities which formerly oppressed the arms and institutions of Rome. Perhaps the same reflections will illustrate the fall of that mighty empire, and explain the probable causes of our actual security.

The Romans were ignorant of the extent of their dangers and the number of their enemies. Beyond the Rhine and Danube the northern countries of Europe and Asia were filled with innumerable tribes of hunters and shepherds, poor, voracious, and turbulent, bold in arms and impatient to ravish the fruits of industry. The barbarian world was agitated by the rapid impulse of war, and the peace of Gaul or Italy was shaken by the distant revolutions of China. The Huns, who fled before a victorious enemy, directed their march towards the West; and the torrent was swelled by the gradual accession of captives and allies. The flying tribes who yielded to the Huns assumed in *their* turn the spirit of conquest; the endless column of barbarians pressed on the Roman empire with accumulated weight: and if the foremost were destroyed the vacant space was instantly replenished by new assailants. Such formidable emigrations no longer issue from the North; and the long repose, which has been imputed to the decrease of population, is the happy consequence of the progress of arts and agriculture. Instead of some rude villages thinly scattered among its woods and morasses, Germany now produces a list of two thousand three hundred walled towns; the Christian kingdoms of Denmark, Sweden, and Poland have been successively established; and the Hanse merchants, with the Teutonic knights, have extended their colonies along the coast of the Baltic as far as the Gulf of Finland. From the Gulf of Finland to the Eastern Ocean, Russia now assumes the form of a powerful and civilized empire. The plow, the loom, and the forge are introduced on the banks of the Volga, the Ob, and the Lena; and the fiercest of the Tartar hordes have been taught to tremble and obey. The reign of independent barbarism is now contracted to a narrow span; and the remnant of Calmucks or Uzbecks, whose forces may be almost numbered, cannot seriously excite the apprehensions of the great republic of Europe. Yet this apparent security should not tempt us to forget that new enemies and unknown dangers may *possibly* arise from some obscure people, scarcely visible in the map of the world. The Arabs or Saracens, who spread their conquests from India to Spain, had languished in poverty and contempt till Mahomet breathed into those same bodies the soul of enthusiasm.

The empire of Rome was firmly established by the singular and perfect coalition of its members. The subject nations, resigning the hope and even the wish of independence, embraced the character of Roman citizens; and the provinces of the West were reluctantly torn by the barbarians from the bosom of their mother country. But this union was purchased by the loss of national freedom and military spirit; and the servile provinces, destitute of life and motion, expected their safety from the mercenary troops and governors who were directed by the orders of a distant court. The happiness of an hundred millions depended on the personal merit of one or two men, perhaps children, whose minds were corrupted by education, luxury, and despotic power. The deepest wounds were inflicted on the empire during the minorities of the sons and grandsons of Theodosius; and after those incapable princes seemed to attain the age of manhood they abandoned the church to the bishops, the state to the eunuchs, and the provinces to the barbarians. Europe is now divided into twelve powerful though unequal kingdoms, three respectable commonwealths, and a variety of smaller though independent states; the chances of royal and ministerial talent are multiplied, at least, with the number of its rulers; and a Julian or Semiramis may reign in the North, while Arcadius and Honorius again slumber on the thrones of the South. The abuses of tyranny are restrained by the mutual influence of fear and shame; republics have acquired order and stability; monarchies have imbibed the principles of freedom, or at least of moderation; and some sense of honor and justice is introduced into the most defective constitutions by the general manners of the times. In peace, the progress of knowledge and industry is accelerated by the emulation of so many active rivals; in war, the European forces are exercised by temperate and undecisive contests. If a savage conqueror should issue from the deserts of Tartary, he must repeatedly vanquish the robust peasants of Russia, the numerous armies of Germany, the gallant nobles of France, and the intrepid freemen of Britain, who, perhaps, might confererate for their common defense. Should the victorious barbarians carry slavery and desolation as far as the Atlantic Ocean, ten thousand vessels would transport beyond their pursuit the remains of civilized society; and Europe would revive and flourish in the American world, which is already filled with her colonies and institutions.

Cold, poverty, and a life of danger and fatigue fortify the strength and courage of barbarians. In every age they have oppressed the polite and peaceful nations of China, India, and Persia, who neglected, and still neglect, to counterbalance these natural powers by the resources of military art. The warlike states of antiquity, Greece, Macedonia, and Rome, educated a race of soldiers: exercised their bodies, disciplined their courage, multiplied their forces by regular evolutions, and converted the iron which they possessed into strong and serviceable weapons. But this superiority insensibly declined with their laws and manners; and the feeble policy of Constantine and his successors armed and instructed, for the ruin of the empire, the rude valor of the barbarian mercenaries. The military art has been changed by the invention of gunpowder, which enables man to command the two most powerful agents of nature, air and fire. Mathematics, chemistry, mechanics, architecture, have been applied to the service of war, and the adverse parties oppose to each other the most elaborate modes of attack and of defense. Historians may indignantly observe that the preparations of a siege would found and maintain a flourishing colony; yet we cannot be displeased that the subversion of a city should be a work of cost and difficulty, or that an industrious people should be protected by those arts which survive and supply the decay of military virtue. Cannon and fortifications now form an impregnable barrier against the Tartar horse; and Europe is secure from any future irruption of barbarians, since, before they can conquer, they must cease to be barbarous. Their gradual advances in the science of war would always be accompanied, as we may learn from the example of Russia, with a proportionable improvement in the arts of peace and civil policy; and they themselves must deserve a place among the polished nations whom they subdue.

Should these speculations be found doubtful or fallacious, there still remains a more humble source of comfort and hope. The discoveries of ancient and modern navigators, and the domestic history or tradition of the most enlightened nations, represent the *human savage* naked both in mind and body, and destitute of laws, of arts, of ideas, and almost of language. From this abject condition, perhaps the primitive and universal state of man, he has gradually arisen to command the animals, to fertilize the earth, to traverse the ocean, and to measure the heavens. His progress in the improvement and exercise of his mental and corporeal faculties has been irregular and various, infinitely slow in the beginning and increasing by degrees with redoubled velocity; ages of laborious ascent have been followed by a moment of rapid downfall; and the several climates of the globe have felt the vicissitudes of light and darkness. Yet the experience of four thousand years should enlarge our hopes and diminish our apprehensions. We cannot determine to what height the human species may aspire in their advance towards perfection; but it may safely be presumed that no people, unless the face of nature is changed, will relapse into their original barbarism.

The improvements of society may be viewed under a threefold aspect: 1. The poet or philosopher illustrates his age and country by the efforts of a *single* mind; but these superior powers of reason or fancy are rare and spontaneous productions, and the genius of Homer or Cicero or Newton would excite less admiration if they could be created by the will of a prince or the lessons of a preceptor. 2. The benefits of law and policy, of trade and manufactures, of arts and sciences, are more solid and permanent; and *many* individuals may be qualified, by education and discipline, to promote in their respective stations the interest of the community. But this general order is the effect of skill and labor; and the complex machinery may be decayed by time or injured by violence. 3. Fortunately for mankind, the more useful or at least more necessary arts can be performed without superior talents or national subordination, without powers of *one* or the union of *many*. Each village, each family, each individual, must always possess both ability and inclination to perpetuate the use of fire and of metals; the propagation and service of domestic animals; the methods of hunting and fishing; the rudiments of navigation; the imperfect cultivation of corn or other nutritive grain; and the simple practice of the mechanic trades. Private genius and public industry may be extirpated, but these hardy plants survive the tempest and strike an everlasting root into the most unfavorable soil. The splendid days of Augustus and Trajan were eclipsed by a cloud of ignorance, and the barbarians subverted the laws and palaces of Rome. But the scythe, the invention or emblem of Saturn, still continued annually to mow the harvests of Italy; and the human feasts of the Laestrigons have never been renewed on the coast of Campania.

Since the first discovery of the arts, war, commerce, and religious zeal have diffused among the savages of the Old and New World these inestimable gifts. They have been successively propagated; they can never be lost. We may therefore acquiesce in the pleasing conclusion that every age of the world has increased and still increases the real wealth, the happiness, the knowledge, and perhaps the virtue of the human race.

ON INDIANS AND NEGROES

THOMAS JEFFERSON

Not unlike Hume and Kant, Jefferson, the American philosophe, *also speculated on the extent to which "the savage" and the slave could live "civilized" and "enlightened" lives. This selection is from the only book Jefferson ever wrote, his 1787* Notes on the State of Virginia.

Hitherto I have considered this hypothesis as applied to brute animals only, and not in its extension to the man of America, whether aboriginal or transplanted. It is the opinion of Mons. de Buffon that the former furnishes no exception to it: "Although the savage of the new world is about the same height as man in our world, this does not suffice for him to constitute an exception to the general fact that all living nature has become smaller on that continent. The savage is feeble, and has small organs of generation; he has neither hair nor beard, and no ardor whatever for his female; although swifter than the European because he is better accustomed to running, he is, on the other hand, less strong in body; he is also less sensitive, and yet more timid and cowardly; he has no vivacity, no activity of mind; the activity of his body is less an exercise, a voluntary motion, than a necessary action caused by want; relieve him of hunger and thirst, and you deprive him of the active principle of all his movements; he will rest stupidly upon his legs or lying down entire days. There is no need for seeking further the cause of the isolated mode of life of these savages and their repugnance for society: the most precious spark of the fire of nature has been refused to them; they lack ardor for their females, and consequently have no love for their fellow men: not knowing this strongest and most tender of all affections, their other feelings are also cold and languid; they love their parents and children but little; the most intimate of all ties, the family connection, binds them therefore but loosely together; between family and family there is no tie at all; hence they have no communion, no commonwealth, no state of society. Physical love constitutes their only morality; their heart is icy, their society cold, and their rule harsh. They look upon their wives only as servants for all work, or as beasts of burden, which they load without consideration with the burden of their hunting, and which they compel without mercy, without gratitude, to perform tasks which are often beyond their strength. They have only few children, and they take little care of them. Everywhere the original defect appears: they are indifferent because they have little sexual capacity, and this indifference to the other sex is the fundamental defect which weakens their nature, prevents its development, and—destroying the very germs of life—uproots society at the same time. Man is here no exception to the general rule. Nature, by refusing him the power of love, has treated him worse and lowered him deeper than any animal." An afflicting picture indeed, which, for the honor of human nature, I am glad to believe has no original. Of the Indian of South America I know nothing; for I would not honor with the appellation of knowledge, what I derive from the fables published of them. These I believe to be just as true as the fables of Æsop. This belief is founded on what I have seen of man, white, red, and black, and what has been written of him by authors, enlightened themselves, and writing amidst an enlightened people. The Indian of North America being more within our reach, I can speak of him somewhat from my own knowledge, but more from the information of others better acquainted with him, and on whose truth and judgment I can rely. From these sources I am able to say, in contradiction to this representation, that he is neither more defective in ardor, nor more impotent with his female, than the white reduced to the same diet and exercise: that he is brave, when an enterprise depends on bravery; education with him making the point of honor consist in the destruction of an enemy by strategem, and in the preservation of his own person free from injury; or perhaps this is nature; while it is education which teaches us to honor force more than finesse; that he will defend himself against an host of enemies, always choosing to be killed, rather than to surrender, though it be to the whites, who he knows will treat him well: that in other situations also he meets death with more deliberation, and endures tortures with a firmness unknown almost to religious enthusiasm with us: that he is affectionate to his children, careful of them, and indulgent in the extreme: that his affections comprehend his other connections, weakening, as with us, from circle to circle, as they recede from the center: that his friendships are strong and faithful to the uttermost extremity: that his sensibility is keen, even the warriors weeping most bitterly on the loss of their children, though in general they endeavor to appear superior to human events: that his vivacity and activity of mind is equal to ours in the same situation; hence his eagerness for hunting, and for games of chance. The women are submitted to unjust drudgery. This I believe is the case with every barbarous people. With such, force is law. The stronger sex therefore imposes on the weaker. It is civilization alone which replaces women in the enjoyment of their natural equality. That first teaches us to subdue the selfish passions, and to respect those rights in others which we value in ourselves. Were we in equal barbarism, our females would be equal drudges. The man with them is less strong than with us, but their woman stronger than ours; and both for the same obvious reason; because our man and their woman is habituated to labor, and formed by it. With both races the sex which is indulged with ease is least athletic. An Indian man is small in the hand and wrist for the same reason for which a sailor is large and strong in the arms and shoulders, and a porter in the legs and thighs.—They raise fewer children than we do. The causes of this are to be found, not in a difference of nature, but of circumstance. The women very frequently attending the men in their parties of war and of hunting, child-bearing becomes extremely inconvenient to them. It is said, therefore, that they have learnt the practice of procuring abortion by the use of some vegetable; and that it even extends to prevent conception for a considerable time after. During these parties they are exposed to numerous hazards, to excessive exertions, to the greatest extremities of hunger. Even at their homes the nation depends for food, through a certain part of every year, on the gleanings of the forest: that is, they experience a famine once in every year. With all animals, if the female be badly fed, or not fed at all, her young perish: and if both male and female be reduced to like want, generation becomes less active, less productive. To the obstacles then of want and hazard, which nature has opposed to the multiplication of wild animals, for the purpose of restraining their numbers within certain bounds, those of labor and of voluntary abortion are added with the Indian. No wonder then if they multiply less than we do. Where food is regularly supplied, a single farm will shew more of cattle, than a whole country of forests can of buffaloes. The same Indian women, when married to white traders, who feed them and their children plentifully and regularly, who exempt them from excessive drudgery, who keep them stationary and unexposed to accident, produce and raise as many children as the white women. Instances are known, under these circumstances, of their rearing a dozen children. An inhuman practice once prevailed in this country of making slaves of the Indians. It is a fact well known with us, that the Indian women so enslaved produced and raised as numerous families as either the whites or blacks among whom they lived.—It has been said, that Indians have less hair than the whites, except on the head. But this is a fact of which fair proof can scarcely be had. With them it is disgraceful to be hairy on the body. They say it likens them to hogs. They therefore pluck the hair as fast as it appears. But the traders who marry their women, and prevail on them to discontinue this practice, say, that nature is the same with them as with the whites. Nor, if the fact be true, is the consequence necessary which has been drawn from it. Negroes have notoriously less hair than the whites; yet they are more ardent. But if cold and moisture be the agents of nature for diminishing the races of animals, how comes she all at once to suspend their operation as to the physical man of the new world, whom the Count acknowledges to be *"à peu près de même stature que l'homme de notre monde,"* and to let loose their influence on his moral faculties? How has this "combination of the elements and other physical causes, so contrary to the enlargement of animal nature in this new world, these obstacles to the development and formation of great germs," been arrested and suspended, so as to permit the human body to acquire its just dimensions, and by what inconceivable process has their action been directed on his mind alone? To judge of the truth of this, to form a just estimate of their genius and mental powers, more facts are wanting, and great allowance to be made for those circumstances of their situation which call for a display of particular talents only. This done, we shall probably find that they are formed in mind as well as in body, on the same module with the "Homo sapiens Europæus." The principles of their society forbidding all compulsion, they are to be led to duty and to enterprise by personal influence and persuasion. Hence eloquence in council, bravery and address in war, become the foundations of all consequence with them. To these acquirements all their faculties are directed. Of their bravery and address in war we have multiplied proofs, because we have been the subjects on which they were exercised. Of their eminence in oratory we have fewer examples, because it is displayed chiefly in their own councils. Some, however, we have of very superior luster. I may challenge the whole orations of Demosthenes and Cicero, and of any more eminent orator, if Europe has furnished more eminent, to produce a single passage, superior to the speech of Logan, a Mingo chief, to Lord Dunmore, when governor of this state. And, as a testimony of their talents in this line, I beg leave to introduce it, first stating the incidents necessary for understanding it. In the spring of the year 1774, a robbery and murder were committed on an inhabitant of the frontiers of Virginia, by two Indians of the Shawanee tribe. The neighboring whites, according to their custom, undertook to punish this outrage in a summary way. Col. Cresap, a man infamous for the many murders he had committed on those much-injured people, collected a party, and proceeded down the Kanhaway in quest of vengeance. Unfortunately a canoe of women and children, with one man only, was seen coming from the opposite shore, unarmed and unsuspecting an hostile attack from the whites. Cresap and his party concealed themselves on the bank of the river, and the moment the canoe reached the shore, singled out their objects, and, at one fire, killed every person in it. This happened to be the family of Logan, who had long been distinguished as a friend of the whites. This unworthy return provoked his vengeance. He accordingly signalized himself in the war which ensued. In the autumn of the same year a decisive battle was fought at the mouth of the Great Kanhaway, between the collected forces of the Shawanese, Mingoes, and Delawares, and a detachment of the Virginia militia. The Indians were defeated, and sued for peace. Logan, however, disdained to be seen among the suppliants. But, lest the sincerity of a treaty should be distrusted, from which so distinguished a chief absented himself, he sent by a messenger the following speech to be delivered to Lord Dunmore.

"I appeal to any white man to say, if ever he entered Logan's cabin hungry, and he gave him not meat; if ever he came cold and naked, and he clothed him not. During the course of the last long and bloody war, Logan remained idle in his cabin, an advocate for peace. Such was my love for the whites, that my countrymen pointed as they passed, and said, 'Logan is the friend of white men.' I had even thought to have lived with you, but for the injuries of one man. Col. Cresap, the last spring, in cold blood, and unprovoked, murdered all the relations of Logan, not sparing even my women and children. There runs not a drop of my blood in the veins of any living creature. This called on me for revenge. I have sought it: I have killed many: I have fully glutted my vengeance. For my country, I rejoice at the beams of peace. But do not harbor a thought that mine is the joy of fear. Logan never felt fear. He will not turn on his heel to save his life. Who is there to mourn for Logan?—Not one."

Before we condemn the Indians of this continent as wanting genius, we must consider that letters have not yet been introduced among them. Were we to compare them in their present state with the Europeans North of the Alps, when the Roman arms and arts first crossed those mountains, the comparison would be unequal, because, at that time, those parts of Europe were swarming with numbers; because numbers produce emulation, and multiply the chances of improvement, and one improvement begets another. Yet I may safely ask, how many good poets, how many able mathematicians, how many great inventors in arts or sciences, had Europe North of the Alps then produced? And it was sixteen centuries after this before a Newton could be formed. I do not mean to deny, that there are varieties in the race of man, distinguished by their powers both of body and mind. I believe there are, as I see to be the case in the races of other animals. I only mean to suggest a doubt, whether the bulk and faculties of animals depend on the side of the Atlantic on which their food happens to grow, or which furnishes the elements of which they are compounded? Whether nature has enlisted herself as a Cis or Trans-Atlantic partisan? I am induced to suspect, there has been more eloquence than sound reasoning displayed in support of this theory; that it is one of those cases where the judgment has been seduced by a glowing pen: and whilst I render every tribute of honor and esteem to the celebrated zoologist, who has added, and is still adding, so many precious things to the treasures of science, I must doubt whether in this instance he has not cherished error also, by lending her for a moment his vivid imagination and bewitching language. . . .

[Ought we] to emancipate all slaves born after passing the act. The bill reported by the revisors does not itself contain this proposition; but an amendment containing it was prepared, to be offered to the legislature whenever the bill should be taken up, and further directing, that they should continue with their parents to a certain age, then be brought up, at the public expense, to tillage, arts or sciences, according to their geniuses, till the females should be eighteen, and the males twenty-one years of age, when they should be colonized to such place as the circumstances of the time should render most proper, sending them out with arms, implements of household and of the handicraft arts, seeds, pairs of the useful domestic animals, &c. to declare them a free and independent people, and extend to them our alliance and protection, till they have acquired strength; and to send vessels at the same time to other parts of the world for an equal number of white inhabitants; to induce whom to migrate hither, proper encouragements were to be proposed. It will probably be asked, Why not retain and incorporate the blacks into the state, and thus save the expense of supplying, by importation of white settlers, the vacancies they will leave? Deep rooted prejudices entertained by the whites; ten thousand recollections, by the blacks, of the injuries they have sustained, new provocations, the real distinctions which nature has made; and many other circumstances, will divide us into parties, and produce convulsions which will probably never end but in the extermination of the one or the other race.—To these objections, which are political, may be added others, which are physical and moral. The first difference which strikes us is that of color. Whether the black of the negro resides in the reticular membrane between the skin and scarf-skin, or in the scarf-skin itself; whether it proceeds from the color of the blood, the color of the bile, or from that of some other secretion, the difference is fixed in nature, and is as real as if its seat and cause were better known to us. And is this difference of no importance? Is it not the foundation of a greater or less share of beauty in the two races? Are not the fine mixtures of red and white, the expressions of every passion by greater or less suffusions of color in the one, preferable to that eternal monotony, which reigns in the countenances, that immovable veil of black which covers all the emotions of the other race? Add to these, flowing hair, a more elegant symmetry of form, their own judgment in favor of the whites, declared by their preference of them, as uniformly as is the preference of the Oranootan for the black women over those of his own species. The circumstance of superior beauty, is thought worthy attention in the propagation of our horses, dogs, and other domestic animals; why not in that of man? Besides those of color, figure, and hair, there are other physical distinctions proving a difference of race. They have less hair on the face and body.

They secrete less by the kidneys, and more by the glands of the skin, which gives them a very strong and disagreeable odor. This greater degree of transpiration renders them more tolerant of heat, and less so of cold, than the whites. Perhaps too a difference of structure in the pulmonary apparatus, which a late ingenious experimentalist has discovered to be the principal regulator of animal heat, may have disabled them from extricating, in the act of inspiration, so much of that fluid from the outer air, or obliged them in expiration, to part with more of it. They seem to require less sleep. A black, after hard labor through the day, will be induced by the slightest amusements to sit up till midnight, or later, though knowing he must be out with the first dawn of the morning. They are at least as brave, and more adventuresome. But this may perhaps proceed from a want of fore-thought, which prevents their seeing a danger till it be present. When present, they do not go through it with more coolness or steadiness than the whites. They are more ardent after their female: but love seems with them to be more an eager desire, than a tender delicate mixture of sentiment and sensation. Their griefs are transient. Those numberless afflictions, which render it doubtful whether heaven has given life to us in mercy or in wrath, are less felt, and sooner forgotten with them. In general, their existence appears to participate more of sensation than reflection. To this must be ascribed their disposition to sleep when abstracted from their diversions, and unemployed in labor. An animal whose body is at rest, and who does not reflect, must be disposed to sleep of course. Comparing them by their faculties of memory, reason, and imagination, it appears to me, that in memory they are equal to the whites; in reason much inferior, as I think one could scarcely be found capable of tracing and comprehending the investigations of Euclid; and that in imagination they are dull, tasteless, and anomalous. It would be unfair to follow them to Africa for this investigation. We will consider them here, on the same stage with the whites, and where the facts are not apocryphal on which a judgment is to be formed. It will be right to make great allowances for the difference of condition, of education, of conversation, of the sphere in which they move. Many millions of them have been brought to, and born in America. Most of them indeed have been confined to tillage, to their own homes, and their own society: yet many have been so situated, that they might have availed themselves of the conversation of their masters; many have been brought up to the handicraft arts, from that circumstance have always been associated with the whites. Some have been liberally educated, and all have lived in countries where the arts and sciences are cultivated to a considerable degree, and have had before their eyes samples of the best works from abroad. The Indians, with no advantages of this kind, will often carve figures on their pipes not destitute of design and merit. They will crayon out an animal, a plant, or a country, so as to prove the existence of a germ in their minds which only wants cultivation. They astonish you with strokes of the most sublime oratory; such as prove their reason and sentiment strong, their imagination glowing and elevated. But never yet could I find that a black had uttered a thought above the level of plain narration; never see even an elementary trait of painting or sculpture. In music they are more generally gifted than the whites with accurate ears for tune and time, and they have been found capable of imagining a small catch. Whether they will be equal to the composition of a more extensive run of melody, or of complicated harmony, is yet to be proved. Misery is often the parent of the most affecting touches in poetry.—Among the blacks is misery enough, God knows, but no poetry. Love is the peculiar cestrum of the poet. Their love is ardent, but it kindles the senses only, not the imagination. Religion indeed has produced a Phyllis Whately; but it could not produce a poet. The compositions published under her name are below the dignity of criticism. The heroes of the Dunciad are to her, as Hercules to the author of that poem. Ignatius Sancho has approached nearer to merit in composition; yet his letters do more honor to the heart than the head. They breathe the purest effusions of friendship and general philanthropy, and shew how great a degree of the latter may be compounded with strong religious zeal. He is often happy in the turn of his compliments, and his style is easy and familiar, except when he affects a Shandean fabrication of words. But his imagination is wild and extravagant, escapes incessantly from every restraint of reason and taste, and, in the course of its vagaries, leaves a tract of thought as incoherent and eccentric, as is the course of a meteor through the sky. His subjects should often have led him to a process of sober reasoning: yet we find him always substituting sentiment for demonstration. Upon the whole, though we admit him to the first place among those of his own color who have presented themselves to the public judgment, yet when we compare him with the writers of the race among whom he lived, and particularly with the epistolary class, in which he has taken his own stand, we are compelled to enroll him at the bottom of the column. This criticism supposes the letters published under his name to be genuine, and to have received amendment from no other hand; points which would not be of easy investigation. The improvement of the blacks in body and mind, in the first instance of their mixture with the whites, has been observed by every one, and proves that their inferiority is not the effect merely of their condition of life. We know that among the Romans, about the Augustan age especially, the condition of their slaves was much more deplorable than that of the blacks on the continent of America. The two sexes were confined in separate apartments, because to raise a child cost the master more than to buy one. Cato, for a very restricted indulgence to his slaves in this particular, took from them a certain price. But in this country the slaves multiply as fast as the free inhabitants. Their situation and manners place the commerce between the two sexes almost without restraint.—The same Cato, on a principle of œconomy, always sold his sick and superannuated slaves. He gives it as a standing precept to a master visiting his farm, to sell his old oxen, old wagons, old tools, old and diseased servants, and every thing else become useless. *"Vendat boves vetulos, plaustrum vetus, ferramenta vetera, servum senem, servum morbosum, & si quid aliud supersit vendat."* Cato de re rustica. c. 2. The American slaves cannot enumerate this among the injuries and insults they receive. It was the common practice to expose in the island of Æsculapius, in the Tyber, diseased slaves, whose cure was like to become tedious. The Emperor Claudius, by an edict, gave freedom to such of them as should recover, and first declared, that if any person chose to kill rather than to expose them, it should be deemed homicide. The exposing them is a crime of which no instance has existed with us; and were it to be followed by death, it would be punished capitally. We are told of a certain Vedius Pollio, who, in the presence of Augustus, would have given a slave as food to his fish, for having broken a glass. With the Romans, the regular method of taking the evidence of their slaves was under torture. Here it has been thought better never to resort to their evidence. When a master was murdered, all his slaves, in the same house, or within hearing, were condemned to death. Here punishment falls on the guilty only, and as precise proof is required against him as against a freeman. Yet notwithstanding these and other discouraging circumstances among the Romans, their slaves were often their rarest artists. They excelled too in science, insomuch as to be usually employed as tutors to their master's children. Epictetus, Terence, and Phædrus, were slaves. But they were of the race of whites. It is not their condition then, but nature, which has produced the distinction.—Whether further observation will or will not verify the conjecture, that nature has been less bountiful to them in the endowments of the head, I believe that in those of the heart she will be found to have done them justice. That disposition to theft with which they have been branded, must be ascribed to their situation, and not to any depravity of the moral sense. The man, in whose favor no laws of property exist, probably feels himself less bound to respect those made in favor of others. When arguing for ourselves, we lay it down as a fundamental, that laws, to be just, must give a reciprocation of right: that, without this, they are mere arbitrary rules of conduct, founded in force, and not in conscience: and it is a problem which I give to the master to solve, whether the religious precepts against the violation of property were not framed for him as well as his slave? And whether the slave may not as justifiably take a little from one, who has taken all from him, as he may slay one who would slay him? That a change in the relations in which a man is placed should change his ideas of moral right and wrong, is neither new, nor peculiar to the color of the blacks. Homer tells us it was so 2600 years ago.

> *Emisu, gar t'aretes apoainutai europa Zeus*
> *Haneros, eut' an min kata doulion ema elesin.*
>
> Od. 17.323.

> Jove fix'd it certain, that whatever day
> Makes man a slave, takes half his worth away.

But the slaves of which Homer speaks were whites. Notwithstanding these considerations which must weaken their respect for the laws of property, we find among them numerous instances of the most rigid integrity, and as many as among their better instructed masters, of benevolence, gratitude, and unshaken fidelity.—The opinion, that they are inferior in the faculties of reason and imagination, must be hazarded with great diffidence. To justify a general conclusion, requires many observations, even where the subject may be submitted to the anatomical knife, to optical glasses, to analysis by fire, or by solvents. How much more then where it is a faculty, not a substance, we are examining; where it eludes the research of all the senses; where the conditions of its existence are various and variously combined; where the effects of those which are present or absent bid defiance to calculation; let me add too, as a circumstance of great tenderness, where our conclusion would degrade a whole race of men from the rank in the scale of beings which their Creator may perhaps have given them. To our reproach it must be said, that though for a century and a half we have had under our eyes the races of black and of red men, they have never yet been viewed by us as subjects of natural history. I advance it therefore as a suspicion only, that the blacks, whether originally a distinct race, or made distinct by time and circumstances, are inferior to the whites in the endowments both of body and mind. It is not against experience to suppose, that different species of the same genus, or varieties of the same species, may possess different qualifications. Will not a lover of natural history then, one who views the gradations in all the races of animals with the eye of philosophy, excuse an effort to keep those in the department of man as distinct as nature has formed them? This unfortunate difference of color, and perhaps of faculty, is a powerful obstacle to the emancipation of these people. Many of their advocates, while they wish to vindicate the liberty of human nature, are anxious also to preserve its dignity and beauty. Some of these, embarrassed by the question "What further is to be done with them?" join themselves in opposition with those who are actuated by sordid avarice only. Among the Romans emancipation required but one effort. The slave, when made free, might mix with, without staining the blood of his master. But with us a second is necessary, unknown to history. When freed, he is to be removed beyond the reach of mixture.

"NEGRO"

Encyclopaedia Britannica

This is the beginning of the entry for "Negro" in the 1798 Encyclopaedia Britannica, *the first American edition of the English project modeled upon the great* Encyclopédie.

NEGRO, *Homo pelli nigra,* a name given to a variety of the human species, who are entirely black, and are found in the Torrid zone, especially in that part of Africa which lies within the tropics. In the complexion of negroes we meet with various shades; but they likewise differ far from other men in all the features of their face. Round cheeks, high cheek-bones, a forehead somewhat elevated, a short, broad, flat nose, thick lips, small ears, ugliness, and irregularity of shape, characterize their external appearance. The negro women have the loins greatly depressed, and very large buttocks, which give the back the shape of a saddle. Vices the most notorious seem to be the portion of this unhappy race: idleness, treachery, revenge, cruelty, impudence, stealing, lying, profanity, debauchery, nastiness and intemperance, are said to have extinguished the principles of natural law, and to have silenced the reproofs of conscience. They are strangers to every sentiment of compassion, and are an awful example of the corruption of man when left to himself.

THE END OF EMPIRE

JOSEPH PRIESTLEY

In his utopian vision of the free future, inspired by the American and French Revolutions, which Priestley included in his Lectures to the Right Honorable Edmund Burke *in 1791, he foresaw the end to Western colonialism.*

The very idea of distant possessions will be even ridiculed. The East and the West Indies, and everything without ourselves will be disregarded, and wholly excluded from all European systems; and only those divisions of men, and of territory, will take place which the common convenience requires, and not such as the mad and insatiable ambition of princes demands. No part of America, Africa, or Asia, will be held in subjection to any part of Europe, and all the intercourse that will be kept up among them will be for their mutual advantage.

THE VIKING PORTABLE LIBRARY